# THE VERI†AS CONFLICT

### A NOVEL OF SPIRITUAL WARFARE

# SHAUNTI FELDHAHN

Multnomah® Publishers *Sisters, Oregon*

THE VERITAS CONFLICT
© 2001 Veritas Enterprises, Inc.
published by Multnomah Publishers, Inc.

International Standard Book Number: 1-57673-708-X

Cover images by Tony Stone Images
Cover design by Chris Gilbert / Uttley DouPonce DesignWorks

*The Holy Bible,* New International Version © 1973, 1984 by International Bible Society, used by permission of Zondervan Publishing House

*Holy Bible,* New Living Translation (NLT) © 1996. Used by permission of Tyndale House Publishers, Inc. All rights reserved.

*The Holy Bible,* New King James Version (NKJV) © 1984 by Thomas Nelson, Inc.
*The Holy Bible,* King James Version (KJV)

*Multnomah* is a trademark of Multnomah Publishers, Inc., and is registered in the U.S. Patent and Trademark Office. The colophon is a trademark of Multnomah Publishers, Inc.

Printed in the United States of America

Library of Congress Cataloging-in-Publication Data
Feldhahn, Shaunti Christine.
The veritas conflict : a novel of spiritual warfare / by Shaunti Feldhahn
    p.cm.   ISBN 1-57673-708-X (pbk.)   1. Women college students–Fiction.
2. Spiritual warfare–Fiction.   I. Title.   PS3556.E4574 V4 2001 813'.54–dc21 2001001088

01 02 03 04 05 06 07 08 09 — 10 9 8 7 6 5 4 3 2 1 0

*For Jeff,*
*My beloved, my friend.*

# Enlarged area of Harvard Yard

AT THE END OF THEIR LONG JOURNEY, although they didn't realize it, the new colonists made a declaration of war.

They poured off the longboat, fighting through the surf toward their new home soil. Men, women, and children stretched forward, crying out, flailing through chest-high water and the final seconds of their long journey. No one noticed the frigid temperature of the water, the sodden weight of their clothes. Every fiber was focused on one goal.

A young husband reached for his wife and son, pulling them close, muscling them through the throng toward shore. His heart stretched as if it would burst. "Almost there! O Lord, we're almost there!"

With a jolt, he felt the sand grow firm under his feet. His wife broke free, scrambling forward.

"We're home, David!" she cried.

He fell to the ground as if to a throne-room floor. All around him, the beach was filled with weary, exultant travelers on their knees, faces in the sand, laughing and crying.

David held his wife and son tight, kissing them, rocking back and forth.

"We did it." His voice was choked. *"He* did it!"

His wife dropped her head to her hands. "O God of our fathers—"

"O God!" David's voice came out in a whisper. "We can worship You freely!" His arm tightened around his young son. "Thank You that Gage will grow up in a land of promise."

The boy squirmed and broke free, running along the beach, captivated by the new adventure. His mother got to her feet, but David grabbed her hand.

"Let him run, Grace. It's been a long time."

Her eyes flickered to a small knot of people standing a few feet away. Several watched the scampering boy with solemn expressions, and several didn't watch at all. Grace turned away, pain on her face.

"It's only been one week. To think that she died just seven days from—"

David put a gentle finger to her lips. "Dear one, they're not second-guessing their decision. Each of us decided it was worth the risk, the sacrifice. What can we give that He has not already given?"

"Attention, everyone!"

Their leader had secured the longboat and was standing where the thin strip of sand melded into a tall forest. He held a weathered book in his hand. "We have a few hours of daylight left. We must get to work." His eyes shone as he held the volume aloft. "And then we must get to prayer."

Once the last were ashore and supplies were hauled to the makeshift camp, the group gathered at the tree line facing the dark ocean.

David stood with his wife and son, joining the hymns of praise as bonfires and torches flared around them. Despite the unfamiliar forest at his back, he reveled in the security of unconstrained worship.

The music died away, and David heard a rustling in the crowd as people began to kneel. He gripped his wife's hand, and they knelt again on the sand. The stillness became tense with the presence of the Holy Spirit.

Their leader's voice rang out, and every heart dedicated the settlement of the new land to God. They claimed the promise that had shepherded their long pilgrimage: "Seek and ye shall find, when ye seek me with all of your heart."

The new colony—and later the new nation—would be founded firmly on the bedrock of faith in their Savior. The stake had been driven.


In the darkness high above the little group, where the flickering bonfires looked small in the blackness, two dark beings brooded. Their territory—held so long with little contest—was invaded, and they had finally withdrawn from earshot of words that pierced like cold fire. They glowered at the many luminous warriors surrounding the little group on the beach. More were arriving by the minute, adding to the numbers of those who had traveled the ocean with the saints of God.

The larger of the two watched each of the enemy arrivals and straightened suddenly as a close-packed convoy hovered directly over the saints—who, he was disgusted to see, were still on their knees. The demon lord gestured to his aide, who dropped down for a better view and returned within seconds.

"It is he."

Without a word, both turned and made off into the night. A team of others took surveillance duty.


A giant with dark hair and serious features hovered above the praying leader of the puritans and received a report of his own. He thanked the messenger and glanced sharply skyward.

His lieutenant was at his side in an instant. "General, should we take action?"

"No. They would learn of my posting sooner or later." Petras gazed into the blackness beyond the little group. He could sense hundreds—thousands—observing them. "They must have suspected we would make a stand here."

Petras turned back toward the huddled group on the beach below them. The responsibility for these saints was his, and a fierce protectiveness stirred in his breast. He put a hand to his sword.

As the people moved quietly back to their camp, Petras took a deep breath and rose skyward. The host moved into position below and around him as he began to glow. Shining brighter and brighter, he rose above the tree line, moving over the ocean, casting a pure and fierce light over the camp of the saints. Like a beacon, the light pierced the darkness surrounding them, penetrating the territory that would be their stand.

Suddenly, the angelic host was struck with a holy dread, and every head bowed to receive the coming of the King.

The Son of Man stood among them, and the light of heaven became blinding. It exploded with power, reaching the entire breadth of the land that was to be forged into a new nation.

The angels watched, breathless, as the light penetrated each tree, each person, each blade of grass, with liquid intensity. Then, with a resonance that penetrated just like the light, the Lord spoke.

"They have asked, and I have answered. My covenant is with them."

Instantly, the light vanished. The angelic warriors were suspended, silent. After a time, Petras stirred, his wings shimmering like gossamer threads against the darkness. His eyes were shining as he pulled his sword and held it aloft in salute to his Liege.

"The battle has begun."

# PART ONE

## THE EARLY YEARS

I further entreat you, Sirs, to cease your praises to me, I am weary of the thanks; it is over doing; I fear it should hurt the instrument, and swell the pride of a naughty heart. Who am I? Christ is my all. Little, very little, I can do for his name's sake, who has died for me and given me good hope through grace, and by his providence put in my power, and inclined my heart to this way among others, of expressing my gratitude for his name's sake, to him be the glory of all.

A LETTER FROM THOMAS HOLLIS, AN EARLY BENEFACTOR OF HARVARD, TO PRESIDENT LEVERET, 23 SEPTEMBER 1720

## Mid-1600s

THE DARK LORD'S EYES CLOSED, and his howl of frustration became a roar. At his outburst, his top generals exerted all their discipline to remain stone-faced and still. Their master began pacing, his heavy step shaking the very air of his dominion.

"When our persecution in England drove them not to simple flight and despair, but to establish an enemy stake on these shores, I knew this battle would be hard." He shot a glance of malice at a high-ranking general assigned to Europe, who stared straight ahead.

"But our attempts at terror and increased hardship have only further driven these accursed people into the arms of the Enemy. And now I find out—" he swung on a recently arrived aide, who stepped back a pace—"that this new college will not simply be a center of learning, but is being dedicated to the quest for *heaven's* truth in all the disciplines?"

The aide trembled a bit but nodded. "Yes, my lord. We believe so."

"With what reason? What makes you think so?"

"The school's…ah…*motto,* my lord."

"What is it?"

The others shared quick glances and looked for a way to avoid speaking the fatal words.

Lucifer grabbed the aide and jerked his face close. "WHAT IS IT?"

"'T-t-truth,' my lord." The cruel fingers gripped convulsively, and the aide gasped in pain. "The university's motto is *Veritas*—Truth. And they are pondering a change to *Christo et Ecclesiae*—'For Christ and the Church.'"

Lucifer drew a taloned finger across the demon's neck. The aide convulsed and, with terror-filled eyes, was drawn into a dark portal that opened just behind him. As it clanged shut on his strangled scream, those who remained could still feel the heat and fear that had blasted from the deep beyond.

Their lord didn't turn to face them. "What shall we do to turn this tide?" he asked, then seemed to lose himself in thought. No one spoke. After several minutes, the dark lord stirred and looked up. "Well, they are searching for knowledge, are they? Searching for wisdom, for *truth*. Well, let them find it—*my* wisdom. I will show

13

them that *they* are the wise ones and that there is no truth.

"They want to establish a nation—a *Christian* body of believers. So how do you change the course of a body? You strike at the head, the mind. The heart may often be out of our reach, while their faith continues fervent, but the head…the head can give us a lot to work with."

He surveyed his minions, taking his time, muttering to himself. His gaze settled on a tall demon, and he snapped his fingers. The demon was at Lucifer's side in an instant, bowing long and deferentially. "Yes, my liege."

"Leviathan, you have always been one of my most trusted generals, and I believe your expertise will be much needed here."

The proud eyes flickered. "As you wish."

"I realize that you are more accustomed to being prince over well-established and large-scale initiatives, but this is a strategic time. We must undermine their roots before their power is firmly planted. That will provide incalculable benefits for all the years to come. To put it simply, you wield our most effective tools, and we need your prowess here most of all."

Lucifer continued, carefully hiding his satisfaction at using Leviathan's own tools against him. "And I trust that in time you will find other areas in this new nation that will also be amenable to your efforts, just as you have in so many places before."

The tall demon straightened, his chest high. "I will take delight, my liege, at demonstrating for our side the *proper* use of strategic tools." He ignored an indignant outburst from the general over Europe. "I hope we may find an avenue to poison the course of this new land."

Lucifer leaned toward his officer. "You already have it. That is why you were chosen. Wait no longer!"

Seconds later the guards posted outside the meeting room were bowled over as Leviathan shot like a comet through the door and began to muster his troops. One guard, a less experienced demon recently come up through the ranks, raised an eyebrow at his comrade-in-arms.

The other guard rubbed his hands together. "Get a good eyeful, my boy. If Leviathan has been assigned, this is going to be good."

"Is…is he—"

"One of the seven deadly princes."

The younger demon blanched. "Which one?"

The older guard smiled, a slow smile of anticipation as he watched the battalion take shape. "Pride."

## Many Years Later...

Laura Grindley watched her husband pace the length of the sitting room. Each lap seemed to increase his tension, winding him tighter than the strings in the harpsichord he thumped occasionally in passing. She remained silent on the divan, arms draped over a small pillow in her lap, stroking the satin brocade.

Finally, he turned to face her, and she opened her arms to him.

He knelt quickly in front of her, wrapping his arms around her waist. "I'm sorry, my love. It wasn't supposed to be this way. I have long sought to avoid dragging you into my burden."

"Don't be sorry. You are doing what God intends you to do." Her hands stroked his thick hair as if he were a child. "You are standing in the gap, standing for what is right, for the truth. How could I not support the only strong beam that is keeping the foundations from crumbling?"

George Grindley hugged his wife fiercely then released her and stood. "I have to go. Whelen Pike will be at the board meeting today, and they will be voting. So I must at all costs be there."


Two hours later, George breathed his third silent plea that the Lord would help him keep his temper...or maybe just that He would send down a lightning bolt and wipe the smug smile off the countenance before him. Either would do.

Whelen Pike was stirring sugar into his teacup. "After all, Mr. Grindley, I was asked to join this board to help whip the business affairs of the college into shape. No offense to the more established board members." He nodded at the other faces around the table. "Or to those lost in the tragic accident at sea one year ago, God rest their souls. But perhaps...well, let us just say what we are all thinking, shall we? We need the bracing reality of true business acumen. We must restore order to the chaos in which we now find ourselves. Begging your pardon for that characterization, of course."

George could see Kingsley, Edwards, and the others already assuming thoughtful expressions as they did all too often under the misleading but clever arguments Whelen Pike brought to the table.

Business acumen? Cleverly concealed fraud and confidence tricks! George had labored at trade, earning his fortune with integrity and pride. He had long sought to be the "trusted servant" to whom the Master would give ever more talents to manage, and his Master had indeed blessed his efforts. Pike, on the other hand, would pick the Master's pocket and show a doubled return by sleight of hand.

George's eyes slid to the easel holding the model of Pike's suggested "revision" to the university's shield. No more flowing banner, no place for the motto *Christo et*

*Ecclesiae.* It was so stark, the triangular talisman somehow emasculated by the absence of its trailing banner. The remaining motto: *Veritas,* alone, out of context. Truth in a vacuum.

"Gentlemen," George said, "we've already been through this. And our previous vote was binding. This board may have only a few remaining members following our tragic losses last year, but such a proposal still requires a unanimous vote. And I cannot and will not allow either the motto or the shield to be altered to lessen the cause of Christ just because certain members believe that doing so will advance the cause of business for an already wealthy university. Those who founded the college were very clear about our ultimate goal. Just because you who remain no longer agree with that goal doesn't mean it should change. Rather, I respectfully submit that *you* should be persuaded to alter your opinions, giving way to the inexorability of the ultimate Truth." He looked directly at Pike. "Truth…in the cause of Christ. There is no other."

Pike arched his eyebrows, pursed his lips, and slowly nodded. "Of course we are willing to alter our opinions…and have, my dear boy. Quite often, as a matter of fact. I consider myself to be an open-minded man and am only seeking the ultimate good of the college after all. I am only seeking to apply the business talents for which I was chosen."

Pike's fingers played with the silver teaspoon, and George set his jaw and tried to match Pike's patience. With a click, the spoon came to rest again on the table, pointing at George. Pike looked around. "Well, gentlemen, I think we've had enough for one day, don't you? What do you say to reconvening next week? I was not prepared to outline my analysis of the university's financial situation today, but next week we could revisit—"

"I think not." George's voice was sharp. "We'll wait until our next regularly scheduled meeting, Whelen." George seethed at the smooth usurpation of his prerogative as chairman. In the next moment he was washed with shame. He was being ruled by pride at Whelen's tactics, opposing a suggestion simply because of the source. He breathed a silent prayer for forgiveness. Then, looking across the table, added a plea for Whelen Pike and his family.

But he was not inclined to back down, especially when he noted the other board members looking thoughtfully at the man. He lifted the gavel and tapped it on the grand mahogany table. "This meeting—and this debate—is closed, gentlemen. We'll reconvene in three months' time."


Whelen Pike spoke a soft order, and his manservant approached to refill his cup. The servant poured deftly, careful to avoid spilling a drop on the small ribbon-tied package that sat nearby. He stopped when his master raised a hand and, stepping back in silent deference, returned to his place against the wall.

Whelen raised the cup to his lips, his eyes on the portrait hanging on the opposite wall. The wooden frame was intricately engraved with leaves and branches. The woman's dark eyes stared into his, their challenge unabated even now so many years after her death.

His lips hardened to a thin line. A torturous death. In the hellfire the hypocrites had accused her of fanning.

Their matriarch should have lived out her life in peace, surrounded by material comforts. Instead, her property had been seized, her family ostracized for generations. That she indeed practiced the dark magic was beside the point. Those who pointed their fingers were no better than she. His fingers tightened on his cup. It had taken them years to come back, and they would not let it slip away. Their mandate would prevail.

He took another sip and closed his eyes. He could feel the vital forces moving, their strength gathering like the thunderclouds. After a long moment of communion, he set the cup on its saucer. He gestured with his hand, and his manservant bowed and departed.

Whelen sourly regarded the small stack of papers wrapped in a blue velvet cover and bound with a slender cream ribbon. Back when he was married he had reveled in the accolades of visitors admiring his wife's eye for detail, her "delightful" adornments to their opulent home. But that was before. He heartily wished he did not have to touch those adornments now.

Best to get it over with, he supposed. Now that she had passed on—he shuddered—to her *reward,* as she had so ridiculously put it, her journal would certainly provide the information he needed. He did not want to wade through pages of sentimental sop, but it would be worth it to find access to the valuable keepsakes she had refused to return.

He pulled the loosely bound pages toward him and opened them at a random spot.

*I continue to pray, O my Lord and God, that Thou would intervene in this family.*
*Down through the generations break through the darkness and open their eyes just*
*as Thou hast opened mine.*

He slammed the volume shut. Thank the gods the little traitor had not been allowed to raise his son.

## Two Weeks Later...

George emerged from the grand house just off the west side of campus, pulling on his leather gloves. A small boy scampered past him and down the steps to the carriage. The doorman gave a subtle assist as the child clambered inside. The young master didn't want any help.

George was halfway down the steps when he stopped and hurried back up. Opening the door wide, he pulled his wife to him and planted a firm kiss, then playfully patted her backside. She shooed him back out the door with a smile.

High above, several dark beings followed the carriage, frustrated as the man and his grandson stopped on a few simple errands. They could see a familiar warrior watching over them—the result of his wife's accursed prayers, no doubt—and several more were always around the university due to the increased warfare over the last few years. Although they were willing to enter direct battle, they preferred to face minimal opposition from the host of heaven. Their support was still too weak. But by direct order, it had to be done today.

Suddenly, their leader came alert and pointed. Their charge was heading for a bridge across the Charles River. Another group of people was strolling across that bridge a few hundred yards ahead enjoying the sunny day. A few boys were jumping on and off the stone railing. The voices of scolding mothers could be heard. With a tight smile the leader barked out his orders.

Heading toward the Anderson bridge, Gael rested a powerful hand on the carriage below him. He had been with this child of God for years on and off and was looking forward to watching the meeting in Boston unfold. He noticed that his charge had his head in his hands, praying for the meeting. Gael joined his prayers, asking God to intervene. He had felt the excitement of the host of heaven when this meeting had been announced; perhaps the tactics of the enemy would soon be countered!

He had barely started praying when he felt a swift, distinctive chill. Gael whipped around, his hand on his sword. Nothing.

He looked ahead at the group of people on the bridge and noticed a commotion. Two children had slipped from a ledge and were dangling above the cold water. Several women were hollering, desperate, leaning far over the verge.

As Gael rose to a better view he could see a skirmish in the air opposite the bridge. Four brilliant warriors were fighting off a second malevolent attempt to yank the children down. The enemy was swarming, suddenly too numerous for the angelic team. The children fell screaming into the water, and Gael reflexively prepared to help his comrades.

· Then he stopped, hovering in the air, scarcely breathing. The instinct honed from eons on the front lines of the Great War was sending an urgent message. He settled to the roof of the swaying carriage, eyes intent. George had seen the fracas on the bridge and was urging the driver forward. Gael turned a full circle, sword unsheathed and held low and ready.

A diversion. Somehow, he was certain.

George stripped off his waistcoat. Through the small front window the driver hollered back that two men had plunged in after the children, who were being swept closer to the opposite shore. The river was swift, and George prayed that God would help him reach them before they were swept from reach. *O God, save those children!* They were scarcely older than his grandson, who had started whimpering as the carriage hurtled toward the bridge.

Gael risked a glance forward—they were almost there, and all attention was focused on the four people in the water. Flashes rose like lightning as the angels fought off the demonic swarm. The other angels were calling for assistance, but Gael didn't leave the carriage.

*ON YOUR GUARD.* The unmistakable voice of the Lord made Gael jump. And something else.

He listened briefly and closed his eyes. The carriage lurched below him, and he could feel the wheels click onto the stone of the bridge. His eyes opened, burning with purpose. Rising to his full height, he spread his wings and raised his sword. The carriage slowed, and George leaned out the door as they swept past, one foot on the running board, calling to the stricken families that he would follow the opposite shore.

From every side, below the bridge and from the air, they attacked. As one, the dark forces turned abruptly from the existing fracas and focused on the carriage. Twenty demons went for Gael and another two for the horse. Gael knew what would happen even as it unfolded: desperate moments fighting an impossibly large ambush, his sword ripping through the demon ranks but not enough, not enough. Huge hands pummeled Gael from every side, swords ripping, pushing him back. He gasped in pain, wings fluttering, trying somehow to reach the front of the carriage, trying to cry for help.

The carriage was moving faster again, picking up speed down the slope, the man of God looking ahead now, still with one foot on the running board, the child wailing inside. In anguish, Gael saw two hulking bodies, faces burning with glee, reach the horse. For just a moment they looked back at him in triumph. Then one plunged his claws deep into the horse's brain.

Laura Grindley slipped from the richly brocaded stool to the floor. Her breath came out in great ragged sobs. Her son Cleon knelt beside her, holding her, equally overcome. Finally, Cleon looked up at the two men seated on the divan opposite them. One leaned awkwardly over the space between them and placed his hand on Laura's shoulder. He explained that it had been instantaneous, the moment head hit cobblestone. They were sorry, so sorry. At least somehow, miraculously, Cleon's son had been saved from the bucking, rampaging carriage. At least he was unhurt. The men on the divan began to pray for the heartbroken wife and son.

A dozen angels stepped out of time, kneeling around the crumpled body of the man of God. The world around them was paused in shadow, the people with half-formed words still on their lips, the crazed horse's legs pointing at the air. Demonic cheering and celebration could be heard, and the countenances of the massive angels spoke of rigid self-control.

One warrior of very high rank stood to his feet. He spoke a fierce word and pointed an upright hand. The demon forces became suddenly silent in swift retreat.

Gael walked across the bridge toward the group. For a moment he paused in surprise at the presence of the ranking angel, then moved forward and dropped to his knees. He stared at his charge, sorrow glimmering in his eyes.

"I don't know what the Lord's plan is this time. Often I do, but this time…" Gael shook his head. "Oh, Petras, we were so excited. And on today of all days."

"I don't know what the Master's plan is either, my friends. But He does all things well, and I'm eager to see what will come, especially since He sent me here. I am sorry for your pain, trusted friend. You served this child of God well. And I know how hard it is to hear the Lord's voice and be aware that your watch-care is at a sudden end."

Gael was silent for a moment, then reached out his large hand and laid it on George's chest. "I have been striving with this godly man's team for over forty-five years." He looked up at Petras, and an intent light suddenly shone in his eyes. "But, like you, I have stood and worshiped at the throne of grace for the ages. Worthy is our Master of our praise and our trust."

"Well said, my friend. Worthy is the Lord; His purposes will prevail!"

A sudden thought hit Gael, and he looked up sharply. "What about his wife? Laura! She'll be—"

"That is being taken care of. Those in your usual company will minister the Lord's comfort to her when she learns." Petras extended his hand to Gael and pulled him to his feet. "We know that their reunion will be all the more joyous on her appointed day. My friend, you did your part well in this darkening time. And it will be your honor to escort him home."

For several minutes, Laura struggled to fight her way out of the dark pit. And then she could feel herself being wrapped in arms stronger than any on earth, arms of infinite love and shared grief. She clung to the almost tangible comfort. Her Father understood the boundless pain. After a few moments, her anguished tears settled.

She looked up. "I pray for him every day. How could this happen?" Her eyes bored into those of the gray-haired man opposite her.

He shook his head. "I don't know. George was in the midst of a spiritual battle; we all knew that. Ever since I married you two, George stood for God against the enemy of our souls. You have endured many attacks over the years. I don't know why God would allow this, but I do know the enemy must have wanted to destroy him for a long, long time." He leaned forward, palms up. "Why would this happen now? I don't know, Laura. I just don't know."

Laura gripped Cleon's hand, and she began to shiver. She remembered the purpose of the meeting George had set out for that very morning. New tears leaked down her cheeks, and she looked up at her pastor with a shattered expression.

"I think I do."

George stood in awe. The blackness had become shimmering, translucent. All around him were majestic beings—beings with half smiles on their solemn faces, as if anticipating a small child's reaction to a wondrous present. He wanted to ask what was happening, but somehow he knew. Instead of pain and sorrow, he felt a thrill of excitement.

One giant angel—they had to be angels—stood beside him. He was shining, wings, garments, and face reflecting a greater glory. George noticed with surprising clarity that the angel's wings were battered and torn, his garments rent in many places. A picture came into his mind of this very being suddenly passing his own still form on the cobblestones of the bridge, and pulling his grandson from the rocketing carriage. He stared at the angel and watched in fascination as tears and bruises began to be healed as light suffused them. The angel stepped toward him and pointed downward.

He looked down and gasped. The streets of Cambridge were fading rapidly beneath his feet. They seemed covered in shadow, under a dark veil. Somehow he caught a glimpse of his wife—how he loved her!—going about some task, singing a song to herself. He could see her clearly despite the shadow. Her hair was falling out of its clasp, tendrils curling lightly on her neck. His heart ached. His beloved, his best friend. He longed to linger, to say good-bye. Yet he also yearned to keep moving, to set sail for a distant shore.

The cherished sight of his wife faded rapidly, but the ache only increased. What was this? It became like a pounding in his chest as he moved swiftly along a brilliant passageway. Then he realized that the ache was drawing him forward, like a magnet searching for its match. George trembled with the intensity of the pressure in his heart, the anticipation of what he would find. He could hear soft voices, laughter, and snatches of singing. At the end of the passageway reflections of shimmering golden colors played off dimly seen figures, distant mountaintops. George could tell there was a crowd waiting for him, a promise of a joyous reunion, but he couldn't yet make out any faces.

Except for one. George drew a shuddering breath as he realized this was the face he had been longing to see his whole life. He thought his heart would burst. George found his feet and began running forward. Incredibly, so did the Other. The ache grew and grew, until finally, at long last, George threw himself into the arms of his Savior. He had come home.

## Fifteen Years Later...

Cleon Grindley sat in a pool of lantern light, his head bent, intent on the parchment before him. It was the early hours of the morning, but he couldn't sleep until he had put these words to paper. The silence of the night was broken only by the scratching sound of his quill pen. Line after line, page after page. The thoughts poured from him, and his prayers became fervent as he knew what the Lord was asking of him and of the others involved. From time to time Cleon would look over at the bed, thankful that his wife and infant daughter could sleep even with his lamp lit.

He stretched and rubbed his eyes, then took a sip of water from the glass on the writing table beside him. It took him a moment to notice that the glass was shaking. The sense of certainty, of heavenly revelation, was so strong that he felt he would burst if he didn't instantly obey his Father's every directive.

He gathered the papers together in the proper order and sat for a moment, letting the tension subside, replaced by awe. The Lord had given him the plan! After so many years of prayer, he believed he knew the answer to his father's long and eventually fatal quest. Cleon prayed anew that he would be a good guardian of the mission.

He leaned back in his chair, lifted the parchment, and settled his reading glasses on his nose.

To the honorable gentleman of Trudburry House, Boston
From Mister Cleon Grindley, Grindley House, Cambridge
Dear Jonathan,

Greetings in the name of the Lord! Thank you for your kind regards on the birth of my latest daughter. Eleanor is beautiful, taking after both her mother and grandmother more than me, thank heavens. Please thank Mary Ann for the fine blanket weaving. It is lining Eleanor's little crib even now.

I have been powerfully influenced by what I can only assume is the voice of the heavenly Father to continue the fight that was begun by my dear earthly father fifteen years ago. As you know, my father counted you among his closest friends and was bursting with eagerness to share with you some "secret plan" on the day he was taken from this life.

Neither I nor my mother had any inkling what the plan was, only that my father believed he had found a solution for "always keeping the name of Christ at Harvard." He was worried—and subsequent events validate his concern—that the board's slipping commitment to the cause of Christ would be solidified in policy in years hence. Now that Whelen Pike has long held the position of chairman, most members truly seem ashamed of the name that is above all names. They prefer to run the university like a business, and deem religion "a bit out of place in the guidance of an institution dedicated to higher learning."

As you know, the inevitable change in the school's motto occurred after a suitable period of mourning my father—since he was the lone holdout against that travesty. The shield was stripped of its banner proclaiming Christo et Ecclesiae. So the earliest motto of Veritas was returned but was given no context, no anchor, no reference to the original meaning that Jesus Christ is the source and end of all knowledge. How anyone can argue that there is truth outside Christ I do not know. My heart aches, and I believe that such a stand has invited a presence into the college that is not of God.

We can already see a change—subtle, but real. Those who do not know Christ feel much more comfortable with the university now, and those who are devout are beginning to feel as if they are somehow keeping their fingers in the hole of a dam. I shiver at times when I walk through the section of Harvard Yard bounded by the president's office. That area is so beautiful, but Whelen Pike's choice of president makes me cautious, and as I walk the paths my spirit rebels as if under the weight of a thousand hostile eyes.

I know you love the school as I do, and you may be shocked to know that there is now another possible change underway. If you look at your ring, you will notice that the shield carries three books with *Ve-ri-tas* written across their spines. You may know that the shield was designed with the top two books facing up and one turned down, signifying that we are searching for heaven's truth in all the disciplines but that much knowledge will be hidden from us.

Well, with the miraculous recent advancements in science, politics, and medicine, Mr. Pike and others are talking openly about changing the tenor of that shield. They are proposing to turn *all* the books up. It seems that man has the audacity to challenge God since we now know so much. We have become so proud, to even consider declaring all knowledge open to us! Does it not seem, sometimes, that we are facing a deadly strategy from the enemy of our souls?

I have to believe that my father sensed this coming, with the simultaneous advent of Whelen Pike's philosophy and the sudden loss of the Christ-fearing board members. (I might add, for no one's consideration but your own, that I have oft been struck by the mysterious nature of both my father's death and the deaths of the other board members, especially in such a short space of time. I don't know if such thoughts have ever crossed your mind.) My father must have known that time, if nothing else, would eventually eliminate his lone stand against the slipping commitment of the board so long as the trustees kept appointing people such as Mr. Pike. All the others would have to do was wait. He was young—only forty-five when he died—but even so, ten or twenty years to retirement would not be a long wait in the general scheme of things. Especially if, as I can't help but suspect, there is more than just Mr. Pike behind this scheme. (In keeping with our family heritage, we have of course been diligent in intercession for the school—and for Whelen Pike and his family—since we recognize that our battle is not against flesh and blood.)

So what was my father's plan? I have been praying for the answer to that question for fifteen long years. And tonight I awoke with such a burning in my soul; I believe I know! Thanks be to God!

Through those of us with positions and means in society there is an easy way of ensuring that the name of Christ always remains in force at Harvard University. If not directing the play, as we would all pray, at least prominent *on* the stage. (I cannot imagine a day when Christ would be taken off the stage entirely, but then I couldn't imagine a day when man would dare to declare that he knew the mysteries of the universe either. I fear the gradual but inexorable erosion of our faith in this country. I realized several years ago that many hundreds of bright young men have graduated from the Harvard from which "Christ and the Church" have been removed. Some have been devout, but not all; and even in those who love the Lord, I have often sensed a dangerous pride at the loftiness of their position. Many of these graduates have gone on to positions of prominence in business and government— often in the governing of our new republic. I worry that bad yeast will corrupt the whole loaf.)

So bear with me, old friend. I am outlining the plan in this letter so that you can pray over the idea before we meet in three weeks' time. If you consider it right, perhaps you can invite several of your friends—such as Messrs. Rutherford and Crist—to join us. You will know who should be considered once you see what I am proposing.

Cleon was jolted from the letter by his daughter's nighttime cry. He listened for a moment until he heard blankets rustling, followed by the unmistakable sounds of nursing. He grinned into the darkness, giving thanks once more for his family. Cleon switched pages and glanced through the notes he had so hastily jotted upon awakening. He would have to rewrite the plan more neatly before sending the letter to Jonathan.

He took a peek over his shoulder at his sleepy wife, then stood at the desk and blew out the light. It could wait until tomorrow.

## Three Weeks Later...

The angels soared upward from the house in Boston, strengthened by the prayers of the saints. Each warrior knew that at some point the existence of the plan would become known, and the battle would begin anew. But for now, they created an impenetrable shield around this place of peace.

In the sitting room below them, eight elderly men knelt on the floor, each covenanting with the Lord to do his part to keep the name of Christ paramount at Harvard. Their words were joyous, resolved. A sense of anticipation filled the air. A younger man also knelt with his father's friends, wiping tears from his eyes.

# PART TWO

## TODAY

In the world it is called tolerance but in hell it is called despair. The sin that believes in nothing, cares for nothing, seeks to know nothing, enjoys nothing, finds purpose in nothing, lives for nothing but remains alive because there is nothing which it would die for.

DOROTHY SAYERS

# TWO

CLAIRE RIVERS RACED DOWN THE DRIVEWAY, her heart pounding. She had watched through the front blinds until the mail truck drove away. There were three large envelopes in the contents of the mailbox. She had seen them—two manila, one white. *O God, O God, please…* She was shaking and glad that her mother had stayed in the kitchen, out of sight of the driveway.

She yanked open the mailbox and hauled out the letters, catalogs, advertisements, and…there! She yanked out one of the manila envelopes by its corner, stared at it, and made a short sound of frustration at the blur of mail-order prose. One of her favorite catalogs—just not today.

She juggled the stack, and her heart suddenly stopped. A burgundy logo peeked at her. She gripped the corner of the white envelope and pulled it out. It was big.

She ripped it open and pulled out the short stack of papers. Then she was screaming, jumping up and down…and being pummeled on all sides by her mother, her brothers, and even the dog.

Through happy tears Claire accepted their hugs and punches. She finally found her voice and weakly batted at her mother's arm, grinning. "So much for not watching me!"

Her mother wiped her eyes on her sleeve. "Are you kidding, Clairie-bell? You didn't actually *believe* me, did you?" She hugged her daughter fiercely, rocking her back and forth and murmuring something in a choked voice.

Claire saw a few neighbors peeking through their windows. "Uh, Mom, can we go inside?"

They trooped into the kitchen, and Claire stood, eyes closed, trying not to cry. *Harvard! O God, I can't believe it!* It had been such a long wait. She could scarcely contain the urge to melt from relief right there in the middle of the kitchen.

"…and here she is!" Her mom handed her the cordless phone. Claire looked at it blankly. Her mom raised an eyebrow, mouthing *Dad*.

Claire tried to pull herself together. "Daddy! Did Mom tell you?"

"No, and I'm going crazy! What is it? Wait…you got accepted to Wheaton didn't you?" A banshee yell came over the line. "I knew it! I just knew it."

"Dad…."

"What?"

"Well, I don't…" Claire looked wildly at her mother, who was going through the stack of mail on the kitchen table.

"You *didn't* get accepted?"

"No, Dad, I mean…I don't know about Wheaton yet." She heard her mother's soft cry and saw her pick up a manila envelope embossed with Wheaton's logo.

She closed her eyes and tried to muster up the same excitement she'd felt just moments before. "Dad, I got into Harvard! *Harvard!*"

A pause. "Wow, Clairie-bell, that's just wonderful. I'm really proud of you!" He cleared his throat. "No matter what, you should be real proud of yourself."

Tears flooded her eyes, and her throat closed. It was the same old thing.

"…and we'll take you out to dinner to celebrate, okay?"

"Yeah, sure. That'd be great, Daddy."


A moment later, Barbara Rivers watched her daughter carefully replace the phone in its cradle and leave the room without a word. Barbara bowed her head for a moment, growing tense, then shoved her chair back from the table. She picked up a dog-eared book from the kitchen counter and headed for the glassed-in porch at the side of the house.


Upstairs, Claire flopped across her bed, one arm flung over her eyes. *What's wrong with this picture? This should be the happiest day of my life!* Her glance fell on the file drawer where months ago she had stashed nearly two dozen college catalogs, a handful of SAT practice tests and score sheets, and her admissions applications to eight schools. Funny. Such a small space to hold so many big dreams.

Claire suddenly breathed an exultant sigh and giggled. She had gotten into Harvard University! She, a middle-class girl from the Midwest! In the eight years since her Christian high school had been chartered, only a handful of graduates had gone on to Ivy League colleges, and she would be the first one at Harvard. Unbelievable.

Claire rolled over and grabbed the threadbare Eeyore that had been her companion since birth. She hugged it to her chest and stared at the other members of her well-loved Winnie the Pooh collection.

At lunch yesterday a bunch of her girlfriends had lamented the closeness of graduation, wishing that high school could last forever. Claire had looked at them like they were crazy.

She knew she was different. It wasn't just the schoolwork and the grades that seemed to come so easily, or the fact that she was just as eager to investigate genealogy or to volunteer at the crisis pregnancy center as she was to hang out at the mall; it was her yearning for *life*. She wanted to see the world, to venture beyond the boundaries of church, school, and family that had defined her for so long. Some of her college-bound friends talked more about finding a husband than finding a career. She wanted to get married someday, of course, but she also wanted to do great things with her life, to make a contribution, to change the world. Her father and mother had always told her she could do anything she set her mind to, and she believed them. They had weathered a few big storms as a family, and she knew she was stronger for it.

Claire twisted Eeyore's floppy ear around and around her finger. As far back as she could remember, her parents had assumed her plans would include their alma mater: Wheaton, the Harvard of Christian colleges. In the last year or two she had tried to drop hints that she might want to look elsewhere, but they never really heard her. She knew they wanted her to go to a Christian college for the same reason they had scraped and saved to pay tuition for her private high school: They didn't want their eldest daughter corrupted by the world.

*Well, maybe I can use a little corrupting!* That thought was followed just as quickly by a sharp sense of shame. *O Lord, forgive me. You know I don't mean that. I just want...* What did she want? She lay quietly for a long moment, fighting with the turmoil that had been her constant companion for the last few weeks. *I just want* more!

She sat up, pounding Eeyore's nose into the floral duvet covering the bed. Her mom and dad might not want to recognize the truth, but it was plain as day that no matter how great a Christian college was, an Ivy League school would open far more doors for her. They needed to trust her and the values they had instilled in her.

But how could she make them see that? Suddenly, she was filled with a piercing fear that they wouldn't see it, that they would present her with a choice between their helping to pay for Wheaton and her paying for Harvard. The whole family had sacrificed to build up a small college account for her, but her father called it the Wheaton fund. What if they weren't willing to use it for a non-Christian school? She could probably get a partial scholarship and a job, but no way could she earn the thirty-five thousand dollars a year it would cost.

Claire jumped to her feet and circled the room. Her foot thumped against something heavy on the floor by her backpack. She bent down, flicking away quiz papers and magazines, and saw her student study Bible. She hadn't picked it up since Sunday.

Claire was suddenly flooded with conviction...and longing. She had so many anxieties, but she hadn't prayed. She hadn't spent time in the Word. She hadn't turned all these concerns over to the Lord. Instead, she had griped and complained and let fear take hold. She dropped her head.

"O God, forgive me. I am so weak."

Claire locked her door, then knelt by her bed.


In the sunroom, Barbara was suddenly flooded by peace. She raised her head from the pillows on the love seat and wiped her eyes. The floor around her was littered with scrunched-up tissues, a silent testament to the hour she had spent praying for her daughter. She didn't know exactly what had happened, but she knew God had heard her prayers and released the burden that had weighed on her since she awakened at dawn.

She had said something about her heaviness of heart to Tom as he dressed for work, but he had been distracted with thoughts of the day ahead. He'd just smiled at her worried reflection in the mirror as he tied his tie and combed his hair and told her not to worry about it.

Barbara shook her head, remembering. Tom was a wonderful husband and father; she just wished he would spend more time reading the Bible and praying rather than just listening to sermons on tape or reading an inspirational book now and then. But she knew his walk had been a long and sometimes rocky road. Barbara prayed often that God would deepen Tom's relationship with Him.

And now Claire. Today was the first time in months she had felt such an urgency to pray for her daughter. It had started in the morning as an undefined uneasiness and had grown throughout the day until the mail came. When Claire walked out of the kitchen, Barbara knew she had urgent business to do for her child.

Over the past few years, the Lord had shown her that when she felt she should drop everything and pray, she should listen. The lesson had solidified one day last year when she suddenly found herself thinking of a missionary friend in the Philippines. His image in her mind was so strong that she stopped washing the dishes and got on her knees. She had prayed for more than half an hour; then the burden of prayer had departed. The missionary's "praise report" arrived a month later, telling his friends that he had evaded a kidnapping attempt by Marxist guerrillas on the very day Barbara had prayed. The experience had shaken and excited her and had renewed her determination to listen to that urging.

Barbara looked up now with that same sense of release and gave thanks to God. Then she picked up a clock and peered at it. She stifled a wince and laughed. She had a lot to do before Tom got home.


Out in the cul-de-sac three large beings met in conference, their attention fixed on the writhing spirit that one angel held in tight control.

"Tell us your name, spirit!"

The demon hissed out foul curses, struggling to get free. His captor winced as a black talon raked across his side.

Another angel of high rank drew his sword. "In the name of the Lord Jesus, tell us your name and designation."

The demon cringed. "I am Pargon, of the troop of Krolech."

The first angel started, eyes narrowing. "What is your assignment?" His grip tightened, and he pointed a glowing sword toward the demon's throat when he hesitated. "The Lord Himself revealed you to us; you have no choice but to comply."

Pargon straightened as well as he could. "I am ordered to bring confusion, fear, distraction, and rebellion to the girl, an assignment I have carried out rather well, I might add." He spat at his captor. "You have no hope against her pride and desire for independence. You cannot force her to do anything outside her will—and she's a strong-willed one, she is."

"What was your assigned goal, Pargon?" The angel kept the sword pointed at Pargon's neck.

"To ensure that her rebellion leads her to Harvard, decimating her family relationships in the process. The previous team was incompetent, but this time will be different. We have known for weeks that she was accepted, and we are waiting to welcome her to our territory with open arms. It has, after all, been rightfully *our* territory since your filthy Leader was officially uninvited. One of the always-growing number of areas that meets that description. How delightful that the prince of this world was instated not just by default but by the active behest of all those delicious souls who enjoy their own rule rather than that of our Enemy." He rubbed his hands together. "Perhaps once your young charge leaves that home she will join the club." The demon cackled, then gasped as the giant sword sent him spinning into space.

His captor's voice boomed after him. "We command you to depart from this family and region and to go where Jesus may send you."

They watched the black dot disappear into the distance, and then the high-ranking warrior sheathed his sword, turning toward his comrades.

"Well met, Gael, Mattal," he nodded to the demon's captor and his silent comrade. "It's been a long time. Report."

"Kai, my friend, you may know that I have been assigned from time to time to Claire Rivers, the young girl Pargon was harassing," Gael said.

Kai nodded. "Yes, actually, I knew you were on her team since before her birth." He smiled as Gael raised his eyebrows but didn't explain further. "Continue."

"She committed to walk with the Lord nearly two years ago, and we have been watching her closely since that time. Other than the attack on the family years ago, the enemy has harassed her primarily with the minor demons that have plagued so many teenagers in this recent age. But they have largely been dealt with through the covering of prayer that surrounds this home."

"The praying mother," Kai said.

"Yes, her mother. Because of that prayer, Mattal and I have been able to counter much of the usual harassment. But things changed a few weeks ago." Gael looked at his comrade.

Mattal nodded, remembering. "One day, a half troop of dark spirits showed up. We were not familiar with them. We...did not know until now that they were from the troop of Krolech. They descended on the house and began what appeared to be a strategic, concerted torment. We could tell they were trying to drive a wedge in the family, and we were outmatched. We joined several battles to protect our charges and were both severely injured. Of course, we were going to call for backup when it all started, but—well—the Lord stopped us."

"Continue."

"By the power of the Lord, we were able to shield Claire from the worst attacks, but many still prevailed. She has been growing increasingly agitated, anxious, and rebellious in recent weeks. Her mother and father believe it a natural part of adolescence—the enemy's version of modern adolescence, that is—and chalk it up to her waiting to hear from colleges. They were not aware of the increasing spiritual warfare surrounding their household."

Gael looked at Kai, his eyes piercing. "Today, without warning, the rest of the spirits departed, leaving Pargon on duty. He was hounding Claire with confusion and fear, and Mattal stirred her mother to pray. When Claire repented and submitted to her Master, the Lord delivered the spirit into our hands. Then you arrived just as we were about to interrogate him."

Gael fell silent, the unspoken question hanging in the air. After a moment of thought, Kai stirred.

"I have been told to brief both of you on why I am here," Kai said, "but I myself know only a piece of the story. I do know that the torment of recent weeks was allowed by the Lord to see whether Claire would submit to Him in her time of need. That is why you were allowed to be outmatched. Despite Claire's sometimes stubborn and strong will, she has a soft heart, and she successfully passed this test, may the Lord be praised. This was necessary because many more tests await her. More than she can possibly imagine."

"Will she be stubborn and go to Harvard?" Gael asked.

Kai smiled, and he looked around to ensure their privacy. "Actually, our Master intends Claire Rivers to go to Harvard. Before her birth I was told that a place and a special purpose had been prepared for her there. A purpose for the ages. *He* has been the one putting the desire for Harvard into her heart since she became a new creation two years ago."

Kai moved forward and placed his hand on Gael's shoulder. "Friend, you know what this means. You are going back to Cambridge."

# *September*

CLAIRE PUSHED OPEN THE DOORS of the science center, a new student orientation program clutched in her hand. She was half-expecting to see yesterday's deserted space, but the center was alive with activity. Hundreds of freshmen milled around inspecting flyers and schedules on the large bulletin boards that lined one long hallway.

Claire stood near the entryway, unsure what to do next. The last twenty-four hours had been unnerving. Immersed in this foreign environment, knowing no one on campus—with the exception of the roommate she had met for ten minutes late last night—she felt like a stranger even to herself. Everything on campus was unfamiliar, and she kept getting lost despite the campus maps. If she couldn't even read the stupid maps, how was she going to survive her studies?

People flowed around her on both sides like a stream around a rock, pushing forward, trying to look like they knew what they were doing. *When unsure, wait and watch.* Her father's words came back clearly as she scanned the room.

In the large common area opposite the bulletin boards, tables and booths displayed large pictures and signs about various activities. Behind the tables, poised and confident upperclassmen answered the questions of the freshmen stopping by. The upperclassmen looked like a whole different breed of person, sort of like—Claire suddenly smiled to herself—kings and queens beneficently bestowing their wisdom on the grateful rabble.

Claire snorted and turned away, breathing a deep sigh of relief. They were just like her, only older. They knew the ropes and she didn't, but that difference wouldn't last long.

She really didn't know what she was looking for. The bulletin boards were a crowded jumble, and she was glad to see that other students looked confused as well. She had expected a few dozen neatly placed announcements and flyers, but there had to be a hundred or more crammed in all over the place. Handwritten announcements. Professional posters. Bright colors. Some of them—crammed with oversized lettering and odd graphics—gave her a strange feeling.

Standing just behind Claire, Gael glared toward the ceiling. Rank upon rank of spirits hovered or perched near the top of the bulletin boards watching intently to see which students were interested in which activities. Several of the booths across the room were so thickly covered that it seemed as if they were swarming with flies. A few other brilliant warriors were visible around the room, tense and watchful on enemy territory.

Gael put a steadying hand on Claire's shoulder.

Claire took a deep breath and moved forward, fingering a few flyers at random. Tai chi class—what was that?—was held every afternoon. A weekly dinner group discussed cross-cultural relationships between Israelis and Palestinians. The history department was sponsoring a special class on Machu Picchu and a holiday study trip to Peru. The anthropology department sought interns to accompany professors on digs, initiatives heralded as "groundbreaking." *At least someone here has my dad's really bad sense of humor.* Her grin died at the next flyer, which encouraged all students to picket the speech of a leading "antichoice bigot" at a church event in Boston.

What else? An intramural crew team for men or women met each morning at the boathouse before class. Crewing on the Charles River! That would be a cool Cambridge sort of thing to do. But *5:30 A.M.!* Yeah, right. Well…the English department offered brown bag lunches every Friday for prospective authors. Nope.

Claire moved to the next board, where a picture caught her eye. What was *that?* She drew back, her hand flying to her throat. A bright fuchsia flyer depicted two naked men—together. Her breath came out in a gasp as, despite herself, she read the advertisement for the upcoming Gay and Lesbian Awareness Day on campus. A petite blonde standing next to her glanced up at Claire's gasp, then peered at the poster. Claire was shocked to hear her laugh.

"Yeah, it's kinda funny to see that on a public bulletin board, isn't it? I mean, to each his own, but I don't see any pictures out here of a man and woman having sex, so why do they want to show two men?" She shrugged.

Claire dropped her eyes from the picture. "Beats me."

"Well, you know how prejudiced so many conservatives are. The gay students probably feel they need to be over-the-top so they don't get silenced." She looked at Claire expectantly.

"You think so?" Claire mumbled.

The girl cocked an eyebrow and moved away.

Across the room another warrior dropped through the roof and into the bustling group. Students walked around and through him, but for the moment he took no notice. Instead, Caliel caught Gael's eye where he stood behind Claire. Gael jerked his head toward the doors at the far entrance to the building, and both angels watched as a young man with curly brown hair walked into the mix of students. The angels straightened as they assessed the massive demon traveling with him. *Katoth.*

The warriors watched the curly brown head push through the crowd and to the Greenhouse Café, the food court that adjoined the large room. The dark presence kept even with every step.

The Spirit spoke, and their attention focused quickly on a young woman with glossy dark hair. She was just gathering her onion rings and soda and heading toward the cashier. A smaller, sinewy demon hovered nearby.

The young man turned the corner. Katoth appeared to recognize his smaller colleague, who sketched a deferential greeting.

The female student glanced up at the young man headed into the food court. He was looking directly at her. She smiled in greeting as he paused, then walked over to her.

"Have we met before?" He cocked his head disarmingly.

"No…I don't think so. But you do actually seem familiar to me for some reason. What's your name?"

"Stefan. I'm a junior."

"I'm Sherry. Nice to meet you."

The angels watched as the pair shook hands, chatting. Another pair of beings talked as well, hovering just above them.

Caliel moved closer to the food court, while Gael returned his attention to his charge.


Claire stood at the bulletin boards and tried to shake off a morose feeling. She just had to find people she could connect with. There had to be something that would interest her.

There! She saw a flyer advertising auditions for an a cappella singing group. And there was another group…and another. There had to be six or seven singing groups at least. She dug into her bag for a notepad and pen, jotting down some of the key information.

"You don't need to do that."

The voice, right by her ear, made her jump. She swung around, coming face-to-face with a wiry student. His hair stuck out as if he hadn't combed it in a while. He stared at her intensely and didn't move.

Claire took her hand down from her rapidly beating heart. "You startled me!" She tried a smile.

The student kept staring. "I said, you don't need to take notes. Those booths over there,"—he pointed at the rows of tables across the room—"have all these flyers available for you to take with you." Someone in the crowd jostled him, and his arm brushed hers.

Claire stepped back a pace. She glanced at the pocket protector in his shirt pocket, a row of five pencils sticking out. A sophisticated HP calculator rested in a holster on his extrawide belt. She looked back up at his face, bemused.

He didn't say anything else, just kept staring.

"Well...uh...thanks for the advice. You saved me some time." She dropped her notepad in her backpack and fought the urge to turn away. She stuck out her hand. "I'm Claire."

He nodded, ignoring her hand. "Yes. I'm Mitch. I'm a physics major. I'm working in the lab this year under Professor Roughton. Do you know Professor Roughton?"

Claire let her hand drop to her side and shook her head.

"Roughton is a giant in physics. He's developed some of the main theories of our day on the flexibility of the time continuum. You should stop by and see me sometime in the lab. I can introduce you to him."

Claire could see Mitch's eyes wandering to her long, curly hair. Her cheeks grew hot, and she stammered to think of a polite negative response. *Help me, God! What do I do here?*

Suddenly someone clapped Mitch on the back, causing him to lurch forward a step.

"Hey, Mitch, are you trying to hog all the prettiest freshmen again?"

The voice belonged to a dark-haired student wearing a striped shirt and khakis. He turned toward Claire. "Mitch and I are in the same lab program. I'm Brent." He thrust out his hand, winking at her above Mitch's head.

Claire returned the handshake. "Claire Rivers."

Brent placed a hand on her shoulder and stepped between her and Mitch. "I saw you looking at the a cappella group flyers. I was just going over to their tables, and I can show you if you like."

"If you don't mind, that would be great." She let Brent guide her away and nodded to Mitch over her shoulder. "Nice to meet you, Mitch." He stared after her for a moment, then turned back to the bulletin boards.

Claire let out an explosive sigh, and Brent started laughing. "You looked like a deer caught in the headlights. I just had to rescue you."

Claire put her hand to her forehead. "Thank you! I didn't want to be mean…."

"Oh, you weren't mean; don't worry about it. Mitch is a one-of-a-kind guy. He's a true prodigy, but has—how shall I put this?—no social skills. He's your stereotypical physics genius who has no idea how to connect to people."

Claire looked up at Brent. "While you, on the other hand, don't fit that stereotype at all." She blushed in dismay. *I can't believe I just said that!*

Brent grinned down at her. "Well, *someone* in the physics department has to be normal!"

They pushed past a large group of people, but Claire hardly noticed. She was focusing on keeping her mouth shut.

"The tables for the choir stuff are mostly on the other side of the room," Brent said. "Over there, see? What else are you interested in?"

"I don't really know yet. I'm just sort of wandering."

"Well, I'm posted at that booth over there, for the *Harvard Lampoon*—well, supposed to be posted, anyway." His gaze was amused, and Claire blushed again. "Go ahead and wander, and if you have any questions, please stop by." He left her abruptly, melding into the crowd.

"Thanks." She shook her head and muttered sarcastically to herself, "'While *you* don't fit that stereotype at all.' Aagh!" Pounding the heel of her hand against her forehead, she turned away.

Behind her, a glowing, invisible giant grinned.

IAN BURKE LOCKED HIS DOOR BEHIND HIM and cut through the backstreets of Cambridge, heading for campus. He stopped to pick up his mail at Harkness Commons, the law school's student center. The long hallways echoed, empty in the week before classes started.

Ian slung his backpack over one shoulder and made the short walk to Old Campus. Brown and gold leaves crunched under his feet, and he stooped to pick up a few early acorns and slip them into his backpack. One day he'd have a wife and a house and all the trappings of the nonstudent life that had eluded him for so long. When that day came, he'd like a Harvard oak tree growing in the backyard.

That day was probably a long way away. He didn't even know what firm he'd be working for next summer or what city he'd be living in, much less who his wife was going to be—or even if he'd have one. He put a firm stop to that common mental refrain. *Lord, You know the plans You have for me…and I'll trust You until You reveal them.*

Robinson Hall loomed in front of him, and he stepped aside from the entrance as scores of people streamed out. Ian was taken aback by how young they looked. This had to be the new freshman class—a bunch of eighteen-year-olds. Ian was only twenty-three, but he felt old by comparison.

He jogged up the steps to the third floor eager to hear the reason for being summoned to Mansfield's office. These hallways echoed also. The dark wood, high ceilings, and oversized doors had once been slightly intimidating but were now as comfortable as home. After the most perfunctory of knocks, he banged open the door labeled Office of Professor William Mansfield.

The man at the desk jerked and dropped a book on the floor, then laughed and put a hand to his heart. "Ian! It's not fair for a young man like you to try to put me in my grave before I'm ready!"

Ian came around the desk as the older man rose from his chair. They slapped backs like father and son.

"Mansfield, I get you every time because you always concentrate so hard. One day that'll get you into trouble." Ian spread his hands as if capturing a vista in front of his eyes. "I can just see it now—you're in a big faculty meeting, Professor Pike calls on you for your scintillating insights…and you stare blindly into space as you mentally review the latest colonial texts unearthed in Boston."

Professor Mansfield snorted. "No, I'd be mentally calculating the odds that Pike would call on me for *anything*. Well, welcome back! Sit down, sit down." He gestured toward a chair then asked about Ian's summer as he bustled around to get coffee and sugar from a sideboard.

Over the rim of his coffee cup, Ian studied his mentor, noticing as always the thick shock of silver hair, sparkling gray eyes, slim reading glasses, and the casual assurance that seemed to rest on the revered professor like a suit of clothes. Ian had met the professor five years before at a dessert party held in the older man's home for the freshman members of the Harvard Christian Fellowship. He had told the awed young people that they might feel like aliens in a strange land and that he would be there for them if they needed someone to talk to.

Even more surprising, he had meant it. The members of HCF had quickly gotten over their reverence for the proclaimed author of more than twenty books, someone they were as apt to see on television as in their classroom. He had told them all to call him Mansfield ("only my dear wife called me William"), and they had promoted him to instant grandpa status. He had invited Ian and many other students to join him and his church family for Thanksgiving and Easter dinners, when the students couldn't get home to their own families. And in Ian's sophomore year the professor had driven him to the airport and sat with him in the terminal when the shattered young man learned he had lost his parents to a driver high on cocaine.

Over the next two years, Ian spent a lot of time helping the professor with administrative chores while asking him questions about everything from colonial history to dating to graduate program options. He had gradually realized he was being groomed for something but never came right out and asked Mansfield what it was. The day Ian stepped into Mansfield's office waving an acceptance letter to Harvard Law School, the professor had offered him a graduate teaching assistantship on the spot. Such a coveted position—TA for the most popular history class at Harvard—was not lightly given, especially to a first-year graduate student.

And the following year, when Ian had stood before a packed classroom of students with blank notebooks and pens at the ready, he had glimpsed the depth of trust his mentor was placing in him. For one fleeting moment he had been terrified at the responsibility he had so cavalierly accepted. Ian smiled at the memory. It had turned out fine on the whole.

"I'm glad you're back," Mansfield said, leaning back in his chair. "We're going to be really busy. A lot has changed over the summer. First, let me brief you on the class size issue." Mansfield pressed his fingertips together. "I have met with the registrar several times about expanding the size of the Introduction to European History class, among others. They have my formal proposal and are considering it right now. I expect to hear something within the week. If, as I hope, the class is allowed to expand, that change would take effect next fall."

"It just seems such a shame to turn down so many students for your classes, especially when Professor Barkson's classes are in a bigger room than yours and are always half full."

Mansfield smiled. "Remember, Doug Barkson was the head of the department for a long time."

"It just seems odd that they don't switch your room assignments, that's all."

"Now *that* is a political hot potato I don't intend to touch! I've asked for the class to be expanded and moved to a completely different venue, like Sanders Theater."

Ian's eyebrows rose at the mention of the famous old classroom, which seated over a thousand students. "That would be cool."

The professor fell silent, staring away with a pensive expression. "On to the next subject. There have been a few developments that will dramatically affect our little task force project. It appears that the Master Planner has been arranging things for us behind the scenes." He swung around to face his protégé. "In the last two weeks I've been asked to both be an official curator of the Harvard Library resources—" he smiled at Ian's congratulations—*"and* to be a permanent member of the faculty's academic steering committee."

Ian let out a whoop and jumped to his feet. "What amazing timing! I don't believe it!" His grin faded as he saw the professor's pensive expression. "Mansfield! Isn't that the committee that decides all the standards for undergrad curriculum and content, among other things?" At the professor's slow nod Ian sat down again and looked intently across the desk. "That would seem to be excellent news. It places you firmly at the table right before the task force report is released. You can actually steer the debate and ensure that they don't just listen politely and sweep the whole thing under the table like before. Why the concern?"

"It's more a concern about who's controlling the table. They've just promoted Professor Anton Pike to chairman." Mansfield glanced across the desk at Ian. Total understanding had flooded his face. "So, my young friend...*you* have a lot of work to do."


Claire sat on the couch in the sitting room of her dorm suite sorting out all the stuff she had collected from the expo. Floral curtains, which her mother had insisted on hanging before she left, fluttered at the window. Matching ones hung in the bedroom she and her roommate shared, but not in the second bedroom that completed the small three-person suite.

The late afternoon breeze stirred the pile of flyers beside her, but she made no move to shut the window. Might as well enjoy the few warm days left before the fabled Boston cold arrived.

The door to her suite was slightly ajar, giving her a partial view of the hallway. Someone stopped at her door and rapped lightly.

"Come in!"

A curly brown head—a very handsome curly brown head—popped around the door. "Hi! Is Sherry here?"

"No. I really haven't seen her today." Claire tried not to stare. "She might be stuck at the Coop getting textbooks."

He pushed the door open a bit more, and Claire found herself looking down, blushing slightly at his smile.

"What's *your* name?"

"Claire."

"That's a pretty name. I'm Stefan. I live in Dunster House, down by the river." He moved as if to depart and then snapped his fingers, remembering something. "Actually, wait a second." He checked the front of the suite door, where their names were written on bright orange construction-paper balloons, courtesy of their resident assistant. "That's right, Mercedes lives here, doesn't she? I need to ask her a question. Is she around?"

"You know, honestly, I have no idea. Hold on."

Claire uncurled herself from the couch and knocked on Mercedes's bedroom door. No answer. She looked toward Stefan and shrugged.

"Well, thanks for trying. Good to meet you. And if you see Sherry, would you tell her I stopped by?"

"Sure thing."

Claire turned back to her stack of flyers, trying not to feel envious. Why was it that some girls just attracted guys like static electricity, while others—like her!—were more likely to be considered a pal?

Sighing, she turned her attention to her calendar. Okay. There were three singing groups she was interested in, an a cappella group and two choirs. She was leaning toward the choirs since she could get academic credit for those and would probably get an A. She noted the audition times, which were coming up quick.

Next she pulled out the flyers related to special study classes and professional clubs. Most had history department labels. The Friday brown bag luncheons featuring well-known guest speakers looked especially interesting. One special-study class involved field trips to early colonial sites, and another—offered in connection with the divinity school—studied the "Origins of World Religion," taking field trips to "religious centers" around Boston. What did that mean?

Claire looked at the final flyer in her stack. What were the chances that her parents could afford another three thousand dollars this semester so she could go on the joint history/anthropology/business department Machu Picchu trip over Christmas break? Claire laughed to herself. What were the chances that her parents would let her be gone over Christmas, *period?*

She shuffled the flyers into a file and pulled a few others out of her backpack. The top flyer advertised the first meeting of the Harvard Christian Fellowship next Friday night at six. She had been delighted to see a booth with the word *Christian* on it.

Other dates were noted in her calendar: a service club that worked in Boston on Saturday mornings, an intramural volleyball league, and a dinner for all students from Michigan. *Maybe meeting some Midwesterners will make this place feel more like home.*

The dorm room door creaked open. A stack of books walked in, eclipsing the trim form of Claire's roommate. The pile was leaning ominously.

"Sherry, what are you doing?" Claire laughed and hurried to help.

Sherry glided faster and faster toward the couch, barely making it before the stack collapsed. Heavy textbooks thudded onto the cushions. Claire's bulletins went flying in all directions.

"Whew, am I glad you were here! If the door was locked, I never would've made it." Sherry grinned and swept up her straight brown hair, fanning her neck.

"I'm very impressed with that balancing act." Claire bent to pick up several of the flyers that were now scattered around the room. "Those things are heavy. Why didn't you get some help?"

Sherry's gentle Southern accent grew exaggerated as she placed a delicate hand against her breastbone. "Oh, I found a sweet young man to help me out." She knelt to gather more flyers into a ragged pile and grinned up at Claire. "He carried the books over here from the Coop, but he had somewhere he had to be, so I figured I could handle getting them up the stairs and into the room." She glanced at the jumble on the couch. "Barely." She handed over the stack. "Sorry about the flyers."

"Oh, that's okay."

"Hey, what's this?" Sherry plucked back the top sheet. "Machu Picchu! The ruins in Peru? Cool! You going?"

"Oh, I don't know. It's over Christmas, and my parents would probably flip—"

"Yeah, I know what you mean."

"—and it's really expensive."

Sherry looked down at the flyer. "Three thousand dollars. Actually, for a flight to Peru, classes, and two weeks of touring, that's pretty good." She gathered up a few books and walked into the bedroom, speaking over her shoulder. "I'd say it's worth it if you're interested."

Claire picked up a few more books and followed her roommate. Of course it would be *worth it,* but who had three thousand dollars lying around?

As she entered their joint bedroom, her eyes flickered to Sherry's loft, noticing for the first time the quality of the structure. It wasn't a bunch of cobbled-together planks like so many other students put up to maximize floor space—it was a handsome, custom-built system complete with drawers and shelves for clothes and books.

Claire helped Sherry slot the textbooks into the beautiful blond wood shelves built into the loft. Claire's books were already organized in brightly colored plastic crates across the room.

Claire eyed the Bible sitting on Sherry's bookcase next to her textbooks. In one e-mail, Sherry had said she went to church in her Georgia hometown. Claire hoped that meant she was a committed Christian.

"Sherry, in one of your e-mails over the summer you said you didn't know your major yet. Which way are you leaning?"

"History, maybe."

"Hey, I'm thinking about history too! Well, either history or biology if I go premed, but I kinda doubt that. I might do biology as a minor." She stepped back from Sherry's bookcase for a moment, staring at the load on the shelves. "How many classes do you *have?*"

Her roommate made a face. "Too many."

"You seem to have a lot more reading than I do."

"I have two advanced classes this semester. I placed out of the introductory prerequisites."

Claire paused, a heavy book in her hands. "Hey, isn't this the Intro to European History text?"

"Yes." Sherry dug a schedule out of her pocket. "I'm in Professor Mansfield's class at…eleven o'clock, Tuesdays and Thursdays."

"No kidding! We're in the same class."

Sherry smiled and dusted her hands off on her jeans. She glanced at the clock. "Want to go get dinner?"

SURROUNDED BY DARKNESS, KROLECH WAITED for a report. The demon's masters were pressing for the latest information on his progress, and he wanted to have good news to relay before he went anywhere near them—especially since he had heard through the ranks that Leviathan himself was due for a briefing on this, one of his prize initiatives.

An aide got Krolech's attention, and he settled before a large map of his territory as several underlings arrived. He carefully allowed his pleasure to show as they spoke in turn about the initiatives underway in each of the different cities. They were clever, these troop commanders—some of the best. Their hold on the area was so tight and their mechanisms so well established that it had become a simple thing to take whatever strategic steps were decided upon. This marriage needed to be destroyed—easy to increase temptations or stress. That family needed to be embittered—easy to ensure that a beloved son or daughter contracted a fatal illness. This business should be undermined—so easy to appeal to greed when integrity was long gone and then, of course, alert the authorities.

They loved doing that. Loved using and destroying those created in the image of the Enemy, the One who had cast them from heaven, who had forever removed them from glory. His human children might be wayward, but they were still His children and He loved them. He reached out to them every day, yearning to draw them to Himself before it was too late. That was all the reason the dark forces needed to hate them; they wanted it to be "too late" for as many of these people as possible. They reveled in turning laughter into mourning and drew strength from the tears of broken men. They particularly loved it when they could use these double-minded children of God against one another—and against Him.

The enemy troops were still a factor, of course, so even the best-laid plans didn't always work out perfectly. But, as in so many other places, this wasn't *their* territory anymore. There were so few residents who feared God anymore, so few prayer warriors, that it now took special effort from the heavenly host assigned to this area to counter the fine-tuned intentions of darkness.

Finally, the city reports wound down. The room grew tense as Krolech pointed toward the center of the map, the center of their plan. The university had been the crown jewel of this handpicked team's success for many years, but these days it was becoming more and more troublesome. It was beginning to remind them of those early days after they had finally gained control of the area, but when there were still enough God-fearing, praying men—and enough Enemy warriors—around to cause serious headaches. With the exception of a few outliers, the years since had been much easier. But now, unexpectedly, the headaches were back.

In the past few years, the praying had intensified again. The Enemy had stirred Christian fellowship groups of every stripe, and they were praying in concert as had happened from time to time in years past.

This time it had started small, sometimes with just a few believers here and there, but it had deepened. And before the dark forces knew what had happened, whole *classes* had been admitted with large numbers of praying Christians! God-fearing chaplains and leaders had arisen to shepherd them. Now, instead of fellowship groups of ten or twenty, there were groups of fifty, then eighty. Dozens of God-fearing men and women now met weekly to pray over the campus. No wonder it was no longer as easy as it had been.

Krolech's eyes narrowed as the reports progressed, and he drummed a heavy beat on the massive table with his fingers. His underlings winced whenever he questioned their efficiency, their results. He was particularly irritated in cases where set plans couldn't be immediately instituted—a student's angelic guard prevented an attack; a faculty member's long-awaited divorce was thwarted by the tender intervention of a praying friend; a classroom debate was no longer effectively influenced by the dark side.

It was an unacceptable situation for a troop of the best and the brightest—and was certainly unacceptable for a key pivot point in the Great War.

Finally, the dark commander barked an order, and his underlings wound up their briefing. They departed quickly leaving Krolech to his thoughts, waiting to see what he would come up with to stem this slow tide.

Krolech brooded for a moment after the meeting. One thing was certain. He wasn't going anywhere near his master until he had managed to polish his crown jewel a bit. He returned to studying the center of the large map, formulating new strategies, thinking, planning. A thought struck him. Come to think of it, it might simply be time to strengthen some old strategies….

Humming to herself, Claire pulled on a light jacket and bounded down the stairs of her dorm and out into the late afternoon. The grassy square in front of her dorm was lined with venerable redbrick buildings and majestic old trees. Harvard Yard. Claire crunched through the leaves, gazing around at the solid weight of history. Presidents had gone to this school. JFK had lived in her dorm, on the floor below her. The students walking and chattering on the paths around her would go on to be senators, multimillionaires, governors, captains of industry. She looked back at her building. *Maybe one day some-one will say, "Claire Rivers lived in that dorm."* She giggled, thinking how preposterous that sounded.

She noticed a tour group across the Yard standing in a loose semicircle around an admissions office tour guide. The guide was pointing out some feature on the wrought-iron Johnston Gate, the giant entrance to the Yard through the twelve-foot walls surrounding the college property.

The tour group broke ranks and trooped across the Yard toward the statue of John Harvard. Claire noticed many young faces in the group. They looked around hungrily, weighing the chances of beating the odds for admittance. She smiled at several, and they looked at her enviously as she passed by.

A dark presence hovered above her head and whispered beguiling words to her. He rubbed his hands together with eager relish. Floating a few feet away, a warrior angel stared at him fiercely, keeping pace with him and the girl. The angel far outmatched the demon for size and strength, but the demon pretended to be unconcerned by his presence. The dark being made no moves of aggression, gave no excuse for the angel to cut short his time with the girl. He just kept speaking those subtle words to her. They were being accepted, and so was he. As long as he was accepted, he had the right to be there.

Claire stepped through Johnston Gate and into the bustle of Harvard Square, heading for the Coop, the giant co-op store that sold everything from textbooks and school paraphernalia to toiletries and furniture. She watched two tourists in the distance taking photographs in front of the famous Out of Town News kiosk. She smiled with inward amusement, pleased to belong to this place.

A steady stream of cars traveled past her, and after a moment she stopped and looked for a place to cross the street. She saw several people in the cars staring out their windows at the picture-postcard entrance to Harvard Yard; she watched their eyes flicker in her direction and take in the backpack she had slung over one shoulder. *They know I'm a student at Harvard.*

The demon above her smiled maliciously and kept whispering.

BARBARA RIVERS TOOK A DEEP BREATH as she watched the red and gold leaves flutter on the branches in front of her. The trees in their friend's backyard were beginning their yearly blaze of color. God's paintbrush at its best.

"Here you go." Tom handed her a tall glass, ice clinking. "Margaret's raspberry iced tea. Perfect for christening David and Margaret's long-awaited deck."

David was busy at the grill, a grin playing on his lips. "Does that officially make us adults, now that we not only have a house, but a house with a back *deck?* I have no more excuses!"

Tom slapped him on the back. "Friend, I hate to tell you this, but I think you officially became an adult last year when Jeremy went to college!"

"Well, at least that makes two of us."

"I've heard the colors in Boston are amazing in October." Barbara's voice was distant. "I wonder if Claire will have a chance to get out and see them."

Margaret set down a tray of hamburger buns on the picnic table and came over to join Barbara. "You know, Jeremy was pretty busy getting acclimated his first semester. It took him a few months to get hooked up with a group of friends and do things like sightseeing. Claire doesn't even start classes until Monday, right?"

When Barbara didn't respond, Margaret rubbed her friend's shoulder. "I know it's hard to have your baby so far away. But she'll be okay; she's a good kid." A grin flashed across her features. "A little headstrong, perhaps, but good."

"Her stubborn streak used to drive me crazy. But I'm kind of glad for it now: It'll serve her well at Harvard. As long as she is stubborn in the right direction. You wouldn't believe some of the things she saw in her first few days there. And I know she wasn't telling me the half of it. There are going to be so many temptations…."

Barbara fell silent, and after a moment Margaret took her hand and guided her to the picnic table. She gently pushed her to a sitting position, then straddled the bench and faced her friend. "Do you remember what you told me about seven or eight years ago, when you were debating whether to put Claire in Christian school?"

"I said that I wanted her *out* of the public school system after I found out that group was conducting assemblies on safe sex and abortion rights and such. She was only ten!"

"Right, but that wasn't all. We had all made the same decision: We wanted our children to learn as much as they could without that sort of pressure *and*...do you remember what else?" She watched Barbara's face closely. "We said we wanted to arm them with a solid Christian education before they went out into the world."

Barbara laughed slightly, remembering. "I know. I just didn't think that going out into the world would come so soon." She made a face at Margaret's sympathetic chuckle, slightly annoyed. "It's all fine for you to say. Jeremy went to a Christian college!"

"Yes, but still, it's college—and he's out from under our wing, making his own choices."

Tom came over and sat down on the bench opposite the two women. He looked at his wife. "Lord knows I wanted Claire to go to a Christian college more than anyone. I wanted some assurance that she wouldn't make the same stupid choices that I had, and I figured Wheaton would give me that. But that wasn't God's plan." Tom reached across the table and took Barbara's hands. "We've always said that we were raising the kids to be salt and light in a decaying world, right? Well, at some point we have to let them go out into the darkness and trust God to care for them. After all, He's had the harder job trusting *us* with them all these years. Us trusting Him should be a piece of cake."

Barbara felt her husband gently stroking her fingers between his. Unexpectedly, her eyes grew red. She looked down at the table. "I know it *should* be. And I know we can't all just cluster in our Christian colleges and churches and clubs. But—"

David set down the tray of cooked hamburgers. "You've said yourself, Barbara, that if all the Christians leave the public schools, leave the secular universities, that we've removed a major influence for positive change of exactly those things we're tempted to run away from. If Christians remove themselves from society, we're like candles glowing brightly in an already lighted room, while the darkness outside remains unchanged."

"I understand that!" Barbara tried to keep her voice even. "And I believe it. Somebody needs to venture out into the darkness and light it up. I just don't know that I want my baby to be the guinea pig."

Tom continued rubbing her hands. "Honey, what you just said is wrong, and you know it. It's not that somebody needs to be out there in the darkness; it's that all of us do. I don't like the idea of Claire being out there any more than you do, but we've trained her up in the way she should go, and we have to let God complete her training on the front lines. If there's anything we should have learned by now, it's that we need to learn how to confront the problems of the world head on, with God's help."

He made a self-deprecating face and turned to their friends. "I've always wanted to protect Claire, to insulate her. But when she said she wanted to go to Harvard, I finally had to stop and think. Maybe if I had been forced to deal with 'real life' earlier in my own life I wouldn't have caused this family so much trouble."

Barbara started to protest, but he shushed her. "You know what I mean."

"I think," Margaret said, "that you need to bring this up at home group on Thursday night and let everyone pray for you and for Claire. I know you've been praying a lot, but all your friends want to get in on the action. After all, we kind of feel that each other's kids are our own."

David finished setting out plates and utensils and took his seat. He held out his hands. "Let's pray now."

The little group joined their hands and hearts, giving thanks for the food and for the opportunity to come before the Throne. David and Margaret asked God to give peace and protection to the Rivers family, especially to the daughter so far away.

HOW DID ANYONE EXPECT TO MAKE SENSE of this stupid map? Claire fumbled with her purse and portfolio while trying to hold the flimsy paper open. The subway lines looked like spaghetti strands, crisscrossing the page at random.

She looked wildly around her at the bustling underground Government Center station. There was the blue line to Bowdoin and the green line to Lechmere. She had gotten off the red line on the subway—the T, she quickly corrected herself—and had to switch to another. But which one?

She looked at the digital clock hanging over a nearby platform. The first day of class had been a blur. She should have taken the time to ask for directions before she hurried from her last class to the Harvard Square T station. She was already late. Not a good way to meet the people who were financing her education.

A distinguished-looking woman in a long, red wool coat walked by, her shopping bags rustling as she passed. Claire turned around. "Oh, excuse me, ma'am! Could you tell me which direction the blue line…?"

The woman shook her head and kept walking.

Claire stared at the map again. Why couldn't the lines just say North or East like any self-respecting highway system would? A younger woman in a tracksuit approached from the other direction. Claire stepped toward her. "Excuse me. Does the blue line to Wonderland go toward the business district?"

"Don't know." The tracksuit turned a corner and was gone.

Claire stared after her. "Gee, thanks for the help."

"Whatcha need, dearie?" Another woman stopped next to her.

Relieved, Claire poured out her dilemma. The woman pointed out her line, and Claire hurried to the correct platform. She stared down the tracks, but could see no lights approaching.

She noticed the hum of a soft drink machine from a nearby newspaper kiosk. She stepped in, bumped from all sides by patrons hurrying in and out. People jostled for space in front of the cashier. The bottles of soda were in the glass case behind him. Where was the line?

Keeping an ear out for the sound of her train, she inched her way forward behind a man in a baseball cap. Suddenly, she was poked by a sharp elbow and found another person between her and the baseball cap.

"Hey!" She tapped the offending shoulder. "I'm sorry, but the line is back there." Several people turned to look, but no one seemed surprised when the line-breaker didn't budge. No one said anything.

Claire's face was red when she finally got to the cashier.

"Whaddaya want?"

"A-a-a Coke, please." The man was turning around with the bottle in his hand when Claire shook her head. "I'm sorry. I meant a Diet Coke."

The cashier heaved an exasperated sigh. "Fine." He switched the drinks, slamming the Coke bottle back into the case, and punched at some numbers on the register.

Claire read the total. A dollar twenty-nine. She handed over a twenty.

"Need something smaller!"

Claire hesitated, confused.

"Smaller! Need something smaller than a twenty!"

"I'm sorry. That's all I—"

*"Fine."* The cashier stuffed the bill in his drawer and slapped the change on the counter. He looked over her shoulder as she scrabbled to keep the coins from rolling away. "Whaddaya want?"

She scurried out of the kiosk just in time to see her train approaching

As Claire prepared to board the train, Gael nodded to another angel slowly going the other direction. A toddling boy and his mother were walking just in front of their unseen watch-carer, the other angel's smile indulgent as the boy stopped repeatedly to explore objects on the floor and on the walls of the kiosk.

The other angel caught Gael's eye and gestured toward his young charge. "This one has been gifted to serve the Prince of Peace as an evangelist." His voice was proud, though purposely muted from any enemy ears.

Gael made a congratulatory gesture. "May his gift be realized. And may the Lord of hosts strengthen you in your work."

The T began to move. Gael folded his wings and dropped into the car. Claire was perched on the edge of a crowded bench seat, her back ramrod straight. She looked at her watch.

*Peace, Claire. God is in control.*

Claire looked at her watch again, her mouth tightening. Gael stood in the swaying car, mingling with the suitcases of an airport traveler, considering his charge. Not only was Claire letting pride have sway; she was not listening, not praying, had not gone before the Throne in days. The Lord of hosts longed to pour out all His love and wisdom on His adopted child, but she was not seeking it.

Gael shook his head. Every member of the heavenly host longed always to be in that golden throne room, to sing holy, holy, holy to the King! And here these children of the King dallied and strayed like that toddler he had just seen, letting anything distract them from going into His presence.

And she wasn't just any toddler, either. Kai's words rang in his head. *Our Master intends Claire Rivers to go to Harvard. Before her birth, I was told that a place and a special purpose had been prepared for her there. A purpose for the ages.* The angel's countenance grew solemn, a subtle gleam appearing in his eye as he pondered his next move.

Claire shifted from foot to foot, staring at the numbers above the elevator doors in the lobby. She picked up her purse, then returned it to the floor. She pulled her zipper up to the neck of her jacket, then down again.

The elevator must have been put into service fifty years ago.

A grandmotherly lady was resting her arm on an ornate railing bolstering the lobby wall. She cast a kind eye at Claire.

"All aflutter today, are we?" Her voice carried the gentle hint of an Irish brogue.

"Yes." Claire kept her eyes on the creeping numbers. *Seven...six...* Suddenly, she shook herself and turned around. "I'm sorry. I didn't mean to be rude." Her smile was sheepish. "I'm trying not to be anxious about this meeting—a meeting that just has to be on the *top floor* when I'm already running late!"

The grandmother smiled. "Maybe God is trying to teach you patience, child."

"Yes. I'm sure He is." Claire forced herself to take a calming breath. "Are you a Christian, by chance?"

The wrinkled eyes lifted in a smile. "I am a servant of the Lord Jesus Christ."

"So am I. And it didn't take me long to figure out that there aren't as many believers here in Boston as I thought there would be. People don't usually bring up God out of the blue. This whole city just seems colder, harder, than I had expected."

The elevator dinged, the doors opening to discharge a group of people. Claire tried not to be impatient as the elderly lady shuffled quietly on board. The doors slowly closed, and Claire punched the top button, looking over at her companion, who nodded for the same floor.

The car began its tortoiselike movement. Claire gritted her teeth, again staring at the numbers above the door.

"In the early days," the old lady said, "this area was the seedbed for great devotion. But that gradually changed as so many became sure that they knew so much. They began to look for enlightenment in so many other places: to science, within themselves, to some counterfeit sense of reason from which almighty God was removed." Her wrinkled fingers caressed the curve of her walking stick. "As if reason that dared to account for the Author of all knowledge somehow didn't count."

Her voice was gentle, almost sad. "Dark became light and light dark, just as Isaiah warned the wicked of Judah. Many people chose to look everywhere except to the only One who is truly able to light the way." She raised her walking stick and poked it toward Claire. "Don't you make that same mistake, my dear."

Claire fought the urge to step back a pace. "I won't. I won't."

"Once you take your eyes off Him, even for a moment, there's nothing to hold on to, nothing to guide you. He is the only unshifting horizon by which you can find your way. Fix your eyes on Jesus, the author and finisher of your faith."

"Actually, that's one reason I'm here. I'm going to a Christian Foundation Office. I have to meet with them once a semester for accountability, to keep my scholarship to college...."

"And where are you in school, young lady?"

"At Harvard, actually."

The response was not the usual awkward nod. Instead, her companion looked at her quietly.

"I, uh, I can't afford the full tuition, and Harvard almost never gives grants, so I was really thankful to get the scholarship." Claire fiddled with her zipper again, looking up at the flickering numbers. "But to keep it, I have to meet with these foundation people each semester. Like I said, it's an accountability thing to ensure that I'm doing well in school, not slipping in my walk—that sort of thing. This is our first meeting. I had my first two classes this morning."

The old woman nodded slowly. "Young lady, God has a special plan for your life. And it's not about you; it's about Him. You must remember that the best accountability of all is to lift your eyes to the hills every morning."

A shiver ran down Claire's spine. She had so disregarded the message of that psalm lately. Had she even read her Bible this week?

Claire's voice came out as a whisper. "I will lift up my eyes to the hills—from whence comes my help? My help comes from the LORD, who made heaven and earth...." Her voice trailed off, her eyes staring at nothing.

"He will not allow your foot to be moved; he who keeps you will not slumber." Her companion's voice was oddly strong. "Behold, he who keeps Israel shall neither slumber nor sleep. He is your keeper, the shade at your right hand. The sun shall not strike you by day, nor the moon by night."

She stood straighter, capturing Claire's eyes with hers. A wizened hand reached out and gently cupped Claire's chin in benediction.

"The Lord shall preserve you from all evil; He shall preserve your soul. The Lord shall preserve your going out and your coming in from this time forth, and forevermore."

*Ding!*

The elevator lurched to a stop. Claire rocked a little on her feet. She made no move toward the doors.

"Thank you," she whispered.

"Remember, my dear: The Lord is your keeper. Spend time with Him; He longs for your company. And He knows your every need. Whenever you're faced with a choice, make sure that you trust in God, not in man."

The doors were creaking open. Claire shouldered her purse. "I will. Thank you."

She stepped out onto the twenty-eighth floor, expecting her companion to disembark as well. She turned to smile at the old lady just as the elevator closed on her last words.

"Remember, Claire." The doors clanged shut.

*Claire!*

For a long moment she stood, swaying slightly, and stared at the elevator doors. Finally, she forced her feet to move toward the signboard that pointed toward the various offices.

*Dear God! What just happened?*


"Can I help you?"

Claire was standing in front of a receptionist's desk. The woman was looking at her with raised eyebrows, and Claire realized that she'd already asked the question twice.

"I'm terribly sorry, ma'am. I'm afraid I was lost in thought about something."

"Yes. You looked it." The receptionist picked up the phone. "Whom are you here to see?"

"Ms. Tabor-Brown. I'm afraid I'm about fifteen minutes late."

"Okay." She tapped out a few numbers and pointed at a comfortable-looking couch. "I'm sure she'll be with you in a moment."

Claire sank gratefully into the soft cushions. She set down her leather portfolio and ran her hand across its soft brown surface. Aunt Trudy always did pick nice birthday presents. She started to unzip the case.

"Claire Rivers?"

Claire started slightly and looked up. A very tall woman was standing on the other side of the table.

Claire jumped to her feet. "Yes. Are you Ms. Tabor-Brown?"

She gave one nod and a brief smile. "Please join me in my office." She turned and set off down the hallway.

Claire scrambled to follow her, hooking her purse strap with one finger and juggling the half-open portfolio and papers with her other hand. She was just catching up to her host when the woman abruptly turned and entered an open door to her left. Claire managed not to bang into her.

The office was sparse and seemed as brisk as her guide.

"Have a seat." The lady closed the door behind her. "Well, let's get right to it, shall we? Miss Rivers, you were chosen by the foundation's national office as one of just twenty participants in our annual scholarship program." Another quick smile. "I have been assigned to be your program officer for as long as you are with us. As you know, the program is both merit based and need based, and we give scholarships only to students going to secular, top-rank schools such as Harvard."

She sat down and folded her hands on the desk. "Our founder likes to support Christian students who will someday be leaders in whatever professional field they pursue, who will raise not only the standard of excellence in their arena, but also that of Christ."

Claire nodded. She had the feeling Ms. Tabor-Brown had said this all many times before.

"As such, a condition of your scholarship is that we meet with you once a semester to monitor your academic progress. We require you to maintain a B average or better and to carry a course load that reflects your dedication to hard work and professional leadership in some field. Do you have your class registration schedule with you?"

"Yes, ma'am." Claire opened the portfolio on her lap, hoping her program officer couldn't see its disarray.

The woman took the yellow paper and set it in the center of her empty desktop. "Let's see. Okay...okay. Monday, Wednesday, Friday...biology at eight in the morning, British literature at ten and—" she looked up at Claire—"is this a school choir in the afternoon?"

"Uh...yes. I'm not 100 percent sure of that one; my final audition is coming up tomorrow afternoon."

"Is that one of your five actual classes this semester?"

"Yes. I get academic credit for it."

Ms. Tabor-Brown raised an eyebrow, and her gaze moved back to the yellow printout. "Then on Tuesdays and Thursdays you have sociology at nine-thirty and European history at eleven. This looks like a good start, although it's a bit unfocused. We prefer to see a trend leading to excellence in a particular professional field." She glanced up at

Claire, and her eyes lightened with a smile. "Of course, we don't expect you, as a freshman, to know exactly what you will be doing with the rest of your life. We just want to see that you aren't taking Basket Weaving 101."

Claire tried to return the smile. *Is she comparing choir to basket weaving?*

"The more you seem dedicated to the ideals of our scholarship, the better chance you'll have of being awarded it again next year, and so on. A multiyear award is hoped for but certainly not guaranteed. Our founder has been known to not renew scholarships for students he believed were not focusing, not cutting it. He is very fair, but he has high expectations and expects them to be met."

Claire's smile was confident, her tension dissipating. "That's fine. I believe Christians should be committed to excellence."

"He believes that, too. In fact, he is convinced that Christians who are well respected professionally can transform our culture at the highest levels. So he has committed his considerable resources to finding and supporting those students who will impact our society for Christ. We believe that you, Claire, are one of those people."

Claire sat a little straighter in her chair.

"Are you able to support your tuition without the scholarship?"

"No." Claire cleared her throat. "No, I'm not. My parents have saved a little, and I have enough for about half the tuition to a state school. But not Harvard, no."

Ms. Tabor-Brown tapped a pencil briskly on the desk. "Well then, we'd better make sure that you don't lose the scholarship." She pulled a brochure out of her drawer. "Here are a few guidelines that you might find helpful."

Claire listened and took notes as Ms. Tabor-Brown talked.

"...as many advanced classes and high grades as possible..." "...must maintain your integrity and a good Christian witness on campus..." "...overcome the many challenges to your faith..."

She focused on their confidence in her and pushed aside the niggling doubts. She'd always been able to cut it before.

MANSFIELD STEPPED AWAY FROM THE CASHIER, a full plate in one hand, a drink in the other. He scanned the elegant tables of the faculty dining room. It always got busy the first week of class.

"Hey, Mansfield!" Several colleagues from his department beckoned to him from across the room. "Join us. We were just debating whether or not your last article in the *Journal of History* was actually a rip-off of Tully's book." They gestured at one of the junior professors at the table, who grinned, shaking his head. "And whether you'll still be assigned to Sanders once the powers-that-be learn the horrifying truth."

"Actually, you jokers need to check your dates. I think my article was originally written when Bill Tully was still in diapers."

Guffaws rose from the table.

"And if the powers-that-be want to see something *really* horrifying, they should've seen your fielding error in that game yesterday, Jack. But I'll leave you to argue about this behind my back." He nodded further down the room. "I might join someone else for lunch."

He skirted tables filled with energetic first-day-of-class discussions. *Father, help me to reach out in Your love this year.* He approached a lone figure at an otherwise empty table. She glanced up from the magazine she was reading, and her eyes narrowed.

"Sharon, mind if I join you?"

She stared at him a moment, then slid a few books off the chair beside her.

Mansfield nodded agreeably and took the seat, silently giving thanks for the food. "So did you have a good summer?"

"What do you want?" She returned her attention to her sandwich.

"Nothing, really. I just saw you down here by yourself and thought I'd see how your summer went."

"It was fine."

"What did you do? Did you go to San Francisco again?"

"Did I go to Sodom and Gomorrah, do you mean?"

Mansfield glanced up at her cynical expression. "Sharon, I really just wanted to hear how your summer went. Honest—no other agenda."

She sighed. "It was great. I got to see Leslie—you knew she was transferred from UCLA to Berkeley?"

"Yes, I believe you told us that last semester."

"Well, we just hung out for a few weeks, had a nice slow pace. She took me to a couple of little restaurants she found. We spent a few days at a bed-and-breakfast on the coast." She smiled maliciously at Mansfield. "Very romantic."

"Sounds like you had a relaxing time. What's the coast like there? I've never spent much time in the Bay area."

Sharon briefly recounted the details of her vacation. Mansfield prayed silently, watching her face.

"…and then Leslie and I and several other friends and their partners went over to meet with one of the city councils about this terrible proposal that would have allowed anyone renting out rooms to students to turn down gay couples, just because of their precious religious convictions." She picked up her coffee cup, muttering to herself. "Of course, come to think of it, you probably would've been on *their* side."

Mansfield didn't speak for a moment. He could feel a muscle in his jaw twitch. *God, give me Your love for Sharon.*

"I would never want to see someone's civil rights violated, Sharon. I would never want a prejudiced person to hurt you or your friends."

"But you agree with that rental proposal, don't you?"

"Well, let me ask you a question."

"Oh, here it comes! This is where you get all judgmental on me, right? If you would've stoned me four thousand years ago, why would you rent me a room today? Something like that?"

"No, nothing like that." His gaze was direct, and he held her eyes until she looked away. "The question is whether or not the people who rented rooms were allowed to turn down *any* type of couple. As I have told you before, I don't agree with the gay lifestyle, but I also don't agree with straight people living together before they're married, or with married people committing adultery, or with any other type of sexual activity outside of marriage. I would hope that a Christian home owner would show the love of God to everyone, but I can see how someone might prefer not to support any lifestyle that God says is outside His best plan for us."

"Well, let's not stray outside of God's plan, by *all* means! Let's just keep us as second-class citizens, keep us back in the days when we felt we had to stay in the closet and deny our happiness because it offended someone's delicate sensibilities! By all means, let's allow people like you to hate us, unchallenged."

"Sharon, why do you think that I hate you just because I disagree with you? I don't hate you. I would like to be your friend."

Sharon took a big swig of her coffee and set the cup down. "I have a hard time being friends with people like you."

"Well, at least you're honest about it." Mansfield raised his glass to her.

"I don't get you, Mansfield." Sharon stood suddenly and picked up her belongings. "I have to get to my lesson plans."

She nodded good-bye and was gone, weaving her way out among the tables. Mansfield took a deep breath. *Gee, that went well.*

Several colleagues passed by his table, giving cheerful greetings, exchanging handshakes. One stopped, plate in hand, to slap him on the back. "You old son of a gun, trying to put me out of business! They're talking about reassigning *me* from Sanders to make room for your class."

Mansfield was chagrined. "Boris…"

"Just kiddin' with ya. I asked to be reassigned next year so I could concentrate on my two smaller seminars."

Mansfield put a hand over his heart, a smile playing on his lips. "Thank goodness. I thought our friendship was doomed."

His colleague slapped his back again and moved away. Mansfield started to dig into his plate again when he felt someone approach from behind.

"Professor, may I have a word with you?" The voice was familiar, rich and resonant.

"Anton." Mansfield nodded as Anton Pike came around to stand beside the table. "Of course. What's up?"

"I need to speak with you about your unilateral request to the registrar to increase the size of your class."

"It *is* my class, Anton. I hardly think a unilateral request is inapprop—"

"The decision to significantly increase class size is more than an administrative decision. You really should've come to the academic steering committee first. The registrar's office sent me their preliminary approval as a formality." He smiled down at Mansfield, his tone sympathetic. "I was forced to tell them to cancel the request and send it to committee. The committee will address the issue of whether it's appropriate to have a megaclass in the history department at a later date."

Mansfield folded his hands together. "And when might that be?"

"Whenever we have space on the agenda, Professor."

"Meaning not while you are chairman, Anton?"

The business professor looked back at him with that same half smile.

Mansfield remained calm. "I'm afraid that 'whenever' is not good enough, Anton. I'll have to appeal this higher up. This issue has been in the works for a long time—long before you became chairman of the academic steering committee."

"And *as* the chairman I can tell you that the final decision on which issues advance to the higher levels of the administration rests squarely with me. Now you could choose to go over my head, but that wouldn't be a good idea." He paused, and his voice took on a casual tone. "You know, I overheard your colleagues back there talking about whether you plagiarized Bill Tully's book."

Mansfield let out a chuckle. "Yeah, right." He glanced up at Anton, and his voice dropped. "You can't be serious. I wrote that article years ago. We were joking about the timing, but no one would ever think—"

"What I would be forced to tell the administration—were the subject to ever come up, of course—was that what I overheard didn't sound like joking. And the article *was* just published. The supposed date of writing could've been changed, although it would be hard to imagine that an esteemed professor such as yourself would resort to such tactics." Anton looked away, his voice distant, his fingers smoothing their way along the chair back. "It's such a shame that even when a charge has no merit, an academic investigation can make life rough on the accused."

*Lord, You are my shield and my buckler. Help me respond to this.* Instantly, Mansfield felt a drawing back, a caution in his spirit.

"Anton, your tactics are inappropriate and demeaning, but if that's how you want to get your way, fine. I will respect your position as chairman of the academic steering committee."

He watched as Anton inclined his head in a nod and moved away, leaving several nearby diners to look at Mansfield curiously. He smiled at them, wondering what they had overheard, and returned to eating. It was several minutes before he realized he wasn't tasting anything on his plate.


"There's no way around it, Anton." The voice on the other end of the line was quiet but intent. "James Statton says we are almost certain to lose the lawsuit. We need over half a billion in cash, and we need it soon."

Anton Pike leaned back in his executive leather chair, twisting the phone cord between his fingers, his mind grappling with the unwanted news his brother was sharing.

"There's no way of funneling the money from the shadow companies?"

"Not now. The money is more than there, obviously, but the regulators will have us under a microscope from the second we file the papers. It would be bad if we tipped our hand."

"That's one way of putting it. Well then, it looks like you're right. We'll have to do an initial public offering on Helion and sell off just enough shares to raise half a billion."

"I'm always right. That's why I'm running the business side and you're just running the substructure."

Anton snorted. "Just the more important of the two. Your side wouldn't make the money if my side wasn't effective, now would it?"

"And your substructure would fall apart if my work didn't keep it attractive, would it not?"

"The chicken and the egg, my dear Victor." Anton relaxed a little and put his feet up on his mahogany desk. "I'm sure our forebears have had the same argument for generations."

"I'm sure." A pause. "So any news on your end yet?"

"It's a little early to be sure, but several students from last year's classes show great promise. And I've already heard the same from our people elsewhere. I'm sure there'll be enough Fellows this year to allow you the next phase of expansion."

"Excellent. And the opposition?"

"In check for now, but still very much there. Today, I narrowly avoided one potential problem that would've greatly expanded the opposition's influence."

"Is that the one I think it is?"

"As usual. There are others, but he's definitely some sort of linchpin in the Enemy strategy."

There was a pause on the other end of the line. Then Victor spoke slowly. "It occurs to me that you may not have the ability to mitigate the blight much longer. We may have to remove the obstacle."

"I don't think that will work. He's too well respected for the usual damage to be credible."

"I didn't say 'move,' brother. I said 'remove.' Permanently."

"Hm. Let's file that away for future reference. It certainly would be pleasing to eliminate the hazard. But that may not be—"

"You and I both know that this is a critical time. Progress has been steady, and any backtracking now is an unnecessary disruption. We must hold—"

He stopped speaking abruptly, and Anton could hear another soft voice in the background. Victor came back on the line. "I need to go. One of the newer Fellows has just joined me for…ah…a private briefing on the status of her business line." There was a rustling on the line. "I'll be there in a moment, Johanna. Why don't you ask Alfonse to get you something from the fridge?"

Anton chuckled. "Johanna. The lovely little graduate from two or three years ago?"

"Four, Anton, four. Give me some credit."

"Oh, I do. I do. How long has this been going on?"

"About three minutes. She has made a couple of unfortunate mistakes, and since she's already here for a team meeting, she offered to come back this evening to discuss how she could make up for them."

"I'm sure she shows great promise as a Fellow, Victor."

"Great promise." There was a click as the line went dead.

Johanna slipped through the side door without turning on the light. With a quick glance around, she headed down the path toward the conference center near Victor's house. She looked up at the sparkling sky and grinned. *Victor.* Not Mr. Pike, not the famous CEO, but Victor.

The ocean wind from the nearby bluffs whipped her light jacket, and she could feel the gentle tingle of sea salt hitting her left cheek. Right where his last kiss had left off. She shivered with remembered pleasure. Would anything in her career path change now that she had consolidated her hold on his affections?

She pondered a moment, frowning. *Consummated* would be a better word; Victor was hardly the monogamous type.

Coarse gravel crunched under her feet. The conference center, with its elegant hotel rooms and meeting facilities, was just a few hundred yards away. The path was not well lit. Annoying for the occasional late-night meetings or midnight inductions held at the house but handy for a hidden getaway.

*If you have to hide, you're doing something wrong.* A fragment of uninvited memory floated to the surface. *Unless the only consequence of discovery is being "It."* She shook herself, annoyed. Why was she thinking of that stodgy old history professor now of all times? His archaic ideas of right and wrong had fueled many a heated debate during his office hours. Heated on her side, that is…he always stayed infuriatingly calm.

Johanna shoved her hands in her pockets and scowled. Even four years out of school he could still ruin her fun. Why had she ever listened to him in the first place?

Another nighttime scene rose before her eyes. She was walking through Johnston Gate, the driving snow stinging her eyes as she crossed Massachusetts Avenue and headed for the small movie theater on a nearby side street. In front of her on the corner, a young woman shivered, holding a baby in one hand and a cup of coins in the other. The baby was wrapped in a fluffy blue bunting, but the woman's mismatched clothes were tattered and she had no gloves or hat.

Johanna fished in her pocket for a dollar and dropped it into the quivering cup. The woman nodded her thanks.

Johanna walked a few steps farther down the more sheltered side street and tripped on her shoelace. As she bent down to retie the offending lace, a car pulled up beside her and a familiar figure stepped out onto the sidewalk. *Mansfield.* She scowled and bent her head to avoid meeting his eyes.

Mansfield didn't notice her, and Johanna watched as he walked back toward the homeless mother. *Probably going to give her a few pennies and lecture her on the conse-quences of premarital sex,* she thought. "What's your name?" she heard Mansfield say.

"M-Maggie."

"And who is this?"

"She be Princess."

"Princess, eh?" The genial voice chuckled. "I thought perhaps she was a little boy."

"They didn't have no pink blankets at the charity closet."

"Maggie, you know that Massachusetts guarantees a place in a shelter to every homeless person, don't you?"

"Yes sir."

"Do you have a place to stay tonight?"

"I'm too late. They close the doors at eight."

Johanna heard shuffling behind her. She started as Mansfield appeared at her side, still talking.

"Well, I know a place that will take you in this evening and get you some help." Johanna watched from the shadows. Mansfield had one hand on the woman's arm, guiding her down the sidewalk. He chucked the baby under the chin. "And will help look after this little one, too. Is that okay? Do you have someone else you'd like to call?"

The woman's glance was scornful. "Ain't got nobody. And ain't got no tokens for the T."

"You don't need the T." He gestured toward his car still idling nearby. "I'll take you there."

The young woman pulled her arms tighter around her baby and stepped back a pace. "Look, man, I don't know what you want, but…"

"I don't want anything except for you and your baby to get out of this weather. This is·a church shelter I'm going to take you to. It's not far from here. And church people run it. They're good people; you'll like them."

The woman peered at Mansfield's face, then at the car. "Well, if it's church folk, I suppose…"

Mansfield's eyes smiled as he ushered the young woman and her baby into the backseat. He folded himself into the driver's seat, and within seconds the car was gone.

Johanna stood slowly, her mind grappling with what she had just seen.

The memory still irritated her.

For the rest of that semester she had taken a perverse pleasure in her office-hours debates with the professor. *Like scratching an itch,* she thought.

She made a face. The pleasure had ended the day three students from that Christian group had walked in during one such session. They had jumped all over her, until Mansfield had asked them to wait outside. When she asked why they were so rude, he apologized but explained that they were passionate about their faith, about Jesus, and that individual Christians sometimes didn't reflect the loving nature of Christ as well as they should.

"What is there to be passionate about?" she had asked scornfully. She shook her head at the memory. Was *that* the wrong question to ask! He had told her the whole Jesus story. She had been eager to escape his office. It was just like that church she'd gone to as a kid: The whole thing made her uncomfortable.

She reached the darkened conference center and hurried quietly to her room. Thank goodness she was an independent adult now and immune to such silver-tongued myths and traditions.

A LITTLE OUT OF BREATH, CLAIRE AND SHERRY approached Room 105 in Emerson Hall. Two minutes past eleven. Two minutes late for the first session of Introduction to European History. They were going to have to figure out a quicker way across campus from their nine-thirty classes if they were ever going to get here on time. They slipped into the back of the room. They had already heard yesterday's horror stories of how some professors, on the first day of class, made an example of anyone walking in even a minute late.

The two girls exchanged relieved glances at the buzz of conversation in the lecture hall. Below them row upon row of seats were arranged in an amphitheater, overlooking a raised platform that held a podium, whiteboards, and multimedia equipment. They found two empty seats together near the top rank of seats.

The room quieted as an older professor and several TAs moved through a side door and toward the platform. All conversation stopped as the silver-haired professor rapped on the podium and turned on the microphone clipped to his belt.

"Greetings, everyone. You are in the class Introduction to European History, which will meet here every Tuesday and Thursday from eleven to twelve-thirty, with occasional sections conducted by my teaching assistants in smaller classrooms. As the airlines say, if you're not in the right place, I would suggest that you depart before the plane leaves the gate." Scattered laughter punctuated the room.

"Let me tell you what we're going to be doing here today. First, I'll tell you a little about myself and outline what this class will be about. Today will be a shortened teaching session: We're only going to cover the first half of chapter one in our text. At the end of the class I'm going to introduce you to my team of assistants, who will be helping to guide this rather large class through the semester." He gestured to the five TAs standing off to the side.

Claire couldn't help staring at the poised men and women on the platform, especially an attractive young man wearing a distinctive striped shirt. She nudged Sherry, who nodded approvingly when she pointed.

"The teaching assistants will provide some of the one-on-one attention that I can't possibly provide in such a large class. Before you leave, we'll hand out a sheet showing how we've divided the class into sections. Each of you will be assigned to the section of a particular TA.

"But first things first. My name is William Mansfield, and this is my fifteenth year of teaching at Harvard." The professor walked slowly up and down the front of the room, recounting his experience in Washington, D.C., moving backward through time. "Before that stint as the president's policy advisor, I spent several years in colonial Williamsburg as a professor and consultant on the original writings of the founding fathers."

As he described his fascinating career, he frequently looked out at the serried rows of desks in front of him. "Now," he smoothly switched gears, "let's begin our overview of European history with the latter years of the Roman Empire." A rustling sound filled the room as one hundred notebooks were flipped open. "Roughly eighteen hundred years ago, the once-mighty Roman Empire found itself in an increasingly troubled situation...."

Claire sat at the piano in the tiny rehearsal room in Paine Hall, intently picking out the notes on the score in front of her. She had only half an hour to familiarize herself with the music before her final audition for the Harvard-Radcliffe Collegium, the school's most prestigious choir. She had breezed through the preliminary auditions last week and had been delighted to see the respect on the choir director's face as he listened to her voice. She had eagerly agreed to commit to the choir if selected.

Nothing was certain until the final list went up, she reminded herself sternly, but wouldn't it be awesome to be in one of the most prestigious college choirs in the country? The director had told the auditioning group that the choir did one national and one foreign tour each year and this year's summer tour was to Singapore, Malaysia, Hong Kong, and perhaps even mainland China!

Claire knew committing to the choir would mean a lot of rehearsals, and she wouldn't have time for any other activities. The choir would be her home, her friends, her study mates. And the rehearsals conflicted with the Friday evening meetings of the Harvard Christian Fellowship, including the first meeting in two days. But there were sure to be Christians in the group she could have a Bible study with or something.

*Knock-knock-knock!* "Claire Rivers, you're up next!"

Claire jumped and grabbed her music. She paced in front of the audition hall, reviewing the soprano line one last time. For some reason she felt a little uneasy and tried to shake it off. Smiling confidently, she listened through the closed door to the muted sounds of the current quartet. Her favorite and best singing style was how the

Collegium did its final auditions—in four-part harmony, with three current members singing the other lines. She paced a bit to stay loose, but the uneasy feeling returned. What *was* that?

She gasped. *I haven't prayed about this! I should've asked if this is what God wanted before I committed to it.* Feeling slightly foolish, she stood in a quiet corner. *Lord, forgive me for not seeking Your face about this. I give this audition to You. May Your will be done, on earth as it is in heaven—*

"Claire Rivers!"

She took a deep breath and walked through the double doors…

…and Gael received his orders. He swept in quietly, taking an unseen position between Claire and the director. His eyes were sympathetic as he gently placed his hands on her shoulders.

Less than five minutes later, Claire walked blindly out the doors, down the hallway, and into the sunny courtyard in front of Paine Hall. What on earth had happened? She hadn't been able to sing one phrase correctly. She had even started on the wrong note after the director had just played it, for crying out loud!

She had sung a few lines off-key until the director had cleared his throat and stopped her. Her face flush with embarrassment, Claire saw the other singers glance at each other. She could practically hear them thinking, *How did* she *ever get this far?*

The director had laughed the mistake off. "You must be a bit nervous, Claire. Don't worry. Just start again."

She had agreed with heartfelt thanks—and proceeded to make even worse mistakes. She couldn't follow the director's tempo—a simple thing she had learned in second grade!—and was off-beat as well as off-key. It was a relief when the director had stopped the piece halfway through. "Thank you, Claire. That will be all. We'll be posting the final choir roster tomorrow."

Out in the late afternoon sunshine, Claire plopped dully down in the shade of a big tree. She watched hundreds of students walk by without really seeing them.

She flopped onto her back, sticks and dry leaves crackling underneath her, mentally kicking herself. She hadn't really liked the other choir or the a cappella group she had visited. Maybe she should've kept her options open until being sure of the Collegium…but no, she just hadn't felt comfortable in those other groups. They had seemed aloof and supercilious, and as much as she wanted to sing, she knew being cooped up with a group of snooty people would be even worse.

Another student from the music program came out of Paine Hall, and Claire looked away and picked up a book. She breathed a sigh of relief when the student walked in the other direction.

She slammed her book to the ground. *Why, Lord?*

To her mind came the image of her last-minute prayer before the audition. The memory stopped her complaints cold. Conviction washed over her. "Forgive me, God. Forgive me for my stupid pride."

A demon hovering above her suddenly received an almighty blow, spinning him high into the air, through the trunks of several trees, and around the corner of a nearby building. He had been soaking up strength and pleasure from the last few minutes of torment he had inflicted on the girl. But now he found himself abruptly tossed out of range.

Muttering viciously, his head throbbing, he worked his way back toward that tree—and found himself stopped short by the massive sword of a watch-care angel.

"You have been cast aside. Take your foul intentions away from here."

The demon growled, furious that weeks of careful strategy had been ripped to shreds in one instant of connection between the accursed girl and his eternal Enemy. Then, looking over the angel's shoulder, he saw the girl pull a yellow piece of paper out of her backpack, and his eyes narrowed. No, he would not force a further approach with the flaming sword at his throat. He might be invited back in soon enough.

He folded his arms haughtily and looked back at his adversary. "You are weak— always so willing to watch out for these pitiful ones who are so double-minded, so willing to work against all you are striving for. You could've been so much more powerful, so much more effective, in the hands of my master."

He glanced over at the girl again and smiled with anticipation, eager for her destruction, her humiliation. *I will win. It is only a matter of time.*

Claire sat up and pulled her yellow class schedule out of her backpack.

Now what? She could technically get away with carrying only four classes, but no way would she face the admonishing gaze of Ms. Tabor-Brown. She needed to put *something* where choir had been. It would be nice to have a class that looked impressive on her freshman transcript. She had always been one of the smartest students in her high school classes and had always felt on top of things. But here everyone had been the smartest person in his high school classes, the most academically proficient, the recipient of the highest grades.

She was determined to prove that a midwestern girl from a Christian high school could hack it with the best of them. If Sherry could handle it, couldn't she? Maybe eliminating choir was a godsend, a message to fill that slot with a really difficult or prestigious class—something that would set her apart from the pack. After all, she had to make sure that she would get that scholarship for next year. And she wanted something that would look good to potential employers, something that would impress all these confident freshmen sauntering by on the paths around her. So many students came to Harvard as if it were their birthright, from Exeter, Andover, or some other exclusive prep school. She wasn't a second-class citizen, and she would prove it.

Above the tree behind her, a dark being smugly moved past the force that had been obstructing him and settled into his old position.

Claire rummaged through her backpack to find the fall catalog of classes. A week ago she had highlighted several dozen classes of interest, then narrowed them down. She flipped through the pages and scanned the other candidates again. Anthropology. Well, there was that Machu Picchu class, but she'd never be able to pay for it. Biology. She already had one, and most of the others required her current introductory class as a prerequisite. Economics. Yeah, right. Maybe later, once she learned the difference between a stock and a bond.

Another few pages. Philosophy. Now there were some interesting sounding classes she hadn't noticed before. *Existential Thought. The Gulf Between Sartre and Kant.* Huh? *Optimistic Humanism versus Nihilism.* She kept flipping.

Religion. Ah. Reading carefully through the descriptions, she felt her spirits perk up for the first time since she had walked out of the music building. She recognized most of the Christian-based subjects, and several on other religious thought—even the advanced classes. Bible Writings and Interpretations—a study of both the Hebrew Bible and the writings of its commentators. Monday, Wednesday, Friday at one o'clock. Perfect!

And—wow—it was an advanced class, a cross-registration class between the college and the divinity school. Wouldn't that look great on her transcript and set her apart from so many of the other freshmen here—that she had the guts to try a graduate-level class as a freshman…in her first semester, no less! *That would be a perfect way to impress the scholarship committee. What a gift from God!*

Claire scanned the short list of religion classes that students were supposed to take before being allowed into this one. Every single one sounded like a class she had taken in high school or at the community college her senior year. She glanced at her watch. She was sure she would need to discuss this unorthodox class request with the registrar, but the office was probably closed by now. Right after her early morning biology class, she would head over there. And she'd be sure to casually mention her choice to the scholarship people.

She flopped onto her back again, looking up at the spreading arms of the tree above her, feeling pleased that she had a direction to pursue.

An acorn bounced off her backpack, and another off her foot. She sat up just in time to catch one in the back of her head.

"Hey!"

"Oh, I'm so sorry!" Sherry stood a few feet behind the tree, laughing and clutching the remnants of her arsenal. "Care to join us for dinner?"

A large group from their freshman dorm was waiting for Sherry, chattering and laughing on their way to Annenberg, the cavernous dining room in Memorial Hall. Claire noticed that her reclusive suitemate, Mercedes, was among them. She gathered her books, and as she approached the group, she watched Sherry drop back to make a smiling comment to a male student with curly dark hair. When he turned his head, Claire saw that it was Stefan.

THE GROUP SETTLED AT A LONG TABLE with their dinner trays, and after introductions were made, Claire bowed her head to give thanks. Out of the corner of her eye, she was pleased to see Sherry and one other girl, Teresa, do the same. The others didn't join in, and there was a lull in conversation. Claire could feel them staring.

Claire felt extremely self-conscious, but when she looked up, she noticed that several of her hallmates seemed more uncomfortable than she did.

"Is there something wrong with the food?" A guy sitting across the table looked at her, puzzled. He peered at the meatloaf on his plate.

"What?"

"Is there something wrong with the food? You guys were inspecting your trays so closely—"

He was interrupted by a giggle from Teresa. "Nothing's wrong with the food, Ben. We were just saying grace."

"What's that?"

"What's what?"

"What's 'saying grace'?"

"You don't know what grace…well, it's…um…" She shot a glance at Claire and Sherry. "Well, it's just…it's praying to give thanks for the food and to ask God to bless it."

"Oh."

"Didn't you ever say grace before meals at your house?" Claire asked.

"I don't think so. No one in our family is really religious. But be my guest. Whatever works for you…"

Stefan laughed and pounded him on the back. "Ben, man, I hate to tell you this, but I don't think it'll work for you. I don't think even God could do anything about that cafeteria meatloaf on your plate!"

The others broke up laughing, and Claire and Teresa giggled despite themselves.


Over a small dinner table in Michigan, Barbara and Tom Rivers and their two sons bowed their heads to give thanks for their meal and to ask the Lord's protection and blessing over the family, their work, their schools, and the daughter away at Harvard. As was the family practice each took a turn. Barbara felt a stirring in her heart, a certain importance about this night, but before she could speak Tom grasped her hand tightly and began to pray. Gratitude washed over her as she listened to her husband's earnest petitions for Claire and her new life. As Barbara joined her prayers silently to those of her husband, she realized she didn't need to say anything.

The freshmen trooped out of the dining hall and broke up into twos and threes as they crossed under the intricate iron portico into Harvard Yard and started down the brick walkway toward their dorm. It was much quieter in the Yard. The brick buildings, oak trees, and manicured paths somehow encouraged decorum.

Claire and Sherry walked side by side, comparing notes about high school.

"Yeah, I figured you were the homecoming queen type," Claire said. "Let me guess: captain of the cheerleading team?"

"Cocaptain, actually."

"Oh, of course. My bad."

"How about you?" Sherry asked. "Drill team?"

"Soccer team."

"Well, well. A jock."

"And choir."

"A geek?"

"Hey!" Claire shoved her roommate, laughing despite the twisting in her gut. "Low blow!"

"So really, you didn't do cheerleading or anything?"

"It wasn't...my crowd."

"Oh." Sherry suddenly looked uncomfortable.

"I preferred to hang with the heavy-metal heads and the shop guys, you know. All that talk of transmissions and oil changes really gets me going."

Sherry's mouth opened slightly. "Wha—?"

"Just kidding."

"Oh, you!"

Claire laughed. "It's funny, looking back on it now. For years I was pretty insecure. I couldn't relate to the cheerleader crowd and didn't really know how to make friends."

"No kidding? You don't seem to have that problem now."

"Thank God! But just you try talking about me behind my back sometime; then we'll see how much of a problem I still have."

Claire looked over at her roommate, trying to figure out how much to say. She wanted to tell her how much God had changed her, how much more she liked the person she had become than the insecure, unhappy, awkward adolescent she had once been. She glanced at Sherry's polished profile, the trendy clothes. But then, Sherry probably wouldn't be able to relate.


"Wasn't that funny tonight with Ben?"

"What was?" Sherry was in her pajamas, brushing her long dark hair in front of the sink, her back to Claire.

"That he didn't know what saying grace was."

"Well, we sometimes forget that many people in this country don't go to church anymore. He just hasn't had any exposure to that culture." Sherry turned around, and her Southern accent grew heavy with sarcasm. "If he'd grown up in the Bible Belt, boy, he'd have seen people saying grace at meals…whether they meant it or not!"

Claire cleared some notebooks off her bed and crawled under the covers. "What do you mean?"

"Well, in Georgia my family always went to church every Sunday and always said grace at meals. But that didn't stop my aunt and uncle from drinking themselves under the table not half an hour afterward, or my brother from hanging out with a bad crowd, or my daddy from carrying on with his secretary…." She turned away.

The room was quiet for a moment, then Claire said, "It…it sounds like you've been through a lot."

"Well, yeah. I guess. But no more than lots of other people. Are your parents still together?"

"Yes, thank God." Instantly, she flushed. "I'm sorry. I didn't mean that to sound…." Claire took a deep breath and tried again. "It must be hard to have divorced parents. I'm just really thankful to God that mine are still together."

"Don't apologize. Actually, my parents aren't divorced. They stayed together and are driving each other crazy every day. Let me tell you, I was really glad to get out of there."

Sherry climbed the ladder to her loft, and Claire listened to the sheets rustling above her for a moment, hoping Sherry would continue. After a moment she sighed and clicked off the light.

"When I was thirteen, a friend took me to a special youth service at another church in town." Sherry's somewhat muffled voice floated down toward her. "I think it was a Baptist church. I walked down the aisle at the end of the night when they called everyone forward who wanted to be made new. I didn't understand half of what the preacher said, but I knew I needed *something* different—needed to know God for real. For a few months I went to Sunday school and church with my friend, and I loved it. I was so happy and felt so…alive, you know? But my mom and dad got more and more annoyed that I wasn't coming to church with them and with the hassle of dropping me off at my friend's house. They made me go back to my old church. Then my friend moved away at the end of the school year."

When Sherry didn't continue, Claire spoke quietly into the darkness. "Did you ever go to a good church again?"

"Not really. But there was a Bible club at school. Nothing like at your Christian school, probably. It was pretty good, when I could get there, but it usually seemed more like a Christian dating club than a Bible study. Not that that's always bad, you know. There were quite a few cute guys to choose from."

Claire laughed. "You do seem to have the ability to attract them. One of these days you'll have to tell me your secret. Seriously, though, can I ask you a question?"

"Sure."

"Well…I want to find a good church. I figure if I don't start looking now, I'll just keep putting it off and putting it off and never do it." She paused. Where was this idea coming from? "Would you want to join me? We could visit different churches on Sunday mornings until each of us found one we liked. It…well, it would be nice to have someone else to hold me accountable and ensure that I get my rear in gear and out of bed on Sunday mornings."

Sherry laughed, and Claire could hear the sheets rustling above her. Suddenly, a white blob that had to be her roommate's face peered over the side of the loft; Claire could hear the warmth in her voice. "You know what? I would never have suggested it, but I think that's a great idea. Maybe that'll keep me on the straight and narrow here. Thanks for asking." The face disappeared abruptly.

Claire stared above her, a grin spreading over her face. *Thank You, Lord! You are so good to us. Help us find a church where we can be grounded in You.*


In the dark of the bedroom, Gael and Caliel exchanged thankful glances and prepared to depart. God's message to these young women had been eagerly accepted.

As they slipped through the wall of the dorm and out into the night sky, they prayed for God's protection over this room, these two precious young people, and the important start they had just made. They knew that others of their number were keeping regular watch over each dorm, and especially over suites such as this one where the enemy had rightful access. They couldn't be everywhere at once, but the Spirit could.

## ELEVEN

CLAIRE SETTLED INTO HER SEAT, smiling at a nearby girl she recognized from the first class on Monday and trying not to yawn. Introduction to Biology: Mondays, Wednesdays, and Fridays. Normally students avoided the 8:00 A.M. classes at all costs, but Claire liked biology and found the smaller class size helpful.

Professor Lyte, who appeared to be in her late forties, arrived, sipping a steaming tall coffee from C'est Bon.

Claire grinned to herself. The Starbucks outlet was closer, but she had soon discovered that few Harvard people would patronize chain stores. The day before, walking between classes, she had overheard one freshman telling another that she had ventured into the local International House of Pancakes out of curiosity but didn't stay to eat. "It was so *pedestrian*," the girl had said. Claire snorted in amusement. She bet that that girl bought school supplies at Wal-Mart when no one was looking.

The girl next to her leaned over and held out her hand. "Hi, I'm Joanne Markowitz. Everyone calls me Jo." She didn't look at all like she had just rolled out of bed for an early morning class.

"Claire Rivers. Nice to meet you." The two girls chatted briefly, watching their biology professor erase the whiteboard at the front of the room.

During the first class, Professor Lyte had seemed friendly but no pushover. She had emphasized that class participation would comprise a large part of the final grade. Claire pulled out the biology text and turned to the section about the origins of life on earth. She had highlighted several segments in her reading and penciled questions in the margins. One benefit of having gone to a Christian high school was that she had some good questions to ask about inconsistencies and holes in the standard evolutionary theory. She knew, for example, that evolutionary theorists used the same word, *evolution*, to describe two completely different concepts, making the obvious "survival of the fittest" process seem linked to the unproven theory that mutations somehow created higher life forms, when in fact the two weren't at all related. She was relieved to have something to bring up that would provide at least *some* class participation points.

Even if it was a controversial question Claire was looking forward to a high-level intellectual debate on the issue. She was curious as to what an academic college discussion on all sides of an issue would look like, since it had been difficult to pull out many different viewpoints at a Christian high school.

Professor Lyte began the lecture outlining the evolution of life from the primordial soup on the newly formed earth billions of years ago. At a good clip she walked through Darwin's process of evolution. She marked an estimated timeline on the whiteboard, detailing when amoebas evolved into more sophisticated beings, when dinosaurs walked the earth, and when the tree of life branched out to include man's apelike ancestors.

Thirty minutes into the fifty-minute class, Claire noticed that the professor had never once used the word *theory* to describe interspecies evolution. It was presented as known fact, with a few details left to be filled in by scientists in the coming years.

"Okay, that's a brief outline. As I said at the outset, this is a quick reminder of the foundations of evolution since I presume all of you had this in high school." The professor capped her marker and turned to the class. "Who has questions?"

Several hands shot up, including Claire's.

Professor Lyte called on a male student in the back and answered a complicated question about the cellular level evolution that was theorized to have started the whole process. She drew several diagrams with question marks beside a few of them.

"That is what we believe the process was, at any rate. There are still some holes to be filled in, as scientists can't yet be sure of the exact order of events." She grinned. "It was a few years ago, after all."

As the students laughed, she pointed to another upraised hand. "Let's try you there, with the marine buzz cut."

The young man cleared his throat. "Well, I was wondering about what you just said—the assumptions underlying this process. You said 'we believe' but aren't sure. But aren't there more than just a few holes in our knowledge of how life started?"

*Darn!* Claire thought, *He's asking my question!*

"I mean, isn't interspecies evolution actually a theory rather than proven fact? There's a great deal of other evidence that shows that it actually might not—"

"First of all, yes, the process of evolution is technically just a theory," Professor Lyte said. "A key tenet of scientific analysis is that for something to be proven, it has to be reproducible. Therefore, evolution is only a theory because we haven't been able to reproduce it as yet. It's been a little hard for scientists to accurately reproduce the conditions spawned by the big bang."

The questioner started to speak, but the professor raised her hand. "Look, you asked about theory versus fact, but let me deal with what I think your real agenda is in asking that question. You're intending to challenge the theory of evolution with what you believe is the better theory of creation. Evolutionism versus creationism, the oldest fight in the Bible Belt." Her tone was humorous, and most of the other students laughed. "Am I correct so far, Mr...?"

"Turner. Doug Turner."

"Mr. Turner, I get this same question every few semesters. So am I on track with what you're really asking in keeping with your personal agenda?"

Claire winced. *Okay, I guess I'm glad he asked my question!*

Doug Turner's face was red, but he spoke up readily. "Yes, ma'am, that's pretty much it. Everyone accepts evolution as fact, but since it really *is* still a theory and there are these other inconsistencies, I wanted to ask a few questions about that." His voice trailed off, and he glanced around the classroom, embarrassed.

Professor Lyte stood still in front of the whiteboard for a moment, then calmly took a sip from her coffee cup and set it aside. She clasped her hands behind her back and began to pace the length of the room.

"Let me tell you one of my only ground rules for this class—and this is for Mr. Turner and anyone else in here who may share his belief system." Her gaze swept the seats before her, and Claire quickly looked down.

"I have three main ground rules." She ticked them off on her fingers. "Rule one, you do your assigned reading diligently before you come to class, so that, rule two, you can be an active participant in class discussions. And rule three—" she turned and focused on Doug Turner—"those class discussions do not include a debate about the validity of the theory of evolution versus any other theory." She held his gaze for a moment, then nodded, satisfied, and turned back to the class.

"We have too much to cover in this class to waste time debating the validity of something that the scientific community has widely accepted for a century of the most rigorous scientific study. This is not a religion class or a philosophy class. This is a *science* class and as such must stick with the facts and not with flights of speculation or personal faith.

"I am not going to spend my class time arguing about this. So as of now, this particular debate will stop and never resume. Here's how rule three works: In all class discussions, in your writing assignments and labs and problem sets—in your *tests*—we are going to treat evolution with the foundational and frankly *correct* assumption that it is the only valid explanation for life on this planet."

Doug Turner started to say something, but she cut him off. "Period. End of story. If anyone can't live with that ground rule, then that person should find him- or herself a different biology class. Or a different major." She paused. "Understood?"

Claire saw that most of her fellow students looked either amused or perplexed by the whole topic. No one seemed inclined to argue. Claire glanced at Doug Turner and felt faintly ashamed of herself.

"Okay then, that pretty much does it for today. Check your syllabus for the next readings. See you Friday."

As the students started rising to their feet, Jo Markowitz caught Claire's eye. She chuckled and nodded toward Doug Turner. "Poor guy, he really got slammed."

"Yes, he did." Claire made very busy about gathering her papers into her notebook and loading up her backpack.

"Well, what does he expect? This isn't some hillbilly church, after all. Welcome to college, mister." Jo gathered up her books and moved away. "See you Friday."

"Yeah, see you."

Claire sat still for a moment, downcast. *Lord, forgive me. I'm such a jerk!* Then she grabbed her backpack and hurried after Doug, who was moving toward the door. She caught the corner of his sleeve, and he looked wary as he turned toward her.

"I just wanted to say thanks, Doug."

His eyes registered surprise, but he didn't say anything. Claire briefly introduced herself and plowed ahead.

"Look, I had a lot of the same types of questions. I'm sorry you got hammered like that."

He sighed, smiling ruefully. "Yeah, well, so am I. I guess it's to be expected. Welcome to Harvard!"

"I had hoped we could get into a good scientific debate on the subject. I'll bet most of these guys haven't ever heard an intellectual presentation of a viewpoint other than evolution. When you started to ask that question, I was glad that we would have a chance to get into it."

Doug snorted. "Are you kidding? This is *Harvard,* Claire. Harvard makes such a thing about tolerance and the freedom to express all viewpoints. Gays, communists, humanists, Buddhists—all are invited to participate in the 'marketplace of ideas.' But get some conservative Christian in here, and the marketplace of ideas is curiously closed. Now gee…why is that?"

Claire was puzzled and it must have shown on her face. Doug's tone softened. "Claire, are you a Christian?"

"Yes."

"So am I…as you probably guessed. Look, I'm sorry to go off like this. I guess I'm just smarting a bit. I was warned about this, but that doesn't mean I know how to handle it. At least there is one other Christian in the class. That's something! It's always good to have an ally."

Claire smiled, trying not to let him see the shame behind her eyes.

At a large secluded house on Nantucket Island, off the New England coast, about two dozen men huddled in conversation. Bay windows overlooked a backyard that ended abruptly in windswept bluffs. The men were long used to the stunning view and took it for granted. They didn't talk sand and surf, but dollars, pesos, and soles. Heavy gold jewelry glittered on fingers and wrists, and heavy bodies fit into well-cut casual trousers and sweaters. On the coffee table, laptop computers jostled notepads for space.

A lone man stood by the windows, eyes scanning the bluffs and the ocean that churned nearly a hundred feet below. Victor Pike couldn't see the forces that moved beyond his dimension of sight, but he could feel them. It was a familiar and welcome presence today.

The discussions and negotiations continued behind him at a brisk clip, punctuated by the swift clicking of a keyboard. After a moment his right-hand man appeared, and he jerked his head toward the kitchen that adjoined the large common room.

The kitchen door silently swung shut behind them.

"Victor, they balked at the first proposal as you expected." His aide spoke with a subtle Latin accent. "But even Mulligan and his people think they can make your counter-offer work." He smiled. "Of course, I did not tell them that this was what you wanted all along."

"Do they recognize that I am still taking all the risk down south? Are they properly grateful for the buffer I provide them?"

"One can never be sure, of course, but yes, I'd say so. That was probably why the bosses agreed to your undisputed control of the international channel."

A slow smile spread across Victor's face. "Excellent, Alfonse, excellent. Go and tell them."

Alfonse stepped back into the room. "Victor Pike agrees to the deal." Carefully restrained nods of acknowledgment greeted the long-awaited announcement, but the players did not exchange words of congratulation. They might have to cooperate out of necessity, but that didn't mean they wished each other well.

Alfonse smiled to himself at the dynamics running just under the surface. "Congratulations, gentlemen. It is a pleasure to continue doing business with you."

When all the hands had been firmly shaken, the men ushered out, and lackeys had collected the coffee cups that littered every conceivable surface, Victor called his leadership team together. Unlike those who had just left, this group grew animated as they outlined plans and projected profits.

Victor pulled Alfonse aside. "Does anyone know when my brother arrives?"

His aide checked his watch. "The Lear should be landing any moment, and we have a car waiting at the airport. Fifteen minutes, max."

"Good. Peru is next on the agenda. Let's wait on that until he gets here. This team will have all day today and most of tomorrow to hammer out the distribution issues before the other Fellows arrive for the joint meeting." He frowned suddenly, thinking. "Of course, Anton will have to go back tonight since he has class tomorrow morning. The joint meeting will have to address recruitment issues once he returns on Friday. Anton says he has some very promising candidates this year."

He looked around at the others in the room, still deep in discussion over the ramifications of the morning meeting. Quite the contrast to those who had just left. These men and women—his Fellows—were younger, trimmer, better looking. Their business casual attire was trendy, not ostentatious, designed for lithe, well-toned bodies. Leather loafers and expensive watches spoke of understated wealth. Even the few women wore little additional jewelry.

Golden boys and girls, Ivy League grads—poster children for the business. Perfect.

Victor turned to his aide. "What day is Anton bringing in the primary candidates?"

"He said he'd stay here Friday night for meetings, then take the Lear back on Saturday morning and pick up about six students, including a few coming in from other universities. They should be back here midmorning."

"Excellent. On Saturday our business will mostly be done, and our team members will have more casual time to talk with the newcomers." Victor walked a few steps toward the windows, gazing out at the slate-colored water. "Here's the only restriction: I don't want the candidates to see the size of our leadership—not yet. Not until they are more committed. Why don't you pick which Fellows would be best for recruiting and assessment—say about twenty or so."

He glanced over at one young man, perched on one of the overstuffed chairs, caught up in a lively brainstorming session with a petite woman. "I think some like Murphy would be particularly good. He's a fairly recent alum, and his business line has been highly successful. And Johanna, of course."

Alfonse pulled a small notepad and pen from his jacket, smiling slightly. "Will do. I'm sure Johanna will be happy to oblige you." Victor raised an eyebrow as Alfonse briskly jotted a few notes. "We'll arrange for those twenty to have lunch with the candidates and take them around the island in the afternoon. I'm assuming we'll do a few of the usual tests?"

Victor smiled out at the windswept bay. "Of course."

# TWELVE

"THIS BUILDING HOUSES THE LARGEST UNIVERSITY LIBRARY in the world." A young man wearing a conservative suit and tie spoke in a low voice as he gestured toward the imposing ranks of books and high ceilings of Widener Library. A small group of well-dressed listeners obediently looked where he pointed. "Widener is also the third largest library in the country."

Not five feet away, sitting at a table between shelves of books, Sherry caught Stefan's glance and rolled her eyes. This was the second such group to walk through the Loker Reading Room in the past hour. She leaned across the table and whispered, "I thought they didn't bring tours in where students were trying to study."

"They don't—not the normal tours. But there are a bunch of VIPs at Harvard for a conference today, so they're touring them privately around the campus." Stefan nodded toward the nearby group, careful not to look directly at them." Don't look now, but check out the tall guy with the silver hair. That's the CEO of one of the largest Internet companies in the world. And that other man in the charcoal suit, I'm pretty sure that's a state governor. And, by the way, the woman next to him *isn't his wife.*"

Sherry casually leaned back in her chair, coughed, and turned her head, getting a fleeting glance of the governor and the woman standing close by his side. She flashed a raised eyebrow at Stefan and mouthed "how do you know?"

They leaned toward each other again.

"I think he said something that made my father wonder when Dad invited him to the conference."

"Whoa! He told the organizers of the conference that he was bringing his *mistress?*"

Stefan sputtered and made urgent quiet down motions with his hands. Sherry grimaced and looked around carefully. The group was still listening to the tour guide's explanation of some point about Harvard's history and hadn't even glanced their way.

Stefan placed his textbook between them and leaned forward, pretending to show something to her. His lips were near her ear, making Sherry tingle. "No, silly, he just said that his wife might not be able to make it and that he would probably be accompanied by someone else."

Sherry looked down at the textbook between them. "Yes, but c'mon—the guy's a public figure and he's *married*. Isn't it awfully stupid to be seen with someone other than his wife?"

Stefan arched an eyebrow. "Have you ever seen his wife? Nobody's gonna blame the guy!"

Sherry started to giggle, unsuccessfully smothering her mouth against her hand.

"Oh listen!" Stefan nudged her with his shoulder. "Have you heard the Widener story yet? You gotta listen to this part."

Sherry sat back and picked up her notebook, studiously staring at it while she tuned her ears to the nearby group.

"…so the young Harry Elkins Widener decided to travel home from England in 1912, bringing with him a massive collection of books and papers. The 1907 Harvard graduate was planning to donate his personal library to the college. Unfortunately for him, he decided to join the maiden voyage of the new luxury liner *Titanic* that was getting so much press."

The group murmured in surprise. Fascinated, Sherry began to jot notes in her European history notebook.

*Story of Widener Library: Harry Elkins Widener, Harvard grad going back to school from England with books. 1912. The Titanic. Oops.*

"Young Harry, like so many other young men, did not get a seat on a lifeboat and was lost in the freezing water. Obviously, all his books were lost as well. Harry's mother, Mrs. Widener, decided to commemorate her beloved son by gifting Harvard with two million dollars to build a library in his name. Two million dollars may not sound like much in today's dollars, but at the turn of the century it was an enormous amount of money—enough to build a monumental facility with sixty-five *miles* of shelves and capacity for three million books."

*Harry drowned. Mrs. Widener (mother) gave $2 million for library.*

"However, her grant to the college had three strict stipulations. One, she decreed that all Harvard students must be taught how to swim." He smiled as several people in the group chuckled.

"Two, that a room be created in the library that would look just like Harry's, right up to having a fresh carnation placed in a vase every morning."

*Three conditions on her grant: 1) all students know how to swim. 2) room look just like Harry's (example: carnation every morning).*

"And finally, that 'not a brick would change' in the library once it was built." The guide paused and looked around at his rapt audience. "For almost ninety years now, the college has been careful to adhere strictly to these stipulations, with the exception of the first. It wasn't that it was an odd request—it was just illegal because it discriminated against physically challenged students."

*3) not a brick of the library would change. Harvard has kept all conditions but #1 (discriminates against disabled students).*

As she wrote, Sherry smiled to herself. Harvard was so funny—they were careful not to label any viewpoint as odd, no matter how strange. But if it was *discriminatory*...well, that was a different matter!

She noticed Stefan looking at her, and she smiled at him. He smiled back, the dimple in his cheek becoming more pronounced. She looked back down at her notebook, trying not to blush.

"...others weren't problems," the tour guide was saying, "but stipulation number three actually presented a *big* problem to the school a few years back. It was clear that we were quickly outgrowing the current confines of Widener, but how do you put an extension on a building that has a formal stipulation that 'not a brick can change'?"

The tour guide smiled and pointed at the large windows set in the east wall of the library. "Well, Mrs. Widener said no *brick* could change, but she said nothing about a *window*. So what we did—as you'll see when we go outside in a moment—was knock out a large window on the second floor and build a skyway. That connected this building to the expansion building—the Pusey Library—that was constructed a few feet away, right next door. Voilà! Any questions before we move on?" The group started to move away.

*Number 3 problem when outgrew Widener. But Mrs. W said 'no brick change'— so they knocked out a* window *to build connection to extension building. Clever!*

"Well, well, young Stefan, is that you, so diligently bent over your studies?"

The Internet CEO had stopped by their table. Stefan rose to his feet and shook the man's hand.

"Hello. Good to see you, sir."

"I thought that was you, son. We're enjoying the conference time. Your father has put together a really good group of people." He turned to Sherry, who was trying not to stare. "And who is your friend here?"

"This is Sherry. We have a class together."

Sherry stood up and shook the offered hand. "Sherry Rice. Nice to meet you, sir."

"My pleasure. Well, I hope we didn't disturb you kids."

Sherry smiled. "No problem, sir. I enjoyed eavesdropping on that story he was telling y'all." She gestured at the tour guide, who was moving the group toward the doors at the far end of the room.

"Well, good. Nice to meet you, Sherry. I'm sure I'll see you later, Stefan."

Sherry noticed that as he turned away, the CEO flashed a thumb's up at Stefan. She quickly took her seat, pleased in spite of herself. She hoped Stefan hadn't seen her blush. She heard his chair scrape the floor as he sat down again.

"It's amazing the people that you know, mister!" she said.

"Well, hey. That's a prime benefit of having a father on the faculty."

In a classroom across campus a TA eyed the seats in front of him. Martin's gaze rested on a young woman, a student with dark hair and eyes, who had made a promising comment during the class discussion on business precepts.

Another student was going on and on about something, but Martin wasn't listening. He caught the professor's eye and nodded toward the girl. The professor subtly nodded yes and returned his attention to the class. The TA made a mark next to her name. Mercedes Ramon.

When the class broke up a few minutes later, Martin walked out past her chair and stopped to chat. After a few moments of banter, he looked at his watch and then gestured down to where the professor was surrounded by a few other students.

"You know, Professor Pike likes to get to know his business students. A few of us were just going to grab some lunch with the professor—want to join us?"

An hour later, Anton Pike sipped the last of his iced tea, listening to the conversation between three students and his TA. The girl seemed a promising possibility. He raised his hand and caught their waiter's eye, making a quick gesture. The waiter nodded.

When the bill arrived, Martin picked it up and then began patting his jacket pockets. "Nuts! I forgot my reading glasses."

He looked across the table and casually handed the bill to Mercedes. "Since you have the least seniority here, looks like you get stuck with bill duty." He grinned over at her. "A crack business student like you shouldn't have any trouble figuring out who owes what, right?"

Anton watched the girl intently. She looked around the table, noting who had which dish, and—

"Huh—he forgot to charge for my lunch." Mercedes was looking down at the restaurant's printout. "The bill is short by probably twelve dollars."

Neither Anton nor Martin said anything. Mercedes glanced around the table. "Tell you what, rather than just me getting the windfall, let's spread the wealth. I'll go ahead and chip in some, and the rest of you can pay two dollars less than you would have otherwise."

One of the other students said, "Shouldn't we tell the waiter his bill was short? He'll get in trouble when he tries to balance his accounts at the end of his shift."

Mercedes waved a hand. "No, no. I used to wait tables; it's easy to just write those things off. You just say there was a problem with the meal so you deducted it from the bill or something. Besides, if he didn't catch it, why should we point it out to him?"

The others pulled out their wallets and started putting cash into the center of the table. Anton leaned back in his chair and smiled to himself. Yes. A very promising possibility.

"WAIT A MINUTE—*WHICH* CLASS DO YOU HAVE AFTER LUNCH?" A cacophony of lunchtime clatter surrounded Claire and her hallmate Teresa as they found an empty table in Loker Commons, the bustling food court and entertainment area underneath Memorial Hall. Teresa brushed crumbs off her chair and unloaded her tray, looking up at Claire for an answer.

"I think its full name is Bible Writings and Interpretations. It's a religion class." Claire smiled at the confused look on Teresa's face.

"That's not a freshman class, is it?"

"Nope. I had so many Bible classes at my high school that they allowed me to waive into an advanced religion class—even one that's cross-registered with a few graduate students at the *div school!*" She saw the slight frown on Teresa's face. "Don't worry. The first two days of material was all stuff I'd had before. I honestly expected it to be tougher than it was." She popped a french fry into her mouth, grinning mischievously. "Other than the fact that we've already had to write a paper it seems fine."

"No way! You've already had a paper? In the first two days of class?"

"Yep. Apparently, advanced and graduate school classes have a lot more writing. It wasn't much, really. Just a two-page overview of issues raised by writers like St. Augustine. Pretty easy, since I like Augustine—even if some others in the class don't!"

Teresa raised an eyebrow in query.

"Well," Claire continued, "I sort of got the impression that a few people in the class aren't exactly thrilled with Christianity and are taking the class more to poke holes than to study the Bible."

"Claire, I'm not trying to give you advice or anything. I don't know you well enough yet, and I may be completely wrong about this whole thing. But just let me mention something, okay?"

Claire nodded briefly, growing irritated by the concern that continued to hover on Teresa's face.

"I know you went to a Christian high school, and you probably know the Bible backward and forward—probably much better than I do. But did you know that the divinity school here isn't a purely Christian program at all? Seriously, it's true. Several people from my high school went through Harvard, and they all say the same thing:

The div school isn't really a seminary to ordain Christian pastors anymore and some-times is actually hostile to biblical Christianity."

"That seems awfully silly, Teresa...."

"I know, I know, but at least check into it. The div school seems to value tolerance and openness to other faiths above all else."

"You mean getting more liberal?" Claire shrugged and glanced at her watch. "I don't mind talking about less conservative theology."

"Look, I'm the last person to get into quibbles about conservative theology versus liberal theology. I go to a mainstream Presbyterian church where my favorite pastor is a woman. That's not the kind of thing I mean. Just...take a look at the div school's class offerings sometime, rather than just those classes cross-registered with the undergrads. Or go to their Web site—it's kinda spooky. It's almost easier to find a respectful discus-sion of Buddhist or Hindu thinking than orthodox Christianity."

"At a *divinity school?*"

"Look, I'm just a freshman. What do I know? But I was warned about that several times before coming here by Christian men and women I respect. They say the same thing is happening at a lot of other schools."

"Well, what am I supposed to do about it? Why are you telling me this?"

Teresa leaned back in her chair, raising her hands slightly in defense. "Look, I'm just trying to help."

"I'm sorry. I know. Keep going."

"All I was going to do was pass along the advice they gave me. They warned that no matter how ready I thought I was intellectually and academically to take a Harvard religion class, to avoid them like the plague until I was also *emotionally* ready. They can apparently be really challenging, especially for younger people like us who aren't as mature in our faith yet, or who don't know how to handle the whole 'tolerance' thing. I would imagine that advice would be doubled for someone taking a class like this as a freshman."

Claire noticed that her voice carried no admiration for the bold attempt Claire was making. Finishing her fries, she grabbed her backpack and stood up.

"Thanks, Teresa. I appreciate your telling me about all that. I guess I'll go find out what this class session holds and see what I think. By the way, are you going to be at the Harvard Christian Fellowship meeting tonight?"

"Wouldn't miss it. I'll see you."

Claire hurried toward class and tried to put her conversation with Teresa out of her mind. There was no way she was going to be a quitter on such a prestigious opportu-nity. What on earth did Teresa mean, anyway, saying she might not be able to handle the class emotionally?

The demon hurrying along above her prodded and poked at Claire with his long fingers, making a suggestion that he knew would fall on open ears.

Claire thought of something. *You know, I'll bet Teresa just isn't used to religion classes. Maybe she's just a little jealous of Christians who know the Bible better than she does. I should have been nicer to her. Maybe I can help her along with that stuff sometime.* Her irritation gone, Claire bounced up the stairs to the imposing Andover Hall.

Seated in a large circle of desks and chairs with twenty other students, Claire listened to her religion TA, Jack DuBois, introduce himself. She had seen him in class on Wednesday, but this was the first meeting of his class section. He was immaculately dressed in black pants, gray long-sleeved shirt, and charcoal tie, setting him apart from the jeans and T-shirts in the circle with him.

He was a student at the divinity school, he said, only a few months away from receiving his Ph.D. He had taken some time off in the middle of his graduate program and traveled, visiting such famous spiritual sites as the Buddhist monasteries in Nepal, the Dome of the Rock in Israel, and the Vatican in Rome. He did a lot of research and writing for the Global Religions Institute at the div school, and had been the TA for Professor Misha Dubrovsky's Bible Writings and Interpretations class for the past three years.

At the Wednesday class session, Claire had spoken briefly with Professor Dubrovsky—a middle-aged man with a thick Russian accent—letting him assess whether this upstart freshman was ready for his class. She had apparently answered his questions to his satisfaction, for he had signed the registrar's slip without fuss and gestured for her to take a seat.

As the class discussion had progressed that day, Claire had been able to make no sense of what the stern-faced professor personally believed. Looking back, she recalled her vague unease when he let several clearly biased student statements pass without comment or balance from another point of view.

She had also been annoyed when several students referred to the "father/mother God" or the "universal cosmic Christ." Two women in the large class actually referred to the "mother goddess." Claire's fertile imagination had wandered for a moment as she pictured a lightning bolt slashing through the classroom and shooting the women across the room. She had elected not to mention that part of the class to Ms. Tabor-Brown, when her program officer congratulated her on the graduate-level course.

Sitting in class now, Claire tried to push her vague uneasiness aside. Jack DuBois was going over his expectations, reading from some notes in front of him.

"As the TA for your section, I will be the primary interface between you and Misha. I'll give you my home phone number for emergencies, but I prefer that you contact me during my regular office hours. I will grade all your papers and will be the main person assessing your readiness for class, your class participation, and so on."

Jack looked over the top of his glasses at the students. "If you want a good assessment of your class discussions, papers, and tests, I strongly suggest that you abide by Misha's class codes handed out at the first class and always remember that we work from the assumption of an analytical, level playing field for all viewpoints. Going from past experience, that may be a sticking point for some of you."

He looked around at the twenty students arrayed in front of him. "Any questions? Good; then why don't we go around and have each of you briefly state your name and major so that we all know who we are. We're going to get to know each other very well in this little section over the next few months."

There were a lot of religion and philosophy majors. When her turn came, Claire said she was considering biology and history but wasn't sure of her major yet.

Jack had been scribbling notes on his class roster, but looked up swiftly. "You don't know your major yet?"

"Uh, no. I'm a freshman. I've had all the prerequisites in high school or at the community college where I took some classes, so Professor Dubrovsky thought he'd let me try it." For some reason she didn't add that she went to a Christian high school.

Jack nodded and gestured to the next person. When they were all through he picked up the book they'd been assigned, St. Augustine's *Confessions,* then glanced around the circle. "Well, let's begin. Although Augustine is billed as a landmark thinker and the *Confessions* as a groundbreaking book in the Christian religion, in actuality Augustine is simply articulating the existing fourth-century belief structure about Christianity and the Bible. For example, he views the Bible as God's literal 'word' to creation, to be used for guidance on everything from large theological points to minor details of life. This was a common belief system for several centuries, especially among the poor and poorly educated masses, right up until the sixteenth and seventeenth centuries, when scientists began questioning that assumption."

Claire kept her head down as she scribbled notes. For the second time that hour, she began to feel uneasy and unsettled. What was Jack getting at?

He had opened the book. "Okay, let's pin down a few references in the *Confessions* that clearly mirror—rather than transform—a classic fourth-century worldview of the Hebrew Bible." As the students began reaching for their copies of the paperback, he paused and raised one hand.

"Before taking examples let's make sure we're all on the same page for this study. Is there anyone here who believes that the Bible is the inspired word of God?"

Claire looked up and raised her hand. All heads turned her way, and the room grew quiet.

For just a moment Claire felt a strange sense of panic. No other hands were raised, and the looks on the other students' faces ranged from astonishment to pity, as if she'd said she had been kidnapped by a UFO or believed the earth was flat. A few students looked down at their desks. One caught her eye and gave a quick warning shake of his head.

Jack leaned back in his chair. "Well, then." He glanced at the student roster, a small smile playing on his lips. "Um…Claire. Why don't you clarify what you take that to mean, just so that there is no misunderstanding here?"

Claire could feel her face growing hot. "Well, I just think that—well—the Bible is what you said. You know—God's inspired Word to the world."

"Defend that statement."

"What do you mean, 'defend that statement'? Defend my personal beliefs?"

"Yes. This is an analytical class, and any statements of personal belief—especially when they fall outside the norm—must be defended intellectually in order to be considered relevant for class discussion. So, Claire, defend your statement that the Bible is the inspired word of God."

Claire took a deep breath, trying to organize her thoughts. "I just know it is. It's so obvious." She grappled vainly for the apologetics pointers she'd heard in high school. "I mean, the Bible is so relevant to everyday life, how else can you explain it?"

"Try again."

"Look, what do you want me to say? I'm just coming from different assumptions, and I can't defend them from the outside like you want me to. I *start* by believing that it's true and go from there."

"Claire, in this day and age no one can credibly base their theology on the Bible. If that's where you're coming from, you'd better be able to think and discuss your theology systematically." Jack directed his attention to the rest of the class. "Well, let's not take too much time with this discussion. I'm sure we'll work through this issue eventually. In the meantime, let's move on with Augustine's *Confessions.*"

He pointed at a woman in a red ethnic-patterned outfit. "You in the red—um, Molly—please provide for us an example of where St. Augustine lays out a classic fourth-century Christian belief system in his writing."

The class swirled around her as Claire sat still and silent. Humiliated and angry, she tried to act pleasant on the surface. She even screwed up her courage to comment on a point in the *Confessions* that she knew backward and forward. But most of the discussion went right over her reeling head.

At the end of class Jack passed back the short papers the students had written on

Augustine. As he walked around the room distributing the essays, he commented on their merit or lack thereof. "Several of you did not appear to have read Augustine's *Confessions* at all. Your low grades reflect my antipathy toward those who do not do their reading assignments. On the other hand, several of you who *did* do the reading clearly did not read the class codes and were marked way down because of it. Those grades can be pulled up by rewriting your assignment. In general, the first paper of the year is always a bit shaky. If you want to discuss your grade or writing technique, please stop by during office hours."

Jack walked in front of Claire's desk and placed her paper facedown on top of her notebook. He handed out the final two papers, then glanced at his watch. "That's it for today. See you Monday."

Claire stared at the paper in front of her. This would be her first grade of any kind at college, and with the way the day had already gone… She turned the paper over.

A big F was circled in red. Claire's stomach lurched. She began taking short, shallow breaths as she read the TA's red pen comments.

*Writing is rambling rather than concise. Reread* Harbrace College Handbook *for a refresher.*

*Did not properly lay out your thesis, so your support arguments carried little weight.*

*Captured Augustine's mindset well. Good overview was diminished by your unfocused conclusion.*

She hadn't even read the *Harbrace College Handbook*. She wouldn't get to that until the second semester freshman writing class.

*Intrinsic quality of paper was a C–. Downgraded to F for inadherence to class code of "level playing field for all viewpoints."*

Under the TA's last comment Claire noticed a few arrows pointing to red circles around words in her paper. Her eyes followed an arrow to a sentence in her second paragraph: "In keeping with Augustine's personal conversion history, the *Confessions* clearly outlines God's control yet His giving of free will to man."

She read the small handwritten insert and gasped aloud. The word *His* had been circled in red and */Her* added. Her eyes flew down the first page, then the next. Everywhere Claire had referred to God as *He,* Jack had changed it to read *He/She.*

Claire flew out of her seat, catching the TA as he stepped into the hallway. She tried to step squarely in front of him. "You failed me on this paper because I referred to God as *He?*" She held up the offending document, her body tense and quivering.

Jack turned toward her with an air of resignation. "Oh, that was you? Hmm, I hadn't put that together before now. Look, Claire—" Jack set his satchel down and took the paper from her hand—"you consistently used the old paternalistic pronoun for God. We stressed in the first class that we have to provide a level playing field for all viewpoints, and the only way to do that is to recognize that students hold God to be many different things. The class codes clearly state that student papers, in keeping with that standard, have to accommodate the broadest possible terminology."

"First of all, Jack, I wasn't in the first class—"

"Well, we can certainly work out a rewrite."

"And second, that totally goes against the personal convictions of a Bible-believing Christian! How can I refer to God as He/She when Jesus Himself referred to God as 'Father'?"

Jack sighed, as if talking to a slow child. "Claire, you're using the Bible as a standard for theology again. That is totally backward from the analytical approach this class must take."

Claire started to say something, but Jack stopped her.

"Look, if you have a problem with this policy, take it up with Misha. Maybe he interprets his class standards more loosely than I do; I don't know. But until I hear otherwise from him, these are the only rules that will allow for a free-flowing, intellectual debate that is unimpeded by personal bias."

Jack picked up his satchel. "Sorry, Claire." He shrugged his shoulders and walked away down the hall.


Claire gathered her things in a blur and walked toward her dorm and up the stairs to her hallway. Was it possible she had actually *failed* her very first assignment because she didn't—and wouldn't—refer to God as She?

And the way all those students had looked at her… Groaning, she propelled herself into her room and onto her bed. Her face was hot with humiliation and anger, and tears leaked onto her pillows.

What a bunch of jerks! What a condescending, infuriating TA! She was never going to make it here. Her first grade, an F! What would her parents think? What would her peers think? She'd never gotten an F on anything in her life!

Suddenly, her hand flew to her throat. What would the scholarship office do when they heard?

She began to shiver. What was she thinking going to Harvard anyway? She was fooling herself to think she could hack it.

More tears came, and she clutched her comforter like a lifeline. *O God, O Jesus, help me!*


With a mighty cry and a sweep of his sword, Gael knocked a half dozen demons aside. He stepped quickly beside his charge, shielding her with his wings. His tone was urgent as he spoke a single word to her over and over, his words cutting through a dark and malevolent fog.


Claire's anguished mental merry-go-round stopped on one thought: *Pray.* She needed to pray. She started to bow her head, then slipped to her knees, almost whimpering. The second she focused her mind on the Lord, the thoughts rushed in like a wave.

She groaned and put her head in her hands...and suddenly knew a small piece of what had happened. She had made the same exact mistake as before when she committed to the choir without first seeking the Lord.

She began to weep again, rocking back and forth. *God, forgive me! I'm so stupid, so prideful. Why do I keep doing that? Almighty God, protect me from myself! Protect me from my pride!*

She thought of all the trouble she had gone to to get into the class and to impress her scholarship committee. She had also oh-so casually let a bunch of her hallmates know that she was taking a graduate-level course. Her face grew hot with humiliation.

*O God,* the tears came again, *You know me. You know my weaknesses and my pride, my fears and my constant failings. Forgive me, Lord. Give me a direction that I can follow, knowing that it is from You. That's all I want.*

For several long minutes Claire stayed on her knees, pouring out her heart, earnestly praying for direction.

Eventually the turmoil passed, but there was no peace. She sensed no answer from the Lord and glumly rested her forehead on the bed. Why was it that sometimes she felt the Lord so strongly in the midst of turmoil, while other times prayer brought about no change at all?


Behind her, Gael stood close watch, sword out, fiercely shielding her from the demons that still sought an audience. He spoke gently to her. *"Patience, dear one. The Lord loves you so tenderly. You must learn to stand in faith, in the evidence of things not yet seen. He is teaching you. Trust in Him."*

These little ones struggled so hard, so unnecessarily. He put a hand on her shoulder. *"Trust, Claire. He is working even now."*


Claire shook off her melancholy, rose to her feet, and stretched. Maybe she'd feel better after the first meeting of Harvard Christian Fellowship that night. Being with other

Christians might help her feel less off-balance in this crazy environment where up was down and down was up.

"It looks like heaven, doesn't it?"

The voice behind her startled Claire, and she jumped, turning toward a smiling male student with a backpack slung over his arm. He was half in, half out of the doorway that she had inadvertently blocked as she stared at the animated crowd in the room.

"Excuse me?"

"I said, it looks like heaven." He gestured toward the students crowding into the large room. There had to be almost two hundred of them. Many were hugging and slapping backs, greeting old friends after the long summer hiatus. "Uh…let's move out of the doorway, shall we?"

Claire looked over his shoulder and saw several other students waiting to enter. She blushed as she allowed the stranger to guide her into the large classroom "Sorry. I just didn't realize there would be so many people here." She stuck out her hand. "Claire Rivers. Sorry about that."

"No need to apologize. I had much the same reaction myself two years ago. And the group has only grown since then. My name is Brad Jacobson."

Claire found a seat to set her backpack on, and Brad set his stuff beside hers. She nodded toward the crowd. "What did you mean, 'it looks like heaven'?"

"Well, for instance…look at those five girls over there."

He pointed to a far corner, where a group of female students were posing, arms around one another, for another girl holding a camera. One student was white with long, silky blond hair. Another was tall and dark-skinned, wearing clothing that looked African. The girls next to her looked Japanese and Hispanic, and the last one in line was white. A flash went off. The girl holding the camera was black too. Claire watched all six girls cheer and huddle around the tall African, who was displaying a diamond engagement ring.

She turned back to Brad. "I see what you mean."

"Every time I see these brothers and sisters in Christ from all different ethnic groups and Christian traditions, these friends coming together and hugging and greeting one another after a time apart, it reminds me of that great reunion we'll all have someday in heaven." He grinned again, reminding Claire of a little boy. "At least, that's what it makes me think of."

"What a neat thought." Claire cocked her head. "So you're a junior?"

"Yep. I'm an economics and history double major, and I'm from New York. What about you?"

"I'm from Michigan. I'm thinking of history or maybe biology." She sighed, her melancholy returning. "But everything is so up in the air right now. It's hard to know. Some of the classes are—well—different than what I thought."

"How so?"

"Well, I have this advanced religion class, which I thought would be good since I had a lot of training at my Christian high school, but practically the first thing they did was start making fun of anyone who believed in the Bible."

Brad snorted. "Ah…let me guess. Bible Writings and Interpretations?"

"How'd you know?"

"Oh, that one is notorious for beating up on Christians." When Claire's eyes widened, he laughed. "Hey, it's just one of the many examples of how this university values tolerance over truth. Did you know that our motto, *Veritas,* is the Latin word for *Truth?* There's a dynamite speaker scheduled to talk about that in a few weeks." He shook his head, bemused. "It makes you wonder how we backtracked so far. Harvard places so much value on diversity, except when it comes to diversity of belief! People who believe in objective truth have a really tough time here because it's just not accepted in the classroom."

"I had begun to suspect that."

He smiled at her, his eyes gentle. "You know, I've been planning to take that Bible Writings class for a while. Probably next semester, once I've gotten good and prayed up…but not before then."

Claire was silent for a second. When she finally spoke, her voice was low, as if she were talking to herself. "I was thinking maybe I should wait and take it later myself. Even though that might look bad to my scholarship committee."

"It's not my place to suggest this, obviously, but waiting might not be a bad idea. I've seen a lot of Christians get really screwed up by that class and others like it if they take it before they're ready to handle it. Scholarship requirements can seem scary, but remember that God knows your every need."

The memory of the old lady in the elevator rose strong before Claire's eyes. *He knows your every need. Whenever you are faced with a choice, make sure that you trust in God, not in man… Remember, Claire…*

Suddenly, a great weight lifted from her mind. She was flooded with peace and knew what it meant. Teresa had been right. Brad was right. *Thank You, Lord.*

She looked back at her new friend. "You know, Brad, I think you were just an answer to prayer."

## FOURTEEN

IAN REACHED THE END OF THE BLOCK AND SLOWED to a brisk walk, his sides heaving. He squinted at his watch in the early morning sun, clicking off the timer. Six miles in forty-four minutes. Not bad, but he'd done better. He wiped his face on his sleeve. He hadn't run in nearly a week, he'd been so busy since classes started. He'd do better tomorrow.

He reached a quaint old road marker and steadied himself against it as he stretched out his calf and hamstring muscles.

He turned down the next street, admiring the beautiful colonial-style houses. Many abutted the sidewalk, but some of the larger—and older—ones had long sweeping driveways. Trees shaded the streets with colors of red and gold.

The early morning was quiet. Only a few distant sounds from Massachusetts Avenue, many blocks to the east near the campus, penetrated the leafy shield. He loved this old neighborhood; it was why he had chosen to live here rather than on campus. After his daily struggles there, this area always gave him much-needed peace.

He stopped and stretched again, admiring a huge colonial-style house rising well back behind a solid iron gate. He didn't remember seeing that house before. He peered into the property through the wrought-iron pattern near the top of the gate. Graceful flint-stone stairs descended from a shiny black door. A handsome gas lamppost burned weakly against the rising morning.

He noticed a gold plaque on one of the tall brick pillars flanking the driveway. *Grindley House. Hmm.* One of the historic houses that dotted that part of Cambridge, he supposed. Many of them were on the National Register for Historic Sites.

"Can I help you?"

Ian started and whirled around. A wizened face peeked out from behind the gate.

He put his hand on his heart. "Whoa! You startled me." He smiled sheepishly. "Sorry to disturb you. I was just stretching out from a run and admiring your house."

The gate opened slightly, revealing an elderly man in slippers clutching the morning newspaper. He was frail and slightly bent, but his gray eyes twinkled. "You didn't disturb me. I was just getting the paper and saw you inspecting my property. I thought I'd find out if you were friend or foe."

"Definitely friend, sir." Ian extended his hand. "Ian Burke. I'm a student at the law school, and I live just a few streets over. You just happened to be where I ended my morning run, and your beautiful house caught my eye."

The wrinkled face smiled. "An esquire-to-be, eh?" He shook Ian's hand. "I'm Edward Grindley. And young man, if you appreciate the family home, you're definitely not foe."

"Definitely not. But just out of curiosity, sir, what would you have done if I was? You weren't planning to fight off a burglar with just your newspaper?"

The smile widened and Edward pushed open the heavy gate a bit more. "No, that wouldn't have been necessary." He made a clicking noise through his teeth and two Doberman pinschers appeared behind him, their teeth bared.

Ian stepped back a pace. Two fierce pairs of eyes followed him. "Uh…well, yes sir. You'd have been right about that."

"Meshach and Shadrach don't like any visitors that *I* don't like. Normally we don't think so much of Harvard lawyers, but perhaps we'll make an exception for you." He turned to the two dogs and murmured something, snapping his fingers. After one last glare at Ian, they backed away and trotted off. "Feel free to drop by anytime. Maybe someday you'd like to see the house."

"Maybe someday I'll do that, sir. Thank you. Well, I'd better get back to my studies."

"You do that, young man. And may the Lord bless your work." Abruptly, he disappeared behind the gate, which clanged gently shut.

Ian stood staring at the gate, a bemused smile on his face; then he turned and headed for home. *I wonder if he's a Christian?*

Anton Pike smiled to himself as he watched the students board the plane. Although they were probably all tickled pink to be riding in a private Learjet, they looked deliberately casual, as if this were something they did every other week. He had selected them well.

Martin boarded right behind him. He drew his longtime TA aside and gave him some instructions for the cabin crew. There was to be no expense spared on this flight; he wanted the students treated with the utmost luxury. Let them see the considerable fruits that came with loyal labor.

Thirty minutes later the wheels touched down on the small strip at the Nantucket airport. He ushered the students from the plane to the four black Lincoln Towncars waiting out front, dividing up the group for the ride. As always, he watched their every move—from the way they treated the drivers to their comfort level in heading off to an unknown destination. *So far, so good,* he mused. They might be able to take all six this year. And there might still be a few more from other schools.

They made their way across the island, the procession winding among quaint homes with gray boarding and white trim. The gray houses grew larger and more elegant as they turned toward an area on the bluffs, their facades nearly hidden behind high hedges and gates. At the end of a long cul-de-sac lined with sand and sea grass, the cars pulled into a circular driveway in front of a three-story home. Dormer windows peeped out from many angles, and a white-railed widow's walk lined the roof. An immaculate green lawn stretched back to the windswept bluffs beyond the house.

Anton noticed the students smile with delight as they stepped from the cars and took in their surroundings.

"Welcome!"

The students turned to see a tall man who resembled their professor walking up from the side of the house. A large but wiry dog trotted at his side. The man threw a thick stick, and the dog raced after it.

Anton stepped forward and clapped the man on the back, then gestured toward the students. "This is my brother Victor, the CEO of Pike Holdings. Victor, these are some of the student candidates for the Pike Fellowships this year."

He introduced them one by one: Nathan the marketing whiz, Tomoki the Japanese genius with computers, Amy the spreadsheet jock…Sergei…Myron…Donelle… He nodded toward his aide. "And of course, you also know my teaching assistant, Martin."

When all hands had been shaken, Victor smiled at the group and led the way through the front door. "You all are in luck today. Some of my highest-level business managers from all over the world are in town for our semiannual strategy meeting. We are taking a break for a few hours, and you'll get a chance to meet some of them. I hope that will be interesting for you."

They passed through the foyer and into the spacious common area beyond. Oak tables, cream sofas, and overstuffed chairs were scattered about. A two-story wall of windows showcased the view of the bluffs. About twenty men and women rose to their feet when the students entered, broad smiles on their faces.

Late that night the same twenty men and women, along with Anton and Victor, huddled around a conference table in one of the secure lower areas of the house. Old portraits and heavy, oddly patterned wall hangings lined the thick stone walls. Whiteboards sat on easels around the room, each section labeled with a name: Nathan, Tomoki, Amy… On the table in front of them, each of the twenty Fellows had a file laden with extensive background information on each candidate.

As the group assessed the candidates, the important factors were listed below each name. The most important factor of all—one they had to get right—was loyalty. Would the candidate be loyal to the organization and its leaders? Each person there had been put through the same secret screening process when he or she had been a candidate. And with few exceptions, they all had proven their loyalty at the deepest levels. Over the decades, the company had made very few mistakes on recruits. It couldn't afford to.

Anton leaned back in his chair, his eyes glinting as he listened to the discussion. The family had done a remarkable job of setting the stage on campus. He had enjoyed playing his part in the long tradition, and had done it well. It was so easy now, every year, to find a good group of malleable students that they could nurture and mold into their own image.

His eyes flickered to several portraits across the room. He had pored through the old records and knew that his ancestors hadn't always had it so easy. But generations of physical and spiritual effort had been paying off handsomely for a long time now, even if temporary nuisances arose from time to time.

One portrait, weathered and faded, stared its usual challenge, and Anton again silently promised that nuisances were all they would allow. The witch-hunts of earlier times were gradually being replaced by tolerance and peace. Judgmentalism was being swept aside by progress, an inexorable evolution. They were getting close.

Anton took a deep breath. He could feel the welcome forces moving just beyond his sight, feel their guiding presence in this room. He basked in their presence for a moment before returning his attention to the recruiting discussion. As long as the guides helped them find the loyal ones, they were fine.

*BEEP! BEEP! BEEP! BEEP!* SHERRY ROLLED OVER, head foggy. *Beep! Beep! Beep!* She found the offending alarm clock and smacked at the ten-minute snooze button. Below her, she heard Claire rustling around; then silence fell.

*Beep! Beep! Beep!* Sherry slapped at the off switch and summoned up a mighty force of will to avoid going back to sleep. "Claire." She spoke in a low tone. Maybe if Claire wasn't awake—

"What? Huh?"

*Darn.* "You still want to go to church today?"

A pause.

"Yes. Yes, I do. Thank you."

Claire moved around the room, gathering her shower things. She looked up at Sherry's unmoving form. "You coming?"

Sherry forced herself to sit up, squinting at the light pouring through a crack in the curtains. Her head hurt, and her voice was hoarse. "Yeah. I'll be right there."

Claire pulled on her robe and headed toward the girls' shower room down the hall.

Sherry backed slowly down the steps from her loft. She peered at herself in the mirror as she passed. Hmm. She *looked* like someone with an almighty hangover. Not that she was going to admit that to her roommate.

She drank a few glasses of water, then reached for her basket of shower things, stifling her irritation. Stefan or Mercedes could have at least warned her about the kick in those drinks.

Thirty minutes later Sherry and Claire slipped into the back of Memorial Church, the beautifully appointed student–faculty church in New Harvard Yard, not far from their dorm. The carillon began to chime just as they slipped into a crowded pew. Like everyone around them, they remained standing.

As the last notes died away, the choir began to sing. Their voices were beautiful, but Sherry took little notice. It was all in Latin anyway.

When the choir had finished, a man wearing a robe stepped up to the pulpit. His resonant voice rang out over the microphone. "The Lord be with you."

*"And also with you!"*

Sherry started at the congregation's loud response. She glanced sideways at Claire and was relieved to see her flipping hastily through the church bulletin. At least she didn't know the liturgy either.

"Lift up your hearts."

*"We lift them up to the Lord."*

"Let us give thanks to the Lord our God."

*"It is right to give Him thanks and praise."*

As the man in the pulpit began a prayer, Sherry looked at the bowed heads around her. The couple next to her had lowered their heads but didn't seem to be praying. In fact, most people in the congregation looked as if they were simply waiting for the leader's prayer to be over so they could sit down.

Precisely one hour later the choir sang a benediction, and the congregation trooped out into the crisp air of New Harvard Yard. Claire and Sherry emerged with the pack. They walked out alone, not having recognized anyone.

They walked a ways down the path without speaking. After a moment, Claire spoke. "So, what did you think?"

"Well, it's a beautiful church."

"That it is."

"And the choir was amazing. But I didn't...I don't know...really *get* much from the service itself."

Claire gave an inward sigh of relief. *Thank You, God.* "I know what you mean." She started to elaborate, but a still small voice kept her quiet. *Let Sherry talk.*

"You know how I mentioned the church my parents went to in Georgia? Well, it reminded me of that. All beautiful on the outside, but nothing much on the inside." Suddenly she giggled. "And I couldn't follow the liturgy at *all!* I never knew what page we were supposed to be on!"

"That wasn't the main issue though, was it?" Claire asked. "I mean, you'll learn the worship style of whatever church you go to. And I've been to several churches with formal liturgies that I loved."

"No. You're right. It wasn't the formality. It was...look, I don't have as much experience with church stuff as you, but I know there has to be *more* than what we heard in there."

"Was it just that a guest pastor was preaching? The regular pastor is supposed to be pretty good."

Sherry pondered that. "I don't think that's it. Did you notice that the preacher never once used the name *Jesus* in his prayers or sermon? I mean, Jesus is the point of the whole thing, don't you think?"

Despite herself, Claire broke up laughing at the childlike expression on Sherry's face. "Yes, I would say Jesus is the point of the whole thing."

"Oh, *I* know how to describe it!" Sherry suddenly snapped her fingers. "You know that old quote 'There was no *there,* there'? That's what I felt like."

"Gertrude Stein."

"Pardon me?"

"Gertrude Stein. Famous author—nineteenth-century graduate of this very school. That's who said 'There was no *there,* there.'"

Sherry pushed her away in playful disgust. "How do you know these things?"

Claire grinned and hooked her arm through her roommate's, steering her toward the dining hall. "What would you say to helping each other stay accountable here?"

"You used that word before. What do you mean exactly?"

"I mean, just—well—agreeing that we'll hold each other to acting like Christians should. That we'll ensure that the other gets up for church on Sunday or that we'll confront each other if we see things that look wrong. You know, like if you see me suddenly wanting to shack up with some guy, you'd better hit me over the head with a two-by-four!"

"Gladly. I've always wielded a mean piece of lumber." She pulled her arm from Claire's and mimicked swinging a baseball bat. "So what would be involved in this accountability thing, seriously? Like we'd report in to each other every day?"

"No, nothing like that! We would just sit down and list out the things that we think are important enough to hold each other to a high standard on—like doing a daily quiet time or living a Christian lifestyle. And then we'd just bring it up if we see the other person slipping. I for one *need* to know that someone is going to call me to task if I slip up—it'll make me less likely to cross that line."

Sherry didn't say anything, just continued walking.

*O God, help her not get defensive. Lord, help me know how to be the friend she needs. I know she wasn't all that excited about going to church this morning. Please place that desire in her heart. Draw her heart to You!*

"What would you say to discussing this over lunch at the beautiful Annenberg Dining Hall?" Claire asked. "Maybe we can say grace over our meal and startle some other poor spiritually deprived student into thinking there's something wrong with the food."

Sherry grinned, her expression lightening. Then she grew serious. "Let's do it." She stopped walking and turned toward her roommate. "I mean it. Let's do that accountability thing. That would be good for me." She started along the path again, her voice light. "And then next week maybe we can find a church where there is some *there,* there."

For just a moment Claire couldn't respond through the tears that sprang to her eyes.

Gael saluted his colleague, and Caliel leaped into the air. His wings became a blur as he left New Harvard Yard and the two girls far below. Boston, then Massachusetts, faded behind him as he sped like a comet toward his destination.

He entered a small town, flying at a moderate pace, taking stock of his surroundings. People were pouring out of church doors and into parking lots. Televisions were tuned to football games, and pillows plumped up for a good nap. A typical Sunday afternoon in Georgia.

Several shining warriors atop a redbrick church waved as he flashed by. The roof of another little church held only dark beings with hate-filled eyes. They hissed at his passing. Caliel read the signboard out front. Today's Topic: Find Your Personal Truth. He shook his head, wondering why the church bothered to keep the cross primly atop the peak of the building.

He descended into a neighborhood of stately homes, eyes flickering in every direction, and found one particular house on a corner lot. Graceful oak trees cast mottled shadows on an artfully landscaped lawn. Caliel could hear the sounds of a meal being served around back.

Caliel headed toward the deck at the back of the house. He cut through the parlor, carefully avoiding several other rooms. He knew the den was lined with souvenirs from business trips to India, statues of many-armed Hindu gods featured prominently in a backlit hutch. Caliel had had several previous run-ins with the occupants of those statues.

He could hear a computer game being played in the study next to the den, the sounds of electronically generated shots, screams, and evil laughter surrounding that part of the house like a fog. Caliel sighed, forming a mental picture of the teenage boy who would be seated at the controls. Several of the demons residing in that game would be out into the room by now, enjoying the sight of their own pictures flashing by on the screen from time to time.

Caliel was careful not to reveal himself as he slipped by those rooms. Hovering at ceiling level, he entered the kitchen. A slim, elegant woman was conveying the final dishes out to the deck, where the rest of the family waited at a long table. A grandmother in a lace collar and pearls sat primly on one side, with two other children, an aunt, and an uncle on the other. Only two chairs were unoccupied.

The woman settled into her seat. "Why don't we say grace? It is Sunday, after all." The others at the table nodded.

A heavyset man at the other end of the table put down the roll he was already chewing on. Turning his head, he hollered through the kitchen. "Trevor! Get in here *right now.*"

A long moment later a sullen teenager shuffled into view, his shirt untucked, baggy pants looking like they'd been slept in.

"Yeah, I'm coming. Keep your shirt on."

The man looked furious but was quelled by a glance from his wife.


Three demons within and around the teenager's body started when they saw Caliel standing quietly behind the woman.

"What are *you* doing here?" one seethed.

Caliel stayed where he was and didn't answer.

The smallest demon jumped on the table and minced his way over to the heavyset man. He poked him in the chest. *"Are you going to take that from your son? He's disrespecting you in front of the whole family! Be a man and stand up to the boy!"*


As the teenager shuffled by, the man rose to his feet. He cuffed his son on the side of the head. "You live under my roof, you'll pay me proper respect. Got it?" He took his son's arm and tried to push him into his seat. The others at the table looked bored, as if they'd seen it all before.

The teenager twisted his arm out of his father's grasp, his hands balling into fists.


*"Yeah, hit him!"* The demons turned now to their host. *"Do it. You don't have to take that from the old man!"* One dark form stepped even with the boy and seemed to dissolve within him. The other demons turned to Caliel, triumphant looks on their faces, and stepped one by one inside the teenage body.

A crazed look appeared on the boy's face, and Caliel could see the unearthly hatred in his eyes. Uh-oh. This had changed in the last few weeks. The angel stepped forward to the woman, prodding her.


As the boy raised his fist, the woman jumped up and grabbed his arm. She started a bit as he angrily swung around to face her, but she spoke sternly enough. "Trevor, now stop it." She turned to her husband. "You too, Stanley. This is getting ridiculous. It's the Lord's day."

Trevor seethed but quieted. He took his seat, slamming his chair forward. His mother settled back down and gestured for the family to hold hands.

"Oh, not grace again!" The words blurted from Trevor's mouth. "C'mon, Mom, it's stupid."

"It's the Lord's day: We give thanks. You know that, Trevor. Now come on." She grabbed the hands of those next to her, and Trevor reluctantly did the same.

She bowed her head. "Lord, we thank You for this food that we are about to receive...."

Caliel leaned forward, his voice dropping to an urgent whisper as he spoke the same words over and over to the woman's mind. *Sherry, Sherry. Your daughter. Pray!*

"...and for this beautiful day, and for family and friends." She lost her train of thought for a moment then resumed her weekly prayer, the words coming by rote. "Bless all of us, in Jesus' name, amen."

"Amen."

Caliel could feel the tide advancing. The door was closing on this family as a possible spiritual support for his charge.

The world of the shadowlands seemed to recede, the world of the spirit becoming more distinct. The family appeared to move in slow motion, passing the silver dishes of turkey, stuffing, and fruit. Only the dark beings within the troubled son were clearly visible, taunting and mocking their foe.

Caliel raised his arms toward heaven, his wings outstretched, shining brightly.

"Lord, there are those in this family who have a simple understanding of You, although they do not understand their need to commit to a relationship with You. O God, I pray that Your grace and mercy would be sufficient for their lack. Keep reaching out to them with Your loving arms."

He felt the desperately tender love of the Lord for these lost souls wash over him and continued to pray that they would turn and receive it while there was still time.

## SIXTEEN

"SO WHAT CLASSES *DID* YOUR FRIENDS TELL YOU TO TAKE?" Claire had spotted Teresa studying at a carrel in Widener Library and walked over, deciding to take the bull by the horns.

Teresa looked up, eyes wide, then smiled. "Hey. You startled me." She cocked her head. "What did you say?"

"I decided to drop the advanced religion class I was telling you about on Friday."

"All right!" Teresa gave her a high five, which Claire, bemused, returned. "This is going to sound funny, but, well…I was praying for you that night, and I felt really spiritually agitated about your class. I didn't know why." She grinned. "But after your reaction to my caution on Friday, I figured I wasn't going to bring *that* up."

"I know, I know. I'm really sorry I got so irritated at lunch. I don't know why. You were totally right."

"Claire, honestly, it's okay." Teresa hooked a nearby chair with her foot and pulled it up to the carrel, gesturing for Claire to sit down. "What was it that you asked me when you walked up?"

"Oh…well, before class tomorrow I somehow need to find another class to make my five, since I'm dropping religion. And since I'll have missed three class sessions, I'm really at a loss as to what course won't leave me hopelessly behind." Claire sighed, feeling rudderless. "On Friday you said something about your alumni friends who went here, who warned you to stay *away* from the religion classes. Did they ever steer you *toward* any other classes?"

"Um…yeah. Do you have a class catalog?" She took the booklet Claire offered her. "It seems to me that you have two choices—to take a class that has content you're already fairly familiar with, or to take a class that doesn't look that hard."

Teresa flipped through the catalog pointing out various options. In the end it came down to two choices: a marketing class or a philosophy/ethics class listing many readings by authors Claire already knew. Both had been recommended by one of Teresa's friends, and both were taught on Monday, Wednesday, and Friday afternoons.

Claire doubted her ability to catch up in the completely new subject of business. After her religion debacle she was a little hesitant to brave the class discussions in philosophy, but finally decided it was probably the best option. She would go by and talk to the professor on Monday morning.

She thanked Teresa and left her to her studies, thankful for her new friend. Why had she ever doubted Teresa's reaction?

*Lord, forgive me. You know what I need even before I ask. Why are You so good to me?*

In a corner nearby, six angels watched Claire as she moved through the stacks, looking for a book and quietly singing a praise song to herself. They closed their eyes and raised their hands, giving thanks to the King of kings for His working in Claire's life.

A high-ranking angel walked up, gently smiling as he looked upon the girl. She had found the book she was looking for and had taken a seat at a study carrel, spreading out her papers before her.

The angel clasped arms with each of his comrades. "Well met, my friends."

"Well met, Kai."

Kai stepped forward and laid a hand on Claire's shoulder. His wings stretched, forming a glistening canopy over her head. He lifted his face to the sky. "Our Master and King, thank You for what You are doing in this girl's life. Strengthen us to watch over her. Strengthen her parents and friends to pray without ceasing, that Your will may be done."

Kai dropped his hand and turned to the others. "So it has begun. She has usually made the right choices, and God's grace has been sufficient in those where she has erred."

"Gael, Etàn, and Metras—" he selected the three angels—"tomorrow, you must ensure her admittance to the philosophy class."

Gael inclined his head. "We received that order, but were curious how it fit into the plan."

"The Lord intends to use that class for many purposes. Primarily it will be her learning ground, her place of testing. And her place of growth, if she cleaves to the Lord." He turned to the fourth angel. "Caliel, my friend, the Lord is pleased with Sherry's progress. But the enemy now circles like a roaring lion. He is anxious to devour both of these young women. Both have provided him with an open door, but Claire's heart is soft. She has repented and been forgiven. Sherry is still leaving the door open."

Caliel's face was drawn with concern. "She is not covered in prayer, Kai. There is no one praying for her—"

"Except Claire."

"Yes, except Claire."

"See that she is stirred to intercede more. And stir others where you can." Caliel nodded. "Claire is already stepping into a praying community, where she can be protected and nurtured. Sherry must come in as well. But it will be her choice. The Lord is knocking; she must answer. And then—she must choose to obey."

Kai turned to an angel who had been standing quietly to the side, observing. Kai inclined his head in deep respect, giving him the floor. "General Petras, are the other pieces of this plan in place?"

"They are. It will be accelerating very soon. You all have your orders."

"We do, General, and we stand ready." Kai's gaze returned to Claire's bent head. He smiled, feeling the love of the Lord for this chosen one. "Now she must be ready."


*Whack!* The computer monitor quivered from the blow as Ian stood by his desk, muttering. "I'm gonna kill this stupid thing!"

The screen was frozen, a document halfway loaded on the screen. Three times in twenty minutes. Unbelievable! He checked his watch, annoyance changing to agitation. Mansfield would be at the restaurant any minute now. Why on earth did this always happen when he was in a hurry?

Ian punched the power button twice, waiting with impatience as the computer went through an infuriatingly slow reboot. He glared out the window of his apartment located on the second floor of a beautiful old house and drummed his fingers against his leg.

For the last few days of working on this project deadline, it seemed as if his computer, printer, or fax were constantly out of sorts. And always at the worst times, too...

Ian smacked his forehead. Of course! It made perfect sense.

Feeling a bit foolish, he tentatively placed his hand on the monitor. "In the name of Jesus, if there are any...uh...evil forces working here, I command you to stop your interference and go!"

His voice grew more assured. "This room and this project are covered by the blood of the Lamb, and you have no place here. Demons, I command you to leave by the authority of Jesus Christ." He paused. "Lord God, I ask for Your protection over this project and ask that the enemy's eyes would be blinded. In Jesus' mighty name, amen."


Four gremlins shot through the walls of Ian's second-floor apartment writhing in pain. They sped away, hands clapped over their ears, trying to get away from that *Name*. The glowing sword of a member of the heavenly host helped ensure their haste.

A few minutes later, Ian ran down the outside stairs that gave access to his apartment, stuffing a sheaf of papers in his backpack. He hopped on his bicycle and sped away.

An hour later, at a Porter Square restaurant a mile from campus, Ian and Mansfield sat in close conversation. Notebooks, papers, and textbooks were laid out on the table. They had been careful to schedule this meeting after the lunch rush, when they would be able to choose a secluded, high-sided booth. For certain strategy sessions both preferred this place to Mansfield's office.

A warrior stood guard on the roof of the restaurant, his contingent of angels hidden but available at a moment's notice. The enemy would have no access to this meeting.

Mansfield scanned the clipboard in front of him. "Which one's next?"

"Um…mathematics. There's probably not much there."

"Probably not, but check the notes just in case."

Ian sipped his lemonade, his eyes flickering between several notebooks and lists. "I think we're clear."

Mansfield made a note on his clipboard. "Philosophy next?"

"Might as well mark every class." He saw Mansfield's stern look and raised his hands defensively. "I'm just saying…"

"If we're going to have any chance at this, we need to be as fair as possible in our report. Just because someone else is not being fair-minded doesn't give us an excuse. Besides, credibility is a hard enough issue without us compounding the problem by overdoing it." Mansfield tapped on a thick sheaf of computer paper covered with print. "Let's just go through class by class."

At his left hand, Ian set a list of classes slated for the next school year. At his right, between him and his mentor, sat the thick sheaf. The four hundred pages of notes and reports were the result of nearly two years of work by a small committee of professors, students, and graduate TAs such as himself. The cover page read "Initial Report of the Committee on Ideological Diversity, Harvard University" and was dated just two weeks before the start of classes.

Ian flipped through both the draft catalog and the report until he came to philosophy. Both sections were long. *Advanced Philosophical Debate…Existential Thought…Philosophy of Ethics…*

"Okay: Advanced Philosophical Debate. Professor Janssen." Ian set the course description in front of his mentor. "The readings look fairly neutral, but—" he flipped open the thick report—"it scored just three out of ten. Nearly all respondents cited specific instances where the professor's ground rules or class discussions actively worked against those with opinions based on objective truth."

Mansfield jotted a few notes as Ian continued his briefing. "See here? Last fall this girl's class was told that 'religious convictions' were not appropriate grounds for philosophical debate. Janssen said they had to come up with some other philosophical structure for debating, for example, which actions were right and which were wrong."

Mansfield frowned but didn't look up from his clipboard. "Well, that's a common enough point: You can't just say, 'Well, the Bible says so,' and expect to win an advanced debate. You need to back it up analytically—"

"Obviously, yes. But this was more the standard problem of there not being a level playing field for different ideologies. Janssen disallowed 'religious convictions,' but these four students describe several times where class debate drew on Buddhist, Humanist, or New Age philosophy in making a point. Only comments based on Judeo-Christian scriptures were disallowed. Obviously, Humanist philosophy involves just as much religious belief as anything else. Although Humanists usually don't think so!"

Ian flipped a page over. "And see this segment where the class debated hot topics like abortion? The syllabus materials the professor picked were all ones that steered the debate into prochoice rather than neutral terms from the outset—the classic case of defining the terms, thus controlling the debate."

Mansfield took the pages from Ian's hand and scanned them. "Hmm, yes." He used a highlighter to mark off a few passages. "Okay, there are some good objective criteria here. Mark this page for copying, and put it in my briefing book. And put the syllabus materials on my list; there are probably a half-dozen classes in philosophy and psychology and sociology that use those same materials rather than more neutral ones when they get to the abortion debate. Let's find those. That's a glaring case of philosophical inconsistency that needs to be addressed.

"And also," Mansfield pursed his lips, tapping the highlighter rapidly against the table, "find me several fair-minded examples of where a class subject may have tended to lean one direction, but where the professor himself was fair-minded and objective about purposefully *eliminating* bias of any kind. I know there are plenty like that. If we give credit where credit is due, they'll be more likely to take our criticisms seriously."

"Good point." Ian made a note, then turned to the next course on the list.

The sky began to darken, and the streetlights had come on before the two men were ready to call it a day. The restaurant was beginning to fill up again as they gathered their papers and books. Their server—a business school student they recognized from the Graduate Christian Fellowship meetings—came by to clear off the table.

They thanked her profusely, and she accepted Mansfield's customary large tip with a smile. She didn't know what their project was, but she was always willing to allow them to sit at that booth for hours, keep her mouth shut about anything she overheard, and seat other patrons out of hearing distance if she could. To them, she was worth her weight in gold.

Ian rode away through the dusky streets smiling to himself. Just a few more weeks. They were almost ready. He couldn't wait to see Professor Anton Pike's reaction.

# SEVENTEEN

"NO, I'M SORRY. I TOLD YOU." The receptionist on the third floor of Emerson heaved an exaggerated sigh and pushed her reading glasses atop her head. It was barely nine-fifteen on Monday morning, and the week was already starting out lousy. This was the fourth student through her doors this morning asking the same stupid question.

The young man in front of her started to say something, and she held up her hand. "Professor Kwong's Philosophy of Ethics class has been full since the first day of registration. I'm sure you know that it's one of the most popular classes."

The student broke in, smiling at her. "Yes, I understand that. What I'm wondering is, would he be willing to at least put me on a waiting list in case someone drops the class?"

"Sorry. The professor doesn't do waiting lists."

"Well, could I at least call back in—"

"Look, young man. I'm sure no one is going to drop this class." She turned back to her computer. "I know you're probably used to getting your own way, but you'll just have to take no for an answer this time."

She shook her head as the student dropped the pleasant facade and stormed out. How rude young people were these days!

Just outside the building, two warriors flashed signals to each other across Harvard Yard. Etàn followed a tall male student who was steering a blue bicycle off of Massachusetts Avenue and through Johnston Gate. Metras tracked with a young woman who was just leaving her dorm, bundled up in a fluffy red scarf against the blustery morning. Both were heading toward Emerson.

Etàn grabbed up a good-sized tree branch and skated it across the path like a stone across a lake. It skidded against the bicycle, entangling itself in the back tires.

The student uttered a short sound of frustration and hopped off his bike to clear away the debris. This was his second delay of the morning.

The angel quickly rose above the trees and scanned another section of campus. Where *were* they?

A hundred yards away the other student hurried along the walkway, her red scarf pressed against her nose. Metras moved in front of her, subtly clearing her a path, speeding her along. A movement caught his eye. Uh-oh.

Another female student was coming the other direction on a nearby walkway and saw her friend in the red scarf. She slowed a bit and called good morning, trying to catch the girl's attention, wanting to stop and chat.

Metras held up a shimmering wing. The bundled-up girl walked right past, never seeing her friend.

He continued to move her swiftly along, casting glances back at his comrade. The timing was going to be tight, and Gael wasn't in sight yet.


A few minutes later, red-scarf was inside Emerson and heading up to the third floor. The bicycle student had seen a female friend coming his way and had detoured to flirt with her. The two colleagues were starting to get nervous when Gael finally swooped up.

"We're moving. It'll be less than five minutes."

"What took so long?" Etàn kept a wary eye on his charge as Metras watched red-scarf's progress through the building walls.

"She stopped to get breakfast in the cafeteria after biology class. I tried to stir her, but one of our adversaries got her chatting with a young man in line." He smiled gently. "She wasn't listening very well. But thankfully she's coming now."

"Five minutes." Etàn started to turn back to the male student, then stopped. "Gael, my friend, do you think our adversaries know of the plan?"

"No, I don't think so. Just making mischief as usual. That was one of the holdups; I couldn't look too eager, or we would have been followed."

The other angels nodded knowingly as they went their separate ways. Such machinations were all too common.


On the third floor of Emerson, the receptionist watched another student come in and groaned to herself.

The girl unwrapped several layers of red scarf from around her neck and smiled at her. "It's cold outside!"

The receptionist kept typing and didn't respond. The girl approached her counter.

"I'm sorry to bother you. Is this Professor Kwong's department? I need to drop his Philosophy of Ethics class."

The receptionist looked up in surprise. "Certainly. Fill this out." She passed a form over the counter, smiling inwardly. That rude young man had been five minutes too early. Whoever walked in next would win the lottery.


Outside, Etàn saw Gael approaching at treetop level, his eyes on Claire. She was only a few feet from Emerson when the bicycle student waved good-bye to his friend and ped-aled the last short distance to the bike rack in front of the building. He hopped off his bike and pulled a locking chain partially out of his backpack.

Etàn sped over and tapped on the backpack. It slipped out of the student's hands and fell to the ground.

The student reached down, grabbed the bike chain, and started to wrap it around the bike rack and his front tire.

Etàn pulled out his sword. He flipped the links this way and that way; everywhere but where the student wanted them to go. The chain got tangled, and the student's hands got cold as he tried to extricate the links and start over again. He poked his thumb on a sharp edge and started muttering to himself.

The student took a deep breath, trying to calm down. This had been one incredibly frustrating morning. He glanced at his watch, irritated. At this rate, he would barely have time to add the stupid philosophy course before he had to make his first class of the day.


Gael spoke forcefully to Claire, and she sped up a little, quickly reaching the heavy doors. She paused at the base of a stairway, trying to remember what office to go to, and reached for the zipper on her backpack.

*No time!* Gael put a large hand on her back, pushing her toward the stairs. *Third floor, suite 300. Hurry.*

She released the zipper and began bounding up the stairs, suddenly remembering.


Outside, the bicycle student had succeeded in wrapping his chain where he wanted it and was fumbling through his backpack for the lock. Where *was* that stupid thing? He could hear it clanking, but the papers and books in his backpack kept shifting and hiding it.

He set his backpack on the bicycle seat and jerked open the zippers on both sides, opening it all the way. He steadied the books and papers so they didn't fall out, looking in every corner. Where was that lock? Did he somehow not put it in the backpack this morning? *Great, just great.*

Slamming the pack down, he finally noticed a glint of steel by his foot. How'd it get down there? He grabbed the lock and snapped it onto the chain.


Gael, hovering at the third-floor level, looked down until he saw Etàn's final signal. Gael nodded and ducked back inside the building's walls. He was just in time to see the red-scarfed girl leave the office and walk away down the hall. He clapped Metras on the back in thanks.

A moment later, they both smiled in relief as they heard soft footsteps on the stairs behind them.


Claire reached suite 300 and pushed open the door. She was out of breath from climbing the stairs so quickly. Why was she in such a hurry, anyway?

A bell clanged quietly, and she approached the counter that separated the entrance area from the offices of the department. A stern-looking woman was typing busily on a computer. Claire noticed her glance at a nearby clock.

"Grand Central Station, can I help you?" She spoke without looking up.

Claire looked around. Was she talking to her? "Excuse me?"

The receptionist turned and faced her. "It's been a busy morning. Let me guess. You're here to try to add Professors Kwong's Philosophy of Ethics class."

"Uh…yes. Is that a problem?" *O God, not after everything else. Please!*

"I've had four other students in here in the last half hour with the same question. I've had to tell every single one of them the same thing: The class has been completely full since day one. It's one of the most popular classes on campus."

"Oh no." Claire found herself close to tears. She looked down at her feet, trying to maintain her composure.

"But you appear to be in luck, young lady. Another student came in here not one minute ago and dropped the class. So there is now room for you." She abruptly handed a short form across the counter. "Fill this out, and you're all set."

Claire filled in the required spaces and handed it back, a wide grin breaking out on her face. "Thank you, ma'am! Thank you so much."

The stern-faced woman nodded briefly.

Behind Claire a bell tingled and she turned. A tall male student walked in. He looked over Claire's shoulder to the receptionist.

"Is this where I go to add Professor Kwong's class?"

"Philosophy of Ethics?"

"Yes."

"I'm sorry, young man. That course is full. The last space was just taken a few minutes ago." She didn't look at Claire.

"Well, that figures. It took me forever to get here and find this room. I must've walked by it twice without seeing it." He shrugged, pulling the door open again. "Oh well. That's the breaks."

The receptionist looked at Claire as the student departed. A semblance of a smile appeared on the austere face.

"I must say, this has been an unusual morning. The fates have been kind to you today. You must have been born under a lucky star."

# EIGHTEEN

CLUTCHING HER ADD SLIP, CLAIRE TOOK A DEEP BREATH and slipped into the philosophy classroom. She felt awkward. The class was fairly small—just thirty students—and they had been getting to know each other for the last week.

"Claire?" A stylishly dressed blond girl approached. Claire recognized her with a start.

"Jo? Right?" When Jo nodded, Claire let out a sigh of relief. "I'm just adding the class, and I'm glad to see that I know *somebody* here."

Jo smiled and gestured toward her row. "There's room over here. C'mon."

While Claire settled into her seat, Jo asked, "Do you have a syllabus? Want to know where we are?"

"I'd love a thirty-second overview."

"Easy." Jo scanned her notes from the first three classes. "Well, much of the course is about the foundations for moral behavior in society. You know, what is right and what is wrong and how do you decide which is which—that kind of thing. Last week we read from a few different philosophers—Descartes, the Bible, St. Augustine, a few others. We read a few things from John Stuart Mill over the weekend since we're talking about utilitarianism today."

Five minutes later Claire listened to Professor Kwong's introduction of the day's topic. "The philosophy of utilitarianism," the professor said, writing on the board, "proposes that the test of right or wrong is what will maximize pleasure for the greatest number of people."

Professor Kwong turned back to the class. He was a handsome man, his dark hair peppered here and there with streaks of silver. "Now, before we dive into the utilitarian perspective, let's review the definition of philosophy so we can ensure that we fit this discussion into the philosophy paradigm. Can anyone summarize the widely accepted definition?"

A guy in the second row, wearing slouchy khakis and shaggy sideburns, made a slight motion with his hand. Professor Kwong nodded. "Karl."

The student read from his notebook, scarcely looking up. "The philosophical method, as defined by Plato and Aristotle, is the 'pursuit of truth through reason.'"

"Exactly. As we said previously, the three principles of philosophy are—" he ticked the items off on his fingers—"A—beliefs cannot be contradictory; B—beliefs must be based on appropriate reasons; and C—a philosopher ought to arrive at the view based on the best reasons. Therefore, in our discussions you must both give your reasons for your beliefs and critically evaluate the reasons that others give for their beliefs."

Claire's thoughts flickered to her biology professor. Too bad she'd never taken philosophy.

Professor Kwong was leaning on the podium, his face intent. "Philosophy is part science part art. It is a common view that science is absolute, but it is not. It is changing all the time. Philosophy is the same—we have to be open to change if someone presents a better reason for truth.

"So now we turn to our first philosophy, utilitarianism, which holds that morality arises from satisfying the most preferences and avoiding the most pain for the most people. Can anyone tell me the genesis of this philosophy?"

A female student in the back raised her hand. "It started in the 1800s in England, with John Stuart Mill and a couple of other philosophers. You had us read those sections from Mill's book *The Subjection of Women.*" She flipped through some papers in front of her. "He said that a prime example of something that *didn't* maximize the greatest happiness for the greatest number of people was the legal subordination of women. So utilitarianism proposed that a 'principle of perfect equality' be instituted instead."

Professor Kwong nodded. "Good, Alicia, good. Okay. So for utilitarians an act is morally right if it leads to the best outcome—as defined by the most happiness for the most people. Mill felt that the emancipation of women would maximize happiness and was therefore morally right. Can anyone tell me how this view of morality differs from some of the philosophies we studied last week—for example, the Ten Commandments? Brad?"

"Well, the Ten Commandments and the Bible say that certain principles must be followed because they are objectively right and true."

As the student started speaking, Claire recognized the voice and craned her neck to see across the room.

*Brad Jacobson! From Christian Fellowship? He's in this class?*

"'Objectively right' meaning...?"

"Meaning that right and wrong were created by God and exist independent of whether they have this or that effect. Something just *is* or *is not* true. Utilitarians focus solely on the results; the Bible focuses on the principles before talking about the results."

Jo raised her hand and got Kwong's nod. "Utilitarians thought biblical philosophies placed too much emphasis on rules. They wanted to help people get out from under that kind of repressive society—which was one reason women were subjugated to begin with—and to allow people to do whatever would have the best results.

Clearly, that philosophy is much more flexible and allows laws and governments to change as times change."

She looked across the room at Brad. "Following certain strict rules may work for *you* morally and that's fine. Whatever works for you. But I think most people these days don't need that. Besides, how can you impose your religiously based standards on a society where some people disagree with you? It's far better to look at things on a case by case basis. What might be right one time could be wrong the next time. Why should you lock yourself into saying something is always right or always wrong?"

Another student chimed in. "Besides, the Ten Commandments are so archaic, who can figure them out? And—let's be honest—who'd really want to? Like I'm really going to covet my neighbor's oxen or whatever anyway!"

The classroom broke up in laughter as the student scratched himself like a country bumpkin, a goofy smile on his face.

Claire's face grew hot as she looked over at Brad. He seemed unaffected by the derision.

The professor shook his head, smiling. "Okay, Tim, thank you for your fine impersonation of Jethro Bodine." More laughter rippled across the room as he called on another student.

"Actually, in my economics class last week, the professor mentioned this. He said the common cost/benefit analysis that's used to make economic decisions was actually derived from utilitarian philosophy. For example, to decide whether to dam up a recreational river in order to generate power, an economist will try to attach a cost or a benefit to each outcome. What's the numerical benefit for the population in leaving the river open for fishing and boating versus having more electricity for their city? That's all derived from this philosophy apparently."

Claire kept her head down, furiously taking notes. So many opinions! Her mind was racing. How was she ever going to get an organized opinion out of her mouth? Page after page filled up in her notebook as she tried to keep up with the discussion. Page after page of reasons why utilitarianism was a solid foundation for moral decision making. There was something about the utilitarian philosophy that didn't sound right, but what on earth was it? She couldn't even catch her breath and think coherently, couldn't formulate any kind of counterargument.

Her attention was jerked back by the professor's next question.

"…was a good overview of the benefits of utilitarianism. Now, what are the holes in the philosophy? Are there any?" He paused, looking around. "Come, come. You can't just blindly accept any philosophy without acknowledging both its positives and negatives. Find some holes! How do we *disagree* that it helps us make good moral decisions?"

*Well, obviously, it has no reference to what God says is right or wrong! How can you even think of morality outside of God?* Claire's train of thought was stopped in its tracks as she saw the professor scanning the crowd, looking for someone to call on. He was looking in her direction. She lowered her head and pretended to be writing in her notebook.

"Let's try…Brad. Why don't you take a crack at this. Give us an example where utilitarian philosophy may *not* determine what is right or wrong."

Claire craned her neck. Brad was turning his pen over and over in both hands, thinking.

"Well, there seem to be a couple of obvious holes in the philosophy. It's fine as far as it goes—it may be a useful exercise to help make some decisions—but as for determining what is ultimately morally right, it doesn't seem to cut it.

"First of all, at the most basic level, how can you even have the *idea* of the 'most good for the most people' without some objective external standard of what *good* is? From a faith-based point of view, the answer is clearly what God says is good, but utilitarianism doesn't acknowledge that and so basically disproves itself.

"Utilitarianism says that the most pleasure for the most people somehow creates moral rightness. But what if what is clearly morally right goes against what the majority wants? For example…well, look at slavery. White people were the majority in America, and they decided that having slaves made them happy. According to utilitarians the happiness of the minority—the slaves—wouldn't be enough to counter the majority view. But slavery was still clearly, morally *wrong.*"

The room was silent for a moment, and Claire grinned to herself. *Great argument!*

Professor Kwong nodded. "Good example. So let's look at two counterarguments. The subjugation of women—a clear moral wrong—was countermanded by utilitarianism. But the subjugation of African slaves in America would not be. How do we reconcile those two opposites?"

Brad spoke up again. "Well, utilitarians used their philosophy to propose that women be made equal with men. *However,* society could've come to that decision just as easily using the Bible's standard of objective truth—which is, after all, what the abolitionist leaders drew on to justify their defiance of slavery—like Phillips Brooks, the famous pastor, and Harvard Overseer, who fought for the rights of slaves."

Claire heard Jo mutter to herself, "I thought the Bible actively *justified* slavery."

Brad was continuing. "The Bible's standard of right and wrong clearly says, for example, to 'love your neighbor as yourself.' And since no one presumably wants to be a slave, loving your neighbor as yourself means setting him free. It also says to 'look out not only for your own interests, but also for the interests of others' and that 'there is neither Jew nor Greek, slave nor free, male nor female, for you are all one in Christ Jesus.'"

"It *says* that? In the Bible?" Jo blurted out the question, astonished.

"Yes, it says that. The last Scripture was—um—Galatians 3:28."

Claire was surprised to see Jo jot the Scripture reference down. "But what about all the Bible stuff about keeping women as second-class citizens? How does that jibe with those passages?"

"Actually, the Bible says nowhere that women are to be treated as second-class citizens. The subjugation of women was much more the tradition of the culture than anything codified as morally right in the Bible. In fact, Jesus and the apostles spent quite a bit of time trying to elevate women's position in society, which was incredibly unusual for that day. I know a lot of people *think* the Bible says women are to be subservient, but it really doesn't."

Jo started to say something else, but Professor Kwong broke in, laughing. "Okay, let's pull the discussion back to utilitarianism, shall we? Does anyone want to comment on the holes Brad raised?"

It was astonishing, Claire thought, to watch how quickly one dissenting opinion could change the tone of an entire debate. She was bemused to see some of the former utilitarianism fans suddenly raising cases where the philosophy didn't adequately determine right and wrong—the Nazis trying to exterminate the Jews or other wars of ethnic cleansing. One student even discussed how medical experiments involving animal cruelty ran counter to utilitarianism.

She also noticed that a half dozen students who had previously sat silent were now speaking up, actively raising dissenting viewpoints. They weren't willing to be the first naysayer, but once someone else had broken that ground, they were suddenly empowered to express themselves.

The discussion heated up as the staunch utilitarians stood their ground. As the opinions flew back and forth, Claire's frantic notes got further and further behind. By the time she finished processing one person's statement, she had missed half of the next person's rebuttal.

She was right on...wait...his point seemed so off, but...I didn't get that...

Her fingers cramped. She sighed and set down her pen with a click. *Forget it. Just forget it.*

Gael turned to Kai, standing in the back of the classroom. "She has never been one to give up. These types of classes..." His voice trailed off, the unspoken question grave in his eyes.

Kai's voice was deep. "Our Lord gave the words to Hosea: 'My people are destroyed for lack of knowledge.' Your charge does not yet have the tools she needs to stand. That is your mandate from On High. She loves the Lord her God with her heart and her

soul, but her mind and strength are still the battlegrounds. Just as it has been for centuries in this nation."

"For centuries that battle has been undermining God's people." Gael's gaze traveled
back to Claire, and his face grew determined. "But not this one."

Kai surveyed the glum carriage of Claire's body. "She has become wrapped in confusion and fear. But she must gain the knowledge to win the fight for her mind. She
must develop the courage to take a public stand. God has not given His people a spirit
of timidity or fear, but of power, love, and a sound mind! God has given her all those
things, but she must learn how to walk in them and how to stand on them. In this class,
my friend, she will learn. She must. She must be ready to fulfill God's mandate on her
life—for the life of this campus, the life of this nation."

"That is why you are here then, commander? Because this young one is—"

"Chosen of God for generations. She has been given the mantle to speak and see
eyes opened, to catalyze change. It is a mantle of power. But she must learn how to carry
it with humility before she learns *of* it, else she will either speak in her own strength,
with no power for transformation, or…she will be destroyed under its weight."


As the students began filing out, Brad crossed the room. Jo looked surprised to see him
coming but smiled pleasantly enough. He smiled briefly at Claire where she sat gathering her books, then turned to Jo.

"I hope I didn't slam you in class. I wasn't trying to…just trying to correct a common misunderstanding."

"Don't worry about it," Jo said. "I was wondering how on earth you can say that
the Bible doesn't preach the subjugation of women when it has all that stuff in there
about wives obeying their husbands."

Claire glanced at Brad with a panicked look. With some surprise she noticed that
he didn't look flustered at all. He was searching through his backpack.

"Well, do you mind if I just address that directly?" He brought out a small Bible.

Jo set her notebook and papers back down. The last few students were straggling
out the door, leaving the three of them alone.

"Hey, Mr. Bible, go for it if you can. I don't think there's another class coming in
after us." She glanced over at Claire. "Do you want to hear this?"

"Uh…yeah." Claire took a deep breath. "Actually, I agree with a lot of what Brad
was saying, about the Bible and all. But I'm still curious to hear his thoughts on this
issue."

Even as she spoke, a thought came to her mind. *Don't just listen. Pray.* As Jo gestured for Brad to take a seat, Claire did.

"Well, since you brought it up, let me go right to that thorny passage you mentioned." Brad opened his Bible and read Ephesians 5:22. "'You wives will submit to your husbands as you do to the Lord. For a husband is the head of his wife as Christ is the head of his body, the church.'" He looked up at Jo. "Is that the subjugation passage you were thinking of?"

Jo rolled her eyes. "Well, *yes*. How can you not say that that preaches the subjection of women?"

"Jo, my friend, I don't know how to break it to you, but you're missing the forest for the trees."

"Look, Brad, I know you're a traditionalist, an old-fashioned guy. I know what you're going to say."

"No you don't. I'm not a traditionalist, not a women's subjugationist, not a communist—not an anything other than a Christian. Let me read more of that passage, not just those two sentences." He moved his finger back to Ephesians 5:18.

"'Let the Holy Spirit fill and control you. Then you will sing psalms and hymns and spiritual songs among yourselves, making music to the Lord in your hearts. And you will always give thanks for everything to God the Father in the name of our Lord Jesus Christ.

"'And further, you will submit to one another out of reverence for Christ. You wives will submit to your husbands as you do to the Lord. For a husband is the head of his wife as Christ is the head of his body, the church; he gave his life to be her Savior. As the church submits to Christ, so you wives must submit to your husbands in everything. And you husbands must love your wives with the same love Christ showed the church. He gave up his life for her to make her holy...'"

Brad skipped ahead a few verses, finger moving down the page.

"'In the same way, husbands ought to love their wives as they love their own bodies. For a man is actually loving himself when he loves his wife. No one hates his own body but lovingly cares for it, just as Christ cares for his body, which is the church.'"

He looked up at the two women. "There's more, but we've already hit the most controversial part. So what do you think, Jo? Still think the Bible preaches that men should rule over the little woman with an iron fist?"

Jo looked a bit confused. "Well, obviously I didn't realize all that stuff was in there about husbands loving their wives as themselves. That doesn't really sound like subjugation, no. But *still!*" She pulled the Bible out of Brad's hand, jabbing her finger at the word *submit*. "It's still based on the condition that the woman has to submit to the man. That is so infuriatingly chauvinistic! It was written by some man thousands of years ago in a patriarchal society—a man who obviously had his own hang-ups and issues. And you read that today and *agree* with it?" She slammed the Bible shut and tossed it back on Brad's desk, glaring at him. Then she turned to Claire and glared at her, too.

*O Lord God, help! And forgive* my *unbelief. You know I have the same doubts sometimes....*

Brad calmly opened the Bible to the same passage. "Well, what is it actually saying that I'm agreeing with, Jo? Where is the first instance of the word *submit?*"

Jo reluctantly took the book back. "Well—hmm. It says 'submit to one another out of reverence for Christ.' So, is that some sort of conditional statement?"

"The first condition is actually in verse 18, where it essentially says submit to God—God's Holy Spirit—first and foremost. Then it says, in verse 21, that if they do that, then wives and husbands will be able to lovingly submit to each other. Those are both pretty important as the first two steps before it ever talks about a wife submitting to her husband. Any husband who is first submitting to God, and is *then* willing to submit to his wife as a partner, isn't going to be keeping her under his thumb. Most of that passage talks about him loving her as he loves himself, and lifting her up so she'll be holy before God—"

"Yes, but then it *still* says, when you come right down to it, that the husband is the head of the wife and she must submit to him! C'mon, Brad! You can dress it all up, but it still says it right there in black-and-white."

"Yes, it does." Brad took a deep breath. He glanced at Claire, who looked back at him, nervous. "Look, before I get into that you need to know that there are legitimate differences of opinion in the Christian community about certain passages in the Bible. Some people believe that some passages were limited to the culture and tradition of the day—that they are not supposed to be applied in the modern day. So keep that in mind here.

"But I think of the Bible as God's inspired Word to us. I tend to think that if God is really God, he knew that our culture and traditions would change and wouldn't have given us a Bible that would gradually become obsolete. So instead of excusing the Scriptures that I think are kind of difficult—like this one—I just decide to trust that God is conveying an unchanging truth and spend some time trying to find out what that message is."

He tapped on the page in front of Jo. "I know that not every Christian will necessarily agree with me, but let me just tell you my opinion on this. Okay?"

Jo leaned back and crossed her arms over her chest. She tossed her blond hair back from her face. "I can't wait to hear this."

*Lord, give Brad Your words. Open her ears—and mine—to hear what You have to say.*

"It all revolves around the relationship between Christ and His church. And this is something, Jo, that you may or may not get, depending on how much you understand about Christianity and what Jesus did for us. How much do you know about the message of Christianity?"

"Just the usual, I guess. Jesus was born as a baby in a manger at Christmas. He preached that people should love one another. Um—He was put to death on a cross and supposedly came back to life at Easter. That's about it." Jo looked as if she were discussing a clinical biology experiment.

Brad grinned. "Not bad. Mind if I expand on that a bit? Because you need to know about the amazing thing Jesus did for us, His church, in order to understand what this passage is saying.

"See, the Bible says that Jesus—God the Son—came to us as a tiny baby because we were lost and in terrible danger. We were constantly choosing darkness over light, constantly trying to make *ourselves* God, and our sin separated us from the real God who loved and created us.

"And that holy God knew that the consequence of that sin could only be death—eternal separation from Him. It was as if He was on one side of a great chasm, our sin placed us on the other, and we could not bridge it on our own.

"But here's the incredible thing: God loved us so much that He wasn't willing to lose us. Like a dad whose children are in danger, He was willing to do anything to save us. So He sent His only Son to live on earth among us and bridge that chasm. That is what *Emmanuel* means—*God with us!* Jesus was fully God but fully human, and He lived the perfect life that the rest of us couldn't. He fully shared our lives and showed us God's love—love for everyone, not just the 'good' people. And then not only did He fulfill the requirement of perfection—He also bore the *consequences* of the sin of the whole world! He died for our sin. He carried all the sin of the world on His shoulders, and when He died, He fulfilled the penalty for all of us. And when He rose from that death—He *did* rise from the dead on the third day—He conquered sin and death forever."

Brad smiled at Jo, who was looking down at her desk, not meeting his eyes.

"The Bible says that anyone who accepts what Jesus has done for them—who believes in Him and trusts Him as their Lord and Savior—will be saved. They just have to accept the gift of grace, forgiveness, and new life that has already been purchased for them at great cost! Then, when the heavenly Father looks on that person He will not see a child who is sinful and lost: He will see a child who is shining with the purity and the perfection of His Son. And those children will not only live in His abundant life here on earth—they will also spend eternity with Him in heaven."

*O God, what a beautiful presentation of the gospel. Help Jo to hear it, really hear it.*

Jo finally looked up. She seemed tense and a little exasperated. "Look, I hear what you're saying. I do. Great story. But what does it have to do with this?" She tapped on Ephesians 5 with her pen.

"Well, to understand my point about husbands and wives, you had to hear that whole story. Read verse—um—" he looked at the text upside down—"verse 25."

"It says for husbands to love their wives like Christ loved the church."

"Okay—so here's my opinion of how to answer your main question. Yes, the passage does say that the wife should submit and that the husband, as the head, should love his wife as Christ loved us. So here's the question for you, Jo: Knowing what you now know about the Christ story, who has the harder job? The wife who has to submit or the husband who has to love his wife like Christ loved the church?"

Jo stared at him, her mouth opening slightly.

Brad looked back and forth between Jo and Claire. "Look, if I were your husband, yes, you'd have to submit to me—but you'd be submitting to a man who was commanded to love you as sacrificially and as fully as *Christ* loves you. Give me a break! Which command is really harder, ladies? Which is the more servantlike? You're afraid of the word *submit,* and understandably so, because it raises all those specters of being kept under a man's thumb, losing your freedom, your equality, and so on. But that's *not* the Bible's model. If you submit to a godly husband—a husband who loves you so much that he's willing to die for you—he's going to be putting your good just as high or higher than his own. He's going to be doing everything possible to serve you and love you. And all you have to do is submit to that—to accept his best heart for you and to honor his God-given desire to lead your marriage in the best and most holy way possible."

Brad took back the Bible. He closed it gently, and Claire watched him rest his hand over the cover for a moment. When he looked up, Claire was astonished to see a glimmer of tears in his eyes. "God's design for a godly marriage is wondrous. And that is why I think this is one of the most beautiful passages in the Bible—even today."

## NINETEEN

## *October*

"OKAY, GOOD EXAMPLE. ANYONE ELSE?" Anton Pike's eyes scoured the room. "The trader must not have thought that his strategy was particularly risky, but it almost brought down his bank. What does this event tell you about the bank's corporate planning process? Anyone?" He called on a male student in the back of the room.

"Well, the corporate culture encouraged traders and bankers to pursue high returns by all means possible, and they didn't seem to have many checks and balances in place. So when this deal started to go sour, they didn't catch it early."

"Exactly, um, Doug Turner, correct?" The professor jotted a couple of notes on the board. "As we discussed in the last class, by definition high returns are given for high risk. What Mr. Turner is pointing out is that if the bank was urging its people to go for the high returns, it should have also planned for the high risk that went along with it. So, Doug, take it a step further. Why didn't they do that planning?"

Doug laughed and ran a hand over his buzz cut. "Well, the bank was insured by the federal government and was also very large. The officers figured that if they took too big of a risk and got themselves into a pickle, the Fed would bail them out. The government couldn't afford to let them fail. And that is what happened in the end."

"Why were they willing to take that risk?"

"They figured, hey—they were playing with other people's money after all. It's the best of both worlds. You take the risk and it works out; you get a great return. You take the risk and it blows up on you; the government takes the loss. Let 'er rip, man!"

Anton looked quickly over at Martin, who jotted a note by the name Doug Turner in his class roster. Neither saw the student's derisive expression as he shook his head in disgust.

Ninety minutes later Martin and Anton casually watched as Doug looked over the lunch bill. Within a minute, he raised his eyebrows and looked up. "That's funny…" He beckoned to the waiter. "Excuse me, sir, you forgot to add my meal to the bill."

The waiter took back the slip of paper, grimaced, and inclined his head. "Thank you for catching that, sir." The waiter looked over Doug's shoulder and caught Anton's eye. The professor smiled slightly and shook his head. *Not this one.*

Claire leaned against a tree and propped her biology textbook on her knees. The sun was warm and the spongy grass comfortable. If the Boston winters were indeed worse than those in Michigan, she'd better get in all the sun she could.

She was deep in a description of the human circulatory system when she overheard the sounds of an impassioned debate. Three people had stopped in the middle of a nearby walkway, their voices raised in disagreement. One of the three was Teresa.

"Look, Sam, I really don't appreciate your judgments."

A young woman was speaking to a genteel-looking male student wearing a sport coat and tie. Teresa was looking back and forth between the two students, fidgeting nervously with her book bag.

"You know nothing about my life," the young woman continued, her tone indignant. "How can you say whether or not I'll go to heaven?"

Claire sat up straighter, watching. *Uh-oh...*

"It's like I told you at lunch. The Bible says all sinners have to repent and accept Jesus as Lord. Simple as that."

"So you're saying I'm a sinner. Me, a sinner." The woman put her hands on her hips, leaning forward. "I spend ten hours a week working with the poor in Roxbury, Sam. How much time do *you* spend?"

Sam shrugged. "It doesn't matter how much time I spend. We're talking about you. Look, I was at that party the other night. I saw what went on. You really need to read your Bible sometime. You were giving no thought to tomorrow, which is exactly what God warns against—"

"Are you telling me God doesn't want me to have any fun?" The young woman gave a sharp bark of laughter. "You all are nuts, you hear me?" She turned to Teresa. "I don't know what kind of Neanderthals you're friends with, but count me out for lunch after class next time."

Teresa smiled in apology and laid a hand gently on the other woman's arm. Claire started praying under her breath.

"Listen," Teresa said, "I'm sorry. I wasn't expecting to get into a theological discussion. Please understand. We have lots of people in HCF coming from all sorts of theological viewpoints. Personally, I believe that people who follow Jesus are supposed to care for the poor and do good things, and I think that we don't do nearly enough. But I also believe that the Bible says we aren't saved by good works. I didn't know that about your Roxbury work, and I think that's great." She hesitated, searching for the right words. "My take, though, is that it doesn't mean as much without following Jesus. Because otherwise it's trying to work your way into heaven, and that's not how God does things. He wants you to know His Son."

The other girl held up a hand. "Let's not go there again, okay? An hour of that is about all I can take."

"Sure. I'll see you later for stats study group."

"Yeah." The girl turned and walked off.

Claire got to her feet but stayed in the shadow of the tree.

"I can't believe you, Sam!" Teresa's voice was low, intent. "I had established a great relationship with her, and I've been praying for her every night. Now in one lunch you totally turned her off."

Sam shrugged. "Look, she asked, I answered, okay? What'd you want me to do?"

"I wanted you to be sensitive to her!"

"You mean compromise the truth. I won't—"

"I'm not talking about compromising the truth! I'm talking about recognizing where she is! She doesn't know the Bible; she doesn't get all the lingo you spouted. She—"

"She was just falling-down drunk the other night. I happened to see her stumbling out of the place—"

"So what? She's not in the body of Christ, and you can't expect her to behave like a Christian!" Teresa paused, waving her hands in a half retraction. "I mean...of course God wants all of us to live according to His ways, but you can't expect that someone who is completely in the world is going to live a godly life without knowing God!"

"See, that argument drives me crazy." Sam's voice rose slightly. "Why *shouldn't* we expect that? It's just a matter of discipline."

Claire glanced around, noticing that other students walking by were giving the two a wide berth.

"Why don't people just not drink?" Sam crossed his arms. "Why don't homosexuals just exercise a little discipline and not have sex? Why should I pander to someone who, with a little effort, could probably live a righteous lifestyle?"

"Are you perfect, Sam?" Teresa's voice was growing weary. "Maybe you're better about things than I am, but you're probably not perfect yet. And I'm certainly not." She jabbed her finger in the direction her friend had gone. "And *she's* not. I really, really want to do what Christ did and meet people where they are."

Sam heaved a sigh. "It sounds good, Teresa, but I think it just encourages sin." He was looking at his watch. "I've got another class. I'll see you at HCF on Friday."

As soon as Sam walked away, Claire shot out from behind her tree.

"Oh!" Teresa put a hand to her head. "You startled me."

"I saw that whole thing, Teresa."

"You did? Well, why didn't you come out and help me?"

"I don't know. I thought…I thought you were doing fine."

Teresa made a face and waved off her irritation. "No biggie. Did you hear all that?"

"I couldn't believe it. Who was that guy?"

"Sam something. He's a sophomore. I don't know his last name." She sighed. "He's in HCF, and I don't think he's particularly good at being gracious with people."

"You don't say." Claire put her arm around her friend and steered her to where she'd left her backpack under the tree. "I could use something to drink. You up for Au Bon Pain? My treat, to apologize for being a wimp?"

Teresa smiled, her tension dissipating. "Sure."

*RAP! RAP! RAP!* THE SOUND OF THE GAVEL brought the loud chatter in the conference room down to a manageable buzz. Mansfield took his seat among two dozen other faculty members as Anton Pike called the meeting to order.

"Welcome back, ladies and gentlemen. I trust your summer ventures have all gone well." Anton smiled around at his colleagues, catching individual eyes, nodding at a few friends. "I'm honored to be serving as the new chairman of this steering committee. As listed on your agenda, we have a few new permanent members with us, but since each of these has served on an ad hoc basis in the past, I trust you all know each other."

A few people nodded their congratulations toward Mansfield and the other new members. Anton tapped the gavel again.

"We've got a lot to cover today, so let's go down the agenda before we start. We need to discuss Harvard's upcoming international project in Russia and which faculty members plan to volunteer…after the break the admissions office wants to update you on their new procedures for applicants…then our main report will be the final conclusions of the task force on alternative lifestyles diversity."

Mansfield looked across the table to Sharon DeLay, the head of that task force, then glanced down the ranks of faculty toward Taylor Haller. In the past few years, Mansfield had befriended Taylor and two or three other faculty members who were vocally homosexual. They had established a mutual respect in spite of their disagreements over lifestyle. Why was Sharon's mind so closed to any possible good intentions on his part?

He leaned back in his chair, staring at the rich mahogany walls, urgently praying that he would be able to respond meaningfully to the task force members without completely alienating them.

The mahogany walls of the conference room could hardly be seen beneath the assembly of demonic forces. Their presence was like a heavy cloud shrouding the entire room. Here and there—behind Mansfield, above another faculty member, by the door—a few angels hovered, their shimmering presence creating pools of light amid the blackness. They were there to protect the saints and watch the proceedings, but this was definitely not their turf.

One high-ranking warrior made his way across the conference room to another comrade by the door.

"Greetings, Etàn. We are, as usual, overmatched."

Etàn clasped arms with his superior. "Overmatched for today, yes. But we are eagerly awaiting the turn of the tide. Kai, we are at your service for the start of the plan."

"Shortly, shortly. You will all know as soon as I get the orders." He glanced around the room. "I admit, patience is hard in such a place."

His gaze fell on the woman seated across the table from the man of God. She and several of those on either side of her were enveloped by dark figures. The talons of one figure dug deep into her neck and head, hate-filled eyes staring at the man of God. Something in those eyes caught Kai's attention.

With a start, Kai recognized the demon. He turned away in pain. They had been colleagues before the Rebellion, comrades worshiping together before the throne of grace. His friend had even somewhat resembled Kai—tall, strong armed, fair haired, the light of the Lord reflected in his eyes.

Unbeknownst to Kai in those ages, his comrade had quietly chafed at the adoration laden on their King, and the restrictions of their covenant. He had wanted his own way, his own pursuits, his own service. During the Rebellion, he had chosen to follow Lucifer in a quest for personal glory. Kai and their other friends had watched, horrified, as he had chosen—chosen!—to be forever separated from the love of God.

Kai's throat closed as he considered the being before him. Some personal glory. His former friend was nearly unrecognizable, the shining armor replaced by garments that seemed to absorb all light, surrounding him with darkness. No longer tall, he was bent and twisted, shrunken from the weight of the load he had chosen. Strong hands that had played the sweetest of music before the throne were now gnarled talons, ready to inflict pain. Clear eyes that once shone with the reflection of Another's glory had turned red and empty in the search for his own.

Kai took a deep breath and looked at the woman who sat unawares beneath the weight of this creature. The assignment of torment was clear, in addition to the bitterness that was hardened by years of willful sin, willful disobedience. In a flash, the Lord showed him a young girl, terrified and sobbing after yet another attack by a once-trusted uncle. No one had known. She had not told, as she had been instructed. Her father lived in another state, and he wouldn't have believed her over his brother anyway. He wouldn't have held her and stroked her hair and lessened the pain with arms that were strong for his little girl.

The secret had tormented Sharon year after year, and the dark forces had converged, right on time, just as the hurt was scarring over. They had twisted her healing pain into bitterness, a rejection of the possibility of loving tenderness in men. She had been kissed by a boy only once, at a school dance, and later vomited in the bushes.

At college, at this very university, Kai saw that his adversary—his former friend—had latched on and fomented Sharon's friendship with another young girl with a secret. He was skilled at these machinations, playing on the loneliness and pain they both shared, whispering lies, eagerly awaiting the inevitable. The two girls had fallen into sin. Both knew it was wrong, but time after time of easing their pain and loneliness seared their consciences. As the years progressed, they went on to other partners. But both became hardened, their emotions distorted, bitterness always near the surface.

Strong emotions shook Kai to the core as he watched this review of Sharon's past, saw the terrible delight his enemy had taken in this destruction of a soul. Trembling with righteous anger, Kai closed his eyes and prayed.

Ten minutes into the presentation of the alternative lifestyles task force, Mansfield felt his temperature rising. He fought hard to maintain an outward posture of polite interest, keeping a firm lid on the opposing thoughts that roiled in his brain. Sharon DeLay and the other task force members had just finished summarizing their findings of "considerable bias inside and outside the classroom against gay, lesbian, transsexual, or transgendered students." They cited example after example of gay students being made to feel unwelcome or uncomfortable, then began outlining their recommendations.

Sharon flipped through a few pages of the thick report in front of her. "As you can see on page four of the executive summary, our recommendations are consistent with the ongoing efforts to promote this diversity at the high school level. We are adapting to the university setting the official resolutions and recommendations from the National Education Association for public schools: implementing programs to increase acceptance of sexual diversity; stocking school libraries with positive learning materials about gays, lesbians, and bisexuals; changing heterosexist language and getting rid of pejorative books on homosexuality; conducting gay-awareness training for students and teachers, and recruiting teachers gay students can look to as role models; introducing gay–lesbian issues into the curriculum, including an accurate portrayal of their contributions throughout history; and so forth. We feel that affirmative steps are critical to rooting out the bias we found at all levels of this university system."

Mansfield sighed as Sharon continued. Although some concern was probably understandable on an individual, personal level, accusations of systemic bias were pretty empty coming from a group wielding so much political clout on campus. But as much as he wanted to point out the inconsistencies, he knew from past experience that their position would become even more entrenched if he opposed their findings. He felt the Lord's gentle restraint on his tongue, so he sat and prayed. Maybe the Lord was helping him save up his political capital for his own task force report at the next meeting.

A woman across the room—Elsa Chasinov, another new member of the steering committee that Mansfield didn't know well—raised her hand in query.

Anton Pike nodded in her direction. "Yes, Elsa."

"I understand that you are concerned about extracurricular bias against those who are living alternative lifestyles. But since this is an academic steering committee only, may I just delve into your findings about the classroom environment?"

Sharon raised an eyebrow. "Well, fine. But keep in mind that the same systemic bias that is evidenced in the classroom breaks out into other areas of campus life. But go ahead."

Elsa flipped through the handout from the task force. "I see where you reference many examples of heterosexist bias outside the classroom, and I see your concluding statement that you did, in fact, find considerable academic bias as well. But I see very few actual classroom examples. Why the lack of classroom-related information?"

"Aha! That lack is the very point!" Sharon leaned forward, tapping on the thick report in front of her. "Our concern in the classroom is less about the *presence* of something and more about its *absence*. There is very little academic support for the person living a nontraditional lifestyle. For example, while multiple textbooks in sociology, philosophy, history, and so forth refer frequently to the traditional ideas of marriage and the husband-wife-child family unit in their stories and anecdotes, almost none carry references to same-sex unions or gay parents of children. Gay, lesbian, and transsexual students reading these books see nothing they can relate to. They feel like outcasts—odd and unacceptable."

"So what you're saying—" Elsa settled back in her chair, clasping her hands behind her head—"is that gay students in my biology and physiology classes feel discriminated against because I don't actively include their lifestyles in my academic curricula? Because my books and research materials are silent on the subject?"

"Exactly. You can understand how uncomfortable it is for *me* to constantly be confronted with this insidious bias in our textbooks day after day, much less for an eighteen-year-old gay student who already feels awkward in an unfamiliar environment and may not yet be comfortable with themselves and their way of being." Sharon's voice grew stronger, and she hefted the report in her hand. "It is obviously unacceptable for a university of Harvard's caliber to let this silent bias continue. We must lead the way for inclusiveness in language and content, to support the choice of the gay lifestyle, for example, as a healthy alternative."

Staring at her face, Mansfield felt as if a cold cloud were descending on the room.

He shivered despite himself and looked down the table. Elsa was pursing her lips, a thoughtful expression on her face. "Hmm. Interesting." Without knowing why, Mansfield found himself suddenly praying for her.

Taylor Haller cleared his throat. "And another thing, if I may?" He glanced at Sharon.

"Please."

Taylor flipped quickly through the task force report. "If you go to page 57, you'll see another issue that is actually far more serious than the silent bias that Sharon is talking about. It actually relates to some content we've found in biology, sociology, and psychology textbooks, including one that you use in your class, Elsa. We've actually found several passages inferring that the same-sex impulse might be the result of pathology from childhood trauma or other wounds inflicted on a person's psyche. You can imagine how frustrating it is to have finally eliminated—after many years of hard work—the archaic medical references to homosexuality as a type of illness, for example, only to have an equally damaging inference pop up in its place." He jabbed his finger hard at the report in front of him. "And with all due respect, Elsa, you have this—this garbage in your classroom!"

Elsa was looking at Taylor curiously. "I'm not sure what you're suggesting. These texts contain the latest medical research on all types of biological and behavioral issues, including the segments that you're mentioning. I mean yes, some of it is controversial, but it *is* outlining rigorous and credible scientific testing and analysis, after all. So we can't really argue that it doesn't have its place in the scientific discussion, now can we?" She looked up, and stopped short when she caught his expression. "Can we?"

Taylor just stared at her and pursed his lips.

"Look, you're not seriously suggesting that…" Elsa's voice trailed off, and her eyes flickered back and forth to the various task force members. Their faces were flat, their expressions stony.

Mansfield could still sense the Lord's restraint on his own participation. He prayed furiously. *O Lord God, break through the darkness surrounding this discussion. Give her the words to say and the courage to say them. Open her eyes to the tactics of darkness, and help her see them for what they are.*

From across the room Kai could see a sword glowing through the infestation, moving toward Elsa Chasinov. Etàn, his giant frame hampered on all sides by the grasping, hissing spirits, came within a sword's length of the professor. The thick hordes would not permit him closer access, but Etàn at least had his mandate from the Lord. He rested the tip of the blade on Elsa's shoulder. The spirits surrounding her retreated slightly from the white-hot light that, for just a moment, blazed forth from the sword.

Elsa held up both hands, palms outward. "Wait a second. What exactly are you suggesting here?"

"We have found," Sharon said, "that in order to have true diversity in academia we cannot be hampered by a bigoted environment. It's important to avoid moral judgments against human beings who pursue lifestyles different from the norm. Obviously, the textbook passages we're talking about make a hurtful judgment when they imply that same-sex attraction arises from some problem in a gay person's past." Her voice was indignant. "As if gay people start out as straight and are *made* to be gay somewhere along the way."

"I'm sorry. I honestly don't understand. Are you suggesting that we eliminate scientific data from the classroom simply because you don't *agree* with it?" Elsa looked around at several other committee members around her. "Are we talking about censorship? Censorship at *Harvard?*"

Other faculty members began to murmur, and Mansfield sucked in his breath. *C'mon...keep going! You're getting it!*

Sharon looked affronted. "Of course not, Elsa! Of *course* we're not talking about censorship."

*Sure you are.* Mansfield quivered with the strain of remaining silent.

"We were tasked," Sharon gestured at her task force members, "with the responsibility of encouraging and protecting an academic environment in which all people can feel included. The university has rightfully decided that we must achieve a goal of real diversity, and as such there are unavoidable choices to be made. Either we are encouraging diversity or we are not. Sometimes, in order to achieve the greater good of real diversity, we have to set aside other things that are also good, such as exploring every little detail of every little scientific avenue of study."

Mansfield's thoughts shouted. *And exactly why is achieving diversity a greater good than learning—at a university of all places?*

"As you yourself said, the textbook passages you are referring to are describing *theories* of behavior, not yet proofs. Wouldn't it be better, given the potentially hurtful impact of the content, to wait until these theories are actually proved—or disproved— by science before including them in your curriculum?"

"But this is *science,* Sharon!" Elsa looked at her colleague, incredulous. "Much of the point of science involves delving into research areas that aren't yet proven. We can't just pick and choose what—"

"Sure we can. We absolutely should keep the greater good in mind."

Mansfield shook his head slightly, exasperated.

Sharon caught the movement out of the corner of her eye and shot a glare in his direction. "For example, would you say—would any of you say—that biology classes in the first half of this century were correct in teaching the medical theory that African-Americans couldn't see well at night, or that their brains didn't work like those of white people? Of course not. It was hurtful to those minority students who attended university and had to listen to that garbage. But it was the *science* of the day!"

Various faculty members nodded thoughtfully, and the room grew silent. Mansfield watched Elsa look around, her brow furrowed.

Sharon gazed calmly at the others around the table, measuring her words. "We as faculty at a leading university in this country must ensure that this same sort of hurtful bias does not continue today."

Mansfield saw agreement in the eyes of many around the table. Elsa drummed her fingers on the table for a moment, then leaned forward and looked at Sharon. "Let me—"

*Rap! Rap! Rap!*

All heads snapped toward the front of the room. Anton Pike set down the gavel and looked at the clock next to the door. "In the interest of time, we need to wrap up this discussion and move to a vote on the proposals before us. I have a conference call in a few minutes, and I'd like to take agenda items for our next meeting before I leave." Pike glanced down at the executive summary. "You outline several recommendations on page 4—eliminating pejorative books and introducing gay/lesbian issues into classroom curricula, for instance. You then conclude that for the next step, the task force should select members of this steering committee to decide how those recommendations would be implemented—in essence, creating a subcommittee to come up with specifics." He looked up briefly from reading the report. "Do I have this right?"

"Absolutely."

"So right now all we need to decide is whether or not to convene the subcommittee to take this to the next step? We aren't voting on any of your page-four recommendations yet?"

"That is correct." Sharon looked around the table. "We're simply asking this steering team to endorse our findings and allow us to continue working to develop an implementation plan. The larger committee can vote on the specifics in a few months."

"Well then, let's have a voice vote." Anton's voice was brisk. "All in favor say aye."

A series of assents rippled around the room.

"All opposed, nay."

Mansfield and a few others—Elsa among them—gave a quiet dissent.

*Bang!* The gavel came down. "The ayes have it, and the motion is carried."

Sharon raised her hand.

"Yes, Sharon, anything else?" Anton glanced at the clock again.

"Just one more quick matter. We would like to send a note from this steering team to the president's office about something we discovered during our research. Over three years ago, the American Gay and Lesbian Alliance provided Harvard with an endowment to fund five scholarships a year. These scholarships would be given annually to seniors who had made significant social and/or academic contributions to the advancement of gay, lesbian, and transsexual rights.

"Unfortunately, the actual implementation of the endowment has gotten bogged down in paperwork in the finance department, and not a single scholarship has been given. For *three years,* seniors have come and gone without these scholarships, and many of these students could have benefited from the funds, I'm sure. This delay is utterly unacceptable, and I would like to send a strong complaint to the president's office."

Anton made a note. "Absolutely." He looked around the room. "Are we in agreement?" When everyone nodded, he rapped the gavel. "Well then, we'll send a note to the president tomorrow."

He pulled a page from his organizer. "Okay. Let's take agenda items for the next meeting, and my assistant will type it up and distribute—" A soft buzz from his pager interrupted him. "Rats, my conference call is on." He strode quickly to the door and handed the paper to someone outside. "My assistant Martin will take any agenda items, in addition to the few I already have listed." Pike slipped out.

Martin went down the list checking off items and adding new ones as various faculty members chimed in. Mansfield prayed furiously, wondering how on earth he was going to bring up the Ideological Diversity Task Force report without raising red flags that would alert Anton Pike.

"…then Professor Gannett will go through the plans for our holiday schedule. And wrapping it up, the committee will hear the final diversity report from the ideological diversity task force. That discussion will be led by Professor…um…Burke."

Mansfield grew still. *How did Ian's name get listed?*

"Any further agenda items?" Martin looked around the room. "Well then, it looks like this meeting is adjourned. Thank you, Professors." He rapped the gavel lightly.

Mansfield remained in his seat as his colleagues began rising and stretching, a slow grin playing across his features. *Well, I'll be.*

## TWENTY-ONE

THE VIEW FROM THE FORTY-FIRST-FLOOR corner conference room was magnificent, but the twelve men and women surrounding the table took little notice. It served its purpose of impressing visiting clients, but otherwise there was little point in lingering on the view. Time was money.

More and more files and spreadsheets cluttered the desk as the group conducted its business. From time to time, people on the conference call chimed in. The participants were all good humored, but the tension in the room was evident. The quarter earnings were due in, and the stakes were high.

Just outside the room, the phone rang at the ultra-tidy desk of an executive secretary.

"Helion Pharmaceuticals." The secretary's pleasant voice dropped a notch. "Certainly, Mr. Pike. I'll get him right away."

She punched the hold button and stood quickly to her feet. One of the new receptionists was approaching, and the executive secretary raised a hand, forestalling the newcomer, as she rapped on the conference room door.

"Mr. Statton? I'm sorry to interrupt. Mr. Pike is on the phone—"

The door was jerked open by an irritated man wearing a gray wool suit, starched shirt, and expensive tie.

"What!"

"Sorry to interrupt. Mr. Pike is trying to reach you—he and his brother. He said they couldn't get through on your cell."

She could hear expressions of consternation on the other side of the door.

The man quickly checked the tiny cell phone on his belt. "He's waiting for our figures. Tell him I'm on my way down to thirty-nine. Transfer the call to my second extension there."

"Yes, sir." The executive secretary watched as he collected several sheets of paper and then headed at a brisk clip toward the elevators. She waited a moment, and then punched the transfer sequence.

The young receptionist leaned casually on the desk. "The boss is a busy man."

"Yes, he is."

"Who is Mr. Pike?"

"The boss of the boss."

"How can someone be the boss of the company president?"

The executive secretary lowered her voice. "Since you're the receptionist on the executive floor, I suppose you do need to understand a little of what goes on. Do you know what a holding company is, dear?"

"No."

"A holding company is a sort of superstructure that owns either partial or full interest in lots of different types of companies. Well, Helion Pharmaceuticals—as huge as it is—is actually a subsidiary of a holding company. And Mr. Pike is the president of that holding company. It's all rather low-key, but that's why when Mr. Pike says jump, they jump."

The young woman's eyes grew big. "So if we're one subsidiary...are there others?"

"I'm sure there are." The executive secretary turned back to her computer, but the young woman didn't notice the tacit dismissal. She was gazing off toward the elevators Mr. Statton had used.

"You know, yesterday I forgot something on my desk when I was leaving. I tried to get off at the thirty-ninth floor to turn around and come back." She looked at the older woman, a frown on her face. "It wouldn't let me. This computer voice said 'enter access key.' I didn't know what it was talking about. Isn't thirty-nine one of the Helion floors also?"

The secretary didn't look up. "Yes, but only a few staff members have access to it."

"But today when I was going down to lunch, there were tons of people that got *on* at thirty-nine. Who works down there?"

"There's no need to concern yourself with that, dear. All you need to know is, when they say jump, you jump."


Two flights down, James Statton held the phone to his ear, taking notes.

"The final papers were filed with the Securities and Exchange Commission last week... Oh yes, Victor, we made sure of that, especially after that stupid blunder last week. The SEC would notice any irregularities in a heartbeat. We went over them with a fine-toothed comb, just to be sure.

"What was that, Anton?... No, the investment bank is working up the IPO figures now. And don't worry; I made sure that one of our Fellows is the principal on the deal." He nodded. "Yes. Brenda. She's very good. And she assures me that her entire team—Murphy and the others—is trustworthy. We won't encounter any further problems from that quarter....

"Well, from a market standpoint, right after the award would be the best time, as long as no leaks hit the street. And with the way this class-action is going… I know, I know." His voice dropped in frustration. "Look, gentlemen, let's bottom line this thing: We are almost certainly going to need the cash for the settlement by January. Obviously, it's your call, but I see no way around it. We can't afford to wait to do the IPO. We have to have the cash in-house within the next two months."

He leaned back in his chair, his face grim. "You know as well as I do that if the IPO doesn't net at least a half billion, we might have to start divesting some business lines. I know taking the company public totally goes against the Cardinal Mandate, but I don't see any other way."

He listened for a long moment, and his face grew thoughtful. "Well, if any of the other presidents have ideas, let me know. In the meantime, I'm doing what I can here to increase our shadow cash flow, but there's no way I can get a big enough jump without tipping somebody off. It's not just the government—there are too many eyes in too many distribution channels."

His face cracked in a tight smile. "It's disgustingly ironic. The Cardinal Mandate is working; the shadow companies are the most profitable they've ever been; but just when we most need the infusion we can't risk it. Not until after the SEC and the market analysts put away their microscopes. And you can't use family money without attracting even *more* attention."

Statton paused and cleared his throat. "And that, gentlemen, brings me to my next problem. We have a liability in our team. I have waited to mention this until I was sure, but I received confirmation today. A young Fellow in my reporting line has let several things slip in the past year or so. And today she told one of our executives here—a man who'd just been fired—of the truth behind the lawsuit."

He winced away from the receiver, and his eyes narrowed at the sharp recriminations from the other end of the line. "Don't lay this at my feet, gentlemen. That is why I'm telling you now. The truth absolutely cannot get out, and neither can we overlook so serious a security breach. It is up to you to decide what—"

He listened for a second. "What? Oh…Johanna Godfrey. She's four or five years out—currently managing the…oh, really? Well, since you know who I'm talking about, that should help your decision." He nodded sharply. "Let me know if you need anything from me. Believe me, Victor, I want to know how this could have happened as much as you do."


"No, he hasn't left yet. I'll transfer you." At her station on the executive floor, the young receptionist punched a few buttons.

A loud crash made her jump in her seat. A thirtysomething man in an elegant navy wool coat went down on his knees on the marble floor of the entryway, trying to scoop files, papers, and personal items back into a cardboard box. Another bulging box sat on the floor next to him.

"Hey," she grabbed an empty plastic bag from a drawer and scooted around the desk. "That won't work. The bottom fell out. Here."

The man took the bag and began clumsily transferring the items.

"You need more hands." She smiled and held the bag open.

"Thank you. That's awfully nice of you. What are you doing here?"

"What do you mean?"

"I mean, you're too nice to be working here."

She laughed.

"I mean it. You just started, didn't you? Well, trust me. You'd do better to leave. This isn't the place for people with a conscience."

"Are you leaving?"

"I was fired." As her eyes widened in shock, the man bent again to the pile on the floor. "Look, whatever your name is…"

"Heather."

"Okay, Heather. You look like a young, idealistic person. I hate to break it to you, but this is not the nicest company to work for. That's why we're losing the big lawsuit."

"What?"

"Oh man, didn't anybody tell you?" He lowered his voice slightly. "Helion developed this wonder drug that calmed down hyperactive kids and kids with ADD. I have an eight-year-old with ADD, and I thought this medicine was a miracle. I thought Helion deserved every penny of the hundreds of millions the drug earned. Turns out, though, that the company knew all along that it was dangerous, that it affected the genetics of any kid taking it, so that *their* kids would be likely to have ADD. And then *they* would need the drug."

The receptionist's lips parted in astonishment.

"Several years ago some outside person—thank God—documented the side effects and warned the world. Of course, thousands of families joined a class-action lawsuit against Helion. The company has fought it in the courts for years, but we're in the final stretch, and we're almost certainly going to lose. When that happens, Helion is going to have to come up with a lot of money to pay the families of these kids."

"Is that why you're having to leave?" The receptionist looked around the empty entryway.

"No. I'm having to leave because they knew I couldn't do this anymore." He slapped several picture frames into the bag, and the receptionist heard one of them crack. "I rose through the ranks, but I was never really in their little group. For a while I bought into the idea that this is just the way business is done, but I woke up when my son was affected. I tried to bring some standards, some sort of integrity, into this business, but I found out that was really not what they wanted."

He finished loading his stuff into her bag. He picked up the box as well, and they stood in the entryway facing each other. His voice was quiet.

"Heather, look. Today I found out that company insiders *knew* about the drug's genetic side effects during clinical testing but suppressed the information. They knew the medicine would make millions, perhaps billions. They knew that children like my son would be genetically altered, but *they didn't care*. They were creating the next generation of customers to line their pockets!"

"How do you know that?"

He punched the down button for the elevator. "I can't go into it, okay? And I know better than to tell anyone on the outside. I have a family."

"Wait—uh—what's your name?"

"Jason Dugan." The elevator doors opened and he stepped inside.

"Wait! Jason!" She slapped her hand against the side of the elevator door. "What's on the thirty-ninth floor?"

Jason's eyes were gentle. With a wry smile, he lifted her hand off the elevator frame and the doors closed, carrying him downward.


James Statton's eyes narrowed, listening. "You want my honest opinion? I think the Enemy has made inroads, and everyone had better come armed with more than just inspiration at the next Nantucket meeting. We're going to need it."

He hung up the phone and crashed his fist against the table. A curse burst from his lips. That class-action lawsuit couldn't have come at a worse time. He sat still for a moment, then settled deeper into his executive leather chair, resting his arms on the thick armrests. He leaned his head against the back of the chair, and his eyes flickered and rolled back in his head before his eyelids slowly closed. The Master would pick his sacrifice.


The sidewalks were crowded as workers poured from revolving glass doorways. The Friday afternoon bustle at the end of the workweek.

They flew noisily into the building—it was their territory, after all—and perched atop the modern art sculpture in the lobby. Their otherworldly eyes peered through the walls as the elevators made their swift descent. They saw the navy wool coat crowded in with others. That one.

The lead demon began to move, then saw the eagerness on his lackey's face. His aide was due a little rejuvenation; he had been in that skirmish last week. The lead demon crooked a finger at him and pointed.

The lackey jumped and headed upward, arriving at the top of the skyscraper in the blink of an eye. A maintenance man was standing by the elevator drive shaft, waiting. The lackey melded into his body.

A smirk crossed the maintenance man's face. He flipped a red emergency stop switch on the drive motor, made a few adjustments to the controls, then pulled out a power tool and went to work on the end of the main cable.

The lackey looked down. Through layer upon layer of floors, he could see the eager eyes of thousands of colleagues. They had all heard. They paused in the middle of their tasks—by the water coolers, in the computers, on the desks—looking upward, watching.

The sound of the power tool was loud. The cable snapped. The sounds of terror, shock, and sadness rolled over the building like a wave. "For the Master!" the lackey cried. And as the sacrifice was completed, the revitalized troops took it in with deep, refreshing breaths then returned to their tasks in a much better frame of mind.

# TWENTY-TWO

THE FIRE CAST A WARM GLOW ON THE RUG in front of the hearth. Johanna Godfrey stretched in relaxed contentment, enjoying the feel of it against her skin.

"Here you are." Victor returned with another glass of wine, his body pale against the shadows of the den. She leaned on her side and accepted the glass, sipping with pleasure. Chateau Lafite Rothschild '66. Her favorite.

Victor ran his hand lightly down her side. "And then, my dear, we'd better get ready. There's a midnight meeting of all the Fellows."

"Tonight?" Johanna's sense of ease dampened slightly. "I didn't hear about it at the session today."

"Perhaps," he kissed her on the forehead, "you were too busy thinking about other things."

Johanna set down the glass and leaned toward Victor, her blue eyes smoky. She pressed into his embrace, and her voice was soft in his ear. "Perhaps."

He ran his fingers down her cheek, her throat. "Time to go."

Johanna descended the last few stairs and pushed open the door to the large ground-level conference hall. It was empty.

"What…?"

Victor brushed past her and headed to the glass doors at the side of the room. He slid them open, letting in the cool ocean breeze that rose from the dark bluffs beyond. He gestured her forward. "They're outside."

He ushered her through the door and into the blackness of the great lawn. It was too dark to see other than a few feet in front of her and Victor on her right side.

At the far end of the lawn, she could finally make out a mass of gray figures waiting, but there were still no lights. A flickering movement caught her attention. Distant black shapes rose against the midnight sky, blotting out the stars. She sucked in her breath. What were those?

She slowed her step, but Victor's grasp was firm on her arm. "Come on. It's almost midnight."

"What's going on?" She tried to wrench her arm free.

Victor smiled down at her. "You'll see, dear one." He propelled her onward.

By the time they reached the edge of the crowd, she was shaking. The gray shapes resolved themselves into people: James, Murphy, Brenda… They reached out and welcomed her into the group, smiling.

She relaxed a little under the attention, still perplexed. It wasn't her birthday…she'd already had her four-year anniversary induction.… Others clapped her on the back or patted her on the arm as she moved forward through the crowd grasping Victor's arm.

They were smiling at her, saying things she couldn't quite make out: "…the knowing of the elders…the Fellows dedicate you…as you are advanced…may the masters be pleased…"

She returned the smiles and nods of her friends. Was she being promoted?

They reached the edge of the bluffs. Victor turned toward her and cupped her chin with his hand, tilting her face upward for a soft kiss. She stepped back, surprised. He had said no one could know of their liaison.

He advanced and cupped her chin again. She looked up into his eyes with a questioning smile. His eyes were black. Pure black. And something else…

She began to tremble and pulled away. Suddenly, rough hands gripped her arms, holding her tight. She looked wildly over her shoulder at the stony faces of two large men she had never seen before. They held her fast as she began squirming in earnest.

Victor watched impassively as she began screaming for help, twisting and scratching. Somehow she broke free and darted toward the crowd. Hands grabbed at her clothing, wrenching her back. She felt the rough grasp of the two men, yanking her hair, pulling her backward and down to her knees.

She was panting, the knees of her elegant trousers soaking in the moisture of the grass. Desperately she sought the faces of her friends among the crowd of Fellows. They had stepped to the front of the group, their expressions hard, cold.

Suddenly she understood. Her heart contracted with bottomless despair.

Large hands were firm on her shoulders, holding her down. With a shuddering breath, she looked up at the sky. The stars were pin-point bright, scattered through the blackness like tiny shards of broken glass.

Victor stood still, staring down at her, his lips parted in a small smile. Someone had handed him a head-high wooden pole that he held like a ceremonial staff. It was intricately engraved with a leafy vine and bore a wicked steel point. *A pike.*

Victor checked his watch and nodded at the men behind her. She raised her chin, defiant. They yanked her to her feet and faced her toward him. Each one took a wrist and pulled outward until she was stretched out between them. She clamped her mouth shut, trying not to gasp in pain.

Victor took a short step forward and backhanded her across her face. Johanna was thrown sideways. The large men faced her forward again, and Victor struck her other cheek. One more time, and she slumped between her captors, her head thick and the taste of blood in her mouth.

Victor stepped back, stretching out the pike toward the hanging figure. "Here we have the traitor, the one unworthy of our sacred trust. She has broken the first article of the Cardinal Mandate."

"The Masters demand a sacrifice," the crowd responded.

"Let this, the first atonement in five years, serve as a pleasing offering to prosper our way." Victor raised his chin and slowly scanned the crowd. "And let this serve as a warning to the younger ones among us who may have been lax in considering the pledges of their blood oath."

He paused and addressed the small group of Fellows at the front of the crowd. "And let this motivate you all to follow the approaching matter with the utmost care. No mistakes." His eyes bored into those of James Statton, emphasizing each word. "No mistakes."

He turned back to Johanna's two captors and nodded. They released their grasps. Johanna swayed slightly in surprise. Suddenly, Murphy and James were beside her, the other Fellows approaching from the front. They began crowding her backward, their hands pushing and prodding, their eyes intent.

She took one step backward, then another. She could feel the cool breeze from the ocean, hear the waves crashing on the rocks below the bluffs. She tried to push against her former friends, tried to shove forward through the crowd, tried to scream. There were too many hands, knocking the wind out of her. No sound came out.

Johanna felt the ground grow soft under her heel, and her mind reeled in terror. Only moments. Only moments.

James grabbed one elbow, Murphy the other.

"No! NO!" Her mind grappled for something, anything to save her. "God, help me!"

The crowd hissed, their faces contorted.

With a flood of emotion, she felt a terrible pain at the utter selfishness of her life, the futility of how it was ending. She twisted and struggled with all her might. "O God, O Jesus! Forgive me!" She tasted salty tears as the final inches gave way. "Forgive me!"

And as her feet left the edge, her mind was flooded not with terror, but with a strange sensation she'd never felt before. She floated downward, a rapturous smile growing on her face as a shining person came into view above her. She reached out and He took her hand, the depth of eternity in His voice.

"Today, my child, you will be with Me in Paradise."

The rocks rushed toward her, pain exploding in her head, a white-hot comet flashing toward an unknown realm. The last of the blackness that her wonder-filled eyes saw was a glimpse of Victor at the edge of the cliffs, screaming in rage.

## TWENTY-THREE

MURPHY BARKER STEPPED OUT OF THE SAUNA, clouds of steam billowing out the door behind him. The air of the locker room was like a cold blast on his skin. He grabbed a thick towel from the folded pile nearby, wrapping it around his waist. The soft terry cloth was monogrammed with KCP—Keppler, Collins, and Preston, the New York investment bank where he'd spent the first four years of his career.

He rubbed another towel over his face and hair, then strode to his locker. Better get back to the desk before the conference call with Mulligan on the Lima deal. Their paperwork had had some dangerous holes again. If their cash flow was going to be of any use to the Mandate, they'd better exercise a little more quality control. They—

"Barks!"

Murphy swiveled. "Hey, Tank, how's it going?" He sat on the bench and pulled on his socks and shoes.

"Much better since we kicked your sorry tails all over the court last night." His colleague opened the locker a few paces down the row and loosened his tie. He grinned sideways. "Word on the street is that you were so distressed this morning you went out and made a few stupid calls on the Mulligan deal when the markets opened."

"Not stupid, Tankton. Well informed."

"What…have you actually talked to Mulligan?"

"You know that's illegal."

"Yeah. So was some of that garbage you pulled in the basketball game last night."

Murphy smiled and closed the locker. "Gotta go. I've got a one o'clock conference call I shouldn't miss."


Two hours later, Murphy finished entering his notes from the call into a secure file. He shook his head in exasperation. For such a longtime Fellow, Mulligan was unusually verbose.

He went on-line and typed in a site name. The screen came up a uniform white, empty. He clicked on a particular corner of the screen, and a small dialog box popped up. He typed in a password and another dialog box floated to the surface: "Verify specifications." He entered several letters and numbers.

The computer hard drive whirred for a moment. The screen read "Entering secure Intranet. Please wait" then changed to "Transmission verified. Please continue."

The glow of the computer monitor was reflected in Murphy's eyes as he clicked through various tasks, uploading the secure file he'd just finished, replying to several directives, and posting responses to colleagues in other locations.

It took over an hour, but he didn't mind. This was his real job.

He was just finishing his last posting when he heard a sharp rap on his office door. He quickly pressed a key and a KCP media report appeared on his screen as the door opened.

His boss looked in. "You in the middle of something?"

"Just reading today's evaluation of the entertainment industry. Good growth potential."

"Not in anything I'd want my kids to watch." His boss dropped a thin file on Murphy's desk. "I need you to go over to the client site for a meeting in an hour. The lawyers need some hand-holding until this Lima pharmaceutical deal goes through. And we need Mulligan's signature on this paperwork today. You obviously won't be able to talk to him yourself, but see if the lawyers can walk it in to his secretary."

"Sure, boss."

As the office door closed again, Murphy made a face. What a sniveling idiot. Groveling to every directive was getting on his nerves.

He punched a keyboard sequence and returned to his original task. A request for a hand-carry from someone in another group caught his eye, and he smiled with anticipation as he picked up the telephone to call for details. He was going to be near that area of the city anyway. What perfect timing.

The rush-hour crowd was thick on the sidewalk as Murphy retraced his steps. They had said it was easy to miss. His eyes flickered to the numbers above the doorways. One door had no number, just a small sign reading Peephole Publications. Bingo.

The door was black with no windows. An intercom panel was set off to the side. Murphy set down his heavy briefcase and pressed the intercom button twice.

"Yes?"

"Tom Smith here. I'm picking up a package from Jenks."

"Great. Come on in, down to the end of the hall."

Murphy heard a slight buzz and a click as the door unlatched. A long hallway stretched in front of him, lit by bare florescent bulbs. Plastic chairs populated a small waiting area at the end of the hallway. Psychedelic murals lined the walls and ceiling. Random stickers and postcards decorated a closed door.

Murphy stood, waiting. The heavy smell of cigarette smoke—and something else—hung in the air. He'd probably have to get his suit coat dry-cleaned before he wore it again.

After a few minutes the door opened and a thin man strolled in carrying a thick manila envelope. He stuck out his hand. "Jenks. Good to meet you." He looked about twice Murphy's age, his hair thin and oily.

Murphy shook the offered hand. "Tom Smith. I'm here to pick up the third-quarter papers."

"Yes." Jenks handed over the package. His eyes were wary. "The usual? Secure courier?"

"Absolutely. Hand-carried. Oh…and I'm supposed to tell you that because things have gotten so busy, it'll probably be a week before they're finished."

"You boys really need to get more people working on it."

"Oh, trust me." Murphy's smile was all teeth. "We're recruiting all the time. And it's in our best interests to process the quarterlies as soon as possible, too, you know. As soon as we do these, your bonus will be deposited."

"Great. Fabulous." Jenks took a cigarette packet from his jeans pocket and tapped a cigarette out. He stuck it between his lips, speaking around the obstruction. "So where do you work?"

Murphy just shook his head, smiling.

"Yeah, yeah, I know. But I can't help asking."

Jenks lit the dangling cigarette and pulled the smoke deep into his lungs. Murphy made no move to leave. Jenks blew a cloud of smoke sideways, watching his visitor.

"You want to watch the shoot? We've got a new girl getting ready right now."

"I thought you'd never ask."


The klieg lights were so hot. Beyond them, in the darkness, the young woman couldn't see the shadowy shapes that she knew were watching.

*Click! Click! Click!* Her back ached from the strain of holding her position. She could feel herself trembling, silky material caressing the backs of her legs. Her fingers tightened, holding the whisper-thin garment together at her collarbone.

She wanted to vomit. Why had she gone this far? Why hadn't she spent her last few dollars on a bus ticket home? She had somehow known that this day, this choice, would come. Perspiration beaded on her upper lip.

*"Cut!"* Jenks peeled away from the blackness behind the camera and set his hands on his hips.

The makeup girl appeared beside her with a giant powder brush. She applied powder to her face, blotting out the offending moisture. The soft bristles continued their work, moving downward. She made a gesture and the young model slowly opened the garment, watching the makeup girl's face as she worked. She was chewing gum, totally uninterested.

The young woman knew the gauzy material barely covered anything, but at least it was *some* type of covering. And what choice did she have, really? Yesterday her super had tossed her neighbor's stuff out onto the sidewalk. "No rent, no room!" Behind the high-up blinds she had shivered, watching. In two days that would be her.

She had pounded the pavement, but there were so many girls chasing so few jobs. She didn't even have money for food, and she couldn't face going back to her mom's trailer park—even if she could get there. The guy who'd offered to be her agent said it was only a matter of time before her breakthrough. And in the meantime he'd offered her a job that would make her rent for the month. Everyone in the industry knew these jobs were a rite of passage. Get with it. What was the problem?

She had stared at the business card a long time before she made the call.

The makeup girl stepped away, and she gratefully pulled herself together again.

"Hmm." The word was soft. "Wait."

Jenks suddenly appeared in the pool of light. "I liked that last view, my dear."

He stopped in front of her, his eyes traveling her length. She didn't move as he pulled the soft material away and down. "Yes, much better."

As he walked back to the camera, she could feel the air conditioning against her skin. She bit her lip and raised her chin. She would not cry.


Murphy watched from the darkness, his eyes hungry and appreciative. These were the perks he liked best.

He spoke briefly to the girl's agent, who was also smoking, a cigarette dangling from limp fingers. "How old is she?"

"Seventeen."

"Old enough." Murphy's gaze never left the pool of light. "How's business?"

"Better every year, my man. Better every year."

## TWENTY-FOUR

THE ROOM WAS SO QUIET, CLAIRE THOUGHT, that you really could have heard a pin drop. Students packed the seats and stairs and every inch of standing room, yet each person at the Harvard Christian Fellowship meeting was enthralled as Professor Mansfield took them through the history of Harvard's early years.

She had been startled to see that the dynamite speaker Brad had referred to a few weeks before was her European history professor. She was delighted to learn that he was a Christian and obviously beloved by the older members of HCF.

"How many of you have felt that the environment here at Harvard was apathetic or even antagonistic toward Christian beliefs and values?"

A forest of hands shot up in the air. Claire looked around. Nearly everyone in the room. It wasn't just her!

"Give me a classroom example, someone." He called on a girl in the front row.

"Well, last year in psychology we learned about how little of the brain we actually use and how many mysteries there are about how the brain functions. They did two class sessions on all the paranormal psychology, psychics, mediums, influencing people by the power of your thoughts, all that sort of thing.

"The professor wasn't a mystical sort of person; it was all just clinically interesting to her. She wanted us to do an experiment where we would try to read each other's thoughts and another where we would actually try to influence another person's actions by a sort of meditation—she called it "programming." I really wasn't comfortable with that, because the Bible says divination is abominable to God, and that seemed to be coming awfully close! But the prof wouldn't budge and said that if I refused to do the experiments, she'd have to give me an F on those assignments."

Mansfield shook his head. "I've heard that sort of thing before. What did you do?"

The student looked uncomfortable. "Well…I went ahead and did it. I couldn't afford to fail. But it just made me uneasy the whole time."

Mansfield turned back to the class. "Her example is just one of hundreds I've heard in the past few years. People often think of Harvard as a main breeding ground for secular humanism in America, and they're probably right. For the last century or more, the spiritual environment at this school has been quite dark and has influenced other universities around the country. The faculty research and social thinking done

here—research that has been more and more influenced by today's humanistic, relativistic worldview—has often spread to institutions all over the country.

"You've all heard the political phrase, during the presidential primaries, 'As New
Hampshire goes, so goes the nation.' Well, it does seem that as Harvard goes, so go the
nation's universities. And because many of the nation's leaders go to these universities,
so goes the nation."

He held up a warning hand. "Now, just so you all don't get too big for your
britches, remember: We all know that what Harvard primarily has going for it is the
name—right?" He grinned at the sheepish looks around the room. "Anyone here that
has been in a classroom at any other challenging college has seen that there isn't a whole
lot of difference between it and Harvard. Here we're just a lot older and—unfortunately—sometimes more arrogant about promoting ourselves and our 'heritage of
scholarship.'"

Mansfield paused, looking around. "Tonight I want to go back into the past and tell
you about the spiritual heritage Harvard has and that you have as Christian students—a
spiritual heritage shared by Christian university students all over the country."

The professor propped some reading glasses on his nose and opened a small
leather-bound book. "Let me read to you from the early *College Laws,* dated just six
years after this school was founded in 1636:

"Let every student be plainly instructed and earnestly pressed to consider well
the main end of his life and studies is to know God and Jesus Christ which is
eternal life, John 17:3, and therefore to lay Christ in the bottom, as the only
foundation of all sound knowledge and learning."

"The official founding purpose of Harvard—and the 'main end' of anyone's life
and studies—was to help students know God and Jesus Christ. This is why an early college motto was *Veritas*—Truth not for its own sake, but, as the eventual tag line
indicates, *Veritas Christo et Ecclesiae.* Truth for Christ and the Church."

The glasses came off, and Mansfield switched on a projector. A picture of an old
Harvard seal sprang up on a screen behind him, its outlines familiar and yet different
from the seal Claire was used to.

He gestured to the screen. "This school has gone through many changes over the
last few hundred years—and those changes have been inevitably mirrored in the motto
and the shield. The early founders of Harvard were Puritans and orthodox Christians
in the Calvinist tradition. The motto *Christo et Ecclesiae,* instituted in the late 1600s,
was the primary motto for over a century. And for much of that time it was representative of the orthodox Christian beliefs of the students and faculty."

Mansfield began pacing the room, and his tone changed. "However, by the mid-1700s, as great strides made in science and other areas of study, we in this new country—especially intellectuals—had begun to grow dangerously proud in our own knowledge. And as we grew more convinced of our own superiority, we grew less convinced of God's. The influence of the so-called Enlightenment began to eat away at the faith's Christ-centered focus. The Unitarian and transcendentalist movements emerged, appealing to those who preferred to define their own faith, rather than bowing to the sovereignty of God and accepting His revealed plan in the Bible.

"Many Harvard leaders considered themselves the intellectual stalwarts of the Age of Reason, but since they lived in a time when having *no* faith was not yet acceptable, many were eager to embrace Unitarianism." He smiled sadly. "Since Unitarians reject the centrality of Jesus, that was the beginning of the end of Harvard as a Christ-centered institution.

"An old book, *Three Centuries of Harvard* by Samuel Eliot Morison, perfectly captured this transition. Morison wrote: 'Faith in the divinity of human nature seemed the destined religion for a democracy, closely allied to confidence in the power of education to develop the reason, conscience, and character of man.'"

Mansfield glanced up at the intent expressions before him. "Once you build a faith in the divinity of human nature, Christ is bound to be removed from the center. And that is exactly what happened. Harvard changed the motto from *Christo et Ecclesiae* back to the very first motto of *Veritas*. This time, however, *Veritas* wasn't referring to Jesus Christ as the source and end of all knowledge. Rather, a return to *Veritas* meant a liberation of reason from religion. Harvard was beginning to transform itself into a modern—and therefore purely secular—university."

Claire listened as Mansfield described the ensuing tug-of-war between those who supported and opposed that change, and the compromise that eventually merged the two mottoes into *Veritas Christo et Ecclesiae.* The students were surprised to learn that it was still the formal motto for the present day, even if only *Veritas* was actually used.

"But it gives me some small hope," Mansfield pointed out, "that the school has not chosen to formally eliminate Christ and the Church from its standard. Just as God says His Word will not return void, so will His Holy Spirit tenaciously pursue those who have once invited Him in. The Good Shepherd will leave the ninety-nine to doggedly seek that one lost sheep."

Mansfield returned his attention to the screen. "In addition to the motto, let me give you another example of how this seal is slightly different than today's." Using a pointer, he tapped the three books spaced in an inverted triangle inside the seal. "Take a look at these three books on the older crest, with the letters *Ve-ri-tas* written across them. Do you notice anything different from the way they appear on the modern version of the seal?"

He waited a minute while the newer students strained to discern any differences. Claire spotted a Harvard sweatshirt on a student across the room, and her eyes flickered back and forth from the sweatshirt to the screen. The books looked the same, except…

Her hand shot up, and Mansfield promptly called on her.

"The third book! That bottom book…in the old seal it is facing down. In today's seal it looks like it's faceup."

"Exactly. The early Harvard fathers included the top books to represent the Old and New Testaments and the bottom book to represent the Book of Life. The presence of books, in the university setting, presumably also came to exemplify the quest for truth in all the academic disciplines. The early founders carefully kept the bottom book turned down to make it clear that, while we can search and study and learn, there will always be limits to human knowledge. There will always be mysteries known only to our sovereign God.

"At some point, however, the university decided to turn that book faceup. Apparently we now know everything there is to know." Indignant chortles sounded throughout the room.

The professor removed his reading glasses and tucked them back into his pocket. When he looked up his jaw was set, and his eyes seemed to bore into those before him.

"I have a warning for you, one borne from repeated and sometimes sorrowful experience while shepherding the members of this Christian Fellowship year after year: Don't ever challenge God. Ever. As you are surrounded by the best and the brightest on this campus, don't give in to the temptation to try to upstage one another. Instead, adopt a mantle of humility and 'let your gentleness be evident to all.' *That* is what will bring the Lord near to you and to this place.

"Otherwise, pride could so easily fester in your hearts and make you more *of* this world and this place. If pride prevails, you may graduate with honors, you may be acclaimed by men, you may achieve worldly success—but you will be pulled away from God. Sin always separates us from God, and pride seems to be a particular trap at many universities." He smiled sadly. "And Harvard University is no exception."

Claire shifted uncomfortably in her seat, recalling the many times she had fallen into that trap in the last few weeks. *Lord, thank You for showing me that. Forgive me, and keep me from my pride!*

A student in the back raised his hand, and Mansfield nodded. "Yes, Sam."

"Professor Mansfield, I see that pride can be a trap, but how do we defend right from wrong without seeming prideful? Society has so twisted things that people don't recognize the truth anymore. Everyone here thinks homosexuality is okay, that getting blasted is okay, premarital sex, cussing—it's all normal! We as Christians *have* to stand up for what's right, but when we do, people accuse us of being judgmental or prideful!"

"I know it's hard to see truth being disregarded. But I'd urge you to remember—" Mansfield swept the ranks of seats with a solemn gaze—"I'd urge *all* of you to remember that our job as Christians isn't always to rail about right and wrong."

He reached for a Bible and held it up so all could see it. "Our job is to speak life instead of death. If you look at the Gospels, Jesus didn't talk much about right and wrong. But His entire ministry was—and is!—about Life instead of death. He built life-giving relationships. And people flocked to Him—everyone except the Pharisees, who were masters at determining right from wrong.

"Let me read you something. I know this is not on the subject of the lecture, but I think it's important to interject here." He popped his briefcase open and drew out a small book. "Some of the writings of Francis Frangipane. Listen to his words:

"My personal attitude is this: I will stand for revival, unity and prayer; I will labor to restore healing and reconciliation between God's people. Yet, if all God truly wanted was to raise up one fully yielded son—a son who would refuse to be offended, refuse to react, refuse to harbor unforgiveness regardless of those who slander and persecute—I have determined to be that person. My primary goal in all things is not revival, but to bring pleasure to Christ."

Mansfield smiled at the intent faces before him. "Our primary purpose is not to defend right from wrong, or truth from untruth—it's not even to defend *Him*. God can do that, remember. Our ultimate goal is to be fully yielded to Christ.

"If we are primarily focused on the obvious sins of the world, we are diverted from *our* sins—pride, a lack of grace, self-centeredness. The list is sadly long, and these failings may be even more fundamental than the immorality of our neighbors. But if we are striving, above all, to be fully yielded to Christ, then He can do whatever He wants through us, *including* reaching our neighbors. Let us not forget that."

A few minutes later, Claire stood and stretched. The student leaders of the group had taken prayer requests and conducted some HCF business. As they released the group for the night, they announced that "dinner is at Chili's—see you there!"

Claire looked around in some confusion. People were putting on their coats and straggling out in groups.

Brad and a female student appeared at her elbow. "Hey there. Want to join us for dinner?"

"Is that what everyone's doing? I was wondering what was going on!"

The other girl smiled at her. "They should've announced it better, shouldn't they?

Most Fridays after HCF, we get together for dinner somewhere. It's the best part of fellowship!" She stuck out her hand. "I'm Alison. It's good to have you here."

Through the crowd Claire saw a face she had been hoping for. "Alison, Brad, can you hold on a second? My roommate is here. Could she join us for dinner?"

"Absolutely."

Claire sped across the room and grabbed Sherry's arm. Her roommate turned, and relief flickered across her face.

"I'm so glad you came," Claire said. "I didn't see you before."

"I came in a bit late and couldn't find you." Sherry glanced around and lowered her voice. "I don't see anyone I know."

"Well, that's easily remedied. Let me introduce you to a few folks."

Claire pulled her along to where Brad and Alison were standing. After the introductions, Claire started pulling on her jacket. "Sherry, these guys are going to Chili's with everyone else. You coming?"

"Uh…actually, I can't. I've already made plans. But thanks."

"Oh?" Claire kept her voice light. "Who are you going out with?"

"Oh, you know, a group of people from the dorm. But you all have fun."

Alison smiled at her. "Oh, we will. Maybe you can join us for dinner next week. HCF's a great bunch of people."

"I'm sure it is." Sherry looked at her watch. "Actually, I've got to run or I'll be late. See you."


As she walked toward the restaurant with her two new friends, Claire was very conscious of Brad's presence. He strolled next to her, talking politely, gesturing for her to go first through doorways and tight spaces. As they progressed through Harvard Square, she glanced at him out of the corner of her eye. He was short with a strong profile, a shock of brown hair, and a stocky build. He wasn't what she would have called handsome, but she was drawn toward his warmth and kindness.

Claire recognized the tall figure of her history professor strolling along beside several students. She tugged on Alison's arm. "What's *he* doing?"

"Professor Mansfield often joins us for Fellowship dinners." She laughed at Claire's shocked expression. "He's a mentor and surrogate grandfather to a lot of students in this group. He's a wonderful guy. You'll love him."

"He's my European history professor!"

"Well, then, you're even more fortunate than most. C'mon, I'll introduce you."

Before Claire could protest, Alison was pulling her toward the next little knot of people. Alison caught Mansfield's eye.

"Alison!" Mansfield smiled and stopped to give her a hug. "I haven't seen you since we've been back this year. How was your summer, my dear? Did you enjoy your internship?"

"I really did—it was fascinating. You were so kind to help—"

Mansfield waved a hand. "It was nothing. I knew you'd do well. Finding good people like you to work on Capitol Hill for the summer makes me look good to my old colleagues in Washington, after all! So you could say I was really doing it for *me.*"

Alison grinned and shocked Claire by punching the professor lightly on the arm. "Yeah, right. Well, for whatever reason you did it, thank you. I had a blast."

Mansfield turned Claire's direction. "And who is this, Alison? You didn't introduce me to your friend."

"Professor, this is a new student, Claire...um, what's your last name?"

Claire held out her hand. "Claire Rivers. I'm in your European history class, actually."

"Well, good. At least, I hope it's good. I shouldn't speak too quickly, I suppose. Are you enjoying the class?"

"Oh, very much! It's my favorite class. I hope it will *still* be my favorite class after your quiz next week."

Mansfield chuckled and motioned to the group to continue walking.


Over dinner, Mansfield talked with Claire and Doug Turner, the two freshmen at his table, about their families, their hometowns, their hobbies, what they thought their majors would be. As he listened with evident interest to their answers, Claire had to remind herself that he was a famous figure. The presence that was so charismatic in the classroom was now warm and humble, focusing intently on them.

Claire found herself describing a hobby she loved but hadn't had time for since arriving on campus: genealogy research. "I just love the investigation aspects. It's like being a detective, trying to put together the pieces of a historical puzzle."

Mansfield leaned back in his chair and folded his hands behind his head. "Well, Claire, if you enjoy historical investigations, we'll have to talk sometime. I always have projects that I need student help on. Why don't you come see me at some point next week?"

"Are you serious?"

"Of course I'm serious. You seem like just the sort that I'd like to have as a research assistant, and it would be a paid job. Why don't you drop by on Thursday afternoon? I have office hours all day, and we'll have plenty of time to talk. Call and schedule a time."

Claire could only nod eagerly. *Thank You, Lord!* She felt a spreading warmth at this unexpected opportunity. Her parents would be so proud of her assisting a famous professor on an academic project. Not to mention a little extra income.

"You'll really enjoy working with this guy, Claire," Brad said. "He's the best. Speaking of all your projects, Professor, how is the *big* project coming?"

"Actually, very well. We've just got another few weeks before the big meeting. You're the prayer coordinator this year, aren't you? I'd appreciate this group's prayers before and during the meeting."

Brad nodded. "You got it. The meeting's down on our calendar, and we'll start praying and fasting in shifts the week before. I think we students sometimes forget how important it is to pray for our professors, to pray for the school. We may not have another chance like this for years. We need to cover this whole thing in serious prayer."

"That will be very important," Mansfield said. "I'm convinced this is a spiritual battle. We'll need concerted prayer and fasting to take back this ground for the kingdom."

Brad glanced at a few puzzled expressions around the table. "Professor, would you mind outlining your project for those who haven't been involved?"

"No, I wouldn't mind. Before I tell you this, though, I'll need your word that it doesn't go beyond this room. A lot of what we're trying to do depends on it remaining quiet until the appropriate time."

Each of the students nodded.

"Harvard considers itself the ultimate 'marketplace of ideas,' and the project I'm leading aims to bring that marketplace into true balance. Let me provide some background."

Mansfield leaned back in his chair and adopted a professorial tone of voice. "Like many universities, Harvard considers itself a leader in society, a first mover on new ideas, new ways of viewing the world. And it probably is. The problem, as I discussed in the talk tonight, is that as Harvard has left its Christian roots behind, it has not simply embraced and encompassed the new ideas; it has actively rejected the old ones. In that way, it is not truly a marketplace for free thought. Some types of thought, such as traditional, faith-based values—actually, Judeo-Christian-based values—are often discriminated against in a way that alternative viewpoints would not be. The same goes for politically conservative viewpoints.

"This school seems to value diversity and tolerance above all, but that tolerance is actually limited in a way that many don't recognize. Anything that can be labeled 'intolerant'—the Christian view that Jesus is the only way to salvation, for example—is simply not acceptable. Not *tolerated*, if you will. It's rather ironic.

"This has resulted, not surprisingly perhaps, in a sort of speech code environment, where only 'tolerance' viewpoints are welcomed, and others are often met with active dislike, if not hostility. The end result is that those with faith-based viewpoints may not share those views as openly as they otherwise might."

Mansfield smiled at the knowing chuckles that came from several students.

"Now, in a strange sort of way you should be encouraged by the existence of tacit speech codes. What that really means is that some people know, deep down, that their viewpoint can't stand up to a fair and open debate. Therefore, they try to keep the debate from happening. They don't even want to think about it. If you can get around that blockage, you've got a great chance of making a lasting point and even changing some minds.

"So, what does this have to do with the project that Brad mentioned? Well, for years now I've felt a calling to try to reintroduce fairness into this marketplace of ideas and to work for kingdom purposes here at this school.

"I have served off and on as an ad hoc member of the steering committee that sets the standards for the undergraduate curricula. Just recently I was made a permanent member. This steering committee is sometimes quite frustrating because it's controlled largely by those who *like* the status quo and don't see a problem. They don't seem to see the fact that students who are not challenged with ideas beyond their comfort zone— such as some of those that are now suppressed in the classroom—are actually learning less than those who are challenged in that way." A small smile played on Mansfield's lips. "But I hope and pray that that's all about to change.

"You see, several years ago the school was on this 'diversity' crusade. They wanted to ensure the diversity of the student body because they know—rightfully—that different types of people bring different viewpoints and enrich the learning experience for everyone. They had plans to increase the diversity of race, of gender, of sexual orientation, diversity of skills and interests. Pretty much every kind of *outward* diversity was championed. However, the school was doing nothing to encourage *ideological* diversity. In fact, as we've discussed, it was actively discouraged.

"So about two years ago I made a case to the steering committee that just as there needed to be task forces that assessed the diversity of race, sexual orientation, and the others, there needed to be a task force that did an empirical study of ideological diversity on campus." He smiled slightly. "A few of the more…obstructionist committee members were not there the day I proposed this, and somehow the others agreed to the proposal with very little debate.

"As the various task forces have conducted their studies over the last few years, we too have been researching, analyzing, and polling students in nearly every class. But we've been much more quiet about it than the other task forces. While some of them provided interim updates, I elected not to. Now, at staggered times over the last year, each task force has finished its research and come out with its final report. Many of the recommendations have been granted. The next—and last—report to be heard is mine. It will be very interesting to see the reaction of the various members of the committee, as they seem to have forgotten that this task force was ever formed."

Alison chimed in suddenly. "That's because you've been so careful to keep it under wraps. I've never seen such a massive project kept so quiet for so long! Whoever compiled all those survey sheets deserves a medal."

The professor laughed. "I'll be sure to tell my teaching assistant that you think so. His latest estimate was that we have good data on almost seventy percent of our undergrad classes and professors here."

"Wow." Brad said. "I didn't realize you'd gotten so far. So are you going to share your results with the students?"

"Probably not, Brad. At least not for a while. I'll be able to share a few things in summary form down the road, but the task force reports are strictly confidential."

"Yeah," Brad muttered. "Gotta hate that integrity thing." The others laughed, and as she watched their good-natured ribbing, Claire found herself smiling. Brad was a really nice guy.

Idly, she wondered if this was what Sherry felt for Stefan. The unbidden thought was like a cold bucket of water poured over her head. The peace that had been growing in her all evening abruptly fled. Her memory replayed last weekend's scene of Sherry stumbling into their room after being out with Stefan.

Claire tried to rid herself of that picture and reenter the camaraderie of this little group around a cozy restaurant table. She smiled and laughed with the others, but that scene, that gnawing sense of concern, wouldn't leave her mind.


Early morning sun poured into the room, and Claire awoke with a start. She quietly rose and stood on tiptoe on her bed, peering over the rim of Sherry's loft.

The comforter was uncreased, the sheets unruffled. Sherry's teddy bear still sat at attention against her plumped-up pillow. He looked like he'd pulled the lonely late-shift duty, watching in vain all night.

"I know how you feel," Claire muttered as she sank back to her covers and stared at the ceiling. She sighed.

*Now what, Lord?*

## TWENTY-FIVE

LYING IN HER BED, CLAIRE WATCHED as her roommate changed into a night shirt and prepared to turn in. She moved around, hanging up clothes, putting books in their place. She never looked over at Claire.

"Sherry, where were you last night?"

Sherry didn't respond immediately, and when she did her tone was cool. "Just out with some friends."

"I was worried about you."

"Don't be. This is a safe campus." She started shuffling her papers into piles.

"Yeah, safe from everyone but cute young men that would just *love* to get their hands on an equally cute southern belle."

Claire was relieved when Sherry laughed. "Okay, you guessed. I was with Stefan. We stayed up really late talking, and I was exhausted. It was easier to sleep on his sofa than come all the way back here."

"Sherry, I have to ask. Did you and Stefan—?"

"Did I sleep with him? Is that what you want to know?" Sherry slammed something down on the desk. "I appreciate your concern, but is that really your business?"

"Um…actually, yes. You did ask me to hold you accountable. And I can't help but wonder when you spend the night in a guy's room!" She jumped out of bed and went over to her roommate. "Look, I don't want to pry, but I care about you and I care about your desire to keep from going down the wrong road. You said that was what you needed in an accountability partner. And if I don't do it for you, then you won't want to do it for me…and I know I need to be held accountable, Sherry. Either we're doing this or we aren't!"

Sherry let out a small sigh. "Yeah." She turned slightly, not quite looking at Claire. "You're right. I'm sorry. You were only doing what I asked you to do."

Claire stepped over and gave her roommate a quick hug. "Sherry, I didn't mean to make you angry. I don't *want* to make you angry. It's not exactly comfortable for me to ask you these questions."

"You need to, though." Sherry's voice was so low Claire could hardly hear it.

"Yes, I do. And you need to do the same for me."

A thousand miles away, a middle-aged woman sat on her prayer couch in a darkened sunroom, hugging her knees to her chest. Barbara prayed for her daughter, prayed for her protection and her wisdom in facing the temptations of college. It never occurred to her to pray, yet, for her daughter to have the strength to help others face those temptations. But God knew. Her prayers ascended to the throne of grace, and His hand moved.

Caliel moved in, and his sword blazed as he hacked away the dark layers surrounding his charge. The layers were hard, but they were no match for the grace of God extended to this young woman. Waves of the deepest eternal love, of a Father for His child, penetrated and lifted the darkness.

Caliel gave thanks to his King for His goodness as he saw the light coming back into Sherry's face. There was unsullied innocence in her eyes despite the desperate hunger for love and completeness. The warrior fervently prayed that she would look for that completeness in the only place where it could truly be found.

As Claire touched her shoulder, Sherry's eyes suddenly filled. "I *want* to do the right thing, Claire. I don't want to screw up."

"I'm glad you don't. I don't want either of us to." Claire hugged her roommate again, then backed off. "Look, Jesus said the spirit is willing but the flesh is weak, right? So we've just got to help each other avoid that weakness. But I need to hear from you that it's okay for me to ask you things like 'Where were you last night?' Otherwise I'll wimp out."

"You can ask me anything you want. Just please…forgive me in advance if I get defensive. I'll try not to be defensive, honest I will. I'll—I'll promise to always answer honestly, anything that you ask. I promise I'll never lie to you."

"That's a pretty serious promise. Are you sure?"

"I may wish I never said this, but *I promise* I'll always answer your questions and answer them truthfully."

Claire stretched out her hand and shook Sherry's firmly. "Okay, roomie, it's a deal. And Sherry—I make the same promise to you."

Moments later Claire lay back in bed and stared at the ceiling. *O God, I don't know if I'm up to this! How did I get appointed Sherry's caretaker? I have so many temptations myself…. What am I doing thinking I can somehow keep her together as well? Please strengthen me for this. Give me love for her, as well as the courage to challenge her. And Lord…please help both of us make the right choices.*

## TWENTY-SIX

THE AUTUMN RAIN DRUMMED ON THE ROOF of the little church as the congregation listened to the pastor's impassioned message. One of the HCF students had recommended this church, and Claire and Sherry had put it next on their church-shopping list.

The little signboard out front had posted this morning's sermon topic: Your Adversary the Devil, 1 Peter 5:8. The preacher grew animated as he paced the length of the stage. "You must not be unaware of the tactics of the enemy, children! The great deceiver may come disguised as a beautiful angel of light, but he wants nothing more than to exploit your anxieties, your weaknesses, in order to destroy you."

Claire looked down at the Bible on her lap, rereading 1 Peter 5:6–9. "Humble yourselves, therefore, under God's mighty hand, that he may lift you up in due time. Cast all your anxiety on him because he cares for you. Be self-controlled and alert. Your enemy the devil prowls around like a roaring lion looking for someone to devour. Resist him, standing firm in the faith, because you know that your brothers throughout the world are undergoing the same kind of sufferings."

The pastor continued pacing, every now and then descending to floor level and gazing out into the congregation. "The enemy of our souls *hates us*. The image is of a prowling lion circling his prey, seeking any weakness, any chance to jump in and attack and destroy. He will send his minions to harass and discourage us, to trip us up, to tempt us as he tempted Eve in the Garden of Eden."

The pastor took a handkerchief and wiped his forehead, then waved the cloth in the air at invisible adversaries. "Just as we know there are angels all around us, servants of a holy God who are sent to help us, we know there are demons all around us as well. They are sent by our enemy to wreak havoc in our lives, to destroy those that God loves.

"But 1 Peter 5 and James 4 give us the answer to these attacks: Humble yourselves before the Lord, resist the devil, and get rid of the sin in your life." His voice grew louder, and he held up his Bible. "James 4:7: 'Submit yourselves to God. Resist the devil, and he will flee from you. Come near to God and he will come near to you. Wash your hands, you sinners and purify your hearts, you double-minded.... Humble yourselves before the Lord, and he will lift you up.'"

Claire sat quietly. She wasn't hearing much that was new to her, but she could see Sherry leaning forward, intently jotting notes in the margins of her bulletin.


Over lunch at a little deli not far from the church, Sherry kept returning to the sermon. "So you mean there are, like, evil things that are seeking to harass us? Real evil beings?"

"Of course. Haven't you read the parts in the Gospels where Jesus casts out demons?"

"I guess so. I just never—I don't know. I never thought much about those parts. It never occurred to me that those—you know—*demons* existed today."

"Just like angels exist, demons exist." Claire looked over the rim of her soda and grinned at her roommate. "Unfortunately."

"You mean there could be angels and demons in this very room, just…hanging out?"

"Yeah, I guess so."

"Whoa." Sherry leaned across the table and lowered her voice. "What do you think they're doing?"

"How should I know? Maybe the angels are standing around this very table, listening to this conversation and laughing."

"No, seriously! Remember what the pastor said about demons trying to attack us? Do you think that really happens? What kind of attack is he talking about?"

Claire shrugged. "Maybe sometimes when you get depressed, that's actually a demon trying to discourage you. Or if everything is just going all wrong one day, maybe those are demons harassing you." She watched her roommate's eyes widen. "Look, I'm no expert. I'm just guessing. No one knows for sure how spiritual warfare really works. We just have to take what the Bible tells us about it and try our best to put it into practice."

Sherry seemed lost in thought, idly twisting the straw in her drink.

"Earth to Sherry."

"Hm? Oh, sorry. I was just thinking. I was wondering how I would know if I was—you know—being attacked. You can't *see* anything, so how do you know?"

"I guess you just have to pray about it and make an educated guess. I wouldn't see a demon under every rock or anything, but they're definitely out there." Claire glanced at her watch and picked up her umbrella. "Look, can we get out of here? I've got tons of reading to do before philosophy class tomorrow."


The rain rapped against the windows of his office as Mansfield set his coffee mug on his desk. His expression was intent as he looked across at Ian. "And then I just sat there, stunned. Pike's assistant never picked up on the title of the task force, and my name wasn't even on his agenda as the presenter! He was so anxious to get going that he wasn't paying attention. If my name had come up, I'm sure it would've caught his notice, but your name was listed instead. It was so strange." He picked up the mug again, wrapping his fingers around its warmth. "Someone is really looking out for us."

Ian whistled under his breath. "So as far as you know, Professor Pike is still unaware of our task force and our upcoming report. Thank God. What a miracle."

"That's right. Let's pray it stays that way. Pray that the enemy's eyes stay blind to this so no sabotage is planned ahead of time." He paused, drumming his fingertips against the side of the mug. "Ian, there is something I want to mention to you. We've worked hard to put together a good report that might open some eyes to the truth, but we went into this with our eyes open. We've always known that this report will probably be unpopular and that, like a battleship, Harvard is big and unwieldy and unlikely to change direction quickly—or even to change at all.

"But over the last few days, the strangest thing has happened as I've prayed for our work. I have felt the Lord's hand so strongly. It's like He's telling me that this report—this meeting—will start something huge for His purposes on campus, whether or not our recommendations are followed. And last night..."

Mansfield rose to his feet and began pacing the room. "Last night I had a dream that just had to be from God. I was looking at a dark, tumultuous sea; it gave me an oppressive feeling. And then I saw the Lord's hand stretched out over the water. He had something like golden sand, or maybe salt, cupped in His hand, just sitting there. I got the feeling it had been sitting there a long time, waiting. But then, as I watched, the breath of God began to blow, causing the grains to scatter toward the sea.

"When the grains hit the black surface, they transformed the sea as far as the eye could see. They illuminated all the water and made it transparent. You could see the creatures swimming in its depths and see the rocks and plants below. The sea became the thing of life and beauty it was always intended to be. And then in my dream I heard the Lord saying, 'The Truth shall set you free.'"

Mansfield paused in his step, looking out the window at the storm. "In church this morning I kept praying about it, and I think God was giving us a gentle message of what He's about to do. In His timing we are somehow—" his voice grew quiet and began to tremble—"somehow going to be a part of bringing this transformation to this lost and hurting campus. To this place that so desperately needs the light of His love. No matter how dark and oppressive it has gotten, no matter how far people have strayed from God and His precepts, His truth can and will break through the darkness." He turned around and pulled off his glasses, wiping his eyes on his jacket sleeve. His eyes were red as he looked at Ian. "I feel like the time of waiting is almost at an end. That we are about to see a master plan unfold."

Ian looked up at his mentor soberly, not speaking. The rain was loud on the windowpane.

"I don't know what the something is that will scatter the grains of salt. But it's out there. I feel it. I *feel* it."

Neither man moved for a moment. Then Mansfield leaned on his desk and lowered himself to the floor. Ian set his notebook on his chair and joined him. And on their knees the two men came into the throne room of Heaven. And God's hand moved.

The two guards scanned the sky, unaffected by the thunder and the cold wind and rain. In the spirit, they were in a place of brilliant light, and their eyes were leaping with anticipation. The news had just arrived: Their orders were about to change, and the battle was about to begin anew.

They tensed as a messenger approached, closely followed by two enemy minions. The enemy spirits shuddered to a halt in midair as the messenger continued inside the walls, the radiance enveloping him. The dark spirits hissed and spat but came no closer.

"Greetings, Etàn."

"Greetings, my friends." Etàn stretched his arms and wings in the brilliant light and sighed in pleasure. "It's always a welcome respite to join you in this place of refuge, even if for only a short time. Maybe I should get injured more often."

"Yes, I know." The lead guard glanced as his sidekick and gave an exaggerated sigh. "As our charges say…it's a tough job, but somebody's got to do it."

"Oh, sure." Etàn laughed. "But since I know that you have to be tired of the easy life—" his expression sobered—"I come with news."

"Yes." Both guards were alert, seasoned intensity replacing humor in an instant. They nodded occasionally as Etàn outlined the plan and conveyed their orders. When he was done, the lead guard spoke quietly.

"Although I've enjoyed my posting here—probably a lot more than you've enjoyed the war wounds of the battlefield—something in me aches to return to the struggle. We are designed for the fight. I'm grateful for the healing time our Master has given me, but I am ready to return." He paused, his eyes bright. "But before I go, we have a long-awaited task to perform."

The three angels turned toward the great house beyond the courtyard, and Etàn's eyes came to rest on a particular tree that creaked and swayed in the storm. He tapped his colleague on the shoulder and pointed.

The angel smiled. "Perfect."

"Meshach! Meshach, come away from there!" An impatient cane rapped through debris that cluttered the hardwood floor, but drew little notice from the whining, pawing dog. "There's already too much junk scratching this floor, and you're making it worse."

The old man stared at the corner where the giant elm had made its unwelcome entrance. In the dim light from a heavily-curtained window, he could see Meshach's backside and tail working furiously as he tried to burrow further behind the tree. A chunk of plaster hit the floor and shattered, tiny pieces skittering in all directions.

That blasted dog was going to destroy what was left of the wall. What was he doing?

Edward Grindley glanced around. No lamps. This wing of the house wasn't wired for electricity and hadn't been used in years; this room—an old sitting room, he believed—had only the one window on the side wall. An enormous, graceful fireplace was set in the other wall, only a few feet from where the tree now adorned the corner. If the tree was going to carve a new hole, at least it could have let in more light.

He shuffled past a few stray branches and rapped his cane against the brick of the fireplace. "Meshach!"

No effect. The dog was giving small strange yelps.

Sighing, Edward leaned hard on his cane and stretched into the corner, his free hand searching for Meshach's collar. He stopped suddenly. What was that? His hand closed around something in the debris. He pulled it out and held it up to the light...


...and the heavenly host erupted in cheers. The long-delayed battle had just been renewed.

## TWENTY-SEVEN

BRANCHES AND LEAVES LITTERED THE WET PAVEMENT as Ian jogged along the sidewalk. He could see his breath and enjoyed the crisp air on his face.

He scanned the street, assessing the damage from yesterday's storm. The news said power lines and trees were down in lots of places around town.

*Whoa!* Ian came to a quick halt in front of a familiar pair of iron gates, which were standing wide open. *That's something you don't see every day.*

A tree had toppled into the corner of the grand old house. Several trucks with winches and cranes stood nearby, and people bustled about. Ian turned away, preparing to continue his run.

*STOP.*

The thought was so loud that Ian jumped. He looked around, his heart racing. Was that…?

*Go back.*

"Lord, is that You?" Ian barely whispered the words. The sense of the Lord's presence was incredibly strong. He began to shake.

"Well, well, young man. Nice to see you."

Ian whirled around and came face-to-face with a pair of bright eyes. Edward Grindley smiled at Ian's expression and beckoned him inside the gates. Edward closed the gate behind them and pointed toward the activity at the corner of the house. "As you can see, young man, the storm seems to have created a hole in my sitting room."

"I'm sorry," Ian said.

"I'm not. I found something I didn't know I had—a false wall with a secret cabinet inside it. It was filled with very old family books and papers."

"How cool!"

"Yes, it is." The old man stared at him for a moment, until Ian became uncomfortable.

"What?"

"Son, I need to ask you a question. Are you a believer in Jesus Christ?"

"Yes, I am. Are you?"

"Yes."

"I thought so, the time we met. The names of your dogs made me wonder."

"Well, young man, I'm just wondering what it is about you that I'm supposed to find out, because as you jogged past, the Lord told me quite clearly that I was supposed to speak with you." On seeing Ian's dumbfounded expression, the wrinkled face lifted in a mischievous smile. "I gather that perhaps the same thing happened to you."

"That…well, that has never happened to me before."

The old eyes twinkled. "It happens to me all the time. Of course, I've had many more years to learn His gentle voice." Edward leaned on his cane and began walking toward the house. "I now know His voice better than that of many of my friends."

Ian matched the old man's pace. "I wish…"

Edward stopped and turned toward Ian, searching his face. "Young man, you love the Lord. It's written all over you. His Word says that His sheep hear their Shepherd's voice and are not fooled by the voice of the stranger. You just keep yourself glued to the Good Shepherd, and you'll thoroughly recognize His voice." He raised his cane, gesturing toward Ian's chest. "I promise you that."

Edward ushered Ian through a small side door and into the damaged wing. The rooms were dark, the hush broken only by the distant sounds of voices and machinery outside. The elegant wooden legs of antique furniture peeked out from under white slipcovers. Large, beautifully framed paintings looked down from the walls. A clock ticked loudly in one of the rooms.

At the end of the hallway, Edward ushered Ian through a door and into the main section of the house. Rose-colored marble covered the foyer floor, and a giant crystal chandelier cast rainbows of light on the cathedral ceiling and walls.

Edward led Ian into a spacious, sunny kitchen. A tall, elegant woman was clearing vegetables off a chopping block and tossing them into a simmering pot. She smiled at Ian as the two men entered.

Edward gestured toward her. "Kathryn, my youngest daughter. She is visiting with me for a few weeks while her husband is out of the country on business." She stepped forward to shake Ian's hand. "Kathryn, this is Ian. He's a student at Harvard Law School. I was just going to show him the materials we found in the wall yesterday."

"Let me get the papers, Dad. Why don't you two sit down? The soup and bread will be ready in a few minutes."

Ian started to protest, but she gently pushed him into a chair at the kitchen table. "I insist, Ian. You must join us." She smiled at his jogging attire. "It looks like you could use some good carbs today anyway."

As she vanished around the corner, Edward chuckled. "There's no arguing with Kathryn. She's a prayer warrior, and she knows you're here for a reason, just like I do."

"But what is the reason?"

"Who knows? Maybe we'll find out today, maybe we won't. But God certainly arranged this meeting, so He's in charge. One way or another, He will let us know."

Kathryn reappeared and set a stack of books and papers in front of her father. They were old and dusty, but Ian could dimly make out a gold-embossed crest on the spines of several volumes. They reminded him of the old tomes he saw from time to time on Mansfield's desk.

Edward pulled out a dark blue clothbound book. It had the look of an oversized desk ledger and was stamped with a gold crest on the front.

"When we first found this stash, I thought it was just a historical curiosity. But as I flipped through this ledger I realized there was far more at stake. I would like to find someone trustworthy at Harvard—if possible, a Christian who holds a position of authority—to whom I can show these books."

He looked at Ian, his eyes piercing. "The Grindley family has had a historic relationship with Harvard University since its founding. A Grindley was a member of the Massachusetts General Court that decided to establish the university, and for well over a hundred years there was always a Grindley family member on the board or in another leadership position.

"Grindleys have always carried a special...mantle at Harvard. We have been Christ-bearers. In the last decades, as the school has become thoroughly secularized, our family involvement has not been as overt or as welcome to the new—ahem—powers that be. Our family had historically been a large donor to the school, but much of our family fortune was given away during the Great Depression. When our wealth left, so did our access to the Harvard leadership. So although many of us have attended the university since then, we have never been welcomed back into the inner corridors of power.

"However, we haven't let that keep us from what we know is a family calling for Christian leadership at this school—it just had to go underground. For decades now our family has maintained a strong commitment of daily intercession for Harvard. We believe there is work going on in the spiritual realm that we may never see, but it is very real, very time-intensive work nonetheless.

"My great uncle—Joseph Grindley Halverson—was the last Grindley family member to serve in a position of leadership. And these—" Edward laid his hands gently on the stack of materials in front of them—"these are his books." He looked at the young man sitting in front of him. "Ian, the spiritual undercurrents at Harvard are strong. If these books are authentic—if they are saying what I think they are—they may be a powerful tool for Truth, in the right hands."

Ian cleared his throat. "Well, it happens that I'm a teaching assistant for Dr. William Mansfield, a senior professor of history. He's a wonderful Christian man with a heart to reach the campus for the Lord." Goose bumps rose on Ian's arms. "Believe it or not, he's also a curator of the library, and he looks at old books all the time."

Edward sat back in his chair. He glanced sideways at Kathryn. "Can you call him?"


The coffee cups were empty, the soup bowls stacked in the sink, as Mansfield's voice quietly filled the sunny kitchen. A series of parchment pages were clipped to a blotter in front of him. He was careful not to touch the brittle edges as he read from the old letter:

> "So what was my father's plan? I have been praying for the answer to that question for fifteen long years. And tonight, I awoke with such a burning in my soul; I believe I know! Thanks be to God! Through those of us with positions and means in society there is an easy way of ensuring that the name of Christ always remains in force at Harvard University. If not directing the play, as we would all pray, at least prominent *on* the stage."

Mansfield's voice was taut with emotion as he turned to the next page and continued reading. The others sat silent, intent.

> "Bear with me but a little longer, Jonathan, as I explain my thinking. As Harvard University grows more enamored with commerce and less with the cross of Christ, what will become the standard of influence? It is unlikely to be, may Heaven forgive us, the fruit of the Spirit or the wisdom of the Lord evident in the character of a man. Instead, as the ages have proven, wherever Christ is not the center (and unfortunately sometimes even where He is) monetary gain often speaks loudest to our sinful natures. Unredeemed man will gravitate toward the benefactors of monetary gifts where he might not toward the Benefactor of all life.
>
> "So this was my epiphany. If we want to ensure that Christ will be purposefully kept before the eyes of Harvard students, let us actually *buy* that assurance. Let us use the splendid financial favors that God has bestowed on us to create endowments for whichever priorities we hold most dear. For example, given my interest in the political arena, I would consider endowing a permanent salary for a Christian professor to teach the art of governing with integrity. Perhaps I should provide for scholarships to young men of faith and character that could use Harvard as a springboard to political leadership in this young nation of ours, but who cannot afford the tuition on their own. Or perhaps, rather than civics I should endow a professorship for

a Christian teacher of science now that advancements are being made so rapidly—students could use the reminder that we must use our knowledge for good and not for evil.

"You can see, Jonathan, that the possibilities are limited only by our financial fortunes and our creativity as to what grants and endowments would make the greatest impact years hence. Now, obviously, there is nothing we can do that can substitute for the power of the Holy Spirit to defend His own name. Psalm 127: 'Except the Lord build the house, they labor in vain that build it. Except the Lord keep the city, the watchman waketh but in vain.' But knowing that the Lord desires His name to be honored at Harvard, we can build and we can watch. And then we can trust Him to take our humble offering and magnify His name!

"I leave this to you to think through until we meet. Based on a notation in my father's ledger, I feel certain he had set aside the initial funds he intended to use for this purpose—the purpose he was hastening to discuss with you on the day he died. In the morning I will go speak with his banker of many years and confirm my hunch.

"I look forward to meeting with you and any friends that you propose in three weeks' time. With great anticipation, I remain your humble servant, Cleon Grindley."

The kitchen settled into quiet, all eyes staring into the distant past. Edward stirred after a moment and gently opened the heavy ledger.

"Dr. Mansfield, if you look here…and here…and here…you'll see large balances that occur roughly three months, one year, and four years after the date of this letter. Each of them is then noted as being transferred to the Harvard administration. And from the books I've gone through so far, each of them appears to be accompanied by a letter and contract with the university, including a stamped receipt."

He pulled out another blue bound book, carefully opening it to a marked section. "This document outlines Cleon Grindley's specifications for the first two grants. See here? 'To be bestowed upon men of the highest Christian faith and character, between the ages of sixteen and twenty-five, who meet the standard of need.'" He looked up at Mansfield and Ian. "This has to be describing those merit scholarships he referred to in the letter." He flipped through a few more pages. "There's another contract here that endows a Chair at the university for a Christian professor of the sciences."

Edward gently grasped Mansfield's arm. Ian could see the wrinkled hand trembling. "The records of Cleon Grindley alone appear to show that Harvard was given the money for several hundred thousand dollars' worth of grants—in today's dollars—for

Christ-centered purposes on campus. And as far as I know, not a penny of it is being used for its stated purpose."

Mansfield fingered the blotter. "As I told you when I got here, Mr. Grindley, these documents are almost certainly authentic. And if they are…" Mansfield locked his fingers behind his head and leaned back in his chair. A slow smile was beginning to play across his features. "…the timing is just about perfect."

"May I ask what you mean?"

"It might take too long to fully explain, but suffice it to say that Ian and I, and dozens of students, have been working hard on a project that we hope could restore some balance to the rather hostile campus environment. The project will reach its climax soon. If this information here is accurate—" he gestured to the pile of old books and papers—"not only is it incredibly important for its own sake; it also comes at a time that might give us a tremendous amount of support."

"I have been praying about this nonstop since we found these documents yesterday," Edward said. "I feel as if we are on the cusp of something extraordinary, something the Lord has long planned for just such a time as this. Just now the Lord dropped a Scripture reference in my mind: 2 Kings 2:19–22. But I can't remember what that passage is. Wait a moment."

He turned awkwardly in his chair, and pulled a Bible out of the dish rack on the counter beside him. He caught Ian's amused expression and gave a sheepish smile. "I had to set it somewhere. Well, it gives new meaning to 'washed with the Word of God,' correct?"

Ian laughed. Edward grinned and flipped through the dog-eared pages. "Okay. Here we are.

"The men of the city said to Elisha, 'Look, our lord, this town is well situated, as you can see, but the water is bad and the land is unproductive.'

'Bring me a new bowl,' he said, 'and put salt in it.' So they brought it to him.

Then he went out to the spring and threw the salt into it, saying, 'This is what the Lord says: "I have healed this water. Never again will it cause death or make the land unproductive."' And the water has remained wholesome to this day, according to the word Elisha had spoken."

Edward looked up at his guests. "Does that mean anything to you?"

After a frozen moment, Mansfield cleared his throat. "As a matter of fact, God told me much the same thing in a dream the other night. Whatever it means, I don't think we should waste any time."

He drummed his fingers on the tabletop a moment, then turned to Ian. "We need to find out if Harvard received other grants and endowments with Christian stipulations. And whether Harvard has in fact never used that money for its intended purpose. It will probably take a lot of time to dig into this properly. At least several dozen hours tracking down the archived documents on Harvard's end."

Ian's brow instantly furrowed, and Mansfield patted his shoulder reassuringly. "Don't worry, Ian, I don't intend to work you into an early grave. But that young woman I met last week in the Christian Fellowship group—I'm thinking she might be a perfect answer to this quandary."

## TWENTY-EIGHT

CLASS HAD BEEN IN SESSION FOR ONLY TEN MINUTES, and already Claire had a headache. She looked down at her notes. Existentialism—There are no objective standards or rules to govern our decisions; all existence is based on individual, subjective choices of which standards to accept or reject from moment to moment.

She knew that this concept was wrong but had no idea how to take it apart. She sat glumly in her chair, listening.

Professor Kwong was writing on the board. "Existentialists conclude that because people freely choose which decisions to make, without guidance from any standards or rules, they are totally responsible for those choices. The downside of total freedom is total responsibility. Existentialists actually note that because individuals are *forced* to choose for themselves, this freedom and responsibility are in some ways a weight they would rather not have. These philosophers say that people are condemned to be free. If people attempt to flee from this freedom and responsibility by embracing objective standards or rules that help them make decisions, they are actually just deceiving themselves.

"This is why so many existentialist writings are so heavy—as you may have noticed from the readings I assigned. In their view, life is simply a series of experiences and choices, so confronting the most difficult subjects—the most extreme forms of human life—will provide the deepest experiences.

"Now, what does this philosophy have to say about right and wrong?" When no hands were raised, he called on a girl in the back.

"Well, it says that there isn't any real right or wrong. It's up to you to decide what is right or wrong in each situation."

"And what are the consequences of those choices? How would this work for moral decision making?" Professor Kwong looked at the back row. "Niles?"

Claire turned in time to see a ruggedly handsome blond student put his hand down. "Well, for one thing we wouldn't be shackled by some outmoded sense of religious guilt."

Claire sighed. *How come the cute ones are all messed up?*

"Existentialism," Niles continued, "says that you as an individual are completely responsible for your choices. Which is *good* because that means you'll be careful with the choices you make. Which means your choices will be the right ones for that situation."

The professor clasped his hands behind his back. "So you agree with the existentialist philosophy?"

"It makes great sense. Every moral decision you come across will probably be a bit different from the last one, and you bear the responsibility for making the right decision in *this* situation."

*But without any standards, how do you know which decision to make?* Almost without thinking, Claire raised her hand.

"Claire?"

"Uh—" she took a deep breath and turned to look at Niles. "I guess what I'm wondering is: If you don't have any standards to rely on, how do you know which decision to make?"

"What do you mean? The same way you make any decision. You just know what's right to do—what's right for you."

Claire shook her head, confused. "But that doesn't make any sense! Without a rule to go by, *how* do you know?"

"Oh, come on. Don't tell me you need a rule to tell you what to do. Suppose you saw a person beating up a child in a store. What's the right thing to do?"

Claire felt herself blushing. "Well, stop them, of course."

"See? You didn't need a rule to tell you that. You just knew."

"But—"

"But what? It's obvious. Just use your human reason."

Claire glanced at the professor. He showed no signs of stopping the discussion. The other students were listening with interest. She screwed up her courage.

"But what about cases where the decision isn't obvious? Like, say that the person isn't beating up the kid but is just giving her a hard spanking in the parking lot. She's the parent, she presumably knows her kid—but you're a little uncomfortable watching it happen. Existentialism says you just sort of...have to make a choice without any standards to go by?"

"And what rules or standards do you refer to for *that* one?" Niles said. "It's not like city code number eighteen hundred says, 'Thou shalt stop a spanking in progress in a grocery store parking lot.' You just have to rely on instinct. What *else* would you rely on?"

*Well, prayer, for one thing.* Claire could see all heads turn toward her, like a classroom version of a tennis match. She wasn't about to say her real answer out loud. Why didn't someone jump in and help her? She shot a glance across the room. Brad's seat was empty.

"Well..." she floundered, then grasped thankfully at a counterquestion that popped to mind. "What happens if *you* rely on instinct and someone else relies on another way of making decisions? You could end up with two completely different outcomes. One of you stops the mom from spanking the child; the other walks on by. How could both be right?"

The heads turned the other way. Claire breathed a sigh of relief.

"Well, obviously, the two different people bear the responsibility for their different choices." Niles shrugged. "What was right for one person wasn't right for the other person, I suppose."

Claire's head was starting to swim again. Her confusion must have shown on her face, because Niles jumped on it.

"Look, the whole point of existentialism is that because different standards supply conflicting advice, you can't rely on some simple rule. You have to make individual decisions case by case. And in this case, what's right for *me* is to stop the mom from spanking her child because I think that's child abuse. But what's right for *you* may be to walk on by and pretend you didn't see anything. Then we both have to live with the consequences of that decision."

The heads turned back to Claire. The silence lengthened until Professor Kwong coughed and took back control of the discussion. Claire could feel Jo looking at her sideways, feel the almost pitying smile on her face. As the professor went on to the next point, Claire sat red faced and glum. How on *earth* was she ever going to handle this class?


Niles stood as the class broke up. Students were chattering all around him, but he didn't join in. He rarely did.

He looked over at the girl as he stuffed his notebook into his satchel. She was pretty cute. Too bad she was so misguided.

He snorted in derision as he replayed their debate over spanking. Everyone knew it was wrong. Except his parents, of course. *Spare the rod and spoil the child.* They had *that* down to a fine art, not that they would ever have done it in a parking lot where anyone could see.

They had beaten him until he was black and blue, and did anyone from their prim and proper church ever lift a finger or ask a question? No, of course not. They were too busy singing their hymns about the Good News to notice the tears of a little boy in the pew beside them. Too busy passing hellfire judgment on others to notice the cancer in their own souls.

All those religious fanatics were so dangerous, clinging together in their churches, schools, and bookstores, hiding behind their little facades of piety. It was all meaningless, all smoke and mirrors.

He stalked out of the room, hardly watching where he was going. The last sermon he had heard at their sickening church was on proselytizing. He had been a teenager, and completely disinterested, but he'd understood the gist at least.

Niles gagged at the idea of spreading such hypocrisy.


"Hey." Claire dumped her backpack on the floor and flopped lengthwise across her bed. She stared over at Sherry, who was logging off her e-mail account. "Let me guess whose e-mail you were reading."

Sherry turned in her chair and shrugged, her cheeks slightly flushed. "I'm sure you'd be right."

"If only someone would write me witty and romantic e-mails six times a day as Stefan does for you…" She grinned suddenly. "I would probably go stark raving mad." She bounced up off of the bed. "I've got to get studying, or I'm never going to be ready for midterms. I have no idea what I'm doing in philosophy, and I haven't even looked at my biology textbook in a week!"

"Yeah, I know what you mean. My literature class is awful. Did I tell you we had to read an entire novel each week?"

"No kidding? That's as bad as that stupid religion cross-reg class I tried to take. And you already had a really tough schedule. You're one of the smartest people I know, but still…"

"I don't know what I was thinking. My accounting class alone was already too advanced. But people keep saying Parkinson is the best, so I figured if the professor was good I could hack it, but now I have all these tests coming up at once…." Sherry's voice died away as she looked at the thick stack of accounting workbooks on her desk.

"Well, listen. Why don't you come to lunch with some of the HCF folks after history tomorrow? Alison and Doug are both business students and I'm pretty sure Alison had that accounting class last year. She might still have her notes."

"You think they'd share?"

"They're both pretty generous. And it's not like there's anything wrong with sharing class notes." Claire grinned. "That *is* why the school arranges study groups for most classes, after all. It's not cheating, not like those files and files of tests that some folks keep!"

"Good point." Sherry stood up, restless.

"So you'll join us for lunch? The others would love to spend some time with my elusive roommate."

"Yeah, sure. Thanks for thinking of me."

A warmth grew in Claire's belly as she watched her roommate's firm nod. *Finally!*

It would make such a difference once Sherry got to know the HCF folks. She just needed friends who would—

"You know what?" Sherry walked toward the phone on the wall by Claire's desk "I'm going to mention this to Stefan. He's no accounting wizard, but since lots of his friends—and his dad—are in the business program, I'll see if he has any ideas, too."

Ian gulped the last of his coffee and rose from his seat. Two women who had been circling the packed coffee area like vultures descended on the table. "Are you leaving?"

"It's all yours."

As he quickly cleared his table, Ian noticed that one of the women had a map and a book about Cambridge under her arm, and he wondered how they had found this little coffee shop. It was tucked away on the second floor of the Coop, the giant bookstore in Harvard Square, and usually frequented by students.

Though a number of students had papers and textbooks laid out before them, several were clearly there to avoid studying. A rack with dozens of magazines stood just outside the coffee shop area. Ian watched a student close a textbook and go pull a magazine off the rack. He smiled to himself as she returned to her coffee. He had fallen into that trap on many a day.

He passed behind her table and his eye fell on the article she was reading. With a start, he looked closer, then quickly made his way over to the magazine rack.

## TWENTY-NINE

THE NEXT MORNING, BEFORE EUROPEAN HISTORY CLASS, Mansfield scanned the article with raised eyebrows. "Well, what do you know. I wonder if they'll win it."

"They're related, aren't they?"

"Oh yes. The CEO, Victor, is Anton's brother. I believe Anton is known to be a sort of strategist and advisor for his brother's business ventures, although he hasn't yet been enticed enough to leave the faculty and go into business with the family."

"Too bad."

Mansfield handed back the magazine. He pushed open the door to the classroom and walked in, nodding to a few students who entered at the same time. "You could say that. Sometimes I think he stays only to be perverse. If the business really is doing that well, you would think he'd jump ship and go triple his salary, wouldn't you?"

"What does their business actually do?"

"It's some kind of a holding company, I think. I don't really know, quite frankly. They have a lot of different business lines."

Ian balanced the magazine on the stack of handouts he was holding. He kept his voice low as Mansfield laid out his notes for that day's class. "The article isn't much help: 'According to leaks on the street, multinational conglomerate Pike Holdings is this year's front-runner for the annual Excellence Award, arguably the most prestigious award in the industry. The Excellence Award typically has the same effect on a business that the Best Picture Academy Award has on a movie—it can propel a little-known business into prime time, quadrupling both their profits and their stock values. Pike Holdings, however, is one of the largest privately held companies in the country, and its stock is not yet offered for public sale. With rumors of the award now circulating, speculation is rampant that the closely held conglomerate may be planning an initial public offering, finally giving other investors a bite of the pie. Mouths are watering on Wall Street.'"

Ian closed the article and sighed. "It's like Psalm 73 where Asaph laments that exactly the wrong people always seem to win."

Mansfield wagged a finger at his protégé. "You don't know that. Be fair. Maybe Victor Pike and his company are completely different from Anton."

Claire yawned, stretching in her seat as the class broke up. She looked around, watching for Alison and the other HCF students who had arranged to meet her and Sherry for lunch.

"Hey, Sherry." Claire waved to her roommate, two seats in front of her. "There's no rush. They'll meet us here in about five minutes." When Sherry didn't look at her, a cold knot formed in her stomach. "Aren't you coming to lunch?"

Sherry slung her backpack over her shoulder. "Can't. I'm meeting Stefan. We'll probably grab some pizza at Loker Commons."

"Hey, you're standing me up! I was looking forward to introducing you to Brad, and Alison, and—"

"Some other time, okay?"

"No, it's not okay. You said you'd come."

"Look, Claire, don't push, all right? I've got things going on, too, you know. Stefan's going to help me study for that accounting exam."

"How's he going to do that? You said yourself he wasn't an accounting whiz." Something in her roommate's face made Claire grow still, the tension forgotten. "No. He doesn't have the questions from the test…does he?"

Sherry's eyes flickered away.

"Don't do it, Sherry. Don't. I know that people sometimes share tests, but it's *cheating*. Come on! You are *so* much smarter than I am. You're smart enough to whiz through anything if you study!"

Her roommate hesitated for just a moment.

"Sherry, I'm sorry I snapped at you. Look, why don't you come to lunch with the gang? It's a great group of people, and you'll love hanging out with them."

"But Stefan's meeting me…"

"Call and leave a message on his voice mail. He'll understand."

"There you are!" Stefan was bounding down the steps at the side of the room. "I was on my way to Mem Hall to meet you and realized your class was right on the way."

Sherry straightened and smiled at Stefan as he scooted down the row of seats toward her. He pulled her to him and gave her a quick kiss.

"Ready to go?"

Claire smiled. "Stefan, Sherry and I were just talking about our previous lunch plans. There's a group of us from the HCF meeting in a few minutes. Want to join us?"

"No thanks. Not my kind of crowd, honestly." As he turned away, Claire caught Stefan sharing a private smirk with Sherry and rolling his eyes in her direction.

"I'm so *terribly* sorry to hear that such nice people are not your kind of crowd."

Claire's voice was biting, even as she knew she was going too far. "But they *are* really great, and they were looking forward to meeting Sherry."

Sherry lowered her head and glared at the floor. A small smile appeared on Stefan's lips. "Looks like they'll have to meet her another time, then." He put his hand against the small of Sherry's back, guiding her out of the row and out of the room.

Sherry didn't look back.

Claire collapsed on her chair and put her head in her hands. *Lord, please forgive me. I want Sherry to like me and trust me, and I just screwed that up so badly. Please, dear Lord…make up for my mistake. Your strength is made perfect in my weakness—*

She heard the soft sounds of someone approaching behind her. A gentle hand was laid on her shoulder.

"Claire? You okay?"

She sniffed quickly and wiped her eyes against her sleeve before turning around. Brad's face was concerned, his eyes gentle. She started crying again.

"I'm so awful, Brad, so unlike how God wants me to be. I totally lost my cool, and now Sherry's not coming…."

As Claire poured out the story, she could see several others quietly gathering around her, their eyes gentle and concerned.

"…so now I may have turned her off from HCF completely. When what she needs *most* is to get connected to Christian friends." She wiped her eyes on her sleeve again, fresh tears threatening to overflow.

Brad fished in his satchel and handed Claire a pack of tissues. "Claire," he said gently, "you've got such a good heart."

Claire's lip quivered. "Brad, please! I—"

"No, I mean it. The only reason you're so sensitive to what you did is because God has given you such a soft heart and such a burden for Sherry. We all get angry sometimes. So did Jesus. How we handle it is the important thing."

Alison crouched down to eye level with Claire. "You can't make someone walk a straight path. You can only hold someone accountable to the extent that they're willing to be held accountable. And you're trying, aren't you?"

Claire looked up at Alison and nodded.

Alison smiled. "All God wants from you is for you to be faithful to Him. You're his servant; you do what you think He's telling you to. But the results are up to Him. Only the Holy Spirit can change someone's heart."

"But I'm so worried that she's not listening to Him."

Brad touched her arm. "And you can't really make her listen, can you? You can only try to model Jesus for her. Why don't we take a minute to pray, okay? That's what Sherry needs most right now."

Without a word, the others sank into nearby seats and began lifting up Sherry—and Claire—before the Lord.

An hour later, Caliel glared across the room at the spirits drooling over his charge. Sherry sat at Stefan's desk, nervously flipping through a textbook. While two demons smirked in the corner another was perched on the desk. From time to time he reached out a hand as if to caress her face. Each time, Caliel barked an order and the spirit withdrew his hand until the next attempt, looking at him with bold eyes.

Caliel longed to draw his sword and wipe the smiles off all their faces, but he was under restraint from heaven. He could carry the message, could urge her to obey, could fight if Sherry herself allowed it—but it must be her choice.

He had heard the deep longing of his Master for this little one, the yearning of a Father for a restless child to be safe and at peace in His care. But Sherry was putting herself in danger. Caliel looked across the room. She didn't know the half of it.

Stefan was half in and half out of the closet, banging through boxes. A dark figure lolled nearby, gazing at Caliel. From hard experience with Katoth over the last few months, the angel sensed another challenge coming. He returned the gaze of his high-ranking opponent, continuing his silent prayers for strength and wisdom. Unlike the mischief makers, or even the lustful Prach over there on the desk, Katoth was an experienced agent of the enemy. And his assignment was generational.

There was a lot of history over there by the closet, with a great deal of Satan's power behind it.

"Found it."

Sherry jumped as Stefan slapped a file down on the desk.

"I knew I had it here somewhere. One of my buddies took accounting with old Parkinson last year. He never changes his tests—too set in his ways. They've taken to calling it Parkinson's disease."

Sherry smiled briefly then stared at the closed folder. She didn't move.

"What's the matter, Sher? Afraid there's an electric shock when you open it? Hidden cameras? Whooo…" He circled her chair, waving his fingers and making a cartoonish ghost sound. "Afraid a lightning bolt is going to come down through the ceiling and *get ya?*"

"Stop it." She turned her back to him. "You're bein' ugly."

Stefan bent down, brushing her hair aside. "I just love it when you talk Southern to me." He buried his lips in the nape of her neck.

Sherry's annoyance fled as tingles ran up and down her spine. She could feel small kisses working their way up her neck and to her ear, feel his hands working their way—

She stiffened and grabbed his hands in hers, lifting them away.

"Still aren't ready, Sher?"

"We talked about that. You know that. Besides, I have to study for this test—" Her eyes flashed back to the file on the desk.

Stefan crouched beside her chair, took her hands, and looked into her face. "Why is this bothering you so much, Sher?" He pushed a wayward lock of hair from her eyes. "I've been worried about you since midterms began. Your tough schedule really seems to have caught up with you. Now, you know how much I admire your guts, but you *are* only a freshman, and it just takes a while to figure out how to juggle it all. By next semester you'll be cruising, and you won't need the help."

He brought her hands to his lips, kissing them gently. "But now you *do* need the help. This way, at least, you won't be unfairly penalized for taking such a demanding schedule."

Sherry's forehead wrinkled suddenly. "I've tried to stay on top of all my classes, but every professor gives so much homework it's like—"

"It's like they each think theirs is the only class you're taking? So they each assign so much work it's impossible to keep up with all of it?"

"Exactly! I mean, it's been driving me crazy that—"

Stefan captured her hands again, and his fingers caressed hers. "Sher, there's no way your professors can expect you to do all this without help. You've got to understand. This is truly commonplace. *Everyone* knows that Parkinson never changes his tests. I'm sure everyone else went out and found their copies weeks ago."


Caliel's face grew hard. *Lies, Sherry.*

He felt her spirit quiver, her senses attuned solely to the fingers moving slowly along her hands. *Sherry, resist.*

Was she even hearing him?

Suddenly, Caliel felt her spirit pull back from Stefan, saw the doubt flicker in her eyes. He lunged toward his charge...and was slammed back by a dark wall. As he stumbled and righted himself, Caliel's eyes bored into those of Katoth, who smiled slowly and whispered to Stefan. The young man kissed Sherry's hand again.

Caliel's face grew fierce. He drew his sword.

Instantly he felt the restraint of the Holy Spirit. Arm poised to strike, he quivered, straining to remain still. It must be her choice to make. Her choice. He expelled a tight burst of frustration.

Katoth's eyes narrowed at the angel's tension, the drawn sword. His lips drew back in a derisive smile. He turned his back on Caliel and his attention to Sherry.

Stefan's eyebrows were raised. "I'm not kidding, Sher. I've run into, oh, half a dozen people in that class, and *all* of them already have the old test."

"But if it's not allowed…"

"Look, you can take some invisible high road on this if you want, but it would be pretty stupid. Everyone else is going to know the questions ahead of time; why shouldn't you? Especially since you're taking much harder courses than they are and have had less time to study. But, hey, it's up to you."

Sherry fiddled with the file folder, running her fingers up and down the edge. "Stefan, I just don't know."

Caliel saw his opening and burst through the dark wall, swinging his sword toward the desk.

"Ahh!" Sherry jumped as the thick manila edge sliced across her skin. The file tumbled to the ground as she popped her bloodied finger in her mouth.

Katoth jerked around and glared at Caliel. He growled an order, and Prach and the other demons came at him from every direction, clawing and cutting. Caliel felt his sword hit its mark many times, but each time his adversaries swarmed back. He gasped as a powerful blow ripped across his side, then another across his face. They were stronger than he had expected.

He was being backed up, slowly, slowly, away from his charge. *Sherry, flee from evil!* Caliel shouted. *The Lord is your light and your salvation. He makes the weak strong. He gives grace to help in time of need.*

His adversaries winced at the words. Katoth growled.

*Sherry, turn your ear from lies. Recognize the Lord's voice. He yearns to rescue you. Choose Him!*

Caliel watched across the room as Katoth circled Sherry, his eyes narrow, hungry.

Stefan's smile was gentle as he applied a small bandage. "That better, clumsy-head?"

"I didn't mean to be such a baby. Why do paper cuts hurt so much, anyway?" Sherry rubbed her bandaged finger, then glanced at the clock on the wall. "Listen, I've got a lot of work to do this afternoon. I should get going."

"I wish you'd stay, but I understand." Stefan bent down and retrieved the file folder and its spilled contents. "At least take this with you. You've earned it!"

"Actually, I was thinking I'd better avoid it like the plague lest it bite me again!"

Stefan's smile wavered for just an instant before he chuckled and started to extend the file again.

Sherry grabbed her jacket from the back of the chair and slipped it on. She picked up her textbooks in one hand, her backpack in the other. Rising on tiptoe, she gave Stefan a quick kiss. "Thanks for the offer, Stef, but I'm serious. I really can't. It just doesn't feel right."

Caliel let out an explosive cry as he soared free of the melee. Sherry was half running down the hall. He hovered over her, watching her back, ensuring that they would not come after her. He winced at the catch in his side but didn't pause. There would be time for healing later.

He caught a hurried image of Katoth's silent fury inside Stefan's dorm room. Caliel took a deep breath. Every instinct screamed at him. This fight was nowhere near over.

CLAIRE LOOKED UP IN SURPRISE as Sherry banged into the room, dumped her backpack and several books on her desk, and turned on her computer.

"Sherry…"

"Look, I don't need any of your garbage, all right? I didn't copy the old test."

Claire crossed the room and gave her roommate a hug, feeling the distance between them in the tension of Sherry's body. "Sherry, all I wanted to say was I'm sorry. I'm sorry I snapped at you—"

"You snapped at *Stefan.*" Sherry turned back to her desk, slinging her jacket down on the pile.

"Yeah. Yeah, I did. I just got really angry when I saw him making fun of me behind my back…with you."

After a moment, Sherry turned. She didn't quite meet Claire's eyes. "I'm sorry about that. Stefan just isn't into religious stuff or religious people. I should have stood up for you, but I was pretty ticked at the time."

"I noticed."

"Yeah, well, I'm over it." She looked directly at Claire, a ghost of a grin playing on her face. "So I won't tell you what he called you after we left the building."

Claire lifted her head. "Well, then, I won't tell you how that makes me feel."

The uncomfortable look returned to Sherry's face, and she began yanking books out of her backpack. "I don't have time to play psychiatrist to your insecurities, Claire."

Claire quivered, heat rising in her neck and face. She opened her mouth to respond.

*Peace, child.*

Her mouth closed with a snap. She turned and walked back to her desk. Sitting down, she stared at the textbook page she had interrupted. After a moment she turned the page, unable to recall what she had just read.

Silence stretched the room, broken only by the small sounds of Sherry putting her things away.

After a time, Claire heard Sherry stop, then sigh. The sound of her light steps approached, and Claire felt a gentle cuff on her shoulder.

"Sorry. That was mean. You've told me about your childhood issues, and I totally took advantage of that to hurt you. I'm sorry."

Claire's breath let out slowly. "Thanks." A smile crossed her face. "And I'm glad you didn't copy the old test."

"So am I." Sherry turned back to her desk and computer. "I'd better get studying."

"Going to try to beat accounting into submission?"

"No, I need to ease into that. I'll start with our history reading. I haven't done it in two classes, and it's getting away from me."

Two hours later, there was a tap on the door to their room.

"Come in." Claire barely glanced up.

Mercedes poked her head in. "Claire, there's someone at the door for you."

"Oh? Thanks." In her socks and sweats, Claire shuffled out to the suite's common area. Brad stood there, looking around curiously.

"Brad? Hey. How'd you know where I live?"

He put on a serious face, rubbing his hands together. "Ve have vays...." Claire rolled her eyes, and he grinned. "No, seriously, I was over here helping Teresa study for her statistics midterm. We were going to knock off for dinner and wondered if you wanted a study break."

"Helping Teresa with stats, huh?" She shivered in mock disgust. "Yuck. Better you than me for *that* subject, dude."

"What, you don't like integrals? Derivatives?"

"I hate that kind of stuff."

"Well then, you'll love stats. Derivatives is calculus."

She grabbed a small pillow off the couch and held it up threateningly, trying not to laugh. "You have the same kind of humor as my cousin from New Orleans, and *he* drives me crazy."

"You have a cousin in *Nawlins?* So do I." He raised his eyebrows. "How do you pronounce the capital of Louisiana, again?"

She shrugged. "New Orleans. Why?"

Brad shrugged back. "Because I pronounce it *Baton Rouge.*"

The pillow flew. He held his hands over his head. "Get *out!*" She pointed at the door, laughing hard. "You are *not* allowed in this room. Git!"

He minced out the door, at the last minute popping his head back in, talking quickly. "If you want to come to dinner..."

She picked up another couch pillow and tried to level her best glare at him. His eyes widened in mock surprise, and his voice quickened.

"...Teresa and I are leavinginfiveminutes. Bye."

He disappeared right before the pillow struck the doorjamb.

Claire giggled as she hustled back into her room to change.

"What was *that* all about?" Sherry was turned in her chair, facing the doorway.

"That was just Brad." She went to her closet and pulled out a pair of khakis. "Goofball."

"He likes you."

"What?"

"He likes you. It's obvious."

Claire put her hands on her hips. "You weren't even out there. How can you say that?"

"Honey, I don't need to *see* it to know these things. He likes you. And you like him. Don't you?"

Claire pulled on her khakis, wrinkling her nose. She couldn't keep a small smile from playing on her lips.

Sherry crowed. "I knew it!" She rubbed her hands together. "Oh, this is good. Okay. What's next?"

"*Dinner* is next. And don't get any ideas. There'll be a group."

"A group…yesss…" She tapped her fingers on the desk, ruminating. "Actually, just lovely Teresa, from what I heard. Now what can we do about that?"

"Sherry." Claire was trying not to laugh.

"How about a Tonya Harding/Nancy Kerrigan sort of thing?"

"Sherry." She shook her head, giggling.

"You know, a well-placed two-by-four to the knee now and then will do wonders for the competition."

"Sherry!" Claire stomped her foot, trying hard to frown. "That's enough now, c'mon. Teresa's a sister in Christ, after all."

Sherry heaved a big sigh, shaking her head. "Yes. Yes, there is that." She brightened and looked up. "I've got it! How about we drug her in the middle of the night and ship her off to a nunnery."

"Okay. Okay, I'm outta here." Claire shrugged into her coat. "Why don't you join us for dinner? Someone said they have that cheesecake you like so much. Cheesecake has *got* to be some sort of brain food."

"Nah. Thanks, though. I'm not even caught up on history. I've got to get to that accounting stuff soon or I'm doomed."

"Well, I won't try to tempt you then. But I'll bring you back some."

"Thanks." Sherry turned back to her desk.

As she left the room, Claire called back over her shoulder. "And don't check your e-mail! You'll be on all night if you do that."

Sherry jerked her hand from the computer mouse. "Okay!"

The clatter of trays and plates surrounded the students as they sat at one end of a long table. The others had made quick work of their dessert, but Teresa's cheesecake was hardly touched.

"I just thought that was how every family lived, you know?" Teresa shook her head. "I would barely make friends, and we would move. But my dad had to go wherever the jobs were. He spoke English pretty well, but since he didn't have much of an education, the jobs weren't exactly chasing him."

"I had no idea you had such a hard childhood," Claire said. "I mean, no offense, but you seem so…*polished.* I would've thought you came from a long line of Ivy League grads—or at least college grads! I would never have guessed that your background was so different from most people here. I *knew* I liked you!" A grin broke out on her face as Teresa laughed.

"When did your dad come over from South America?" Brad asked.

"I think he was twenty. He had met my mom when she was on a summer missions trip there. They wrote letters every week, and the next year he got a visa to visit her in the States. He never left. No matter where we move to, the first thing he puts up on the wall is a copy of his citizenship oath."

"It sounds like your dad is a very special person," Claire said.

"Yes, he is. He's a gentle man who loves the Lord with all his heart. Dad has worked so hard all his life to put a roof over our heads. And he has never, *never* complained." Her lip quivered slightly. "He taught us to be grateful for everything we had, even when all we had was each other."

"How many brothers and sisters did you say you have?" Brad asked.

"There are three of us." She smiled slightly. "When we landed in Chicago, Dad knocked on the door of every private school he could find to try to get us the education he never had. We were in the inner city, but there was this really good Catholic school nearby where we could work to help pay the tuition. We all wanted to do so well, to make our dad proud. Believe it or not, my older sister is at Yale, and my younger brother was just accepted here also. Partial scholarships for all of us."

Brad and Claire both exclaimed aloud.

"Three kids from inner-city Chicago, first-generation Americans, going to Ivy League schools?" Claire said.

Brad leaned forward. "What about your mom? What's she doing?"

Teresa grew still. She didn't speak for a moment.

"That's okay, you don't need to get into it if—"

"No, it's okay. I'd kinda like someone here to know, actually." She paused and looked at Brad and Claire. "It's sort of hard to explain, but…well, about seven years ago my mom started working part time, and my dad—after working two or three jobs at a time—finally got a fairly stable job. We were so glad that he could finally stop killing himself. And we even built up a little bit of savings. See, we had moved to Chicago because Mom got a job at a bank that would pay for health insurance. We'd never had health insurance before, and—"

"You'd never had health insurance? Ever?" Brad said.

"Nope."

"What'd you do if you got sick?"

"We just had to make do. Dad actually had a chronic heart problem, but—before we got the insurance—couldn't even afford the cheap community clinic nearby. Once he had this terrible chest pain, and Mom insisted on driving him to the emergency room. He got there just in time. About five minutes later he had a heart attack. We were all crying. I was only ten and so scared. But God was watching over us big time. There must've been angels clearing a path through the traffic or something, because normally it would take us twenty minutes to get to the hospital; that day it only took ten. Thank God." She shivered.

"So anyway, the reason we'd moved to Chicago was because Mom's bank job would pay for health insurance—which we needed, obviously. And then Dad got us into that Catholic school. And with the two jobs we finally saved a little money. Everything was going so well for a while.

"And then, a coworker of Mom's convinced her to play the Lotto. At first it was no big deal; she'd buy tickets on a lark whenever those huge jackpots got built up. But somewhere along the way she got hooked. She started playing every day on her way home from work and didn't tell my dad. She started spending a dollar a day—just one ticket a day. But soon it was five, then ten."

She glanced at Brad and Claire. They looked back at her soberly. "Fifty dollars—sometimes a *hundred* dollars—would just vanish into thin air *each week*. Dad started having trouble paying the bills but didn't know why. He didn't know that Mom was drawing down our savings account."

Teresa fiddled with her fork, her self-assurance vanishing. "And then she started going to casinos. Sometimes when she was supposed to be at work, she'd take a day trip on the free bus out there. These casino companies make it so easy, so seductive. Mom was always convinced that the next dollar—the next one—would finally win back all the money she'd lost.

"Before we knew it, she…she ended up gambling away our life savings and getting us deep into debt. She knew it was wrong, knew it would devastate us, but she was like a junkie or something. She was willing to do anything to win that money back and not have to face us with the truth. To tell us that all of Dad's hard work…"

Claire reached sideways and took her friend's hand in hers. Teresa's eyes grew red, and she looked hard at the table, her jaw muscle working. A teardrop wound its way down Teresa's cheek. She brushed it away and pressed the heels of her hands into her eyes. After a moment, she looked back up.

"My mom was terrified about losing all our money, and she had nothing left to gamble away to try to get it back. So she…she decided to take some of the bank's money and gamble with that. They found out of course and convicted her of theft and embezzlement. She served some time in prison and will be on parole practically forever."

Claire squeezed Teresa's hand. Her eyes were bleak as she looked for a long moment at her friend. "What is your mother doing now?"

Teresa smiled sadly. "Oh, she's been out a few years, and she's doing her court-mandated community service. She can't ever get another good job, not with a felony conviction. She realizes how much she screwed up her life—and ours—and she's living under a lot of guilt. She's going to Gamblers Anonymous and living with her parents in Detroit. I really believe it will be okay in time, but right now it's a long road back. Real life doesn't work like the nice, neat movie endings."

Brad shook his head. "Teresa, I'm so sorry. I had no idea. We're honored that you took us into your confidence. Thank you for sharing all of that."

"How's your father handling all of this?" Claire asked.

"Oh, he's…he's doing okay. God has always been so faithful, and Dad knows how to lean on Him. Better than the rest of us, sometimes."

"Teresa," Claire leaned forward. "What are you not telling us? There's something else. Isn't there?"

Her friend's eyes filled again. "It's just that Dad lost his health insurance when Mom lost her job. The doctors…" she bit her lip, struggling to keep her emotions in check, "The doctors still need to watch his heart, but now he can't afford the visits, and I *know* he skips his heart medicine to pay for things the kids need. I keep telling him to take his medicine and not to worry about us, but he's so stubborn where we're concerned."

When Teresa fell silent again, Claire said, "Thank you for telling us that story. You should mention this to the HCF prayer team, too."

Teresa let out a long breath and smiled at the concerned expressions on the faces of her two friends. "Maybe I'll do that. Thanks for listening." She straightened in her seat and glanced at her watch. "Wow, we've been forever. I've got to run a book back to the library before nine o'clock. Brad, would you mind waiting a few minutes before starting up on stats again?"

"No problem. I'll walk Claire back and meet you there."

Teresa grabbed a takeout box and neatly transferred the untouched cheesecake into it. She held it out to Claire. "Why don't you take this back to Sherry?"

Claire smiled her thanks and began shrugging into her parka as Teresa dashed out the door.

With a satisfying thump, Sherry closed the massive history textbook. She eyed the clock, then the next set of materials on her desk. Her fingers drummed a beat on the words *Generally Accepted Auditing Standards* on the cover of a slim workbook.

She stood and stretched and noticed the rumpled comforter on Claire's bed. She restretched the heavy blanket over the pillow and righted the ragged Eyeore doll. Claire was so attached to that pitiful thing.

She found a jacket that needed to be replaced on its hanger, shirts and pants to be stored in their drawers, jumbled papers that needed sorting.

Finally she crossed the room again and stared down at her desk. The screen saver on her computer flickered to a new cartoon picture: Snoopy checking his e-mail.

*I should check to see if the TA sent something about the test.*

In a moment she was on her Harvard e-mail account. Nothing from the TA but three e-mails from friends back home and two from Stefan. One was a joke about paper cuts. She smiled as she pressed reply and started typing.

*Rap, rap, rap!*

"Come in!" Sherry called, her fingers busy on the keyboard.

The door swung open, and Mercedes popped her head in. "Hey."

"Hey. Two seconds." Sherry hit *send* and swung around. "What's up?"

"Well, since we just missed dinner at Annenburg, some of us were going to grab something at Au Bon Pain in the Square. Want a study break?"

Sherry squinted at the clock across the room. "Oh my gosh. Is it nine o'clock already?"

"A few minutes after."

Sherry smacked her head. "I can't believe I was on the computer that long!"

"You've been studying way too much. Come take a study break before you fry your brain."

"Um…I should probably get to accounting. I've got the midterm tomorrow—"

"Well then, you will definitely need a caffeine fix." She jerked her head toward the hallway. "Come on."

Slowly, Sherry rose from her chair, eyeing the stack of notes she needed to wade through. Her stomach growled a little. "Well…I haven't had dinner yet…"

"Perfect, then."

"But I haven't started accounting."

"Oh!" Mercedes snapped her fingers. "I meant to tell you…hold on." She disappeared from the doorway, and Sherry could hear her banging a few file drawers in her room. She walked back in, holding out a thin, stapled sheaf of papers.

"Here you go. Someone in my finance class gave me a copy of this, since I'm probably taking Parkinson next semester."

Sherry just stared as Mercedes strode across the room and pulled out the bottom drawer of her desk.

"I'll just stick it here, and if you want it you know where it is." Mercedes turned around, her smile bright. "Ready to go?"

# THIRTY-ONE

BRAD SEEMED DEEP IN THOUGHT as he and Claire left the warmth of the dining room and hurried across the dark stretch of grass in front of Memorial Hall. When he finally spoke, his voice was quiet.

"Do you mind if I ask you something, Claire?"

"No, go ahead."

"What was that all about back there? Most of the folks here—like me—can't really relate to Teresa's background, no matter how empathetic we want to be. But you...you seemed to know a lot about what Teresa was saying."

"We had something similar happen in our family, Brad." Her voice was short. "That's why."

Brad stopped walking, and she could feel his penetrating gaze. She stopped beside him and looked down.

"You don't have to tell me," Brad said. "I'm sorry. I shouldn't have—"

"No, it's okay. Like Teresa, I'd kinda like someone here to know. Although I don't want everyone—"

"You don't need to worry, Claire. If you want to tell me something, that's fine. If you don't, that's fine. It won't go any further."

"Compared to what Teresa has gone through, it's nothing." She took a breath, then plunged ahead. "When I was in junior high, my family declared bankruptcy."

Brad made a short sound of surprise, and Claire smiled wryly. "See, my dad had gotten hooked on credit cards. It sounds stupid, but it seems a lot like Teresa's mom and her gambling addiction. These credit card companies were *throwing* themselves at him, sending preapproved cards with limits of thousands of dollars. He started using the cards for convenience but ended up spending way more than we made. I don't know all the details, you know, but it became a stretch just to pay the minimums each month, and eventually we couldn't even afford those. And the more he got himself in debt, the more the card companies seemed to like him."

Her smile turned sour. "Isn't that crazy? Now that I'm older I understand that the card companies make more money off of people who get themselves in too deep. It just seems so irresponsible of them."

Brad didn't say anything for a moment. "Well, it might have been irresponsible of the card companies, of course, but why was your dad—"

"Look, I'm not defending what he did. He was wrong, and our family has been paying for it ever since. I cried my heart out when some men came to take away our stuff and loaded my bike on their truck. And even now I'll probably never get a student loan because of the bankruptcy. So I'm not saying they made him spend the money. I'm just saying that it seems stupid and heartless of the credit card companies to send four or five applications each *week* to someone who already has ten credit cards! It's like they know they're enticing someone who already has a problem, and that's just where they want them. It makes me shiver just thinking about it again."

She resumed walking, and Brad matched her stride. "Thanks for telling me. So if you don't have student loans…"

"I've had to bust my tail looking for scholarships." Claire grinned suddenly. "And since Harvard gives hardly any scholarships, figuring out how to afford this school has been really interesting! My mom and dad did have a small college savings account that was enough for freshman room and board, but my main source of tuition right now is from a private foundation."

"Thank God." Brad shook his head. "What a shame if you couldn't have found a way."

"I know. Just think of all the people I would never have met. Like you." Claire was glad the night was too dark for Brad to see the blush that filled her face.

He looked over at her with a brief smile and continued walking.

"What about you? Do you have a scholarship? Loans?"

"Nope. My mother lives in a penthouse suite overlooking Central Park in New York City. She's paying for school."

"Wow."

"She's a master at making deals. She said she'd pay for school *if* I went to Harvard or Yale rather than some Christian college like Wheaton."

Claire laughed aloud. "My dad said the exact opposite. He thought if I went to Wheaton maybe I'd be protected from the world and have the moral education to avoid the kinds of decisions he made."

"Different perspectives. My mother doesn't have much use for Christianity. She would get so irritated when I'd invite her to church."

"What about your father?"

"I've never had a real relationship with my father. My parents divorced when I was a baby. He was never particularly interested in us, I guess."

*O Lord God, You have spared me from so much pain that others face…*

"And since my father's family were prim and proper churchgoers—one of those gothic churches on Madison Avenue—Mother refused to have anything to do with that stuff. Even after God transformed my life."

The front of Claire's dorm rose tall in the darkness before them, and Brad slowed his step. "Mother was definitely not happy about my YWAM mission year, I'll tell you that."

"What?"

"You didn't know? Yeah, I did a year with Youth With A Mission between high school and college."

"No kidding! That must've been interesting."

"It was. I was in a small team that actually spent the year in San Francisco instead of Nepal or El Salvador or somewhere." He laughed at Claire's raised eyebrows. "Hey, San Fran is a major mission field with a lot of unhappy intellectuals searching for anything to give them contentment."

"Not to mention a city with a pretty difficult homosexual agenda, right?"

"That's true." Brad looked away for a moment, distracted by something. His voice was distant. "But mostly just a lot of tortured people searching for meaning in life. A lot of New Age junk. I learned a lot about thinking on my feet in the middle of a challenging crowd."

"So *that's* why you always seem able to handle yourself in philosophy!"

"That, and sitting under my pastor's teaching every Sunday in New York. He was a great apologist. Also, I've had a few more years of practice here than you have. It takes a while, but it just sort of clicks eventually. You'll see."

"Just thinking about it makes me queasy."

The double doors to her building banged open, and light spilled out along with five chattering students, heavy backpacks hefted over their shoulders.

"Well," Claire stepped back a pace, "I should get back to midterms. And I need to get this cheesecake to Sherry before it freezes."


The small lamp cast a pool of light over the book and papers on the desk, but Sherry could see little beyond it. She could hear the sounds of Claire's breathing and see the blankets curled up in a pile on the side of the bed. She was sure Claire was in there somewhere.

The digital clock beside her clicked smoothly over. 1:30 A.M. *Ugh.* And she still had two more sections to go over in the accounting book. One was easy, but the other…there was no way she'd be able to figure out this accrual accounting thing before nine o'clock in the morning.

Before she knew it, her hand was reaching down to the bottom drawer. Maybe she would just peek at *that* part of the test. She lifted the stapled pages to the desktop, then stopped for a second, wavering. It was almost as if voices were ringing in her head, her brain telling her to stop.

*It's only going to be that one part. If everyone else has a copy of the whole test, I'm actually doing pretty well to only look at that one section.*

At the whispering sound of turning pages, Gael came over and put his hand on Caliel's shoulder. "Courage, friend."

"We prayed; the saints prayed. The Logos says 'Lead me not into temptation.' And she *wasn't*... She was even steered away. But she chose temptation anyway. All on her own!" Caliel's eyes burned. "How can they do that! I do not understand it no matter how many times I see it. How can they look square in the face of the King of kings and thumb their nose?"

Gael stood beside Caliel, watching the young woman copy line after line into her notebook. The room was quiet except for the scratching of her pen.

"He cannot let her unwise choices stand unchallenged," Caliel said. "He is a loving Father. And whom the Lord loves, He also disciplines. He will bring His discipline, either soon or years down the road. But it will come."

Caliel paused as he heard the voice of the Lord. He listened for a moment, his gaze tender on his charge. "Her heart must remain soft to receive it. I will continue pricking her conscience. She must not let it become seared. Must not allow herself to choose this constant, wayward action. Because when the Lord delivers a child from a seared conscience...."

Gael watched his colleague's silent, ageless struggle. "But if a hand sins, it is better to cut it off and throw it into the fire than lose the whole body to the fires of hell." He clasped Caliel's arm in respect. "I pray that need not happen. But it is far better than the alternative, my friend."

"The Lord knows every instant of her struggle, every thought, every choice. And He loves this one so much. I pray that she will see His outstretched hand."

## THIRTY-TWO

SHERRY PUT DOWN HER NUMBER TWO PENCIL and closed her test booklet. Five minutes early. She got to her feet and walked the booklet up to the proctor at the front of the room. The woman hardly looked up as Sherry handed it over.

The buildings were a blur as Sherry hurried back to her dorm. The proctor would be calling time right about now. Why did she have this insane urge to go back and rip up her test and spill out her crime? Everyone did it. It was the most public secret on record.

She took the stairs two at a time and fled into her room, wondering if there was anywhere she could hide from this urge to confess. Her mouth was dry. She jerked open the small refrigerator, looking for a soft drink, and saw the untouched cheesecake Claire had brought her last night while she was out with Mercedes.

Sherry slammed the refrigerator shut and whirled around, trying to escape the terrible weight in her mind. Her eye fell on Claire's Bible, open on her bed.

*This must be one of those demonic attacks that preacher was talking about!*

Claire found Sherry sitting in front of her computer, staring at the screen.

"Hey." Claire dumped her backpack on her bed and her mail on her desk, and went over to Sherry's desk. "What's up? Don't you usually have class now?"

"Skipped it. I needed to take a nap."

"Not surprising. You must've been up all night. I could use a nap myself, but I have philosophy class in half an hour. Some hot-shot guest lecturer whose writings are really bizarre."

When Sherry didn't smile or respond, Claire walked back toward her desk. "How'd the accounting test go?"

"Fine."

"Just fine? After all that—"

"It was fine, okay?" Sherry stood up and climbed the stairs to her loft bed. She lay down with a sigh, facing the wall.

Claire stood across the room, staring up at her roommate. She forced the words out of her mouth. "Sherry, I'm sorry to bug you, but I have to ask…"

Sherry didn't turn, didn't respond.

"Sherry, you awake?"

"Yep."

"You know what I'm asking, darn it. Just tell me!"

"Fine. I used the old test. Is that what you wanted to hear?"

Claire closed her eyes and took a deep breath. "I thought you said you didn't copy Stefan's test."

"I didn't."

"Well, where'd you get it?"

"None of your business."

"Sherry—"

Sherry rolled over and sat up, staring down at Claire with angry eyes. "Look, Miss High and Mighty, I've got two papers due tomorrow and a test next week. I haven't slept more than four hours in the last four days. I'm exhausted," her voice choked, "and I've got enough other attacks going on without *you* condemning me." Tears started leaking from her eyes, and she flopped back down on her bed.

*Help, Lord....*

Claire stepped up on her bed and grasped the side of the loft. "Sherry, I have too many logs in my own eye to be judgmental about yours. The only reason I'm asking about this is that I care about you. God's rules aren't there to oppress you; they're there because He knows what's best for you and the consequences that breaking those rules will have for you down the road." She paused, considering. "What do you mean when you say other attacks are going on?"

"I don't know, Claire, okay? I just feel..." She sighed and sat up again. "I just feel...not right, you know? Like someone's hammering on my brain. I'm going crazy with the pressure. It's like that Bible verse about the devil prowling around and trying to discourage you, like you said."

"When did this start?"

"During accounting." She made an explosive sound of frustration. "I mean, the stupid test was—"

"Sherry, I really don't think you're under demonic attack. I think this pressure in your head is your conscience, not the devil. It's God's way of trying to get through to you before—"

"Hey, I don't want to hear it. I really don't." She descended the stairs from her loft. "What's really right or wrong here, anyway? If everyone does it, is it really wrong? Wouldn't I be more wrong to be the only one *not* doing it?" She walked back over to her desk and sat sideways in her chair, not looking at Claire.

"Come on, you don't believe that! First of all it's ridiculous to believe that everyone does it. But more importantly, if it's cheating it's still not right!"

"Look, Claire, maybe what's right for you isn't right for me. We all have to walk our own paths." She swung around toward Claire and thumped her chest. "Maybe it's time to do what's right for me for a change!"


Prach sighed in delight. He looked over at Caliel and Gael, their swords out but impotent in the face of yet another human choice. Ah, just as in the days of old, just as in the master stratagem of the Garden, the model of all his work. He snickered, flaunting his success.

These sickening humans were so easy to influence. This one had made her choice, and he would seal it soon. Now if only he could get his hands on the other one…. He looked hungrily at Claire, watching her pleading face, and shook his head. The Spirit of the accursed Enemy was strong on her and was growing stronger every day. He itched to work on his charge with no interference.

Claire finally grabbed her backpack and headed for her philosophy class. Prach smiled. Maybe his colleagues there would have better luck at confusing and intimidating her. He returned his attention to the dark-haired one, rubbing his hands together, anticipating his next move.


"So in his landmark book *Rocks of Ages,* how does Gould define religion?" Author and guest instructor Leyla Lemoine barely glanced out at the watching students. "He defines religion by *contrasting it to science.*"

Claire doodled in the margins of her notepad, her face tight, half her mind still on the argument in her room. She wasn't in the mood for this class today. Professor Kwong had told them to expect a luminary in the world of current philosophical thinking; he hadn't told them to expect a New Age diatribe.

"This is similar," the guest speaker was saying, "to my own little philosophical construct as outlined in my recent writing—I believe you have a copy of my most-published article in your materials. We can know religious beliefs only through faith. All else we learn through scientific analysis."

She paced the floor, walking like a cat on her toes. "Stephen Gould explains that science and religion are in conflict, because each claims to have knowledge of the world but each tells a very different story. The Bible says the world was created in seven days; physicists tell us that the universe burst into existence fifteen billion years ago and has continued to expand ever since."

She paused and held out her hands, palms up, as if they were two balances of a scale. "The Bible," she lifted her right hand, "tells us that God specially created humans in His image, and then created animals, which—religion tells us—we must accept purely on faith. But scientists," she held up her other hand, "have proven through empirical evidence that life evolved slowly in a long process and that the appearance of humans was essentially due to chance."

Claire set down her pen and crossed her arms, frustration showing all over her face.

"As Gould points out, science and religion ask very different questions in the process of knowledge, with very different methods for answering those questions." The instructor balanced her hands back and forth. "Where science questions 'how the heavens go'—how does the physical world operate in a predictable and understandable fashion—religion asks 'how to go to heaven.' Where science calls upon evidence and reason to answer its question, religion calls upon faith, tradition, and religious authorities to answer its question."

Her smile was rueful, and she shook her head. "Ah, religion. But then, I suppose some people still believe in God, or we wouldn't be bothering to discuss it, right?"

Claire's face grew red. She glanced across the room to Brad. He was sitting calmly, taking notes.

The instructor crossed to the whiteboard at the front of the room and drew two columns, one labeled Science the other Religion. In each she quickly wrote a few words summarizing the points made so far.

"We also see that science and religion have very different standards for deciding which answers are the correct ones. Science asks if the theory makes empirical predictions that can be independently verified. Religion asks if your belief or claim contradicts Scripture, religious authority, or tradition."

She turned back to the class. "As Gould points out, there is even an example of this tension in the Bible itself in the parable of Doubting Thomas. Several days after Jesus' public execution Thomas was told by the followers of Jesus that He had risen from the dead and appeared to them in person. Thomas said, understandably, that he would not believe them until he had *seen* and *touched* Jesus and His wounds."

Ms. Lemoine gestured with her marker to the Science column on the board. "Thomas, in other words, was being a scientist, asking for empirical evidence of a claim. But then, the story says, Jesus showed up and rebuked him for his doubt. Why was that?"

The instructor paused, looking out at the students. "Thomas had asked the correct questions, tried to use the proper methods of inquiry, and applied the appropriate standards for searching for the truth, *if—*" she held her finger up dramatically—"if he were doing science. But, as Gould points out, his methods were inappropriate for religion. That, ladies and gentlemen, is why Jesus rebuked him!"

Claire's mouth dropped open. *That's ridiculous…that…that…* Her mind wouldn't work.

"We can see from these few examples," the instructor continued, "that science and religion cannot be synthesized. Of course, religion has its place in life, offering rules for how to live and such things. But science and religion posit wildly incompatible routes to knowledge and truth. As such, I take Gould's comments one step further. They inevitably contradict each other, and they cannot both be true."

Claire watched, dumbfounded, as the guest speaker took questions from the audience. No one else seemed to object to her theory. Claire felt as though all the water chutes in a dam had been opened at once, and all the water was thundering downstream, blowing away every obstacle in its path. She had no idea how to jump in without getting herself killed.

"…well, then that would be something to consider further. But like I said, since they contradict each other, science and religion cannot both be true."

Out of the corner of her eye, Claire saw Brad raise his hand.

"If that is the case," Brad said, "then what is true, Ms. Lemoine? You say they cannot both be true—but if there *is* no God who created a specific, objective, moral order of absolutes, then there is no such thing as true, and you cannot make that statement. Furthermore, if there is no true, both of Gould's seemingly incompatible definitions of science and religion might make perfect sense together."

The guest instructor had folded her arms after the first few words and stood behind the podium, looking at the young upstart.

"It's a figure of speech, young man, a necessary terminology we must employ even though there obviously *is* no such thing as absolute truth in—"

"And I hate to point this out," Brad's voice was apologetic, "but the whole religion-versus-science question is…well, it's sort of a silly one to begin with. I mean no disrespect to you or Mr. Gould. It's an honor to have an author of your stature in our class, and I do appreciate your willingness to instruct us. But I think I should point out the straw man that seems to have been set up at the beginning of this discussion."

"What straw man?"

"From the very beginning, Gould defines religion as the opposite of science. That's a straw man—a construct designed to be shaky from the beginning and therefore easily torn down. He sets science versus religion as if they have to be incompatible, which they don't. It's ridiculous to say—" he gestured to the columns on the whiteboard—"that science depends on reason, but religion depends only on simple-minded faith, as if religion didn't also depend on reason and intellectual knowledge as well."

Leyla Lemoine was standing with crossed arms, her foot tapping a double-time beat on the floor. "What is your name, young man?"

Brad looked her in the eye. "Brad. I'm a junior."

"Well, young Brad, how is it that you have earned the right to criticize your instructors for intellectual dishonesty, to pretend to know more than a well-respected author like Stephen Gould?"

"As I said, Ms. Lemoine, I mean no disrespect to either of you. And I'm only a student; obviously I have many things to learn. Maybe I misunderstood you. But you were talking about something I strongly believe, and it *sounded* like you were teaching incorrect information as if it were true. I felt that I had to raise this point."

"Ah." The instructor's smile was all teeth as she turned to the class. "We have an absolutist in our midst—a person who believes there is actually such a thing as absolute truth. Truth with a capital *T*. Most thinking people in this day and age acknowledge that truth is relative, that there *is* no such thing as ultimate, absolute truth."

Brad raised his hand again. She called on him with an amused shake of her head.

"Ms. Lemoine, are you sure about that?"

"About what?"

"That there is no absolute truth?"

"Of course I'm sure." Her congenial expression tightened. "Brad, I am growing tired of this petty—"

"I'm sorry to point this out," Brad broke in, almost apologetically, "but you just contradicted yourself."

Muffled giggles sounded throughout the classroom.

"If there is no absolute truth, you can never claim that something is absolutely true—such as saying that you're completely sure of something." He smiled politely. "Don't you think so?"

Claire watched as the instructor struggled to keep her cool and to maintain control of the class. She looked over at Brad. *How does he do that?*

A male student sitting near Claire raised his hand. He wore a thin multicolored friendship necklace. Claire knew him only as Jarvis, who came from somewhere in the Caribbean.

As soon as he was called on, he turned tentatively toward Brad. "I do not want to be offensive, but I do not understand how you come here and preach the fundamentalist beliefs with a clear conscience. You cannot impose your views on others who disagree with you." His slight accent was thick with indignation. "I saw similar argument to yours in a talk show over summer. A television evangelist was guest on the show. He was causing the guilt, judging those who are different. And he also say there is absolute truth. But then talk show host point out that maybe there *is* real truth but since we can't really know what it is or who has it, the important thing is that you follow your heart wherever it leads. And that will lead you to the real truth. Follow your desires—"

"Yes, yes." Ms. Lemoine was nodding vigorously up front. "As I say in chapter 4 of my book *Shame No More,* if we can reach into the core of our being, touch and recognize our inmost desires—and act on them without fear, shame, or self-censorship—then that is our means to what is right for us."

*But what if those inmost desires are wrong?* Claire tapped her pencil eraser furiously against her desk. She saw the instructor's eyes searching the seats for the next student comment and lowered her head. *No, no. No way.*

Ms. Lemoine was studiously ignoring the section of the room where Brad sat. Jo Markowitz slowly raised her hand, and Ms. Lemoine beamed at her. "Yes, Jo."

"Ms. Lemoine, I loved your book—"

"Thank you."

"—but actually I had a question about that very part of chapter 4." Jo flipped through a hardcover book until she found the page she was looking for. "You talk about 'chipping away at the morass of expectations, traditions, societal mores, and self-judgments until you come to the inner sculpture within the stone: the Desire.' You say, 'If we can learn ourselves the way a sculptor learns the silent block of marble, finding and following our most perfect desire, we will achieve our true personhood.' We will, in other words, achieve what is highest and best for us."

Jo looked up at the instructor. "But I don't actually agree that you *have* one perfect inmost desire to follow. Don't we all have many desires, and aren't some of them contradictory? I *really want* to be a size eight, and I *really want* to eat all the ice cream in the cafeteria."

Laughter broke out across the classroom. Jo shrugged, waiting for an explanation.

Claire's eyes narrowed, her mind hardly registering Ms. Lemoine's response. *How come I never think of things to say until ten minutes afterward?*


That evening, when the usual group from their hallway trooped over to Annenberg for dinner, Claire fell in step with Sherry.

"I'm sorry about this afternoon. I probably came across as judgmental, and I really didn't mean to."

Sherry walked a few paces, then shrugged. "No big deal. We're just different people, that's all. So is your big meeting with Professor Mansfield tomorrow or another day?"

"Tomorrow."

A few buildings passed as the two roommates walked side by side in silence.

"You know, I was talking to someone the other day about this great church that's just one stop down on the T. There's supposedly some Harvard and MIT students there. Should we try it on Sunday?"

Sherry shrugged again. "Okay."

Sherry and Claire pulled even with two other students walking just in front of them. They were laughing and joking, and Sherry joined in without missing a beat. Claire watched the surface chatter, her hopes seizing on the new church possibility. *At least that's something…*

After a few moments, Sherry looked back over her shoulder to where Claire was walking alone a few paces behind. Claire watched her hesitate; then Sherry fell back in step with her roommate.

"Look." She looped her arm through Claire's. "I'm sorry to be irritable. It's just the more you push, the more I want to get away. So I have an idea. On Fridays Stefan and his friends always go down to a restaurant in Boston. Why don't you join us Friday night? We'll probably leave—oh—eight o'clock, so you'll have plenty of time to finish up with HCF before we go. What do you say?"

"Well…" Claire pursed her lips, then looked up with a short smile. "Okay. I don't know any of Stefan's friends, but I think it'd be good to meet them."

"Great. Friday."

"Thanks."

*Lord, if this is an opportunity, help me make the most of it.*

## THIRTY-THREE

MANSFIELD HEARD A HESITANT KNOCK ON THE DOOR and glanced at his watch. "It's three o'clock already. That'll be the new research assistant I was telling you about." He jumped up and swung the door open. "Come in, come in. Claire, isn't it?"

"Yes sir. Claire Rivers." She haltingly stepped into the room, shaking Mansfield's hand.

"Claire Rivers, this is Ian Burke, my TA."

"Nice to meet you."

Mansfield guided her toward a chair then returned to his seat and pulled out his notes from the Grindley meeting.

Ten minutes later Claire sat perfectly still, trying to digest what she had just heard. Hundreds of thousands—maybe millions—of dollars in unused Christian grants and endowments!

"How can—" her voice was hoarse, and she cleared her throat. "How can Harvard *do* that? It sounds like…something weird is going on. It sounds like they've taken the money but never used it as the donors directed."

"It sounds like that," Mansfield said, "but we cannot jump to conclusions. Things are not always as they seem. Perhaps they took the money and did establish the requisite professorships or scholarships for many years, but something legitimate interfered. Maybe the family changed its mind but never recorded it. Or perhaps the university even returned the endowment funds for some reason and canceled the contract."

"Or perhaps the university just decided it didn't need to abide by an antiquated Christian contract anymore," Ian's smile was sardonic, "and decided to appropriate the funds for its own purposes, without telling anybody."

"All right, all right." Mansfield turned to Claire. "This, my dear, is why you're here." He chuckled at her startled expression. "I need a research assistant, just on a temporary basis. Ian is deeply involved in another project and cannot spend the time poring through records to investigate this further. But we absolutely need to know whether or not the Grindley endowments remain unused, as it appears, and whether or not other families did in fact provide grants and endowments with Christian stipulations. If you're interested, we'd like you to spend some time researching these old grants and endowments for us.

"We believe that the Lord may use this to give us some leverage for a very important meeting in two weeks, so we need you to piece together as much as you can before the meeting. We'll pay you the standard rate the department offers its research assistants *if* you'll agree to make yourself available beyond the usual minimum ten hours per week. This may take a few more hours than that, since I'll need your briefing one week from today."

Claire's skin tingled. What an amazing opportunity! *O God, don't let me screw this up!*

She looked up at the professor. He was regarding her soberly, his eyes searching hers. Suddenly, she was very aware of the gravity of this project, of the eternal importance it could carry. Her smile died, and she sat up straight, steadily returning the professor's gaze.

"What do you want me to do?"

Mansfield pulled forward his pages of notes, tossed Claire a notebook and a pen, and started talking.

The headlights of Mansfield's car created warm pools in the blackness as he turned right out of the Everett Street Garage and headed home. The street was deserted, the residential buildings of the Law School rising dark on his right as he passed.

He reached the end of Everett Street and turned right onto Oxford, the two-lane road that ran parallel to Massachusetts Avenue, the other natural border of the main campus. Mansfield peered down the dimly lit street ahead.

The road ended abruptly in front of him, his headlights shining on the open expanse in front of Memorial Hall. Mansfield braked heavily to take the difficult left-hand curve from Oxford Street onto Kirkland, careful not to slip on the slightly wet pavement.

He shook his head, annoyed, as the lights of campus receded in his rearview mirror. The reflector posts that were supposed to warn nighttime drivers of that ninety-degree curve kept getting taken out by inattentive drivers. People complained, but the reflectors rarely got replaced. Mansfield hoped it wouldn't require a *student* getting taken out for the complaints to be taken seriously.

He slowed when he saw the flashing taillights of a car along the side of the road. The white Bonneville was listing to the right, the back tire flat. One woman was trying to jack up the car; another wielded a flashlight. Mansfield recognized one of them and pulled over.

When he approached, the woman at the jack looked up in relief, then her expression changed to annoyance.

"Oh. It's you."

"And hello to you too, Sharon." Mansfield nodded pleasantly. "Can I do anything to help?"

"Yeah. Call a tow truck." Sharon DeLay stood up and kicked the tire jack now lying on the ground. "Stupid thing is bent."

The woman with the flashlight held out her hand. "I'm Leslie. Thanks for stopping."

"Nice to meet you. Sharon has told me quite a bit about you." He bent down and picked up the jack. "I know a trick with these things. Let me give it a try." He knelt, sighing internally. His trousers had just been dry-cleaned. With a deft positioning of the jack, he began cranking up the car.

After a moment he looked back at Leslie. "You're teaching at Berkeley, right?"

"That's right. I'm up for tenure next year."

"Congratulations. They must like you, to be up for tenure so soon."

Leslie gave a self-deprecating shrug. "I hope so. I think they just needed another woman on tenure track, quite frankly. But I'll take it however it comes."

"I'm sure you deserve it. I read one of your articles in the *Journal of American Medicine* this past summer." Mansfield ignored the look of astonishment that came over Sharon's face. He left the jack and began removing the tire nuts. "It was quite good. You're doing some groundbreaking work with genetics out there."

"It'll be interesting to see what comes of it. The research areas here in New England decided not to pursue the next logical step in genetics research—too much furor over the reaction of the religious right or something. I don't know what the big deal is."

Mansfield just smiled as he got up and pulled the spare tire out of the Bonneville's trunk.

Sharon squared off in front of Mansfield, crossing her arms. "Mansfield is a well-known evangelical conservative, Leslie. I'm sure he could tell you why he thinks it's a big deal."

"Really?" Leslie said. "I've never met an evangelical conservative intellectual before."

"Really? Well, I've never helped a lesbian geneticist change a tire before."

Leslie guffawed, slapping her hands together, but Sharon scowled. Mansfield smiled in her direction, his eyes twinkling with genuine warmth. "I'm just kidding!" He finished bolting the spare tire and cranked the car down.

Leslie squeezed Sharon's shoulder. "Hey, lighten up, hon." She looked back to where Mansfield was wiping his hands on a handkerchief. "Sharon's a little testy these days. You'll have to forgive her, she—"

"Hey!"

The three started and turned toward the road. Taylor Haller was leaning out of a car's passenger window. Mansfield could dimly see another man in the driver's seat, looking over curiously.

"What's up?" Sharon walked over and stuck her arm through the open window and shook the driver's hand. "Hey, Randy. How you doing?"

"Need any help?" Taylor asked.

"I think we're set. Mansfield here rode in on his white horse just in time."

Mansfield finished wiping his hands and joined Sharon at the open window. "Hey buddy." He clapped Taylor on the shoulder. "You still up for squash tomorrow?"

"Eight A.M. as usual, unless you oversleep again."

"Hey, that only happened once!"

"I don't know." Taylor shook his head in mock concern. "I think you're losing it, Mansfield. One of these days I *am* going to have a shut-out." He looked at Sharon and Leslie, who had also drifted over to his car. "My goal in life is to have one game—just one—where I keep Mansfield from scoring a single point. But so far he just refuses to act his age!"

"Yeah, for an old geezer I don't do so bad." Mansfield paused, then cocked his head. "Wait a minute…aren't you supposed to be going on that international aid trip tomorrow? The one to Russia with the other faculty volunteers?"

Taylor shook his head, the jesting manner dying away. "The economic crisis has gotten so serious that Harvard put off the trip until the holidays so we can stay longer. That way we'll be able to get out into the really bad areas where we're most needed. In some ways I'm not looking forward to it. What some of their people go through is heart-wrenching." He looked up and grinned. "So no dice. You can't get out of the game that easily."

The man in the driver's seat said something, and Taylor turned his head, listening. He looked back out the window towards them. "Randy says if we don't hurry up we're going to be *trés* late."

Mansfield, Sharon, and Leslie stepped back from the car. "See you."

It only took a moment for Mansfield to slot the punctured tire and tools into Sharon's trunk and close the lid. He turned around to find Sharon watching him.

"I don't get you," she said.

"What?"

"You play squash with Taylor. Someone you despise."

Mansfield tried not to laugh. "I don't despise Taylor. He's a friend! At least usually. When he trounces me, I avoid him for days."

"But you—"

"Look, I know this is hard for you to understand, but just because I disagree with someone's lifestyle or don't share the same beliefs doesn't mean I can't be friends with him."

"Why not? Most of you guys just like staying in your little cliques. You have your church picnics, and your church softball leagues, and your church bookstores, and your church schools. You all cling together behind your stained-glass windows, and you only come out to snipe at what everyone else is doing wrong."

Mansfield looked away, then spoke quietly. "It's a difficult balance we try to walk, Sharon. We try to live with conviction on matters of ultimate truth, but we *should* be doing it in the same loving way that Jesus would. I'm sorry we've been judgmental when we could instead get to know people where they are and affirm the selfless efforts of people like Taylor." He saw the scorn in her eyes change to wariness. "Please forgive us, Sharon. We're all a work in progress, of God's grace working through us. We—"

*CRASH!*

They spun around to see Mansfield's taillight and bumper go flying, a sport-utility vehicle backing off from the rear of his car with a screech of metal. Mansfield bellowed and started forward, Leslie and Sharon right behind him. The SUV pulled out, squealing away from the wreck at high speed.

Mansfield ran into the street, shouting for the driver to stop, trying to get a look at the license plate. He heard Sharon's warning shriek, the sound of squealing brakes, and turned to see another SUV bearing down on him, tires locked and skidding on the wet pavement. He dove sideways, feeling the wind of the vehicle's passing, the tires whizzing by as he somehow rolled out of the way.

He rose to one knee, adrenaline pumping through his system. How on earth had he escaped? The vehicle swerved to a stop a few yards down the road. A head jutted out the window and the driver swore at him, then made an obscene gesture and pulled away.

Mansfield stood to his feet and put his hands on his knees, breathing heavily. He looked at Sharon.

"Thank you. I would've been toast if you hadn't yelled." He straightened and patted her gently on the shoulder. "Thanks."

Sharon stared at him for a moment, then nodded sharply and turned away.


As Sharon walked back to her car, a dark presence perched on the limb of a nearby tree watched with narrowed eyes. That was close. The wall she had spent years building under his attentive care had almost cracked.

The demon stood and paced along the thick branch. If that first SUV hadn't been so close, the tired driver so easily diverted into the cursed man's car, the foul attempt might have worked. He scowled, glaring at Mansfield and the powerful warrior angel standing right behind him. Too bad the second SUV hadn't been just a fraction closer;

the man would have taken himself out. Etán would have had to make the SUV fly to do anything about it.

He would have loved to take credit for eliminating the irritating thorn in his master's territory! His mind wandered a moment and he puffed his chest, thinking about the glorious honors he would have received on the streets of darkness. Leviathan himself might have honored him for such a prize.

He watched Mansfield finish his inspection of his shattered bumper and wave good-bye to the two women. As the man drove away, the demon left the branch and dropped to the ground, still reveling in the honors ceremony playing in his head. The diversion of that SUV had been quite skillful, if he did say so himself. Perhaps he should wait before reporting this almost-success to his superiors. Perhaps next time he could report the real thing.

## THIRTY-FOUR

"YOU SURE YOU CAN'T PLAY?" Alison twirled a basketball in her hands, disappointment clear on her face. "It'll be girls against boys; we could use another girl."

"I don't want to leave the ladies in the lurch, but I already made plans." Claire looked toward the small group of HCF students dressed in sweats and sneakers stretching out and shooting hoops just a few feet away.

Her attention was caught for just a moment as Brad and Teresa went one-on-one under the basket. Teresa was giggling as Brad tried to slap the ball from her hands. Brad was joking around, intent on getting the ball back. Teresa on the other hand…

Claire watched her hallmate's face, then smiled to herself. She'd have to see what she could do about that.

Claire wrenched her attention back to Alison. "Sherry invited me to go downtown with Stefan and their friends. Frankly, I'd rather hang out with you guys, but I figure it's important to keep that connection with Sherry, you know?"

"Totally understand. Get out of here, then. I'll see you Sunday at the crew races."

Halfway across Harvard Yard, Claire glanced upward and stopped dead in her tracks. The sky was blazing with stars. The Milky Way stretched from horizon to horizon, a bracelet of unfathomable depth adorning their little corner of the universe. The Yard was quiet, deserted. Claire sank to the ground, her gaze fastened on the remarkable display.

"I will lift up mine eyes to the hills, from whence cometh my help." Her voice was a whisper, and she closed her eyes. "O God of the universe, help me to honor You in all I say and do. Help me not to get so focused on myself that I lose sight of Your glory and power."

She opened her eyes and stared again at the marvelous expanse. "Lord, You created such vastness that my little brain can't even comprehend the tiniest piece of it. And you hold these trillions of stars together simply by a word of Your power! O God!" Her voice choked on an immensity of feeling. "I ask for Your protection here in this place. I ask You to steer me through these difficult waters. Give me Your mind, Lord, and Your heart for all these people You've put in my path. Forgive me, Lord, for all the ways

I get in the way of Your plan. Help me be more like You."

The sound of approaching students broke Claire's reverie. She stood quickly and set off toward her dorm. She brushed by the loud group of ten or twelve going the other direction. One person slammed into her.

"Oh, sorry!" The girl lurched, giggling, and continued on.

Claire watched over her shoulder as the girl laughed and listed heavily toward the young man walking next to her.

Claire sighed and headed home. She took the dorm stairs at a good clip and arrived at her suite just as Sherry was welcoming several of Stefan's friends.

"And here's my roommate, Claire!" Sherry reached out and tugged her into the center of the crowded room, hugging her briefly. "Glad you made it back in time. Claire, this is…" she gestured at the dozen or so people scattered around the room. "Well, this is everybody."

Claire laughed and waved. "Hi, everybody."

She heard a few chuckles, but several people just stared and turned back to their original conversations. She turned to Sherry with a raised eyebrow, then headed toward their bedroom. "I'm just going to change."

"Oh, no need to, really."

"But under this jacket, all I have on is a casual sweater."

"Whatever you're wearing is fine, honestly."

"Sherry, where are we—"

"I don't know exactly where we're going. I think we're going to wander down Landsdowne Street until we find a place we like."

"But are we going to dinner or is this—"

Her words were drowned out as someone called out to the crowd. Suddenly, everyone was noisily piling out of the room and heading down the hall.

Claire followed, closing and locking the door behind her. She caught up to Sherry in a chattering group of people and walked silently beside her roommate as the students headed toward the Harvard Square T station.

As they pushed through the turnstiles, they heard the T approaching. The mass of students hurried down the escalator toward the platform as the train pulled up. Its doors opened with a hydraulic *whsssh.*

"Hurry it up!"

A good-looking blond student—who looked familiar, Claire thought—ran to the wide doors and held his hand against the doorjamb, beckoning to the others who were racing for the train.

Claire was in the middle of the pack that dashed through the doors, breathless and laughing. All the seats were full, so the students filled in the empty center spaces around the poles. Sherry and Stefan were last, stepping through just as the doors tried to close on the blond student's arm. He yanked his arm out of harm's way and whacked Stefan on the head.

"What you thinking, man?" The student laughed, but his eyes showed irritation. "You run faster than that!"

"Just wanted to see if you'd risk your life for me, my man, that's all."

Sherry caught Claire's gaze and rolled her eyes. "Niles needs to lighten up. He's an old buddy of Stefan's. I don't know *how* the two of them have stayed friends." Sherry turned and tapped on the blond student's shoulder. "Niles, I want you to meet my roommate, Claire. Claire, this is Niles. He's a junior."

Claire let go of the pole she was gripping and reached to shake his hand. "Do I know you? You look really familiar."

Niles raised an eyebrow. "You're in my philosophy class."

"You're in Kwong's class?" Claire had no sooner asked the question than the memory of a difficult existentialism debate rose in her mind. She dropped her eyes, embarrassed, masking the movement by clutching a pole for balance.

Niles laughed and slapped Stefan on the back. "Your friend and I had a definite difference of opinion on the right thing to do when watching child abuse in a parking lot."

"Hey! I didn't define it that way, you did. You came up with the example!"

"Yeah, yeah." Niles waved a dismissive hand and turned to Stefan. "You know, that reminds me of this article on 'community values' I read the other day when I was writing an editorial for the student newspaper."

"How's that coming, by the way?"

"The writing's okay—as an opinion columnist I get to mouth off on whatever the heck I want to—but the research for this piece just drove me crazy. I don't get how *anyone* can believe this garbage that the religious right puts out. They actually believe that harassing perfect strangers with propaganda on their outdated beliefs is okay. It's the most ridiculous—"

Claire flushed and gripped her pole tighter as Niles continued his diatribe. She glanced at Sherry, who was looking away, embarrassed.

Claire let go of her pole and walked down the aisle toward a seat that had been vacated. She sat down, sighing. She didn't know how to defend herself against such venom, and didn't want to listen to it.


The students, bundled up against the cold, turned the corner onto Landsdowne Street, and Sherry pulled even with Claire.

"Sorry about that. Niles really has it in for Christians. I should've warned you."

Claire walked a few paces, trying to think of something eloquent to say. "Bummer."

Stefan ran up and grabbed Sherry from behind, lifting her off her feet and swinging her around and around. She shrieked and giggled until he set her down.

"Well!" Stefan clapped his gloved hands together. "Where should we go?"

A couple behind Claire shouted out a suggestion. The others booed and catcalled.

"Okay, okay." Stefan held up his hands. "I propose we go to…" He swiveled slowly, his arm and hand extended. "That one!"

Several people immediately set off toward the chosen doorway, which was painted black. The sign beside the door read *La Nuit*. Hours of Operation 7 P.M. to 3 A.M. No minors.

Claire sighed. *I'm guessing this isn't a restaurant.*

Sherry followed her gaze, then tugged on Stefan's arm and whispered something in his ear.

Stefan straightened and snapped his fingers. "Right, right. Hey Niles! Come back here a sec."

Niles shuffled back, and Stefan said something in a low voice. Niles nodded and reached for his wallet. He pulled out a small laminated card and flipped it to Stefan. "She was fine with it as long as Sherry's roomie doesn't lose it."

Stefan caught the card and handed it to Claire. "Hear that? Don't lose it. Niles's girlfriend is a big German woman who could kick your tail." He grinned and slapped Niles on the back, and they set off down the street toward the black-painted door.

Sherry started after them, but Claire grabbed her arm.

"Sherry!" Her voice was an urgent whisper. "No one said anything about using a fake ID. I thought we were just going to dinner or something."

"Don't be such a scaredy-cat. The bouncers here don't care. I was here just last weekend and they barely looked at my ID."

"I'm not scared. It's just—"

A shout interrupted her. "You girls coming or what?"

Sherry flashed a smile in Stefan's direction, then looped her arm through Claire's and pulled her toward him. Most of the others were already through the doorway.

"Yeah, yeah, hold up! We're coming."

Claire's thoughts were in a jumble as she allowed herself to be propelled toward the club. Stefan and a few others fell in behind her and Sherry as they approached the bouncer, who wore all black, three earrings, and a ponytail. Sherry started a round of bright chatter with Claire as she handed the man her card and got his nod. He barely inspected Claire's ID before waving her through and taking Stefan's.

The inside of the club was dark and loud. A heavy beat seemed to pulse the very walls. Sherry pushed through throngs of people dressed in black, various types of drinks in their hands. Claire followed, keeping her roommate in sight with difficulty. She could feel the beat through the soles of her feet.

Sherry stopped at an oversized corner booth already filled with half their group. The others were piling their coats on a nearby chair.

Claire leaned toward Sherry, raising her voice above the music. "How did we manage to get a table?"

"Stefan called ahead. All that stuff outside was just kidding around. We figured we'd come here. The club saves this table for him if he asks."

"How often does he come here?"

"Probably two or three nights a week. Here or one of the other Landsdowne Street clubs."

"Three nights a week!"

"Or more. Usually Thursday, Friday, and Saturday. And since he's always with an entourage, the clubs roll out the red-carpet treatment. He is," she raised an eyebrow, "a *very* good customer."


An hour later Claire sat at the booth talking with several of Stefan's friends. Half the seats were empty, their occupants on the dance floor or at the bar. The table was littered with beer bottles, mugs, and shot glasses—detritus of long-winded discourse on who slept with whom, who kicked whose tail on the squash court, which fabulous companies were pursuing each graduating student, which stocks in their huge portfolios were up, which were down.

Claire nodded, smiled, made appropriate comments in the right places, and felt alone.

One student was expounding on yesterday's argument with his girlfriend, currently out on the dance floor with Niles.

"...so I say to her 'Give me that, you idiot,' and when she finally does, all it is is a Macy's catalog!"

The others roared, slapping their hands against the table. Claire obligingly laughed at the punch line of the long story.

The speaker took a swig of his beer. "It must be her Midwestern genes. All those primitive prairie folk, you know." He paused, then looked around the table. "Oops. Is there anyone here from the Midwest?"

"I'm from Michigan." Claire grinned into her soda as the others chided the red-faced jokester. "Where are you from?"

"I'm from New Yawk."

"Where in New York? Manhattan?"

"Yes sir. Right near Central Park."

Another student slapped him on the back. "His parents have a penthouse the size of Harvard Yard. Jimmy usually drops that bomb only when he's trying to get someone in bed."

Jimmy shoved him away, laughing and cussing fluently.

Claire took another sip of her drink. Jimmy put down his beer and gestured toward the dance floor.

"How about you and me take a turn out there, hey?"

Claire started to protest, then reconsidered. "Okay."

She allowed Jimmy to grab her hand and pull her toward the crowd in the lowered dance floor. She stared around at the sea of black dresses, black trousers, black turtlenecks. She had on the yellow-flowered sweater and black pants she'd been wearing all day.

Jimmy pulled her into the crowd and up to where Stefan, Sherry, Niles, and several others were moving to the heavy beat. Stefan and Sherry were locked together in a sensual dance. Jimmy moved close to Claire, and she could smell the alcohol on his breath.

He was a good dancer even with the unsteadiness of four beers. Claire loosened up a bit as the music changed to a familiar piece, and Jimmy put an arm around her waist. He swayed slightly, and his hand slipped downward. Claire stepped back in time to the music, causing his hand to drop away. She could feel the warmth flooding her face. Thank God this place was so dark.

After a few minutes the music switched again. Claire enjoyed the rhythm, the tempo, the energy of being a part of the pulsing crowd. But even as her body joined in, her mind was oddly distant. She watched the others around her, watched the glazed eyes, the dripping sweat, the couples locked in a primal mating dance. Her eyes drifted beyond the dance floor to the tables and ledges laden with empty bottles and glasses, to the corner booth where six people were still engaged in shallow, self-centered conversation.

She sighed, her heart hurting for them.

## THIRTY-FIVE

THE SPIRAL STAIRCASE INSIDE THE COOP stretched gracefully upward beside her as Claire ran her fingers along shelves of books, looking for her next philosophy reading assignment.

She stopped at the appropriate section, scanned the row, then plucked out a large paperback. *The Humanist Manifesto—I and II.* She sighed and headed into the Coop's coffee shop. *Yippee.*

She placed her order and waited, looking around at the scattered tables. She did a double take, squinting into the far recesses of a corner area.

"Tall latte with Irish Cream."

She started and took the tall cup proffered over the counter. Sipping gingerly, she ventured back into the corner.

"Hey."

Brad looked up and smiled. He put down the student newspaper he was reading and moved several textbooks from the other chair at his table.

Claire took the seat. "Does the paper have our advertisement in there about the big study break HCF is hosting in two weeks?" She looked at the strange expression on his face. "Don't you know what I'm talking about? The Fellowship is putting on this Saturday barbecue for anyone on campus who wants to come. Isn't that a great idea for outreach?"

She peered more closely at his face. "What's wrong?"

"I know about the barbecue." He sighed and tapped the paper. "And yeah, they have our advertisement. But some columnist wrote a nasty opinion piece about it... actually, about the whole Fellowship."

Claire set her cup down hard. "What?"

"It's really unfortunate. This guy isn't even trying to be objective."

"Who wrote it?"

Brad peered at the byline. "Um...Niles somebody. Niles? That's—"

"The guy in our philosophy class. He's a friend of Sherry's boyfriend. I was out with them last night, and he was going on about Christians. It was just hateful. Totally unthinking."

Brad laughed. "That's ironic. That's exactly what he accuses us of."

"How can he *say* that?"

"Let me read you a few selections." Brad looked down, running his finger across line after line of text. "He starts by talking about how misguided fundamentalist Christians are—that's how he describes the Fellowship by the way, even though there are tons of people in HCF from all different streams of the church. We have to be misguided, you see, for believing and trying to convince others to believe something so 'patently bizarre.'"

"Oh, of course."

Brad started reading aloud.

"Their private beliefs wouldn't bother me so much if they didn't feel compelled to impose them on those with no desire to listen. I don't mind if someone wants to pursue his peculiar belief system in private, just please don't beat me over the head with it and tell me its 'good for my soul.'

"Thankfully, not all Christians are of this stripe. Many of my classmates attend various churches in the area and willingly acknowledge the already obvious fact that they don't have a corner on 'truth.' But the fundamentalists, or evangelicals, are dangerously zealous, intolerant, even hateful, illustrating the adage that the deeper the religious belief, the more unsafe one becomes to oneself and others.

"I decided to take it upon myself to examine the peculiar brand of evangelical Christians that we have here at Harvard. So one Friday night I arrived incognito at the meeting of the Harvard Christian Fellowship as if I were just another lost sap looking for 'answers,' as one of their leaders so snidely put it."

Claire stared into her coffee cup, her stomach churning, as Brad skipped down the page. "Oh, here's a nice line.

"Why is it that people singing incomprehensible lyrics about blind faith have the gall to claim entitlement to the answers we truth seekers will spend the rest of our lives pursuing? Their blind passion is commendable, I suppose, in the same way that a beer-bellied Packers fan could be commended for painting his face and torso green and yellow and standing shirtless in the freezing rain. It's brave but not sensible. And it's certainly not right to ask everyone else in the stadium to make similar fools of themselves."

Brad shook his head. "Here's the nice attack on our barbecue."

"In the next two weeks you will see flyers and posters everywhere inviting you to a free barbecue on the lawn between Mem Hall and the Science Center. Be forewarned. HCF will use free food and friendliness the same way a Venus's-flytrap will use its attractive scent: as bait to lure and trap unwary unbelievers."

Brad slapped the paper down on the table and nearly glared at Claire. "And this part is what really gets me." He leaned on his elbows, reading.

"As a final capper, the organizer of this little soiree is HCF member and anti-choice activist Alison Rodenberg, who as we speak is trying to organize an 'Ivy Leaguers for Life' rally at the state capitol. My friends, don't be fooled. This group is unsafe, their proselytizing is an affront, and I urge all right-minded students to exercise their right of free speech and picket their transparent attempt to impose their arcane values on others."

He looked across the table in silence.

After a long moment, Claire closed her mouth. "That's…that's…"

"Worse than usual," Brad declared dryly.

"What's his problem?"

"I don't know, but it's certainly going to create a problem for us. Alison told me about this an hour ago, and we agreed that if we're picketed we're going to have to set up some sort of tent so those who want a study break don't have to see the people shouting at them. And we'll probably need a security guard to keep the picket line at a reasonable distance. I don't know now if anyone will come, but we can't just call it off. We can't set a precedent of discontinuing outreach plans because of harassment. Alison and I are meeting tonight to talk about it."

Claire took a slow sip of her latte. "How is Alison?"

"She was pretty upset."

"I can imagine. It's so unfair!" She slammed the cup down on the table. Hot liquid spurted from the opening in the plastic cover and onto her hand and wrist. "Ahh!" She grabbed a napkin and wiped off the scalding liquid.

Brad jumped up to grab other napkins and returned in a hurry. "You okay?" He knelt beside her and gingerly pressed a napkin to the back of her hand, then wiped the table.

Claire looked at the concern on his face as he worked. "Thanks. Sorry about that."

"It's no trouble. What were you about to say when you decided to test your heat tolerance?"

"I was just thinking that Niles is so mad at those who 'proselytize' just because all his nice, moderate churchgoing friends don't claim to have the truth. I bet those people aren't even Christians!"

Brad looked down at his long-empty coffee mug. After a moment he raised his eyes and caught her gaze. "Do you mind a kind rebuke, Claire?"

Claire wrinkled her nose.

"Nothing bad, trust me. It's just…it's hurtful—and I think wrong—if we question people's faith without knowing anything about them. John said in his first epistle that 'everyone who believes that Jesus is the Christ is a child of God.' And Paul warns us not to jump to conclusions about 'whether or not someone is faithful.' If Niles's friends claim Jesus as Lord and Savior, we can't judge where they are in their faith. That's God's job."

Brad gestured in the general direction of the campus. "You know how people in the Fellowship come from all different streams of the church? Like Teresa comes from a mainline denomination whereas Alison comes from a charismatic church? Well, in the same way I'm sure there are sincere believers on campus who may be uncomfortable with HCF, or with outward displays of religion, but who will still spend eternity worshiping around God's throne." He put his hand to his chest. "I may disagree with their theology and think they're dead *wrong* about not claiming ultimate truth, but does that mean they don't have a relationship with Jesus?"

Claire didn't meet his eyes. His voice was gentle. "We have to be very careful. They may or may not, but we don't know. But we do know that God meets people where *they* are. We have to do the same."

There was silence for a moment, then Claire looked up. "I'm so awful sometimes, Brad. I'm really only a baby Christian myself. Why do I go around judging people?" She let out a long breath. "Forgive me. You're totally right."

"Nothing to forgive, believe me. All of us are a work in progress." Suddenly, he was overtaken by a yawn. He covered his mouth a bit sheepishly and lifted his mug. "And right now I'm a sleepy work in progress. I'm going to get a refill. Be back in a second."

Claire watched him stand in line and wait for his order. The girl behind the counter lit up when he smiled his thanks. Just like Teresa had during their little basketball skirmish last night. A small smile played on Claire's lips, and she drummed her fingers on the tabletop, her eyes narrowing.

"That's better." He slid back into his chair. "I'm addicted to this stuff."

"Can I ask you a question? A personal question?"

"I already know what you're going to ask." He glanced around, then back at her, his voice a hoarse whisper. "It was Professor Plum in the library with the candlestick."

"Cut it out." Claire tried not to laugh. "This is serious."

Brad sat back in his chair and took a careful sip from his mug. "Okay. Shoot."

"You're not dating anyone, are you?"

"Not right now."

"I think that someone in the Fellowship likes you. I know you're a nice, reserved guy and have never done anything to encourage her, but I'm quite sure she likes you and about 80 percent sure that she'll be talking to me about it."

"Claire…"

"No, no, let me finish. I'm wondering if you want me to sort of…broker an introduction, you know."

"Claire!"

"Since I've gotten to know you pretty well in the last few months, I thought you might want me to give her a few insider tips on what you were thinking." She cocked an eyebrow. "Or maybe you want a few tips on what she's thinking?"

Brad took a slow sip, looking at her over the rim. Then he smiled. "Thanks for offering, but no."

"Oh, come on! Teresa's really cute. She— Oh!" She slapped her hand to her mouth. "I said her name, didn't I?

"Yes, you did."

"Well…shoot. Well, the cat's out of the bag anyway, so what do you say?"

"Look, I appreciate the thought. I really do. But the answer is no. I don't do things that way."

"But—"

"Claire!" Brad set the mug down hard, and she stared at him, disconcerted. He stood to his feet. "Look, thanks and everything. But please don't play matchmaker." He shrugged into his jacket and dropped a dollar bill on the table. "I've got to run. I'll see you tomorrow at the picnic."

"Sure."

He started away. Claire reached up and grabbed the arm of his jacket. He turned slightly. "Brad, I'm sorry. Is anything wrong?"

"Other than our Fellowship being attacked by a mean-spirited article?"

She didn't drop her hand. "Yes."

His eyes searched hers for a long moment. Then he smiled and jerked his head toward the door. "Let's go for a walk."


They headed down JFK Street toward the river. Saturday shoppers crowded the sidewalks, and Brad kept a light hand against Claire's back as he steered the two of them through the throngs.

They left the crowd behind and strolled quietly along the street, facing into the wind. They crossed Memorial Drive at the light and turned left onto the sidewalk that ran parallel to the river. The usual Saturday crowd was thinned by the cold. A giggling couple whizzed by on Rollerblades.

"Claire, I don't know you all that well yet, but I'd like to get to know you better."

"I feel the same way about you."

"That's good, because I have something to tell you." He looked sideways, then back at the path. "This may be hard for you to hear. I have a…very difficult personal struggle that some of my close friends know about, but it's not something I desire to share with the whole group."

Claire pursed her lips. "Okay."

"I have struggled my whole life with the fact that I have never been attracted to any woman."

It took Claire's mind a second to process what she had just heard. Her lips parted in shock. Brad stopped walking and turned toward her. His eyes were vulnerable and sad.

For one interminable moment, she felt suspended, as if she couldn't breathe. Then she stepped forward and wrapped her arms around her friend. "I'm sorry, Brad." She felt him hug her in return. "I'm sorry. Thank you for telling me."

She heard him choke something into her shoulder, and she kept her arms where they were. After a long moment, he released her and stepped back, wiping moisture from his eyes. He smiled in self-deprecation.

"Sorry. It's so hard sometimes to see what everyone else has and to not have it. I pray every day that God will deliver and heal me. I love Him so much. I only want to live a life that's pleasing to Him."

Claire took a deep breath, her voice tentative. "So you haven't…"

"No. No way. I've stayed as far as possible from that lifestyle since God says it is displeasing. I may be struggling, but I would never describe myself as gay. I've never done anything—" He looked down at the ground. "It's sort of weird to be talking about it with a girl."

"We don't have to if you—"

"No. This is all part of the friendship thing. It's just that most of the people who know are guys. I'm in an accountability group with my roommate and several of the other guys in the Fellowship. Their job is to ask me all the tough questions."

"Well, I'm glad you have that. That must almost be a relief."

"It *is* a relief! And one of the rules I've asked them to hold me accountable on is to not date right now, or at least to not go out with any girl without telling them first. That's why I told you no about Teresa. I just don't think it's a good idea at this point."

They walked another few paces in silence, drawing near a footbridge that stretched across the river. Claire looked at the small nameplate. *Weeks Memorial Bridge.*

"I've always wondered what this bridge was for," she said.

"Well, look." Brad gestured across the river. "See those buildings over there? That's the business school. The MBA students can use this bridge as a shortcut to get to this side of the campus. And see here on this side—" he turned all the way around—"that's Dunster House right behind us."

"Oh, that's where Stefan lives. Sherry's boyfriend."

"Ah. Right." He gestured at a nearby side street. "If we follow that street all the way up, we'll run smack into the middle of campus." He looked at his watch. "Speaking of which…"

"Yeah, I should be getting back, too."

As they headed up the narrow street, Claire ventured a tentative smile. "Can I ask you another question?"

"As long as you don't mind that I may not answer."

"That's fair." Claire looked sideways at her friend. "How…does this happen? You know, becoming someone who struggles with this issue?"

"Well, there are lots of theories. For men, it seems to start as a very young boy, with a lack of emotional and physical affection, a lack of bonding with a father figure." He glanced sideways as they walked. "Make sure you understand what I mean. It's not that if you don't have the father bond, you'll necessarily struggle with this issue. It's just that most men who do struggle with this have that one thing in common."

"Oh."

They walked on a bit longer. Claire's memory began replaying the derisive comments she had heard in HCF from time to time about the gay agenda and the militancy of the gay lobby on campus. She bit her lip, thinking. Brad had been quietly sitting there the whole time. Even if he disagreed with the gay groups at Harvard, how must he have been hurt by that tone of derision? How many times had *she* unconsciously said something without realizing how it might hurt her brother in Christ?

She cleared her throat, wondering about something else. "A lot of people here say the reason homosexuality should be considered normal is that it's genetic."

"Yeah, I know. It's not genetic. The research is pretty clear. But let me tell you something. It *feels* genetic. When it begins as a very young boy, it sure feels inborn."

They crossed another street and headed up a hill along a one-way road. Multistory buildings rose on either side.

Brad breathed a long sigh. "This issue really is an example of the sins of the fathers being passed down from generation to generation, as the Bible says. My father basically abandoned me out of selfishness, and look at the ramifications of his sin in my life. That's why it takes so much prayer and discipline—and most of all, just pure deliverance by the power of the Holy Spirit—to overcome this." Suddenly, his eyes grew fierce, and he slapped his fist into his palm. "I have met men who've been delivered from this, and by the grace of God, I will be healed!"

"Do you want to get married someday?"

Brad stopped walking and swung toward her, his face incredulous. "Do I want to get married?" He drew a shuddering breath. "More than anything in the world, Claire. I want to experience that covenant joy that God created for His children. That's why I will not—*will not*—let myself slip up in this struggle. I believe God will heal me, and I will not give the enemy a foothold in my life!"

As they resumed walking, the sound of traffic grew louder, and they stepped out from between two buildings onto the sidewalk along Massachusetts Avenue. Dozens of cars were whizzing by. Across the street rose the wall that bordered the south side of the main campus.

"Where're you headed?" Brad asked.

"I'm just going back to my dorm."

"You'll be okay?"

"Yeah, sure."

He stepped toward her, enfolding her in a hug. His voice was soft. "Thank you."

Claire found herself blinking back tears. "Thank you for telling me even though I'm a girl."

He stepped back, smiling ruefully. "It was a good experiment."

"Glad to be of service. Anytime." She caught his eye and her voice sobered. "Seriously. Anytime."

Brad inclined his head in acknowledgement, then turned away, walking down the row of shops toward Harvard Square. Claire stared wistfully at a giggling couple approaching from the other direction, their arms entwined around each other's waists. They brushed past Brad as if he wasn't even there.

## THIRTY-SIX

THE EARLY AFTERNOON SUN WAS BRIGHT in Claire's eyes as she and Teresa walked along the riverbank. The weekend throngs were thick despite the chill; the crew races always drew a crowd. Out on the river, several crew boats approached from upstream.

The girls stopped talking and watched as several eight-man boats sculled by. The men in the long shells were pulling hard, the coxswains barking their commands. The elongated oars dipped and pulled, dipped and pulled, in a strenuous but graceful beat. The boats seemed to skate over the water.

The crowd grew thicker as the girls approached the Weld Boathouse. They were supposed to be right here somewhere.

"Claire! Teresa!"

She turned and saw Doug Turner waving. He had a prime spot right by the boathouse. Teresa and Claire walked over and said their hellos to the dozen or so people spread out on the blankets. There were three or four new faces, people who weren't in HCF who had been invited to join the group for its annual picnic at the Head of the Charles crew race.

Claire found a spot on the blanket, wishing Sherry could have come. She'd been too hungover from last night.

She started to look for a plate and lunch fixings. A hand stretched out with an already-prepared sandwich, and she looked up in surprise.

Brad smiled and plopped down beside her. "I saw you guys coming. I knew you and Teresa were both the peanut-butter-and-jelly sort."

"Thanks." She smiled at her friend and punched him lightly on the arm. "I was starving."

They sat in companionable silence while Claire munched on her sandwich.

Brad twisted a blade of grass in his fingers. "So how's your supersecret project for Mansfield coming?"

"Oh, going in circles."

Brad raised an eyebrow.

"I spent two days just fighting red tape. But I think I've finally figured out where to look, and I'm going over there on Monday. I've got until Thursday to finish the project, so it should be okay." She grinned sideways. "Unless I fail out of school because I don't study for my tests."

Claire glanced at the clock by her bedside and started. Nine o'clock already. How was that possible? She hadn't even had dinner.

She returned her attention to the photocopied pages in front of her. Her hands were practically shaking as she typed the latest notation into her laptop. It had taken a few days, but she had done it. She had had to go through layers of red tape for her "historical research project"—as she had described it to desk clerk after desk clerk—but she had finally managed to find the documents Mansfield was looking for.

She had looked through file upon file of old typewritten pages, mimeographed sheets, and handwritten ledgers. And buried within all of that was gold. What on earth were they going to do with all of this? She couldn't wait to tell the professor what she had found.

Claire finished typing and hit print. She stood and stretched, watching the pages glide neatly onto the tray. It was probably more information than the professor would want to go through, but she figured it was better to err on the side of too much detail. She could always verbally summarize it for him.

She knew there was a lot more she hadn't yet found, but Professor Mansfield—Mansfield, she quickly corrected herself—wanted a status report as soon as she was done with her classes.

*Classes!* She hadn't done the homework for either philosophy or Mansfield's European history class. For a fleeting moment she considered asking him for an extension, then quickly discarded that idea. Now was not the time for Mansfield to question her ability to handle this project.

The door to their room creaked open, and Sherry came in, giggling, Stefan right behind her. He was tickling her, playfully whispering something in her ear. He broke off suddenly when he caught sight of Claire. Sherry looked over at her and blushed.

"Hey."

"Hey," Claire said.

"We missed you at dinner."

"Yeah. I had to work on this project. I didn't even notice."

Sherry glanced back at Stefan, then looked at her roommate. "I thought you had a study group or something tonight."

"Oh man! You're right...I completely forgot. My biology TA was doing a review before the test next week." Claire looked at her watch. "I guess I won't miss that much of it if I run."

She pulled the pages off the printer and stuffed them and a few notebooks in her backpack. She disconnected her laptop from the printer and carefully slotted it into her pack as well.

"Um…" she looked around the room and grabbed her history textbook. "I'll probably go to Widener for a few hours after the review session so I can get that history paper finished. Can I still borrow your notes for the day I missed?"

"Yeah, sure." Sherry disengaged herself from Stefan and looked through the stacks of books on her desk. "Here you go. All the notes are dated, so you can find the right day pretty easily. Hope you can read my handwriting."

"Thanks." Claire shrugged into her jacket. "I probably won't be back until pretty late. I'll try not to wake you."

"No biggie. I need to blow off steam from all those midterms, so I might be out late anyway. We'll probably go over to Stefan's suite for a while."

As Claire headed for the door, she saw Stefan reach to pull Sherry back toward him. Claire hesitated and looked back over her shoulder. Sherry glanced up and Claire's eyes bored into hers. Sherry hesitated for just a moment, then dropped her gaze.

Claire turned back toward the hallway, an odd pain in her chest. As the door to her suite closed behind her, she bowed her head for a moment, then headed down the stairs, her prayers fervent and no bounce in her step.

<br>

Two hours later, seated at her carrel in the A basement of Widener, Claire read through Sherry's four pages of history notes for the day she had missed.

At the end of the fourth page, Sherry had drawn a double line and below the line, another set of notations continued in a different pen. *The next day's notes, probably. I already have those.*

She quickly scanned through them to be sure, then suddenly jumped to her feet, nearly knocking her chair over backward. She picked up the notebook, still reading, and an unbelieving grin broke out on her face. Claire felt in her pockets for some loose change, eyes scanning the shadowed rows of books and shelves. She couldn't wait to get to that meeting tomorrow.

<br>

Sherry pointed the remote at Stefan's television, turning up the volume a notch, and moved back to where he was sitting on the floor by his bed. She scooted back between his outstretched legs and leaned against his chest.

"Is that better?" She glanced over her shoulder as she spoke.

"Much, much better." He put his arms around her, pulling her tight against him.

"This way my hallmates won't hear you when you holler for help." He dropped his lips to her ear, nibbling. "Not that you would want to, of course."

She giggled, tingles racing down her neck. He tugged at her shirt buttons, and for a while she enjoyed his ministrations.

After a while she took a deep breath, weakly batting at his hands. "Stop…stop."

"Do you really want me to?"

Sherry didn't respond. Her breathing was suddenly shallow.

He massaged her shoulders. "Well, well. Cat got your tongue? Or have you finally decided?"

"Stefan…"

He placed his hands on her shoulders and turned her in his direction. She slowly rotated until she was facing him.

"Sher, it's time to take our relationship to the next level."

Sherry started to look down at the floor, and Stefan placed his hand gently under her chin, tipping her face up. He looked into her eyes. "You know that I love you. I want to be with you." He ran his fingers along her check, her neck, her back…

She closed her eyes. His touch was feather soft. Her voice came out in a whisper. "I love you, too."

"Then show me."

Stefan got to his feet. He stood, looking down at her, and held out his hand. "Show me that you love me, too." Longing filled her eyes, and his voice softened. "There's nothing wrong with following your heart, Sher. You know you want to. Don't keep yourself from what you've wanted for so long. Don't keep yourself from me."

He held out his hand again.

For an embattled moment every muscle of Sherry's body, every quiver of emotion, cried out to satisfy this desperate longing, while her mind and spirit screamed a warning to flee.


Caliel strained at the dark wall, crying out to his wavering charge, trying to break through the barrier she had built. He could see the barbed claws hooked into the young woman, the terrible anticipation on the faces of his adversaries.

The words of his King, the dreadful sadness, rang in his head.

*Her choice…*

Caliel called out to her again as scenes of other times, other choices, other consequences, flew through his memory.

*Her choice…*

Her choice to keep herself for the holy covenant of marriage. Her choice to avoid the consequence of such a sacred loss. Her choice to wait for the unmatched delight of God's perfect gift.

*Her choice!*

Caliel watched Sherry reach up and let Stefan pull her to her feet. Stefan sat her gently on the bed. Her voice sounded faint through the dark barrier. "What if your roommates come in…? What if somebody knocks…?"

"Don't worry. My suitemates are gone for hours. Nobody will know."

Katoth leveled a triumphant glare at Caliel and spoke tauntingly, his words spilling over onto the young man's lips.

"Nobody will know."

And as Sherry made her choice, the demons crowded into the room, raucous and cheering as they watched. Obscene words and gestures filled the air.

Caliel stood, a silent sentinel across the room, his head bowed in pain.

## THIRTY-SEVEN

"SO FAR I'VE FOUND AT LEAST THREE INSTANCES of grants and endowments with Christian stipulations that aren't being used as intended."

Mansfield, Ian, and Claire sat at a large booth at the restaurant in Porter Square, again secure in the circumspect service of their favorite waitress—and even more secure, did they but know it, in the protection of unseen warriors.

Claire had notes and photocopies laid out, her laptop ready for further reference. Her hands trembled a little under the table, and she clasped them together, hoping her nervousness didn't show. Although she tried to look and sound professional and matter-of-fact, she experienced a thrill as she watched her revered professor take notes on what she was saying.

"I…um…I've gone through enough of the documentation on each grant that I can be *fairly* sure about its history. But I've never done this kind of research before, so I can't promise that I've seen everything about each one. Also, I've gone through a bunch of records to find these three grants, but there are still a lot more documents out there. There could be a lot more to find." Her expression was hesitant. "Do you want me to tell you what research I've done so far, or give you the details on what I've found?"

Mansfield's pen was poised over a legal-sized notepad. "Just cut to the chase for now. Tell us about the three examples. I don't want a lot of details yet. Just the basics."

"Okay." Claire breathed deeply as she shuffled through several pages. "There were several grants given around the time of the Cleon Grindley letter. I don't know whether all of them were in response to his plea or not, but several were explicitly Christian. As you asked, I started by looking up the names Rutherford and Crist, since he mentioned those in the letter."

Claire passed a sheet of paper to Mansfield. "Here's a summary of a grant from a Robert Angus Crist, a Boston resident, given eleven years after the letter was written. I'm assuming it's the same Mr. Crist that Cleon Grindley referenced."

"That's probably safe to assume, for now."

"Well, he left twenty thousand dollars—that must be three or four hundred thousand in today's dollars—to be used for 'special lectures by a luminary of the day, a person of evident Christian character, on a topic that will edify and encourage the student body in their pursuit of the Christian faith.' He also stipulated that 'these lectures must take place every few years, but never less than once every three years.' There was some legalese in there about 'in trust' and 'on behalf of the estate,' so I bet he left this money for Harvard in his will." Claire's voice grew tentative. "Is…is this the sort of information you want, Professor?"

"Yes, yes, go on." Mansfield's voice was sharp, and he didn't look up as his pen scratched across the page. For a moment, Claire's heart was in her throat. "I can't believe this. This is great. Just great information you've found. Keep going."

Claire breathed a quiet sigh of relief as she handed over the next paper. "This next one—"

"Wait a minute. What was the dispensation of the Crist lectures?"

"The dispensation?"

"Yes, yes. You know—the outcome. What happened to the money? Were the lectures ever given?"

"Hold on…." Claire pulled up a file on her laptop. "Okay. Apparently, the Crist lectures were given pretty regularly until just after World War II. But even before then they didn't necessarily adhere to the standards Crist set out. For a while they seem to have gone every two or three years, but then that started to slip to every five or ten years, or even longer. There were a few here in the seventies, but none since. And the topics— well, as you can see on your paper, some of the recent topics hardly seem to meet the Christian criteria Mr. Crist specified."

"Civil Rights and the Political Process." Mansfield raised his eyebrows. "Ethics of the Scientific Academy?" He looked up from the notes, his lips curving. "Surely not your standard evangelistic message."

"No." Claire gestured at the other page before him. "Do you want to go on to grant number two?"

"Please."

"Another one I found was given shortly after the Grindley letter, so I'm guessing it might be another of his father's friends. The Rice family endowed a salary for a professor to teach a subject of Harvard's choosing, but the professor had to be a Protestant Christian attending a Baptist, Presbyterian, or Congregationalist church. Isn't that odd?"

The professor pursed his lips. "Not really. Those were some of the only denominations back then. The Rice family probably believed that being specific was the best way to ensure their wishes would be followed, and a truly Christian professor would be hired." His voice slowed. "Unfortunately, today that level of specificity is probably the biggest roadblock to the use of that grant. So has this Baptist, Presbyterian, or Congregationalist professor ever been hired? Even back then?"

"Not that I can tell…but again, I'm not sure I'm finding everything there is to find in these records yet."

"All right. Let's go on to the next one. No, wait. Before you do that, what did you find out about the Grindley grants? Didn't he also endow a professorship?"

"Yep." Claire spoke from memory, not even consulting the laptop. "He endowed a salary for a Christian science professor, as well as those scholarships for young men 'of the highest Christian faith and character.' He said that candidates for the science teaching position would be required to show evidence of strong Christian faith *and* to commit to teaching science from a Christian perspective. Perhaps that explains why his professorship grant was quietly dropped about fifteen years after his death."

Mansfield stretched and shook his head. His forehead was creased. "Good grief. Well, let's go onto the last one you've found."

Claire pushed another sheet of paper in her professor's direction. "I haven't come across any more grants from the Grindley group, so to speak. Like I said, it'll take a lot more time to go through all the records. But this third grant I found is really interesting. This money was given about twenty years earlier than the Grindley letter, so obviously it was unrelated. Apparently, the widow of a minister—a woman who was from a wealthy family—left a grant for scholarships for Christian seminary students at Harvard. Mrs. Donaldson detailed what kind of students the money could go to. It was set up as a trust that would pay Harvard a certain amount of money each year.

"Apparently, the money has been spent by the divinity school every single year, but never for the stated purpose. At least with some of these grants it looks like the money has just been sitting there, earning interest, being used neither for its intended Christian purpose nor any purpose at all. Or if it was used—like with the Crist lectures—there was sometimes an attempt to adhere to the conditions of the endowment. With the Donaldson scholarships, the divinity school has been spending the money year after year without even trying to look like they were adhering to the standards."

Ian whistled. "Boy, that is crazy." He glanced over at Mansfield, noting his professor's somber expression. "Mansfield, what's wrong? I would've thought you'd be glad for the credibility this will give our concerns."

"Will it? I had really thought this could be the breakthrough."

"Why can't it be?"

"Well, look, there are a few things here that make our point that legitimate Christian stipulations have been abused—like the div school spending the Donaldson scholarship money for completely unrelated things. But frankly, some of these stipulations do us more harm than good because they look hopelessly outdated and illegitimate. I'm quite sure that someone is going to protest that Harvard would be foolish to follow these old-fashioned stipulations—saying that a professor must be Baptist, or assuming that all students are young men. These conditions might help make the point that our religious point of view is old-fashioned and out-of-touch, having no place in a modern university."

Suddenly, Claire remembered what else she had brought to this meeting. A warmth settled in her belly, a feeling of certainty overtaking her.

"Professor, let me ask you a question." Her voice was strangely strong. "Do you think anyone would think it foolish or out-of-touch for a university to spend millions of extra dollars to build a second building rather than expand an original one, simply because nearly a hundred years ago the building's donor stipulated that 'not a brick could change'? Do you think anyone would think it foolish that Harvard would place a fresh carnation at the empty bedside of a person long dead simply because a grant required it to?"

Mansfield raised an eyebrow. "Yes, I imagine that plenty of people would think it foolish."

Claire grinned as she handed over a photocopied page from Sherry's notebook. "That's perfect then."

Mansfield rapidly scanned the notes, his eyes widening. He smacked his hand flat against the tabletop and let out a whoop, then handed the page to Ian, who was protesting his ignorance. "Widener Library!"

A few people at nearby tables looked in their direction. He lowered his voice to a loud whisper. "I'd forgotten all about that. They were so careful to adhere to every letter of an old-fashioned grant stipulation that they knocked out a window just so they could say that 'not a brick changed'!" He clasped his hands, his voice dropping suddenly. "O Lord, thank You for Your goodness."

None of them could speak for a moment. Claire's eyes tingled as she fought back emotion. *Thank You, Father. Thank You for letting me be a part of this.*


"Time to pray." In the great room, every head bowed. Several of the HCF members slid off the hard classroom chairs and to their knees. Every thought, every prayer was focused on the King of kings and Lord of lords, asking for His help and blessing on Professor William Mansfield and the long-awaited efforts of the coming week. And as children of the King, they were immediately ushered into the throne room.

Hundreds of angels stood silent, worshiping. Amidst the furor of the daily battle for the lives and souls on campus, the holy hush of this place was like a balm. They could feel the Lord's Spirit among them, feel His overwhelming love and delight in these precious children.

Somewhere amid the sea of bowed heads, a lone male voice began to sing. *We are standing on holy ground.* Harmonies sprang out as other students joined in. *And I know that there are angels all around.* The heavenly host lifted their hands in praise, their resonant voices carrying through eternity. *Let us praise Jesus now. We are standing in His presence on holy ground.*

A deep hush overtook them. As the children of God began to pray aloud, one person here, another there, the Son of Man appeared among them. And, as so many times before, the One they loved and served with full devotion laid His hands on each bowed head, interceding for them before the throne of grace.

And so the week of prayer and fasting began, not by human might or power, but by the Spirit of God.

## THIRTY-EIGHT

## November

SHERRY SLIPPED OUT OF DUNSTER HOUSE, catching the heavy door before it closed loudly behind her. The early morning air was cold and the courtyard quiet, the only sound the splashing of crews on the Charles. She paused in the entryway and watched the river's misty surface through Dunster's tall iron gates. Two shells were sculling by, their coxswains calling a steady beat.

As soon as they passed, she moved quickly toward the exit at the other end of the courtyard, yawning. No sane person would get up this early. Unless they were doing the "walk of shame," of course.

As she stepped through the arch of the G entryway, the street in sight, Sherry heard quick steps on the other side of the door. For a second she panicked, then she straightened and kept walking. No way would it be someone she knew.

The door opened with a squeak, and another young woman hurried out, wrapped in an oversized sweater and sweat pants, gloves in her hand. Their eyes met.

Her face flushed slightly. "Hey." She pulled on her gloves, heading for the exit.

Sherry looked down. "How's it going?"

They stepped out through the arch and went in separate directions. The other girl turned right toward the bicycle racks between Dunster and Mather House next door. Sherry hurried up DeWolfe Street toward Massachusetts Avenue and Harvard Yard. It was still early enough that Claire wouldn't be up.

Claire woke slowly, stretching in her bed. She heard creaks from the loft above her, and knew Sherry was awake. She spoke on a yawn. "Aren't Saturdays the best?"

"You said it. What time is it?"

"Almost eleven."

"Man." It was Sherry's turn to yawn. "I zonked out after—" There was a sudden pause and then another yawn. "I haven't slept that sound in ages."

"What time did you get home?"

"Oh, I don't know."

"It must have been pretty late. I didn't hear you come in."

"Mmm." Sherry climbed down from the loft. "So what are you doing today?"

Claire forced herself to sit up. "A bunch of folks from HCF—Brad, Alison, Doug, and whoever—are going into Boston for lunch. The guys want to check out some sports superstore that just opened down by the ball field." She rolled her eyes. "The girls decided to ditch them and wander down Newbury Street instead."

"Really?"

"Have you been there yet?"

"No, but I've been dying to go. Someone told me it's the best place to shop."

"That's what I heard. Not that I have the money to actually *buy* anything."

Claire watched as Sherry went to her computer. There were probably already three e-mails from Stefan or his friends, when they'd just seen each other last night.

She made a face. Yesterday Sherry had already made plans with Stefan's gang and again hadn't come to HCF. She hadn't joined them at the restaurant, as she had said she might "if she could get away." She hadn't come over to play pool at Alison's place afterward. Claire had been one of the last ones to leave, vainly hoping that Sherry might still show up. And who knows what time she got home.

She jumped out of bed and went over to Sherry's desk. "Hey, why don't you come to Newbury Street with us?"

Sherry turned her head slightly, her eyes still on the computer screen. "I don't know...."

"Look, we're probably leaving around noon. We'll take the T and find someplace for lunch, and then just wander. What do you say?"

"Maybe some other time. Mercedes and some of the others asked me to go play volleyball with the dorm team, so I'll probably do that."

"Well, what about church tomorrow? Remember that church down by MIT that I told you about last week? I really liked it."

Sherry stood up and tapped the keyboard, closing the e-mail program. "Yeah, maybe."

"Maybe?"

Sherry brushed past her. "Well, you don't have to get all snippy about it. I just don't know how I'll feel tomorrow, that's all."

"Should it matter how you feel? Shouldn't you try to make church a habit, so you'll go even when you don't feel like it? Or if you don't go to church, shouldn't you at least go to the HCF meetings so that you get plugged into the Christian community and make friends who will encourage you and help you grow in God?"

Sherry opened her closet, reaching for her shower caddy. "Look, I know I should, but something always gets in the way, and—"

"Only if you let it! Don't you think there are some mornings when I don't want to go to church? But I know I need to. Like I need to go to HCF. And once I do that, suddenly I find that I *want* to be there."

"Well, that's the difference between us, then. I just don't *want* to be there, I guess." She turned toward Claire, facing her roommate for the first time. "I'm just not like you."

"But we agreed to keep each other accountable. You said you'd—"

"It just seems kind of silly now. I—" She turned back to her closet, reaching for her robe.

"Sherry."

"Yes."

"Is there something you need to tell me?"

"What do you mean?" She went to her dresser and began searching a drawer for clean clothes.

Claire sank down to her bed. "You know. The accountability thing, to live a Christian lifestyle. Have you and Stefan…?"

"Nothing's happening, Claire."

"Why…uh…why were you so late?"

A pause. "One of Stefan's friends—do you remember Niles from the other night? Well, he was having a really tough time with his girlfriend. She broke up with him and he needed girl advice. He was a mess. So I spent half the night talking with him."

"Well that was nice of you. And I'm glad you're sticking to your guns with Stefan."

"Yeah." Sherry turned, clothes draped over her arm. She smiled slightly and headed for the door. "Well, I'm going to get a shower. If Mercedes asks, tell her I'll be done in a few minutes."

The door swung shut behind her. Claire stared at it for a minute before rising and getting her own shower things ready. She worked slowly, turning over the conversation in her mind. At least Sherry hadn't slept with him. That was something.

Where had she put her towel? She searched the room with her eyes. Her gaze stopped by her bed, where her Bible and journal were peeking out from under the dust ruffle. She walked over and pulled them out. Then she looked at the clock.

She hesitated just a moment, then set the shower stuff down and climbed back into bed, plumping up the pillows behind her. She opened the Bible to Philippians, where she had left off days ago.

*How many days has it been?* Her mind turned backward to the day of that stupid guest instructor in philosophy. Alison had heard her and Brad talking about it at dinner.

"I can solve your angst for you," Alison had said. "Read Philippians and think of how Paul could write about rejoicing in a filthy prison. He was persecuted and tortured and imprisoned for his faith. We're only laughed at. What a deal!"

Brad had held up his hand. "And remember that often people who are derisive have a totally wrong impression of what Christianity is, and have never heard a good presentation of the gospel. Once someone gets to know you and hears your heart, that usually changes things."

Claire opened back to where the shiny maroon ribbon lay between the pages. Her eye fell on a familiar passage in Philippians 2.

Continue to work out your salvation with fear and trembling, for it is God who works in you to will and to act according to his good purpose. Do everything without complaining or arguing, so that you may become blameless and pure, children of God without fault in a crooked and depraved generation, in which you shine like stars in the universe as you hold out the word of life.

She opened her journal and began to write. *Lord, forgive me for so totally ignoring You. I want to shine like stars in the midst of this crooked and depraved place...*

The words filled page after page as she came before her Father. *This isn't hard, Lord! Why don't I do this more often?*

An image of her berating Sherry just minutes before rose before her mind's eye. *Shouldn't you try to make church a habit so that you'll go even when you don't feel like it?... And once I do, suddenly I find that I want to be there....*

Claire groaned and fell face forward into her comforter. *I'm such an idiot. Lord, how do You put up with me? Thank You that You are greater than my weakness!*

She heard footsteps coming toward the door, and she bowed her head, her voice a whisper. "Lord, I promise You: I will lift my eyes to the hills *every morning*, whether I feel like it or not."

She jumped out of bed as Sherry came in, her head wrapped in a towel. She felt oddly jubilant as she made the bed and got ready to meet her friends. One thing she knew: she had made a promise to God, and she'd better not break it.

"So why is it that we expect to have it easy in this life?" The young pastor stood ne the altar, his Bible open in his hand. "Peter says we are aliens and strangers in world."

Claire sat in the last pew, her coat folded on the empty space beside her. She coming in late and was doubly irritated at having waited in vain for Sherry to home. She should have known her roommate would stand her up.

Sherry insisted that nothing was going on with Stefan, but it was *not* a good idea to keep putting herself in these positions, no matter how many of Stefan's wayward friends needed a shoulder to cry on or advice on relationships.

"Our perspective is all wrong." The pastor had stepped to the podium. He took a quick sip of the water tucked behind it. "We have to realize that this world is not our home. We are made for a completely different place."

He set his Bible down and moved out from behind the podium, searching the congregation with earnest eyes. "The analogy Peter uses is this: We are underground espionage agents working and living out our daily lives in hostile territory. We work for a completely different government than the one we're living under! Not only that, but we are under specific orders to infiltrate the place we're living and turn the allegiance of its citizens toward another kingdom!"

Claire sat up straighter. *That's good...*

He held up a warning hand. "Nobody misunderstand me: I am *not* talking about an earthly government. In the very next verses, Peter clarifies that we are supposed to honor and pray for our earthly government leaders, no matter what our political differences. No—I'm talking about one of two spiritual governments: the one that governs the realm of light that we were made for and the one that governs the realm of darkness that we currently live in. Obviously, our God is more powerful than all the forces of the enemy, but long ago in the Garden we made our choice as to which realm our earthly bodies would live in."

Claire opened up her journal and began taking notes.

"Should it surprise us when we encounter roadblocks? Of course not! Did the good-hearted citizens with the resistance in Nazi Germany expect their lives to be nice and easy? Of course not! They expected heartache and trouble. They even expected casualties."

The young pastor picked up his Bible again and held it up. "This Book clearly tells us that the world we are living in is not our home. There will be times when the evil one—the prince of this world—sends his agents to attack and demoralize us. There will even be times when the evil one takes out one of our fellow espionage agents. We mourn, of course, but we *shouldn't be surprised.* Instead, we should redouble our efforts with the espionage tools we've been given: love, prayer, the Word of God, service, truth, hope, faith, gentleness, kindness, self-control.

"So ask yourself these questions. When you encounter trouble, how do you react? When you are opposed, do you slink back to your secret bunker and hide? Or do you stand firm in the job *your* King has entrusted to you in this dark place, knowing that 'at the proper time we will reap a harvest if we do not give up'?"

Claire shifted uncomfortably in her seat, thinking of all the slinking and hiding she'd done since arriving at Harvard.

The pastor flipped back to 1 Peter 2. "'I urge you, as aliens and strangers in the world, to abstain from sinful desires, which war against your soul. Live such good lives among the pagans that, though they accuse you of doing wrong, they may see your good deeds and glorify God on the day He visits us.'" His eyes were penetrating as he searched the pews. "Ask yourself again: When you're tempted, how do you react? Do you give in to the ways of the kingdom you have infiltrated?"

*Ouch.* Claire's mind flitted to the fake IDs.

"Or do you so thoroughly shine God's radiance, purity, and love that the kingdom you have infiltrated is turned to *His* ways? And how often do you stay in touch with the King who is your real commander in chief? Do you get His direction every morning, or are you out there in dangerous territory on your own, ignoring His urgent signals?"

Claire had kept her promise to the Lord that morning, but how many days had been wasted by her lack of prayerfulness? She gripped the Bible in her lap tighter. *I promise Lord.*

"How do you react when you're busy with your daily life and come across someone's urgent, now-or-never sort of need? Do you tell the oppressed prisoner of the dark world that you're busy now but you'll come back to your underground espionage job at two o'clock next Tuesday? Or do you prayerfully rearrange your daily life to fit the calling of your *true* job? I have news for you, dear saints." He leaned forward on the podium. "Ministry is *always inconvenient.*"

Claire heard soft grunts of acknowledgment all around her. The pastor again stepped out from behind the podium and walked to the edge of the platform, holding the open Bible in his hand.

"And finally, how do you react when trouble comes? When something terrible happens that you don't understand? Do you shake your fist at your King and yell 'Why?' Or do you love and trust your King with all your heart, mind, soul, and strength and remember what He said when you took the job: 'In *this world* you will have trouble. But take heart! I have overcome the world.'"

The pastor slowly closed his Bible and gazed out the back windows that shone in the morning sun. His voice was soft. "When my time as an underground espionage agent in this dark world is over and I finally get to go home, I want nothing more than to hear my King say, 'Well done, good and faithful servant! Enter into the joy of your Lord.'"


Claire walked out of the church and onto the sidewalk, hands deep in her pockets, her bright blue scarf a fluffy barrier against the cold.

She thought of the week ahead as she headed for the entrance to the T. She had so much homework to read for philosophy, some really oppressive humanist stuff she'd started before but hadn't had the heart to finish.

*Lord, if You want me to be an espionage agent that will stand and fight for Your Kingdom, please help me learn how. Because right now that bunker is looking pretty darned good.*

## THIRTY-NINE

"MIND IF I JOIN YOU?"

Claire looked up from her book, startled, the clatter and hum of the Greenhouse Café impinging again on her consciousness. Ian Burke was standing next to her table, holding a tray and looking at her curiously. Had he asked that question twice?

"I'm sorry!" Claire moved her backpack and lunch plate out of the way. "I was just..." She gestured at her novel before closing it and moving it aside.

"I don't want to interrupt anything." Ian had an amused glint in his eye. "Are you sure...?"

"Oh no! I mean...yes...I mean..." She made a comical face. "You'd think now that I'm at Harvard, I'd learn how to talk. You're not interrupting, and please join me."

Ian slid into the seat. "What are you reading?"

"Just something silly."

"What? Now I'm curious."

Claire hesitated, then held out the book. "It was my grandmother's. It's not as old as the Grindley House books, but I still love this old hardcover edition. The new paperback version just doesn't...have as much character, or something."

Ian tipped the book sideways, squinting at the faded typeface on the spine. *Pollyanna.* Hm. I've never read it."

"You're kidding."

"Nope." Ian handed the book back. He bowed his head briefly, then began digging in to his food. "I'm a pretty imaginative person, and lots of people have accused me of being Pollyanna-ish because I'm too pie-in-the-sky with things sometimes. But I've never read the book. Why?"

"Well...it's a classic. And one every Christian should read, I think."

"Really? How so?"

"Because you—" Claire caught herself and looked across the table, trying to maintain a professional reserve. She had almost started addressing him like one of her peers instead of her TA and supervisor. "Well, partly because of the misperception of what *Pollyanna-ish* means. See, the reason that word tends to have a negative connotation— in the world's eyes—is that the character of Pollyanna is trying to literally do what the Bible says: to rejoice and be glad in all things."

Out of the corner of her eye, she saw Ian's lips part in surprise. "In the book," she continued, "Pollyanna's father was a pastor who taught her to always be glad, and the entire book is about how this glad little girl impacted her world simply by doing what God says to do."

"I had no idea." Ian looked impressed. "I'll have to read that sometime."

"It's just a children's book, but it's so uplifting that I have to read it from time to time to remind myself how to act when confronted with things that are hard to be glad about. Like the stupid philosophy class that I have at two!"

"What's wrong with your class?"

"It's hard to explain." She sighed, the lightness in her spirit vanishing. "I just feel like every time I walk into that class my brain is going to be tied in knots. I feel like I'm getting steamrolled, like I have no idea how to defend what I believe—or even to think through what others believe—in time to defend my position. Sometimes I even find myself second-guessing what I know is true!" She made a face. "I guess I'm not making much sense."

"No, you're making perfect sense. Would you mind a few comments?"

"Please."

"You're talking about Kwong's class, right? I had it when I was a sophomore. And believe me, I understand completely. *Any* philosophy class can tie anyone's brain in knots, until you learn how to stand on your feet—" a grin flashed across his face—"and even after, sometimes!"

Claire shook her head. "I never thought I'd say this, but I just don't know if I'm up to it. You know, intellectually. There's this other Christian guy in the class—Brad—and he always seems to have these great arguments during class discussion, like he's able to keep up with the debate. I just don't know if I can—"

"Don't say it." Ian leaned forward. "That's the big lie. Think about it: Would you be feeling just as dumb if you shared the secular viewpoint of most of the philosophers and other students? Of course not! Everything you said and thought would fit just perfectly into the flow of what you were hearing all around you, and you'd probably feel much more at ease. Instead," he rapped sharply on the table, "you have to *work*. You have to *think*. I'm afraid that some students are able to coast along, without ever learning how to truly analyze dissenting opinions and evidence, because it's never presented to them. There's a lot of stuff that's not politically correct, so it's simply never included. Alternatively, of course, as you've no doubt seen, it's simply bashed down without a true debate whenever it dares to rear its head."

"Yeah. I've seen the bashing part."

Ian laughed aloud. "Honestly, Claire, in terms of your development as a student, this may be the best possible thing for you. As a TA, I see it all the time—where a very smart person is just intellectually lazy because he or she has been confronted with only agreeable opinions. You're going to have to learn how to truly analyze things where other students may be able to coast." He gestured toward *Pollyanna* in her backpack. "That's something you can be glad about, isn't it?"

Claire's voice was thoughtful. "I guess… But, well, let me ask you this. Our class today is on something called 'situation ethics' and—"

"Ah, the old name for moral relativism. You're in for some fun today. Go on."

"Just what I need. More fun. Anyway, we had to read pieces of the *Humanist Manifesto* and a few other articles, and it's just so…*ick.*" She wrinkled her nose. "I don't even know how to describe it. 'There is no God.' 'There's no such thing as absolute right or wrong.' 'All ethics are made only by man, for men.' 'Everyone must decide their own standard of behavior.' Do you know how much material there is on this? It's like four inches thick! I don't even know where to *start* defending what I believe."

"Well, at least you haven't given up." Ian drummed his fingers on the table, thinking. "Okay. Let me tell you four things I do when I'm in debates like that. Number one, get analytical. Ask yourself, *What are the assumptions here?* Figuring out the unspoken assumptions behind the worldview can make or break your debate.

"Usually when a professor or a student says something or asks a question, there are two parts to the statement: an assumption and the question itself." He leaned forward, jabbing his finger against the table for emphasis. "Don't answer the question before you figure out what the assumption is! For example, if someone says, 'Well, that's right for you, but not right for me,' then the unspoken premise is that there is no absolute truth. And if there is no absolute truth, then anything goes. Why can't I take a hammer and bash them over the head? Hey!" Ian sat taller in his seat, puffing out his chest and slapping his hand to his breastbone. "It was right for me!"

He shook his finger at her. "Very few people, by the way, will agree with you when you make that argument. Most people who think they're relativists really aren't. They just want the freedom to do what they want to do without guilt, but they don't want anyone else—enjoying their own guiltless freedom—to bash them over the head with a hammer."

Claire laughed. "Okay. What's number two?"

"Number two is the follow-up. If number one is *uncover assumptions,* number two is *question assumptions.* You have to work backwards to show them the logical conclusion of whatever it is they're saying. Wherever possible, try to catch intellectual inconsistencies. If someone says, 'There are no absolutes; everything is relative,' one fun tactic is to then ask, 'Are you sure?'" He chuckled as comprehension dawned on Claire's face, remembering Brad's classroom debate with Leyla Lemoine. "Of course, if they are *sure* about something, that itself is an absolute, isn't it?"

Ian waved his hand. "But that's just a simple example, and that will resolve very few discussions. So you'll want to first get their permission to ask questions about their statement. That will set a much better tone for the discussion, believe me!

"So, suppose you've got this perfectly sincere friend who says there are no absolutes. Now that you have his permission, you can ask him, 'Do you believe there is a God who created the universe?' If he says, 'Oh, I believe in God,' then he is being intellectually inconsistent—since most people would argue that if there is a creator God, He has created moral absolutes.

"But if he says, 'That's right; there is no God like that,' then he's at least being consistent, and the next logical step is to say, "Okay then, so you believe we humans just appeared by random chance.' They'll probably agree. Then the last step is to say, 'So you believe we're just cosmic garbage, a collection of chemicals with no ultimate meaning in life.'

"That's an example of a very effective strategy: Find a logical but ridiculously extreme conclusion of what they're saying, and that will point out the absurdity of the initial assumption. Most people, frankly, haven't given it that much thought. And like I said, very few people are comfortable agreeing that they have no ultimate meaning or purpose, that they're merely a collection of chemicals. Now some hard-core secular humanists will actually agree with that, believe it or not! They say we have no free will, no spirit beyond what we can see, no *soul*, since none of those things can be scientifically seen and measured."

"They say we have no soul? No meaning in life?" Claire shuddered. "How awful. You'd think those people would see little point in living."

"Actually, some atheists have taken their own lives for that very reason."

"It's so sad!" Claire exclaimed. "Why do some people fight so hard against believing in God? You'd think people would want to believe in someone who lovingly created them, someone who gives their life meaning and purpose."

"I know." Ian shrugged. "People try so hard to create these—these *intellectual constructs,* when the truth is so much easier. I don't get it. The only thing I can think is that people don't want to face the fact that believing in God comes with believing that He has a way for them to live, and they'd prefer to do their own thing."

Claire's thoughts flitted to Sherry.

Ian was smiling slightly. "Mansfield showed me this quote from Aldous Huxley, the author of *Brave New World.* He was an agnostic and wrote something like—and I'm paraphrasing here—'I was an unbeliever, not because I could find a way to discredit Christianity, but because I wanted to sleep with my girlfriend.'" Ian raised his glass in a toast. "At least the man was honest!"

Claire smiled and was about to ask a question when Ian held up a warning hand.

"Keep in mind that I'm describing people's beliefs as if they were a nice neat package that you can understand if you work hard enough. In actuality, a lot of people themselves don't really understand what they believe. It's often a confusing mix of beliefs picked up here and there that may not even make sense together, and they often don't want to bother thinking about it. I've seen the same thing with Christians, actually. The key is whether or not the person is truly open to the discussion and willing to examine himself and his beliefs honestly."

"That makes sense. So is there a number three?"

"Yep. And a number four." Ian drained his glass and set it back down. He looked at the clock on the wall. "And then you have to go or you're going to be late. The third thing I try to do in these debates is to put myself in their shoes so that I can start to love and talk with them where they are, as Jesus would, and so that they understand me better. That goes for a student *or* a professor. You need to speak their language and use their lingo, which will help them hear you. For example, if they're ridiculing you, nicely object in principle to their 'bigotry' or their 'intolerance,' and point out that they would never make fun of a black student or a gay person." He grinned. "You might actually see the lightbulb go on over their head. And since phraseology like *people of color* is so popular, call yourself a *person of faith*.

"You also need to make that distinction, quite frankly, since so many people nowadays associate the word *Christian* only with politics or rigid rules or the religious culture of our country, rather than with heartfelt belief in Christ. And keep in mind—maybe even jot down—the main points that you want to say, or you may get your brain scrambled in the midst of their counterresponse."

"That's good. What's the last one?" Claire looked at the clock and started to gather her things.

"Claire…"

She paused and looked up. His face was serious.

"Number four is…have the courage to speak the truth in love. It takes guts, Claire. Guts to publicly defend an unpopular position, especially when you're defending yourself to a professor. But 'always be prepared to give an answer for the hope that is within you.' And when you speak for the Truth, *pray* for those you're talking with and trust the Holy Spirit to give you the words to say. But always, always speak in love. If they're abusive—and trust me, Claire, they sometimes will be—respond with the grace that Christ showed, and you will be blameless before God and man."

"Ian, I just don't know if I—" She heard a gentle chuckle and broke off, looking back at his face.

"Claire, I don't know you very well, but I think you'll do just fine. It's important to know how to defend what you believe. But in the end, arguments and words rarely change someone's mind. What changes minds is the building of relationships. Let them be intrigued and drawn by your winsome manner. By the beauty of a quiet and gentle spirit."

He nodded briefly in parting, and was gone.

Claire stood staring after him then shouldered her backpack, breathing a silent prayer. She *was* going to learn how to deal with this class.

She was about ten steps along before she realized her thoughts weren't on the class. She shook her head firmly. And she was *not* going to fall for her TA.


"So Paul Kurtz, the author of the *Humanist Manifesto II*, contends that one does not need God-given moral absolutes to champion basic moral virtues such as 'fairness, kindness, beneficence, justice, and tolerance.'"

Professor Kwong was walking around the classroom, looking intently at his students. "Of course, other humanists question why these should be considered virtuous without a deity to provide a standard of virtue. But Hall and Tarkunde get around the religion problem by positing that we animals developed the idea of morality during the evolutionary survival-of-the-fittest process, since morality is important for a properly functioning and therefore stronger society. They argue that religion is not necessary for ethical standards." He gestured toward the back row. "Niles?"

Niles was sitting alone in a section of chairs, his face tight. "I would argue that not only is it not necessary, but it's usually the religious people anyway who are *against* virtues like fairness and tolerance. They just want people to live by their rules, whether or not they're beneficial for *them.*"

Claire shook her head, sighing at the spite in his voice. How was there any basis for morality *without* God?

A girl in the front row raised her hand, then turned and looked at Niles in irritation. "Come off it, Niles! You're just as bad as the right-wingers; everything is so black and white with you." She looked back at the professor. "Look, it's obvious to me that the humanists are way extreme in their philosophy. But I'm glad, at least, that they brought up this issue of morality. It's always bugged me that religious people think they're the only ones who are ethical or moral. Are you saying I'm not a moral person just because I don't happen to believe in God?"

Claire cast an uncomfortable look in the speaker's direction. That *was* actually the logical conclusion of her own earlier thought—even if it was subconscious. But there were plenty of secular people who were good and moral. She sighed again, wishing this whole thing could be a little more simple.

"See, but that's exactly what I mean," Niles said. "There are many ways to live ethically. That magazine article you put in our packet from that atheist author just ripped the carpet out from under the religious right on this."

Kwong walked to the podium and set his reading glasses on his nose. "'For the religious right to contend that they are for love and peace—when they oppress the gay community and judgmentally make my daughter feel guilty for wanting to move in with her boyfriend—is the height of hypocrisy. When will they learn that all people are precious and worthy of fulfillment and self-actualization, wherever that self-actualization is found?'" He looked over the top of the glasses at Niles. "Is that the article you're referring to?"

"Yes."

When no one else jumped in, Brad slowly raised his hand. Claire watched several students share derisive looks toward her friend. *God, I can't handle that!* Would anyone ever like her if she were as bold as Brad?

Brad turned and addressed Niles. "Obviously, I disagree with that author—"

"No, really?" Niles's tone was scathing.

"First, as an aside, I understand what she thinks about the religious community, but unfortunately she is misinformed."

"Is that so?"

*What's his problem?* It gave Claire some minor satisfaction that several other students also glanced at Niles in annoyance.

"Unfortunately, there are some so-called religious people who are terribly judgmental," Brad said, "and some who seem to delight in rules and regulations. But that is counter to how Jesus said we were to act. It's one thing for a person of faith to stand up for the truth, but quite another for that person to do God's job. If someone needs to change, only God can really convince them of that. It's hard as a Christian to see anyone be judgmental and hateful in the name of a compassionate and loving God. Most true believers aren't perfect, but they are loving and kind, people who try to befriend the hurting and oppressed just like Jesus did. But even when they aren't loving, you have to remember that they are just fallible people, not God.

"But that wasn't my primary point." Brad looked back at Professor Kwong. "What I was going to say is that the author contradicts herself. She says she's an atheist and mocks Judeo-Christian religious beliefs, but later in the article says that people are precious. But how is that possible? If we're all just the product of random chance rather than of a loving Creator, then we're a bunch of cosmic trash. And if we're just a bunch of cosmic trash, then how can she say we're precious? It doesn't make sense."

Claire sat up straighter in her seat. *Just like Ian said...!* She uncapped her pen and began scribbling notes in the margins of her notebook.

Two women in the row in front of her began murmuring to each other. One of them raised her hand.

"But Brad, you have to admit that religion does come with strict rules, and religion does often make people feel guilty and trapped. I'd prefer to think of myself as precious—even if it's just in my own mind—and pursue what makes sense for me. Shouldn't I be able to pursue whatever actions will be valuable for my self-actualization, even if they don't conform to the religious rules of the day?"

"Well, Bethany," Brad said, "I guess my thought is—it may feel good to tell yourself you're precious rather than cosmic trash. But if in truth we're really not precious and beloved creations of God, and if I'm not subject to anything other than what self-actualizes me, then maybe it makes me feel good to oppress you. It *self-actualizes* me to oppress you.

"If I'm a soldier in Nazi Germany and get self-fulfillment and esteem from causing the death of a Jewish victim, who's to say I'm wrong? Not society—it was deemed to be good for society at the time. Not outside observers—for if all those Jewish people really are just cosmic trash in the process of evolution, then there's nothing inherently precious about the human lives being lost. And since humanists say morality is only a social construct created by men during the process of evolution, in the grand scheme of things the Jewish killings are ultimately only a matter of whether or not the Nazi society would be strengthened or weakened by them."

Claire looked from the perplexity on Bethany's face to the straightforward appeal on Brad's. She looked down at the notes traveling along the margins of her notebook. *So that's how that works.*


Niles slammed out of class, furious. He couldn't believe that Kwong had allowed the class to deteriorate like that. Kwong never had come back to him, although he'd raised his hand several times.

His mind churned as he headed to pick up his mail, his thoughts black. No one really appreciated him or recognized the critical importance of what he had so thoroughly thought out.

The mailbox area was crowded, and he waited impatiently to get to the latest batch of useless activity flyers, administrative announcements, and...

*Ah.* He smiled as he pulled the small stack from his box. A now-familiar-looking cream-colored envelope was on top. He slit it open. At least somebody appreciated him. The note, as usual, started without preamble.

Niles, we continue to be impressed with the effectiveness of your column in
the student paper. Yesterday we saw a number of students gathered around
one of the posters announcing your protest rally. They seemed highly appre-

ciative and interested in joining the effort. Keep it up! You are doing a good work, one we only wish we had time to do. The campus owes you a great debt.

The letter was signed, *Your fans.*

He straightened in satisfaction. Just the boost he needed. He only wished they'd sign these notes so he could get in touch with them.

VERITAS FORTY

THREE MINOR SENTRIES LOLLED AROUND the faculty conference room, one atop the great portrait that looked down the length of the polished table, another drumming on the door with his fingertips. Yet another sat in one of the leather swivel chairs, enjoying the ride as he twisted it this way and that.

None of the vile sons of Adam were around to see the chair bouncing and turning, seemingly of its own accord, so they might as well have some fun. Of course, it was also fun scaring the wits out of an impressionable human every now and then with a well-placed manifestation.

His mind played over the memory of a recent haunting he'd done at a house in Boston—the barest hint to the terrified residents that a murder victim had returned. He laughed at the thought. His colleagues had arranged the murder all right, and he had *so* enjoyed replaying the event in artful creaks and distant, otherworldly screams. Many years ago he tried to merely create fear, but these days their orders had expanded to include anything that drew attention to the paranormal—ghost tours, séances, channeling. That was fine with them; they—and their master—reveled in the adulation. It made them strong. And even better, it made their adversaries suffer.

He twirled the chair again. He liked ghost duty and was eager to get back to it. This guard stuff was boring, especially when territory was so firmly held, so uncontested by those weakling forces of the Enemy.

*"EN GUARDE!"* The spirit jumped to the ceiling at the loud voice not two feet behind his head. He whirled and came face-to-face with a warrior of high rank, his garments shining, his skin and hair glowing like burnished bronze. He held a sword in one hand and a writhing demon—one of the complacent sentries—in the other.

The startled spirit's eyes flew to the doorway, where a dozen young men and women—*Christians!*—were entering the room. Closely following them were two ranks of Enemy warriors. The third sentry was casually pinned by another pair of giant hands.

He pulled his sword, yelling a battle cry of blasphemy against their King. The bronze giant blocked his blow, ripped a hole in space, and flung him and his comrades through it. "Go to your chosen fate!"

Kai stepped up behind the giant angel, surveying the now-uncontested room. "General, as you can see, the ground is clear and the enemy was prevented from getting a message out."

"Make sure the saints have time and protection to lay the groundwork. Each of these precious ones has been fasting all day, just as their colleagues have been praying and fasting in rotation all week. Give them as much time as they need."

"Yes, sir."

Petras looked around the room, meeting the eyes of each of the warriors chosen for just such a time as this. "It has been a long time, my friends. But with the Lord's power, this ground will be retaken for His glory!"

The angels cheered. Petras drew his sword, extending it over the heads of the students. "Let us seal this place and protect their work." Instantly, the room was enclosed within an arc of brilliant light, as the students began to pray.

Some of the young men and women sat and prayed silently. Others walked around the room, praying aloud in turn. Two students moved along the polished table, laying hands on every chair and praying for the occupant. Every now and then the students would join in snatches of a hymn or worship song, coming in unity before the throne.

And as they prayed, the warriors received their orders, moving to their assigned places in the room or departing for a strategic posting. Their faces were shining, their swords at the ready.

Sharon DeLay walked down the hall, nearly whistling. For some reason, she'd been in a great mood all day.

A demon flew behind her. He'd been in a terrible mood all day, ever since *that* had shown up. He glowered at the glowing warrior whose extended sword prevented him from sinking his claws into his prey. He was under the restraint of the Holy Spirit. He could feel it, and it irritated him nearly to distraction. At least they were almost there.

Sharon waved to Elsa Chasinov, and the two of them chatted in the hallway for a moment before making their way into the conference room.

The demon smirked and looked up at his tormentor as he flew through the wall—and straight into a blazing cauldron of light. The demon shrieked and clawed at his eyes as he shot back out into the hallway. What the heaven was going on?

Fifteen minutes later, amidst a sea of collegial chatter, Anton Pike tapped the gavel and tried to get comfortable in his seat. Something was wrong. He felt sick, but didn't have the time to excuse himself and meditate. He was anxious to get this meeting over with. He had too many balls in the air as it was, and he needed to get with Victor soon to finalize their latest staffing decisions.

He tapped the gavel again, this time a little too loudly. "Let's get started, shall we? I know we all have a lot to do today, and I'd like to keep things short." He took a stack of papers and split it, passing the sheets to his left and right. Then he looked down at his copy.

"I'll just run through our short agenda for today. First we'll hear from a representative of the finance committee. Cheryl Crenshaw, the newly appointed director of the office of finance, will summarize the projections for next semester's budgets. She'll tell you what resources you can expect to receive so you can plan for teaching assistants, your sabbaticals, and the like." He grinned as he nodded toward the guest speaker. "Remember, we *like* Cheryl."

Chuckles resounded around the room as he continued. "Okay, after that we have just some routine business: We need to send a few cases of cheating to the Honor Committee—" he glanced down the table—"Marvin, is there something special there, or can you just go ahead and skip that presentation?"

"That's fine." Marvin looked cheerful.

"And we need to hear from Howard about some of the schedule conflicts that might arise during the holidays," he glanced at another professor, who nodded. "And then we'll take a minute to talk through the latest proposal for reducing grade inflation. I know we're all sick of the subject, but the president's office wants to know whether we should hire a consultant." He looked down at the final line on his agenda. "And finally, we have the last of the diversity task force reports. Professor Burke will address the subject of ideol…" Anton's voice faltered, and he cleared his throat. "Um…ideological diversity?"

He looked around at the faculty members. "There must be some mistake. There's no Professor Burke on this committee." He scratched through that line with his pen. "I'll just drop that from the agenda until we determine—"

"Actually, Anton, that's my report." Mansfield leaned back in his chair and reached for a stack of bound materials, which he hefted to the table. "Sorry about the mix-up. I don't know how my teaching assistant's name got listed instead of mine, but let me tell you how delighted he was to be promoted to full professor."

The other faculty members chuckled. Anton plastered on a jovial smile.

"Well, Mansfield, you certainly seem to be well prepared. Do you have a copy of the report for every faculty member?"

Mansfield nodded.

"Good, good. Since I'm sure we're all quite pressed for time, why don't you just pass those out at the end." He smiled around at the other members. "We can all read the task force conclusions for ourselves and then discuss them at some future date."

Anton picked up his pen and gestured toward the first speaker. "Well, Cheryl, why don't you—"

"Excuse me, Anton." Jack Sprague, at the far end of the room, spoke up. "Sorry for interrupting, but I think it's important to actually *hear* all the task force reports."

Elsa Chasinov nodded. "Frankly, I don't have time to read the bloody thing, so I'd prefer just to hear the presentation and make a decision based on the verbal recommendations. That would be a great deal easier."

Others nodded their agreement.

Anton forced a laugh. "Of course, I totally understand. But I'd really like to help Mansfield and his people a little more, since they're the last in a long string of these reports. We've heard so many of these things that the recommendations all sound the same after a while." He mimed writing down a boring proposal. "'Convene a subcommittee to figure out how to implement the task force recommendations.' It would be so much better if we all just read the report and came prepared to talk about it at a later date."

"It might be better, but let's be realistic," Mansfield said. "We're all very busy, and few of us are going to take the time to read through this thing." He hefted it in his hands and grinned. "Heck, *I* don't even want to read it, and it's my report!"

"But since we're all busy today, I was just thinking that—"

"Look," Sharon DeLay said, a little irritated, "we all have midterms to grade, and the next meeting will be even more pressed. Let's just take some time now and be done with it."

Anton forced himself to nod pleasantly. "Sure, then." He gestured at Cheryl Crenshaw. "Sorry for the sidetracking. Please go ahead, Cheryl."

He returned his attention to the papers in front of him, not hearing a word the finance director said. Out of the corner of his eye, he watched Mansfield listen and take notes. *That blasted man.*

A mile across campus, but adjacent in spirit, a group of students sat in a quiet dorm room, oblivious to the raucous noise of other students clattering in and out of the building on a beautiful Friday afternoon. Their heads were bowed, and their prayers were fervent as they interceded for the meeting that was in progress.

Claire lifted her face to the sun outside the window, her spirit exuberant. She had the strangest feeling that a race was being run. *Go, God, go.*


"Before you open the reports in front of you—and at the risk of teaching the teachers— let me ask you a question that will set the stage." Mansfield looked around at the expressions before him: attentive, interested. Usually the faculty members couldn't wait to leave.

He was filled with a sense of peace and breathed a quiet prayer of thanksgiving. He could feel the prayers of those interceding for this meeting.

"Let's go back to the reason why we're doing this exercise of increasing diversity to begin with. Why does Harvard—and other schools—place such an emphasis on diversity? We all know it's a good thing, but what purpose are we trying to serve?"

One of the professors leaned back, clasping his hands behind his head. "Well, we want to purposely include those who may have been excluded in the past."

"Yes, clearly. But *why* are we making such an effort? Are we just doing it to be nice?"

The professor smiled, and his voice grew magisterial. "Ah, I see what you're getting at. No, of course that's not the only reason. Fundamentally, we recognize that pulling together students of all races and backgrounds will enrich our environment in a way that might not have happened organically."

Mansfield tried not to smile at the professor's pompous tone.

"Studies show," the man continued, "that those students who are exposed to many different experiences and beliefs learn far more than those who are not."

"Exactly." Mansfield clasped his hands together, punctuating his point. He rested his elbows on the table and looked intently around the room. "As all of us have seen, a classroom learning environment is fundamentally better when, for example, I have a poor student from the inner city who is willing to speak up during a discussion of the Great Depression. The other students' experiences and assumptions are challenged, and everyone learns more. I'm sure you all agree."

Most of the heads nodded. Mansfield blocked out the peripheral sight of Anton Pike's set face and hard eyes.

"As we all know—and have been trying to do—we must go beyond fostering diversity of race alone in order to achieve a fertile learning environment. Since different life experiences and beliefs enrich our classrooms, having a wealthy black student isn't much more helpful than having a wealthy white student. But having that inner-city student, regardless of race, who knows what it's like to use food stamps and hear gunfire outside—now *that* will stretch and enliven everyone else in the classroom."

He tapped sharply on the document in front of him. "That, ladies and gentlemen, offers a starting point for our discussion of ideological diversity. Simply put, ideological diversity is diversity of *belief*—so as you can imagine, it's probably the most fundamental way of ensuring a fertile learning environment."

Mansfield noted that curiosity was growing more evident on the faces of some faculty around the table. Others looked cautious. He smiled agreeably.

"What our task force has found over the past two years is similar to what Sharon talked about with the alternative lifestyles task force: the absence of one whole point of view."

He nodded respectfully at Sharon. She looked at him, her eyes narrowing.

"But in this case, the lack is even more egregious and pervasive—a widespread, active suppression of diversity. Where Sharon was concerned that class materials never mentioned the gay point of view, what we have found is that certain other—much broader—points of view are either twisted incorrectly, never mentioned at all, or mentioned and mocked. These points of view are those that could be described as conservative or those that are faith based."

The room began to buzz, and Mansfield continued quickly. "Harvard prides itself on being a marketplace of ideas, but unfortunately that marketplace is set up in a way that de facto excludes a massive amount of input. This report lists thousands of cases where students were prevented from learning because of bias against those with faith-based or conservative belief systems. The evidence for this prejudice was so overwhelming that we could probably consider it systemic."

The room erupted in protest. Sharon DeLay sputtered, "It is the bigoted religious conservatives that have oppressed other points of view for so long—how can you argue that they're the ones being suppressed?"

Taylor Haller's mouth was hanging open in astonishment. "Are you trying to tell us that you Christian right-wingers need special protection? Because let me tell you—"

"I am not saying that conservative and faith-based points of view need special protection any more than, frankly, the gay point of view needs special protection."

Sharon looked affronted and opened her mouth to respond. Mansfield leaned forward. "What I *am* saying is that all points of view should have equal access to the marketplace of ideas—including those that don't happen to be politically correct.

Sharon, you said several weeks ago that we didn't know what it was like to be a lesbian professor having to deal with textbooks that never make mention of the gay lifestyle. Well, you know what? You're right. I don't.

"But neither do you know what it's like to be a person of faith in an environment that is so hostile." He looked directly at Taylor. "Within the last minute alone, you called me a right-winger." He looked back at Sharon. "And you implied that I was bigoted and purposefully oppressive of others. All because I'm coming from a faith-based point of view. Both of those statements are wrong, and they hurt."

He looked around the table, trying to catch the eyes of his colleagues. "And they are very common on campus. If those statements are hurtful toward me, an experienced senior professor secure in my beliefs and my standing at this university, imagine how oppressive they are to your average eighteen-year-old person of faith."

"Excuse me, Mansfield…"

Mansfield turned to see Elsa Chasinov raising her hand.

"If I can interrupt here?" At Mansfield's nod she continued. "I don't want to be disrespectful of religious people, but I have to point out the obvious: *Diversity* usually means actively including those with some sort of minority status. You can hardly consider Christians in America to be the minority."

Mansfield prayed furiously as he responded. "Elsa, I know it may not seem apparent to you, but that is exactly what I'm saying." He heard grunts of astonishment around the table. "When I talk about people of faith, I'm not speaking of those who simply attend church now and then. That's a superficial measurement, and I agree that those people are in the majority in this country. Rather, I mean those for whom faith is an all-encompassing part of life. Probably the closest example I can come to is a comparison with those living an alternative lifestyle."

He turned to Taylor and Sharon, who looked surprised. "Some gays define themselves by their sexual orientation, embracing the gay culture, the gay lifestyle, and a set of gay-centered belief systems. It's not a perfect parallel, but a person of faith does much the same, choosing to live their life by a set of beliefs that others may not understand or appreciate. As a Christian I have a relationship with Jesus Christ that I try to live out day by day. That's what defines me, what gives meaning to my life."

The others around the table began to look uncomfortable, even embarrassed.

*Rap! Rap!* The sound of the gavel made Mansfield jump. Anton Pike smiled. "I'm sorry, folks, I shouldn't have let this discussion deteriorate into a debate on religious beliefs of a personal nature." He looked at Mansfield, his smile vanishing. "I had hoped that all the task forces from this committee would conduct their work in a professional, objective manner. But I think we've had quite enough of your personal platform for today, so why don't we just conclude—"

"Excuse me, Anton."

Anton Pike glared at Taylor Haller's interruption.

"Mansfield is right, you know. We are doing to him what we would hate someone doing to us: totally devaluing his opinion from the start, not giving him a chance to explain his admittedly uncomfortable viewpoint." He turned to Mansfield, his face serious. "Please continue. I may not agree with you, but that doesn't mean we should silence your opinion."

Anton tapped the gavel again. "I must respectfully disagree, Taylor. I had hoped that we could be out of here in good time today, and it's clear that this discussion will take a while. I propose, again, that we read Mansfield's report and come back to it later if necessary."

Mansfield could feel the tide turning. *Please, Lord, help!*

Swiftly and with the utmost grace, Petras moved behind another chair. His voice was resonant as he spoke to its occupant. At his gesture, three other heavenly messengers took up position near several other faculty members. The Lord knew those who were open to the Spirit.

Jack Sprague raised his hand.

Anton sighed. "Yes, Jack?"

"I know you're eager to conclude the meeting, Anton, but let's remember that this is a formal task force report, the result of years of work. Their conclusion that Harvard allows systemic bias is pretty inflammatory, and I would like to hear what evidence they have to back it up."

A half dozen other heads nodded, and murmured assents could be heard throughout the room.

For a fraction of a second, as if in slow motion, Mansfield watched as a furious, terrible expression altered Anton's genial countenance. In the next instant it was gone, replaced by a flat calmness.

Anton settled back in his chair. He picked up his pen, poising his arm to write. His eyebrows cocked in a pleasantly surprised expression. "Very well, then. If that's the desire of the committee, I'll be delighted to finish hearing the report of this task force today."

"Thank you, Anton. If you'll turn to page two in your report..." As Mansfield began to walk the committee members through his executive summary, he wondered if any of them could sense the danger vibrating in the chair at the head of the table.

"Oh, you'll be sorry. You and your stinking King. You—" Foul perversions poured from the lips of a massive dark presence at the head of the table.

Krolech was being held in tight control by five of the troop's largest warriors, their garments flaming with the brilliance of the room. The restraining order must have come from the accursed Enemy Himself. Despite his anger, Krolech allowed himself some small satisfaction at the tension so evident in the angels nearest him. If they had been like those slimy humans, the simpering members of the heavenly host would have soiled themselves in fear by now.

He snarled, trying to get comfortable within his host's body. There was no one to help him, his incompetent colleagues having been prohibited. He was there only because he totally possessed the human vessel, even if he couldn't currently direct him. At least—he smiled to himself—his host was more than devious enough without him.

The demon's red eyes watched the Enemy's human lackey at the other end of the table, picturing all sorts of delightful ways to rip him to shreds. One of the angels immediately put his hand on his sword and leveled a challenging stare at him.

Krolech slowly turned his head away. As soon as the angel returned his attention to the dialogue in the room, however, he returned to his brooding over the disgusting parasite. There must be some creative way to fix this problem.

His attention was drawn back to the room as several professors asked congenial and interested questions of the man down the table. Those professors had been the charges of *his troop!* He growled again, rage boiling inside him.

The accursed son of Adam would not get away with this.


In the little room across campus one student was reading the Twenty-third Psalm. "'…your rod and your staff, they comfort me. You prepare a table before me in the presence of my enemies….'"

Claire suddenly gasped, and several students raised their heads to look at her.

"What's wrong?" Brad said.

"I don't know. I don't—" Claire began to tremble. "Danger. There's something…dangerous." She looked wildly around the room, so overwhelmed that she wasn't even concerned about looking foolish.

Alison leaned toward her, her voice urgent. "It doesn't matter whether you understand it. Maybe God is trying to tell you something because there's some specific thing we need to pray for."

Claire pressed her hands against her temples. "I just felt such danger…and…and *anger.*"

"From Mansfield?" Brad's eyebrows rose skyward.

"No—no. It was—evil—"

Alison started and glanced quickly around the group. "We haven't prayed against backlash from the enemy. We can't just pray for this meeting; we have to pray for what comes after it!" She bowed her head and closed her eyes tight. "Lord, forgive us for being so focused on the immediate outcome that we're forgetting about the bigger picture."

As each of the students petitioned God for His protection over Mansfield and the project after the meeting, Claire slowly relaxed. Her agitation diminished, then gradually vanished altogether.

*Whew. I wonder what that was all about?*


Krolech's rage turned to sharp pain as a giant sword pricked his neck. An angel—the idiot Etàn—was standing before him, holding the weapon at his throat.

"Whatever you are planning, foul Krolech, you can forget it. The Spirit of God binds you and commands your obedience to His directives regarding this man."

The angel gestured toward Mansfield, who was now standing at a whiteboard at the side of the room, totting up some inane statistics. It infuriated Krolech to no end that his troops weren't there to prod derisive rebuttals from the fools around the table.

"He may be protected for now, *friend,*" Krolech said, "but we all know that restraints are sometimes lifted. And when it is—" he gave a long sensuous laugh—"we'll be ready."

He looked up at Etàn's intent face and smiled wickedly. "I look forward to taking another of your charges, Etàn. I will win in the end. I am larger and stronger. This territory is, after all, mine. There will come a day when I will again operate freely, and then you and your petty band will be no match for me. You know that, don't you?"


Etàn's knuckles grew white on the sword. Krolech was a legend, a massive territorial spirit, and—the truth could not be denied—was indeed larger and more experienced in warfare than he. But—he drew a slow breath and held himself erect—the Lord was *God.* He had more power in His tiniest finger, His tiniest thought, than all the armies of Satan combined. And God had chosen Etàn and his team to be on the front lines of this battle. A glint came into his eye, and he stared down his massive foe.

"You're forgetting yourself, Krolech. No matter what happens in this battle, there will come a day when *God* will operate freely as well. And then you and your petty band will be no match for the fires of the great pit. You know *that.*" His steely eyes looked through the demon and into eternity. "Don't you?"

Mansfield was standing at the whiteboard, gesturing with a pointer to a table of numbers. "As you can see by these statistics, the conclusion that we lack ideological diversity is not just an opinion; it is empirically verifiable."

He looked at the faces around the table. His colleagues were watching with mixed emotions, varying shades of agreement or disagreement evident on their faces. Across the room, Cheryl Crenshaw was examining the numbers with interest.

"Now, looking at these statistics, some observers might conclude that Harvard is trying to suppress certain points of view." He smiled at the affronted expressions on the faces around him. "I disagree. There are actually many cases where Harvard has attempted to be sensitive to faith-based beliefs. For example, you may recall the controversy over annual student fees for the health center, some of which go for pro-choice education and abortion referrals. Our administration has gone to considerable trouble to allow students with prolife convictions to opt out of paying that portion of the fee. I think the evidence is clear that we're not looking at some active antifaith conspiracy.

"I believe instead that Harvard's difficulty with ideological diversity arises simply from the overwhelmingly one-sided composition of Harvard's administration and faculty. Most individuals in academia—professors, researchers, administrators, and the like—describe themselves as politically and socially liberal." He smiled slightly. "Now, just because one is a political liberal doesn't mean one is antifaith. But without a concerted effort to counter the lack of diversity, it's understandable that the collective worldview of these educators would in time spill over and dominate—and frequently bias—the classroom setting, teaching materials, textbooks, and the like."

The conference room began a slow buzz of disagreement. Many of the faculty members looked uncomfortable. Irritation showed on several faces.

A professor on the other side of the room raised his hand. "But, Mansfield, if what you're saying is true, what are we supposed to do about it?" His voice carried a hint of exasperation. "Personally, I would hope that a professional, highly educated instructor would be open-minded enough to keep their classroom objective. But if you really think that a professor's ideology works its way into the classroom without his or her knowledge, then by definition you're not going to be able to change that."

"Untrue!" Mansfield rapped the pointer against the table. He saw surprise on several faces and forced himself to keep a rein on his emotions. "I have sat here and listened to recommendation after recommendation on increasing diversity in this university—both inside and outside the classroom. The essence of my proposal is no different: Be aware of the bias, and actively work to counter it.

"For example, if your class is discussing a political hot button and you know you're politically liberal, you need to try especially hard to pull in the viewpoints of conservative students. Now, most of you may already be doing this—or think that you are. But let's be honest." He pointed to the statistics on the board again. "It's rarely a level playing field. I know that most of you are fair-minded enough to make an effort, but are you really working at it? Do you go beyond just calling on a conservative student once in a while?"

He cocked an eyebrow. "For example, when was the last time you included materials in your syllabus that you totally disagreed with ideologically?" He leaned on the table, looking around. "And I'm not talking about some token paper that makes the other side look stupid, either. You need to spend *extra* effort, *extra* time, to respectfully bring in these neglected or even oppressed viewpoints. You might call it affirmative action for the classroom.

"We should have the same level of effort for ideological diversity in the twenty-first century that we did for racial diversity in the twentieth. It's just as critical—perhaps more so, from a university's perspective—because it strikes at the heart of academia, at the heart of how our students learn to *think*. That, after all, is the primary skill students will take away from their college years.

"In just five years very few of my students are going to remember what year the Magna Carta was signed." He clasped his right hand to his breast and sighed. "Much to my everlasting regret." Several around the table laughed. Anton Pike's expression darkened, his lips pressing together.

"They may not remember what they learned about the Magna Carta, but every day for the rest of their lives they will use what they learned about how to *think,* how to process information, how to analyze. What service are we doing them if we refuse to allow them to analyze between conflicting opinions?"

There was a long pause; then Elsa Chasinov spoke up, looking around at the other professors for support. "I understand that you truly believe what you're saying, Mansfield, and your passion is commendable. But I have to respectfully disagree with your conclusion that other ideologies are suppressed. You should see some of the arguments students in my science classes get into, about all sorts of things. And yes, I may have my own worldview, but it is—as my colleague noted—an open-minded worldview. You'll have to come up with a much better argument than—"

"Elsa," Mansfield leaned with both hands on the conference table, looking directly at her, "in your biology classes, when was the last time you allowed an intellectual discussion of evolution versus intelligent design?"

The room broke up in a clamor of exclamations and disbelieving laughter. Mansfield breathed an urgent prayer as he saw Anton raise his gavel. He rapped on the table with his pointer, and his voice rose above the din. "Ladies and gentlemen, just how *open-minded* are your worldviews right now?"

The clamor quieted abruptly, the loud disbelief momentarily suspended.

"Elsa, when you or any of our science professors prohibit discussion of the holes or inconsistencies in the theory of evolution, aren't you just as guilty as the seventeenth-century church officials who prevented a fair hearing on Galileo's 'heretical' theory that the earth revolved around the sun?"

"That's ridiculous, Mansfield, and you know it!" Elsa looked like she was trying not to laugh. "Galileo was a scientist who was obviously correct in his theories, but the creationists of today are just simple-minded—" Elsa broke off, a strange expression on her face.

"Just simple-minded, religious, nonscientific people who are obviously incorrect in their theories? So we don't need to talk about them? Is that what you were going to say, Elsa?"

Elsa's cheeks were pink, but she held herself straight in her chair. "Yes, as a matter of fact. Something like that."

Mansfield's lips twitched. "Do you see my point, Elsa?" He looked around at the others. "There's actually quite a bit of interesting scientific research on the intelligent design theory, but few students are allowed to even hear about it, much less ask questions about it. Look, I'm not talking about something radical here. *Of course* evolution is the predominant scientific theory of the day, and *of course* it's going to dominate our science classes. But when there are credible scientists also studying intelligent design, why is that discussion not even allowed for ten minutes of one semester?"

He gestured to the elegant trappings of the conference room. "This is one of the greatest thinking universities in the world! Why shouldn't we have an intellectual discussion on the issue? Is it perhaps because it requires some sort of religious overtone, and we're no longer comfortable mixing science and religion?"

Taylor spoke into the uncomfortable pause that followed that question. His expression was thoughtful. "That's an interesting point. If I'm honest with myself, I have to say that I am discomforted by students who say overtly religious things in my classroom."

"If I might add to that," Jack Sprague said, "I must admit to seeing this issue in a different light. Each of us believes strongly in the 'rightness' of our position, whatever that might be. And that's fine. But when that translates into suppressing—or worse, mocking—the beliefs of others, we've gone too far." He raised a warning hand. *"How-*

*ever*, it's one thing to avoid mocking an unappealing belief. It's quite another to actively include those beliefs when they may not be at all appropriate for an intellectual class-room discussion. I am most definitely not comfortable with the idea of using our classrooms as a religious platform."

Mansfield inclined his head. "Absolutely. I'm merely trying to level the playing field so that—"

*Rap! Rap!* The gavel cracked against the table, and Anton's voice was congenial as he looked at his watch. "Well, now that we all respect one another's positions, I move that we wrap up this discussion. We—"

"Excuse me, Anton." Mansfield's voice was calm. "I'd like to have a few more min-utes to present my recommendations and ask the steering committee to act on another issue of relevance. If that's acceptable to my colleagues, of course."

Several murmured assents could be heard.

Anton laid down his pen and adopted an amiable expression. "By all means, then."

Mansfield stepped to his place at the table and flipped through the thick report. "If you'll turn to page 6, you'll see our conclusions."

As pages rustled in response, he read several bullet points from the executive sum-mary.

"'In summary, it appears that the same environment that discourages conservative and faith-based ideologies at the classroom level is an outgrowth of higher-level admin-istration policies—perhaps unrealized—that tacitly favor humanistic, secular ideologies.'" He looked up from the final sentence, which he knew by heart. "'This bias, ladies and gentlemen, is verifiable, should not be tolerated in an esteemed institution such as Harvard University, and can begin to be addressed with a few simple actions on the part of the faculty and administration.'"

A chuckle rose from the chairman's seat, and Mansfield looked up, irritated at the interruption.

"My dear colleague, before you continue I just have to make an observation." Anton leaned back in his chair, clasping his hands behind his head. "It is fascinating to me that you would make the claim of such a pervasive bias in an institution that so val-ues diversity. Frankly, your conclusion says more about *your* perspective than about any real problem at Harvard. Perhaps you are so steeped in your fundamentalist culture that you see true respect for diversity as some sort of bias or bigotry against your worldview. But that's the exact opposite of the truth."

Anton leaned forward, his voice measured and reasonable. "You see, Dr. Mansfield, hiding behind your claim of bigotry is the underlying assumption that *your* beliefs are inherently entitled to preeminence; therefore, anyone who dares to challenge that assumption must be biased."

Anton placed his reading glasses on his nose. "That being the case, I believe we have spent more than enough time on this topic, and I know we're all pressed for time." He didn't look up. "I move for a vote on Dr. Mansfield's recommendations without further delay. Do I hear—"

"Excuse me, Anton!" Mansfield slapped his hand against the table. Several heads turned swiftly in his direction. "First of all, I haven't yet presented the recommendations—or my other important findings—so how can we vote on them?"

"They are written in—"

"And second, I must address your accusation that I find bias just because people won't accede to my supposed belief of superiority." His voice quavered, righteous anger burning in his chest. "No, *no*. I want Harvard University to be a true marketplace of ideas—*including* religious and conservative ideas. You, Mr. Chairman, want it to be secular, without religious input, as if that would be neutral.

"The same argument," he continued, turning back to his colleagues, "is often made in public high schools when people oppose religious input because of the separation of church and state. But the absence of religious input does not create neutrality. Instead, it leaves only one worldview standing: secular humanism. And secular humanism is *itself* a religion. It carries just as many beliefs about the order of the moral world, the existence of a deity, and so on as any of the other major world religions.

"Therefore, the absence of so-called religious input is not neutral but is instead actively hostile to faith-based points of view. And therefore you, Mr. Chairman, are guilty of exactly what you accused me of: You believe that the secular worldview is inherently entitled to preeminence, that it should be our default ideology."

He slapped his thick report down on the desk. "I am not proposing action because I assume Christianity is inherently entitled to preeminence—although I do believe the absolute truth of the Christian gospel will win in the end—but because I believe we must allow a true marketplace of ideas and because squelching a whole stream of thought leads to both bias and an intellectual deficit. That's why my primary recommendation is to convene a subcommittee—just like the other subcommittees from the other diversity task forces—to determine specific ways to counter this disturbing trend."

Mansfield looked around at his colleagues. Jack, Elsa, Taylor—all the faculty members looked like people who had sat just a bit too long on a prolonged car ride. Jack stirred, murmuring something about moving to a vote. Others doodled with their pens, avoiding Mansfield's eyes.

Anton leaned forward and raised his gavel. An instant later he paused and looked around at the awkward silence in the room. He closed his mouth and sat back in his chair, a small smile playing on his lips. Mansfield could practically hear his thoughts: *"All the more rope to hang himself with…"*

Mansfield pulled something off his finger and flung it to the table, where it clanged and skittered along the polished surface. Everyone jumped slightly, their attention sharpening on the spinning signet ring. One by one, they looked up at Mansfield's solemn face.

"That ring has a crest on it, a motto that's been part of our unequaled heritage for hundreds of years." Mansfield picked up the ring, turning the face toward his colleagues. "*Veritas*. Truth. We have a struggle for truth today, ladies and gentlemen, a struggle for *veritas*. We have thousands of young, impressionable seekers of truth come through these doors every year looking to visit and perhaps even make a purchase from the marketplace of ideas. My question is this: Will we allow all ideologies an equal spot in that marketplace?"

He breathed a silent prayer as he reached into his briefcase and pulled out a bulging folder. "Ladies and gentlemen, it seems clear that right now this argument doesn't carry much weight with you. You truly don't believe there's much evidence—despite the numbers—that we face a systemic problem with suppression of ideological diversity." He placed the folder on the table and looked at his colleagues. "I have here the smoking gun that proves you are wrong."

He began to bring out one item after another: a yellowed sheaf of parchments, a small clothbound book, an old leather-covered folder. He laid them side by side on the desk in front of him.

"At our last meeting this committee—at the urging of the alternative lifestyles task force—sent a strongly worded request to the president's office to expedite the release of certain scholarships for gay students that had been endowed three or four years ago. Remember? These materials here, ladies and gentlemen, document grants and endowments given for *faith-based* purposes, enormous sums that have gone unused or misused for decades or—in some cases—even hundreds of years."

Mansfield noted with satisfaction the astonishment on many faces around the room. He was careful to avoid glancing in Anton Pike's direction.

He held up each item, outlining the donor and their Christian directives—the Crist lectures, the Donaldson scholarships, the Grindley professorship. He described which moneys had sat unused, which had been misused.

Jack Sprague raised his hand. "But, Professor, you can't seriously be suggesting that Harvard University hire a professor to teach creation science or some such thing just because a devout donor in the eighteen hundreds endowed a chair for that purpose?" He looked around at his colleagues. "Would we keep an instructor on staff to teach about UFOs just because someone long dead thought they were interesting? I mean, it's quite understandable that you'd like Harvard to look into these lost endowments, but to require adherence to such outdated, eccentric stipulations would be crazy."

"Really, Jack?" Mansfield's tone was amused. "Have you ever heard of a little library expansion project that painstakingly cut out Widener's upstairs window, just so 'not a brick could change'?"

"But that's diff—"

"Is different? Why? Why is Harvard willing to adhere so closely to Mrs. Widener's stipulations and not those of Grindley or Donaldson? In fact, why has Harvard forgotten that these grants and endowments even *exist?* Unlike your UFO example, actively considering a faith-based approach to scholarship is something that hundreds of other universities do every day. Why can't Harvard take up that mantle and do a better job of it—even if it's just in one class out of hundreds? Why have they so thoroughly forgotten these grants? Is it because—perhaps, just perhaps—this college has such a systemic problem with a lack of ideological diversity that it doesn't think the purpose of those endowments even needs to be considered anymore?"

Sharon was sitting back in her chair, clearly annoyed. "Mansfield, give me a break. Of course they don't need to be considered anymore. Those stipulations were clearly for another day and age. No one really believes that only men should receive scholarships or that anyone actually *believes* creationism anymore. These stipulations serve no purpose in the modern university. And because it serves no purpose for those funds to just sit there, of course this institution should feel free to reallocate the money."

"Really? So you're saying that we should, in essence, feel free to pick and choose which beliefs are right? Well then, by all means, let's just put out a missive to all of Harvard's current donors explaining that we'll feel free to reallocate those funds as soon as we disagree with their conditions. In fact, that means the endowment for gay scholarships will be free for reappropriation whenever the pendulum of popular opinion swings back the other way and it no longer becomes politically correct to support nontraditional lifestyles." He nodded pleasantly.

*Wham!* Anton's gavel hit the table with such force that several people nearly started to their feet. Anton stood and pointed the gavel at Mansfield. "That is enough of your disrespectful, agenda-driven threats, Professor Mansfield. It is intolerable that you would use this committee as a forum for your hate speech, and it calls into question whether you belong on this steering committee at all. We cannot abide by—"

"Excuse me." Cheryl Crenshaw's quiet voice spoke from the side of the room. There was a rustling as all heads turned in her direction. She slowly stood to her feet. "I apologize for interrupting, but coming from the finance arena I believe you may be missing something. Our esteemed colleague brings up an important point. We cannot afford for donors to think their gifts may be misused. Our endowment is the backbone of everything we do here. No matter how old-fashioned an idea may seem to us, if we accept a gift it is traditionally thought that we must abide by it. Therefore—"

"Are you seriously suggesting that we hire a professor to—"

"All I'm suggesting, Mr. Chairman, is that we cannot so cavalierly dismiss the concerns of the ideological diversity task force. In fact, since the nation's popular opinion is apt to change over time—as Professor Mansfield suggested—this task force may have saved this university significant heartache and money in litigation, fines, or other discrimination charges. I believe you should send this to the administration to be resolved in due time."

"Ms. Crenshaw," Anton's voice was smooth as glass, "we appreciate your input, but I must point out that the academic steering committee has traditionally operated under the jurisdiction of Harvard's president and the other officers. I think we can all agree that this is a matter for an officer of the university rather than an administrator—"

"Normally, perhaps, but in this case you have both." Cheryl Crenshaw smiled at the group, an eyebrow raised in amusement. "It will be announced tomorrow that I am the new chief financial officer of Harvard University."

As the committee members murmured their congratulations, Mansfield could hardly contain himself, watching Anton struggle for self-control.

"Therefore, Mr. Chairman," Cheryl said, "I hope this committee will choose to send the matter of these faith-based grants and endowments to the administration, so that this matter can be more fully explored." She turned to Mansfield. "Unless you believe you should first do more digging in the files and approach the administration once you have further information on these examples."

"No!"

Mansfield and Cheryl turned to see Anton holding up a stiff hand. He dropped his arm and laughed awkwardly. "No, that won't be necessary. I think we already have more than enough information to vote on sending this matter to the administration for its review. All in favor say aye."

A chorus of voices chimed in. "Aye."

"All opposed, nay."

Several strong nays were heard.

"The ayes have it, and the motion is carried." Anton rapped his gavel against its stand.

Mansfield shook his head, bemused. That was the quickest battle he'd won in years.

Murmurs of conversation began to rise around the table. He looked at the report in his hands. Somehow he had to move to a vote on his task force recommendations.

"Mr. Chairman." Cheryl's calm voice cut through the other voices in the room. "I would also like to make an informal suggestion to this committee. Now that this issue has been formally presented on the record, it may not be long before someone else gets hold of it. I don't imagine that the press would find out or that they'd care, but we can't take the risk that they find out on a slow news day." She smiled. "It's your decision, but I'd urge you to establish—for the record—some type of immediate good-faith effort to actually resolve these lost endowments."

Mansfield grinned to himself. Her soft-spoken manner was deceiving.

"And what would you suggest, Ms. Crenshaw?" Anton said, his voice clipped.

"Well, one thought might be to provisionally honor one of those endowments that could be quickly implemented without controversy. Such as the—" she turned toward Mansfield—"the Crist lectures, I believe you said the name was?"

Mansfield nodded.

"We'd have to establish that the facts are as Dr. Mansfield described, but if so it seems likely that you could choose someone to give a Crist lecture by the end of this year, even while the administration of the endowment and the organization of future lectures is being worked out. The finance office could almost immediately release funds to a Christian student group to cover the cost of publicizing and organizing the lecture. That also keeps it limited enough that we could choose not to continue the lectures if the endowments turn out to be invalid or some such thing."

Mansfield watched heads nod around the table.

Jack leaned forward. "I agree. Anton, I move that we provisionally endorse the Crist lectures, put our action in the minutes, and file the record of this meeting with the administration. In the interest of time and simplicity, I move that we ask Professor Mansfield to either give a Crist lecture by the end of this semester or appoint someone else to do so. I also move that we approve the ideological diversity task force's recommendation to form a subcommittee to look into their proposals and take volunteers to serve on that subcommittee." He raised his hand. "I'd like to volunteer for that subcommittee."

Jack kept his hand up, and his gaze swept around the table. Mansfield looked on, his head spinning, as four or five hands were raised. Several others chimed in, "Second the motion."

Anton's hands were balled into fists, his knuckles white, a pen clenched in one fist. "Very well. All in favor of Jack's proposal say aye."

Mansfield caught Jack's eye with a nod of thanks as a round of ayes rose from the table.

"All opposed, nay."

There was silence.

Anton's voice was strained. "The ayes have it, and the motion is carried." He banged his gavel against the table. "This meeting is adjourned."

Without a word he strode from the room.

Ten minutes and much backslapping later, Mansfield walked out the front doors of the building and breathed a heartfelt prayer of gratitude. The administration would probably take years to resolve such a big issue, but what a first step! As soon as he got to his office, he would call his faithful HCF prayer warriors with the news.

He turned the corner of the building, passing the side entrances at ground level. Suddenly, the skin prickled on the back of his neck. He turned his head just slightly. Anton Pike was standing in the deep shadow of an entranceway watching him pass.

Mansfield looked straight ahead. He found himself quickening his step. What was going on?

He remembered the danger he'd felt early on in the meeting, the chairman's knee-jerk reaction against any further investigation of the old endowments. His sense of peace fled. Maybe the detective work wasn't over after all.

# FORTY-ONE

IN A DORM ROOM ACROSS CAMPUS, THE PHONE RANG. The head of every tired but faithful prayer warrior came up with a jerk. They looked at the phone, their expressions intent, as it rang once more. Finally, Brad leaned over and pulled the phone toward him.

"Hello?"

In an instant, the expression on Brad's face changed to jubilation. He jumped up, still listening, and began relaying the conversation, one ear still against the receiver. The others cheered and began high-fiving each other.

Above their heads, the heavenly warriors clasped arms in thanksgiving. Gael looked down at his charge just as Brad called out to her.

"Claire, Mansfield says to call Ian. He wants you both in his office right away."

Gael watched as Claire hurried to gather her things and make the call.

Another angel, of many years experience, approached. "The prayers of the young saints are effective!" he said.

"And our battle is fully underway, my friend. Our first hand has been played, and the enemy is now considering their counterattack."

Claire hung up the phone and hurried out the door. Gael prepared to follow her.

"Vigilance, my friend. The enemy does not yet know of the role your young charge will play in the great battle."

Gael's head snapped around. "What?" He glanced back at Claire as she headed down the stairs and out the door.

The other angel smiled. "Go. All will reveal itself in due course."

Coffee cups littered the desk in front of Ian and Claire as Mansfield looked up from his notes.

"If Pike wanted to steer us away from something, I have to think there must be something else there to be found. Something that he knows might make even more difference in our attempt to create a level playing field for faith-based viewpoints."

He tapped his pen against the palm of his hand for a long moment. Claire sat quietly, trying to contain her thrill at being privy to the inner circle.

"I'd love to think that the administration will see the injustice and move on it quickly," Mansfield said, "but this grant thing is a big deal with lots of legal angles. I think it's more likely we're entering a waiting game that may take years. That said, I also think we should use this waiting time to do a little more digging and find what it is that Professor Pike doesn't want us to see. Ian, what's your time like?"

Ian pursed his lips. "Well, if you want to know the truth, I've spent so much time on the task force project that I'm really behind in a couple of classes. If someone else can do most of the legwork, I can put in a few hours in the next week or two. But once I have to start studying for finals…" He sliced his hand through the air. "I'm done."

Mansfield looked at Claire. She tried to keep her breathing even. "Claire, I'm going to need to hire a permanent research assistant who can fill in with Ian and continue working on this. I was very pleased with the work you did before, but it's a slightly different thing hiring a permanent assistant. Before I proceed, I'd like to ask you a question. Would you share with us how you came to know the Lord? We'd like to get to know you a little better, my dear."

Claire cleared her throat. "Well, I guess it started with my parents. Mom and Dad went to Wheaton, but we only went to church off and on as I was growing up."

Her voice was soft as she told of her childhood in a nominal Christian home, and of the Christian schools that at first left her cold and untouched. She described her father's poor financial decisions, the bankruptcy, the resulting struggles, and the eventual spiritual reawakening that had gently dawned on the whole family.

"I always believed in God, but religion was a private thing for me. I didn't like to talk about it, and I didn't understand the Jesus thing at all. But after my mom—and then my dad—recommitted their lives to Jesus, I began to see a difference in them that I couldn't explain. I began to *want* to know what it was about Jesus that had given them this newness. But here I was," she smiled ruefully, "an involved student at a Christian high school. I was too embarrassed to ask anyone about it. Then came the retreat."

Claire looked off into the distance. "I went with the church youth group to a wilderness camp in the Porcupine Mountains. You know—one of those places with team-building exercises like rope courses and rappelling down rocks and such. There was an amazing camp counselor there—Miss Gana. She was originally from Nigeria, and she was such a beautiful person. She had such a strong relationship with the Lord and was articulate and firm in her convictions. She made every student feel like they were the most special person there. I'd never met anyone like her."

"One day," Claire looked down at her hands, "we were going down this mountainside, and a rockslide started above us. She was the last person in line, right behind me, and she threw me down and lay on top of me as this mass of rocks came crashing down. Several big rocks smashed into her."

Claire's eyes misted up. "I was knocked out, but really only scraped and bruised. And most of the others had gone around a bend and were fine, but Miss Gana—" After a moment, Claire took a shuddering breath. "Miss Gana was not fine. They got her down from the mountain and to the hospital, but they said her internal injuries couldn't be repaired."

Claire started crying. "She asked to see me at the end. She told me that God had a special calling on my life. She said that she knew I'd never committed myself to Jesus and that He wanted my heart and my soul." Tears dripped onto Claire's folded hands. "I prayed with her in that hospital room. She…died. In the middle of the night."

The room was silent. After a moment, Mansfield pulled a tissue out of a box and handed it to Claire. The two men waited while she wiped her eyes and blew her nose.

Claire smiled slightly, wadding the tissue into a ball. "Sorry to get all emotional." She aimed for the wastebasket and made it. "But you did ask."

"I don't know how you could tell that story *without* getting emotional," Ian said. "She saved your life and then she—well—she saved your *life.*"

Claire sighed. "So that's my story. My parents gave me a Bible, and I started reading it and…well…here I am. Just this struggling person trying to figure out what God's calling is for my life."

"A special calling, from the sound of it," Mansfield said.

"I don't know about that. I've always wanted…well, never mind that. But I feel like I'm so knocked around here that I can't get my footing. It's hard to know what God wants me to do."

Mansfield smiled. "A common sentiment, my dear. Just remember that it's all about God. He's the potter, and we're the clay. It's His right to use us for His perfect will— whether these earthen vessels are used for a common or noble purpose." He stood to his feet. "Claire, I'm asking you to consider joining our little team on this project."

"Really?"

"Yes, really."

"But I'm only a freshman!"

"Yes, and Ian here was only a sophomore when I realized the extraordinary spirit and gifting that God had placed in him." He smiled at her, and she felt herself flush. "Normally it's true that a research assistant would generally be an upperclassman, but in this case…well, let's just say you're already well versed in the issue, and I'd prefer to bring in as few people as possible on a matter as delicate as this."

His gaze turned serious. "However, there are a few things you should carefully consider before you accept this position. I usually have quite a few balls in the air, and thus

I require a high level of professionalism in my assistants. I consider this a job, like any other job. If you say you'll do something, I consider it done. If you say you'll work certain hours, I'll depend on you to be here. I realize your primary job at Harvard is to study, but I'm looking for a person who can handle both study and work. In return for this extra commitment, I pay my permanent assistants slightly more than the department average."

His eyes bored into hers. "Are you able to commit to that, or do you want some time to think about it?"

Claire sat for a moment and let out a soft breath. A prayer coursed through her thoughts, and with a thrill of recognition, she knew what her answer should be.

"Professor Mansfield." She stood to her feet and held out her hand. "It would be an honor to work for you."

He shook her hand and smiled. "Done."

She saw Ian's grin and tried not to blush.

Mansfield gestured for her to take a seat again and picked up his notes. Claire listened carefully as he described their next steps. "Go to the archives...go to the financial offices and see if the resource staff have suggestions...make sure you check with me every few days...be discreet." He looked up at Claire. "Please show Ian the ropes for how you researched the older documents so he can head up this project."

"Yes sir."

The meeting broke up and Mansfield left for another appointment. Claire compared notes with Ian on when they would make the first move. They said good-bye, standing in the long, echoing corridor of Robinson Hall, the Friday evening shadows creeping in the large windows at each end.

"So I'll see you on Monday at three?" Ian asked. "At the steps of Widener?"

"Okay. See you then."

Ian smiled down at her. "It'll be a fun project."

"Yes." Claire's stomach flip-flopped suddenly. She ducked her head and walked down the hall.


She climbed the stairs to her dorm room at record pace and arrived out of breath. The hallway was empty, the suite quiet, all the others presumably at dinner. She was missing the HCF meeting, but what a small sacrifice for the events of this day!

Claire sat on her bed, then flopped backward, arms out. Words of praise and thanksgiving suddenly sprang to her lips, and she didn't feel foolish for speaking them aloud. She closed her eyes and let a simple worship song spill out. "You have been faithful.... You have been good...."

After a moment, she reached underneath the bed and drew out a wooden jewelry box, beautifully decorated with angels and streaks of light. A portion of Psalm 91:11 was engraved along the lid: "He shall give His angels charge over thee…."

She opened the box and poked through the jumble of earrings and necklaces. She pulled out a small, worn piece of notepaper and carefully opened it up. The notepaper bore the insignia *Marquette Memorial Hospital, Marquette, Michigan.* The handwriting was uneven but clear.

My dear Claire,

What an extraordinary day. I believe I shall soon be with the Lord, and nothing gives me greater joy. The doctors say they cannot stop the bleeding, but I have no family except my brother—whom you met in the hospital— and I am only too ready to leave this dark place and go dance in the light.

But before I do, I must tell you something. Claire, when I said that God had a special calling on your life, I was not just speaking of the special purpose He has for all of us here to be His ambassadors to this world that so desperately needs His love. I meant a truly anointed calling to draw people to Himself.

On the mountain waiting for the paramedics, I don't know if I was conscious or unconscious, but I saw what I can only describe as a vision of some kind. I saw a great assembly of people spread out in some sort of open place, a rather dark place. It's hard to describe, but there were thousands upon thousands facing a stage. And on that stage was you.

Claire gripped the paper harder, reading the familiar words as if for the first time.

I don't know how old you were—I sensed that you were older—and I don't know what you were saying, but you were speaking to the crowd. And as you spoke, it was as if there was a light shower of something like golden rain. It fell into the darkness in the crowd, and each place it fell, the darkness turned light and started to shine.

The handwriting grew more uneven.

They are telling me I am tiring myself and must stop. I just said that's silly if I'm going anyway!

So anyway, Claire, I saw individual people in the massive crowd, and on many a golden cross appeared on their chests—like the cross that used to be on the armor of knights in the middle ages, you know? It was as if they were marked in some way as they listened to you and as the golden rain fell.

Dear Claire, I don't have the gift of interpreting these things, but at least something seems clear: You have a role to speak out and see others be affected by God. You must cling to Him, Claire. If in your future there is a fight against what God has for you, you must cling even more strongly to Him. Psalm 91 says that He will send His angels to protect you, but it also says that that protection is for "he who dwells in the shadow of the Most High." So dwell there, Claire.

Do not let the darkness distract or discourage you. He has a special purpose for you. Stand fast in the faith, and I will be part of that great cloud of witnesses cheering you on.

Claire folded the note and fell sobbing to her bed. "O God, O God... I am so weak, so feeble! Who am I that You should regard me? Who am I that You should give me *any* special calling? God, whatever You have for my life, I yield to You." She paused, wiping her tears on her pillow. "And God...just don't let me mess it up!"

# FORTY-TWO

"HEY. DID YOU HEAR ABOUT THE CRASH?"

Claire looked up from her desk, her mind still trying to process the nuances of protons and neutrons. Sherry was standing half in, half out of the bedroom.

"What?" Claire could hear the television in the lounge area of their suite and a lot of voices talking at once. She had thought it was just another Sunday evening procrastination session.

"A jumbo jet crashed just outside Chicago about nine o'clock this evening. The news said it was one of the worst air disasters ever. Something like—" Sherry leaned back into the common area—"how many, you guys?"

Several voices could be heard beyond the door. "Four hundred."

Sherry turned back to her roommate. "Four hundred people on board. All presumed dead. The plane crashed right beside one of the Great Lakes. I forget which one."

"How awful."

Claire went out into the lounge area. Several of her hallmates were coming into the room, joining others watching the news. There were hurried shots of crying people, glimpses of the rainy nighttime weather outside O'Hare, cameramen jostling each other, reporters shouting questions.

"Sir, how did you find out that your wife…?"

Claire watched the ravaged faces, sick to her stomach.

"Sir, would you like to say anything to the airline…?"

"How do you feel about this tragedy…?"

"How the heck do you think they feel?" Torri was perched on the arm of the couch, her face tight as she yelled at the screen. "I hate those blasted reporters."

Stefan was sitting against the coffee table. Sherry sat next to him and leaned into his shoulder.

Teresa was also there, teary-eyed. "Those poor people. God comfort them."

"Yeah, right." Mercedes snorted, leaning against the wall near her room. "Like God cares, even if He does exist."

Claire's head snapped around. Teresa glanced in her direction, her eyes red, before responding to Claire's suitemate. "He does care. Just because we don't know why something happens doesn't mean—"

"Don't give me any of your religious trash! How—"

"Cut it out, Mercedes. You always harp on the fact that you don't believe in God, but I know that God exists and He does care. Now is not the time for—"

"Give it a rest, Saint Teresa. In the face of *that,*" her finger jabbed toward the screen, "how can you even *begin* to argue the existence of a loving God?"

Stefan stirred a bit. "Hey, Mercedes, tone it down would you? Her religion is how she deals with tragedy—all the people on that plane are now in a better place, that sort of thing. We all find our truth and our comfort in different places." He nodded several times, his voice kind. Sherry was looking up at him, a thoughtful expression on her face. "It's important that people pursue whatever works for them."

"I don't mind it when people practice their religion in private," Mercedes said. "Just don't get in my face about it."

Teresa stood up. "And you're not in *my* face? So it's only nonreligious people who are allowed to broadcast their private opinions? But if a person of faith wants to do so, it's called getting in your face?"

Claire stood up straighter. *That's a really good point.* Why couldn't she ever think of good comebacks like that?

Mercedes' eyes narrowed. "I don't think anyone here wants to hear your fundamentalist judgments at a time like this."

Teresa glanced again at Claire, her eyes pleading.

A strong sense of conviction overwhelmed her. *You do not know how to respond, because you never take the risk and try. Set aside your pride, child. Trust.*

Claire glanced at the pictures of the hellish nighttime crash site, shots of the initial flames playing and replaying on the screen. Several verses flashed through her mind. *"The prince of this world..." "Your enemy the devil prowls around like a roaring lion, looking for someone to devour. Resist him, standing firm in the faith..."*

Should she say something?

In a flash Claire somehow knew that she was being presented with a choice, a life-changing decision. The next level in her walk with God, or retreat and self-protection. It was stark and obvious, staring her in the face. And she had to choose.

"And besides," Mercedes was continuing, "you can't even answer my question about how a loving God would do something like this."

"I think you're confusing God with Satan." Shocked, Claire realized those words had come out of her mouth. All heads turned in her direction, and she noticed some of her hallmates looking embarrassed for her.

For one split second she faltered, but then a surge of confidence overtook her as the argument took shape in her mind. "We've all seen both good and evil in the world. God is completely good and loving, but there is also a being of pure evil in the world. God doesn't delight in causing planes to crash; but the evil one sure does." She gestured at the television screen. "Would you say that looked like the work of a good and loving God? Or like the work of an evil being that loved killing and destroying?"

Torri was openly staring, her eyes incredulous. "But God is supposed to be all-powerful, right? So He may not have *caused* it, but…"

"…but He certainly *allowed* it." The professor took a swig of brandy. "How can you reconcile that, Mansfield?"

Across campus, the fire was crackling in the Faculty Club, the crash scenes flickering on the television in the background. Mansfield cupped his coffee mug in his hands and settled farther back into the overstuffed chair, considering his colleague's question. After a moment he looked up. Jack Sprague was swirling the liquid in his glass, waiting.

Mansfield had learned not to get into it with those who had no desire to listen, but Jack seemed genuinely interested in the debate.

"Jack, let me restate your question. You're basically saying that if there is a good and loving supreme being—whom I call God—why didn't he prevent this airplane crash? Correct?"

"Essentially, yes."

"By asking that you're assuming that if there was a God, He would be big and inscrutable and powerful enough to somehow, mysteriously stop the airplane from crashing."

"By definition of what I understand God to be, yes, of course."

"Then let me ask you a question. If there is a being powerful and inscrutable enough to be able to mysteriously stop the crash of a jetliner, isn't such a being also inscrutable enough that you and I aren't going to be able to understand Him and His ways?"

Mansfield watched his words sink in. Jack's eyes flickered slightly.

"Jack, we can't have it both ways. Either we acknowledge that God is powerful *and* mysterious enough that we can't understand why He allows certain events to happen, or we say that God wasn't powerful and inscrutable enough to have stopped the airplane from crashing, in which case we can hardly get mad at Him."

Mansfield took a sip of his coffee, watching his colleague over the rim. The other man was pursing his lips, replaying Mansfield's argument in his mind.

"Not only that," Mansfield said, "but let me give you a completely different reason. Assuming that God is all-powerful, would you really want to live in the sort of world where He was constantly changing the laws of physics? In order to keep anyone from getting physically hurt, He'd have to be altering the law of gravity one minute, the law of thermodynamics the next. When you walked out the door in the morning, you'd never know whether you'd keep walking on the sidewalk or float right out into space. Do you really want to live in such an inconsistent world, a world where a deity was constantly playing with your mind? It would be terrible."

Jack leaned back in his chair. "I don't know. Having no killer hurricanes or earthquakes sounds pretty good to me."

"Really? The same law of gravity that causes a ball to bounce also causes killer landslides. God could interfere with natural laws—and probably does, at times—but if it were constant, we'd be completely unable to learn and function rationally. Think about it: We'd never know the consequences of any little action we took during the day. We wouldn't even have the knowledge we needed to put our coats on when it got cold! And then, because we never learned how to function, God would have to be constantly altering the natural laws to protect us. We'd never mature beyond intellectual and emotional babyhood."

"Hm." Jack looked at him for a moment, then stared vaguely into his brandy snifter, as if it held the answers to the mysteries of the universe. "Professor Mansfield, you got me. Those are very…well…hm."

Mansfield chuckled, settling back in his chair. "Jack, my friend, there's hope for you yet."

# FORTY-THREE

IAN STARTED UP THE STEPS TO THE MASSIVE DOORS of Widener Library. Students dotted the steps, talking, reading, eating a late sack lunch, or just enjoying one of the last sunny days before Boston's winter arrived. He stopped beside a figure sitting halfway up the steps, engrossed in a book.

*"Pollyanna?"*

Claire looked up, startled. She smiled and slipped the book into her backpack. "No. This week's reading for philosophy." She stood up and slung the backpack over her shoulder. "Ready to start?"

Thirty minutes later, deep in the building's archives, Claire finished describing how she had gone about looking through the initial documents.

"So then you take the grants you thought looked like possibilities and cross-reference them," she tapped a dusty shelf of card files that lined a back wall, "with this section of the old card catalog…"

Ian made a face when she was done. He looked around at the dozens of old bookcases lining the infrequently visited room. "Wow. Not easy. I'm amazed you found what you did."

"Well, it takes a while, but I find it fascinating." Claire sat at one of the long tables in the center of the room and opened up her research notebook. "That's why I got into genealogy research in high school. I did a lot on the Internet, of course, but what I really thought was cool was going down into the basement archives of libraries and looking at the old county records of births, voting records, and all that. Really interesting."

"I'll take your word for it." Ian picked up his notebook and pen, gesturing at the card files and bookshelves. "How about you take the A to M section on that end of the room, and I'll take N to Z?"

"Sure thing." She walked to the far side of the room and began scanning the shelves, making notes and muttering to herself as she worked.

Ian stood staring at the rows of massive bookshelves in front of him. *Lord, if You want me to find something special about these grants, You're going to have to guide me to it.*

288

He picked a row at random and walked between the bookshelves. The faint smell of must rose from the old tomes. *Mansfield must love it down here.* He reached up and picked a book at random. *Genealogy and Heritage of the John Telling Family: From the Revolutionary War to the War of the States.* Hmm. Great bedtime reading.

He replaced the book and ran his hands along the textured spines of several others. Well, he wasn't getting anywhere like this. He walked to a section of the room and pulled out an oversized ledger. He sat at the long table, the ledger open in front of him, and began taking notes on pages and pages of endowment lists.

The room was quiet for a long while, the gentle hum of the climate control system the only noise besides rustling pages and scratching pens.

The sound of approaching footsteps brought Ian back to the room. The door creaked open, and Ian's eyebrows rose as a familiar head peered inside.

"Mansfield? What are you doing here?"

Mansfield stepped inside the room, closing the door behind him. "I was in Widener for a meeting and thought I might find you in this section. Have you two found anything yet?"

"No, we really just started the research part about an hour ago. It took Claire a while to explain the whole complicated process in a way that my little brain could understand."

Across the room Claire giggled.

"Ah, I see." Mansfield rounded the table and came to stand behind Ian. "What are you working on here?"

"Just one of many lists of people who've given endowments or grants. I think these donors are from the 1700s mostly. Some of these lines have a short summary of the grant's purpose, but many don't, and they're really hard to read. I just finished the *N*s and *O*s and was starting on the *P*s. It's slow going."

Mansfield looked over the list on Ian's notepad. "Not many *O*s, I see." He looked closer. "A donation of Bibles for chapel services—Oakley Ostrich, of Philadelphia? Heavens, what a name!"

Claire's voice carried from behind a bookshelf. "Sounds like a colonial zookeeper, or something."

Ian snorted on a laugh, and Mansfield chuckled.

"From what you've done so far," the professor asked, "is there anything promising?"

Ian shook his head. "Honestly, this could take days, and we've barely started." He flipped to the next page and began scanning.

"Yes, yes." Mansfield sighed. "I'm too eager, I suppose. But if you could've seen Pike's reaction—"

Ian gasped, all his attention suddenly riveted on the page.

"What?"

Ian bent forward, nose close to the page, his finger following a line of cramped writing as he spoke. "I've been looking mostly at the summary lines for anything that might be a Christian stipulation." He looked up at his mentor, a strange expression on his face. "But maybe we should've been looking for something else."

Ian shifted the heavy ledger so Mansfield could see it. He could hear Claire approaching from the other side of the room. He rested his finger beside a particular notation. "What do you make of that?"

Mansfield squinted at the writing, then patted his jacket pockets and pulled out a small magnifying glass. "Well, I'll be…"

Claire had stopped in front of the table. "What? What?"

Ian swiveled the ledger around, and Mansfield handed her the magnifying glass. She bent down and examined the faded script.

"Contribution to the—wow, this handwriting is bad—the endowment for the Pike Fellowships…" her voice slowed suddenly. "Given by Talbot Pike of Cambridge, Massachusetts." She looked up at the two men. "Pike!"

"Is that just coincidence?" Ian asked. "Could there be any connection? Pike is not an uncommon name. There have to be thousands—"

"In Cambridge, Massachusetts? Involved at Harvard?" Mansfield stepped back from the table and began walking slowly along its length. "I suppose it's possible, but it seems unlikely. Anton Pike has been here for nearly fifteen years, although he's much younger than I am. I wonder if there have been other—"

He stopped walking and a strange look appeared on his face. "Oh."

"What?" Ian and Claire said together.

"I just remembered. Decades ago I did my postdoctoral work here. I took several economics courses, and one of them almost ruined my record. There was one professor that just…well, I prefer to avoid going into the sordid details, but let's just say I empathize with every student who's ever been treated unfairly by his instructor. My memory is fuzzy, but I'm almost positive that professor's name was Pike." Mansfield drummed his fingers on a chair back, his tone dubious. "But I never would've thought about a connection to our friend Anton."

"Besides, what does this have to do with anything?" Ian asked. "So there was a Pike that gave money to Harvard hundreds of years ago. And a mean ol' Pike who tried to fail you in economics. And a mean ol' Pike who's a business professor today." He paused. "And who is also the chairman of the academic steering committee."

"As I remember," Mansfield's eyes stared into the distant past, "my economics professor Pike—his first name was William, come to think of it, because I was annoyed that he had my name—was in some sort of leadership position at Harvard, too. Maybe more in the graduate school, though. I just can't remember."

Ian flipped to a clean page of his notebook and began jotting down notes. "So we have those three: Talbot, William, and now Anton. But I still wonder what that has to do with anything."

"Do you think," Claire said, "that there's something about the Pike family—if it is one family—that Anton Pike didn't want you to find, and that's why he acted so strange about further investigation of the grants and endowments?"

Ian nodded. "Makes you wonder, doesn't it? But how would we find out?"

"Well," Claire said, "if I was doing a family genealogy investigation, the next thing I'd do would be to cross-reference whatever information I had. So I'd cross-reference these names and find out if there were any other Pikes on the Harvard faculty."

She pulled the ledger toward her. "Come to think of it, we have another trail to follow right here!" She tapped on the line they had been examining, her voice intent. "This Talbot Pike, whoever he was, gave money to endow the Pike Fellowships. If that's some sort of scholarship, perhaps it still exists today. And if we find out about that, I bet we can work backward in time and find out what Anton Pike was worried about!"

She looked up at them, and her expression changed to one of consternation. "Or…not. I'm sorry. I get carried away sometimes. I—"

"Claire." Mansfield crossed his arms and stared at her.

"Yes?" Claire's voice came out on a soft squeak.

"That is a brilliant idea."

"Really?"

"Yes, really." Mansfield put his hands on the table and leaned toward her. "As I think I told you yesterday, as well." He straightened up and looked down at Ian. "If you all agree, I suggest that we set aside our search for Christian grants for the moment. The issue is with the administration, and there frankly is no hurry unless we find something even more important, which is unlikely given our personnel constraints and the size of the task."

He smiled at Ian's relieved look. "Given this new trail—I think you called it that, Claire—I suggest we follow it in three ways. First—" he nodded for Ian to take notes— "check whether there are other Pike donations recorded in these old records and what the donations were for. Second, check the modern records for scholarships and such and see if there is still a Pike Fellowship at Harvard. Third, find the archives for Harvard's staff lists and see what you can find out about other Pikes who worked here." He pointed at Ian. "You keep checking this ledger for Pike grants—"

"Oh goodie."

"And Claire, you check for anything else in this room about Pike donations. I'll pop upstairs and ask if the archives for faculty lists are in this building somewhere. Then perhaps one of you can go over to the financial offices and see about the Pike Fellowships."

He glanced over to see if they understood, nodded once, and vanished out the door.

Claire and Ian looked at each other and shrugged. Claire went over to the card catalog, and Ian turned back to the ledger. He perused each line carefully, thankful that Mansfield had left his magnifying glass.

*Peterson...Philbrick...Perry...Patterson... They must have been using some logical system to arrange these names, but darned if I know what it was.*

"Aha!"

Ian looked up at Claire, who was standing at the card files. She was holding up a tan index card triumphantly. "I thought it might be here!"

"What?"

"A faculty list from the 1700s."

"No kidding!"

"Well, that's what it looks like, anyway." Claire hurried over to the bookshelves on the far side of the room. She disappeared into one row, her voice floating back to Ian at his table. "You can never tell with these things until you actually find the document."

Ian turned back to his ledger. *Preston...Pierce...Pryce...* He heard rustling and saw Claire returning, a stack of books in her hands.

"I think these might have some faculty lists." She set the stack down across from Ian and flipped open the first cover, looking at the table of contents.

"Aren't you supposed to be looking for more Pike donations?"

Claire's head shot up, her mouth open in consternation.

Ian chuckled. "Just kidding."

"Not funny, Ian!"

"Sorry. I'm sure Mansfield will approve."

"I hope so." She bent back to the book.

"Claire..." When she looked up, Ian smiled reassuringly. "Mansfield may be famous, but he's a brother in Christ and a very kind person. You've already impressed him, which is unusual for someone he hasn't known long. If you work hard for him, you could have a great opportunity to continue in the future. You don't need to worry. Just be yourself."

He picked up the magnifying glass and looked back at the yellowed page. And there it was...*Bertram Pike.* He started and bent closer to the page. "I think I have another one. This one's really faded, but...oh, man! I'm sure it says something about Pike Fellowships!"

Claire set down her book and came around the table behind him. "Let me try?" Claire took the offered magnifying glass. "I can't read the first three words, but that...yes...it says something about some amount of sterling for the Pike Fellowship at...um...Harvard College."

"Can you read the city where Bertram lived?"

"The first letter is *S*. It's not Cambridge."

"Somerville?"

"Could be. Right next door!"

"*Was* there even a Somerville in the 1700s?"

Claire shrugged. "I have no idea. But even if there wasn't, that's another Pike and another note about these Fellowships." She walked back around the table. "This is amazing. You know, given how hard this sort of research is, we could've looked for weeks and not found a thing. I kind of feel like God is setting this up."

"Yes. Thank You, Lord, and if there's more to be found, help us find it!"

"Amen."

Claire sat down and began flipping through the books, again muttering softly to herself as she worked.

Ian glanced over at her once, amused. She was kind of cute. Too bad she was so young.... He returned to his task, the soft rustling of pages a nice background noise.

After a while the rustling stopped. He glanced up. Claire was bent over a slim book with a navy cover, reading something intently. There were half a dozen books just like it beside her elbow. She pulled another book off that stack and opened it to a particular page. He started to return to the ledger.

"You're not going to believe this." Claire's voice was soft.

His head snapped up, and he raised his eyebrows.

She flipped the two books around so he could see the covers. "These are the printed documentation of decades of Harvard instructors and classes and board members and officers, all that sort of thing." She held the books open, showing him several pages. "See here, and here—two other Pikes, one of them on the board."

Ian slowly sat back in his chair. He stared around the quiet room then across the table at her solemn expression. "I'm getting the creeps."

"Me, too." She pulled the books back. "Can we pray for a minute?"

"Gladly." Without thinking, he reached across the table and grabbed her hand. He felt her tight grip, the tension in her hands. "O God, we don't know what's going on here. But, Lord, You do. Please guide us and protect us. We've asked You to help us find anything there was to find. Well...now we've found something. And we don't know what it means or what to do with it. Help us, O Lord."

He paused, and Claire picked up the prayer. "Father, thank You for the opportunity to work for You. Thank You for being with us. I also pray that You would send Your angels to surround and protect us. And please, Lord, help us dwell in the shadow of the Most High, as Psalm 91 says. Amen."

Claire looked up. "I think we need to be praying about this a lot more."

"I agree. There's something going on here—"

The door creaked suddenly, and both students jumped.

Mansfield stared at their expressions and laughed. "I didn't mean to frighten you!"

"It wasn't you that frightened us." Ian gestured Mansfield over. "Take a look."

Mansfield took a seat and looked over the documents. After a moment he grew very still. "We need to pray about this."

"We did."

"I'll bet." He pushed his chair back from the table and leaned forward, his elbows on his knees. For a long moment, he rested his forehead in his hand, his eyes closed. Ian and Claire waited respectfully.

"First of all," his voice was quiet, and he didn't lift his head, "I don't know what all this means, but I feel like we're seeing the patterns of an intricate web being woven behind the scenes. And it doesn't give me a good feeling." He sighed and straightened in his chair. "I think we'd better look for the modern-day Pike Fellowships as soon as possible."

Ian glanced over at Claire. "This is actually a pretty good week for me. I could do it tomorrow after class. Next week things start to get much more dicey."

"Tomorrow and Wednesday would be sort of hard with my schedule," Claire said. "I could go during lunchtime, but that would only give me about an hour. But please go without me if you need more time."

Mansfield chuckled. "No, my dear. Clearly, you have a gift for this sort of thing."

"How about you and I go Thursday after history class lets out?" Ian looked at Mansfield for confirmation. "*If* Claire can spend a few days digging around to find the right office and contacts beforehand so we don't have to waste any time. Then we can grab lunch after class and head over to the appropriate place as soon as we're done."

"I think lunch is a good idea," Mansfield said, "and it will give us a chance to discuss this more thoroughly. And Claire, I agree with Ian. You need to do the advance work to find out the right office before you all go over there."

"I don't think I can until after my philosophy class on Wednesday." At Mansfield's raised eyebrow, she said, "I know you asked me to be available for this job, and I *could* do it earlier if I had to. But we're debating abortion during Wednesday's class, and I really want to make sure I'm well prepared."

"Ah, understandable. Well, just make sure it gets done. There's something going on here, and I have a feeling we need to move quickly. And one other thing. Will you be prepared for my test on Thursday?"

Claire straightened abruptly in her chair and slapped a hand to her forehead.

"I was afraid of that." Mansfield grinned and glanced over at Ian. "Why doesn't my TA here give you a quick review of the material once you're done here? I've seen from your class participation that you've kept up well with all of the readings, and I don't want your test performance to suffer simply because you're working for me."

"Thank you, sir."

Mansfield stood up, and both students rose to their feet as well. "Thank you both for your dedication. I think we're on God's trail, and I look forward to seeing where it takes us."

# FORTY-FOUR

THE BROWN GRASS CRUNCHED UNDER HER FEET as Claire hurried across Harvard Yard. She was eager for the shelter of Emerson. Like everyone else who had to be out on such a bitter day, she had her parka hood pulled tight over her head.

She smiled as she remembered Ian's comment from the night before, as he walked her back to her dorm through the biting wind: *"Maybe this weather is why some Bostonians always look grumpy."*

Their review session last night had been a surprise; he had spent much more time on it than she expected. Not that it wasn't an appropriate thing for him to do, she thought hastily, being such a conscientious TA and all. She had spent so much time on Mansfield's project; it was nice of him to recognize that she hadn't had much time with her history books.

Their time in one of the secluded booths at Loker Commons had gone so quickly that neither of them had noticed the sky growing dark outside or the clock ticking past the time the food court closed. Naturally, they had figured they should have a pizza delivered while they continued studying.

*Naturally.* Claire giggled, even as her mind grappled with the surprising events of the previous night. Ian had been the perfect picture of reserve; friendly but polite. Even the matter-of-fact pizza dinner had been somewhat businesslike. But then he had insisted on walking her back to her dorm. What was *that* all about?

*Boys,* she thought, *are a different species.*

She reached the imposing facade of Emerson and wrenched the heavy doors open just enough to slip inside. Several people were hurrying quietly through the echoing hallway. The eleven o'clock classes had already started.

*Nuts. Of all the classes to be late for…*

She slipped into the back of the giant auditorium. Ian was down on the stage in front, going over arrangements for Thursday's test. Mansfield was turning around from writing on the whiteboard. She tried to steer her eyes away from the podium as she cast around for an empty seat.

The room was packed. No one wanted to miss the last class before the test. Where on earth was she going to—

In a frozen moment, she saw the one empty seat. First row center, right in front of the podium. She groaned slightly and slunk down the steps to the ground row, sure that every eye was focused on her.

As she hurried to her seat and slid into the chair, her backpack brushed the books and papers on her neighbor's desk. They fell to the floor with a crash, and papers went skittering across the tiled floor to the base of the stage. She jumped to retrieve the materials, dropping her own half-open backpack with a bang. She apologized under her breath and sat back in her seat, wincing as she looked up at the stage.

Mansfield and Ian were standing side by side right at the edge, their arms crossed, looking down at her.

"Well, well, Miss Rivers," Mansfield drawled in his best Southern accent, "how nice of you to join us."

Her face red, Claire stood up slightly and sketched a half bow to the class, which broke up into good-natured laughter.


"So as we can see, the close of the Middle Ages saw a gradual but inexorable shift from a theologically based paradigm to a science-centered paradigm." Mansfield was in the last ten minutes of his lecture, wrapping up the Middle Ages before Ian's test review. "From a day in which the idea of God was paramount and people would believe something simply because the church said it was so, to a day in which something had to be demonstrated and proven to the people's satisfaction.

"Prior to that change, discussion and argument—and fiat—were the only ways to defend a set of beliefs. But with the advent of the scientific method, theories were hypothesized and then proven by scientific testing. The scientific method—" he turned briefly to the class—"I would write that down, by the way—is still the one we use today.

"As you'll remember from your reading, the last gasp of the previous system came in 1634, when Galileo was condemned by the pope and forced to recant—under the threat of torture—his scandalous contention that the earth revolved around the sun. In 1600 another unfortunate astronomer, Giordano Bruno, had been burned at the stake for sticking to that theory. Galileo, under the same threat, was forced to declare that the earth was, indeed, the center of the universe. He then lived under house arrest for the rest of his life.

"Then, in 1687, Sir Isaac Newton wrote his masterpiece, *Principia.*" The professor walked back to the podium and briefly held up an old tome. "Using mathematical physics, *Principia* provided an accurate working model of the planetary systems and proved—contrary to what the church was declaring—that the earth was not the center of the universe.

"That was the beginning of the end of the church's dominance over every area of people's thoughts and lives. Before Newton, the church—remember, a weighty, all-encompassing institution since the conversion of Constantine—would say 'X is true,' and the people accepted it. After Newton, the church said 'X is true,' and the people said 'Prove it.'

"This one shift brought about the end of the Middle Ages. The Catholic church lost much control over the intellectual and cultural life of Europe. And as people began to question long-held scientific ideas, philosophers arose to question long-held moral notions as well. Descartes—'I think, therefore I am'—in his philosophy of rationalism proposed that our human *reason* was now the only reliable source of knowledge. Spinoza suggested applying mathematics to understand the world. And so on.

"The first of these philosophers—like Newton himself—were devout Christian believers trying to delve deeper into the mysteries of God's moral laws. But as the years progressed from the Newtonian discrediting of the church, each succeeding generation went from producing philosophers of faith to producing openly skeptical atheists. The first such philosopher of that new age was David Hume, the self-titled 'extreme skeptic.'"

Mansfield wrote a few notes on the board. "In the mid-1700s, Hume coined the philosophy of empiricism, which basically says that human reason is important, but since it is based on the input of our faulty human senses, we can never really *know* anything for certain, including about our own existence and especially about the existence of the supernatural." Mansfield looked back at the busy pens of his audience and grinned. "You don't need to write this down; it's context only. I'll leave the memorization of the specifics to your philosophy classes."

He chuckled as relieved sighs rippled among the students. "What's important is that you distinguish this time as one of those key turning points in history that you recognize only in hindsight. Hume was the first to acknowledge that since his philosophy was counter to theistic thought, it was more honest to explicitly abolish any pretense of Christian belief or practice. The other philosophers had said, 'We can't prove it, but there is a God.' Hume said, 'We can't prove it, and there isn't.'

"This major switch led to the rise of determinism, a philosophy that is de rigueur in some circles today, which states that because a cause determines every action, there is no such thing as free will or even responsibility. An upright citizen, for example, became so because he had a good home and schooling, and an alcoholic thief became so not because he chose to but because of his terrible home environment and alcoholic father."

Claire, sketching notes just to be on the safe side, raised an eyebrow. *For goodness' sakes....*

"The logical application of this philosophy states that there is no difference, then, between Martin Luther King Jr. and Adolf Hitler: An atom went one way in King's brain, another in Hitler's, and that's what caused their different belief systems and actions."

A few astonished chuckles arose from the students around Claire. She smiled to herself. *See, when you're not entangled in philosophy class mindbenders, everyone else thinks this stuff sounds crazy, too.*

Mansfield was walking back to the podium, whiteboard marker in hand. "Finally, naturalism was the ultimate philosophical outgrowth of the evolution from the theological to the scientific methods. Naturalism declares that only nature exists, that the supernatural realm—everything from the idea of a supreme being to the concept of the mind or the soul—is simple fantasy.

"Naturalism," he wrote the word with a flourish, "is the philosophy that underlies and is essentially synonymous with secular humanism, the preeminent worldview or religion of today's secular culture—and certainly the preeminent view among academics. The primary consensus of humanism is that human reason and the scientific method are the only sure means of arriving at knowledge and that all beliefs, values, and mores are made by men and for men, with no real absolutes, and certainly with utter rejection of the idea of God. And that—" he capped his marker with a click—"brings us back to where we started.

"So, ladies and gentlemen, you can see that in just the few hundred years following Newton, the theological foundations that had underpinned Western society for over a thousand years—indeed, had informed all manner of theistic cultures even prior to that point—were completely replaced by the scientific and humanistic doctrines of today."

*Where is he going with this?* Claire fidgeted and chewed on the end of her pen. *It almost sounds like he's saying humanism is the ultimate end point. But he wouldn't believe—*

"So the church took an extra-Biblical stand—a stand that was never discussed in Scripture, and which we now know was untrue—and the history of Western civilization was changed forever. Nontruth ultimately will be discredited." He smiled slightly. "Something that the humanists of today, who declare that there is no mind or soul or anything not measurable by science, might want to keep in mind."

Amidst a few startled chuckles from the audience, Mansfield glanced quickly at his watch. "And…I think that is where we have to stop. Ian Burke will conduct a classwide review, and of course each of your TAs are available for your section reviews tomorrow. I'm sure they've already told you the times. See you Thursday."

Claire relaxed into her seat, waiting for the review session to start. Her eye traveled down the last page of notes. Rationalism, empiricism, determinism—unbelievable what a bunch of twisted "isms" these philosophers could come up with. Why did everyone have to make it so complicated, when it was so easy?

She reached into her backpack for the small Bible she had begun to carry with her. She flipped to the first chapter of 1 Corinthians, her finger following the page down to verse 20. *"So where does this leave the philosophers, the scholars, and the world's brilliant debaters? God has made them foolish and shown their wisdom to be useless nonsense."*

She snorted to herself. *You can say that again.*

As the class broke up, Mansfield descended the stairs from the stage and beckoned her and Ian over. He spoke without preamble. "I got a call from Edward Grindley this morning. He wants me to come over tomorrow afternoon. I'm not sure why. I'm planning on briefing him on our progress."

He looked at Claire. "So just to be sure we're on the same page, are we still on track with your timing? You'll be sure to get that advance work done tomorrow afternoon after your class?"

"Yes sir."

"Good." Mansfield was buttoning up his coat. "Well, I'm off. I'll see you Thursday for the test."

Standing side by side, Ian and Claire watched him move out through the departing crowd. It took him a few minutes to get to the door. Every student seemed to want his attention to say hello or ask him a question.

Ian spoke without looking at her. "Just because he's your favorite professor, don't expect him to go easy on you on the test." He grinned. "Or me either, for that matter."

Claire flushed. "I wasn't expecting you to."

"Good."

They stood there a moment longer, watching the classroom gradually empty. Claire hugged her notebook to her chest, wondering if she should leave. She didn't really want to.

"Well, I'd better get going." Ian gestured toward the stage, where papers and books were stacked neatly by his backpack. "I've got a lot of prep work to do before the test."

"Okay." She hesitated, then blurted out the words on her mind. "Thank you for helping me review that material last night."

"Well, we can't have you failing out now, can we?"

Claire shook her head, then made busy about gathering her notebook and papers into her backpack. "I should get out of here. I'll see you Thursday."

"Lunch with Mansfield after the test?"

"Yes."

She smiled at him, then walked up the steps toward the doors in the back of the room. She forced herself not to turn to see if he was watching.

At the back of the room, Kai turned to his team. "The first thread must be pulled. He will have less than thirty minutes."

A cadre of angels nodded and sped off, each going his separate way.

As the young woman headed for the door, Gael saluted his superior with a grin and prepared to depart.

Kai chuckled and clasped his arm. "This is going to be interesting, my friend. The Master's hand is at work!"

"And as the man of God told his class, Truth *will* win!"

Kai's expression sobered. "Yes. It will."


Ian watched Claire go, a smile playing on his lips. He shook himself out of his reverie. What was he thinking? She was still too young.

He bounded up the stairs to the stage and gathered up his things. Within minutes he was heading out the door, walking the half-mile to the law school campus. It was about time he got to some actual law school business!

He pushed through the lunchtime crowds at the Hark and headed for the mail slots that lined the crowded common area of the student center. He checked his little cubicle and groaned. It was stuffed full of flyers. How long had it been since he'd checked it? He didn't have time to deal with this.

He pulled out the crunched mass and plopped himself down on one of the sofas in the common area. He might as well just go through it now and get it over with. Ninety percent of it was going in the trash anyway.

Page after page flipped by under his impatient fingers, and the discard pile grew. Activities, happy hours, intramurals, service projects. He stopped briefly at that one, glancing at the date on the bottom of the page, then grimaced. The project in question had happened a week ago. He flipped more pages.

Apartment listings, recruiting...

He backtracked quickly to the cream-colored recruiting newsletter. Jobs were good. He scanned the flyer. He had probably missed these sessions, too.

Suddenly, he started to his feet, looking intently at the clock on the wall, then back at the cream pages in his hand. He gathered the pile of discarded flyers and threw them in a trash can nearby, then grabbed his satchel and ran for the door.

The company that founded the Excellence Awards was recruiting in Pound Hall, right next door, until one o'clock. It was already after that. His mind flickered to the article about Pike Holdings being the front-runner for the prestigious award. And now here they were on campus. To cap it off, the recruiter was someone he knew, a guy from the law school's Christian Fellowship who had graduated the previous year. Could this possibly be coincidence?

He hurried to the listed classroom and threw open the door. Empty. The clock read 1:05.

Ian made a sound of frustration and started to throw down his satchel. Then he stopped, half in, half out of the room, and forced himself to think. Maybe the career services office knew where to find the recruiters. Maybe…

"Ian!"

Ian swung around to see a familiar face approaching down the hallway.

"D. J.!"

The two friends clasped in a bear hug, slapping each other hard on the back.

Ian stepped back, relief washing over him. "Man, am I glad we didn't miss each other. Do I have some questions for you!"

"What, you angling for a job next summer?"

"Nothing like that. I just have a question for this research project I'm doing. You remember Mansfield?"

"The history prof?" D. J. chuckled. "Who wouldn't? You still his TA?"

"Yes. Listen, do you have time for lunch?"

D. J. looked at his watch. "Hmm. I've really got to catch a plane. We're getting ready to choose the Excellence Award for this year, and you wouldn't believe the stuff that's going on." He hesitated, then nodded. "I can probably squeeze in an hour."

"Long enough."


Ten minutes later the two friends sat at a deli window counter, looking out at the traffic on Massachusetts Avenue and conferring quietly. Ian was giving D. J. an overview of the past few weeks.

D. J. listened, munching on a BLT, as Ian described the downed tree, Edward Grindley, the old records. His face registered astonishment as Ian described Claire's findings on the unused Christian grants and endowments. And he grew increasingly interested as Ian outlined—without using names—the odd finding that a current, hostile professor seemed to be a member of a mysterious family involved from the earliest years of Harvard.

"How weird is that?" D. J. glanced at his watch. "So who is this hostile professor? Who's the family?"

"Anton Pike."

D. J. stared into Ian's face. After a frozen moment, he glanced around the bustling deli, then back at Ian.

"Let's get out of here."

Ian raised an eyebrow, but followed his friend out the door and a few steps down Massachusetts Avenue toward the Cambridge Common. D. J. marched right out into the middle of the frozen park, then swung around to face Ian.

"Do you have any idea what's going on with the Excellence Awards, or is this just pure coincidence?"

"The only thing I know is what I read in the business magazines. They said Pike Holdings was up for your award this year."

D. J. laughed without humor. "Yeah, they're up for it. And my bosses would kill me for telling you this, but they're going to get it, too. Unless we can track down evidence that corroborates some negative rumors we've heard."

"What?"

"Look, I need your word that this doesn't go beyond your little team working on this."

"You got it."

"Okay." D. J. took a deep breath. "As you may know, our company has two business lines—two profit centers, if you will. One is the side that does the Excellence Awards, the other is a major business magazine."

"I didn't know that, but okay."

"The business magazine gives us the investigative tools we need to make the determination about the Excellence Award. Since that award is a huge deal in the marketplace, we have to be sure we get it right." His eyes bored into Ian's. "Or at least be sure that we don't get it wrong."

A blast of wind shot across the Common, and D. J. shivered as he pulled on a pair of gloves. "This year, I think everyone in our office just assumed that Pike Holdings would get the award. Even though everyone knows that one of its main subs is losing a big lawsuit—the Helion case—everyone recognizes that that sort of thing happens. It doesn't affect the fundamental stability of the business going forward. And Pike Holdings has managed to be incredibly profitable even during recessionary years. It's really a business marvel.

"My bosses felt that Pike Holdings was long overdue for the award and that it was essentially the heir apparent for this year. All that was left was the official decision, which was supposed to be made internally last week." He leaned toward Ian. "And I think someone inside may have told the Pike folks that, because their company promptly timed their initial public offering so they'd be out into the market raising money just a week after the award date."

"Wow."

"Yeah, wow. Believe me, whoever the informant is, he's now on thin ice. Because things may be changing. We haven't decided yet who gets the award."

"What do you mean?" Ian cupped his gloved hands over his frozen nose.

"Several strange things happened in the last few months. Mary—one of our investigative reporters—was getting an early start, writing our cover story on Pike Holdings for the award edition. She was trying to get a handle on why the companies in the conglomerate have been so incredibly profitable, so resilient. The kind of thing that our readers are dying to know, right? But since Pike Holdings isn't listed on the stock exchange—it's privately owned by the Pike family—they don't have to disclose much financial information to the public, or to regulators like the SEC. Until they go public with an IPO, they can keep their books and their management practices mostly private.

"But for *our* purposes, we would never give an award to a company that wouldn't let us look at those things, and they knew it. So Mary had this great idea. Since they were planning an IPO, they'd have to start increasing their disclosure at some point. So we told them they might as well start with us, since we promised them confidentiality, and the article wouldn't come out until right before the IPO anyway."

"It sounds like it was pretty much a done deal that they were going to get the award."

"Yeah. But that's when things started to get strange. Mary was pushing for their numbers and they apparently had their accountants working furiously to present us something a little more detailed than the normal baloney. They couriered over a package of hundreds of pages of stuff—from their investment bank, I think—and Mary started looking through it. She's a financial whiz, so she goes right to the spreadsheets that talk about these amazing earnings." D. J. crossed his arms over his chest. "And on one line of one statement, buried deep in a really messy spreadsheet, was this notation: 'Flow-through from Peephole Publications.'"

"The pornography magazine? Are you telling me…?"

"I'm not telling you anything. We have no idea what it means. Because about one minute after she saw that, and was still sitting there at her desk trying to find any other notations like it—which she didn't—two men showed up from the investment bank politely requesting the package back. When she came out to talk to them and to protest, they produced a court document ordering it to be returned as 'proprietary financial information accidentally released.' She didn't let on that she'd seen anything strange, but she didn't get a chance to copy a thing. The two men followed her back to her office and removed the entire package. She'd had it for about thirty minutes, max. The next day she got another nice neat package that looked exactly the same, except the spreadsheets had been organized a little better, and—guess what—that notation was gone."

Ian's voice was dry. "Imagine that. Is that porn magazine one of the conglomerate companies Pike Holdings owns?"

D. J. blew out his breath in frustration. "No. That's why this is so bizarre. Of course, the market doesn't always look kindly on 'sin stocks,' so mainstream companies rarely go near them. Pornography, gambling, alcohol—even tobacco, sometimes—are often privately held, or if they *are* listed on the stock exchange they usually aren't part of a big, well-known conglomerate. It's usually much more quiet. The reports Pike Holdings filed with us—and which they have presumably now filed with the SEC—show no ownership of any such company. Pharmaceuticals, entertainment companies, publishing, finance, international trade, yes. Skin flicks and porn rags, no."

"So what do your bosses think that notation meant?"

D. J. threw up his hands in frustration. "They don't know what to think! Mary went straight to the top and briefed our president on what she'd found. After we confirmed that the second packet had no such notation, our president called over to the investment bank. They said she must have misread something. Since we don't have a copy of the page we can't prove anything. It's really Mary's word against theirs."

"Tough on her."

D. J. gave Ian a sardonic smile. "It would be except for one thing."

"What's that?"

"We can't afford to discount her story and then be wrong." He looked at the dawning comprehension on Ian's face. "We've been doing these awards since the days of J. P. Morgan and Rockefeller. Our choice moves whole markets. The Federal Reserve has to consider the impact of our choice on interest rates, for pete's sake! If we give an award to someone who turns out to have been cooking their books...well..." he gave a dry laugh, "our credibility—and our *survivability*—will rank somewhere below the Flat Earth Society. If you want to know the truth, our bosses have been in a tizzy ever since Mary walked into the president's office."

Ian's mind raced through the events of the last few days. "I sort of feel like we're being set up here. This conversation we're having cannot be a coincidence."

"No."

"What's our next step?"

"Whatever it is, we need to move fast." D. J. tilted his head back, frowning up at the sky. He looked back at Ian. "In order for the award to be processed properly, a cover story written, and all the legal technicalities done, we usually have the recipient chosen by last week. Obviously, that didn't happen. My bosses have worked out that our last possible date is this coming Monday. For weeks we've had reporters and contacts out practically sweeping the sidewalks to find out *anything* we can to help us make this decision. We have a sort of alternate winner picked out that we can substitute at the last minute if we have to."

"Why not just do that now?"

"Because it's a poorly researched choice." D. J. sighed. "We were so sure that we were picking Pike Holdings that we didn't really investigate other options. And the market will be able to tell we didn't do a fair job. We're sort of caught between a rock and a hard place."

"I can see that. But frankly, I can't imagine that our project will have any bearing on yours. It's just a little weird, that's all."

D. J. glanced around the frozen park. "Well, the fact that we're even standing out here in thirty-degree weather talking about this is a little weird. But I know what you mean." He looked down at his watch. "I've got to get out of here. With all this, I really can't afford to miss my plane. Look, Ian, I'm not going to mention this to my supervisors. Not yet. There really isn't anything here that we can put our finger on. But that said, if you find anything by the close of business on Friday, it might make all the difference in the world. And it wouldn't make me look so bad to my bosses, either."

As D. J. strode away toward a row of taxicabs in Harvard Square, Ian whistled softly to himself. Thank goodness Claire was doing that advance work tomorrow afternoon. What on earth was going on?

# FORTY-FIVE

SHERRY SMACKED HER ALARM AND BLEARILY SAT UP IN BED. She could hear faint music, the tinny strains accompanied by a quiet voice. Her groggy eyes searched the empty room. A weak strand of light trickled in from the window. Even *it* didn't want to be up this early.

"Claire? What the heck are you doing?"

The voice abruptly stopped, and the door to their closet creaked open. Claire popped her head out and took off her Walkman headphones. "Good morning." She was fully dressed and wide awake. She smiled up at her sleepy roommate.

"What the sam hill are you doin' in there? It's not even seven o'clock yet."

Claire's smile grew sheepish, and she stepped out of the closet. "I know. But I've been up since before five finishing my philosophy homework. Our class is discussing abortion today, and we have to write a two-page essay arguing for the view that's opposite what we believe."

"Well, that seems like a decent idea, actually. It forces everyone to see the other point of view." Sherry yawned and started down from the loft.

"Yes, but that means I just spent an hour writing reasons why people should be able to kill their unborn babies. I still feel sick just thinking about it. Anyway, after I was done with the reading and the essay, I just felt icky. I needed to spend some quiet time in worship." She grinned at Sherry and jerked her head back toward the closet. "It's kinda hard to find places to do that in this room, but I discovered that those boxes in there make a perfect seat. The boxes, a closed door, and my Walkman, and I was set."

Sherry yawned her way over to the sink, where she grabbed her shower stuff. "I've got to get moving, or I'm going to miss my eight o'clock. If you're gone when I get back, uh, have a good class."

Claire watched Sherry disappear out the door. She still didn't know what her roommate believed.

She sank down to her bed, her mind's eye turning backward in time, staring at two years of memories as a crisis pregnancy center volunteer. She had comforted the desperate unwed teenagers, the single moms who would lose their jobs if they had a child, the women who believed the mantra that it was their choice but who thought they really had no choice. She had cried with the women who had gone through previous abortions and sought God's healing after years of secret desolation, had broken down in front of a friend who'd just had the procedure, anguished by the thought of a fragile infant's brutal end. She had held hands and rubbed aching backs, found clothes and arranged housing, contacted adoptive parents and listened for hours.

And most amazing, she had trembled with inexpressible joy at holding in her arms a tiny squalling bundle that—but for God's meeting the vulnerable and scared where they were—would never have arrived on the earth.

Claire rocked back and forth on the bed, her knees against her chest. Today in class how could she convey God's heart for both the little ones and their mothers? Her mind was starting to swim at the thought of the day's discussion.

Prayers coursed through her mind as she began gathering up the materials on her desk, and within moments she was overwhelmed by a peace and love that she knew could come only from God. She smiled to herself and rubbed down the goose bumps on her arms.

When Claire arrived at her philosophy classroom that afternoon, the room was buzzing as usual, but she immediately noticed a difference. A group of eight female students were sitting side by side in the back row like a panel of judges. They reminded her of a line of soldiers, guns at the ready to protect each other's flank. The eight usually agreed on most issues raised in the class, especially those affecting women. She looked down the row, noting that Jo Markowitz was with them.

Claire found a seat, nodding hello to Bethany at the next desk. She flipped through the reading materials again, skimming the case examples the authors had come up with to illustrate the abortion issue. *Imagine there is a world-class violinist strapped to your body and sharing your organs for nine months; you don't want him there but he'll die if you disconnect him: what do you do…? Imagine that "people seeds" come flying through the air, and even though you've put up screens against them, they come in your windows anyway, take root in the carpet, and grow people who are for nine months totally dependent on you. What do you do?*

Her head started to swim again. She looked across the room at Brad, who was laughing and talking to the person in the seat next to him. *God, I don't know how to hold my own! Please help me! Help these people understand Your ways.*

Coughing emanated from the front of the room, and all eyes turned to Professor Kwong as he brought the class to order.

Ten minutes later things were deteriorating fast. The professor had asked each of them to place their names on a grid—posted at the front of the room—to indicate what they believed about abortion: morally right, wrong, or neutral; should be legal, illegal, or somewhat restricted. All the cards were now on the table, and everyone knew where everyone else stood.

"But you didn't *ask* for the world-class violinist." Keesha, one of the "eight amigas," as Claire had begun to think of them, was looking across the classroom at a Harvard athlete who had come out of the closet as one of just five prolife people in the room. "And frankly, I'm pretty offended that you're harping on this, Eric, since as a guy it's not *your* body that's being invaded without your consent."

So far, nearly everyone in the class had made it clear that men were not allowed to have meaningful opinions on this—unless they were prochoice, of course. The other four prolife students were all men. Claire twisted and untwisted the cap on her pen until she feared it would crack. She hadn't raised her hand yet.

Keesha turned back to Professor Kwong. "Honestly, Professor, this one is a bad metaphor because we're talking about a *potential* violinist, not an actual one."

Professor Kwong inclined his head slightly. "If that is your view, then apply the philosophical analysis to the people seeds example instead."

"Well," Keesha said, "it's basically the same. You didn't ask for the people seeds, but they are in your house, your property, and you want it back. Under the existentialist model of reason, you should be able to say that you don't have to take the responsibility for these potential people."

Claire's mind was racing. *Wrong, wrong, wrong.* There was something *wrong* about the people seeds example, but she couldn't pinpoint what it was.

The professor called on another raised hand.

"And another thing," the next student argued, "is that you even took steps to prevent the people seeds from coming in. You put up screens!"

*Wrong, wrong, the example is wrong.*

Professor Kwong walked the front of the classroom. "So that says something about consequences and responsibility to you? Something about the determinist philosophy as well, perhaps?"

"Absolutely. You have even less responsibility for the unwanted people seeds that were flying through the air if you tried to keep them from coming in."

*No, no, no.* Claire closed her eyes, trying to create a tiny reprieve from the turmoil in her spirit. *God, what is wrong about that case?* Her racing thoughts suddenly focused...*question assumptions*...and the answer settled in her mind.

Slowly, she raised her hand. Professor Kwong's eyebrows lifted at the unusual source, and he immediately called on her. "Claire?"

A few of the eyes in the classroom flitted to the board, noting her status in the pro-life camp.

"Actually, I understand where you are coming from. But I think you're leaving out one very important ingredient." Claire's spirit quailed slightly as she saw the look on Jo's face. "You are saying that because the people seeds flying through the air were unwanted and even protected against, that you shouldn't have responsibility for the people growing in your house."

Claire took a deep breath. "But as a metaphor for unplanned pregnancies, it is wrong in a very subtle but important way: The people seeds don't just come flying through the air. Instead, the case should say that you took a bucket of people seeds and dumped them over your house."

She saw several expressions register surprise, and a surge went through her. "That would entirely change the equation and tip the scale of whether or not you felt responsibility, wouldn't it? You may have put up screens, you may not want the people growing in your carpet—but doesn't it make a difference when you made the choice to pour the people seeds over your house to begin with, knowing there was a possibility this would happen? You could have chosen abstinence—you didn't *have* to put yourself in that situation."

Her voice stopped. She didn't trust herself to continue speaking.

Keesha's face was red. "That's ridiculous! How can you—"

"A moment, please." Professor Kwong interrupted. "As I said at the beginning, with an issue that begets opinions as intense as this one, you must adhere to the class rules. No interruptions. Raise your hand, and you will be called on to speak." He nodded in her direction. "Go ahead, Keesha."

"I was just trying to point out that for those women who are raped, they have no choice in the matter. They didn't 'pour a bucket of people seeds'!"

Claire raised her hand and got the go-ahead. "That's very true, but let's be realistic here. The vast majority of women seeking abortions are not rape cases. If you want to bring up the utilitarian lingo, I'm trying to get at the issues affecting the majority." Even as she said it, a seed of an idea was forming in her head.

Keesha looked affronted and received the professor's nod. "Well, as someone said a few weeks ago, the utilitarian perspective doesn't account for the oppressed *minority*—such as the enslavement of people of color—who are oppressed by those holding the power! What about those women who *aren't* the majority cases, who are raped or who are oppressed by a boss who'll fire them if their pregnancy becomes known? What about the single mothers who will be destitute if they have another child? What about them? Where is the compassion for them?"

Professor Kwong looked at Claire and said, "Let's see this line of reasoning through, between you two. This is a good discussion; keep going."

The tiny thought had flowered. *Help me do this right, Lord.*

"So what you're saying, Keesha, is that, just as in the slavery situation, we need to look out for those who are the most oppressed by those holding the power—"

"Exactly. We—"

"We must look out for the rights of those who are the most marginalized, most vulnerable in their situation? Those who feel scared and alone and ignored and powerless?"

"Yes, that's right."

Claire leaned forward, staring steadily into the other student's eyes, her voice soft. "Keesha, I know of no one who is more marginalized, more deprived of her rights, more vulnerable and powerless, than a tiny baby with no ability to defend herself from those who hold the power over her life."

The room broke up, sounds of disgust and annoyance coming from many seats before she had even finished speaking. Keesha's face was red. Several people looked away, or down at their desks. Others rolled their eyes and whispered to each other. But several people were looking at her with changed expressions, indrawn, their eyes thoughtful.

Claire saw the professor open his mouth. She spoke quickly, trying to catch as many eyes as she could. "Roughly one hundred and fifty years ago, we came to the realization that slavery—although it was widely accepted, integrated into our culture, *and* legalized by the Supreme Court—was a terrible injustice and must be abolished." Hisses and low catcalls began to sound around the room. "The nation affirmed that blacks were people with rights just like everyone else and stated that one human being should not have the power to completely own and control the life of another. We need to—"

Professor Kwong held his hand up. "Okay, let's bring this discussion back on—"

Claire's voice was hurried—"realize that unborn babies are people, too, with every bit of the right to expect compassion and advocacy from us as black slaves did back in the 1800s."

Keesha shouted at Claire, drowning the professor's attempts to regain order. "What a bunch of garbage! How dare you compare the oppression of my people to this issue? It's the other way around! You are again trying to have the power over my body by telling me that I can't do with it as I want. You want to force me to be enslaved to an archaic system of thought that we thankfully abolished back in 1973, when we finally managed to liberate women from enslavement to the biologic product in their uterus."

It was Claire's turn to grow red, her voice choked. "A baby is not a 'biologic product'—it's a little person with a heartbeat and a brain and the ability to feel terrible pain."

Murmurs began spreading, and Claire again raised her voice in a pleading question. "Why do we fight so hard to save premature babies if they aren't precious human beings that we're desperately trying to keep *alive?* It's a *child!*"

Keesha slammed a book closed on her desk, her face set.

"Keesha," Claire blurted the words out, "do you know how the main abortion-facilitation group got started? Margaret Sanger founded Planned Parenthood back in the thirties and forties in order to contain the population of the 'unfit and the feeble-minded' in the slums!" She saw several horrified angry looks around her and plowed ahead. "It wasn't about helping women! Sanger said we had to protect 'racial health' by preventing the reckless spawning of 'human waste'! I know that's hard to believe, but I can show you—"

The class was buzzing again, several people hissing in her direction, and the professor finally went to the podium and rapped on it. "Class! *Ladies and gentlemen!*"

The classroom quieted abruptly.

Professor Kwong stood for a moment, leaning on the podium and staring around the classroom. Claire looked down, trying desperately to keep her emotions under control.

"I think," the professor said in a level voice, "that we had better bring this class discussion back to the matter at hand."

He stood at the lectern for a moment, flipping through the day's reading materials, before he began speaking again. The tension in the room gradually lessened as the professor lectured on various philosophers' and writers' viewpoints on abortion.

Claire half-listened, still trembling slightly, as he began again taking questions.

"But what I don't understand," Jo Markowitz was saying, "is why people make such a big deal of the right to choose what you do with your own body. By giving women the right to choose, it's neutral. We're not *forcing* anyone to have an abortion, and we're not *forcing* anyone to go through nine months of pregnancy. If it's not right for you, just don't participate. What's the big deal?"

Professor Kwong turned from the whiteboard, where he was jotting various notes, and raised his eyebrows. He pondered a moment, then called on Niles, across the room. Niles was again sitting alone at the very end of the row.

"That's the thing that really bugs me about the antichoice fundamentalists, actually. They're trying to impose their values on us. I don't care if they find it wrong for them—that's fine; they don't have to make that choice. But that's the point—it's their *choice*. And I might encourage my girlfriend to make a different one. As Jo said, allowing choice is therefore neutral."

The professor shook his head. "Actually, that is an incorrect statement. One cannot say that allowing the choice is necessarily neutral, since the so-called prolife position is that the product of conception is in fact a living human being. Obviously if the fetus is a living human being, then allowing the woman the choice of an abortion is no more neutral than allowing a person the choice of killing someone they prefer not to be burdened with." A few gasps and annoyed exclamations sounded from various corners of the room, but Professor Kwong's lecturing tone continued apace. "So then the philosophic discussion becomes a different one—whether or not it is appropriate or inappropriate to allow the choice of such a killing."

He clasped his hands behind his back and bounced on the balls of his feet. "A pro-choice author and professor at Princeton University—Peter Singer—argues that assigning intrinsic moral significance to birth is arbitrary and illogical, that a child grows into personhood as it becomes self-aware, and that both abortion and infanticide are defensible before that point."

Claire raised her hand. "So this professor argues that killing a living, breathing infant is okay?"

"That's correct, depending on the circumstances. He candidly says that a fetus is a living human being just like an infant, but argues that the termination of both is morally negligible if it would make the parents happier—such as if the infant was disabled in some way—since both the fetus and the infant are incapable of regarding themselves as distinct people with lives of their own to live."

The class had gotten very quiet. After a moment, Brad slowly raised his hand. "That position makes me want to vomit, but it *is* more intellectually consistent. It's much more honest to argue that if you can terminate a fetus before it's born, you can terminate a baby after it's born. What difference does a few days or weeks make, after all?"

Keesha jabbed her hand into the air. "This whole discussion is ludicrous. It's still my body. How dare you—a man, no less—say that I should not have the choice of what to do with my body? Whether the fetus is alive or not is irrelevant. It's still *my body.*"

Several of the eight amigas squirmed slightly in their seats, looking down or away.

"And furthermore," Keesha was saying in a hard voice, looking at Brad, "you fundamentalist chauvinists are trying to rip away a basic right of women. You won't even admit that allowing choice is the most neutral and fair option. You'd rather force your paternalistic views on us! You want us to return to the back alleys, the days of shame, the days when women were likely to *die* from some quack performing the procedure with a rusty coat hanger. Like we said earlier, we're not forcing anyone to have an abortion—if it's not right for you, just don't do it!" Her voice rose to nearly a shout. "How *dare* you be so oppressive, so intolerant!"

Brad, along with several other students, raised his hand. The professor was about to call on someone else, when Brad said, "Professor, may I respond to that accusation?"

He turned to Keesha, addressing her directly for the first time. "You say that allowing choice is neutral, you say that I'm a chauvinist, you say that I'm intolerant. But in fact you, Keesha, are the intolerant one!"

Several people who had been looking down at their books or whispering to each other broke off and turned to stare at Brad, whose normally reasoned voice was quavering with indignation.

"*You*, Keesha, aren't even being intellectually honest—with yourself or anyone else. As the professor pointed out earlier, allowing the choice to have an abortion is not neutral. Even by *thinking* that it's neutral, you're saying that my view—that the fetus is a living baby and no one should be allowed to have an abortion—is totally irrelevant and doesn't need to even be acknowledged. You're saying that my Christian fundamentalist beliefs are worthy of scorn and ridicule. You're saying that the worldview of 'if it's not right for you, just don't do it' is better than a worldview proclaiming that there are absolutes and that some things are truly right or truly wrong. You're stating the incredibly sexist belief that a man should have absolutely no input into the fate of a baby that he is, after all, half responsible for. You called me paternalistic and chauvinistic just because I believe—and say—that abortion is the taking of a human life and is morally, absolutely *wrong*. How dare *you* be so intolerant, Keesha!"

Brad settled back into his seat and wrenched his gaze back to the professor. "I'm sorry, Professor. I guess I just got tired of being attacked and having my viewpoint derided and oppressed." His voice dropped to a clearly audible mutter. "Us paternalistic, chauvinistic, fundamentalists have feelings too, you know."

The class broke up in explosive laughter, like air bursting from a balloon. The professor's lips twitched, and he glanced at his watch. "Well, I think we're going to have to let that be the last word."

Claire had never seen so many students exit the room so quickly. The sound of the professor's voice—reminding them of an upcoming paper—was drowned out by a waterfall of shuffling papers and a stampede of feet out the door.

Behind her, she overheard two women gathering their books, talking under their breaths. "What a jerk! That self-righteous attitude…"

Her face grew hot and angry. Neither of them had said anything in class, and here they were denigrating someone who'd had the guts to— She turned around, but they were already making their way down the row.

Downcast, she watched them go. *God, did we accomplish* anything *today?*

She made her way across the room to where Brad was stuffing his backpack. Two of the prolife students slapped him on the back as they moved toward the door.

She was about to speak when she heard a soft female voice.

"Brad?"

Both she and Brad turned. Bethany was standing a row above them.

"Yes?" Brad looked wary.

Bethany's manner was reserved, but her voice was warm. "Listen, I just wanted to let you know something. I've been prochoice a long time—abortion has always made me vaguely uneasy, but I've never been able to get past the issue of controlling my own body. But now…well, I'm leaning toward the prolife position."

Some astonishment must have shown in Brad and Claire's eyes, because she hurried on. "It's not, no offense, because of any argument that you made or anything you really said. It's because of how they respond to you. Keesha may be a know-it-all, but she's not usually mean. But today, and with all the other things that people said, well, I just couldn't help but think that if they were so irrational, they must have something to hide." A brief smile flitted across her lips. "I was glad you told her off at the end."

"I didn't mean for it to come across like that," Brad said. "I'm afraid I got a little carried away. I should apologi—"

"No way! It was good to hear you defend yourself for once. You always let people beat you up. I may not completely agree with you, but you should stick it to 'em once in a while."

"Believe me, Bethany, I would love to. I just have to be careful about it. That's all."

"Why?"

"Well…" Brad paused, considering her open demeanor, her frank gaze. "I used to be a very different person. I used to argue all the time—I *had* to get my way, *had* to sneak around and manipulate things for my benefit. Then, a few years ago, I made a faith commitment that changed my life. And God transformed my personality."

"Look," Bethany held up her hand. "I don't want to get all personal here. I just—"

"Don't worry, I won't go into it. I was just answering your question." He pursed his lips. "Anyway, when I became a Christian, God really remade me. I wasn't angry all the time, wasn't so bent on getting my own way. But—" he smiled ruefully—"enough of that old stuff was left in there that I didn't necessarily look like Jesus, either. Jesus said that if someone strikes you on the right cheek, turn to him the other also. In essence, don't retaliate—even when it may be fully deserved. So I've got to really watch it in class—in this whole school, in fact—or the old me could come crashing back in. And that wouldn't be good for me or anybody else."

Claire watched Bethany's face and felt a sudden urge to pray for her. *Lord, open her eyes; open her mind. Help her have ears to hear.*

"What would you say," Bethany asked slowly, "to someone who wasn't expecting to be pregnant, but who was…and thought that abortion might be wrong…but whose life would be ruined if she went through with the pregnancy?"

"Well," Brad looked a little uncomfortable, but his voice was kind. "First, I'd tell her that I cared about both her and the baby. I'd tell her that I would do anything I could to help her carry the baby to term and find adoptive parents or whatever she wanted to do at that point."

"What if…what if she knew she *should* carry the baby, but felt she had no choice but to have an abortion?"

Claire reached out and touched her classmate's arm. "Bethany…" She looked over at Brad. "May I?"

Brad nodded relieved assent.

She turned back to Bethany. "I would tell…this person…to realize first and foremost that she's not simply carrying a fetus—as some people prefer to call it. She's carrying a beautiful, tiny baby." Claire's eyes searched the young woman's face. "Then I would sit with her for as long as she wanted and tell her about all the amazing services available to help her. I'd tell her that she's not alone, and need never be alone through this process."

Tears began to form in the corners of Bethany's eyes. She blinked them away, holding her head higher.

"I would tell her," Claire continued, "that God created her, and loves her, just like God lovingly created the baby. I'd tell her about the amazing tiny person developing inside of her: the heartbeat, the little arms and legs, the miracle that God has fashioned."

"But what if she didn't have any choice?" Bethany asked again, her words despairing. "What if her life would be ruined?"

Claire laid a soft hand on Bethany's shoulder. Her eyes were kind. "I would tell her, Bethany, that she *does* have a choice. She just doesn't like it very much."

Bethany drew in a shuddering breath. "But—"

"And as for her life being ruined? What I have found, really, is that when we say 'It will ruin my life,' in most cases what we really mean is 'It will be a huge inconvenience.' What we really mean is 'I'll have to drop out of school for a year' or 'I'll have to quit my job or get another one' or 'I'll have to move back in with my parents.' Those are all inconveniences—real ones—but when you think of what's hanging in the balance, just inconveniences. Rarely does going through with a pregnancy actually mean that one's life will be ruined. But I can tell…this person…many ways in which abortion will ruin both her life and the life of her little child."

Bethany stood very still, tears leaking unchecked from her eyes. Claire stepped up to her row of seats and hugged her.

"I'm so scared." The words were almost a whisper in Claire's ear. Bethany pressed a shaking hand against her mouth. "So scared."

Claire glanced over at Brad, who also climbed over the row and hugged the tearful woman. They gently sat her down then settled into seats on either side of her.

Claire took her classmate's hand. "Bethany, do you have anyone helping you?"

"No." The voice was still a whisper. "Nobody knows. Only my boyfriend."

"What does he say?"

"He wants me to get an abortion. To 'take care of it,' he said." Bethany took a half-used pack of tissues out of her backpack and gave a tearful smile. "I've been going through five of these packs a day."

Brad and Claire smiled and waited while she blew her nose.

"The problem is," the tears were coming again, "I just can't shake the feeling that I'd be doing something terrible. I know I have the choice, and I know it's my body and no one else can tell me what to do with it, but—" She looked over at Claire. "But the other day I was walking down Mass Ave, and I saw a bumper sticker: Some Choices Are Wrong, it said. I was so furious at the time, but I couldn't get it out of my mind. Yesterday I figured that even though I've missed two periods, I should ask the student health center to confirm whether I was actually pregnant. As soon as the test came back positive, they handed me this pamphlet on places to get an abortion." Her voice was very small. "I don't know what to do."

Claire smiled at her new friend. "Here's what *we're* going to do. In a few minutes, you and I will go get a snack off-campus somewhere, and then I'll go with you over to a place in Somerville, just a few stops down on the T." At Bethany's cautious look, she chuckled slightly. "Don't worry. It's a pregnancy resource center with a medical clinic and counselors and caseworkers that have lots of experience helping people like you. I used to work in a place just like it back home in Michigan."

Bethany laughed slightly. "I thought you sounded pretty professional."

"Hey, listen. I may have done this before, but that doesn't mean I don't care, Bethany. I do." She sat back a bit. "I care about both you *and* the beautiful little life forming inside of you right now."

As the three of them gathered their things, Claire was quietly exultant. *God, and to think I was wondering if this class had any effect at all! What a privilege to serve You! Thank You, Father.*

She arranged to meet Bethany by Johnston Gate in ten minutes and watched her compose herself and leave the classroom. *O Father God, help her to do the right thing.*

She said good-bye to Brad, pulled on her parka, and headed for the door. Suddenly, her thoughts flitted to a biology problem set she had to turn in at the Science Center by three o'clock. But wasn't there something else…?

She stopped dead in her tracks. Mansfield's project! She was supposed to be doing all that advance work right now!

She glanced at her watch, her heart sinking, and raced for the door. She could just make it to the Science Center and back to Johnston Gate in ten minutes. She shook her head.

She would be there for Bethany. But what timing.

# FORTY-SIX

A WHOLE HOST OF GREMLINS CONVERGED on the young woman as she hurried down the stairs of the Science Center, her eyes looking for the correct office. They swarmed through the hallway, tripping her, blocking her vision of the doors, which, they noted with delight, were already laid out in a confusing manner.

Maybe if they delayed her enough, their Masters' purposes for the other girl would prevail.

She found the right office and entered a maze of cubicles. One of the demons sped ahead toward the first desk and poked a long finger through the occupant's computer.

The screen froze up just as Claire approached.

"Excuse me, where is the biology lab's de—?"

"Oh great!" The worker stood and whacked her computer screen. "I didn't save it! This piece of—" She turned and growled at Claire. "It's down at the end on the right."

Claire disappeared, then came hurrying back. "Excuse me, I hate to bother you."

The worker looked up from fiddling with her keyboard, animosity plain on her face. Claire swallowed, but didn't back down.

"Where's the nearest phone?"


Claire stood at a campus phone in the Science Center, drumming her fingers on the wall beside her, notebook ready. The phone was ringing endlessly in her ear. She looked at the clock at the end of the hallway. Bethany would be standing by Johnston Gate already, and it was freezing outside. Would she change her mind?

The phone kept ringing. Would these people ever— She heard a click and sighed. "The number for Ian Burke, please."

She shifted from foot to foot, looking at the wall clock again. Her attention came back to the receiver. "What? I guess it's B-U-R-K-E." She listened a moment longer, then her voice grew alarmed. "No…wait!…not Greg. Don't connect me! It's *Ian* Burke. I-A-N. No, *B* as in *boy*. B-U-R-K-E." She waited, drumming her fingers harder. "Uh, sir, I'm kind of in a hurry… Well, yes, as a matter of fact you could say it was a matter of life and death! Please, sir, I know his number is listed!" She closed her eyes, listening, her voice faint. "No, sir. I really do need your help. Thank you very much, sir."

*God, help me keep my patience, and keep Bethany standing there...*

She grabbed her pen and scribbled the number, then dialed. In a moment, she was speaking hastily to his voice mail.

"Ian, it's Claire. I'm so sorry, but something really urgent has come up, and I'm not going to be able to find the right office for us to go to tomorrow. I can't explain over voice mail." She gave a short sigh of frustration. "I know you were counting on me, and I'm really sorry I didn't do it sooner. But I had this class and... Look, I'll explain a bit more tomorrow. I don't know if *you* might possibly be able to do the advance work or not, but I'll be back tonight probably by dinnertime, and if you need to call me, you have my number. Hopefully this won't be too much of a problem. I'm really sorry." She glanced up at the clock again. "Oh my gosh, I've got to run. I'll try to call you later tonight."

Claire hurried toward the exit, parka over her arm, stuffing her notebook into her backpack as she went. What would they say to her? Was she ruining her reputation with Mansfield?

Her pastor's words rose in her mind: *Ministry is always inconvenient...* She smiled ruefully, zipping the heavy backpack closed. *You don't say.*

She pushed through the doors into a blast of freezing rain and headed for Johnston Gate at a half-run. She fumbled for the zipper of her parka, trying to get it hooked on the run, and jerked it once, twice.... *Come on, you stupid thing.*

She yanked a third time and the backpack fell off her shoulder. It hit the ground and broke open, a gaping rip running the length of one side.

Claire grabbed the pack in her arms, trying to keep books from falling free. She muttered under her breath, "I didn't sign up for this, Lord!" The next instant a curious feeling overwhelmed her, and her lips suddenly twitched.

"Yes. Yes, I did."

She forced herself to pause. She set the backpack down, took a deep breath, and calmly zipped her parka and drew the hood over her head. Then she carefully picked up the broken pack in both arms and continued at a good clip toward the gate. *Please let Bethany be there....*

She rounded the corner. *Oh, thank God.*

Bethany was standing forlornly in the shadow of the tall wall. She was wearing a long trench coat and hugging her arms to her chest, a small purse dangling over her arm.

"It's freezing out here, Claire." Bethany's teeth were chattering. "It's going to snow."

"I know. I'm sorry. It took me longer than I thought."

"I don't know if I want to do this. I just have so much going on and—"

Claire held up her hand. "Look, I totally understand, but can we at least get out of this cold?" She began to steer Bethany toward the Harvard Square T stop. "I'll make you a deal. Let's go down to the T and wait for the train to Somerville. We can at least grab a quick snack and talk about what you're thinking. I think we'll both be more coherent when our noses are thawed."

Bethany sighed, but Claire could see a resigned look in her eyes. "All right. But I reserve the right to not get on the train if I change my mind."

"Deal."

The T stop was deserted and blissfully warm. Claire pulled off her parka and set down her gaping backpack on a concrete bench.

"Nice bag," Bethany said.

"It's the newest style. Everyone's going to be doing it soon." Claire took a long scarf out of her coat pocket and wrapped it around and around the pack. "It looks like we might have a long wait. I bet we just missed a train."

Bethany's voice was quiet. "Claire, don't you think I should have the right to choose what I do with my own body?"

Claire paused in her movements for a split second, then kept working. "Well, it sounds good, Bethany, but is it really your body that we're talking about? Do you remember those cases today, about the people seeds in your carpet and the world-class violinist that's strapped to you, sharing your organs for nine months?"

Bethany nodded.

"Well, just like the people seeds example, the illustration of the violinist is really misleading. The violinist isn't sharing your organs: He has his own!"

"There." She tucked in the scarf ends and tested the pack to ensure it wouldn't fall apart again. Then she took a seat next to Bethany on the bench.

"The question isn't should you have the right to choose what you do with *your* body, but should you have the right to choose what you do with *someone else's* body. The little baby growing in your womb has its own lungs, heart, its own circulatory system. It probably even has a different blood type from yours. He or she is a whole, separate person."

"Yeah, yeah. I know you *say* that, but right now all I feel is that I'm being invaded without my consent. Shouldn't I have the right to say what I do with my *own body?*"

Her voice was becoming angry, and Claire took a deep breath. It would make such a difference once Bethany saw an ultrasound, saw the slow somersaults of a little figure, the tiny head, the delicate arms and legs—all silent appeals from a precious life needing protection.

Claire paused, praying furiously, and a thought popped into her mind. *Don't answer the question until you figure out what the premise is.*

"Um, do you mind if I ask you something about that?"

Bethany shook her head, and Claire found herself shaking. *God, I've never done it this way before. Give me Your words.* She sat on her hands and looked sideways at her friend. "When you say the right to do what you want with your body, what do you mean by *right?*"

"What?"

"Just humor me on this, okay? I just want to understand where you're coming from."

"Whatever. I guess I mean…you know…the ability to choose my own path. It's my prerogative."

"So you're saying you should be autonomous, the ultimate authority for your life."

"Duh!" Bethany was laughing now. "Of course!"

"But don't you think you're leaving something—or *Someone*—out of the equation? Have you considered what it would be like if everyone lived the way you just said you wanted to? Being their own authority?"

"But that's what we have now. Everyone lives their own life, according to what's right for them. I don't get where you're going with this."

"Just humor me. Have you taken any modern history classes that covered dictators like Stalin or Mao?"

"Yeah, last year."

"Well, then you know that the last century was the bloodiest in history because all these dictators said that their definition of reality should prevail and that they should be their own authority. I read somewhere that those regimes caused the deaths of over one hundred and fifty *million* civilians, while doing what was right for them."

"Give me a break!" Bethany sprang to her feet, her face incredulous. "Are you comparing me to some Communist dictator who puts people into death camps?"

"No, of course not. I'm just asking where the limits are, where does your line of reasoning stop? I know you just want to control *you*, and Stalin's bunch wanted to control *other people*, but if you follow your earlier statement to its logical end, you're saying the same thing. You both are saying that you are the ultimate judge of what's best for you." She smiled ruefully. "Those regimes just happened to think that what was best for them was to remain in power over the dead bodies of anyone who disagreed with them. But if each of us is our ultimate judge, who's to say those governments weren't right?"

"But…" Bethany paused, her expression unreadable. "But everyone knows murder isn't right."

"Sure. But what they did is logically consistent with the idea that they should have the *right* to be the ultimate decision maker over their lives. Look, I know you don't want to make that connection, but—"

"You know what? I'll bet those deaths were from religious wars; that's what I think." Bethany folded her arms over her chest, nearly glaring at Claire. "All these religions that are so sure they're right that they're willing to kill someone to convert them! How can all you religious people say there's only one path, anyway? There are paths to God in every religion. No one can tell someone else their path to truth."

"Well, first of all, I'm pretty sure those killings were ideological, not religious. But second, what do you mean by truth?"

Bethany set her hands on her hips and frowned at her questioner. "Look, I understand what you're saying about Stalin, but it works the other way, too. Whenever anyone tries to enforce some sort of absolute on others, it causes immense misery."

"That's a good point, but I'm not talking about *forcing* acceptance of the truth on anyone. You're perfectly welcome to disagree with me; I just think you'd be silly to do so if what I'm saying is true." *Am I making any sense here?* Claire's voice grew tentative. "Have you ever heard of Pascal's wager?"

Bethany shook her head.

"I learned this in high school, so forgive me if I mangle it. Pascal essentially said that in rejecting the claims of Jesus, you're making a terrible gamble. He said that if Christians say there is a heaven and hell, and we're wrong, we don't lose anything when we die. But if nonbelievers say there *isn't* a heaven and hell, and *they're* wrong—they are in huge trouble when they die."

Bethany sighed and sat back down on the bench. "I honestly just don't get all you people who pick right and wrong out of some old book, or say there's only one way to God." She glanced sideways. "You're in that Christian group that's having the barbecue on Saturday, right?"

"Yes."

Bethany turned to face Claire, clearly perplexed. "See, I totally agree there's a God, but I don't claim to have the only path to Him. Don't you think God is bigger than we can understand—"

"Absolutely, but—"

"—and doesn't it make so much more sense to acknowledge that God has put something of Himself in *all* religions, *all* paths? It's like—" She thought a second, then snapped her fingers. "Like school!" Bethany stood up again, restless, thinking on her feet. "As we go through grade school, then junior high, then high school, our teachers are instructing us in things when we're ready for them, piling up new revelations as we expand our knowledge. We learn a little from history, a little from math, a little from science…but we don't pretend that any one subject will bring us to ultimate truth. That's what God's like. He releases truth to us little by little as we can grasp it.

"It's like that old proverb of blind men feeling all different parts of an elephant and arguing that the elephant had to be described as the tail, or the trunk, or the leg, when in fact the elephant was so much more than the little piece they could feel." Bethany's voice grew earnest. "We have to synthesize what all the religions have learned about God through the ages. We can't get stuck on any of the bits and pieces that think they're the be-all and end-all. For Christians to say there's only one way to God is like a math person saying you only need math to be educated!"

*Question assumptions*...Claire thought for a second; then suddenly her eyes opened wide. She could practically hear the Holy Spirit giving her the words to say. She shivered, rubbing down the goose bumps on her arms.

"Bethany, I just realized what's going on. Our major difference is in our view of God. You think there's a lot of overlap between religions, and you view God as a sort of vague deity, a big, mysterious force that's out there in the ether somewhere."

"Yes, I suppose so."

"See, I view God as a person. He's someone who loves me, a perfect Father who created me and wants me to love Him back. He wants a relationship with me, like any good Father would. Just because I can't know and understand all of Him doesn't mean that I can't *know* Him!

She cocked her head. "The elephant analogy says that the men feeling the elephant were blind. But we're not blind men! The Bible says God wants His children to seek Him and find Him where He can be found. And in the Bible, He's already told us what the whole 'elephant' looks like—He's told us how He can be found: through Jesus. Not through living a good life, but through His Son."

"See, that's the kind of absolute that just drives me crazy," Bethany said, drawing back. "You don't have a monopoly on Truth! How can you say that Jesus is the only way when—"

"I didn't say it, Bethany. He did."

"But the other religions all say God has lots of ways—"

"God can't contradict Himself. He wouldn't say 'This is the only way' to one group and then say 'Oh, there are lots of different paths' to another group, would He?"

She saw Bethany's irritation and smiled in a conciliatory fashion. "Look, I totally agree that other religions make some good points. But it's not about a 'monopoly on Truth.' All real truth is from God, and it's not like other religions have found *none* of it! It's just that they are incorporating glimpses of the real Truth, picking and choosing which to accept or reject rather than accepting the whole thing."

Bethany stopped pacing and folded her arms across her chest. "Where does God actually say there's only one way?"

"Jesus said it point-blank. He said, 'I am the Way and the Truth and the Life. No one comes to the Father but through me.'"

"But that's so *ridiculous!* It's so exclusive! It excludes anyone who follows another religion, anyone with a different viewpoint, even people who try their whole lives to be good, moral people!"

Claire smiled. "Well, first of all, don't get mad at me. I didn't make the rules. He did."

"Well, fine. I'll get mad at Him, then."

Claire smiled gently. "But if He's the kind of God I described—Creator of the Universe, the one who fashioned you in secret just like He's fashioning this tiny baby inside you right now—don't you think He has the right to make the rules?"

Bethany stopped. Her eyes narrowed. "Well, if you look at it that way, okay. But I don't know that I want to believe in a God who would send good people to hell. It's too…too *mean.*" Her voice became plaintive. "I thought God was supposed to be loving!"

Claire sighed in relief. She'd heard someone respond to that argument before. Confident, she started to open her mouth.

*No, child! Pray.*

She choked on her intended words and coughed roughly, bending over, her mind furiously racing. *Lord, forgive me! What is it I'm supposed to say?*

Bethany sat on the bench and patted Claire on the back. "You okay?"

"Yeah, yeah." Claire coughed again several times. "Sorry."

She patted her chest, feeling the choking sensation subside, and looked over at her friend. Bethany's eyes were concerned. With a glimmer of surprise, Claire felt her own defenses crumble. She hadn't even known they were raised.

After a pause, Claire spoke from her heart. "Bethany, let me answer what you said in the only way I know how. God isn't mean. He's loving, gracious, and kind and so merciful to us that we can't even fathom it. Yes, He is Lord—He makes the rules, and we don't—but He is also a friend. The most faithful friend you'll ever have. And yes, He's a judge. He says that the wages of sin is death—eternal separation from Him. But He's also so merciful that all you have to do is accept what Jesus did for you and you'll be saved—" She gasped, her mind seizing on a new thought.

"What?" Bethany put her face close to Claire's. "You look like you've seen a ghost."

"No, I've seen the light." Claire put her hand to her forehead. "I've been a Christian three years now, and I never thought of this before."

"What? *What?* You're even making *me* curious!"

"You know how you thought Christianity was so exclusive and intolerant? Well, I just realized…it's actually the most *inclusive* religion in the world!"

"How's that?" Bethany's voice was flat.

"Every other belief system requires you to meet some standard in order to go to heaven, or achieve nirvana, or whatever their equivalent is. But with Christ—" she leaned toward Bethany, her eyes intent— "*anyone* can go to heaven. Not just the good people! Every other faith is *so* much more exclusive that it *is* actually mean. They say you have to be good to go to heaven, but who knows how good you really have to be? What they're saying is that you might die and find out, 'Oh, sorry! You're only allowed two hundred lies in a lifetime, and you told two hundred and *one*. Too bad.'" She jerked her thumb downward.

"Do you see? In Christianity there is one—only one—step, and everyone knows what it is: Give your life to Jesus. The good, the bad, the rich, the poor—they're all God's children. He knows that none of us is going to be as good as He requires—which is perfect—so He made a way for anyone to be saved!"

Bethany still looked wary, but Claire hardly noticed. "All the other religions say we have to earn our way to God, but in Christ, God freely comes to us! So many people think you have to somehow work your way into God's heart, but in reality He's an unconditionally loving Father who simply wants your love."

She shook her head in wonder. "Last year I read a perfect example—in the last words of Buddha versus the last words of Jesus—of just how opposite all other religious philosophies are to Christianity. Buddha's last words to his disciples were 'Keep striving'—and that's exactly what so many people think they must do. But Jesus' last words on the cross were 'It is finished.' God Himself has done it all."

Her thoughts were suddenly wrapped up in silent praise. She heard a sigh and turned to see Bethany's head flop down into her hands.

"I'm just so confused. I don't know what I think anymore." She lifted her head and looked at Claire, a wry smile on her lips. "Are you sure you're a freshman?"

"Look, Bethany…I'm just your average Christian trying to find my way. I don't have all the answers to all your questions. I just know that I have met Jesus and that He is real. He's alive, and He is *the* answer. Once you've met Jesus, no one can convince you of anything else. That's the reason the early Christians didn't recant when they were thrown to the lions. Nothing anyone could say or do could change the Truth they knew."

Bethany sighed again, shaking her head. "I just don't get it."

"Maybe you don't get it because you've never met Him. He's not a concept—He's a person! Why don't you try talking to Him? Ask Him to meet you. I promise He will."

There was a sudden movement of the air inside the station, and the two women could hear the distant approach of the train.

Claire stretched and stood up. "Well, that's us."

Bethany didn't move.

A sudden chill came over Claire. She had almost forgotten their original purpose in all the discussion. *O dear Lord…* Had she unwittingly alienated her?

For a long moment, neither student spoke. The train approached at a rush, the cars squealing on their rails as they slowed into the station.

*O Lord, speak to her….*

Bethany suddenly stood to her feet, looping her purse over her arm. She glared at Claire. "Well, are you coming, or are you going to just let me find this place by myself?" A quick grin flashed across her features.

An answering grin broke out on Claire's face. She grabbed her decrepit backpack and hustled the two of them onto the train.


The two young women didn't notice the giant figures that formed a cordon all around them as they rode. They didn't notice the protection all around them as they disembarked and walked several blocks through an unfamiliar neighborhood just as it started to snow. And they certainly didn't notice the zone of brilliant light that surrounded the small building as they entered, one face nervous, one hopeful.

Within minutes the Spirit was speaking to the heavenly host, and they sprang into the air in delight. Yet another little one would be saved and… They paused as they listened eagerly to the next revelation, then burst into spirals of triumphant praise. Another captive would be set free!

## FORTY-SEVEN

"COME IN, COME IN. QUICKLY." Edward Grindley held the door open for his visitor, squinting at the biting wind and tiny snowflakes that swirled into the foyer and onto his robe and slippers.

Mansfield gladly stepped into the warmth of the house and shook off a light dusting of snow from his hat and shoulders. He could hear the welcome crackle of a fireplace somewhere nearby.

He reached out and shook the hand of his diminutive host. "Thank you for calling, Edward."

Edward Grindley leaned lightly on his walking stick and smiled. "Thank you for coming, and on such a day, at that." He fingered the collar of his robe. "I apologize that I'm not better dressed, but I'm not feeling well. I'm napping as much as I can, and, well, this is one of those days when I will consider myself 'robed in righteousness.'"

Mansfield laughed. "No apologies necessary! I envy you. However, I don't want to disturb you if you're not feeling well."

"Nonsense, nonsense!" Edward's eyes twinkled. "I must speak with you."

He suddenly turned his head and coughed several times, leaning more heavily on his walking stick. His eyes closed, and he winced. After a moment, he turned back to his guest, smiling despite his evident pain. "Besides, Dr. Mansfield, as you can see, if we waited for a day of perfect health, I fear we would have to arrange a meeting in the heavenly realms."

"Let's hope that day is a long way off, Edward."

"Hmm. Yes." Edward moved toward an open doorway off the side of the foyer. He gestured for Mansfield to follow.

The doorway opened into a warm room in deep greens and browns, the flames in a giant fireplace casting a friendly glow on sofas, chairs, and overstuffed ottomans. There were no windows, and two walls were lined with floor-to-ceiling bookshelves, rolling ladders running on tracks along their lengths. A grand piano sat in one corner, its cover open, musical scores spilling out of a folder on its polished surface.

Mansfield smiled in delight as he entered the room.

"My study," Edward said.

"It's perfect."

Mansfield walked over to one of the bookshelves and ran his fingers along the spines of several gold-leaf hardback books. *"Huckleberry Finn, The Swiss Family Robinson, A Tale of Two Cities...*all collectors' editions." His gaze shifted to the fireplace, noting the framed print of Harvard's old crest above the mantel. He turned back to his host, good-natured envy on his face. "This would be my favorite room."

Edward smiled. "It is."

He settled into a large high-backed chair near the fireplace and gestured for Mansfield to take a seat on the sofa nearby. He leaned over and pressed a button on the table at his right hand. Within moments, a pretty girl appeared in the doorway.

"You okay, Grandpa?"

"I'm doing fine. Lacy, this is Professor Mansfield from Harvard—"

"Hello, Lacy." Mansfield nodded in her direction.

"—and I'm wondering if you would hang up his coat in the hall closet and bring us some warm drinks." He turned to his guest. "Would you like hot chocolate? Coffee?"

"Hot tea, if you have it." Mansfield looked over at the girl. She nodded and disappeared. The professor glanced back at his host. "She's lovely."

Edward smiled. "Thank you. She looks just like her mother." His eyes twinkled. "Her mother is my *granddaughter,* so she's actually my great-granddaughter."

"Good heavens."

"And no, I'm not going to tell you how old I am just yet. You'll find that out in due time." His expression suddenly became serious, and he paused a long moment. "I need to tell you why you are here."

Lacy came through the doorway and around the sofa, setting a tray on the coffee table in front of Mansfield.

"Ah, thank you, my dear," Edward said.

She poured hot water from a small teapot for Mansfield and handed a steaming mug of hot chocolate to her great-grandfather. She showed Mansfield the small containers of tea bags, lemon slices, cream, and sugar, then smiled and departed.

Mansfield turned to Edward with a bemused expression on his face. Edward laughed. "We always have guests of one sort or another in this home. All the children learn early on how to be good—and discreet—hosts."

Edward sipped at his mug, then cupped it carefully in his hands. "Professor Mansfield, I asked you here today because I need to tell you a story."

"Please call me Mansfield. Everyone else does."

"Very well." Edward looked into the fire. "In 1636, as you know, the Massachusetts General Court chartered Harvard College. As I believe I told you when we first met, a Grindley was a member of that body. And that man's son was one of Harvard's first board members. The story I have to tell you relates to him.

"Gage Grindley was, according to all accounts, an exceptional man, a man after God's own heart. His very name means 'pledge'—'one who dedicates his life to God.' Unlike many of his contemporaries, Gage never had a period of youthful wanderlust and rebellion before reaffirming his faith. It was always there, steadfast, unwavering. He came over from England with his mother and father as a youth, and by the time his elderly father was voting to establish an institution of higher learning in the new colony, Gage was ready to assume some leadership in the endeavor.

"I won't bore you with all the details of his writings from that time, but I myself have read them. All the Grindleys have read them from the time they make a personal commitment to Jesus Christ as their Lord and Savior."

Mansfield raised one eyebrow slightly, but didn't comment.

"Gage Grindley was instrumental in establishing the Christian purpose of Harvard. He believed that extensive learning across all the disciplines was extremely important for the development of a free New World, but he—like his peers—recognized that intellectual development would be empty unless it occurred in the context of seeking God's knowledge, God's truth."

Edward gestured to the crest that hung above the fireplace. "Hence, *Veritas*. Gage Grindley apparently was an early advocate of that motto. He thought it perfectly synthesized the goal of finding God's truth in all the disciplines, as well as encouraging the goal of seeking—and finding—the truth of the gospel of Christ. All of the founders were passionate about that. As one of the earliest charters said, 'through the good hand of God,' Harvard hoped to educate the 'English and Indian youth of this country in knowledge and godliness.'"

The old man took a careful sip of the hot chocolate, then set the mug on a side table and picked up a slim book. "Gage Grindley eventually became the chairman of the Harvard board of directors. He was sworn in on a frozen autumn morning, much like this one. And that night…well, I'll let you read his own words. They start on page 2."

He held out the book. Mansfield rose and took it from the wrinkled hand. The book was a good-quality paperback, its cover a nondescript burgundy with gold borders. There was no title, but the words *Property of the Grindley Family: not for outside audience* were printed on the bottom right corner.

Mansfield settled back onto the sofa and began to read as directed. He was looking at a printed excerpt of Gage Grindley's description of the day he was sworn in as chairman of the board.


The ceremony completed, I retired to the president's office for a short meeting with the other board members. That done, I gratefully headed for home, Betty looking lovely at my side.

I recall thinking, at the time, how impossibly blessed I had been by the faithful providence of our Lord. To have been entrusted with the task of this young "college in the wilderness," as well as the gift of such a wife and family—well, my heart was filled to overflowing with thanksgiving.

When we arrived at home in the darkness, Hattie had the children all ready for bed, and we set about tucking them in. Little Amanda's fever had abated, and I visited with my daughter for a long spell, reading her a story until her little eyes drooped and closed.

I ventured downstairs, lamp in hand, and went into my study to wait for Betty and our usual time of evening devotions. (We had found that our tempers were much improved and any problems of the day much diminished when we made time each night to spend in the Word of God and in prayer. The servants knew that this was our custom and had retired to their part of the house, which is why the events of that evening were not witnessed by anyone else.)

Betty came in, her flaxen hair shining in the light of the fire, and we knelt by the hearth, prepared to come before the Lord.

In that instant a bright light filled the room, a light that seemed like the very sun itself. In a moment of what I can only describe as holy terror, a giant figure appeared before us, shining with the glory of God. He wore a brilliant tunic, a shining sword at his side, his face, hair, and eyes blazing with what seemed like fire.

We fell with our faces to the floor, unable to speak, or even—for the moment—think, so great was our fright. In a small portion of my mind even then, however, I was able to summon capacity for the rueful thought that *this* was why the biblical angels always led their messages with "be not afraid."

And sure enough, when our heavenly messenger spoke, "Do not be afraid" was first on his lips. He waited while we lifted our faces from the floor and looked up at him. We were clutching each other, still kneeling, but our initial terror had begun to drain away, replaced by wonderment and even a joy deeper than I have ever experienced. So deep that I felt my chest could not hold my heart.

"I come with a message from almighty God," the angel said. "Your endeavor of this time is more important than you can know. This nation has been dedicated to Him, and this college has been dedicated to serve His purposes. Through the years this college will be raised up in stature and influence; thus the enemy desires to take this territory. This will be a ground of great struggle."

His voice was like the thundering of the seas, filling the room. I could feel the strong presence of the Holy Ghost there with us and began to tremble. Beside me, Betty clutched my arm, her face pale but riveted in wonder.

The heavenly messenger continued. "The King of kings desires his children to stand and fight for this important ground. There must be generals to lead this fight in love, wisdom, humility, and courage. You, Gage and Elizabeth Grindley, have found favor in His sight. Your family will be established as ambassadors of Christ here in this place, in every generation to come, that His Glory may go out from here to the nations."

My soul quaked as he spoke, and I fell again to the floor, sobbing. To think that such a sinful wretch as I had found favor of almighty God was more than my feeble mind could grasp.

"The Lord makes this promise to you," the angel continued. "Your household will be a place of refuge, and He will raise up your offspring to succeed you in this fight. As your children and your children's children follow Him, seek His face, and learn to walk in His ways, your household will follow Him all the days of their lives."

Beside me I heard Betty weeping, felt her body trembling as she whispered "Thank You, O Lord God" over and over again.

The angel's face grew fierce, and his voice deepened. "Tell your children: The time will come when men in this place will not endure sound doctrine, but to suit their own desires will gather teachers around themselves who will say whatever their itching ears want to hear. They will turn their ears and eyes away from Truth and shall turn to fables and concocted myths. As in days of old, they will have eyes but will not see, have ears but will not hear. The gospel is veiled and seems like foolishness to those who are perishing."

The angel drew his sword, holding it upright in a strong hand. The trappings of our little room seemed to vanish into the background, and we were surrounded by the brilliant light.

"Therefore!" The angel's voice rang out. "God Almighty in His mercy gives your family this anointing: Your children and your children's children will be salt that seasons this place to keep it from decay. In every generation that walks in His ways, your family will be a lamp set on the lampstand, that those who come near might see the light, that the hidden things will be disclosed to them."

Again I began to shake, still on my knees beside my wife. The angel watched us with a somber but compassionate gaze. Much to my shock, the mighty messenger suddenly knelt before us and looked into our eyes.

"Your descendants have been given the mantle to speak and see eyes opened, to pierce the veil of blindness woven by the evil one. What the listeners do from that point on will be up to them. Thus, your family has this charge from the Lord of hosts: Be prepared in season and out of season to give an answer for the hope that is within you. Pray unceasingly. With great patience endure hardship, keep your head in all situations, and speak always in love."

I was startled to see the great face lift in what looked like a solemn smile. He stood to his feet and clasped his sword. Almost unconsciously, Betty and I also stood, still surrounded by the otherworldly brilliance.

His voice was a trumpet call. "By living a life worthy of the Good News of Christ, and by setting forth the Truth plainly, you will commend yourselves to every man's conscience in the sight of God. For you preach not yourselves but Jesus Christ as Lord."

His eyes bore into ours as he quoted from Paul's second letter to the Corinthians: "'And when the hearers of the Word shall turn to the Lord, the veil shall be taken away.'"

And in a flash, the great visitor vanished.

We stood silent, seemingly suspended in time. The room was quiet. We came back to our senses, staring unseeingly at the pictures on the walls, the rocking chair in the corner, the woven rug beneath our feet.

For a long time neither of us spoke. We started to peer sideways at each other and then threw ourselves into each other's arms, laughing and crying, shouting and talking, all at once. Then, just as quickly as the jubilation came, it was stilled in sober decision. We both sank back to the floor, holding each other tightly, and committed before our Lord to uphold those purposes with which He had so specifically charged our family.

The text stopped suddenly. Mansfield stared at the page, transported to that long-ago room where a couple knelt in solemn covenant.

Mansfield stirred, and looked up at Edward Grindley. His host was watching the fire, listening to the soft pop and crackle of the flames.

"A bit later in his memoirs," Edward spoke quietly, without turning, "Gage Grindley ponders what the angel really meant. He cannot picture a time when Harvard's Christian purpose, or the Puritans' hard-fought freedom of faith in the New World, would be undermined by those with itching ears. He seems offended that a time might come when any person at Harvard would reject sound doctrine." Edward turned from the fire, a rueful smile on his face. "How times have changed."

Mansfield handed back the book, and Edward set the volume on his lap and folded his hands on its cover.

"Dr. Mansfield—excuse me, Mansfield—since the middle of the seventeenth century, the Grindley family has endeavored to take seriously the words of this messenger of God."

"I would hope so!"

"Not just as a fuzzy exhortation and motivation to do great things for God, but as a blueprint for what our role is and how we are to fill this 'mantle' the angel described. Over time we have established many ways to do that. Of course, the most important is fostering a personal relationship with Christ from a young age and living a life that reflects His purity and love." He held up a cautionary hand. "Obviously, we as individuals could undermine our calling through willful disobedience, but so far God has been gracious to this imperfect family of sinners, and we have mostly tried to live in a way that glorifies only Him."

Edward returned his attention to the fire. The leaping flames cast a playful pattern on the Harvard crest above the mantel. "After an individual's faith commitment is made in this family, even from childhood we learn sound doctrine and apologetics in order to winsomely counter those 'itching ears.' We have intercessory teams that pray for Harvard and its students and faculty, to do battle in the spiritual realm against the plans of the evil one. We have sent many of our family members to Harvard and—as I mentioned—have traditionally taken roles of servant leadership whenever given the opportunity.

"We use this house as a true place of refuge, helping those in need and hosting those the enemy would seek to kill, steal, and destroy. We strongly emphasize service to others—especially those who oppose us—to concretely demonstrate the heart of Jesus Christ, the Good Shepherd.

"In order to preach the Word, and always give an answer for the Hope that is within us, we teach even our youngest children a simple statement that captures in one sentence the essence of the gospel: that we are more lost and sinful than we ever dared believe, but are more loved and accepted than we ever dared hope."

"That's beautiful," Mansfield said.

Edward smiled. "The gospel is beautiful." He rested his head against the high back of his chair and closed his eyes. "'For we do not preach ourselves, but Jesus Christ as Lord, and ourselves as your servants for Jesus' sake. For God, who said "Let light shine out of darkness," made His light shine in our hearts to give us the light of the knowledge of the glory of God in the face of Jesus Christ.'"

He opened his eyes, looking at his visitor with bright eyes. "He is our all. Without Him, we are nothing."

For a long moment, neither man said anything.

"It sounds," Mansfield said quietly, "like your family is doing no more than all Christian families should affirm as their common practice."

"Yes, absent the specific responsibility for Harvard—which is given to us for no other reason than His undeserved mercy—that is true. But we are weak and sinful, and perhaps it takes a visit from a warrior angel to get the idea across."

Mansfield chuckled. He paused again. "Edward, you're a man of purpose, and I am honored that you would share this private story with me. Why are you telling me this?"

Edward's eyes suddenly twinkled. "I knew you would get around to that question sooner or later." He patted the book on his lap. "We believe God was speaking the literal truth when he said there would be a Grindley descendent as an ambassador of Christ at Harvard for every generation to come. We therefore have tried to keep track of the ever-widening circle of Grindley descendants so that we would know when someone with the Grindley mantle was at Harvard, but—as you can imagine—after more than three hundred years, it's a big job.

"The direct Grindleys—those with the family name—we have largely been able to keep track of. A percentage of those—as well as some other close relatives—are in what you might call the inner circle, who know of our God-given heritage and calling and actively pray for His purposes at Harvard."

"How many people is that, if you don't mind my asking?"

"No, I don't mind. I would imagine—oh—we're at about three hundred now."

"Three hundred! In just the inner circle?"

Edward chuckled. "Oh yes. Remember, we have thousands upon thousands in our extended family. The inner circle are just those—whether sharing the Grindley name or not—whose commitment to Christ is firm and who have been raised up from childhood to participate in our special calling. There are many thousands of other Christians in our line who do not know."

He pursed his lips. "Unfortunately, as I mentioned when I first met you, as our family fortune diminished during the Great Depression, so did our access to Harvard's highest corridors of power. We have had several dozen students at Harvard since that time, as well as two professors, but no board members or anyone else in policy leadership."

The old man rubbed his hands gently over the cover of the book, his expression sober. "In the last few decades, our fight has dramatically increased, and our access has diminished. We have seen the need for anointed ambassadors of Christ become more and more urgent, but there has been no one with the Grindley mantle raised up to speak out and pierce that veil as God promised would happen in *every* generation!

"In the spirit, we have felt that the enemy has become stronger and stronger, fed by the increasingly dark climate of pride, greed, and a purposeful drawing away from

holiness and the things of God. The evil one has—partly through his work in the edu-
cational system—largely succeeded in establishing secularism as the politically correct
norm in this country, rather than faith-based convictions.

"Thankfully, to counter this, children of God from all around the world have been
brought here to be candles shining in the darkness, and the level of prayer has dramatically increased—as it always does during troublesome periods. But I also feel a
responsibility, as the direct heir of Gage Grindley, to find those with this special anointing to speak out and see eyes opened, to speak the Truth and have people *hear* rather
than think it foolishness. I know that our God has promised such a person—multiple
persons!—in every generation, and He is faithful!

"Recently I realized that I could not simply wait for our great-grandchildren to
reach an age when they could apply to Harvard. I came to the conclusion that God
might already have someone with that mantle in place and that it was my responsibility
to go out and find those individuals and tell them of their special calling, that they
might step into the role God has for them."

Edward looked at Mansfield with mirthful eyes. "In fact, when I went back
through our history, I found quite often that there were Grindley descendants at Harvard who were Christians but who had never heard of the special calling God might
have on their lives."

Mansfield was fascinated. "When will you start looking through the documents
and such?"

"We already have found our Grindley, and that is why we need your help."

"I'm afraid I don't know of any Grindleys at Harvard."

"Oh yes, you do."

"Who?"

"You."

Edward flipped the book open, his eyes amused at Mansfield's astonished expression. "We have a service that tracks our family tree and publishes an update every ten
years or so—it's far too large for a nonprofessional to do it." He held the book out to
Mansfield, pointing at a particular page.

Mansfield slowly took the book, which was open to a family-tree diagram that
spread across two pages. He saw the names of his paternal grandparents and parents, a
vertical line, and then in a neat typeface like all the others "William David Mansfield,
1935–__" Beside his name a line stretched to another box: "Mary Bradford Mansfield
(née Bradford), 1936–1992."

Edward's quiet voice floated into Mansfield's consciousness. "You are not the only
Grindley descendent we have currently found at Harvard, but you are the only one we
are approaching. At various times throughout our history, we have sought out people

like you and offered support and instruction about our heritage. Some don't get it, but it's interesting that—even among those with no knowledge of our family calling—there is a very high percentage of Christians in our extended line. God really does bless the children of the righteous man to the thousandth generation."

Mansfield grappled with the revelation, a bemused smile on his face. "What is it that you want me to do?"

Edward leaned forward, his face intent. "You now know that you, Dr. Mansfield, have an awesome responsibility. Do not give the Crist lecture to someone else; speak out yourself. Even though your willingness to bring in others is admirable, *you* have an anointing that must be released. God must have a great plan to use this as an opportunity to speak out at Harvard—not about history, but about *His Story*. It presumably won't be an enormous crowd, but God can do anything. And, as the angel said, 'When the hearers of the Word shall turn to the Lord, the veil shall be taken away.'"

"How did you know I was asked to do the Crist lecture?"

Edward sat back, his old eyes twinkling, "I have my sources, cousin. I have my sources."

# FORTY-EIGHT

"WHERE WERE YOU?"

Claire's heart sank as she heard the edge in Ian's voice. She gripped the receiver tighter. "I'm so sorry…"

"Don't apologize. Just tell me what happened."

"I don't think…" She closed her eyes, her emotions drained. She just wanted to go to sleep. "I don't think I can."

A pause. Ian's voice was quiet. "What?"

"I don't think I can tell you. I was helping a friend with something personal, and I don't think I should talk about it."

"Claire, you have a job. If you're going to keep this job, we have to depend on you. Three days ago you were assigned a task—a fairly simple one—and I didn't find out that you weren't doing it until tonight. And by then, all the offices I could have called were closed."

"But—"

"I can't spend time calling around tomorrow morning. I have class. Can you do the advance work tomorrow morning before Mansfield's class?"

Claire's voice was quiet. "I have class at 9:30, and then Mansfield's test at 11:00. I'll have to do the advance work in the afternoon."

"Well, if that's the case, it looks like we're not going to be able to start the research until Friday. And that means that anything we find is going to have to be investigated next week, which will be too late. I just found out there's something going on that's even more strange than we thought, but we have to know something by this Friday." Claire heard a short sigh on the other end of the line. "I'm sorry to get irritated. But this is really frustrating."

"I know. I'm so sorry."

"Yeah." A short laugh. "Well, I'll see you tomorrow in class. Good luck on the test."

"Okay."

There was a click, and Claire put down the receiver slowly. She crept to the bed, not even bothering to change her clothes, and crawled under the covers. She pulled Eeyore tight to her chest and curled up into a ball.

*God, I know I made the right decision. Thank You for Bethany and the choice she made. O God, defend me with Mansfield and Ian, and help me still do well on the test.*

She thought of all the heavy books stacked on her desk, and her eyes opened with a jolt. She groaned, then jammed her face into her pillow. *And God, help me find a stupid backpack tomorrow before class. And give me a way to find that information for Mansfield in the morning!*

God cared even about the little things, she told herself. Her prayers trailed off as her weary mind drifted into sleep.

Across the room, the gaze of a giant angel was gentle on his charge. "Trust, Claire. The plans of God Almighty are perfect."

Gael watched from above as the class broke up, the test takers stretching in their seats. The professor left by the side door, and the young woman tentatively approached the unsmiling TA on the podium.

The angel kept an eye on the smirking enemy forces in the room, as the two young people exchanged words. Gael shook his head at the tone Ian was using. That was not going to get them anywhere. And with the events playing out today...

Gael took a position above the young man, speaking urgently to him. *"Tell her about D. J."*

"You won't know until *when?"* Ian's voice was sharp as he looked at Claire.

"I'm sorry, Ian. I tried. I even left my sociology class halfway through and called around. I think I found the right office—over in one of the finance areas—but they said I need to talk to the resource director, and he wouldn't be back until three o'clock. I've left a message for him to call me then."

A short sigh. "Well, thanks for trying."

"Ian, I wish I could explain. I think you'd—"

"That's okay."

Gael tried speaking his message again, but the young man didn't even pause. "And we're obviously not going to worry about lunch today. Mansfield said he'd take the opportunity to get in on some meeting he should be at, and I'm going to try to catch up on my studying. Call me tonight with where we're meeting tomorrow. I'll explain the whole thing then."

"I will. Definitely."

Gael watched in frustration as Ian nodded and walked out the side door. Claire headed back to her desk. Several HCF students came up, and one clapped her on the shoulder.

"You okay?"

"Oh. Yeah." Claire smiled. "Just got a lot to do."

"Well, can you do it after lunch?" At Claire's nod, the student began steering her out the door. "We're meeting up with the gang for lunch at Annenberg to talk about the barbecue on Saturday."


Gael shot across campus, pulling up near several angels in conference on the lawn by Memorial Hall, the lunchtime crowd like city traffic at rush hour.

Gael gave a respectful, if brief, salute to his commanding officer. "Kai, she intends to go to Annenburg with the other saints. Has the second thread been pulled?"

"Yes, by the good hand of God, the unraveling is beginning at this moment." Kai pondered. "Annenburg will not work." He looked at the lunch rush in and out of the building.

Gael followed his eyes. The traffic through the main doors was heavy as students headed for the Sanders Theater classroom or Annenburg dining hall. Gael shifted his view to the outside steps that led to the basement of Memorial Hall. He tapped Kai's shoulder, drawing his attention to the relatively clear stairway. "Loker Commons has a television near the food court."

"Good. Make it so." Kai turned to one of the other angels. "Metras, go to the law school and ensure the timing will work. Listen for the Spirit's direction when the press conference starts."

He turned back to Gael. "Do not delay. Once you know the number of saints who will be eating with Claire, call for reinforcements to hold a table."

"Gladly. I'll even get in on the action myself."


"Nuts." Claire and seven others approached the throngs heading for Annenberg. "We're never going to sit together."

She felt a tug on the sleeve of her coat. Doug Turner was pointing toward another set of stairs. "Anyone up for pizza?"

The group hurried down the outside stairs and through the doors. Claire frowned at the packed tables near the food court, trying to stifle her impatience. Maybe she should just go back to her room.

"I don't think—"

Suddenly she spotted a large group rising from some nearby tables that had been pushed together. They began gathering up trays, empty glasses, and burger wrappers. She hurried over.

"Are you all leaving?"

A tall young man smiled down at her. "Absolutely." He gestured to the tables. "Be our guest."

Claire beckoned to the others standing by the doors. Her friends pushed through the tables, passing the outgoing group with nods and thanks.

Teresa pulled up next to her. "How do you always *do* that?"

Claire shrugged, a genuine grin growing on her face.

Ten minutes later, Claire thankfully tucked into her food. Doug cocked an eyebrow at her, a humorous expression on his face. "You're weird, you know that?"

"Hey! Everyone uses a fork and knife to eat pizza." The others at the table looked on in amusement as Claire cut another piece and used the fork to pop it into her mouth.

"Not everyone where I come from, babe. In fact, in my uncle's pizza parlor, that could get you tossed out the door on your hind end."

"Your uncle owns a pizza parlor? Cool. Where?"

"In Lansing, Michigan."

"No kidding? I didn't know you were from Michigan!"

"Really? I thought you did. I met you at the Michigan students dinner during orientation."

"You were there?" Claire bit her lip as several of their friends guffawed. "I totally don't remember meeting you."

Doug smiled slightly. "Well, I remember meeting you."

Claire watched the fleeting look on his face and ducked her head before the others saw the flush on her cheeks. Out of the corner of her eye, she saw Teresa grinning into her soda.

A commotion of some kind erupted from the lounge area beside the food court. Several students came hurrying out of a side room that held a giant television screen, gesturing for friends at nearby tables to join them.

Doug caught one such student on the fly. "Hey—what's going on?"

The young man delivered the news with great relish. "It's wild! The FBI just busted an investment banker for embezzlement—some guy who graduated from here just a few years ago." The young man moved toward the lounge, speaking over his shoulder. "The networks are all interrupting their shows and talking about it. CNN's on in the lounge."

Claire, Doug, and the others glanced at each other, then rapidly pushed back their chairs and piled toward the side room, mingling with the dozens of other students who were pressing into the small space, staring at the large screen on the wall.

The television transitioned from a commercial to CNN's musical introduction, and the camera tightened in on the good-looking male and female anchors sitting behind their long desk.

"Good afternoon." The woman's face was intent. "Thank you for joining us. I'm Dylan Keelan."

"And I'm Bob Hummer."

A logo appeared on the screen beside his head, the gold letters *KCP* intertwined on a black background.

"Let's go right to our top story," he looked down at some notes. "This morning, rumors hit the street of a possible federal investigation into the business practices of venerable investment bank Keppler, Collins, and Preston."

A switch of view, and the female anchor spoke, a picture of a young man appearing in the air by her head. "Roughly one hour ago, FBI agents arrested this man, Murphy Barker, a banker and strategist with KCP, in connection with a drug-running operation in Peru. Mr. Barker, who graduated from Harvard University with honors just four years ago, is being charged with insider trading, embezzlement, money laundering, and possibly drug trafficking."

The small lounge room began to buzz, the students talking over the sound of the anchor's voice.

*"Quiet!"*

A woman sitting in the front of the room was holding up her arms for silence, her face intent on the screen above her.

The male anchor turned toward the camera. "Since the rumors began this morning, KCP's stock price has taken a beating. After the arrest, KCP executives decried the actions of their associate and asserted that any embezzlement will have no material impact on their earnings this quarter. They have vowed to cooperate fully with the federal investigation."

"Wait a moment." He pressed his hand against his earpiece then looked back into the camera. "Okay. We will now go live to a press conference with the U.S. Attorney for the southern district of New York, who just a few minutes ago left the investment bank after meeting with KCP officers."

The scene switched, and the camera showed a man in a trench coat answering reporters' questions on the sidewalk in front of the massive KCP doors.

"…we do have some evidence that Mr. Murphy Barker had a long-standing connection with this drug cartel. In fact, it's possible that Mr. Barker specifically took the job at Keppler, Collins, and Preston in order to infiltrate Wall Street on behalf of the cartel."

The room of students began to buzz again, this time in whispers, all eyes riveted on the screen.

"Mr. Barker primarily worked in the division of KCP that did mergers, acquisitions, and financing for pharmaceutical companies worldwide. The records are very difficult to follow, but it appears that the drug kingpins were intending to finance his MBA when he entered business school next fall."

A reporter shouted a question, and the U.S. Attorney responded, his expression sober. "Well, we think the reason was that once he got his MBA, he could return to his 'undercover' work at a higher level. One last question."

The U.S. Attorney called on the last reporter and leaned forward, trying to hear over the traffic noise. He stood straighter and looked back at the larger group. "We don't know exactly how he originally got involved with the cartel. The records are spotty, and unless Mr. Barker cooperates fully—which he is not currently doing—it's possible we'll never know the full connection. One possibility arises from the summer internship Mr. Barker did in Peru after his sophomore year at Harvard. It's possible that he got hooked up with the cartel then, completed his major in business, and went off to Wall Street to work for his real bosses."

The U.S. Attorney's expression turned ironic as he looked into the cameras. "It used to be that businessmen became criminals; Now it appears that criminals are becoming businessmen." He held up a hand. "Thank you very much." He pulled up the collar of his coat and stepped quickly to a waiting car. The cameras followed him as he folded himself into the car, and was gone.

The shot returned to the CNN anchors, who explained that they would be back after a short break. The small lounge room broke up in a flurry of discussions and excited gestures. Claire watched as the woman in front stood up slowly, her expression blank, and begin to make her way back through the crowd.

Claire caught her eye as she went by. "Pretty weird, isn't it?"

The woman paused and looked at her, then back to the television screen. "Yes, it is. I'm really blindsided by this. I was in school with Murphy, and I was in Peru with him on that sophomore trip—"

Doug's head whipped around. "Are you serious?"

"Yes." She looked unsettled and her face was pale. "Look, I should be going. I have to write my third-year paper and—"

"Are you a grad student?" Doug gestured toward their abandoned table. "Please. Join us for a minute. Can I get you a soda or something?"

Claire scooted ahead to the food court and brought back a tall glass of ice. "What would you like—water, Coke…?"

"Oh, um, a Diet Coke would be great. Thank you."

A minute later Claire was back with the drink. "Here you go."

"Thank you." The woman looked at the others around the table and smiled slightly. "I guess I'm pretty out of it. Sorry."

Doug smiled and held out his hand. "That's okay. I'm Doug."

"I'm Patrice."

Doug introduced the others around the table, and they nodded and murmured greetings.

Claire caught her eye and smiled briefly. "It must be awful to have one of your friends from school do something like this."

"Yeah. Well, Murphy was never a close friend, but we did know each other. We had a lot of business classes together, plus the two Machu Picchu trips."

"Machu Picchu?" Claire sat back in her chair, startled.

"Yeah. See, we were both majoring in business and had an interest in international finance. He knew I was into Latin American stuff—I speak fluent Spanish—and he told me about the class on the history of the Incas that went down to Machu Picchu over the holidays."

"I remember seeing that during orientation."

"Yeah, they do it almost every year. Anyway, I think the news got it wrong. I don't think he ever did a summer internship there, but he did go down during two winter breaks."

"Was that when he got mixed up with these people the DA was talking about?" Doug asked.

Patrice clenched her fists, her voice rising. "I don't know! I just don't know. But I knew there was *something* strange going on. He and Stefan would go off every weekend and—"

"Wait!" Claire stretched her hand flat on the table. "Who did you say?"

"What…Stefan? Yeah." Patrice laughed sourly. "The favorite son. It drove me crazy that I was a senior and this little pip-squeak freshman was running rings around me just because his daddy was on the faculty."

Claire went cold, barely noticing the good-natured protests from the other "little pip-squeak freshmen" around the table. "Excuse me," she broke into their dialogue. "What is Stefan's last name?" Claire saw Doug and the others looking at her curiously. "And what do you mean 'his daddy was on the faculty'?"

"Oh, you know. That business professor who taught my multinationals class. Stefan was his son, and boy was he arrogant. He—"

"But what was his *name,* Patrice?" Claire rose to her feet.

"Oh, man, I don't remember. *P*-something." She must have seen the expression on Claire's face; she looked up at her curiously. "Well, okay, don't get all upset. Hold on…he taught multinationals, finance, maybe corporate strat—Pike!" She snapped her fingers, even as an icy jolt shot through Claire. "Right, Professor Pike. Because Stefan and Murphy were as thick as thieves in Peru doing some independent study project or something for him, although personally I think Stefan was just out for a good time—"

Claire grabbed her coat and backpack while the others picked up with questions about Murphy Barker and the Peru trip. She had a feeling of complete unreality as she pulled on her gloves.

"Hey." The voice was close by her head.

Claire jumped and turned toward Doug's concerned face. His voice was quiet. "What's going on?" The other students at the table were still in animated discussion with Patrice.

"I don't know, Doug. Something weird, and I can't talk about it. It has to do with this research project I'm doing for Professor Mansfield."

"Okay." Doug folded his arms across his chest. "But this is more than just worry about a research project. What's wrong?"

Claire suddenly found her eyes misting. "I honestly don't know, Doug. Just—just pray for my roommate, Sherry, okay?"

"Sherry?"

"Yes!"

Claire took a step toward the door, then noticed the fleeting hurt look on Doug's face. She forced herself to stop and turn toward her friend.

"I'm sorry, Doug. I'm really worried—as you can tell." She lowered her voice. "Look. I've been worried about Sherry because she's letting her boyfriend influence her—you know—away from God. And now I find out that her boyfriend was friends with the investment banker that just got arrested."

"Stefan Pike is Sherry's boyfriend? I didn't know that."

"There's a lot more to it than this, but I can't go into it. Just pray for her, okay?"

"Yes. Okay. Get out of here." Doug shooed her toward the door.

Within moments Claire was through the doors, walking as quickly as she could toward her dorm.

## FORTY-NINE

CLAIRE TOOK THE STAIRS TWO AT A TIME, then slowed as she approached the door to her suite. She didn't know exactly what was wrong, just that something was.

Claire entered the suite and saw Sherry's sweater thrown over the couch, heard the music through the half-open door to their shared bedroom.

She pushed open the door. Sherry looked up from her desk. "Hey."

"Hey." Claire forced a smile as she shed her coat. "How's your day?"

"Fine. Hey, you got a phone call from a guy in some finance office. The resource director, he said. I wrote it down. He said he was back early from a meeting and was about to leave town for a week, and if you wanted to talk to him you have to call by 1:30."

Claire looked at the clock by her bed. 1:25. *O Lord...*

She hurried to her desk. As she picked up the phone, she saw Sherry pulling on a sweater. "You going somewhere?"

"Yeah. Stefan and I are heading down to Boston to walk around Fanueil Hall. We'll probably have dinner down there somewhere."

Claire looked at the clock, closed her eyes in a desperate prayer, and hung up the phone. "Uh, look, can I mention something to you?"

"Yeah." Sherry was looking in the mirror, straightening her collar.

"Stefan's last name is Pike, right?"

"Yeah."

"He's gone to Peru on the Machu Picchu trip, hasn't he?"

"Yeah. He's gone every year."

Claire took a deep breath. "Did you know that one of his friends—an investment banker named Murphy who graduated a few years back—was just arrested for a drug-running scheme he hooked up with on that trip?"

"What?" Sherry swung around.

"I just saw it on CNN." Claire shot a desperate glance at the clock and picked up the receiver. "I have to tell you more, but can you possibly wait a sec while I call this guy back?"

"Nope. I'm almost late as it is. You want to say something, say it now." She looked at Claire, her arms folded across her chest.

Claire set the receiver back down. "Sherry, it's just that you've been…different in the last few weeks. You aren't interested in HCF or church, you're over at Stefan's at all hours, or out with his friends…none of whom are Christians."

She shot a glance at her roommate. Sherry's lips were pressed together in a tight line. Claire straightened. "I'm concerned that Stefan's drawing you away from God. That—"

"Don't be. You just look out for yourself. I can take care of myself."

"I'm sure you can. I'm not trying to be your baby-sitter."

"Oh, really?"

"Yes, really. But I *am* your accountability partner, and I'm concerned about what I've seen with Stefan. Take this thing with his friend from the Peru trip. There's some weird stuff going on related to the Pikes." She held up the receiver to the phone. "That's even what this research for Mansfield is about, why I have to go talk to this finance guy right away. How well do you really know Stefan Pike, anyway?"

Sherry's voice was droll. "Oh, I know him *very* well."

Claire's intended words caught in her throat. She looked into Sherry's eyes. "I gather there's something you haven't told me about your relationship with Stefan."

"Nothing that's any of your business." Sherry stepped to her closet and pulled out a coat. "Claire, I appreciate your concern. Truly. But if you're implying that Stefan could be mixed up in some drug-running scheme just because a friend of his was busted—"

"That's not what I—"

"—then that's quite insulting." Sherry zipped up her coat and pulled some gloves from her pocket. "I'm going now."

Claire stood up, reaching for her roommate's sleeve. "Sherry, if you'd just listen a minute!"

Sherry swung around, her face close to Claire's, her eyes angry. "I think I've listened quite enough. I can't believe you would seriously impugn the guy I'm in love with just because you saw some news report about a former classmate he probably hardly knows. What a ridiculous…unfounded…mean-spirited…" She jabbed her finger toward Claire. "You will do anything to tear Stefan down in my eyes, and I think I've had quite enough."

"I'm not tearing him down—"

"Just stop." Sherry held up a hand. "I'm sure when you think about it, you'll realize how stupid you look right now. I'm leaving. You can apologize later for being so ugly."

She swept out the door with a bang.

Claire let out a shuddering breath. She hung her head, rubbing the back of her neck. In the next instant, her head shot up. The clock read 1:33. She grabbed the slip of paper bearing Sherry's neat handwriting and punched the numbers. Her hands were shaking as she listened to the ringing. *O God, Mansfield's going to fire me. Please help me catch this guy!*

The ringing stopped and she heard the telltale clicks and pauses of a voice mail system.

"You've reached the desk of the resource director. I will be out of the office from…"

*O God, O God, what do I do?*

"…but leave a message and I will call you back as soon as I return. Thank you."

*Beep!*

Claire hesitated, then pressed the zero button on her telephone.

"Front Desk. Can I help you?"

"Yes, I was trying to return the resource director's call, but I just got his voice mail. Has he actually left yet?"

"I'm sorry, but I do believe he's already left for the day. Can I take a message?"

Claire's stomach twisted. "No. I don't suppose that you'd be willing to check and make sure he's actually left…would you?"

A pause. "Well, if you'll hold on a moment, let me get rid of some of these calls, and then I'll walk back to his office."

Claire held the line, listening vaguely to the soft music as she tried to think of how she would tell Ian and Mansfield about her failure.

The phone clicked. "Well, young lady, you're in luck. He was just walking by my desk on the way out. He's in a bit of a hurry, but let me transfer you."

*Thank You! Thank You!*

Claire heard a male voice come on the line. "Is this Claire Rivers?"

"Yes sir. Thank you for taking my call. Sorry to catch you on the way out, but—"

"I'm afraid I'm going to be away for the next ten days or so. The good news is that the type of information you're looking for *is* here in our computer system, but once I lock my resource room you won't have access until I return. Our security procedures are strict."

"Oh, sir, I don't want to be any trouble, but this is a really time-sensitive research project. Is there *any* way someone there can let me in?"

"I have a clerk, but he's not authorized to let anyone in before I get their access letter."

"Well—" Claire gripped the phone tighter—"how about if I came over right now? Would you be willing to leave your office open and have the clerk take my access letter and show me around? Then he could lock up after I leave today?"

"Hmm." Claire could hear a drumming noise on the other end of the line. "You aren't easily dissuaded, are you?"

"No sir."

"Did you say that Dr. Mansfield authorized this research?"

"Yes sir."

A pause. "Well, let me tell you what. Technically I'm supposed to be present while you look at the system, but I'd be willing to make an exception as long as I can personally log you in."

Claire jumped to her feet.

"If you get over here within the next ten minutes, I'll hold the door open for you. But after that, I'm going to lock it and leave. I'm already late."

"Thank you, sir. You're a godsend!"

A dry chuckle. "Well, I don't know about that, but I'll take whatever I can get. Hold on a moment."

The voice became muffled, and Claire could hear some talking in the background. His voice came back on the line. "My clerk will also be in and out, and he's willing to police the research so that confidentiality is protected."

"Thank you so much, sir! I'll be right there."

Claire stuffed her research notebook into her backpack, grabbed her coat, and hurried out the door. A vague sense of unease arose as she locked the door, fumbling with her keys. She was embarking on this without Ian and Mansfield. She was just a freshman! What sort of upstart would they label her?

Exactly nine minutes later Claire arrived at the proper office, out of breath and looking at her watch.

The receptionist pressed a button on the phone. She grinned, looking up at Claire's flushed face as she spoke into the intercom. "I think she's here, sir."

A disembodied voice rose from the box. "Lucky girl. My hand was on the door-knob. Send her back."

"I'm assuming you're Claire Rivers," the receptionist said.

It took a second for Claire to answer. "Yes, ma'am."

"Sign here." She held out a clipboard. "And indicate which senior faculty member is requesting this information. The records are private, so we have to have that authorization. I'll also need to see your authorization letter."

"Yes, ma'am." Her breathing was coming easier. She scribbled her name and Mansfield's in the appropriate places and handed over the note he had written.

The receptionist perused the note, took back the clipboard, and jerked her head. "Down that corridor. The last room on the left. The one with all the boxes."

Claire headed down the corridor. *All the boxes?* She was passing glass-fronted offices on the left and rows of cubicles on the right. There were a lot of office workers around but very little noise.

A short man with wiry white hair stepped halfway out a doorway, beckoning to her. She quickened her pace and held out her hand.

"Thank you, sir! Thank you so much—"

"Yes, yes, yes." He shook her hand once then steered her into a glass-fronted room with a hand against her back. He couldn't have been any taller than she was. "No accolades needed. Let's just set you up here and get me on my way."

Claire looked around in surprise. One whole side of the long, narrow room was stacked floor to ceiling with cardboard boxes.

His eyes followed hers. "We're modernizing." He hurried her to the opposite end of the room toward a bank of computers. "All those records are finally on-line. Took two years. Those are going to storage. Sit here."

He pulled out a chair in front of a terminal, propelling Claire into the seat. She looked up at his intent profile, his wild mop of hair.

"What do I...?"

"Just wait. I must log you on. Write down the instructions." He smiled as his fingers flew over the keyboard, pulling up several different programs and typing in his private passwords.

Claire pulled a notebook and pen out of her backpack and listened carefully to his instructions, writing as fast as she could.

"...the printers are over there, and if for some reason you need to get onto Harvard's intranet you can do that here." He patted another terminal. "The one you're at is not on-line, so no one can hack into it. The one you're at, by the way, also contains our proprietary alumni database. Much more extensive detail than the one you'll find on the intranet, but it's also a lot more difficult to use, so I don't recommend it." He stared at her from under bushy brows. His eyes twinkled. "Got all that?"

"I hope so. What happens if I need help?"

"My clerk is around. He's supervising the moving of those boxes. He'll be back for another load at some point. The movers will be working all weekend."

Claire took a deep breath. "Okay."

"I hope you find everything you need. I'll be back Monday-after-next if you need anything more."

"Thank you, sir."

The director smiled, nodded, and grabbed an attaché case off a nearby desk. "Good luck, miss." He walked quickly down the long room and out the door. Claire watched through the glass in the upper half of the wall as he hurried along the corridor, heading toward the exit like a short Albert Einstein with a briefcase.

Claire let out a breath and turned back toward the terminal. She tapped tentatively, then with more confidence, as she perused screen after screen of scholarships, student grants, work-study programs. There were many listings to check, but the time flew by under Claire's eager fingers. She pulled up the next section, typing in the usual query: Pike Fellowships.

And there it was. Her lips parted as the screen flickered. "One category found. Processing." A small hourglass appeared in place of the cursor, and then a summary screen appeared. Claire squealed in triumph as the bold heading appeared at the top of the page. "Pike Fellowships, Private Scholarship."

She forced herself to take a deep breath, then leaned forward, biting her lip hard as she scanned the page. It was packed with text. She began muttering to herself, reading the stark, technical summary.

"Private scholarship. Endowed. Restricted. Unpublished; no applications. Description on file: Controlled by the Pike Trust, granted to juniors and seniors of the proper character and standing. Full tuition. Stipend case by case. Crosstrust cooperation necessary with the following universities."

Claire's eyes flickered down the list of mostly Ivy League schools, and the names and phone numbers of the appropriate contacts. Then there was a bunch of technical information about banks, investments, and other legal language. There were also links to more details. At the very bottom was the line, "All recipients chosen by designees of Pike Holdings. Current designees: Anton Pike, Victor Pike."

She leaned back in her chair. "What is Pike Holdings?"


Sherry grabbed Stefan's hand as they headed down the escalator toward the T. She held it tight, her thoughts indignant. What a ludicrous, mean-spirited attack. The nerve of Claire!

They arrived at the platform. The track was empty, but the area was crowded with people. Stefan leaned against a railing to wait, and Sherry backed into him, inviting him to put his arms around her. He did, holding her hands and rubbing his thumb softly along her fingers. She could hear the train approaching.

"When you were on the Machu Picchu trip, did you ever see anything strange going on?" Sherry asked.

The thumb stopped moving. "What?"

"Claire was just telling me about some guy who was on that trip a few years ago, who got arrested in New York, and—"

"What!" He swiveled her around, staring into her eyes.

The train arrived in a rush, the doors smoothly opening. She tugged him toward the doors. "Come on, I'll tell you on the train."

He hung back, his face tense. "Claire told you what?"

Sherry pulled on his arm, moving him through the doors and onto the train. "She just said that she saw some friend of yours busted on CNN for drug-running."

"Do you remember his name?"

"M-something. Sounded like it could be a—"

"Murphy?"

"Yeah, that might've been it. She—"

He started for the doors just as they closed in his face. He turned slowly, and Sherry was taken aback by the dark look on his face.

"How did Claire know that Murphy was a friend of mine?"

"I don't know. She said she was doing research or something, and this had come up. I wasn't listening very closely. I was too angry that she was implying something bad about you."

"Well." A rigid smile appeared on Stefan's face, and he put his arm around her, steering her toward an empty seat in the back of the car. "Why don't you sit down and tell me what you do remember."

She sat in a single seat tucked back in the corner of the car. He stood over her, asking soft questions. She gave soft answers: Claire had been upset…Murphy was arrested for drug-running or something…Claire questioned how well Sherry knew Stefan…she was doing some sort of research on the Pikes…

"Keep going."

"That's pretty much it. I'd taken a phone message that she was in a hurry to return—her research for Mansfield on something—and I had to meet you."

"What message?"

"I don't really know."

"Well, you took the message!" Stefan slammed his fist against the bulkhead of the train car. Sherry started to her feet.

"Sit down."

Sherry looked into his eyes, quivering slightly, but stayed standing.

His voice was soft as he leaned his face close to hers. "You took the message. What did it say?"

"What's going on, Stefan?" Her voice was shaky. "What's wrong?"

"What did the message say, Sherry?"

She sat down and took a calming breath. "I'm not telling you anything until you tell me what's going on."

A fleeting rage crossed Stefan's face, and then he sighed and shrugged. "I'm really not supposed to talk about this, but I suppose with you it's okay." He glanced around before he lowered his voice. "One of our main pharmaceutical competitors has been trying to get us in trouble with the regulators for years, and they've just stepped it up. They're trying to harass us by impugning our people and inviting audits and investigations by the government, trying to get us shut down. And now they seem to have set up poor Murphy."

"But…he doesn't work for your uncle. Claire said Murphy was an investment banker."

"Well, yes, he is. But he's *our* investment banker, so to speak." He cleared his throat. "He works for a big investment bank in New York that represents us, and he's one of our bankers. So by setting him up, this competitor is really harassing us."

"Oh."

"And…I hate to say this, but we've discovered that Mansfield is actually working with this competitor as a consultant."

"Oh!"

Stefan crouched down by her seat and looked into her eyes. "So you see, there's a possibility that Claire is an unwitting pawn in a devious strategy concocted by our competitor. So you can see why I really need you to remember what that message said."

"Yes. What a shame. Well, let me think. This guy called…" She closed her eyes, reciting the words as they came to mind. "He said Claire had left him a message asking if she could come over to his office, but he was leaving earlier than expected, at one-thirty."

Stefan glanced at his watch. As Sherry told him the caller's title and office, Stefan's mouth tightened into a hard line.

"I kinda got the impression she was in a hurry to get over there. She may be there right now."

Stefan stared at the dark tunnel outside the windows as the train wound its way toward their stop in Boston. He muttered to himself.

Sherry sat back, relieved. Thank goodness she'd been able to remember that message!


Claire sat straighter in her chair. She'd have to worry about Pike Holdings later. She clicked print on the summary screen. Across the room she heard the paper going through the printer, and she put her notebook back in her backpack. Easier than writing it all down, that was for sure.

She looked at the details on the monitor one more time, then started paging through the other screens on this scholarship. She muttered under her breath, frustrated. But after a few minutes, her eyes lit up. *Aha!*

It took just a moment, and she was eagerly scanning the Recipients section. The screen was filled with a list of years the scholarship had been granted. She frowned slightly. The record was shorter than expected, starting in 1985. *Probably since they computerized the records.*

She swung around in her chair and stared at the cardboard boxes behind her. If more was in there, she'd never find it. She turned back to the computer, sighing. But that nice old man had said the boxes contained only records that had been modernized, so the information had to be here somewhere.

At least they now knew the old Pike Fellowship was being granted in the modern day. She just needed to work with what she had. But where to start? She felt unsettled, rudderless. Suddenly, she sat upright in her chair. She hadn't told Ian where she was!

Claire walked down the corridor toward the receptionist's station. "Excuse me."

The receptionist looked up in surprise.

Claire smiled. "I'm sorry to bother you."

"It's no bother." The receptionist pressed a few buttons on her telephone and smiled. "What can I do for you...Claire Rivers, right?"

"That's right. I need to make a phone call about this research. Can I use one of the phones in the office or...?"

The receptionist gestured to a telephone on the side of her desk. "Dial 9 to get out."

"Great."

Claire dialed Ian's number, turning away slightly from the receptionist's friendly gaze. The phone rang several times, then Ian's voice mail picked up. *Rats.*

Her voice was soft. "Ian, this is Claire. I hope you get this message soon. Listen, you're not going to believe what happened. I found the right place, but ended up having to rush over here before it closed because they were going to be closed for the next ten days. And I found the records we were looking for. It looks really promising, but I wanted to be sure I called you so you could come over here."

She described the location of the office and how to find the resource room, then glanced at her watch. "I hope you get this message soon. It's two-thirty now. I'm a little uncertain as to how to proceed, and this place closes in a few hours. See you soon. I hope."

She hung up the phone and asked the receptionist to keep an eye out for her research partner. "And one other thing. When will the clerk be back?"

The receptionist looked at a list on her desk. "Oh, not that long now. He's probably taking a coffee break."

"Okay, thanks."

Within minutes Claire was back at the terminal, pondering her next move. Available class years were displayed on the screen in front of her. *1987...1991...2000.* She randomly picked *1989* and clicked on it.

Three names popped up. There were a bunch of technical codes—letters like *FN* or *MT*—beside their names, but no other identifying information, and no dollar amounts of their scholarships.

She called up recipients from another year. Six names and the codes. None of the names were familiar.

Sighing, she went to another list, from four years before. Six names again.

*Murphy Barker*

*Johanna Godfrey*

*Gregory Granville III*

*Soraya Maljanian*

*Paolo Ramirez*

*Heather Stephenson*

She stared, aghast, at the first name on the screen, then slapped her forehead. She should have thought to check that before!

She pressed print again and went to pick up the page from the printer, leaving the first still in the tray. She started to sit back down, then suddenly headed for the terminal the resource director had said was connected to Harvard's intranet.

*I wonder where all these grads are working now?*

THE TRAIN SLOWED TO A STOP IN BOSTON, and Stefan grabbed Sherry's hand and pushed through the thick crowd toward the exit, incurring irritated glances from other travelers.

Sherry smiled sheepishly at the other commuters as Stefan cut into the line waiting for the long escalator up to ground level. He pulled her onto the motorized stairway, then reached into his pocket and pulled out a slim cell phone and checked the signal.

Stefan swore and shook the phone, as if that would bring up a signal. He looked up the steep escalator at the slowly growing square of daylight above them, then gazed intently at the phone's small screen. "Come on, you piece of junk!"


Claire hummed to herself as she tapped out her name and password on the second terminal. In a moment she was on-line. She fumbled around for a minute before figuring out how to access the alumni database that listed the names, phone numbers, and current employment of Harvard graduates.

She smiled. You could do anything through Career Services. They made sure their alumni network would be open to all Harvard job seekers! This was probably a lot more user-friendly than the proprietary alumni database the resource director had mentioned. She typed in the first name on her list. The screen flickered, and his name appeared, one of a huge list.

*Murphy Barker.* There were several lines of information below his name, including his graduating class, major, employment data, and contact data.

She looked for his employer. Keppler, Collins, and Preston.

She snorted. *Not anymore.*

There was a short summary in the work experience section—he was in investment banking, specializing in pharmaceuticals.

*Oh, is that what they call it now?*

Below that was space for lots of data, but most of the lines weren't filled in. His work address and phone number were there, but his home spaces were blank. There was a work e-mail address listed, but nothing else…home e-mail, pager, cell phone, all blank.

She considered for a moment, then pressed print.

She looked at the Pike Fellowship printout from Murphy Barker's year and typed in the next name on the list. *Johanna Godfrey.*

The list smoothly scrolled down to the *G*s. Unlike Murphy, this girl listed lots of data. Her home information, e-mail addresses, pager, and cell phone were all listed. She even listed two work numbers.

She looked at the employment section. *Helion Pharmaceuticals.* Never heard of it.

Claire printed the page, then typed in the next name. She yawned, stretching. Was this even the right path to pursue? Ian had better get here soon.

She leaned forward, only half-interested, as she scanned the summary for Gregory Granville III. She looked at his Bel Air home address, then back at his name. She gave a cynical snort. She'd bet anyone ten bucks that he insisted "the third" be used on everything.

Her eyes sought *employment,* and her eyebrows rose. Mr. Gregory Granville *the third* was working at a well-known Los Angeles publishing company, helping to manage, the summary said, a small division of a popular weekly magazine. *Cool job, at least.*

She peered more closely at the sparse contact information on the screen. A second work number was also listed, but that had to be a typo. It had a New York City area code. She shrugged as she pressed print. Who knew, these days. Maybe Mr. Granville was a real hotshot, and the company gave him an office on each coast.

Claire got to her feet and grabbed the few pages off the printer. This wasn't getting her anywhere.

She hesitated, then sat back down. She entered the last few names and printed out the data for each. One was in a company she'd never heard of, doing hotel management. Another was in an industrial supply and distribution business. The final name worked for a credit card company.

She stood again, staring at the screen. If there was something Anton Pike didn't want them to find, it wasn't here.


They crested the top of the escalator, and Stefan drew Sherry rapidly by the hand out into the afternoon light. She hurried along behind him, a strange sensation growing in her gut.

He stopped abruptly and she slammed into his back, giggling. "Stef—!"

He turned, the phone to his ear, and held up his free hand. Then he pointed to a bench off the path of pedestrian traffic. "I'm going over there to make a quick call."

He paused, listening, and his mouth tightened. Sherry could hear a voice mail system picking up. He punched a few more buttons and put the phone to his ear again.

He smiled briefly. "Why don't you get us a map from the information counter over there?" He gestured toward a nearby kiosk as he started to walk away. "I'll just be a couple minutes."

Sherry stalked toward the kiosk, picked up a map, and got her bearings. They were just a few minutes' walk from Boston Harbor and the famous Fanueil Hall and Quincy Market shopping areas. Her mind began to turn with ways Stefan could make up for his behavior on the train.


Across the river in Cambridge, Ian stopped walking in the middle of the path. His class-mates flowed around him on all sides, but he didn't notice. The skin on his neck prickled, and he had a sudden urge to pray.

*What, Lord?* Immediately he knew. Go home. Go home.

He turned and made tracks for home. The urge to pray grew stronger, and he broke into a half jog as he crossed Massachusetts Avenue and headed west toward his apart-ment.

The jog became a sprint as prayers for protection, for guidance, for *anything* coursed through his mind. What was going on? He bolted up the outside stairs to his second-floor apartment and stared around the room, half expecting to see some sort of disaster.

The room was hushed, quiet. But not normal. The tense feeling did not dissipate, and Ian walked into the center of his living room as if some monster would jump out at him.

He took a deep, slow breath and spoke aloud. "Lord, please show me what's going on. Please show me what I'm supposed to do."

He turned a slow circle, scanning every corner of his studio apartment. His eyes fastened on the telephone sitting on the kitchen counter. The message light was blink-ing.


Stefan stood still, the phone pressed hard to his ear. The bench sat vacant nearby. No way could he sit down.

He listened a moment, then spoke quietly. "Sherry said she was probably over there right now. She wasn't totally sure, but there aren't that many areas in that building to check, so you can probably find her pretty easily."

Another pause. "I don't know. It's already two-thirty. She could've been over there for an hour for all I know." He held the phone away from his ear. "Don't get mad at *me*, Father. I'm trying to save our tails here." He glanced across to where Sherry was looking at a map. "I've got to go. If I don't get back, Sherry's going to start asking questions again."

He hesitated, then spoke haltingly. "Look, don't...*do* anything, okay? We just can't afford that kind of trouble right now. There's too much else going on, especially now that Murphy has fallen." He listened briefly, then sighed in exasperation. "I've got to go. Good-bye."

He hung up the phone with a click. His thoughts roiled. Impulsively, he turned and kicked the bench, hard.

Standing right beside him, a dark presence watched with narrowed eyes. What was *this*? Katoth growled an order, and several lackeys jumped to attention.

"What is this weakness, this faintness of heart? This is the heir! What accounts for this?"

Several demons shot wary glances at each other. The heir was Katoth's territory, as it had been for generations. If there was a problem, he was the one who should know the answer.

Katoth looked around at them, knowing full well what they were thinking. His face contorted with rage. "What accounts for this!"

A lanky demon stepped forward, and his features bore the scars of long experience. "My lord, if I might suggest—"

"Speak!"

"The record of this family may bear some clues. I have been long in the service of Krolech. My memory is faint, my lord, but I recall a dispute from a time long past. It involved an ancestor of the heir."

"What dispute?"

The lanky demon bowed. "I beg your mercy, my lord. As I said, my memory is faint, and I was involved only on the periphery. I'm afraid I'm not the one to fill in the holes."

"Meaning that you probably know very well what the news involves but do not want to be the bearer of bad news." Katoth narrowed his eyes. "A wise choice."

The other demon inclined his head and stepped back into the ranks.

Katoth swept the others with a hard stare. "You would all do well to emulate your comrade's loyalty to me. His fealty will be rewarded." He turned to an aide. "Get me the records."

He turned to watch, brooding, as Stefan returned to Sherry's side with a charming apology and set off toward the harbor.

Claire wandered out to the front desk, papers in hand. The receptionist was sipping from a bottle of soda and reading a newspaper.

"Can I ask you another question?"

"Sure."

"Do you know what the difference is between your proprietary alumni database and the one that Career Services puts out?"

The receptionist leaned on her elbows, thinking. "Well, not entirely. But I do know that the Career Services one has less information in it."

"Why?"

"Well, they ask the alumni what they want listed. If an alum doesn't want to be bothered at home by some Harvard senior looking for a job, he won't list his home number."

"Ah."

"And our proprietary database has a lot of extra information that may or may not be totally accurate because we add to what the alums actually tell us."

"What?"

The receptionist rolled her eyes. "Yeah, I have to do that all the time when alumni call in to check on the status of their student loan payments or something. Our phone system here is set up to recognize the number someone is calling *from*. And if they tell me they're calling from work and our proprietary database doesn't have that number listed, I press a button and—bingo—we now have a second work number for them. Of course it could be that they're at a consulting project or something, not their main number. That's why we can't release that database to anyone without high-up authorization." She smiled. "Like yours."

Claire thanked her and started to walk away. What was she supposed to do? Where was Ian?

"Oh, by the way, the clerk just called in. He's on his way back."

Claire smiled. "Great."

"Hey listen, you look like you could use a break. Do you want a soda or some coffee?"

"You know, I really could use something with caffeine. I'm a bit rudderless until Ian gets here."

The receptionist vanished into a small doorway near the entrance, then reappeared with a cup of coffee in her hand. She beckoned to Claire. "Cream, sugar?"

Claire nodded as she entered a tiny kitchen. "Both would be great."

"Why don't you just fix it how you like it." She gestured to where the fixings were as she headed back out the door. "I can't be away from the phones."

"Thank you."

Claire set her papers on the limited counter space, balancing her Styrofoam cup on top of them. She stretched up to the shelves for the sugar and brushed the balancing cup. It tipped and coffee cascaded all over her papers, the counter, and down to the floor. Infuriated with herself, she jumped back and grabbed some napkins.

Her voice rose in frustration, although there was no one else to hear. "Do I have some sort of coffee curse or something?"

.

A tall man with dark hair approached the receptionist's desk. "Is Claire Rivers in here?"

The receptionist looked up and smiled. "Yes, sir. And you must be Ian Burke."

"That's right. Where is she?"

"Right in there." She gestured toward the door to the kitchen. "She's getting some coffee."

The newcomer chuckled. "We wouldn't want to interfere with that, would we?"

"No sir."

"Why don't I just go wait for her where she was working."

"Okay." The receptionist told him where to find the proper room. "And sign here, please."

The man signed in and headed down the corridor.

Within moments, a young, preppy man pushed a moving dolly through the door. He was followed by three other men in work clothes. One had a dolly, and the others left a wheeled flatbed right outside the doorway.

"Hey." He nodded to the receptionist. "Sorry we're late."

"No problem." Her phone rang, and she spoke quickly, reaching for the handset. "And you have someone needing help in the resource room, by the way."

"Okay."

The young man headed down the corridor, trailed by the three movers. He poked his head in the appropriate doorway and spoke to the dark-haired man sitting by one of the terminals. He was rummaging through a backpack, looking for something.

"Hey, I hear you need some help."

The man put the pack down and turned toward the terminals. "No, I think I've got it. Thanks."

"Okay. We're going to do one more load on this move. I'll be at my desk if you need anything. Ask one of these guys to get me."

"Great."

The young man shrugged, gave a few orders to the movers, then headed back to his desk.

The movers began transferring boxes, ignoring the man at the terminal and griping about Sunday's Patriots game.

Claire dabbed at the sodden papers, trying to get a handle on her anger. She finished cleaning up the mess and tossed the dripping pages in the small wastebasket. Impulsively she bent down, separating the pages with her fingers. Were there any dry spots?

She shook one page free—it had been in the middle of the stack—and tore off the sodden part. The top half, listing the six recipients from Murphy's year, was relatively dry. She stuffed it in her pocket, washed her hands, and headed out of the kitchen. She'd have to reprint the others.

The receptionist was juggling phone calls, but caught Claire's attention, mouthing the words at her. *He's back.*

"Great." Claire headed down the corridor, passing three men rolling boxes toward the door. She entered the glassed-in room, and a tall man rose from the chair in front of the terminal.

She walked over and held out her hand, smiling. "I'm so glad you're back. The resource director said you'd be able to help me. I wasn't sure what I was doing."

His eyes flickered, and then a smile appeared on his face. "You seem to have found quite a bit, young lady." The pages from the printer were lying on the desk beside him. The terminal screen showed the Pike Fellowship recipients from Murphy Barker's year.

"I don't know about that. I feel like I was going in circles."

"Why don't you tell me what you're looking for, and what you've found, and then we'll go from there."

"Sure." She allowed him to steer her toward the seat he'd just vacated. "What's your name?"

"Call me Tony."

"Okay, Tony." She reached into her backpack for a pen, then looked up into his face. His eyes were very dark.

Ian ran down the echoing hallway, looking frantically at the numbers on the doors. Some movers, in the middle of a coarse locker-room joke, were slowly steering a flatbed loaded with cardboard boxes toward a service elevator.

He asked a quick question, and one of the movers pointed.

Ian shot through the doorway and pulled up at the receptionist's station, fairly gasping. "Where is Claire Rivers?"

The receptionist looked startled. "Who are you?"

He tried to catch his breath. "Ian Burke. She asked me to—"

She folded her arms, a sardonic expression on her face. "Since Ian Burke is already back there, I doubt you're him."

"What?" Ian lost his breath again. His voice grew more urgent. "Where are they?"

"Last door on the left, but…hey!" She jumped up, shouting after him as he sprinted away. "You can't just—!"

He didn't stop, and she quickly punched in some numbers on her telephone. "Hello, security?"


Ian slowed as he approached the last room on the left and stopped a few feet short of it. He could hear two voices, one male, one female. Everything sounded collegial, but this pressure, this intensity, continued to increase until he felt that his head was about to explode.

He forced himself to stop and think, praying under his breath as he looked at the maze of cubicles on his right. He slipped down one row, then worked his way back toward the resource room. He stopped in the shadow of an unoccupied cubicle directly across from the large glass window and slowly leaned out until he could see inside the room.

Claire was standing by a bank of computer terminals, talking animatedly to Anton Pike.

His face blanched. *She doesn't know what he looks like!*

Ian drew himself back into the cubicle, praying hard. *O God, show me what to do. What is going on here? Make a way out of this, Lord.*

The sense of danger increased, and he stood and squared his shoulders.


"Why don't you show me what you found?"

"Okay."

The tall man's closeness made Claire a little uncomfortable. She swiveled slightly in her chair. "It started with these old files we found. We—"

"Excuse me!"

One of the movers was approaching from the doorway, his face intent.

"I'm sorry, but we're going to have to ask you to leave immediately." Two other moving men pushed dollies through the door behind him. One began picking up boxes and transferring them to his dolly; the other advanced toward the bank of computers.

Claire started to her feet, and the speaker stepped forward, picking up Claire's back-pack and dumping it in her arms. He pointed toward the door. "We're moving and reorganizing and must disconnect all these terminals."

"But the resource director said we'd have the rest of the day!" Claire turned toward her companion. "Tony, can't I have just a little—"

She stopped at the look on his face. He was staring at the moving man with glazed eyes, flinching backward.

The moving man took her arm, and Claire found herself propelled toward the door. "I'm sorry, miss, but your time is up."

"But—"

As Claire was deposited outside the door, she stared up at the serious expression of the man who had held her arm.

"What—"

"Claire!" Ian shot out from a row of cubicles, grabbed her arm, and hustled her down the corridor. His voice was low. "Thank You, God."

She tried to pull him to a stop. "What is going *on*, Ian? What is *with* everybody?"

"What is going on," he hissed in her ear as he dragged her past the startled recep-tionist and out the office door, "is that you were about to explain our project to Anton Pike."

Her knees buckled, but Ian didn't stop. She found her feet and allowed herself to be propelled down the hall and toward the stairs. Her face was very white. Only once they were hurtling down the stairs did she squeak out a question.

"That was Anton Pike?"

"Yes."

"I thought he was the office clerk."

They reached a stairway landing, and Ian paused, listening for footsteps. He looked back over her shoulder and up the stairs as he spoke. "At some point you're going to have to explain why you thought that, but right now all I want to do is get you out of here."

He pulled her onward. "Thank God you walked out of that office when you did."

"Well, they wouldn't let me stay!"

"Who wouldn't?"

"The moving men."

Ian stumbled on a stair, and caught himself. "What moving men?"

"What do you mean, 'What moving men'?" Claire gestured wildly up the stairs in the direction of the office. "The moving men! The big guys who came in and told us they were closing early and to get lost!"

Ian was staring at her openmouthed.

She put her hands on her hips. "The ringleader pushed me out the door, and then *you* grabbed me and nearly wrenched my arm out of its socket and… What is *up* with you?"

Ian leaned hard on the railing. "Claire, I don't know how to tell you this." His lips began to twist in a disbelieving smile. "But there were no moving men."

She narrowed her eyes. "Huh?"

"You walked out of that office on your own. The only person in there was Anton Pike."

## FIFTY-ONE

MANSFIELD LOOKED FROM ONE TO THE OTHER, the amazed expressions on each face. Then he leaned back in his chair and stared at the darkening sky outside his window.

"Well, praise God for His protection and His supernatural ways! I must say I'm jealous. I've always wondered what it would be like to meet an angel."

"So what do we do now?" Ian turned to Claire, his voice earnest. "Do you have any thoughts?"

Claire grinned. "You don't have to be *that* deferential just because you got so crabby with me."

"I'm sorry about that. If you would've just told me earlier about helping your friend…but I understand why you thought you couldn't."

Claire smiled at him, then turned to Mansfield. "Should we call Ian's friend at the Excellence Awards?"

"I'm afraid we don't have anything more to give him. Right now all we know is that there's definitely *something* going on. But we don't know what."

"But at least we now know there's something to be found," Ian said. "That's huge. Anton Pike wouldn't have gone to such great lengths to interfere if there was nothing there."

He turned to Claire. "Whatever it is, you've probably already seen it." At her startled look, he shrugged. "To you, it was such a small thing that you didn't even notice its significance, but to him it was glaring out like a spotlight. His reaction tells us there's definitely something there! I'd like to go over everything you saw with a fine-toothed comb, but we obviously can't unless we get access to that computer again."

"Yeah." Claire sighed, dejected. "I remember only one of the other alumni names besides Murphy's. That's it. And without the names, we can't re-create the alumni records obviously."

Suddenly, she sat straight up in her chair. Mansfield and Ian looked at her, curious. She reached into her pocket and pulled out a torn piece of paper as if she'd just struck gold.

"You're not going to believe this." She explained what it was.

Ian stood up, his body tense. He poured himself a cup of coffee at Mansfield's sideboard and turned. "I'm no businessman, but I think I've got an idea." He leaned against the sideboard, explaining his thought.

Mansfield listened and after a moment nodded, his voice decisive. "Go ahead then. Let's see what happens."

Ian hesitated. "One final thing. I'm a little concerned about you, Claire. Anton Pike knows you were snooping around, and your roommate is the girlfriend of his son. Surely this has got to get awkward. I've met Stefan a few times, and neither he nor his father are to be trifled with. And honestly, I really had a sense of danger. It was like something was chasing me over there."

"What are you proposing?" Mansfield said.

"I don't know, but I don't like the idea of her being alone—"

Claire raised her hand. "Excuse me, do I have any say in this?"

"It depends on what you want to say."

"Very funny. Look, I appreciate your concern, honestly. But Ian, you should be the first to remember that I'm not in any danger." She preened. "I have three enormous bodyguards, remember?" Within half a second she berated herself. Why was she rejecting an offer to be bodyguarded by Ian, of all people?

Ian laughed and started to object. Mansfield broke in.

"Ian, I take your sense of caution seriously, but we have to remember two things. First, Claire is right. God clearly has gone to great lengths to protect her thus far— even if only from spilling the beans. And second, since Pike has no idea what we know or don't know, he'll be watching to see if we do anything differently. Why don't we just continue this investigation—as quickly as we can—and reevaluate as we go?" He stood to his feet. "Believe me, if I think there's any need for concern, I'll be quick to move on it."

The two students stood and walked to the door. Mansfield held it open for them.

Claire reached up and hugged him. "Thank you, Professor."

He shook his head. "I keep telling you to call me Mansfield." He grinned and shooed them out the door.


Ian and Claire headed down the hallway, trailed closely by a contingent of warriors on high alert. Their faces were set, their guard up. The unraveling was beginning, and resistance was expected.

Three angels stayed behind, near Mansfield's office. Etàn gave several orders. Time was short, and there was much to be accomplished. He watched the man of God, his expression fiercely protective. God's ways were perfect.

In his home not far from campus, Anton Pike punched the buttons on his cordless phone. Within seconds he was speaking with his brother. He did not sit down, just paced the length of his den. His voice was low, furious. After three lengths of the room, he was standing near his desk finishing his description of the day's events.

He smashed his fist down onto the desk, his face livid.

Krolech crashed his fist into the center of the map, causing his principal lieutenants to jump. Katoth, standing directly in front of him, narrowed his eyes but did not flinch.

Krolech growled something unintelligible under his breath, then stuck his face in Katoth's line of sight and growled again.

"What I want to know is why all this is happening now! Is all this just accidental, or is this a concerted enemy plan?"

None of his aides said anything. The enemy never did anything "accidental," and he knew it.

Krolech looked at the map, the crown jewel, and let out a roar that shook the rafters. He swung on his troops. "Leviathan—Leviathan *himself* has asked for a report. And what can I tell him?" His voice grew sarcastic. "Oh, nothing but the fact that my *entire plan* is in danger of unraveling because some novice freshman—guarded by three warriors—just *happens* to stumble across the interweaving of our tapestry!"

He began to pace. "My plan has worked brilliantly, unexposed, for years! It has delivered this jewel into our hands, this jewel that is a cornerstone of the master's strategy for this land. And now these—these *saints,*" he spat the word, "have suddenly exposed the pattern."

Katoth inclined his head, his voice deferential. "My lord, you cannot be sure of that. She didn't tell you anything that she uncovered, and there was nothing in her backpack. She certainly didn't leave with anything. It's likely that she did not even see the significance of her findings. In fact, if she *had* understood their significance, we would probably have been routed by now. This was an incursion, but nothing more. We can ensure that they no longer have access to the information."

Krolech paced some more, his eyes glistening. "See that they don't. And have your troops watch closely to ensure that nothing is released. We may have to move quickly. And I think it's about time that you take full possession of your charge. I'm disappointed in these unexpected weaknesses in the heir."

Katoth's eyes flickered, and Krolech saw it. He drew his lieutenant aside.

"Speak."

Katoth's eyes were shadowed, enraged. "I have tried many times, my liege. But there is always an unexplained resistance. He is fully aligned with our cause—you yourself inducted him into the family mandate when he reached manhood—but..."

"But?"

"But I have been looking at the family records, my liege. And there was a small detail that I was not briefed on when I began this assignment."

Krolech made no sound, just stared hard at the other demon.

"I was not informed about...the praying ancestress."

Krolech lashed out with a ready claw, and Katoth, anticipating, ducked the swing.

Krolech clenched his fists and let out another roar. "One woman! One failure! The generations are dedicated to our master, and *one traitor* can cause this much pain for generations to come! She prayed for her children's children, and for their children and—" he pressed his claws to his forehead—"it is like a thorn in my mind!"

He swung on his lieutenant, his face fierce. "The heir *must* commit. The chain must not be broken. We must have him!"

"I am at your command, my liege."

Krolech stared at the map, placing all the chess pieces, and a slow, terrible smile began to spread across his features. "Because he must become the figurehead one day, we cannot consolidate our hold through the sort of action that ordinarily cements our relationship. However, we can get him as close as possible to observe the power he will wield."

He drew Katoth over to the map and placed a black claw on a particular spot. "I think this will do very nicely. And it will certainly solve several problems."

Katoth rubbed his hands together. "Good. Good."

Krolech turned and addressed the troops, explaining, diagramming, giving orders. When he had finished and dismissed all but Katoth, he turned to his lieutenant.

"We will not answer Leviathan's query until this is taken care of. But by then we will be the heroes."

Ian and Claire approached a dorm room door plastered top to bottom with magnets of sports teams. Ian found a spare inch between baseball magnets and rapped on the door. He waited a second and rapped again.

A distant voice sounded inside. "Yeah, yeah, keep your panties on."

The door was wrenched open, and an unfamiliar student stared at them. "Yeah?" He was wearing only boxer shorts.

Ian tried not to laugh at Claire's expression. Her voice came out in a squeak. "Is Doug here?"

Ten minutes later, Doug Turner sat, openmouthed, as Claire summarized the events of the last few hours. They were in the student lounge on the ground level of Doug's dorm. Their voices were low, even though no one else was in the room.

"This project is pretty confidential," she concluded, "so we'd appreciate it if you didn't mention it to anyone."

Doug nodded, clearly trying to assimilate what he'd been told. "So what do you want from me?"

"Well, we need a business whiz. Mansfield said you were really good at corporate stuff since you'd worked for an investment firm. He suggested you."

"Really? I knew I liked that guy."

"Well, now you need to deliver," Ian said. "Where should we start?"

Doug thought for a second, then pursed his lips. "I've got a hunch. Come on."

He led them back up the stairs to his suite and pushed through the door. Claire followed, hesitant, as the entranceway opened up into a long hallway leading to several bedrooms.

There was stuff on every square inch of floor—wrinkled clothes, sports equipment, and dirty dishes all jockeyed for space. Doug headed down to the second doorway, beckoning them along. By the time Claire reached his room, she figured she had stepped on at least two pairs of underwear. Ian trailed behind her, looking amused.

Doug ushered them into his small room and closed the door behind him.

"How can you *live* like that?" Claire blurted out, motioning toward the mess outside his doorway.

"Hate to tell you this, Claire, but I've been to several guys' rooms that are *worse.*"

He sat at his computer. In a moment he was on-line, his fingers busy on the keyboard. "I'm checking what comes up when I look for data on Pike Holdings." He waited only a few seconds, then frowned at the information appearing on the screen. "This doesn't tell us anything."

"Print it anyway," Claire said.

Ian glanced over at her, amused. She made a quick face back at him.

Doug was already looking at a laser printout. "Nope. See here? Privately Held. Those are the magic words for confidentiality. Only public companies—companies listed on the stock market—have to disclose detailed information. Pike Holdings doesn't list its financials, or even its subsidiary companies."

"But even if it did," Claire said, "it's not going to publicly list owning something like that porn magazine company—" Claire snapped her fingers a few times—"what's its name?"

"Peephole Publications?" Ian and Doug spoke simultaneously, then looked at each other, grimacing.

Claire raised an eyebrow. "I'm not *even* going to ask why you both know that."

Ian shrugged. "Suffice it to say that a lot of Christian men have had to be delivered from temptation. That stuff is pure evil."

"So, as I was saying—" Claire tried to get back on track—"if Pike Holdings went to such lengths to keep some sort of relationship with that magazine secret, then it's not going to be disclosed in whatever source you're checking."

"Yeah, obviously." Doug gestured to his screen. "What I'm looking at, by the way, is a common resource for investment people. It lists summary financials for a lot of companies, as well as ownership information, shareholdings, market valuation, all that kind of thing. Even private companies are in here since everyone has to disclose their ownership, at least. And some private companies even list financials in case they're thinking of doing a private placement, for example."

"I have no idea what you just said, but it sounds good," Claire said.

Doug grinned and turned back to the screen. "Let's work backward. Give me the names on that list of Pike Fellowships. I'll check the Career Services database again. It'll take just a second to pull up the companies those people work for."

Claire read them off as, one by one, Doug pulled up the same screens Claire had seen earlier. They printed everything out, just to be safe.

Doug continued to fiddle with the computer, muttering something about an idea. After a moment he gestured to the pages on the printer. "So is this everything you lost when you ran out of the office this afternoon?"

"No. This doesn't include what I got from the internal database the resource director logged me in to. And of course, there was probably a ton more in that database that I never got around to before those big glowing men with wings threw me out."

"I can't believe you're joking about that!" Ian's voice was stern, but it was clear he was trying not to laugh. "This is serious!"

"I know, I know." Claire held up a hand. "But it's also kind of cool. So humor me."

Doug's voice rose from the computer. "Guys…"

Claire and Ian were behind him instantly, leaning over his shoulder and looking at the screen.

Doug was looking at a page labeled Helion Pharmaceuticals. "Murphy Barker just worked at an investment bank, right? And the bank is a partnership without public ownership, so that's a dead end. But when I checked Johanna Godfrey's employer, this Helion Pharmaceuticals place…my hunch was right." He tapped the screen. "Ignore all these financials and things. This is what you need to look at. Helion is a wholly owned subsidiary of—" his finger traced a line down the screen to a small line of print—"Pike Holdings."

He looked around at them. "Gee, you don't seem surprised. Well, let me show you the rest." Doug toggled to another screen. "See where this alum works? Big hotel management company? Wholly owned by Pike Holdings." He toggled again. "Credit card company. Pike Holdings." Another screen flashed up. "Publishing. Pike Holdings. I checked all of them. They're all the same."

Ian straightened, stretching out a kink in his back. "So every one of the recipients of a Pike scholarship in Murphy Barker's year is working for a Pike Holdings company."

"What does that mean, though?" Claire asked. "Wouldn't it be normal to go work for the company when they essentially gave you the scholarship?"

Doug tilted his head. "Yeah, but four years after graduation… I don't know."

"Most of my friends who graduated last year are already looking to switch jobs!" Ian said.

"That's because they're all working eighteen-hour days at those sweatshop law firms," Doug said.

"True. But there's lots of turnover in businesses, too."

"Guys, can we pull it back here?" Claire was trying to pace in the small room and not getting anywhere. "What does this mean? Is this anything that would help the Excellence Awards?"

"Hmm…" Ian pondered. "I guess it would be worthwhile to tell D. J. tomorrow that we're still finding a few things. This will interest him for sure, but it doesn't really tell his bosses anything."

"Check Peephole Publications for a second." Claire gestured at the screen. "Who's their owner?"

Doug shook his head. "You won't find anything that way." He typed something in, then ran his finger down to a list of unfamiliar company names. "See? They have outside companies as owners, but you won't find out who the people behind those companies actually are. Ten to one these are all just shell companies, incorporated so another company can anonymously hold Peephole stock without socially conscious investors getting indignant. That's one way of getting around the stigma of owning sin stocks. Whoever these owners are, they probably aren't public companies. More likely to be just wealthy individuals who like sin stocks' rich profits."

Claire sighed and plopped down on Doug's bed. "I guess this isn't going to get us anywhere."

There was a long pause; then Ian stirred. "Don't say that yet. I sort of feel like we're being led step by step down the trail God wants us on. Let's all just sleep on it tonight, and I'll call D. J. tomorrow. They probably have until Monday, after all."

They said their good-byes, and Ian walked Claire back to her dorm. Ignoring her protests, he insisted on escorting her up to her room and even glanced around to make sure things looked normal. No one else was home.

She walked him to the door, and he shook a finger at her. "You have my number. Let me know if anything strange happens when Sherry gets back, okay?"

"I will." She looked up into his tired eyes. "Thank you, Ian."

He smiled. "Good night."

The door closed behind him, and Claire stared at her empty suite. She shivered, then reached for the television remote. The television sprang to life, the news flashing with pictures of the day on Wall Street.

The news provided welcome background noise as Claire changed into sweats and unloaded her backpack. She took the pages from Doug's printer and stored them out of sight in her philosophy textbook, then stood the textbook in one of her plastic book crates.

She wandered back into the living room and stood, remote control in hand, about to change channels. Suddenly, she started and looked closer. There was a taped shot of a young, well-dressed man in handcuffs being led into a car and driven away.

Was that...?

The picture repeated itself as the announcer turned to another man sitting at the anchor desk. "Bob, why don't you tell us what this scandal might mean for KCP?"

The man turned toward the camera. His full name, followed by the words *Market Specialist,* appeared at the bottom of the screen.

"Well, in the past twenty years, we've had plenty of examples of what happens when a rogue trader—or, in this case, a rogue investment banker like Mr. Barker—decides he wants a bigger piece of the pie."

Claire grabbed her cordless phone and sat on the couch, punching in Ian's phone number. After a few rings his voice mail picked up, and she spoke quickly, not wanting to miss what the commentator was saying.

"...so it's not a huge market problem, but it casts a pall. And since perception *is* the market, it certainly isn't good for KCP or even the companies KCP represents." He turned to the news anchor. "I was just on the phone with some inside sources at KCP, actually, and they said they're a little concerned about the possible impact on Helion Pharmaceuticals, for one."

Claire bolted to her feet. "What?"

"Really, Bob? Why?"

"Well, my sources indicate that Mr. Barker was in the middle of working with Helion—he was in the pharmaceuticals area, as you know—on their rumored IPO. The company needs all the cash it can get to resolve its impending lawsuit. The higher-ups in the bank aren't sure whether in fact some of Mr. Barker's misdeeds might have come at the expense of Helion. They're checking into that now. Because that, of course, raises the specter that the investment bank itself could be liable for the harm caused by its employee."

Claire's telephone rang right by her hand, and she jumped. "Hello?"

Ian's voice was amazed. "I walked in about a second after you left your message. Do you believe this?"

"Murphy worked *at* KCP, but worked *for* Helion?"

"Well, he was Helion's banker, working on this IPO they were talking about. But that other woman on your list—Johanna Godfrey—she actually worked for Helion itself."

He paused, and Claire could hear him talking to himself. "So these mysterious scholarship recipients don't just work for companies owned by the same holding company; they actually work together in some way." Another pause, and his voice returned to normal. "This can't be a coincidence, but I still don't see how it gets us anywhere."

Claire started to jump in when his call waiting beeped.

"Hold on a second."

Claire waited through the silence, watching the continuing coverage.

Ian came back on the line. "You're not going to believe this."

Claire took a deep breath. "We're going to have to stop saying that."

"D. J. is on the line. He's going to conference the three of us together."

After a few minutes of introductions and explanations, D. J.'s voice grew thoughtful.

"Well, it raises more questions than it answers, but my bosses are really gun-shy, and this development puts me over the edge. I think it's time to tell them a little of what you've found—if that's okay with you."

After a moment, Ian cleared his throat. "Sure. Once that happens, though, we've entered a whole new ball game. We're potentially impugning a perfectly innocent company in a way that could drastically affect its financial future. We've got to be pretty darned sure of our research."

"That's true," D. J. said. "Because once I share this with my bosses, the seed is planted. It can't be taken back. So that means you have to come up with something more—to either clear their name or confirm your suspicions—in the next few days, before we choose the award for this year."

"So what should we do?" Claire asked.

"I think my bosses need to hear this," D. J. said. "They care about our credibility even more than the credibility of an innocent nonrecipient. So I'll give you tomorrow to see if you come up with anything more, but at close of business I'll alert them to the potential issue on the horizon. Then you'll have the weekend to dig some more. But remember, for this issue to be settled one way or another—in a way that's honoring to

God—we have to essentially *prove* or *disprove* these concerns. And if you prove them, well, this company will have a lot more to worry about than just losing an award."

Claire put the phone down and sat for a long time, wondering what to do next. The sound of approaching voices startled her out of her reverie, and she stood up quickly, nervous.

She berated herself as she heard Mercedes' familiar voice and the jangling of her keys. Claire went into her bedroom, closing the door behind her, and sank to the floor by her bed.

"O God, what is going on?" She poured out her heart to her heavenly Father, thankful that He, not she, was in charge.

## FIFTY-TWO

THE NEXT DAY SEEMED TO PASS IN A DREAM.

Sherry never came home, and Claire left for class before her roommate returned in the morning. Claire stuck to her normal class routine, saying hello to Jo Markowitz in biology, walking the paths of Harvard Yard, giving Bethany a quick hug after philosophy—all the while pondering how else to investigate a company that didn't want to be investigated.

She unsuccessfully conferred with Doug right after biology class let out.

"I haven't been able to think of a thing."

There was the quiet noon conference with Ian, the meeting with Mansfield, and the visit to the business library to see if any of their resources showed anything more than Doug's had. Nothing.

The day was unseasonably warm, the sky a perfect blue, but Claire couldn't rid herself of this unsettled mood.

"I feel like I'm spinning my wheels," she said to Ian as they conferred in the entryway of the Science Center. "Like there's something really important just around the corner, or already staring me in the face, and I'm not seeing it."

"Why don't we walk back over to the office you were at yesterday and see if we can talk our way in? We don't have anything to lose."

They trucked over and approached the receptionist. She was no longer smiling.

"Listen, I don't know what was going on yesterday or who you people really are, but I'm afraid you can't come in here anymore. We received an angry call from Professor Pike's office yesterday afternoon telling us that we could be prosecuted for divulging private information."

"But we had authorization from Professor Mansfield!" Claire said. "Can't we at least speak to the resource director's clerk and—"

"It doesn't matter if you had authorization from God himself!" The receptionist was quivering with indignation. "On Monday, at Professor Pike's direction, the college is starting a wholesale investigation into our security practices, which we'll have to spend ages dealing with." She slapped a two-foot-high pile of files on her desk. "I have all these forms to fill out and all this administrative garbage to go through just because you decided to try to get around our security procedures."

Claire's heart sank. The receptionist had been so nice to her. "We weren't trying to get around anything, honest. Everything we've told you is true. I'm so sorry we created extra work for you."

Ian stepped forward, pulling out his billfold. "Let me show you something." He flipped the wallet open and pointed to his driver's license.

The receptionist sighed, then leaned forward and looked at the name. She paused, and stared back up at him. "Well, if you're really Ian Burke, then who was back there yesterday?"

Claire started to answer, then felt Ian's restraining hand on her arm.

"I think the better question," he said, sympathy in his voice, "is why on earth they're investigating you, when you did nothing wrong?"

At the receptionist's irate agreement, Ian sighed and shook his head. "Listen, we still have a lot of research to do back there. Is it possible that we can at least talk to the clerk?"

"He's not in the office for the rest of the day. Still moving boxes."

"Would you possibly," Claire blurted out, "be willing—"

The phone rang with several incoming calls.

"—to leave him a note saying that we dropped by and showed you Ian's identification?"

The receptionist stared hard at Ian and Claire, then shrugged before reaching for her phones. "If I can get around to it, I'll try. But I can't promise anything. Sorry."

Claire started to protest, but Ian steered her firmly out the door.

"Look." He turned to her in the empty hallway, his voice low. "That receptionist has been ordered not to let people back there. She's not authorized to change that order, and we don't want to get her in trouble. Besides, we have no idea whether it would even help: You didn't recognize anything big the first time, and we don't know what else is on that computer."

"Yeah." Claire was still antsy, shifting from foot to foot. "So now what do we do?"

"I think we have to call D. J. and tell him no progress yet." He smiled. "And then we come back here tomorrow morning—before your HCF barbecue—and see if the clerk is around. The resource director did say they'd be moving all weekend, right?"


Claire stood off to the side, trying not to eavesdrop as Ian used a pay phone to call D. J. After a few minutes, he hung up and stuck his hands in the pockets of his jeans, rocking back and forth on the balls of his feet.

"Well, that was interesting."

"What was?" Claire was fairly bouncing up and down.

"They got a phone call this afternoon. Someone from Pike Holdings called for a private little meeting with his boss. Seems they wanted to have an off-the-record discussion about whether they're still a front-runner for the Excellence Award."

"No kidding!"

"No kidding. Someone over there is nervous for some reason. To prepare for the meeting, D. J.'s boss walked around and asked everyone if they'd heard anything on the street, so D. J. went ahead and told him about our project. Apparently his boss took it very seriously. So in the meeting with Pike Holdings he told Pike's people that," he imitated a pompous voice, "they had some concerns that needed to be further investigated before they could make a decision."

"Oh boy."

"Yep. Which means that now it's not just us that are wondering what's going on."


Victor put the phone gently in the cradle and leaned back in his chair. His face was set, hard. This was threatening to spin out of control, and it had to be stopped. Now.

He rose from his desk and went out the door of his office through the living room—now shadowed, its empty sofas looking out over the darkened stretch of lawn—and down a set of stairs. Not the stairs leading to the conference center on the ground floor, but another stairway, longer and steeper.

The air grew cooler, and he flicked on a light, illuminating the stone walls of the hallway. His footsteps echoed as he headed for one particular door.

He pushed the door open and paused, taking in the blackness. Then he flipped a switch. A single spotlight shone on a dark portrait hanging on the wall, the beam so focused that the rest of the room was pitch black. That was exactly what he wanted.

He moved along the polished conference table and slid into a chair opposite the large round speakerphone system embedded in the center. He reached down under the table and pressed and pulled until something clicked. He pulled the speakerphone out of its cavity and set it aside, turning back to the table in anticipation.

A pentagram was engraved into the lowered center of the table. Five holes held five votive candles, which he lit. Then he took his seat, staring at the portrait opposite his chair. The blackness seemed to press in on him as he closed his eyes.


An hour later two men walked away from the conference center hotel rooms, their steps purposeful. They got into a waiting car and headed across the island. There were still a few night flights left to the mainland.

"It's not here tonight."

Claire stared at Brad, uncomprehending. They were standing in front of the usual HCF meeting room, and Brad was telling each arrival to go to some other building Claire had never heard of.

Brad glanced at Claire and started to repeat himself. Then he stopped. "Are you all right?"

"Yeah. Just a lot on my mind, that's all." She gestured at the closed doors at Brad's back. "What's going on?"

"The meeting is at Phillips Brooks House tonight. You didn't get the flyer?"

"Flyer?" Claire said, feeling stupid.

Brad motioned to the table beside him. A stack of brightly colored flyers proclaimed "HCF meeting at the famous Phillips Brooks House." A map was printed at the bottom of the page.

Claire shook her head. "I haven't checked my mailbox in a few days…" Had it really been just two days since she walked out of her dorm room for that abortion debate? It seemed like weeks.

"Well then, here you go." Brad handed her a flyer.

Claire just stood there staring at the paper.

Brad raised an eyebrow. "On the other hand, the meeting has probably already started." He laid a tentative hand on her arm. "How about I walk you over there?"

He taped a flyer to the door behind him, then steered Claire out of the building and across campus.

"You still with me?" Brad asked.

"What?" Claire looked up, startled.

"Whatever is going on with Mansfield's project must be a big deal. Hopefully you can put it all aside and worship."

Claire sighed. "I think I need to."

The cheerful lights of Phillips Brooks House rose before them. It was, Claire thought, somewhat like a real multistory brick house, unlike the other houses, as the school called the sprawling upperclass dorms.

The heavy front door was propped open, and light spilled out. Through the clear night air, she could hear a guitar accompanying the soft singing of many voices. She caught a glance of students crowded into a large front room, sitting or standing in every available space, all looking at some point beyond Claire's view.

Without warning, Claire was overwhelmed with sadness, joy, foreboding—a deep sense of purpose. She stopped walking and stood very still, trying to come to grips with the inexplicable barrage.

Brad also stopped, not saying anything. After a few moments he reached out and lightly gripped Claire's shoulder.

"You okay?"

Claire took several deep breaths. "I don't know what's wrong with me. It's like I suddenly have four people's worth of emotion trying to fight to the surface."

She took another breath and let it out slowly. She looked back up at the open doorway, the friendly lights, the familiar profiles inside. "Let's go in."

# FIFTY-THREE

THE STUDENTS LISTENED, QUIET AND ENTHRALLED, as Mansfield outlined the initial findings on the old Christian grants and endowments. The door had been closed to the cold, and a fire crackled in the fireplace behind him. The sofas and chairs were pushed back along the walls, making room for students to sit on the soft rugs in the center of the room.

"But keep in mind," he cautioned all the young faces looking up at him, "that we have no idea where this will go from here. I spoke to Harvard's new chief financial officer yesterday, and she hasn't seen any indication that the administration is planning to investigate the issue anytime soon. We will simply have to wait for a response and go from there."

Several students raised their hands, and Mansfield called on Sam, who was sitting on a crowded couch along one wall.

"Doesn't it seem just totally unfair to you?" Sam's outrage was reflected on the faces of many around the room. "It's like they're stealing money—pure and simple."

"I know it seems like that to us. But there are likely many complex issues involved in this—not the least of which are the legal questions—and the administration is probably so far removed from a faith-based worldview that it might view this as an unnecessary and trivial nuisance."

"Trivial!" Another student stood up, her voice incredulous. "That money is a hard, cold symbol of our credibility here on campus. Imagine what a difference it would make to have a science professor who actually addressed some of the credible scientific theories that are consistent with the Bible. Imagine what a difference it would make to people like that guy who wants everyone to picket our barbecue tomorrow. Maybe then all the people wed to their secular, relativistic mind-sets wouldn't be quite so ready to harass us!"

From her position by the door, Claire could hear sounds of frustration and indignation all over the room. Several people didn't join in the talking but seemed indrawn, nervous.

She squirmed, thinking about her own barbecue work slot tomorrow. Would Jo Markowitz or Bethany walk by and give them a wide berth? Would her hallmates see her being picketed and roll their eyes?

"Let me address that, please." Mansfield's voice cut through the grumbling, and the room quieted in a matter of seconds.

"Tomorrow by Mem Hall, you will be cheerfully providing a service for any student who needs a study break. Anyone can come and get free hot dogs and hamburgers all day. They can take the food and split, or they can hang out and socialize, maybe even play some volleyball. There will be no strings, no—as the young man put it—proselytizing. As you all know, the college forbids organized proselytizing. But of course we want our friends to recognize that what we do, we do out of God's abundance in our hearts. We will, in other words, be evangelizing with our very lives. And we might very well be picketed because of it."

A student in the corner spoke up, her voice tentative. "Will you be there with us, Dr. Mansfield?"

The professor smiled. "Of course. At least for part of it. The young reporter who wrote that article sees evangelism as something sinister, almost as a personal affront. Our reaction tomorrow—in fact, our reaction to any controversy—can either substantiate his ridicule or show it to be completely baseless."

Doug Turner raised his hand. "What I don't get is why they can't see that we're doing something fun *for them!* Why do they have to make it so complicated?"

"You have just asked one of the main questions we all ask when people are resistant to the gospel: Why are people so resistant to something so beautiful, so *right?* Why can we give a perfect apologetic to a friend in class and get nothing but an uncomprehending stare in return? Why don't they get it?"

Mansfield stirred from where he was standing by the fireplace. He took a brass poker from a rack of hearth tools and shifted the logs. Several glowing pieces fell inward, their embers scattering.

"A few years ago," he said, poking at the embers, "I was snowed in after a conference in Colorado. Several colleagues and I were stuck in a little inn for two days. It was a charming place, with a cozy den, a fireplace much like this one, and—thankfully—shelves of books to entertain bored people stranded in a snowstorm."

The students chuckled as he continued. "A colleague showed me a book by a female author I'd never heard of. He explained—quite passionately—that the novelist wrote fantastic historical fiction, that her research was impeccable, and that readers were transported into whatever time and place she was writing about.

"Now, I read a great deal, but I had never even seen her name. But my colleague was so enthusiastic, that I took the book and read it." He smiled. "And I loved it. So I took down another one, and I loved that one, too. And then the strangest thing happened. I began to see that author's name everywhere. When we finally flew out two days later, I saw a whole row of her novels on the fiction shelf in the airport bookstore. I started to see her books advertised in magazines and on the bestseller lists in newspapers. Had that author just become popular? No—I had been staring right at her books in the stores for years. So what had happened?"

Mansfield reached for his Bible, flipping to a particular page. "Matthew 13:13 and 16. 'Therefore, I speak to them in parables, because seeing they do not see, and hearing they do not hear, nor do they understand…. But blessed are your eyes for they see, and your ears for they hear.'"

He looked up at the students. "What had happened with that novelist was simply that I hadn't been tuned in. I saw but didn't have eyes to see. Just like your classmates, my colleagues, and those people who will probably picket you tomorrow. They have ears but do not hear, eyes but do not see. First Corinthians says, 'The natural man does not receive the things of the Spirit of God, for they are foolishness to him; nor can he know them, because they are spiritually discerned.'

"Remember that tomorrow during the barbecue, and in every class, every late-night dorm discussion. What is so stark and clear to you, they truly *do not see*. You can't force a spiritually blind classmate to 'get it' any more than you can force a physically blind classmate to appreciate a beautiful view. But you can pray, and you can watch for where God is working. Watch for those people who ask the questions, where God may be stirring their spirit. God may be giving them eyes to see."

Claire's mind flickered to her conversation with Bethany in the T station and then to the derisive looks she'd seen toward Brad in class. She slowly raised her hand.

"But, Professor Mansfield, can I ask a question?"

"Certainly."

"Doesn't that just give us an excuse to *not* share, to *not* try, because we know most people in our classes aren't really listening?" She sighed. "I'm only a freshman, and I'm already tired of people rolling their eyes behind my back. I would love to just give up and say, 'They aren't going to get it.'"

Mansfield's gaze was kind. "Believe me, I understand. More than you know. But God doesn't give us the option of backing out. We're told to be witnesses for Him, and we have to take our cue from those the Bible has given us as role models. Do you have your Bible with you?"

"Yes."

"Why don't you read 1 Corinthians, chapter 4, verses 10 through 14?"

Claire reached for her bag and pulled out a small pocket Bible.

"'Our dedication to Christ makes us look like fools, but you are so wise! We are weak, but you are so powerful! You are well thought of, but we are laughed at.

"To this very hour we go hungry and thirsty, without enough clothes to keep us warm. We have endured many beatings, and we have no homes of our own. We have worked wearily with our own hands to earn our living. We bless those who curse us. We are patient with those who abuse us. We respond gently when evil things are said about us. Yet we are treated like the world's garbage, like everybody's trash—right up to the present moment. I am not writing these things to shame you, but to warn you as my beloved children.'"

She stopped reading and looked up. Her smile was wan, but real. "Okay. I get it."

There were chuckles around the room as Mansfield turned back to address the group. Claire stared at the words on the page before her.

*God, make me willing...*

"Tonight," Mansfield was saying, "we meet in this house for a reason. How many of you don't know the story of Phillips Brooks?"

A large percentage of the crowd—including Claire—raised their hands.

"Phillips Brooks was a graduate of Harvard and a preacher at Trinity Church. He was a beloved figure here, intimately involved in the life of Harvard. Even though he turned down all requests to become a professor, he did serve on the board of overseers. He felt strongly that true Christian faith, a vibrant love affair with God, and purposeful obedience to God's will, would show itself through action—through caring for the poor, through evangelism, through service to one's fellow man.

"Interestingly, the students responded to his challenge with passion and fervor. One of Harvard's most effective organizations ever—the Harvard Young Men's Christian Association—was founded in 1886. It became the largest organization in the college's history, and a shining beacon for fellowship, service, and evangelism.

"This building," Mansfield gestured at the rafters, "was built as a memorial following Phillips Brooks's untimely death at the turn of the century, a permanent residence for the YMCA. The outpouring of support, of love, of grief, at the death of the beloved man led to a spiritual awakening on campus. Now, as you may know, this house primarily holds the offices of the student volunteer clubs on campus."

Mansfield reached for a sheaf of papers at his side.

"As you prepare for tomorrow—and for every class, every debate, every conversation from here on out—let me read you the challenging words from Phillips Brooks's address to the freshman class of 1883. This exhortation could apply to those—whether Christian or not—at any college in the nation." Mansfield looked down at the paper.

"He who comes here...must feel himself drawn up and on to live his fullest and to give himself to obedience to truth and fellowman and to God. If any do not do so, if there is any man so false to the spirit of this place that he grows timid or grows reckless here, that he seeks freedom in sluggishness, or thinks that freedom means self-will instead of loyalty to the Eternal Master, if there is any man of whom this place makes a skeptic or a profligate, what can we sadly say but this: that he was not worthy of the place to which he came.... The man whom the college ruins is not fit for the college. He should have gone elsewhere."


As the students walked down the steps of the building heading for the usual evening of food and fellowship, Claire noticed that many were walking in silence. Perhaps they too felt the weight of the challenge, the pensiveness of the day to come.

Claire hung back as the room gradually emptied. She conferred briefly with Mansfield and agreed to touch bases midway through the morning, at the barbecue. He had, he said, some further ideas for their research.

She gave him a quick hug, and then Teresa and several others pulled her toward dinner.


Stefan and Sherry were bundled up in thick coats, about to leave his room, when there was a loud knock on the door. Stefan swung the door open, and his father stepped into the room.

"I must speak—" Anton Pike saw Sherry and broke off.

"Hello," Sherry said, her eyes curious.

Stefan made no introductions. He turned to Sherry with a smile. "Can you do me a favor, Sher? I need to chat here for a second." He held up his car keys. "Can you go warm up the car and tell everyone to go ahead? Ask Niles to take them in his truck. We'll drive tonight and meet them there."

"Are you sure that's a good idea? It'll be pretty crowded down—"

"Just go warm up the car, Sherry. Now."

"Fine." Sherry snatched the keys from his hand and stalked out, slamming the door behind her.

Anton stared after her, his eyes brooding. He turned to his son. "You're letting your control slip. Your power will degrade if unused."

"My control is just fine, father. What are you doing here?"


Ten minutes later Stefan walked to his car. It was running, and the heat was on. Sherry sat in the passenger seat, looking sullenly out the window.

Stefan got in and slammed the door behind him, his face tight. He steered the car away from the curb, not speaking, anticipation, anger, and fear swirling in his brain.

Late that night Claire stared up at the empty loft in the darkness above her, then turned on her side with a sigh, praying for her roommate, for Stefan.

She could see the brilliance of the full moon through a gap in the curtains at the window. It traced a shimmering ribbon across her floor, right up to her bed. Her skin prickling, Claire stared up at the lovely example of God's visible hand in the world.

Her voice came out in a whisper. "The heavens declare the glory of God; and the firmament shows His handiwork."

She closed her eyes, listening to the next verse of the psalm in her mind. *Day unto day utters speech, and night unto night reveals knowledge.*

A warmth came over her as she snuggled into the blankets. She felt God's closeness, His protection. And something else. A sense of purpose. She was washed with the same feeling she had sensed earlier that night.

*What is it, Lord?*

There was no answer, and her tired, overwhelmed mind retreated into sleep.

The moon grew larger outside her window, and the shimmering path came alive, soft images of the past few months dancing before her.

She watched her struggles and timidity in class, her worries over how she would look, what people would think. Her heart sank at Doug Turner's dejection during his lonely evolution debate, at Sherry's averted eyes following Claire's angry response to Stefan's mockery.

The images switched to a plane crash on a rainy night, and she saw herself faced again with that essential choice—stand or retreat. Then Bethany's confused face rose before her mind, and she somehow saw more than before—she saw herself in the quiet T station, talking, and as Bethany listened an invisible hand drew a small gold cross on her chest.

Claire began to shake, tears leaking from her eyes as she saw a very pregnant Bethany kneeling, crying, beside a tousled bed. Claire heaved great sobs, watching a tiny baby girl come forth, held up squalling to her mother's outstretched arms.

The scene switched again. Claire was on a mountainside looking out through unfamiliar eyes. She was laboring to breathe, pain racking her body. She felt the worried hands of teenage hikers and looked with great effort at the unconscious girl beside her. Her eyes opened with a gasp. A great, shining being with wings outstretched stood beside the girl. His eyes gazed into hers, his tender look telling her all she needed to know about the imminence of her own homecoming.

Claire's eyelids flickered. The shimmering ribbon transformed again becoming a shining filament that illuminated the very corners of the room. She turned her head and exhaled in awe at the same great being standing at attention right by her closet.

"I bring a message from the Lord of hosts."

"What is it?"

"The Lord says, 'My child, you already have the answers that you need. The battle is joined, and the trumpet is sounding. Be not discouraged, nor be afraid, for the Lord your God will go before you. But you must stand. And when the time comes, you must speak. And the Lord will make the barren water clear and pure, and healing will begin.'"

Claire's heart ached for her Master. "What does it mean?"

But the great being vanished. Claire took a shuddering breath. The moon receded, the Lord's words growing distant.

She reached out anxiously as the moonlit path grew faint, her heart yearning for her Home.

The answering thought was gentle, almost amused. *Not yet, little one, not yet.*

She turned on her side and snuggled deeper into her covers, her own thoughts growing as faint as the stream of moonlight through the curtains.

She spoke to the Voice in her mind. *May the words of my mouth and the meditations of my heart be pleasing in Your sight, O Lord, my rock and my redeemer.*


Her eyes opened. The morning sunlight was creeping softly through the curtains.

She sat bolt upright in bed. Her gaze went directly to her book crates in the corner. She knew. Somehow she knew.

Shivering slightly with the chill of the morning, she got up, padded over to the corner, and pulled out her philosophy book. With eager fingers she slipped out the pages from Doug's printer, each printed sheet bearing the data for one of the six recipients of the Pike Fellowship.

Sitting cross-legged on the bare floor by her window, she laid each of the six pages in a row. Murphy Barker and his classmates stared up at her.

She got up and grabbed a yellow highlighting pen off her desk, then sat back down. The floor was cold, but she didn't even think about turning up the thermostat. Her eyes were riveted on two pages in front of her.

She used her highlighter to mark a line on Johanna Godfrey's page and one on the page of Gregory Granville the third. Their second work numbers. She grinned briefly to herself. Mr. hotshot Granville came through for her this time.

The phone numbers were the same.

## FIFTY-FOUR

CLAIRE FIDDLED AROUND THE ROOM FOR A WHILE. It was too early to call anyone. She took a shower, ate a breakfast of Pop-Tarts, and packed up a few things she needed for the barbecue that morning.

Then she stood in the middle of the room, wanting to go out, wanting to *do* something with what she'd found. She forced herself to walk over to her bed and sit down. She had maintained her commitment every day thus far, and now was not the time to let it lapse. She pulled out her journal.

Within moments she was deep in prayer, pouring out her heart, seeking direction. She *felt* His enveloping love this morning. A soft song of praise played on her lips, then another, and another.

After a time Claire raised her head, at peace. The impatience was gone. God was in control.

She looked at the clock. It was still a bit early on a Saturday morning to call Ian or Mansfield. She got up and aimlessly straightened her room. Then, on impulse, she picked up the phone and dialed Ian's number.

She listened to the ringing, wincing as she pictured him being awakened from some much-needed sleep.

The phone clicked. "Hello, you've reached Ian Burke…"

She stared at the phone in surprise. Where was he? She collected her thoughts and left a message; she had figured out the answer but didn't want to leave details on voice mail.

"You know what?" she continued in a rush. "I think I'm going to head back over to the resource director's office to see if I can somehow get access to that terminal that has all the detailed alumni information on it and get some concrete evidence. It's not like I know what else to do. It's pretty early, but maybe the clerk will be there moving boxes. You never know."

Ian slowed to a rapid walk, then stopped and bent over, taking in deep mouthfuls of air. After a few moments he straightened, walking again to work out the stitch in his side.

The air was cold and crisp, and puffy white clouds scudded across a light blue sky. It was going to be a beautiful day.

He rounded a corner and entered a now-familiar side street. The tree branches overhead still formed a graceful canopy, even bare of leaves. He approached the tall iron gates and, startled, heard them creaking open.

Edward Grindley's eyes twinkled at him. "Right on time, young Ian."

Ian stared at him in frank astonishment before walking over. "I'm convinced you have security cameras watching the neighborhood the way you always know I'm here." He shook the old man's hand, chuckling. "What are you doing up so early?"

Edward put a hand on Ian's back and steered him inside the gate. "My security camera is called the Holy Spirit. He wouldn't let me sleep this morning, and now I know why." He looked up at the young man. "How about some breakfast?"


Claire walked up to the building, her hands deep in the pockets of her parka. The campus was quiet, the early morning mist still rising off the grass.

And there was a small moving truck pulled up to the building's door.

Her steps quickened with anticipation as she looked inside the empty truck—no one there—and then made her way up the stairs and down the echoing hallway. There was a flatbed outside the familiar door.

"Hello?" Claire called out. The receptionist's station was vacant. She stepped through the doorway, looking around the deserted area. She could hear the faint sound of banging and grunting down the corridor. The sounds grew louder as she cautiously approached the glassed-in office at the end of the row.

Three moving men were trying to maneuver a very large crate onto a dolly. One of them dropped a corner on his foot and swore fluently.

Despite herself, Claire grinned. No angels this time.

When the crate finally rested on the outmatched dolly, she stepped to the door and rapped on it, clearing her throat. All heads turned to look at her. She hesitated as one man's eyes traveled down her figure and up again.

"Um...I'm looking for the clerk."

The mover with the wandering eye left his buddies and walked toward the doorway, his gaze intent. She held her breath, on the verge of retreat.

When he got just two feet away he stopped, looked over her shoulder toward the maze of cubicles, and hollered. "Hey, buddy! You got someone here to see you." He leered down at her startled face and sauntered back to his work.

She turned to see a young man in khakis and a sweater fast approaching.

"Can I help you?"

"I hope so."

Claire blurted out her story as quickly as she could—the needed research, the authorization, the long hours at the resource director's computers, the aborted effort to finish. She gestured toward the rank of computers along the wall. "Is there any way you could let me back on? We have a sort of deadline that we have to meet, and I really need to look at—"

"Sorry. Your shenanigans got us into a lot of trouble the other day, and I don't think anyone here is excited about helping you now." He turned to go back to his cubicle.

"But we didn't do anything wrong! I have my access letter right here. We even stopped by yesterday to—" She broke off, her heart sinking. "Didn't the receptionist tell you?"

"Tell me what?"

"That we stopped by to prove that we hadn't lied about Ian Burke."

"No, she didn't, and since now I can't be sure that you're even telling the truth about *that*, I certainly can't just accept your access letter." He paused, and his tone moderated. "Look, I can see this is important to you, and I'd be willing to put my annoyance aside to help you. But since I wasn't here yesterday…" He shrugged, turning back to his cubicle. "I've got a lot of work to do. I'm sorry."

Dejected, Claire watched him walk back to his cube. He disappeared from sight, and Claire heard him tapping on his keyboard. She turned and walked back down the corridor. How were they ever going to—

"Claire?"

She stopped and looked behind her. The clerk was standing in his cubicle in the middle of the room, his head just visible over the partition.

"Come back here a minute."

Claire found her way through the maze and to his cube.

"Yes?"

He gave her a bemused look, then crossed his arms. "I just checked my e-mail, and there's a note from the receptionist. She says all the extra security work she's got to do is a pain in the behind, but that you were very pleasant to deal with when you and the real Ian Burke showed up." He made a good-natured gesture of exasperation. "Oh, come on then." He stepped out of the cubicle and led Claire toward the resource room.

A host of gremlins peered over the tops of cubicles, boxes, and filing cabinets as the clerk ushered Claire into the big room and began logging her on to the computer. Through the window, the gremlins could see the two chatting, but they did not approach. The presence of a nearby warrior forestalled any thought of eavesdropping.

"We must report this!" one hissed. "Krolech himself will want to know."

Several others shook their heads, and a fierce—if quiet—argument began.

"She was not supposed to get access!"

"She may not find anything."

"And what happens if she *does* find something, and we have not reported it?"

The argument grew louder. One of their number slunk unnoticed out of sight and sped away. A few minutes later the arguing group suddenly quieted. A senior demon advanced and stood before them, his face hard.

"Report."

After some hemming and hawing, the gremlins explained the quandary. He turned and looked into the room where the meddling girl was now tapping away at the keyboard. The clerk and the moving men were nowhere in sight, but she was not alone.

The senior demon leveled a hostile stare at her giant guardian. The guardian stared calmly back.

"For now," the senior demon said, "keep an eye on her. I will consider who should be told. We must find a way to learn what she knows. If necessary, one of you will go in and take a look at the terminal. Report to me on a regular basis as long as she is in this office."

As he glided away one of the gremlins let out an invective-filled complaint under his breath. The others—their disagreements temporarily forgotten—growled in one accord. No way were any of them venturing into that office.

They were going to have to make other arrangements.


"Kick out crusaders! Kick out crusaders!"

Brad stared sourly at the ten protesters not five feet from his grill.

The Fellowship had worked all morning to set up half a dozen picnic tables and four grills on the open lawn between Mem Hall and the Science Center. They had bought hundreds of hot dogs and hamburgers, procured fruit, cheese, and crackers by the bucketful, and set up tables laden with free soda. The Lord had provided them with a perfect Indian summer day.

And these stupid protesters were keeping everyone away.

Alison had left at a run to try to get the promised security help from the administration—who, after all, had authorized their barbecue. Brad had finally offered to cook each of his coworkers a hamburger. He could at least do that while they waited.

Several of the protestors were purposeful, intent. But others had the grins of cheerleaders at a pep rally. From time to time, they would look over at Brad cooking his hamburgers and smirk.

Brad momentarily wondered if his sharp tongs could be put to another use.


Stefan yawned, locking the door behind him. Sherry would probably wake up soon, but she could find her own way back to her dorm room after her irritating behavior last night.

He was half surprised that she'd agreed to stay over, but of course took full advantage of that indecision without meaning much by it.

He had awoken right on time and had showered and dressed.

His stomach rumbled as he headed across campus toward Loker Commons. If he was going to have to wait a while, as ordered, he might as well have breakfast doing it.


With a feeling of complete unreality, Claire printed page after page from the Pike Fellowships database, and the proprietary alumni contact database.

It had taken a while, but she had checked Pike Fellowship recipients from ten randomly selected years, and at least six or seven of them had the same second work number as Johanna Godfrey and Gregory Granville III. Those individuals must have called in at some time from that number, and it became listed—unbeknownst to them—in this proprietary database.

She pulled each page off the printer, carefully highlighting the telltale line, although, she had to admit, she still didn't know what it was saying.

The movers rattled around in the background, but she hardly noticed.

## FIFTY-FIVE

IAN HURRIED DOWN MASSACHUSETTS AVENUE toward the meeting spot, enjoying the clear air. What a great day for the HCF barbecue. He followed a path away from the road and toward the open area in front of the Science Center and Mem Hall.

Even from this distance, the location of the barbecue was obvious. A small group of sign-waving protestors paraded near the HCF tables.

Rather than approaching directly, he walked down the path in front of the Science Center, a little off to the side, and stood near the sharp corner of Oxford and Kirkland.

"Ian."

He turned quickly. Mansfield was climbing out of his car, stopped in a temporary spot on the side of the road. Ian could see a folding table and a few barbecue tools in the backseat.

The two men greeted each other warmly, then Mansfield turned toward the drama on the lawn beside Mem Hall.

Ian crossed his arms, tense. "I spoke with Edward Grindley this morning. He woke up this morning with an urgent need to pray. He wants us to call him later today."

"We'll do that."

"And I got a message from Claire."

The professor took his eyes off the beleaguered HCF students and looked at his TA.

Ian's face was tight. "She sounded pretty excited, but she wouldn't tell me why. She said she figured out the answer—whatever that means—this morning and was going to try to get a little more evidence. But she didn't tell me what. She asked me to meet her here."

"When?"

"In about fifteen minutes."

"I wish she'd told you more. It sounds promising. If she's not here in good time, then we need to reevaluate." Mansfield put his hand on Ian's shoulder. "I'm sure she's fine."

His attention returned to the HCF students. "Come on. Let's go show our support and see if there's anything we can do. We can get the stuff out of the car later."

As they walked up, Alison approached the group from the other direction. She was closely followed by a security truck carrying a bunch of maintenance men and a large folded tent.


Niles marched and shouted with fervor. He was tired after a night downtown, but he was not about to take a rest now. These proselytizers were unsafe, and it was his duty to rid the campus of their practices. People were noticing. Their message was being heard.

Perhaps now people would take him seriously.

He watched Alison walk back to the tables, followed by the truck. Maintenance men started unloading something heavy from the truck bed, and two security guards jumped out of the cab. He gestured to his people to shout louder. They had a right to protest, and they were going to exercise that right.

Alison was looking in their direction, talking with the guards, gesturing, her face sheepish.

Good. He wanted the proselytizers to be embarrassed. Wanted them to be humiliated that their tactics of harassment and fanaticism were being exposed.

Out of the corner of his eye, Niles saw two female students pass by on the nearby path. They were looking at the protestors and their signs curiously, as if they were exhibits in a zoo. His face reddened, and his shouts grew hoarse as the tendons stood out on his neck.

All these students just walking by. Not one truly appreciated what he was doing for them, the safety and tolerance he was ensuring.

A female security officer finished conferring with the zealots and stepped up to his group.

"Excuse me." Her voice was no-nonsense.

He would have preferred to keep shouting—just to make a point—but the others all stopped quite readily and listened.

"The Harvard Christian Fellowship group has a proper permit to conduct a prescheduled activity on these grounds. I also show that a notice of protest was filed. Who is the spokesperson here?"

Niles stepped forward. "I am."

"Good, good." She clapped her hands together. "Here's what we're going to do, just so this is all orderly. We're going to set up a half-tent—sort of a heavy canopy—for the HCF group so that people are free to visit their barbecue tables without harassment. And you all are going to maintain a distance of at least one hundred feet from the front of the tent."

As the protesters groaned and complained, the officer raised her voice and pointed to an area in the direction of Harvard Yard. "We'll set up a post for you over there."

Niles balled his hands into fists and took a leveling breath. "You can't do that. We have a right to be here!"

The officer crossed her arms. "Oh really? Why do you think so?"

"Because I have first amendment rights!"

"Well then, you and your first amendment rights can go stand over there."

She started to walk away, and Niles saw red. She hadn't even *listened* to him! The maintenance men were already swarming around the selected spot, shouldering heavy metal poles, tying ropes to large weights, straining to erect the bulky tent.

"We have rights!" he shouted after her, noticing with satisfaction that everyone within hearing distance was turning to stare.

"We have freedom of speech!" He waved his arms as she and the second security guard—a rather large man—approached with narrowed eyes. "We have freedom of association! And we have freedom to tell these radicals that they must take their loathsome attempts to convert people elsewhere!"

The female guard looked at Niles and said, "Your distance is now one hundred and fifty feet."


The movers finished hefting the round of boxes into the truck, then turned to head up the stairs. One more load.

A heavyset man in a blue coat slipped around the side of the truck and gestured one of the movers aside just as he was about to enter the building. Another man in a black coat stood a short distance away, scanning the area with intent eyes.

The blue-coated man conferred with the mover for a minute, then took out his billfold and held out some cash. The moving man gave a quick glance around, then took the cash and stuffed it in an inside pocket of his work jumper.

The mover quickly reentered the building and walked nonchalantly into the room where his buddies were packing up stray boxes. He drifted toward the end where the girl was working and picked up a long box.


Claire started as one of the moving men tripped and dropped a long slim box on the desk right beside her. Papers went flying.

"Sorry about that, darlin'." He straightened the papers and leaned toward her. "Didn't frighten you, did I?"

"No." His lascivious eyes made her nervous. She gave a brief smile and turned back to her terminal.

He picked up his box, then walked slowly behind her chair. She could hear his breathing behind her neck and tensed. She relaxed slightly as he continued on to the other side of the room, picked up more boxes, and carried them out of the room and down the corridor.

*Ugh.* She shivered. *What a creepy man.*


The moving man loaded his boxes onto the flatbed, then told his comrades he was going to take a bathroom break. They nodded and turned back toward the office as he walked away.

The mover greeted the blue-coated man with a crooked smile and pulled a piece of paper halfway out of his pocket, then pushed it back in. He said something, shrugged, and held out his hand.

There was a long pause. Whatever he saw in blue-coat's eyes, the mover quickly plucked the paper out of his pocket, handed it over with a brief statement, and scuttled back up the stairs.

The recipient called black-coat over and unfolded the piece of paper, holding it so his comrade could also read it. Both pairs of eyes went directly to a place halfway down the page where—amidst a jumble of text and numbers—a line of yellow highlighting stood out.

With a low growl, blue-coat tucked the paper into his pocket, then spoke briefly with his comrade. He made a short but urgent cell-phone call and received the authorization.


One of Niles's friends pulled him over to the picket line the female security officer was setting up. She pointed to a pathway separating the protestors from the white canopy now rising from the lawn. She said something to Niles, gesturing. He didn't hear it.

She nodded to the others, took a last look around, and walked back toward the barbecue.

Through a film of rage Niles watched the proselytizers smugly arranging their tables under the tent. Even in the short time the protestors had stopped chanting, several students had ventured under the canopy for hot dogs and soda.

Most of the freeloaders walked right back out again, paper plates in hand, and went on their way. But some stayed. He could see them sitting at the tables, foolishly chatting with the students working the barbecue.

The protesters held their signs up and tried another chant, but Niles could tell their resolve was weakening. The tent was in a prominent spot by Mem Hall, and the picketers had been relegated to a corner of the lawn.

A stream of people came from Harvard Yard heading for the science center. One person walked over to the protestors to cheer them on, but most students just ignored them. A few shot derisive looks in their direction.

Niles watched as two of his picketers glanced at each other, then handed back their signs and walked away.

"Come back!" He ran to stop them. "Back to your posts!"

"Come off it, Niles," one said, moving away. "We tried."

The other followed his friend. "No one cares, man. We're busted. Take it up with the administration."

Niles glanced back at the other picketers, who were again marching along their allowed space. Seething, he took a few steps toward the tent and stood squarely in the middle of the path that served as their dividing line. Students flowed around him, but he didn't notice.

The barbecue tent now boasted a large sign inviting people in. Several more students had ventured under the white canopy.

He could see that right-winger Brad flipping burgers at the very back of the tent, talking with a young woman holding a bag of hamburger buns. The tall professor was walking around, patting shoulders, smiling and encouraging the illicit display. Near the front of the tent, Alison took a seat at a picnic table, sipping a drink and talking with two students.

Niles looked closer, his hand tightening around the picket sign he still held. Those were students from his marketing class! How had they fallen for this? He watched one accept a plate of cheese and crackers with a word of thanks.

He snapped the sign across his knee. They were *thanking* them! Was anyone thanking *him* for exposing their tricks, for warning the campus how unsafe these people were? No! They walked right into the Venus's-flytrap and *thanked them!*

He turned back to the protestors. They were all gone. A pile of signs littered the ground.

The two men waited for several minutes, impatient, until the three movers returned, closed the back doors of the truck, and drove away. Then they climbed the stairs at a rapid pace and walked side by side down the hallway toward the appropriate door.

Blue-coat stopped short of the door and gestured to black-coat, who slipped inside the office and cast a quick glance around the empty reception area, the deserted cubicles.

"Clear."

The two men strode down the corridor to the glassed-in room. They could hear typing. Black-coat reached inside his jacket, and they stepped quickly to the doorway.

The clerk, sitting in front of one of the computers, looked up in surprise. "May I help you?"

Blue-coat dissembled with an effort, forcing a casual smile. "Actually, yes. We're supposed to pick up our niece, and I'm afraid we're late. Is she still here?"

"Man, what a bummer. You just missed her. She left less than a minute ago."

"Do you know where she went?"

"I think she said something about a barbecue, but I don't know where it was."

Blue-coat tried to catch a glimpse of the computer screen behind the clerk. He let his brow furrow in apparent concern. "By any chance do you happen to know if she found what she was looking for?"

"Well, she was pretty excited about something." The clerk smiled, shrugging. "I'm sorry I can't be of more help."

Blue-coat made a subtle gesture to his comrade. They stepped inside the resource room door and closed it.

The clerk looked startled as blue-coat advanced, smiling, his hand going to his jacket.

"No, you've been a great help."


Claire looked at her watch, annoyed, and picked up her pace. Why did janitors always insist on doing their scrubbing in a way that blocked the most convenient door out? And always when she was in a hurry and couldn't afford the extra few minutes' detour.

She forced herself to calm down. The precious printouts were safe in her backpack, and the only reason she was so anxious was her eagerness to show Mansfield and Ian.

She breathed another prayer of exultation, her spirit almost giddy. They were close to an answer. She could feel it!


The two men left the building at a run and jumped in their nearby car, faces tight, intent. The girl could not tell anyone what she had found. There was a small parking lot in front of Memorial Hall that would work perfectly.


Stefan slipped out the door to Loker Commons in the basement of Mem Hall and walked up the outdoor steps toward ground level. A small parking area was on his left, and a large white tent rose on the lawn not far in front of him. When he was just above eye level with the ground and could see the tent clearly, he stopped.

He leaned against the wall and folded his arms. He'd been ordered to watch this "learning event," and contribute his energy. He wished his father had told him what was planned.


Niles's pickup truck was in a parking garage all the way up by the law school. He didn't even notice the walk there, and before he knew it, was in the truck on Everett Street, passing the law school dorms.

Someone strolled across the street in front of him, and he slammed on his brakes, swerving. He rolled down the truck window and shouted an obscenity at the top of his lungs. The pedestrian made a hand gesture and deliberately slowed his pace.

Niles stomped on the gas. The pedestrian leaped between two parked cars as Niles's heavy bumper barely missed him. In his rearview mirror Niles saw with satisfaction that the pedestrian had run back into the road, shouting something after his truck.

These idiots thought they owned the road. Niles's thoughts grew blacker. He pictured mowing down the smug pedestrian, pictured the self-righteous face plastered on the street. He replayed the image in his mind as he turned onto Oxford Street.

In the distance, a white tent rose at the end of the road.

Black rage pressed in on him, and he slowly pressed down the gas pedal, feeling the slow surge of power.


The two large men pulled up with a jerk in front of Memorial Hall, jumped out of the car, and headed toward the white tent on the lawn.

No sign of the girl, but they couldn't see inside the canopy from this angle. Blue-coat gestured, and his comrade ran ahead to a good vantage point.

Black-coat scanned the cheerful crowds under the canopy, and his eyes narrowed. The girl was off in a back corner talking to the professor. How could they get both of them to leave the tent? He gestured blue-coat over.


Coming out from Harvard Yard, Claire could see a tentlike canopy ahead. Her angle blocked a full view, but she could see Alison sitting at a picnic table in the front.

She looked in vain for protesters. Across the lawn, she saw Mansfield's car pull up to the small lot in front of Mem Hall. Ian got out and began to lug a folding table out of the backseat. His face was worried.

She smiled. He was probably worried about her. She quickened her step, heading toward him rather than the tent.

Mansfield turned, smiling, as Claire appeared at his side.

"Claire!" He put a grandfatherly hand on her shoulder, looking down into her face. It was shining.

He went rigid in surprise and started to drop his hand.

"Don't." She gently patted his hand.

The squealing of nearby tires caught his attention, and suddenly the happy commotion in the tent became distant, pausing in a blink of time.

The voice by his side was clear. "Don't be afraid, William David Mansfield."

Mansfield forced himself to take a shuddering breath as he stared down into the otherworldly eyes. He couldn't speak. Excitement, trepidation, longing washed over him.

The young woman's gaze was solemn. "Your Lord is calling you home. You have run the race well, Dr. Mansfield, and there is much awaiting you. The enemy's schemes are evil, but God will use them for His good."

Mansfield kept his hand on her shoulder, and his words came out as a whisper. "Can you tell me more?"

"Your great work here has been to expose the schemes of the enemy, to open the eyes of the blind to the glorious light of the gospel of Christ. You were born to that purpose, and you have been faithful. The Master's hand is now pulling the final threads of what the enemy has woven around this place. Those schemes are about to unravel. Your sacrifice will be the final thread that the Lord transforms. He will use it to weave a garment of righteousness."

Mansfield looked around at the cheerful silent throng of students, the half-flipped burgers poised over an immobile fire. His senses seemed magnified by the suspended motion. He saw Alison paused in earnest conversation, looked through the tent flap to where Ian was half out of his distant car. With vision that was somehow not his own, he saw Brad and Teresa talking by the grill and also dancing together under a larger tent of white. Tears appeared in his eyes.

"You will still be able to see them, you know. Still pray for them." The young woman's eyes smiled up into his. "And William David Mansfield, you also will receive a robe of righteousness this day."

"Praise be to God!" Tears leaked down his cheeks. "I am ready to meet my Lord."

"God is with you, my friend."

The motion in the tent snapped back into being, the squealing of tires loud in his ears. Mansfield smiled, triumphant, and his fingers tightened on the young woman's shoulder.

Claire ran up beside Ian as he lugged the table out of Mansfield's car.

"Boo."

Startled, he nearly dropped the table. He turned swiftly, then sagged in relief. "Thank God! I—"

The squealing of tires interrupted his words. The two students twisted to see a large pickup truck speeding the final feet of Oxford Street. It was not slowing for the turn.

The students under the front canopy were talking, laughing as the truck leaped the curb and plowed into the back of the tent. It mowed down the heavy tarpaulin, snapping metal poles like twigs before it finally crashed into some immovable object and stopped.

"NO!"

Claire screamed as she watched the students scatter, screaming in horror. The tent was collapsing around those inside, trapping them in the folds of heavy fabric, under tables, thick metal poles. She could see bodies straining to get free. The truck stood grotesquely in the middle of the collapsed tarpaulin.

Claire ran forward, Ian right behind her, stumbling, scrambling, for the tent. She passed hysterical students running the other direction.

One of them was yelling, "Mansfield! Mansfield! O God, Mansfield was back there!"

Claire started crying, pushing through a growing crowd. Students were running toward the scene from all directions, dozens of hands outstretched, pulling at the massive tarpaulin. People were shouting, "Call 911!"

Claire saw someone pull Alison from the wreckage of a picnic table. She was gasping for air, her face pale, holding her side. The helping hands laid Alison down on the ground just as Claire fought her way up to the tent.


Ian was grabbed by hysterical hands.

"O God, help me!"

The girl—he didn't know her name—fell back to the ground, crying out in pain, her thigh pierced by the sharp tines of a barbecue rack.

He looked at the hot metal and knelt beside her, ripping off his windbreaker. "Hold still."

He was shaking and started praying under his breath as he wrapped his hands in the folds of his jacket. He grabbed the metal rack and pulled it free in one fluid motion.

The girl screamed, panting, her hands grabbing at his sweater. Ian had tears in his eyes as he laid his hand on her head. "You'll be okay. It'll be okay." He looked around as another female student ran up.

"Teresa!"

The girl fell to the ground and embraced her friend, who started crying. "Brad was back there! O Jesus, help us!"

"They said Mansfield was, too!" the newcomer cried. Her words caught the attention of three students who were running toward the scene.

"Professor Mansfield?" All three went rigid with horror.

A young woman nearby pressed her hands to her face, tears filling her eyes. "O dear God!"

The word spread quickly, and Ian could hear wails of disbelief.

He was jostled by a heavy body brushing past.

"...took out Claire...good..."

Ian froze and strained to listen over the chaos around him. He got a glimpse of a man in a black jacket speaking in a low voice to someone out of his view. "Claire only talked to the professor, and they both went down. I'd say we're secure."

The other voice was even lower. "Go and watch. I'll stay here. Make sure they're both dead. And grab the evidence if you can."

The black-jacketed man began working his way around the perimeter of the crowd.

Ian jumped to his feet, his blood running cold. He started praying aloud as he tried to fight his way through the throng.

"O God! Help me get her, Lord!"

Suddenly a path opened in front of him. He ran forward, anxious eyes scanning the dreadful scene. Emergency personnel had begun to arrive from the fire station across the street from Mem Hall, and firemen were tunneling through the collapsed tent, carrying limp forms from the wreckage. Several men had wrestled the driver out of the truck and to the ground.

Several still lumps lay under the tarpaulin, near the car. Ian wanted to vomit. He forced himself to breathe, his eyes wild as he looked around.

Claire was kneeling beside Alison, holding her hand, shaking.

He ran up and grabbed her from behind. "Come with me!"

She turned, her face wild. "They say Mansfield was standing right there! Right there, Ian!"

Ian reached down and pulled her to her feet. She fought him, beating on his chest, but he held her until she was able to listen. He whispered in her ear, and her eyes went wide, searching the crowd.

He grabbed her hand, and they broke into a run toward Mansfield's car. He scooped up her backpack and shoveled her into the passenger seat, then ran around to the driver's side.

"We can't just leave them!"

"We have to!" Ian shouted as he jumped into the driver's seat. "They were trying for *you*, Claire!"

He turned the keys in the ignition and peeled away from the building.

He did not see the man in the blue coat run toward the lot and stare after them.

MANSFIELD TREMBLED AS HE WALKED TOWARD the radiant throne escorted by a solemn honor guard.

He *couldn't* approach that Glory, and yet…he could. He looked around at the shining faces of the loved ones lining his path, their gleeful smiles, their delight at his reaction. Rank upon rank spread behind them, those predecessors—he somehow knew—of his godly heritage. All gathered in the throne room to watch him approach the King.

Mansfield closed his eyes, inexpressible joy leaking down his cheeks. His heart stretched as if it would burst. And yet…it was as if his capacity for love had been expanded, able to hold more pure feeling than ever imagined in the shadowed lands.

The honor guard stopped. He was there.

He took a breath and raised his face toward his King. Instantly, he was on his knees, quaking, his face to the throne-room floor.

There was a long pause. And then he felt a gentle touch on his shoulder, heard those words his heart had been longing for his whole life.

"Well done, my good and faithful servant."

The Son of Man knelt beside him, arms outstretched, and Mansfield threw himself into His embrace.

His Savior's voice was strong and tender as he rocked his child, a laugh bubbling up just under the surface.

"Enter into the joy of your Lord!"


Ian made another quick turn, looking behind him in the rearview mirror. No one was following them.

His hands began to shake on the steering wheel, and he started taking fast, shallow breaths. His whole body was cold, his mind grappling with the unfathomable.

A group of students rushed past on the nearby sidewalk, heading in the direction of Mem Hall. Tears were streaming down their faces.

He turned into a deserted side street near the college and stopped the car with a jerk. He slammed the gearshift into park, put his head and arms on the steering wheel, and wept. Beside him, Claire had her head in her hands, shuddering with sobs. He reached over, and she clung to him, her fingers clenching and unclenching on his sweater.

They pulled apart after a time, Claire wiping her eyes on the sleeve of her jacket.

"I think he's dead, you know." Her voice came out in a whisper. "The people back there weren't moving. The firemen said that most of the ones they brought out were unconscious but okay. But they said there were a few…" She broke down again. "O God, why?"

Ian's voice was husky. "Lord, we don't know why this has happened, but we know You are on Your throne. God, show us what we're supposed to do."

He took a deep breath. As if a switch had been flipped, an unearthly peace descended on him. There would be time for mourning later. Right now they had to figure out what to do. For one thing, they had no doubt about the importance of the information Claire carried.

He turned toward her, grabbing her by the shoulders. "What was it?" His voice was urgent. "What was the answer you found?"

Claire stared at him, her eyes widening, then scrambled into the backseat where Ian had thrown her backpack. She fumbled with the zipper and pulled out the precious pages. She handed him one of the sheets, pointing, explaining quickly.

"This *must* be it, but how they knew I had them I don't know." She turned to put the papers back in the pack, and screamed.

Ian spun in his seat. Stefan Pike was running toward the car, stumbling down a gentle incline behind them, looking above and behind him, his eyes wild.

"Go! Go!" Claire yelled.

But Ian didn't go. He wasn't supposed to. He opened the car door and got out.

"*Ian!*"

Stefan saw him and ran up, gasping. "Help me! Help me."

He saw Claire in the backseat, her mouth open, yelling at Ian. He reeled back and turned to run, but Ian grabbed his jacket, wrestling him back against the wall lining the street. He slammed him hard into the brick. Stefan began to struggle, and Ian slammed him back again and again, shouting for an explanation.

Suddenly, he felt Claire's hands pulling him away, heard her shouting at him to stop. He heard Stefan whimpering.

"Help…me…"

Ian gave Stefan a final shove, yelling at him. "What is going on?"

Stefan started whimpering again and batted at his chest, his head, his shoulders. "Get them off me; get them off!"

Ian and Claire looked at each other in alarm.

"What, Stefan?" Claire said. "Get what off you?"

"These claws! *His* claws!" he wailed. "I don't want him! I don't want him!"

Ian swallowed hard. "Stefan, you're seeing something in the spirit that we can't see. What is it?"

Stefan closed his eyes, quivering in place. "There are arms coming over my shoulders from the back and claws digging into my chest. He's on my head and shoulders!" Stefan began to bat his head, hard. "I don't want him!"

Ian could hear Claire praying under her breath.

*O Lord, help us…*

"Stefan, you have a demon on you," Ian said. "We'll pray for you, but you must renounce him."

Stefan's eyes were wild. "I renounce him! I don't want him!"

Ian stepped forward, speaking under his breath. "God, help me do this." He laid his hands on Stefan's shoulders, and his voice grew strong. "Evil spirit, the Lord rebuke you! We bind you in the name of Jesus and proclaim that you must go from this man's life."

Stefan whimpered, his head hanging, his voice a whisper. "I don't want you…"

"He has renounced you, and we tell you to go in the name of Jesus!"

Stefan raised his head, and Ian looked into his eyes. They glazed over, and his body began to sway. Ian caught his arm, and Claire leaped to open the car door just as Stefan collapsed. Ian maneuvered him into the backseat and closed the door.

"What do we do now?" Claire said.

Ian cleared his throat. "I think God told me what to do. We need to take him to the Grindley house. This is all part of the plan."

Claire ran around to the passenger side. "We need to go by my dorm on the way."

"No way."

"I left the printouts of the other pages in my room this morning. They're hidden in my philosophy book, but I don't want to leave them there."

They got into the car, and Ian pulled out of the side street and onto a main road, scowling. "Why'd you leave them?"

A series of emergency vehicles—ambulances, police cars, a truck and crane—sped past them sirens blaring.

"How was I to know all this was going to happen!" She gestured toward another side street. "If you pull in here, you're really close to my dorm. You can't park—they'll tow you in two seconds flat—but you can wait for me."

"I'm not letting you go up to your room alone!"

"I have to, Ian. I'll only be a second. If I'm not back in five minutes, come get me."

"This is ridiculous." Ian pulled down the street she indicated and stopped the car with a jerk. "Someone just tried to kill you—and probably *did* succeed in killing Mansfield—" His voice choked, and he yelled at her. "There is *no way* you're going up there alone!"

"I'll go." Stefan spoke quietly from the backseat. He pushed himself into a sitting position. "I'll watch her back."

Ian turned around in his seat. "What?" Stefan's face was pale, but his eyes were clear.

"Look, I've got a lot I need to tell you guys. A lot you need to know. Let me walk her up and back." He paused, looking at Ian. "Unless you want me to stay with the car?"

Ian wavered. Stefan was watching him with earnest eyes. He sighed. "Claire, are you okay with this?"

Claire looked back at Stefan. She hesitated, then smiled. "Yeah, I'm okay. Let's go."


The phone rang in Anton's den, and he snatched it up, a tight smile on his face. "Yes."

"Do you have your television on?" Victor said.

"You know I do." Anton looked over at the flat screen on his wall—scenes of emergency crews, crying students, a truck being lifted by a crane. He gave a momentary grimace as the camera panned to three students kneeling in anguished prayer.

"The professor is dead."

"Ah, as I thought." Anton closed his eyes, a small smile playing on his lips. He grasped for the familiar surge of power. His eyelids flickered when it did not come. After a moment he cleared his throat. "Our path is clear, then?"

"Not quite. I just received the report from my men. The girl got away."

"Of all the stupid, incompetent…!" Anton jumped up and stomped around the den. "What sort of—"

"It was an Enemy ruse, brother." Victor's voice was deadly calm. "Even more than the one that snatched her from your grasp on Thursday."

"Explain." Anton stood still in the middle of the room, his eyes narrowing as Victor relayed the story told by his men. "An Enemy ruse, as you said."

"Yes. And more than that." Victor paused, and for the first time his voice was tense. "The Masters now say she is a chosen one in the Enemy line."

"*Now* say! Where was this knowledge before?"

"Carefully hidden by the Enemy. But to steal her away, they could hide it no longer."

There was silence; then Victor spoke again, his tone careful. "And there is another problem. Stefan did not stand. He must commit, must be brought in before it is too late. He still does not hold the key to the organization, correct?"

"You know he doesn't. Not until he commits."

"Good. We must stop this now."

Anton paced again, and as he stalked the room he seemed to stretch, to grow more agile. He closed his eyes and his face contorted, his body writhing as the familiar surge finally came.

His eyes opened, staring outside the room, and a smile of great satisfaction spread over his face. "Ah, yes." His voice came out on a soft hiss. "The young one is heading for her dorm. We must take her. I see it now. Merely eliminating her would have been wrong. But a sacrifice to our Master—a sacrifice of the chosen offspring in that lineage—will ensure our hold. And we will deal a deathblow to the Enemy's pitiful attempts to reestablish His. Our mandate will again be secured."

Krolech stopped pacing and turned to Katoth, who was standing at rigid attention.

"Go. Now. She must be brought in, unharmed for the moment. Kill the man. The evidence must not get out. And do not fail this time to reestablish your hold on the heir. Your ineffectiveness is disturbing. This weakness in him, this frailty, must stop."

"My liege—"

"And I don't want to hear any more about the ancestress!" Krolech jabbed his finger in the direction Katoth had come. "It is *your* charge. Now go!"

Claire and Stefan hurried the short distance to her dorm. Stefan began rubbing his temples, his forehead wrinkling.

"What's wrong?" Claire asked.

"Sherry." He muttered something unintelligible. "Can I tell Sherry?"

Claire looked at him anxiously as he continued talking under his breath. He seemed disoriented, confused. As they approached the back door to her dorm, Claire's skin prickled, and she looked behind them. Nothing.

She used her card key, flung open the door, and came face-to-face with Sherry, who was walking out.

"Claire!" Sherry hugged her roommate. "Thank God you're okay! Did you hear about Mansfield? Everyone's gone up to Mem Hall!"

Claire swallowed and tried to push inside the entryway, to get out of public view. Stefan was close behind her. "Yes, I—"

"What are *you* doing here?" Sherry's hands were on her hips as she stared at Stefan.

"Sherry, I have to talk to you." He put a hand on her arm, but she wrenched it away.

"I have no interest in speaking with you after—"

Claire cleared her throat. "Ah, listen, I have to get something from my room. Is anyone else there?"

"Yes. Mercedes is home."

Claire wavered, looking at Stefan, then forced herself to start up the stairs.

Stefan looked up at her, then back at Sherry. A new entreaty was in his voice. "Can you wait a minute? I'm supposed to go with her, and—"

"You're supposed to go with *her?* What sort of fool do you take me for?"

Claire ran up the stairs to her floor and started down the empty hall. She heard a television playing in the lounge but no other voices.

*"Again, in our top story, grief and shock on the Harvard University campus today as the trend of senseless student killings graduates to the college level..."*

The door to the lounge was half open. She peered through the crack. The television was playing to an empty room, the floor littered with boxes of tissues and other scrunched-up talismans of collective grief.

A photo of Mansfield appeared on the screen. Claire pulled back in shock. He was wearing a formal faculty robe, standing on a stage and waving to a clapping crowd of students.

*"The venerable Harvard professor Dr. William Mansfield, appears to be among those killed or injured by a student known to be angry over..."*

Claire stepped back, quivering, her hands to her face. She forced aside the thoughts that screamed for retreat. She couldn't break down now.

She turned and ran for her room.

Mercedes rose from the couch as Claire rushed in and closed the door behind her. She leaned against the door, her skin prickling again. The very air seemed dark.

Her suitemate's eyes stared into hers as the door to Claire's bedroom opened, and two men stepped through the door.

"NO!" Claire twisted, fumbling for the doorknob. Rough hands grabbed her from behind, turning her around, reaching for her face.

She fought them, scratching and kicking, as they pinned her against the wall. One grabbed for her hair, a white cloth in his hand. She smelled something sweet.

Through terror-filled eyes she saw Mercedes standing in the middle of the room, just watching.

"Help me!" Claire screamed at her as she ducked her head and tried to kick away from their grasp. Mercedes stood, unmoved, as Claire was wrestled to the floor. She had a strange, eager smile on her face.

Claire gasped in pain as the men shoved her to her stomach, one fumbling with the white cloth, the other tying her hands behind her back. Out of breath, Claire raised her head and looked up at Mercedes, her voice weak.

"How could you?" she gasped. "How could you?"

The white cloth found her face, and Mercedes disappeared into black.


Gael cried out as another sword found his side. There were too many of them!

At his back he heard Etán and several others clashing with dozens of dark, eager figures. The enemy troops had been terribly invigorated by the pain and grief filling the campus.

Gael's face was set as he fought off yet another determined attack. There would come an hour, soon, when the tide would turn, when the prayers of the nation would pierce the dark wave. But during this period of fresh anguish, raw despair, the enemy troops were at their strength.

And now the dark ones had learned that Claire Rivers was one chosen by the Lord of hosts for His purposes! Of course they would seek to drive a blow to the Father's heart of their great Enemy.

Gael and the others were beaten back, slowly, slowly. Just like at the tent, when wave upon wave had come from nowhere! God's voice had boomed loud with their orders then, and every anguished member of the heavenly host had bowed a knee, trusting in His purposes.

But what was God's purpose here? Through the thronging mass, he could see his unconscious charge being searched, the men arguing over their next steps.

She hadn't listened!

Gael felt a pain greater than the ripping blows of his foes. He had failed to keep her from this headstrong mission. He hadn't known of the waiting ambush, but he had been sure that the enemy would grow desperate, and he had been right.

He felt the strengthening touch of the Spirit of God. There would be more desperate battles ahead, but the Lord of hosts would continue to transform what the enemy meant for evil.

Gael sought assurance from his king as to Claire's fate and heard only silence. He stood straighter, wielding his sword with renewed strength. His task was set before him. He did not need to know.

## FIFTY-SEVEN

THE SATURDAY CROWD WAS THICK AS TOM AND BARBARA RIVERS walked arm in arm through the enormous Michigan shopping mall. Barbara looked through the many display windows, her thoughts as rambling as their leisurely lunchtime conversation. This blouse would be a perfect Christmas present for Grandma, that game for her youngest son.

She shook her head. They needed to pray about their finances first, before they made their gift-buying decisions. She perused a sparkling housewares display, her mind vaguely reaching for that of the Father.

A second later, Tom turned to say something to her and stopped cold when he saw her face. "Honey, what's wrong?" He gripped her shoulders. *"What's wrong!"*

Her face was pale, her body trembling. "Claire…Claire…O Lord." She stared at her husband's white face and pressed a shaking hand to her lips. "We need to pray. *Right now."*

Tom dropped his few packages, and without a further word, the husband and wife hugged each other, their prayers fervent. People flowed all around them as they cried out to the Lord. Several shoppers stared and gave them a wide berth. But others watched, their gazes sympathetic.

They pulled apart slightly, and a woman came up to them, shaking her head. "You heard, huh?"

"Heard what?" Barbara asked.

The woman bit her lip, then pointed at an electronics shop across the walkway. Dozens of people stood, staring at a bank of television sets all showing the same scene. Several people were walking away, clearly upset.

Within minutes, Barbara and Tom were in their car, speeding away from the mall, praying aloud. Over and over, Barbara used her cell phone to punch in the numbers for Claire's room. No answer.

Ian drummed his fingers on the steering wheel, looking at the campus gate right by the car. Three minutes. If they weren't back in *one,* he was going after them.

He could hear more emergency vehicles passing on the nearby road. He flicked on the radio. Jazz music. Mansfield's favorite. He choked, tears again prickling his eyes, as he turned the tuner, looking for a news station. He heard the word *Harvard* and stopped, his finger hovering over the dial.

"*...comment by college authorities on the deaths and injuries.*" There was a pause, and then a different voice, starting midsentence.

"*...can now confirm that most—if not all—of the victims were associated with a student Christian group here on campus, and that the young man driving the truck was Niles LeJames.*"

The announcer came back on, his voice grave. "*This senseless killing appears to have undeniable religious undertones. Mr. LeJames was well known on campus for his strong views against Christian proselytizing and had led a protest rally at the site of the killings earlier in the day. Stay tuned after the break for excerpts from an article written by Mr. LeJames just a few weeks ago.*"


Stefan ran after Sherry as she brushed out the door and stalked away.

"You're not listening, Sher!"

She walked a few more paces on the tree-lined path. He grabbed her by the shoulders, turning her toward him.

She slapped his face. Hard.

"I do not want to stand here and listen to your superspiritual garbage!" she hissed under her breath, looking around. "You're as bad as Claire! I don't care what you say you *saw*. This conversation is *over.*"

She turned and hurried away. Stefan put a hand to his head and leaned against a tree trunk, his eyes glazing. Then, with a start, he turned and took a step toward the dorm.

Two large men stepped out the door carrying a long, heavy duffel bag between them. One had his free hand stuck inside his jacket.

Stefan stood still in the shadow of the tree as the two men looked around. One of them cursed under his breath. "Where did he go?"

Stefan's eyes narrowed, and he stepped out from beside the tree. "Over here."

The man in the blue coat turned and snapped to attention as Stefan walked over.

"We've got the girl. We're not sure where the evidence is. We need to take out the man."

"Leave Ian Burke to me." Stefan's voice was curt.

"Okay." Blue-coat tossed him a small packet of white cloths. "We'll rendezvous at your father's house in one hour. If we don't meet you there, we'll see you on the island later tonight." Blue-coat's eyes bored into his. "It *will* be tonight."

"Yes." Stefan straightened. "Understood."

Blue-coat hesitated. "Are you sure you don't need help?" He looked over to his comrade then back at Stefan. "Let us settle the girl, and then one of us will meet you at the man's car."

Stefan shook his head. "I can handle it." He turned and walked toward Ian's car. Out of the corner of his eye, he could see blue-coat staring after him.


Ian glanced at his watch, and his face tightened. He unbuckled his seat belt and got out of the car just as Stefan came running through the campus gate toward him. Alone.

"Get back in!" Stefan gestured frantically. "Get back in the car!"

"Where's Claire?"

Stefan yanked the passenger door open and jumped in. "They took her!"

"*What?*" Ian turned toward the gate.

"They're on their way to get you! Come on!"

Ian wavered then jumped in and slammed the car into drive. He pulled out of his parking spot, tires squealing, just as a man in a black coat came charging through the gate. The man ran a few paces after the car then stopped, staring, in the middle of the street.

Ian kept one hand on the wheel, and with the other reached over and grabbed Stefan's neck, his fingers digging in.

"What happened!"

He released his grasp with a shake and turned his attention back to the road, pointing the car toward the Grindley House.

Stefan slumped in the seat. "I'm sorry. I'm sorry. There were two of them. And they were armed. There wasn't anything I could do."

Ian had tears in his eyes. "What are they going to do to her?"

"I don't know...."

"You don't know!" Ian slammed on his brakes, swerving to a stop in the middle of the road. Behind him other cars screeched to a halt, horns blaring.

"It's your family that took her!" Ian jabbed his finger at the door. "Get out of this car!"

"No...no...don't make me. They want me. Please, I can help you."

Ian closed his eyes, struggling for self-control. He forced himself to pray, hearing the quiet, urgent voice of the Lord.

He pressed on the gas again, and for the next few minutes they rode in silence, Ian's mind roiling. One thought—stronger than all the others—was pulling him, drawing him like a crane and a winch. *Get to the Grindley House...get to the Grindley House....*

The other ideas fought for supremacy. They should call the police.... They should notify the college....

His lips pressed together. And what would they say? That—on a day already chaotic with so much tragedy—the authorities should investigate whether a prominent business professor had arranged a mysterious kidnapping?

He could see their disbelieving eyes now.

Suddenly, Stefan stirred beside him and started to mutter. Ian glanced over. His passenger was whimpering, holding his head. "No...no..."

Ian sped up, praying furiously as he turned onto the familiar street. He could see the gate ahead, standing wide open. Despite himself, his lips twisted. That security camera at work again...

More whimpers. He looked over at Stefan's face and started to pray aloud.

"In the name of Jesus, evil spirit, I command you to leave this man! Leave this car!"

He turned the wheel, bumping over the edge of the Grindley driveway.


In a flash, Katoth was flung aside. He howled in rage and pain as he smacked against the impenetrable barrier, the stinging prayers of the saints. The car continued on without him. He could see the backpack bouncing around in the backseat.

Behind him, his troop also arrested their progress, hovering, their eyes red and furious.

Katoth watched a score of warriors swarm over the car, watched several women run from the dreadful house, pulling the heir from the passenger seat.

Their prayers! Their prayers!

He roared his rage, holding his head. He pictured Krolech ripping him apart piece by piece.

He stilled. A deadly calm came over him.

It wasn't over yet. The heir could still make his choice. Why would he choose weakness and frailty over the power he had already seen, the dynasty he could command?

Katoth turned to his troop, barking orders even as his thoughts sped ahead. It was time to take some precautions.


Ian stepped through the front door, laying down Claire's backpack and standing aside as two women half-carried Stefan inside. He heard the swift tapping of a cane and turned to see Edward Grindley coming toward him across the foyer, deep sorrow in his grandfatherly gaze.

Ian stepped forward and hugged the old man, then broke down at last in wracking sobs. He slipped to one knee and felt gentle hands on his head and shoulders.

"Mansfield was my *father.*" He whispered to the air. "Why did You take him, Lord?"

Edward kept his wrinkled hands lightly around Ian's shoulders until Ian's tears shuddered to a stop. He looked down in benediction and put his hand under Ian's chin. "The enemy of our souls is the author of death and destruction. But the Prince of Peace transforms what is intended for evil into good. He is transforming the blackest of tragedy into a pearl of great price."

He kept a quavering hand on Ian's arm as the young man rose to his feet. Ian's eyes couldn't leave Edward's face.

"God's purpose is already beginning to unfold, young Ian. There is a wave of anguish, of soul searching, sweeping this campus." He gestured to the three women still standing quietly in the foyer. "Here in this house, we have felt it. The prayers of the saints have grown fervent. We have already received several hundred phone calls, e-mails, faxes, telling us that a breakthrough is coming, that this campus is shaken to its core."

He steered Ian slowly into his den. The television set in the corner played silent pictures of the Harvard campus, scenes of grief.

"Within one hour after the news hit, Memorial Church was overrun with students kneeling at the alter, praying, crying. In every dorm, in every building, students and faculty are grasping for something beyond themselves, searching for something to make sense of the senseless. And, as people watch, the scene is being repeated across the nation."

Ian looked dully at the television then swung, alarmed, toward the old man. "Edward, they took Claire! That accident…they were trying to kill her too!"

"Who is Claire?"

"She was the one doing most of the research on the endowments project, and then we started finding all this other stuff on the Pikes. She—"

Edward gripped his arm. "What is her name, Ian? Her full name?"

"Claire Rivers."

Edward reeled, and several hands reached to steady him.

He looked up at Ian, an odd expression on his face. "There is even more going on than I suspected. God will reveal it in due course. Before we can know what we are to do about your friend, I need to hear the full story of this day." He gestured toward the fireplace. "Come sit down."

Ian cleared his throat, his voice tight, as he allowed himself to be steered toward the sofas around the fireplace. "Do they know how many are dead?"

"They probably know, but they haven't released a formal list. The authorities cordoned off the scene, and it took a while to remove the truck without hurting any-one who might have been trapped under the tent."

"But on the radio they knew Mansfield was dead."

Edward nodded, his face sober. "He was the first one hit. There is already specula-tion that the death toll would have been even higher if Mansfield hadn't been standing in that exact spot. As for the other casualties…well, some students on the scene reported what they saw, but it's not all accurate. There was much confusion over who was in the tent. My daughter has a partial list on the hearth."

Ian went immediately to the list, then he spun around, holding the list in disbelief. "This says Claire Rivers! What—"

"That's what I've been wanting to tell you."

Ian looked up. Stefan was standing in the doorway, his face grave.

Edward took a long, careful look at the young man as Ian, jaw clenched, explained who Stefan was and how he came to be there. He was about to elaborate on their inves-tigation when Edward raised his hand, then crooked his finger at Stefan. "Why don't you sit on the couch here and tell us what's going on." Edward turned to Ian. "Both of you." He gestured at one of the women standing in the foyer. "Kathryn, why don't you join us?"

In a moment, they were all seated by the warmth of the fire. At Edward's nod, Ian explained the events of the morning and afternoon, trying to keep his tone calm as he described Claire leaving for the dorm and Stefan returning without her.

Edward said nothing, just turned to Stefan and raised an eyebrow.

Stefan took a deep breath. "I'll explain a little more in a minute, but first I have to tell you what I saw at the tent. At my father's order, I was watching your barbecue, standing on the Loker Commons stairs. He told me this was to be a 'learning event' that would help shape my powers within our family dynasty."

Edward Grindley made a small grunting noise, and Ian, confused, looked over for an explanation.

The old man smiled sadly. "The enemy often creates a terrible counterfeit to some-thing God has ordained. Harvard has a godly heritage, so the enemy desires to raise up those who will be his agents in this place. You might call Stefan's family a dynasty that has committed itself to the enemies of God for many, many generations."

Ian straightened, putting a hand to his head. "The old Pikes!" He explained briefly what they had found in their research.

Stefan was looking at him, openmouthed. "How did you—? Never mind. We don't have time." He turned back to the larger group. "From my angle, I could see through the tent and into the back corner. Right before the truck hit I saw Mansfield talking to Claire."

Ian stood up, his voice rising. "What kind of trick are you trying to pull, Stefan?"

"Ian, sit down and listen," Edward said. "This is all part of it."

Ian took his seat, quivering, as Stefan continued.

"I watched Mansfield talking to Claire and then—" he closed his eyes, and his whole body shuddered—"and then suddenly it was as if a switch went on in my brain and I could see a whole different picture. I was looking at the lawn, the tent, the students at the barbecue, but superimposed on the whole scene were—" He began panting, no longer looking at his listeners. "Were…these huge, shining men…and these terrible, dark beings with dreadful faces. They were fighting. It sounded like a battlefield. And I looked down and saw these arms coming over my head and shoulders, claws digging into my chest."

His hands clutched at the fabric on the front of his shirt, and he squeezed his eyes shut. "I couldn't get them off! The claws started to burn, and I tried to tug and yank at them, but my hands just went right *through* them, and they stayed latched in place. Then I heard tires squealing. And I looked up at the tent and saw that Claire wasn't Claire at all, but a giant man with huge wings! He looked over at me with this fierce look on his face just as the truck plowed into them! It was like he could see that *I* could see!"

Edward's voice was a little shaky. "And then?"

"And then I saw Mansfield. He was shining, surrounded by these giant beings, and…another man was coming toward him." Stefan looked up, and his eyes were red. "The other man had his arms outstretched, and the expression on his face was—" Stefan's voice choked. "I've never seen anything like that."

He closed his eyes. "I wanted to run toward him. But this…this burning started in my chest like nothing I'd ever experienced. I ran and ran, trying to get away from it."

The fire crackled in the background. Ian cleared his throat. "And that's when you saw us."

Stefan didn't speak, just nodded.

Edward leaned forward. "What you saw, Stefan, was the reality behind the veil. There's a whole world out there that we cannot see, that's more real and more powerful than this one. There's a great war going on, and it has two sides." His voice grew strong. "And you need to decide this day whom you will serve."

"I know that my father—my whole family—is involved in something mystical I don't fully understand. I know many things about the business that I need to share with you." He looked up at Ian; then his eyes flickered downward. "But I haven't been involved in the spiritual ceremonies; I haven't taken the blood oath. There has always been some weakness holding me back."

Edward tapped his cane against the floor. "'Some weakness!'" He harrumphed. "That's called the Holy Spirit, young Stefan! The word of God says that He has set eternity in our hearts. Even people with a generational curse such as yours have the choice to listen to the tug of God. That's why God opened your eyes to something that most of us will never see. I'm thankful for that 'weakness' of yours!" He leaned forward, his face intent. "But you must make a choice. Will you renounce not just this evil spirit over your life, but also your selfish *control* of your life?"

The fire crackled in the background as Edward explained the gospel to the young man.

Ian watched Stefan's face, could see the wavering, the longing, revulsion, fear.

"The man you saw with Mansfield at the end," Edward finished, "was Jesus. Mansfield made his choice and will spend eternity with Him. Where will you spend eternity, young Stefan?"

Stefan stared at him for a long moment. Then he held up his hand. "Look, this is a lot to assimilate all at once. And I'm not sure I believe that it's as easy as you say for someone like me—"

Ian jumped in. "It doesn't matter what you're like, Stefan. It—"

"Look, I'm just not ready. But I don't...I don't want to see Claire hurt. I have an idea of what is planned, and," he shuddered, "we have to stop it."

"If you mean that," Ian said, "then tell us what's going on with the Pike business. That may be the only leverage we have."


Barbara Rivers knelt before their fireplace, the swift pop of the flames an urgent backdrop to her prayers. Tom was beside her, and David, and Margaret. More people were arriving all the time.

With every phone call to their home, every quavering question, the same answer was given: Come over and pray.

The room filled with people—sitting quietly on chairs or on the floor, walking around the room, praying silently or aloud. It didn't matter. Their prayers filled the air like incense ascending to the throne.

All around the country, the same. Amid the grief, the uncertainty, the shock at another massacre, another senseless tragedy, the prayers came forth. Prayers were whispered from shaking lips that had not prayed in decades; knees were bowed that had never before hit the floor. On television, on the radio, pastors who were interviewed about the tragedy called for prayer, awareness, repentance.


And on a stricken college campus, the students repented.

In a dorm room filled with people, Jo Markowitz sat, stunned. There were no more tears left in her eyes.

A friend walked up and put her hand on Jo's shoulder. "The news just said a memorial service is scheduled for Dr. Mansfield and the others on Monday. They said Brad was taken to the hospital over an hour ago. They don't know anything else." Her voice weakened as she tried to dredge up vain encouragement. "He could still be okay."

Jo nodded, dully. "I made fun of him, you know. Not as bad as Niles, but after class I would join the others in ribbing him behind his back. Maybe we egged Niles on. Maybe he wouldn't have done this. Maybe it's our fault…"

"Don't be silly."

Jo grabbed her friend's hand and looked up at her face. "I thought the protest was funny! But would I want to be made fun of? Don't we share some responsibility?"

## FIFTY-EIGHT

CLAIRE'S EYES FLICKERED OPEN. HER HEAD POUNDED. She was lying on a thick carpet, her nose in the soft weave.

She stiffened, trying to stuff down terror as memory flooded back. She moved a bit and, despite herself, let out a low groan. She could feel every nerve ending in her legs, her throbbing arms. She flexed her fingers. Her hands were still tied behind her back.

She managed to maneuver her legs around and roll over.

Anton Pike was standing about two feet away, looking at her, a nasty smile on his face.

She stifled a scream and closed her eyes. A frantic prayer shot through her mind, and she took a deep, quivering breath before opening her eyes again. He was no longer smiling. His face was contorted, inhuman. He bent down and slapped her hard across the face.

The violent motion flung her head sideways and her mind reeled. They were going to kill her. They were going to kill her. She began to pant in short, panic-stricken gasps.

Anton knelt and pulled her chin around so that she faced him. He stuck his finger in her face, and his voice came out on a hiss. "No prayers. No prayers to your God in this house."

In an instant of fierce will, Claire stared belligerently into his eyes. "Lord God, I ask for Your protection over me in this house—"

He reared back and slapped her again, and tears leapt to her eyes. But she didn't stop.

"Jesus, I love You—"

Anton roared, holding his head, and shouted out an order.

Claire struggled to a sitting position—"and I know that He who is in me is greater than he who is in the world!"

The door opened and two men came running in.

"You will not win!" Claire shouted. "You *will not win!*"

In a flurry of motion she was again pushed to the floor. She did not fight this time as one man reached into his pocket and brought out a white cloth. She closed her eyes and prayed even as the sweet, cloying scent was brought to her face.

And in a flash, she was overwhelmed by a strong sensation of power. Her eyes flickered as she slipped under, giving her the barest glimpse of a strong, noble figure kneeling, watchful, by her side.

As they prepared to move her, Gael had his orders. They had come straight from the throne. He still did not know what was to happen, and his ability to work would be limited as he ventured into the dark strongholds, into a place he had never been before. But the Lord of heaven and earth had ordered his access, and the dark ones had no choice. Gael would stay beside his charge.

Stefan was surrounded by open mouths as he laid bare the secrets of Pike Holdings. He had explained to Edward and Kathryn what Ian already knew—Pike Holdings owned companies in many types of industries: pharmaceuticals, entertainment, publishing—the list was long.

He had been given a large pad of paper and with a black marker had drawn a chart. A box labeled Pike Holdings was at the top with a line down that branched into three other boxes below labeled PHARM, ENT, PUBL.

"There are many more," he said, gesturing to the three boxes, "but this will give you the idea. Essentially, the company is a conglomerate made up of two parts. First, there are the surface companies." He tapped the three black boxes. "Mainstream companies with prestige, clout, and the potential to impact our culture in a chosen direction."

"Hm," Edward grunted. "Let me guess what that direction is."

"I'm sure your guess would be right. The pharmaceuticals push for everything from overuse of hyperactivity drugs to the legitimizing of cloning and genetic manipulation. The entertainment companies spread—as religious people are always screaming about—a worldview that is less values driven and so on."

All the religious people in the room cocked their eyebrows as he blithely turned back to the chart.

He picked up a different marker. In green ink, he drew a dotted line down from each of the three PHARM, ENT, PUBL boxes. Then, at the end of the dotted lines, he created new boxes. Ian's eyebrows rose as Stefan labeled them DRUGS, GAMBLING, PORN.

Stefan turned back to the group. "The second part of the conglomerate is what no one on the outside knows. We call these the shadow companies, and they are where we get our large, resilient earnings that the analysts are always going on about. Some are legal businesses, some not, but we secretly own or majority control all of them. These are companies that get stronger and more profitable as traditional morals weaken.

"For example," he pointed at the DRUGS box, "a legitimate pharmaceutical company, or perhaps an international trading firm, will use its distribution network to shuttle around illegal drugs for staggering profits that can then be funneled upward as needed to boost the work of the top level companies.

"Do you know what a drug operation can make in return on investment? It's staggering! Five thousand dollars' worth of heroin or coke in Peru, for example, would probably bring—oh—one hundred thousand dollars on the streets of any city in America. Or more!"

Edward's face grew hard, and he spoke almost under his breath. "And every dollar represents another ounce of addiction, another ounce of life stolen from a man, woman, or child."

Ian leaned forward, tapping the chart. "So a reputable publishing company might work with a shadow company like, say…Peephole Publications?"

Stefan—and Edward and Kathryn—looked at Ian in shock.

Ian recounted his conversation with D. J. about the Excellence Award, their reporter's accidental glance at a tantalizing clue in a spreadsheet, the immediate retraction of those records. He watched Stefan carefully as he explained that the company was waiting for more research, for the "smoking gun" that would either prove or disprove their growing suspicions.

Stefan shook his head once or twice as he listened, but he didn't seem agitated about all the findings that had already been released, and showed no signs of backing down from his explanation.

*Surely he must know that by sharing this with us, it could be the end of Pike Holdings.* Ian watched Stefan fiddle with one of the markers in his hand. *Why is he doing this?*

Edward leaned back in his chair, ruminating over Ian's revelation. "Where do the Pike Fellowships come in?"

Stefan made a green stick figure in each of the original black boxes. "Each recipient of a Pike Fellowship is a person that my father and uncle have chosen to be a liaison between the surface and shadow companies. Ostensibly, these people are rising stars in their company, hotshot managers of a legitimate business purpose. But in reality their job is to secretly manage the connection with the shadow companies. Each of the Fellows—as they are called—has also bought into the spiritual side of this scheme and has taken a blood oath of loyalty to our mandate, either before or upon graduation."

Edward cleared his throat. "So what we're saying is this: Satan gradually undermines the moral foundation of our country, raising up thinking that denies God, denies the existence of absolute truth or values. And Pike Holdings is secretly upheld by businesses that all prosper as the 'anything goes' worldview spreads." Edward looked around at the little group. "It's devilishly brilliant."

"And then," Ian gestured at Stefan's drawing, "the money from those shadow companies is used not only to funnel profits into mainstream companies that can gradually influence our culture in a chosen direction, but also to finance the education for people who will run those companies."

Stefan sighed, looking down at his hands. "That's about it."

"So how do we prove it?"

"You don't." Stefan looked up, a rueful smile on his face. "That's the problem. There's no proof. They have had years to come up with a structure in which their control of the shadow companies is very real but impossible to trace."

"It sounds like the Mob."

"There are some similarities. But instead of their control being based on guns or knives, it's based on much less...*visible* means of persuasion."

Ian shuddered at the tone in Stefan's voice. He looked around the room. Edward was watching Stefan with a measured gaze. Kathryn was sitting quietly at the end of a sofa, observing, her lips moving from time to time in silent prayer.

Stefan continued quietly. "I know there must be something that ties Pike Holdings to all the shadow companies, but I have no idea what it is. I know, for example, that they have several office 'stations' around the country that they use as coordinating centers for all the underground paperwork and all that. I heard something once that made me think that each Fellow is assigned a desk at those offices if they need it. But I have no idea where those offices are, or how you'd even find them. I'm sure they look like legitimate, normal businesses from the outside."

For a suspended moment, Ian's gaze traveled to Claire's backpack, sitting in the corner of the room. Then he looked back at Stefan. "Would one of those offices perhaps be in New York City?"

Within moments, the incriminating pages were being passed around the room, every eye intent on the identical number that was highlighted on a half-dozen pages.

Ian looked down at the sheet he was holding. The highlighted number was followed by several neon exclamation points drawn with the yellow highlighter. This must have been the first record she found.

His fingers tensed, crinkling the paper, and he bowed his head in pain. How were they going to get her back? What was happening to her now?


Claire awoke again on an airplane. This time, she was lying on a bed. Her eyes opened wider. A bed on a plane?

She sat up, trying not to wince at the pain in her head. She was on a narrow cot lined with bed rails, in a tiny room near what sounded like the back of the plane. She tried to lift her hand to feel her jaw, but didn't get very far.

She stared sourly at the bands tying her wrists to the bed rails.

Why wasn't she afraid? All of the terror she had felt earlier seemed to have drained away. She breathed a quiet prayer of thanksgiving.

*Thank You, God!* She paused. *And please get me out of this mess!*

For many long minutes she sat and prayed for rescue, for Ian and the members of HCF. Her thoughts turned to her parents, and tears burned her eyes as she thought of their fear, their questions. *Please God, be with them....* She prayed for Sherry and Stefan and her non-Christian friends on campus.

She was still sitting up, testing the strength of her bindings, when the door opened and Anton Pike walked in. She rattled the bed rails as she looked up at him. "I'm guessing this room isn't frequented by voluntary guests."

"Untrue, my dear Claire. It's quite helpful to have a place to catnap on long flights."

"Don't call me your dear Claire. I'm a child of almighty God. And *you* are being used by Satan."

"I will call you anything I please, my dear." He reached out, lacing his fingers through her hair.

She stiffened, her heart pounding again. Were they intending more than just murder?

With a swift move, he clenched his fist in her hair, pulling her head back so that she stared up into his face. She could feel his warm breath.

"It's really too bad that our sacred purpose prevents me from taking full advantage of your...situation, my dear. The most pleasing sacrifices are pure."

He shoved her back down to the bed and released his hold. Then he was out the door. It closed behind him with a click.

Claire buried her face in the sheet, shaking anew, trying to pray. Sacrifices! Sacred purpose! Tears again burned her eyes as she whispered to the wall. "O God, save me! Don't let me be used for Satan's purposes!"

Her racing thoughts stilled again. Better to die trying to escape than be sacrificed to Satan.

*You are MY vessel, child. And I am with you.*

She gasped, grasping for the tender touch, holding tightly to His presence. No matter what happened, Satan would not get the glory from it.

The pitch of the plane grew steep, and soon she could feel the wheels touching down. The plane taxied for several minutes, then stopped.

Within moments, one of the men was standing by her side untying her bonds. He stepped back. His voice was pleasant as he crossed his arms. "We can do this the easy way or the hard way. Which'll it be?"

Claire stood up, a bit unsteady on her feet. She walked out the door, leaning on the wall from time to time. She walked through a luxurious cabin, eyeing leather-covered seats, tables, even a good-sized television set.

By the time she reached the door, her equilibrium had come back. She looked out the hatch. The plane was parked inside a large hangar. The hangar door was half open, and she could see distant figures—workmen, other travelers—walking around in the twilight.

The large man's partner—the one in the blue coat—was positioned at the bottom of the stairs, eyes watchful. A limousine sat not far away. There was no sign of Anton Pike or the pilots.

She walked down the stairs with shaky steps, wanting both men to think she was less steady than she was. The man by the stairs had his hands in his pockets against the cold; the one behind her hadn't climbed down yet.

At the next-to-last step she took a deep breath. Now or never. She bounded down the last two stairs and sprinted past the startled thug, heading for the open hangar door, shouting.

She watched several outside maintenance men turn their heads in her direction. Then...no! They were closing the door! She shouted for help as the door clanged shut, sealing out the light.

She turned, halfway to the door, panting, looking for another way out. The big men hadn't even run after her. She watched Anton get out of the limousine and say something curt to them. They nodded, and blue-coat jogged toward her.

Frantically, she ran toward the door again, eyes scanning for another exit. She heard the steps of the man behind her and started to whimper. "No..."

She sprinted around a few parked cars, spotting a small side door, but she didn't get there. Blue-coat grabbed her from behind, pinning her to him, her arms tight across her chest.

Claire let her knees buckle. Startled, blue-coat released his grip as she fell to the floor. He cursed loudly as she scored a brutal kick to one knee and started to scramble away. She only got two feet before the other one arrived.

They carried her, kicking and screaming, back to the limousine. Blue-coat was limping, and when they got to the limo he nodded to his partner and they dropped her. She hit the ground hard, and blue-coat kicked her in the side.

"Enough."

Anton Pike stood by the open limo door, a smile playing on his lips, looking down at her pitiful struggles to breathe. He made a gesture.

The man who had released her bonds in the airplane retied her wrists, this time in front. He pulled the bands tighter than before, whispering in her ear. "I guess you chose the hard way."

He climbed in the back of the limo and hauled her in after him, dumping her on the floor. Anton climbed in after her, amused, and closed the door. Then he rolled down the window and looked at blue-coat, who was rubbing his knee and muttering under his breath.

"Go and apologize to the mechanics for our niece, who unfortunately suffered a seizure of some kind. If anyone asks questions, pay them off. Make sure they get the picture; there can be no more questions. Then get the bags and meet us at the house."

Blue-coat nodded and turned away.


Edward looked carefully at every paper, asked a few more questions about the surface companies, then fell silent, praying. The fire popped in the background for several long minutes. Then Edward stirred.

"Why are you telling us this, young Stefan?" As Stefan opened his mouth, Edward leaned forward and looked him hard in the eyes. "The real reason."

Stefan pursed his lips "I have to be honest with you. If it was just a matter of money, I'd have kept my mouth shut and enjoyed my life. But—" he hesitated, and Ian got the idea that he was struggling for words.

"But I don't want to be a…pawn of Satan." Stefan stood up and went to stand near the fire. "I know that Satan is real. I've seen the things he does. I've seen my family's delight in it. But always…always something twists inside me when I'm asked to develop my powers, my knowledge of the black magic."

"If you know Satan is real, do you know God is real?" Ian asked.

"Are you kidding? Of course I know God is real."

"Then why won't you accept Him?"

"There's something…inside me…that is sickened at that thought."

"Be careful saying that—"

"No." Edward stood carefully to his feet. "That makes perfect sense. Satan has been invited into his family. Stefan, you need deliverance. Real deliverance from a curse that has spanned the generations. We don't have much time, but this has to be done. And God has a purpose here." He looked into Stefan's eyes. "Are you willing?"

Stefan swayed, then leaned against the fireplace, gripping the mantelpiece hard. "Yes. Do it quickly, before I lose my resolve."

It didn't take long. They began to pray, and within moments Stefan was on the floor, writhing, his teeth clenched against the blasphemies that kept erupting from his lips. The three Christians stood over him, laying hands on him, joining their experienced prayers with his feeble ones, casting out, binding, and sealing the work that had been done.

Ian's eyes flickered to the doorway of the den. There were at least a dozen people in the foyer, their eyes earnest, some kneeling, some standing but all praying for this young man. Where had they come from?

In the end Stefan whimpered and let out a long sigh, then relaxed into the floor. After a time, he raised his head and sat up. He had a bemused smile on his face. "I feel…clean." He pressed his hands to his body, the smile widening. His voice grew exultant. "For the first time in my life, I don't have this dark *thing* hanging over me!"

"There's only one problem, Stefan." With great effort, Edward knelt in front of the young man. "You are now swept clean of something that has been hanging over you your whole life. But the Bible says that unless someone new comes and inhabits the empty house, Satan will come back stronger than before. You need to choose, Stefan, whom you will serve."

Stefan sat back on his heels and took a deep breath. "I…I'm just not ready yet. I know everything you've told me is true. But I need a little time."

"We don't know how much time any of us have, young man. I pray you make your commitment before it's too late."

He made a move to get up, and all three people in the room jumped to help him. He stood to his feet and looked at Ian. "And now, I say we quickly call your friend D. J. Then we must seek God about Claire Rivers before it's too late."


D. J.'s voice, over the speakerphone in the center of the kitchen table, sounded dazed. He took down all the information and said he'd call back. Within minutes, the phone rang.

"The cross-reference phone directory found the telephone number you have. It's on the thirty-ninth floor of a building on Avenue of the Americas in midtown Manhattan, not far from our office." He read them the street address. "Does that mean anything to you?"

"No." Stefan shook his head. "But remember, I haven't been all that involved in the business stuff yet. I haven't even visited most of the business locations."

"Wait!" Ian was shuffling through papers. "I thought I saw Avenue of the Americas…yes!" He held up the page of contact data for Johanna Godfrey. "This woman works for Helion Pharmaceuticals, and that's the same address!"

There was a pause, and the sound of pages turning on the other end of the line, then D. J.'s voice again. "Good grief. You're right. What does that mean? Could the thirty-ninth floor be one of these coordinating offices you were talking about, Stefan?"

"I guess so. I don't really know."

D. J. paused, then spoke in a slow and deliberate tone. "If what you say is true, this isn't just a matter for the Excellence Award. It's a matter for the FBI, the Securities and Exchange Commission, and the government regulators. Gentlemen, thank you for passing all this information along. I'm sure our magazine will appreciate the scoop. I'll keep you informed. Right now, I have to go give my bosses a heart attack."

There was a click and he was gone.

Stefan was staring into the cup of coffee Kathryn had made for him. "So when can we talk about Claire?"

"Kathryn has notified the authorities of Claire's abduction, but with everything else that is going on I don't think we should rely solely on them." Edward glanced over at Ian, that odd look again on his face. "I've been praying this whole time, and I believe I have some answers. But first, there's something you need to know. Claire Rivers has a special heritage, a godly calling on her life that has been passed down for generations."

"What do you mean?" Ian asked.

"I cannot explain in full, but it is enough for you to know that she is an extended member of our family." Ian looked at Edward in shock as the old man continued. "In fact, so was Mansfield."

Ian's head swam as he watched Edward gesture toward Stefan. "In a way, Stefan and Claire both represent the current generations of a long struggle over this campus, a long conflict for the truth of God to prevail. Stefan is aware of his lineage; Claire is not—just as Mansfield was not until recently. Both Mansfield and Claire were placed here by the hand of God for a particular purpose. Mansfield fulfilled his calling. Now Claire must do the same."

"But—but they have her!" Ian said. "And they're going to kill her!"

"I believe that God will protect her. We—"

"Everyone keeps saying that, and it's about to drive me crazy!" Ian stood up, his fists clenched. "They kidnapped her! Where was her protection then? Where was Mansfield's protection, or the other students'?"

Edward rose unsteadily to his feet. He leaned on his cane and put his free hand on Ian's arm. "We cannot know mysteries that are inherently unknowable. God has not given us that power, and for that I am grateful. It's better simply to trust that, though He slay me, yet will I trust in Him."

Ian's eyes grew misty again, his voice dropping to a whisper. "How can you know that God will protect her? That she has a purpose here?"

Edward shuffled to the kitchen counter, where his Bible again lay in the dish rack. He found a passage and began to read.

"'The men of the city said to Elisha, "Look, our lord, this town is well situated, as you can see, but the water is bad and the land is unproductive."'" His finger skipped a line. "'Then he went out to the spring and threw the salt into it, saying, this is what the Lord says: I have healed this water.'"

Ian's thoughts flickered to Mansfield's strange dream, the hand of God dropping golden salt in a dark sea.

Edward was watching his face. He smiled slightly. "I believe God will use young Claire Rivers as His instrument to make the dark waters clear."

Ian closed his eyes, his heart aching for her. "We have to get her back."


A tall man with dark hair rose from his couch as Anton and his henchman escorted Claire through the door. She walked in quietly, her hands tied before her.

"Welcome, Claire Rivers." The tall man inclined his head. "My name is Victor Pike, and I will be your host for the short time you are with us."

Claire raised her chin. "Where am I?"

"On the island of Nantucket. A charming little island filled with people who know nothing of our purposes here."

"What are those purposes?"

"Tsk, tsk." Victor shook his head. "Not for your ears, my dear. It is enough for you to know that you now have a part to play."

He turned and walked toward a door. Claire was prodded forward. Victor led the way through the door and down some steep stairs. Claire was grateful her hands were in front of her so she could grasp the stair rail from time to time.

A light was flicked on. Stone walls rose on either side of a narrow hallway. Claire shivered from more than cold. Victor led the way through another door, turning on all the lights.

Claire stepped into the room, and her skin crawled. A pentagram was carved into a long table in the center of the room. Claire glanced around. Wall hangings, pictures— a dark portrait of a woman seemed to leap out at her.

Victor stared at the portrait of the woman for a long moment. Anton came and stood beside him. Then they both turned and looked at Claire.

Victor walked toward her on soft feet, his eyes intent. She took a step back and bumped against the henchman standing behind her. He gripped her upper arms, holding her in place.

Victor reached out and gripped her chin. She tried to flinch away, but his grip was strong as steel. He turned her head this way and that, looking at her as if he were a wolf eyeing an exhausted deer after a long hunt, a still-breathing prize.

"Yes." The word was soft. He turned his head and spoke to Anton. "The Masters have revealed it. These are clear waters indeed. Not like the brackish water in which they tortured her." His glance flickered to the portrait.

He released Claire's chin and stepped back a pace. "It will be a perfect atonement, a perfect sacrifice. We have never gotten our hands on one of the enemy dynasty. This will surely be a pleasing offering to our Master, a curse to stop the work of the Enemy in his tracks. The college will be ours, a place of peace and tolerance again."

"Enemy dynasty?" Claire blurted out. "Peace and tolerance? What are you talking about? You're all crazy!"

Victor and Anton stared at her in disbelief. Then Victor threw back his head and laughed.

"She does not know! Oh, this is good. Much better that she was not killed with the others."

Anton was staring at Claire with a tight smile on his face. He crossed his arms, keeping his eyes fastened on her as he spoke to Victor.

"We must not get complacent, brother. There is an…unsettled feeling. We may be seeing a backlash. Like that terrible unforeseen wave after the high school shootings a few years ago, when so many students were lost to the Enemy. We must not let that happen here!"

Victor nodded, his gaze thoughtful. "Another reason for the sacrifice. Unless, of course, the Enemy daughter wants to renounce her calling and her God and offer herself to our Master. That might be equally effective for our purposes."

At Claire's offended look, he leaned closer and rubbed his finger down her cheek. "Think about it, Claire. If you turn, you will not suffer this chosen fate." His eyes bored into hers. "And you *will* suffer."

A Scripture flew into her mind. She straightened and spoke directly into his face. "'O Nebuchadnezzar, I don't need to defend myself before you. If you throw me into the blazing furnace, my God is able to rescue me. But even if he doesn't, you can be sure that I will never serve your god!'"

Victor winced backward, revulsion and rage on his face.

"We have our own scriptures, Claire Rivers," Anton said. "And we will be praying them over you tonight." He looked at the henchman standing by the doorway. "Unbind her and lock her in. We must prepare."

The two brothers left the room as the large man untied Claire's wrists. As he closed the door, all lights went out but the one that shone on the woman's portrait, plunging Claire into darkness.

She charged toward the door, feeling for the light switches. She flicked them on. Nothing happened. The blackness pressed in. A cold, clammy feeling began to crawl up her legs, her arms, her head.

"In Jesus' name, leave me alone!" she shouted to the empty room.

Instantly, the clammy sensation vanished.

For several long moments she fought to keep her breathing steady, fought an elemental fear of the dark. In order to get into the light, she'd have to get near that satanic symbol in the middle of the table, and that was not going to happen.

"God, I know You're with me here in this place." Her voice dropped to a whisper. "O Father, come near me now."

Her mind turned to a story her mother had told her about one of the nation's war heroes who was locked up as a prisoner of war for several long years. He'd been in solitary confinement for nearly two years, and when his captors pulled him out they had expected him to be insane. Instead, his face shone like that of an angel. He'd spent two years singing hymns of praise, reciting Scriptures, and—as he said—"communing with the Lord Almighty."

She faced the blackness, tears prickling her eyes. Well, she might not have two years. And she might be seeing the Lord face-to-face soon. But until then she would commune with the Lord almighty.

She got down on her knees, and began to sing.

The kitchen was crowded, every eye on Stefan as he described his uncle's home on Nantucket Island. He had explained that Claire was certainly being taken there, was probably already there in the house on the bluffs.

Ian watched as another man slipped into the room. Where were they all coming from? They asked pointed questions, probing, gleaning all sorts of details Ian would have never thought to ask.

What was the layout of the house, the bluffs? Would the island authorities cooperate or be unwilling to help without further proof? How many people would be on the property?

A tall young man leaned forward, catching Stefan's attention. "So where would they conduct a ritual sacrifice? I hate to even ask this, but it should be considered."

"Probably on the edge of the bluffs. I know there were some ceremonies downstairs in the conference room, but I think those were mostly the blood oaths, and I never saw them."

"Midnight sacrifice?"

"Almost certainly."

"Would the subject be alive when taken?"

As Stefan nodded, Ian couldn't help himself. "You seem to know a lot about this!" he blurted toward the stranger.

The man turned toward him, his eyes serious. "It's wise to know the ways of one's adversary, although I don't recommend it unless you're well protected in prayer."

"Ian, this is my grandson, Gage Grindley," Edward said. "He is named for a patriarch of our family who came over from England with the early settlers."

Gage stretched forward and shook Ian's hand. Then he turned back to Stefan. "What do they do with the body?"

"They're good at making things look like an accident, or disposing of the body so that it's never found. The person just disappears and becomes a footnote in a missing person's file somewhere." He pulled one of Claire's highlighted pages off the kitchen table. "For instance, this woman is dead. She ended up on the rocks below my uncle's home. Oh, her body was found somewhere else—a tragic rock-climbing accident in the Poconos, I believe. But that's not where she died."

Gage nodded slowly, then glanced at Edward. "I doubt the police will have a search warrant in time."

The group conferred some more; then Edward rapped his cane against the floor.

"It's time!" He rose from his chair. "Ian, we have a five-seater plane, and we can be on Nantucket in little over two hours. We must not delay. Who should go?"

Ian jumped to his feet. "You're not going without me!"

"The others have more experience, Ian."

"She's *my friend.*"

Ian didn't blurt out the next words that sprang to his mind, the cry of his heart, but Edward saw it in his eyes. The old man nodded slowly before turning back to the group.

Stefan stood up. "It's my fault that Claire is in this mess. I should go."

Edward didn't demur. "Two more."

"*Two* more?" Ian said.

"Yes." Edward's smile was amused. "We do want to be able to bring Claire back." He looked toward his grandson. "Are you willing, Gage?"

"Of course, Grandfather. And I'd like Aunt Kathryn to pilot the plane. She can stay in contact with those here and coordinate the intercession."

Ian stared at her, bemused. She gave a quick smile back.

Edward looked around and gave a sharp nod. "Let it be so."

As one accord, every knee in the room bowed before God almighty.

Ian prayed silently, the Word of God running through his mind. *Those who are with us are more than those who are against us…*

Somewhere in the background a clock chimed eight. Edward rose to his feet, looking at the four travelers.

"God be with you."


Krolech was giddy, reveling in the worship as Anton and Victor made their slavish preparations before him and his minions. He had sent word to Leviathan of the important offering to be made this night, the surge of power to come soon, very soon.

Ah, could anyone but a lord understand the sweet stench of a sacrifice? And to think that it was being made to him! Would this give him the leverage he craved to unseat his masters?

The girl was the key. He felt it. He would stand before Leviathan himself with legal right, having proved himself lord over greater realms than a mere college town!

He mulled over his ambition as he watched Katoth relaying his orders to his troops. Katoth had stayed very much in the background all day, brooding over the fate of his charge.

Krolech's eyes narrowed. He would not take the blame for the loss of the heir. The sacrifice of the Enemy daughter would protect him from the wrath of Leviathan or… Lucifer himself. After the sacrifice, Katoth was on his own.


In a dark room underground, Gael watched as Claire sang.

"Jesus, lover of my soul, let me to Thy bosom fly…"

Her voice created shimmering waves in the air, no longer black but crystalline, shimmering in the spirit. Claire raised her hands, her face upturned to the God she knew was there, watching her.

"Other refuge have I none; hangs my helpless soul on Thee.
Leave, O leave me not alone; still support and comfort me.
All my trust on Thee is stayed, all my help from Thee I bring;
Cover my defenseless head with the shadow of Thy wing."

Gael watched the young woman hesitate, then look at her watch. Almost ten o'clock. He saw a great shudder go through her body. Then she put her face in her hands, trying not to cry, rocking back and forth, praying, praying.

Wings outstretched, Gael put his hands on her head and sought the Lord anew. He stood still, listening, as the message was given.

# FIFTY-NINE

THE HUM OF THE MOTOR MADE CONVERSATION DIFFICULT as the little plane flew across the black straits to Nantucket Island. The group conferred and planned as best they could, saying a quick prayer as the plane touched down and taxied to the area reserved for private accounts.

Stefan pointed to a darkened hangar, shouting something to Gage over the noise of the rotor.

As promised, those in Edward's house had called ahead. A car and a boat were ready for them along with various tools requested by radio during their airborne planning session.

Ian was silent, pale, the urgency he had stuffed down for so long starting to rise again. He tried to listen as Stefan described the switchback path that rose from sea level to the top of the bluffs, but it was hard to concentrate. It was all he could do to pray coherently.

As they drove away, Ian looked back at Kathryn standing beside the plane. Her lips were already moving in earnest prayer.

And skimming invisibly over the water toward the island, the troops came in.

The car bumped to a stop as Ian and Stefan pulled up near a beach access, a half-mile from the house. Gage had left them thirty minutes before to pick up the boat at the marina. He would anchor the boat at a small pier Stefan had indicated on the map.

"It's getting pretty late," Ian said. He squinted into the darkness. "Is this the right path?"

There was no answer, and he looked over at his partner. "Stefan, is this the right one?"

Stefan glanced dully out the window. "Yeah."

"Well, let's go."

As Ian pulled their simple gear from the trunk, Stefan began muttering to himself. Ian looked at him sideways, a bit anxious, as they walked down to the beach. He glanced at his watch. "We've got forty-five minutes."

The area was dimly lit by a sliver of moon behind scuttling clouds. Ian put a pair of binoculars to his eyes and stared at the nearby spot where the land began to rise into the distinctive steep slope of ocean bluffs, cut out here and there into sheer cliffs. Perched on one such cliff, not far away, Ian could make out a series of buildings.

He pointed. "Is that it?"

He looked behind him. Stefan was holding his head. Ian grew cold.

"Stefan...are you okay?"

"Yeah, yeah, I'm okay."

Ian shoved the binoculars in his pack and turned to face him. "Stefan, you're scaring me, buddy. You need to pray."

"Yeah, pray for me."

"No. *You* need to pray. You need to make a commitment to Christ. If you don't, there's nothing to keep your old friends from coming back home."

He stared into Stefan's disoriented eyes. *"Please,* Stefan. This is your eternal life we're talking about."

Stefan wavered, then stood straighter. "I can handle this. They won't come back, and we don't have time anyway. Come on. I've got an idea." He set off toward the bluffs, and Ian scrambled to keep up.


Fifteen minutes to midnight.

The door creaked open.

Claire was on her knees. She looked up, trying not to shake as Victor and Anton Pike walked in. They wore black robes, their eyes again insane, unearthly. In Anton's hand was a pike with a sharp steel point.

She tried to catch her breath, but couldn't, tried to pray, but could find only one word. *Jesus...Jesus...* This was it. This was it.

The two henchmen pushed past the brothers, grabbed Claire, and dragged her out the door and up the stairs.

The night was freezing cold, her jacket poor defense against the biting wind. Her entire body trembled as she was dragged across a dark lawn. Her meager struggles were futile. She had long decided that if she were to get out of this, it would be a miracle straight from heaven.

The men stopped several feet short of a cliff and turned, facing her toward the dark house.

Victor and Anton appeared, and following them came a strange procession. More people, some robed, some not. Other than the moon, there were no lights. She could not tell the size of the crowd.

The two brothers stopped in front of her. At Victor's nod, each henchman grabbed one of her wrists and pulled outward, stretching her between them until she felt her sinews would snap. Despite herself, she cried out in pain.

"You…will…not win," she said, trying to breathe.

Anton smiled, a lecherous, dirty smile. "Perhaps you believe, even now, that your friends will save you."

He barked an order, and there was a rustling in the crowd.

Claire saw someone being pushed through the throng, then thrown on the ground before her.

"*Ian!*" Tears leapt to her eyes. "O Lord God, no!"

Someone else pushed his way forward, and she looked up.

"Hello, Father." Stefan's voice was flat, emotionless.

A satisfied smile appeared on Anton's face as his voice hissed out. "The heir returns…"

Ian looked up at Claire, speaking quickly. "Don't stop praying, Claire! Don't stop—"

Stefan kicked him in the side, and Ian arched his back in pain. Victor walked over as Stefan and another man hauled Ian to his feet. Victor made a gesture, and they pulled outward, stringing him between them. Claire heard him clamp his mouth on a groan.

Victor spoke in a high, almost gleeful voice. "You also can join our little ceremony." He turned back to stand by his brother, and the two men faced their captives with proprietary looks.

Victor glanced at his watch. "Let us begin."

Anton planted the pike in the ground, its metal tip glinting. Then he began an eerie chant, which spread to the crowd.

Claire began to tremble again as the sense of evil deepened. It was entwining itself about them, lacing through the crowd, staring out of Anton's and Victor's eyes.

She looked over at Stefan, intent on his task, in something like despair. How could he choose this?

When the chant was well underway, Anton held the rod aloft and cried out words Claire didn't fully understand, shouting about "the family symbol of our ancient line."

Hanging between the two henchmen, she looked at Ian, somehow comforted by his presence. She remembered his words and began to pray, quivering, in a small voice that could not be heard over the chanting.

It didn't matter.

Anton's otherworldly eyes opened wide. He screamed and pointed the pike at her. "Stop!"

She tensed for a blow.

Suddenly, he looked above and behind her, and his eyes narrowed. "What are you doing? You cannot interfere!"

Anton was gaping at an empty spot in the air, Victor beside him. Claire looked at Ian, confused. He also was staring at the astonishment, the anger on the faces of their captors.

A tiny warmth began to glow in her belly.

*He shall give His angels charge over thee...*

Anton held the pike aloft, shouting upward. "This is our territory!" He pointed at the crowd, which shifted, murmuring uneasily, behind him. "These are our possessions! Our rightful ownership." He curled his fingers tighter around the pike. "The symbol of our honor! Our power!"

Claire's eyes widened as Anton's face contorted into that of a raging beast.

He jabbed the pike upward and roared at the sky. "I *will* use it for the sacrifice!"

He hefted the weapon, pointed it toward Claire, and reared back.

Suddenly, there was a roar of wind, and Anton, Victor, and the entire crowd screamed and flinched back, covering their faces as if scathed by a blinding light. Anton dropped the pike as though it had turned red-hot. Each henchman put a hand to his face, holding Claire's wrist with only one hand.

In an instant, as if in slow motion, Claire twisted her wrists away and downward, breaking their grip. She fell backward, scrabbling, watching as Ian also twisted free. She picked herself up and ran headlong from the crowd, away from the house, parallel with the bluffs, into a grove of trees.

They didn't come after her.

There were no other footsteps. She turned in her flight, looking over her shoulder, calling for Ian.

He was on the ground, surrounded.

In despair, she watched as Stefan yanked him to his feet.

Anton's voice rang out. "Do you want to watch, Claire? We will kill him and then find you. If you come back now, perhaps we might spare his life."

Ian tried to yell something to her, but a punch to the stomach silenced him. She could hear him coughing, trying to get air.

She pressed a shaking hand to her mouth. "O God, what do I do?"

Ian dropped to one knee, coughing, gagging.

*God, thank You for getting Claire away. Don't let her come back!*

He was again yanked to his feet. Anton and the man beside him—it must be Victor Pike—were arguing with each other, pointing at the pike on the ground. Ian winced as Stefan and the other man again wrenched his arms outward.

*Stefan.*

Ian looked sideways, trying to catch Stefan's eye. "It's not too late to commit, Stefan." His voice was low enough that the other man wouldn't hear. "It only takes an instant."

Stefan's eyes flickered, but his grip didn't loosen.

"You said you didn't want to be a pawn of Satan. You can still choose light instead of darkness."

Stefan turned his head and stared at him. There was a sudden vulnerability in his eyes, the vulnerability that had vanished right before he betrayed Ian to the guards.

Ian looked into his face and could see the struggle, could see the desperate young man who had earlier broken down and asked for help. Had it only been that morning?

"God wants you, Stefan. Remember the man you saw with Mansfield?"

Stefan's eyes flickered again.

"Remember Jesus? You were longing for Him. He loves you. Turn to Him!"

*"NO!"*

Ian's head snapped around at the almighty roar. Anton, his eyes wild, snatched up the pike, took two charging steps toward Ian, and threw. The pike whistled through the air.

Ian closed his eyes. *Jesus…*

He heard a sickening grunt, and his eyes flew open. Stefan was standing face-to-face with him, infinity in his eyes.

Ian looked down. A spear point protruded from Stefan's front. Ian grabbed his shoulders, holding him up. "No…Stefan…"

A slow smile spread over Stefan's face as his eyes went opaque. "I…commit…"

He became too heavy to hold and slid to the ground, his eyes staring past Ian. "It's You."

The whisper died away, and there was no longer anyone there.

Ian looked up. Anton, Victor, and the others were staring at Stefan in horror.

In an instant the crowd was thrown into confusion, Anton and Victor seeming to collapse in on themselves. The others scattered, screaming, fighting unseen enemies.

Ian jumped to his feet, backing away, running for the trees. Nobody even noticed.

"Over here!" Claire called out to Ian as he ran, eyes wild, searching the blackness of the trees.

He ran up and enfolded her in his arms, holding her so tight she almost couldn't breathe, whispering tear-choked words in her ear.

"Thank You, God! Thank You, God!"

A dry voice interrupted him. "Can we get out of here?"

Claire jumped, turning swiftly. A tall man was standing at the edge of the bluffs.

Ian looked up and sagged in relief. "Gage, thank God." Ian pulled Claire forward. "Come on, it's okay. I'll explain on the way."

SUNLIGHT POURED IN THROUGH THE FRONT WINDOWS of the den, the friendly fire crackling as Edward beckoned Claire inside and closed the door.

An hour later she emerged, a bemused look on her face and a small burgundy-covered book in her hands. Edward was right behind her.

Ian stood up from his seat in the foyer and stepped forward. "I'm told I'm not allowed to ask, so I won't bother."

Edward inclined his head toward him, his voice amused. "There will come a day, young Ian, when you will have the right to know."

Both young people blushed at the look he gave them.

"It's all arranged," Edward continued. "The leaders of HCF are in agreement. Claire will be the student speaker at Mansfield's eulogy tomorrow. The memorial for the others will follow shortly thereafter. Oh, and I almost forgot to tell you, Claire. Your friend Brad is listed in serious but stable condition. That's all we know right now."

He coughed, leaning on his walking stick with both hands. "And on another matter, I have it on good authority that a certain magazine will soon break the news of a major government investigation into Helion Pharmaceuticals's business practices."

"Just Helion?" Claire asked after a moment.

Edward sighed slightly. "They must have guessed Stefan had told us something, or that you had found something in your research. By the time the agents got a search warrant this morning, the thirty-ninth floor of that building was filled with information incriminating only Helion. The managers there are apparently taking the fall to save the entire holding company."

"After getting so close…"

"You never know," Ian said. "They can't have covered their tracks *that* thoroughly in such a short time."

Edward nodded. "All in good time. We'll see. All in good time."

"I have a question for you." Claire struggled for the words. "When we were on that cliff last night, and Anton Pike tried to kill Ian…and hit Stefan instead… What happened? Why were they suddenly so powerless?" She stared up into the kind eyes, seeing a glimpse of the professor she already missed so much. "Why did the whole thing collapse then, and not before? Why did we have to go through that?"

"I can't give you the answers, Claire. Only God can do that."

"I understand. I'm just wondering—"

"My best guess is that the willing act of Stefan—their 'heir'—giving his life for Ian was so Christlike in love and power as to demolish evil strongholds."

His eyes glinted. "And I think there's an additional possibility, taken from the book of Jude." He recited a passage from memory. "'And I remind you of the angels who did not stay within the limits of authority God gave them but left the place where they belonged. God has kept them chained in prisons of darkness, waiting for the day of judgment.'

"Remember that although the evil one is prince of this dark world, he can do nothing outside the boundaries God places on him. It certainly sounds like a mighty angel last night delivered a message that Satan's sacrificial weapon was not to be used on the children of God. But the spirit possessing Anton overstepped his limits."

Edward folded his hands over the head of his cane, looking with clear eyes at both students. "God knew what would happen, and knew these events would cripple part of the enemy's hold over this place." He smiled, his voice wistful. "Young Stefan made the right choice."

Claire clutched several pages in her hand as she ascended the stairs to the outdoor stage in front of Memorial Church. The day was clear, the weather still unseasonably warm. Just as it had been on Saturday.

She crossed the platform, every fiber attuned to the thronging crowd, the steady red eyes of a dozen television cameras, the supportive presence of her parents and several friends in the front row. She wished Sherry had chosen to be here.

Claire approached the podium and the president of the university stepped back with a solemn smile, gesturing her forward. A gentle prayer coursed through Claire's mind as she laid the slim sheaf of paper in front of the microphone and looked up.

New Harvard Yard was packed with people. The chairs extended all the way back to the steps of Widener Library. She had been told that thousands more squeezed into this space for commencement ceremonies, but right now she couldn't imagine it.

Her throat tightened as she looked out at those who had come to pay their respects to Professor William Mansfield. People from all over the country. Students and faculty, senators and secretaries, luminaries and the unknown. A former U.S. president and his wife sat, their eyes sad, in the front row, surrounded by the secret service.

The faces looked up at her.

And behind the veil, many other faces watched as the young woman stepped into her calling. God's hand was poised.

"We are here today," she began, "to honor a man who loved much, and was loved much in return. Many of us were on the receiving end of his simple, unconditional love. Today, I want to talk to you about the reason for that love.

"Professor Mansfield, as anyone who took his classes knows, often said that we must strive for *Veritas*, for Truth. Many people here knew that when Mansfield said *Truth*, he didn't mean some abstract construct. He meant the perfect truth of God that he found in his Christian faith."

There was a soft rustling in the crowd as the words sank in. The faces stayed quiet, upturned, respectful.

"However, even though Mansfield modeled *Veritas* for us, I think most of us don't know what that really means. What is Truth? One kind of truth that we search for at Harvard is greater knowledge of facts and accurate information about our world. That is part of what truth is. But it's not all that Truth is.

"We Christians like to think we have been striving for Truth—meaning, we think, an objective, moral, natural law in the universe, set up by almighty God. That is indeed part of what Truth is. But it's not all that Truth is."

She smiled, her voice sad. "As Mansfield pointed out to the HCF group one night, we have often fallen into the trap of thinking of truth as 'right instead of wrong.' And unfortunately, we have often acted as the caretakers of right, counting up all the ways that others are wrong. Right versus wrong is indeed part of what Truth is. But it's not all that Truth is."

Claire looked out over the sea of faces. "Why are there so many thousands of us here today? Would there be, if what Mansfield represented was right instead of wrong? No. That would not necessarily inspire hope, love, and great devotion. In fact, people who speak of right versus wrong—such as people of faith—are sometimes labeled narrow-minded legalists. As people who are judgmental. As those who—" she made a comical face—"take all the fun out of life."

The laughter died away as her expression sobered. "Or, all too often, such people are labeled hypocrites because we are imperfect people who also do wrong. There's no way to sugarcoat it. Although we're supposed to live in purity as Christ lived, so that others can see Him through us, our lives are always going to be an imperfect reflection at best, and a tarnished, warped image at worst.

"The young man who killed Mansfield," she struggled with the words, "was driven by such a warped understanding. He did not adequately experience the love of Christ from those of us on campus. For if he had experienced it—if we had reached out to him as Jesus would, to break down the walls of hatred and rage—he would never have done what he did. Instead, we succumbed to temptation, attempting to survive a challenging environment by protecting ourselves. But Niles didn't need us to protect ourselves. He needed us to *be* as the Good Shepherd to him. And for that failing—" she swallowed, looking down, her voice dropping to a whisper—"I must ask for Niles's forgiveness."

A murmur ran swiftly through the crowd, looks of disbelief on many faces.

And with that murmuring came a gentle hand.

Gael stood behind his charge, his eyes intent, watching the crowd. Suddenly, on the chest of someone in the audience, a gold cross appeared as if on a shield. Then over there, another. Then another. And another... The field grew.

Eyes were being opened, ears unblocked, just as the Lord had promised.

Gael turned toward Kai who stood nearby, watching the shimmering crosses shine through the shadows.

"Her special calling, as you said, to accomplish God's purposes."

"If she had remained silent," Kai answered, "God would have still accomplished His purposes. The very stones would have cried out." He smiled. "But she has chosen to stand, and is stepping into God's will for her. Her obedience is not just for Harvard's sake; it's for hers. God is pleased with this young one."

"...so, then, what is the Truth that Mansfield lived? Mansfield's struggle was not for right versus wrong. It was for *life instead of death*. It was for the abundant life Jesus meant when he said, 'I am the Way, the Truth and the Life; no one comes to the Father but through Me.'

"If you—all of you gathered here—want to honor his memory today, this week, this semester, ask one of the members of HCF sitting around you, wearing the silver crosses on their lapels, how they came to know the Truth. And in their answer you will hear what Truth is: not just right, not just an objective moral law—but life. These people have been given new life."

She looked out at the crowd, gripping the sides of the podium hard. "And two days ago, Mansfield was given...new life."

She felt tears prickling her eyes and let them fall. "And the reason I can't keep from crying is not just that I miss a professor and friend I had come to love—whom all of us loved—as a friend and surrogate father." She looked up, closing her eyes. "It is because I can picture him now, standing before the Lord he loved so much that he was willing at any time to lay down his life for another."

Her eyes flickered open, and her voice softened to a whisper. "'And this is how we know what love is: Jesus Christ laid down His life for us. And we ought to lay down our lives for our brothers.'"

She looked across the crowd, her voice strengthening. "You are all here today because Professor Mansfield showed *Veritas* by laying down his life every day just as Christ did."

Claire paused, running her hands over the smooth wood of the podium. There was silence in the crowd.

"Over one hundred years ago another man beloved to this campus passed away unexpectedly. The Reverend Phillips Brooks. In an outpouring of love and grief, hundreds of students carried his casket for miles, from Trinity Church in Boston where he was a pastor, across the Charles River, through Harvard Yard, and on to the Mount Auburn Cemetery west of campus."

In a warm den, watching on television, Edward Grindley gave a soft sigh. Gage Grindley turned and looked at his grandfather, his eyebrows raised.

"My grandfather was there then," Edward said, "and he spoke of the funeral procession lining the streets, the revival on campus, the credibility given to evangelism, the progress made in Christian outreach and service. But within a generation—" he smiled sadly—"it was back to business as usual. And look where we are today."

"It sounds as if you don't think all this will serve much purpose," Gage said.

"No, Gage, there's always purpose in God's ways. But we must do our part; we must so live the life of Christ that we transform our culture—not merely impact it. Just as this culture has gradually gone away from Christ, so will it change back only gradually, as hearts change."

Gage's voice was soft. "But in a world that is not our Home—"

"—there will still be sin," Edward finished his grandson's sentence. "There will still be the daily choices in which we show ourselves all too frail. Only Jesus Christ can actually transform, and the only time that will fully happen is when He returns in glory riding on the clouds of heaven."

He looked back at the screen. "But even if this country is never transformed back into a Christian culture, I believe God is using this time to create a place where—for a season—eyes will be opened, and people will be faced with a choice of what they really believe. A marketplace of ideas." He smiled at the thought of Mansfield's oft-repeated words. "And Truth will win."

"Behind me, in Memorial Church," Claire said, "lies Professor Mansfield's casket. And we too will carry it to its final resting place. But rest assured—that is not where he is! He has been welcomed into eternal Life. And with the words of Phillips Brooks's address to the eager young members of an entering freshman class, let me encourage you to seek that Life."

She cleared her throat, trying to keep her voice steady.

"The great hunger everywhere is for life. All things are reaching up towards it. All living things are craving an increase of it. Into this world comes Christ and announces himself as that world's Savior and satisfier, in virtue first of his bestowal of vitality… 'I come to you here that you may live, that you may have life, and that you may have it more abundantly.'

"So speaks the Christ to the student. And with great trust and great hope and happy soberness, giving himself into the power of whatever is diviner than himself, believing truth, rejoicing in duty, the student goes forward into ever-deepening life. Of such life, and of brave, earnest students entering into its fullness, may this new year of the old college life be full."

Out of time and space, a contingent of angels stood around a man with twinkling eyes, his silver hair and character-lined face now, somehow, ageless looking. His eyes were fastened intently upon the young woman speaking to the assembly. He had his arm around a trim woman, and she too watched as if she knew the characters on the Great Stage.

The man glanced behind him and smiled. A great crowd spread to the horizon, also watching the great moment in His story, watching the king's hand at work.

The watchers cheered as each golden shield appeared. From time to time someone would clap in rejoicing as the eyes of someone they knew, perhaps someone they had prayed for, were opened. The man smiled, watching a golden-haired grandma do a spontaneous jig as her grandson—the shield bright on his chest—broke into tears, trying to hide them from his neighbors.

Amid the joyful clamor, he saw a dark-skinned woman standing to one side, a curious little smile on her face as her gaze alternated between the young woman on the stage and the gold crosses shining in the crowd. For just a moment, the man caught her gaze, and she nodded slowly, her eyes twinkling. Then she pointed back toward the crowd.

He turned and stared at the back of the memorial assembly to where a woman stood alone, her bristling manner evident in the arms firmly folded across her chest. A moment later he was shouting, pumping his fists in praise as he saw the golden sign appear.

Joy glimmered in his eyes as he hugged his wife. What mercy, this quiet hope for a new beginning! He closed his eyes in wonder. How astonishing that the King would have used him for such a purpose.

The couple turned back to watch the speaker. The young woman was finishing her remarks. She paused for a moment with head bowed then stepped from the stage, her back straight, her gaze clear.

Suddenly, the man and woman heard a sound like a soft rolling of thunder. They turned and saw the crowd dropping to their knees, heads bent in reverence.

The Son of Man was approaching. He was watching the scene before Him with pride, His eyes glistening. Love unbearable swelled inside them as the man and wife too bowed their knees, their hearts yearning, aching, for His lost children.

Mansfield raised his eyes and gazed into the eternal face. He stopped, breathless, as he saw the expression of a Father who knows that His prodigal is already at the gate.

"They have asked, and I have answered." His voice was like the ringing of the seas. "My covenant is with them."

Multnomah Publishers®

The publisher and author would love to hear your comments about this book. *Please contact us at:*
www.multnomah.net/veritas

# A Note from the Author

This story is a work of fiction, but it does incorporate elements of fact. I would like readers to know which pieces of the fictionalized story are based on real issues and which most decidedly are not.

- First and foremost, unless otherwise specified, no characters, groups, or organizations in this book (other than Harvard itself) are based on real people or organizations. Claire Rivers, William Mansfield, Anton and Victor Pike, Ian Burke, and the others are figments of my imagination, as are the Pike Fellowships, the Pike Fellows, Pike Holdings, and the subsidiary companies mentioned. In a university as large as Harvard, it is inevitable that some real people will share the surnames of my characters (for example, as I write this there are seven individuals with the last name of Mansfield at Harvard, at least two of whom are professors), but my characters were not based in any way on those individuals. Similarly, the Grindley and Pike families, and their dynasties of good and of evil, are fictional and are not based on real people. While I am quite sure that Harvard is a spiritual battleground, the concept of a specific family's evil influence on its evolution is purely fictional.
- I have changed or simplified certain realities at Harvard in order to avoid confusing the reader. For example, in reality there are several different undergraduate Christian fellowship groups on campus, which I have combined into a fictional group named the Harvard Christian Fellowship. Also, there is no governing body on campus known as the "Board of Directors," and I have purposefully left out any reference to the real governing group known as the "President and Fellows of Harvard College" to avoid reader confusion with the purely fictional "Pike Fellows." I have also simplified or consolidated various facts about Harvard life, which only a Harvard student would presumably notice. (For example, most dorms don't have hallways; they have entryways. Don't ask.)
- All elements of the spiritual realm scenes are purely educated guesses, and I ask for readers' grace in recognizing that fact. No human can know what goes on behind the veil, and I am thankful that those answers are left in God's hands. All I can do is try to keep those scenes consistent with the Word of God and humbly acknowledge that I have probably gotten some elements wrong. (For example, do angels have wings? The Bible is silent, except where it depicts the cherubim and seraphim with wings. With no clear answer, I used them as a default and gave the angels wings.) Furthermore, I absolutely do not want to imply that people are somehow puppets of spirit beings, which is why I

included scenes showing several different kinds of spiritual influence: for example, angels as messengers, demons as tempters, *and* people (such as Sherry) making terrible choices with no other influence except their own sin. One thing that writing this book has taught me is that it is very difficult to put on paper that which is inherently unknowable.

- Based on many years of research done by others, my story includes a fictional account of the very real Christian grants and endowments at Harvard. That is, although the grants and endowments are true, this book is a work of imagination based on historical fact. The grants issue continues to be researched and new information uncovered, most notably by Kelly Monroe, a Harvard chaplain who wrote *Finding God at Harvard: Spiritual Journeys of Thinking Christians.* (If readers want to research the current disposition of Christian endowments at their own school, a good place to start is the library reference desk or the archives; ask for any books outlining the school's endowments, grants, or bequests.)

- Furthermore, I have tried to portray the historical facts of Harvard's Christian background as accurately as possible in a fiction setting, using research by Kelly Monroe and Harvard Law School graduate Victor Jih, whose legal analysis of the endowments issue was invaluable, as well as others. This includes the simplified but real issue of the changed motto and shield, the quotes from Harvard donor Thomas Hollis and pastor Phillips Brooks, as well as the true story of Reverend Brooks's funeral procession.

On a final note, as with many secular universities (including those originally founded for Christ), Harvard's environment is quite challenging for people with strong biblical convictions. Although my experience was limited to the graduate school arena, my understanding is that these difficulties extend throughout the undergraduate and graduate levels, including the divinity school. One reason I wrote this book is that when I was at Harvard, I had no idea how to defend what I believed, and I got hammered in my classes, as did many of my friends. My prayer is that the "relationship apologetics" in this book will help others learn how to defend their faith in a winsome and effective manner, while still building relationships with those they actively disagree with.

It is important to emphasize that although Harvard's environment can be challenging, it is also filled with well-meaning, intelligent, nice people who are making many great contributions to our world and simply do not understand how difficult it can be for people of faith. As in every school, every business, every corner of these shadowlands, they do not have "eyes to see."

I'll bet most of us have met people like that—whether in a classroom or around the workplace watercooler—but many don't really know how to build bridges to them, how to pray for them, how to present an effective apologetic that can break through that blindness. Many people think that learning how to defend their beliefs is too hard, unattainable, or boring a pastime. None of those fears are true. In my case, I learned fascinating, effective apologetics simply by listening to the Sunday sermons of my New York pastor, Tim Keller of Redeemer Presbyterian Church. For those of you without the benefit of Tim's weekly teaching, I would highly recommend that you glance through one or more of the books I list below.

Just give it a chance, and you will find that learning basic apologetics is not only attainable; it is a relief! It's a relief to be able to respond well rather than stammering and stuttering and later avoiding such conversations at all. Just be sure to pray as you engage in these newly informed conversations so God can speak through you. And ask the Lord for wisdom as to which individuals are truly open to the discussion, who might have been given eyes to see. If an individual is still blinded, continue to build a grace-filled relationship with him, as Jesus would, and ask the Lord to open his eyes.

May God equip you for His work, that the body of Christ may reach such mature unity in the faith and in the knowledge of God's Son that we will all measure up to the full stature of Christ (Ephesians 4:12–13).

*Grace and Peace,*
*Shaunti Feldhahn*

# OTHER READING

I found several resources particularly helpful as I wrote this novel.

Monroe, Kelly. *Finding God at Harvard: Spiritual Journeys of Thinking Christians.* Grand Rapids, Mich.: Zondervan, 1997.

Budziszewski, J. *How to Stay Christian in College.* Colorado Springs, Colo.: Nav-Press, 1999.

Noebel, Dr. David A. *Understanding the Times.* Eugene, Ore.: Harvest House, 1994.

Noebel, Dr. David A., J. F. Baldwin, and Kevin Bywater. *Clergy in the Classroom: The Religion of Secular Humanism.* Manitou Springs, Colo.: Summit Press, 1995.

Lewis, C. S. *Mere Christianity.* San Francisco: Harper San Francisco, 2001.

Budziszewski, J. "Office Hours." *Boundless.* Webzine distributed by Focus on the Family. www.family.org or www. boundless.org/2000/regulars/office_hours/.

There are many other resources that readers might find helpful, depending on their personal style. While this is by no means an exhaustive list (and I haven't read some of these cover-to-cover), other new or classic books include:

McDowell, Josh. *More than a Carpenter.* Wheaton, Ill.: Tyndale, 1987. (This little book was the first "defense of the faith" book I read as a Christian, and I highly recommend it for believers or seekers.)

McDowell, Josh. *Evidence That Demands a Verdict.* Nashville, Tenn.: Thomas Nelson, 1999.

Copan, Paul. *True for You, But Not for Me: Deflating the Slogans that Leave Christians Speechless.* Minneapolis, Minn.: Bethany House, 1998.

Zacharias, Ravi. *Can Man Live Without God?* Dallas, Tex.: Word, 1996. (As well as his other books, his works are highly valuable for those willing to spend the time to work through them.)

Noebel, Dr. David A. and Chuck Edwards *Worldviews in Focus* (Book and journal for students. Summit Ministries, which teaches students classroom apologetics, is very helpful. See www.summit.org.)

Sire, James. *Chris Chrisman Goes to College.* Downers Grove, Ill.: Intervarsity, 1993.

Geisler, Norman and Peter Bocchino. *Unshakable Foundations.* Minneapolis, Minn.: Bethany House, 2001.

Chamberlain, Paul. *Can We Be Good Without God?* Downers Grove, Ill.: Intervarsity, 1996. (Tim Keller recommended this to me.)

Murray, Michael J. *Reason for the Hope Within.* Grand Rapids, Mich.: Wm. B. Eerdmans, 1998. (Also recommended by Tim Keller.)

Kreeft, Peter and Ronald Tacelli. *Handbook of Christian Apologetics.* Downers Grove, Ill.: Intervarsity, 1994.

Monroe, Kelly. Upcoming book *Veritas Forum* (working title). Downers Grove, Ill.: Intervarsity, not yet published.

French, David. Upcoming book *Fighting the Good Fight* (working title) Nashville, Tenn.: Broadman & Holman, not yet published. (This book includes a description of David's fight to help the beleaguered Tufts University Christian Fellowship group that was kicked off campus for sticking with their biblical convictions.)

Zacharias, Ravi. Upcoming book series Conversations with Jesus. Sisters, Ore.: Multnomah, not yet published.

# ACKNOWLEDGMENTS

This book comes to you courtesy of the prayer and hard work of dozens of people, and this space is too limited to properly thank them all. However, I would like readers to know of several whose contributions helped shape the final product. Also, in a work of fiction that incorporates elements of truth, a number of publications and people must be acknowledged. (If I have inadvertently left anyone out of this list, I ask in advance for your grace and understanding.)

## CITATIONS:

Information on Harvard's Christian heritage and Phillips Brooks quotes were taken from *Finding God at Harvard* by Kelly K. Monroe (Grand Rapids, Mich.: Zondervan, 1996).

Other information on Harvard's history, the excerpt from the college laws, and a legal and historical analysis of Harvard's religiously-restricted grants and endowments is taken from Victor Jih's white paper: "In Harvard We Trust: The Legal Issues Concerning Religiously-Restricted Endowment Funds," Harvard Law School third-year paper, April 12, 1996.

The letter by Harvard donor Thomas Hollis can be found in the Jedidiah Morse book *The True Reasons on Which the Election of a Hollis Professor of Divinity in Harvard College Was Opposed at the Board of Overseers* (Charlestown, 1805), 5. Cited in Jih, 11.

The Dorothy L. Sayers quote is drawn from her speech "The Other Six Deadly Sins," (pamphlet edition, London: Methuen, 1943, 23).

Samuel Eliot Morison's quote about "faith in the divinity of human nature" is drawn from *Three Centuries of Harvard* (1963,) 86–7. Cited in Jih, 7–8.

The quote from Francis Frangipane is taken from his book *The Stronghold of God* (Creation House Press) 112–3.

Information on humanism is partially drawn from *Understanding the Times* by Dr. David A Noebel (Eugene, Ore.: Harvest House, 1991,) 114, 194–214.

The initiatives and recommendations of the National Education Association regarding diversity of sexual orientation can be found in several places, including NEA 2000–2001 Resolution B-9. "Racism, Sexism, and Sexual Orientation Discrimination" (www.nea.org/resolutions/00/00b-9.html), and the article "Understanding Gay and Lesbian Students through Diversity" on the NEA's 2000–2001 New Member CD (www.nea.org/bt/1-students/gayles.pdf). It is helpful to read through both of these resources in order to understand the NEA's position.

Information on Stephen Jay Gould's philosophy is drawn from his book *Rocks of Ages: Science and Religion in the Fullness of Life* (New York: Random House, 1999).

The words to the song "Holy Ground" by Geron David are copyright 1983, Meadowgreen Music Company/Songchannel Music Company (ASCAP). All rights administered by EMI Christian Music Publishing.

The "people seeds" and "world-class violinist" hypotheticals used in the abortion debate are drawn from Judith Jarvis Thomson's article "A Defense of Abortion" *The Rights and Wrongs of Abortion: a Philosophy & Public Affairs Reader*. Cohen, Nagel, and Scanlon, eds. (Princeton University Press, 1974).

Information on Peter Singer's views, as outlined in the abortion debate, was drawn from several sources, including his book *Practical Ethics* (Cambridge University Press, 1979). See addendum for several pertinent quotes.

Information on Margaret Sanger's views and eugenics background, as outlined in the abortion debate, was drawn from several sources, including her books *The Pivot of Civilization* (New York: Division of Maxwell Scientific International, Inc., 1922) and *Woman and the New Race* (New York: Truth Publishing Company, 1920), as well as from the American Life League (www.all.org/issues/pp04a.htm). Planned Parenthood denies Sanger's prejudicial outlook, and we were unable to find all of the quotes that the American Life League and other prolife organizations attribute to Sanger. However, the quotes reprinted in the addendum are taken directly from her writing, and her motivations and eugenics-oriented strategy appear obvious.

The biblical concept of having "eyes to see" and the illustration of seeing an author's works on the bookshelves for the first time is drawn from a Lynn Buzzard article in the devotional *What Does the Lord Require of You?* (ed. Lynn R. Buzzard, Geneva School of Law, 1997. Current publisher, Advocates International). Used by permission.

The idea of tragedy in a collapsed tent was partially sparked by the Dick Francis novel *Proof* (New York: Ballentine Books, 1985).

The words to the hymn "Jesus, Lover of My Soul" are by Charles Wesley (1707–1788).

The idea that Jesus' ministry was not about right versus wrong, but about life instead of death, is partially drawn from a presentation by Chris Blake of *Charisma Life* magazine.

## PERSONAL AND PROFESSIONAL ACKNOWLEDGMENTS:

My heartfelt thanks goes out to all those whose strong shoulders helped carry this book, including:

- The faithful members of my book prayer team: Alison Lambert Darrell, Kristen Lambert, Margaret Treadwell, Betty Dunkum, Lara Johnson Grant, Martha Carter, Nancy French, D. J. Snell, Natt Gantt, Tade and Ruth Okediji, Andy

Stross, Steve Blum, Kathryn Lindstrom, Scott and Tammy Beck, Connie and Chris Stover, Judy Hitson, Lisa and John Nagle, Lon and Katherine Waitman, Lisa and Eric Rice, Debra Goldstone, Kate and Greg Allen, Barbara Hoffman, Roger Scarlett, Allan Beeber, Barb Bowlby, Betsy Beinhocker, and especially my prayer partner Lilliana Colgate.

- The many precious friends whose help with everything from baby-sitting to sharing their stories to editing my manuscript kept me sane and on track to meet my deadline, especially Lisa and Eric Rice, Margaret and David Treadwell, Jennifer Wheeler, Nancy and David French, Vernadette Broyles, Karen Jensen, David Goodwin, Jane Joyner, Anne Crist, Sarah and Hannah Rice, and all the members of our church small group. Thanks also to Anna Afshar and to the Lambert family for hosting me during my Cambridge and Nantucket research trips.
- Those at We Care America and the Joseph Project 2000, especially Dave Donaldson, Matt Hotchkiss, Don McKee, and Jennifer Shuler, for their support and patience, giving me the ability and space to work on this book.

The contributions of numerous people helped shape the final product in significant ways. My grateful professional acknowledgment goes to:

- Jill Coyle, my tireless, talented, patient research assistant, and her husband, Danny. I've never seen someone who could come up with a solution to so many unrelated, sometimes bizarre questions exactly when needed: How tall are the walls around Harvard Yard? What's a good apologetic response to the question of evil? What's the difference between determinism and empiricism?
- Lisa and Eric Rice, who shared their professional skill as screenwriters to help shape the story line.
- A wonderful nanny and all-purpose sounding board on the manuscript, Heather Stevenson, and her successor Corrie Hughes.
- Kelly Monroe for sharing her years of research on Harvard's Christian history, the shield and mottoes, and the real religiously restricted grants and endowments; and Victor Jih, for sharing his legal analysis of the endowments issue.
- The Christian students and chaplains at Harvard who sat for interviews and provided many helpful ideas and examples. My special thanks goes to one individual (you know who you are) whose comments helped me see things in a new light.
- Tim Keller at Redeemer Presbyterian Church in New York for his extensive apologetics insights and arguments, including but not limited to: the "plane

crash argument" on the existence of evil, all responses to the secular "you are precious" or "self-actualization" arguments, and the defense that Christianity is in fact the most inclusive religion in the world.

- Pastor Erick (and Elizabeth) Schenkel for shepherding me and Jeff through Harvard and for the "underground espionage agent" analogy, which has recently become all too real in their work.

- Johnny (and Anne) Crist for exemplifying a heart of unity and for the "ministry is always inconvenient" principle.

- Chuck Edwards of Summit Ministries for reviewing the draft manuscript and coaching me on campus apologetics, especially for teaching me the questions to ask ("Question assumptions...").

- John Perrodin at Focus on the Family for reviewing and providing comments on the draft manuscript.

- The host of other individuals who made specific contributions to the final product: George and Laura Grindley, who helped brainstorm the beginning of the story and let me use their names; Roger Scarlett and Katie Scarlett, who connected me to Summit Ministries; John Pittard, whose videotaped debate between the Harvard-Radcliffe Christian Fellowship and the Secular Society helped shape my apologetics scenes; Carissa Niemi for her willingness to share her story, and Becky Loechel for arranging it; Carter Roughton for sharing his classroom apologetics advice; Bill Lambert for providing a way to observe a real-life e-mail debate on life and faith, as well as the (I would say erroneous) idea that Christians desiring a level playing field are actually assuming preeminence; Professor Kenneth Smith at Georgia State for sharing his philosophy syllabus materials, particularly the Stephen Gould summary; John Kingston for his help on St. Augustine's writings; John Holcomb and also the attorneys at Davis Wright Tremaine for their legal advice.

- Calvin Edwards, my book agent and adviser (special thanks for standing shoulder-to-shoulder with my husband in his own God-sized task at World2One), and Nerida Edwards for her help on the vexing NEA question.

- Frank Peretti, Randy Alcorn, and C. S. Lewis for their inspiration and for opening up a whole new world in Christian fiction that this humble work is only the latest attempt to do justice to.

- The Multnomah family, especially Don Jacobson for his faith, encouragement, and vision, and my editor Rod Morris for his skill and patience with a novice novelist.

Finally, my unending love and gratitude to:

- My parents, Dick and Judy Reidinger, and parents-in-law, Bill and Roberta Feld-hahn, who came all the way from China and Michigan, respectively, to baby-sit round-the-clock so I could meet my deadline. Special thanks to Mom for her thorough reading and insightful edits. If this book reflects even a little of the Father's heart, much of that will be because of the love instilled by my earthly father and mother.
- Morgen Claire, for being such a sweet-tempered little baby and putting up with her mommy being tied to the computer for the last two months of the process.
- My beloved husband and best friend, Jeff. What can I say, dear heart? How can I possibly thank you for the hundreds of hours of prayer, of encouragement, of foot-washing service to me even during your own most busy time with the start up of World2One and our voyage into parenthood? Even half of the plot twists were your idea. This book is yours, just as I am and always will be.
- My God, my Master, my Friend. You are so faithful, even when my faith falters. My prayer is that you would take this stumbling sacrifice of love and use it for the building of your Kingdom. But Lord, who am I, to even attempt such a task? The cry of my heart is the same as that of Thomas Hollis, Harvard's first donor, who said it better than I ever could:

*Who am I? Christ is my all. Little, very little, I can do for his name's sake,*
*who has died for me and given me good hope through grace, and by his providence*
*put in my power, and inclined my heart to this way among others, of expressing*
*my gratitude for his name's sake, to him be the glory of all.*

# ADDENDUM

To ensure that some of the quotes used in the classroom debate on abortion are documented, and to provide a direct reference for readers' further research, I am printing several excerpts from published works by Peter Singer and Margaret Sanger. (My grateful thanks to my research assistant Jill Coyle, who spent dozens of hours tracking down this difficult—and in Sanger's case, often out-of-print—information.)

Peter Singer has published many works that outline his views, including *Practical Ethics* (Cambridge University Press, 1993).

Page 171: "Finally, a newborn baby is not an autonomous being, capable of making choices, and so to kill a newborn baby cannot violate the principle of respect for autonomy. In all this the newborn baby is on the same footing as the fetus, and hence fewer reasons exist against killing both babies and fetuses than exist against killing those who are capable of seeing themselves as distinct entities, existing over time."

Page 186: "When the death of a disabled infant will lead to the birth of another infant with better prospects of a happy life, the total amount of happiness will be greater if the defective infant is killed.... Therefore, if killing the hemophiliac infant has no adverse effect on others, it would, according to the total view, be right to kill him."

Page 188: "...in discussing abortion, we saw that birth does not mark a morally significant dividing line."

Margaret Sanger published many works outlining her views, including her approval of eugenics (the "science" that Hitler employed in his quest against the "inferior" Jewish race). As previously noted, Planned Parenthood denies any prejudice or racism on Sanger's part and also states that they should not be judged based on the objectionable motivations or purposes of their founder. Some Sanger quotes:

From *The Pivot of Civilization* (New York: Division of Maxwell Scientific International, Inc., 1922).

Page 102: "...when we realize that each feeble-minded person is a potential source of an endless progeny of defect, we prefer the policy of sterilization, of making sure that parenthood is absolutely prohibited to the feeble-minded."

Page 104: "Eugenics seems to me to be valuable in its critical and diagnostic aspects, in emphasizing the danger of irresponsible and uncontrolled fertility of the 'unfit' and the feeble-minded...."

Page 134: "The result [of charity] has been the accumulation of large urban populations, the increase of irresponsibility, and ever-widening margin of biological waste."

Page 176: "It [eugenics] sees that the most responsible and most intelligent members of society are the less fertile; that the feeble-minded are the more fertile…. Are we heading to biological destruction, toward the gradual but certain attack upon the stocks of intelligence and racial health by the sinister forces of the hordes of irresponsibility and imbecility?"

From *Woman and the New Race* (New York: Truth Publishing Company, 1920). Page 4: "While…providing the human tinder for racial conflagrations, woman was also unknowingly creating slums, filling asylums with insane, and institutions with other defectives. She was replenishing the ranks of the prostitutes, furnishing grist for the criminal courts and inmates for prisons. Had she planned deliberately to achieve this tragic total of human waste and misery, she could hardly have done it more effectively."